STAR WARS

THE NEW JEDI ORDER

EDGE OF VICTORY II
REBIRTH

Also by Greg Keyes

THE NEW JEDI ORDER

EDGE OF VICTORY II
REBIRTH

GREG KEYES

THE BALLANTINE PUBLISHING GROUP • NEW YORK

A Del Rey® Book
Published by The Ballantine Publishing Group

www.starwars.com
www.starwarskids.com
www.delreydigital.com

ISBN 0-345-44610-0

Manufactured in the United States of America

First Edition: August 2001

10   9   8   7   6   5   4   3   2   1

For Gina Matthiesen

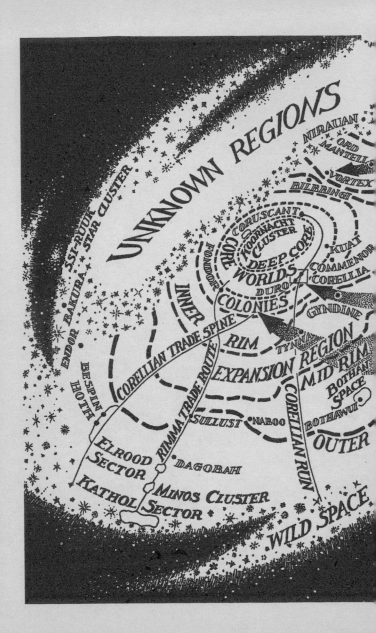

STAR WARS: THE NOVELS

44 YEARS BEFORE
STAR WARS: A New Hope

Jedi Apprentice #1–2

32 YEARS BEFORE
STAR WARS: A New Hope

Cloak of Deception
Darth Maul: Shadow Hunter
Star Wars:
Episode I
The Phantom Menace

22 YEARS BEFORE
STAR WARS: A New Hope

Star Wars:
Episode II

20 YEARS BEFORE
STAR WARS: A New Hope

Star Wars:
Episode III

3 YEARS AFTER
STAR WARS: A New Hope

Star Wars:
Episode V The Empire
Strikes Back
Tales of the Bounty
Hunters

3.5 YEARS AFTER
STAR WARS: A New Hope

Shadows of the Empire

4 YEARS AFTER
STAR WARS: A New Hope

Star Wars: Episode VI
Return of the Jedi
Tales from Jabba's Palace
THE BOUNTY HUNTER WARS:
The Mandalorian Armor
Slave Ship
Hard Merchandise

The Truce at Bakura

6.5–7.5 YEARS AFTER
STAR WARS: A New Hope

X-Wing: Rogue Squadron
X-Wing: Wedge's Gamble
X-Wing: The Krytos Trap
X-Wing: The Bacta War
X-Wing: Wraith Squadron
X-Wing: Iron Fist
X-Wing: Solo Command

14 YEARS AFTER
STAR WARS: A New Hope

The Crystal Star

16–17 YEARS AFTER
STAR WARS: A New Hope

THE BLACK FLEET CRISIS
TRILOGY:
Before the Storm
Shield of Lies
Tyrant's Test

17 YEARS AFTER
STAR WARS: A New Hope

The New Rebellion

18 YEARS AFTER
STAR WARS: A New Hope

THE CORELLIAN TRILOGY:
Ambush at Corellia
Assault at Selonia
Showdown at Centerpoint

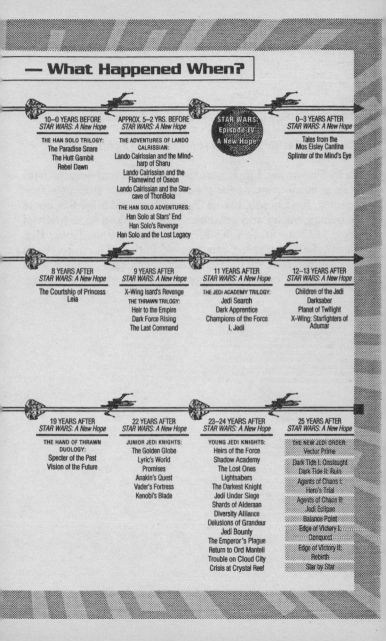

— What Happened When?

10–0 YEARS BEFORE
STAR WARS: A New Hope

THE HAN SOLO TRILOGY:
The Paradise Snare
The Hutt Gambit
Rebel Dawn

APPROX. 5–2 YRS. BEFORE
STAR WARS: A New Hope

THE ADVENTURES OF LANDO CALRISSIAN:
Lando Calrissian and the Mind-harp of Sharu
Lando Calrissian and the Flamewind of Oseon
Lando Calrissian and the Star-cave of ThonBoka

THE HAN SOLO ADVENTURES:
Han Solo at Stars' End
Han Solo's Revenge
Han Solo and the Lost Legacy

STAR WARS: Episode IV A New Hope

0–3 YEARS AFTER
STAR WARS: A New Hope

Tales from the Mos Eisley Cantina
Splinter of the Mind's Eye

8 YEARS AFTER
STAR WARS: A New Hope

The Courtship of Princess Leia

9 YEARS AFTER
STAR WARS: A New Hope

X-Wing Isard's Revenge
THE THRAWN TRILOGY:
Heir to the Empire
Dark Force Rising
The Last Command

11 YEARS AFTER
STAR WARS: A New Hope

THE JEDI ACADEMY TRILOGY:
Jedi Search
Dark Apprentice
Champions of the Force
I, Jedi

12–13 YEARS AFTER
STAR WARS: A New Hope

Children of the Jedi
Darksaber
Planet of Twilight
X-Wing: Starfighters of Adumar

19 YEARS AFTER
STAR WARS: A New Hope

THE HAND OF THRAWN DUOLOGY:
Specter of the Past
Vision of the Future

22 YEARS AFTER
STAR WARS: A New Hope

JUNIOR JEDI KNIGHTS:
The Golden Globe
Lyric's World
Promises
Anakin's Quest
Vader's Fortress
Kenobi's Blade

23–24 YEARS AFTER
STAR WARS: A New Hope

YOUNG JEDI KNIGHTS:
Heirs of the Force
Shadow Academy
The Lost Ones
Lightsabers
The Darkest Knight
Jedi Under Siege
Shards of Alderaan
Diversity Alliance
Delusions of Grandeur
Jedi Bounty
The Emperor's Plague
Return to Ord Mantell
Trouble on Cloud City
Crisis at Crystal Reef

25 YEARS AFTER
STAR WARS: A New Hope

THE NEW JEDI ORDER:
Vector Prime
Dark Tide I: Onslaught
Dark Tide II: Ruin
Agents of Chaos I: Hero's Trial
Agents of Chaos II: Jedi Eclipse
Balance Point
Edge of Victory I: Conquest
Edge of Victory II: Rebirth
Star by Star

The author would like to thank the following people:

The Flying Rat Toli club, for support during a dark time.

Shelly Shapiro and Sue Rostoni for timely help, advice, and hard work at every stage of the process. My fellow authors—Troy Denning, Jim Luceno, Elaine Cunningham, and Mike Stackpole for helping me try and get things right. Thanks also to Michael Kogge, Colette Russen, Kathleen O'Shea, Deanna Hoak, Ben Harper, Leland Chee, Chris Cerasi, Enrique Guerrero, Eelia Goldsmith Hendersheid, Helen Keier, and Dan Wallace. And again, to Kris Boldis for his support. It's been a blast, everyone!

DRAMATIS PERSONAE

Anakin Solo; Jedi Knight (male human)
Booster Terrik; captain, *Errant Venture* (male human)
Cilghal; Jedi healer (female Mon Calamari)
Corran Horn; Jedi Knight (male human)
Colonel Gavin Darklighter; Rogue Squadron (male human)
Han Solo; captain, *Millennium Falcon* (male human)
Jacen Solo; Jedi Knight (male human)
Jaina Solo; Jedi Knight (female human)
Kae Kwaad; master shaper (male Yuuzhan Vong)
Kam Solusar; Jedi Master (male human)
Kyp Durron; Jedi Master (male human)
Leia Organa Solo; former New Republic diplomat (female human)
Luke Skywalker; Jedi Master (male human)
Mara Jade Skywalker; Jedi Master (female human)
Nen Yim; shaper adept (female Yuuzhan Vong)
Nom Anor; executor (male Yuuzhan Vong)
Onimi; Supreme Overlord Shimrra's jester (male Yuuzhan Vong)
Qurang Lah; warleader (male Yuuzhan Vong)
Tahiri Veila; Jedi student (female human)
Talon Karrde; independent information broker (male human)
Traest Kre'fey; admiral (male Bothan)
Tsavong Lah; warmaster (male Yuuzhan Vong)
Vergere; familiar to the deceased Yuuzhan Vong priestess, Elan (female Fosh)

PROLOGUE

Blood, drifting in starlight.

That was the first thing Jacen Solo saw when he opened his eyes. It had beaded into what looked, in the dim, like polished black pearls reflecting the ancient starlight filtering through the transparisteel a meter or so away. He noted absently that the spheroids were all spinning in the same direction.

He was spinning, too, very slowly, through the little nebula of blood. Even in the negligible illumination he could tell he was only a few centimeters from a wall.

From the ache in his leg and skull, he had a good idea where the blood was coming from. It was cold, too, but the air seemed stuffy.

What was going on?

Outside the window, something large and irregular moved to block the stars, and he remembered.

Tsavong Lah, warmaster of the Yuuzhan Vong, clicked the obsidian-sharp talons of his new foot against the living coral of his command chamber floor and considered it in the pale light of the mycoluminescent walls.

He might have had the foot the cursed *Jeedai* took from him replaced with a clone of his own, but that would have been not only dishonorable but personally unsatisfying. That an infidel had taken something from him was bad enough; to pretend that the wound had never happened was unthinkable.

But a hobbling warmaster would lose respect, especially if he had not made the sacrifice himself.

The pain was fading, and feeling was coming into his new foot as the nerves learned their way. The four armored digits of a vua'sa now made up half his stride.

The choice was an homage to the most ancient traditions of his office. The first warmaster created by Yun-Yuuzhan had not been a Yuuzhan Vong, but a living weapon-beast he named vua'sa. A Yuuzhan Vong challenged the vua'sa to single combat, triumphed, and took its place. Even now, Vua was a popular name among the warrior caste.

Tsavong Lah had bade the shapers grow him a vua'sa. Though the creature had been extinct since the ancestral home planet was lost, its pattern still existed in the deeps of shaper memory-qahsa. They had made it; he had fought it and triumphed, despite having to fight on one foot. Now Tsavong Lah knew the gods still deemed him worthy of his station.

And from the cooling corpse of the vua'sa, he had a new foot.

"Warmaster."

Tsavong recognized the voice of his aide, Selong Lian, but did not look up from the examination of his prize.

"Speak."

"Someone petitions for words with you."

"Not my expected appointment?"

"No, Warmaster. It is the deception-sect priestess Ngaaluh."

Tsavong Lah growled in the back of his throat. Worshipers of Yun-Harla had failed the Yuuzhan Vong of late. Still, the sect was powerful, and Supreme Overlord Shimrra continued to favor the antics of those who worshiped the Trickster goddess. And since Yun-Harla oversaw the elevation of warriors and had possibly aided him in his fight with the vua'sa, he perhaps owed the goddess a favor, as well.

"Let me hear her words," he said.

A moment later, the priestess entered. She was slender, her back-sloping forehead narrower than most, the bluish sacs beneath her eyes mere crescents. She wore a ceremonial robe of living tissue grown to resemble a flayed skin.

"Warmaster," she said, crossing her arms in salute. "I am greatly honored."

"Your message," he snapped impatiently. "I have other business waiting. Harrar sent you?"

"Yes, Warmaster."

"Speak, then."

"The priestess Elan, who died to further the conquest of the infidels—"

"Who failed her task," Tsavong Lah reminded.

"Just so, Warmaster. She failed, but died nevertheless in the cause of the glorious Yuuzhan Vong. The priestess Elan had a familiar, a sentient creature named Vergere."

"I am aware of that. Did it not die with its mistress?"

"No, Warmaster. That is what I have come to tell you. It managed to escape the infidels and make its way back to us."

"Did it."

"Yes, Warmaster. She has communicated to us much of interest concerning the infidels, things she learned in their custody. Much more she knows and will not tell except to you, Tsavong Lah."

"You suspect an infidel trick? An attempt to assassinate me, perhaps?"

"We do not entirely trust her, Warmaster, but determined to bring you her words so you might decide how to treat her."

Tsavong Lah inclined his heavily scarred features. "It is good you did so. She must be interrogated and examined by the haar vhinic, of course. Afterward, have her brought to my ship, but keep her far from me. Tell her I will need further proof of both her intelligence and intentions before she may stand before me."

"It will be done, Warmaster."

He gave the priestess the sign of dismissal, and she immediately departed. Good. A priestess who knew her station.

His aide immediately took her place at the red-flanged receiving portal. "Qurang Lah has arrived, Warmaster," he said. "And the executor, Nom Anor."

"They will see me, now," Tsavong Lah pronounced.

Qurang Lah was his crèche-brother, a less elevated version of himself. His face was cut in deep hatch marks, and the gash of Domain Lah, while not as deep as the warmaster's ear-to-ear cut, was still a clear marker of his lineage.

"*Belek tiu,* Warmaster." Qurang Lah saluted with crossed arms, as did the much slighter executor by his side. "Command me."

Tsavong Lah nodded at his crèche-brother, but fixed his gaze on Nom Anor. The executor's one real eye and the venomous plaeryin bol that occupied his other socket stared unblinking back at him.

"Executor," Tsavong Lah rumbled. "I have taken your latest suggestions under advisement. You are certain they are ripe for conquest?"

"The hinges of their fortress are weakened, Warmaster," Nom Anor replied. "I have seen to it personally. The battle will be a quick one, the victory easily secured."

"I have heard this from you before," the warmaster said. He turned his attention to the warrior. "Qurang Lah. You have been briefed in the matter. Have you anything to say?"

Qurang Lah revealed his sharpened teeth. "Conquest is always desirable," he said. "However, this seems a foolish time to move. The infidels tremble before us; they fear to counterattack; they dare dream our bloody path ended with Duro and that we might be satisfied to live in the same galaxy with abomination-using vermin. This is to our advantage; the shipwomb produces their doom, but it must be given time. At this moment, our fleet is thinly scattered, more thinly than the infidels know. One misstep now, before the shipwomb again swells our fleet, could be costly indeed."

"There will be no cost," Nom Anor asserted. "And the moment to strike *is* now. If we wait longer, the *Jeedai* will have more time to act."

"The Jeedai." Tsavong Lah snarled. "Tell me, Nom Anor. With all of your infidel contacts and all your self-proclaimed expertise in manipulating them, why have you been unable to bring me the one Jeedai I desire above all others—Jacen Solo?"

Nom Anor did not flinch. "That is a most difficult task, as you know, Warmaster," he admitted. "Certain elements among the *Jeedai* and their allies have gone rogue. They no longer answer to the senate, or any other body where we have allies. That is my point; when you told the infidels that we would cease our conquest if the *Jeedai* were delivered up to us, it was a brilliant strategy. It gave us time to build our force and secure our territories. It gave us many *Jeedai*. But Jacen is kin to Skywalker, the master of them all. He is the son of Leia Organa Solo and Han Solo, both worthy opponents who have managed to vanish for the time being. I have strategies that will uncover them; even now, a plan unfolds regarding Skywalker and his mate Mara and that will bring the others running, Jacen included."

"And this place you wish to feel the talons of our might? This involves the *Jeedai*?"

"It does not, Warmaster. But it will throw their senate into desperate confusion. It will give us the leverage we need to end the *Jeedai* threat forever. As of now, the government of the New Republic still refuses to make it policy to outlaw the *Jeedai*. In one stroke I can change that, as well as build us a new fortress overlooking the Core. But the time is now; if we wait, we will lose our opportunity."

"Nom Anor has counseled us ill before," Qurang Lah said.

"This is too true," the warmaster returned. "But it chafes me not to strike, to pretend quiescence so long. The number of *Jeedai* the weak-kneed infidels have given us has declined lately. We were humiliated at Yavin Four. There must be atonement, and Yun-Yuuzhan craves the scent of blood."

"If you wish it, Warmaster," Qurang Lah said, "I shall lead my fleet. I never shrink from battle when my duty calls."

"Hurr," Tsavong Lah murmured, considering. "Nom Anor, you will implement your plan. Qurang Lah will command the Yuuzhan Vong forces, and you will advise him how to proceed. If your advice is again flawed, there will be a more serious reckoning. If it is good, as you assure me it will be, you will atone for your recent mistakes. Do you understand?"

"I understand, Warmaster. I will not fail."

"See you do not. Qurang Lah, have you anything else to say?"

"I have not, Warmaster. My duty is clear now." He snapped the salute. "*Belek tiu*. The infidels will fall before us. Their ships shall burn like falling stars. As I speak it, it is already done."

PART ONE

THRESHOLD

ONE

"You've had worse ideas, Luke," Mara Jade Skywalker reluctantly admitted, nodding her head back so the sunlight fell on her face and her deep red-gold tresses trailed behind her. Posed that way, eyes closed, framed against the blue line of the sea, her beauty closed Luke's throat for a moment.

Mara's green eyes opened, and she looked at him with a sort of wistful fondness before arching a cynical brow.

"Getting all fatherly on me again?"

"No," he said softly. "Just thinking how ridiculously lucky I am."

"Hey. I'm the one with the hormone swings. You aren't trying to one-up me, are you?" But she took his hand and gave it a squeeze. "Come on," she said. "Let's walk a bit more."

"You sure you're up to it?"

"What, you want to carry me? Of course I'm up to it. I'm pregnant, not hamstrung. You think it would be better for our kid if I spent all day lying around sucking on oorp?"

"I just thought you wanted to relax."

"Absolutely. And this is relaxing. Us, all alone, on a beautiful island. Well, sort of an island. Come on."

The beach was warm beneath Luke's bare feet. He had been reluctant to agree to going shoeless, but Mara had insisted that's what one did on a beach. He found, to his surprise, that it reminded him pleasantly of his boyhood on Tatooine. Back then, in the relative cool of early evening—one of those rare periods when both blazing suns were nearly set—sometimes he would take his shoes off and feel the still-warm sand between his toes. Not when Uncle Owen was looking, of course, because the old man would launch into an explanation of what shoes were for in the first place, about the valuable moisture Luke was losing though his soles.

For an instant, he could almost hear his uncle's voice and smell Aunt Beru's giju stew. He had an urge to put his shoes back on.

Owen and Beru Larses had been the first personal casualties in Luke Skywalker's battle against the Empire. He wondered if they had known why they died.

He missed them. Anakin Skywalker may have been his father, but the Larses had been his parents.

"I wonder how Han and Leia are doing?" Mara wondered aloud, interrupting his reverie.

"I'm sure they're fine. They've only been gone a few days."

"I wonder if Jacen should have gone with them?"

"Why not? He's proven himself capable often enough. And they're his parents. Besides, with half the galaxy after him, it's better he stay on the move."

"Right. I only meant it makes things worse for Jaina. It's hard on her, doing nothing, knowing her brother is out fighting the fight."

"I know. But Rogue Squadron will probably call her up pretty soon."

"Sure," Mara replied. "Sure they will." She sounded far from convinced.

"You don't think so?" Luke asked.

"No. I think they would like to, but her Jedi training makes her too much of a political liability right now."

"When did the Rogues ever care about politics? Has someone said this to you?"

"Not in so many words, but I hear things, and I'm trained to listen to the words behind the words. I hope I'm wrong, for Jaina's sake."

Her feelings brushed Luke in the Force, running a troubled harmony to her assertion.

"Mara," Luke said, "my love, while I'll believe you when you say picking up parasites on a strange beach is relaxing—"

"Nonsense. This sand is as sterile as an isolation lab. It's perfectly safe to walk barefoot. And you like the feel of it."

"If you say so. But I forbid any more talk about politics, Jedi, the war, the Yuuzhan Vong, anything like that. We're out here for you to relax, to forget all of that for a day or so. Just a day."

She narrowed her eyes at him. "You're the one who thinks the whole universe will collapse unless you're there to keep it spinning."

"I'm not pregnant."

"Say something like *that* again, and I'll make you wish you were," she said, a bit sharply. "And by the way, if we do this again, it's your turn."

"We'll play sabacc for it," Luke responded, trying to keep a straight face but failing. He kissed her, and she kissed him back, hard.

They continued along the strand, past a rambling stand of crawling slii, all knotted roots and giant gauzy leaves. Waves were beginning to lap on the beach, as they hadn't earlier, which meant they were on the bow side of the "island."

It wasn't an island at all, of course, but a carefully landscaped park atop a floating mass of polymer cells filled with inert gas. A hundred or so of them cruised the artificial western sea of Coruscant, pleasure craft built by rich merchants during the grand, high days of the Old Republic. The Emperor had discouraged such frivolity, and most had been docked for decades and fallen into disrepair. Still, many were in good enough shape to refurbish, and in the youth of the New Republic, a few sharp businessmen had purchased some and made them commercial successes. One such person, not surprisingly, had been Lando Calrissian, a longtime friend of Luke's. He had offered Luke use of the craft whenever he wished it. It had taken Luke a long time to call in the offer.

He was glad he had done it—Mara seemed to be enjoying it. But she was right, of course. With everything that was happening now, it was hard not to think of it as a waste of time.

But some feelings could *not* be trusted. Mara was showing now, her belly gloriously rounded around their son, and she was suffering from all of the physical discomforts any woman did in that situation. Nothing in her training as an assassin, smuggler, or Jedi Knight had prepared her for this compromised state, and despite her obvious love for their unborn child, Luke knew physical weakness grated on her. Her comment about Jaina might just as well have been about herself.

And there were other worries, too, and a pocket paradise wasn't likely to help her forget them, but at least they could take a few deep breaths and pretend they were on some distant, uninhabited world, rather than in the thick of the biggest mess since before the Empire had been defeated.

No, strike that. The Empire had threatened to extinguish liberty and freedom, to bring the dark side of the Force to ascendance. The enemy they faced now threatened extinction in a much more literal and ubiquitous sense.

So Luke walked with his wife as evening fell, pretending not to be thinking of these things, knowing she could feel he was anyway.

"What will we name him?" Mara asked at last. The sun had vanished in a lens on the horizon, and now Coruscant began to shatter the illusion of pristine nature. The distant shores glowed in a solid mass, and the sky remained deep red on the horizon. Only near zenith did it resemble the night sky of most moonless planets, but even there was a baroque embroidery of light as aircars and starships followed their carefully assigned paths, some coming home, some leaving home, some merely arriving at another port.

A million little lights, each with a story, each a spark of significance in the Force that flowed from them, around them, through them.

No illusion, here. All was nature. All was beauty, if you had eyes willing to see it.

"I don't know." He sighed. "I don't even know where to start."

"It's just a name," she said.

"You would think. But everyone seems to believe it's important. Since we went public with the news, you wouldn't believe how many suggestions I've gotten, and from the strangest places."

Mara stopped walking, and her face reflected a sudden profound astonishment. "You're afraid," she said.

He nodded. "I guess I am. I guess I don't think it's 'just a name,' not when it comes to people like us. Look at Anakin. Leia named him after our father, a gesture to the person who became Darth Vader, as a recognition that he overcame the dark side and died a good man. It was her reconciliation with him, and a sign to the galaxy that the scars of war could heal. That we could forgive and move on. But for Anakin, it's been a trial. When he was little, he always feared he would walk the same dark path his grandfather did. It was just a name, but it was a real burden to place on his shoulders. It may be years before we learn the full consequences of that decision."

"For all that I admire your sister, she is a politician, and she thinks like one. That's been good for the galaxy, not so good for her children."

"Exactly," Luke said reluctantly. "And whether I like it or not, Mara, because of who we are, our child will inherit part of our burden. I'm just afraid of placing an extra one on his shoulders. Suppose I named him Obi-Wan, as a salute to my old Master? Would he think that means I want him to grow up to be a Jedi? Would he think he had to live up to Ben's reputation? Would he feel his choices in life constrained?"

"I see you've thought a lot about this."

"I guess I have."

"Notice how quickly this takes us back to the things you said we weren't supposed to talk about?"

"Oh. Right."

"Luke, this is who we are," Mara said, stroking his shoulder lightly. "We can't deny it, even alone on an island." She dipped her foot in the wavelets lapping onto the beach. Luke closed his eyes and felt the wind on his face.

"Maybe not," he admitted.

"And so what?" Mara said, playfully kicking a little water on the cuff of his pants. But then her face grew serious again. "There is one *very* important thing I want to say, now, before another second passes," she informed him.

"What's that?"

"I'm really hungry. Really, really hungry. If I don't eat right away, I'm going to salt you in seawater and gobble you up."

"You'd be dissapointed," Luke said. "It's fresh water. Come on. The pavilion isn't far. There should be food waiting."

Luke and Mara ate outside at a table of polished yellow Selonian marble while the blossoms around them chimed a quiet music and released fragrances to complement each course. Luke felt ridiculously pampered and a little guilty, but managed to relax somewhat into the mood.

But the mood was broken during the intermezzo, when the pavilion's protocol droid interrupted them.

"Master Skywalker," it said, "an aircar is approaching and requesting admittance through the security perimeter."

"You have the signal?"

"Most assuredly."

"Transfer to the holostation on the table."

"As you wish, sir."

A hologram of a man's face appeared above the remains of their meal. It was human, very long, with aristocratic features.

"Kenth Hamner," Luke said, a sense of foreboding pricking up his scalp. "To what do we owe this pleasure?"

The retired colonel smiled briefly. "Nothing important. Just a visit from an old friend. May I come aboard?"

That's what his words said. His expression, somehow, conveyed something altogether different.

"Of course. Link to the ship's computer, and it will land you somewhere appropriate. I hope you like grilled nylog."

"One of my favorites. I'll see you soon."

A few moments later, Hamner appeared from one of the

several trails leading to the pavilion, accompanied by the droid.

"You two make me wish I was young again," Hamner said, smiling, looking them over.

"We're not so young, and you're not so old," Mara replied.

Hamner offered her a short bow from the waist. "Mara, you're looking lovely as ever. And my deepest congratulations on your upcoming event."

"Thank you, Kenth," Mara returned graciously.

"Have a seat," Luke said. "May I have the droid bring you something?"

"A cold drink of a mildly stimulating beverage perhaps? Surprise me."

Luke sent the droid off with those rather vague instructions and then turned to Hamner, who was now seated.

"You didn't come here just to congratulate us, did you?"

Hamner nodded sadly. "No. I came to give you a heads-up. Borsk Fey'lya has managed to secure an order for your arrest. The warrant will be served about six standard hours from now."

TWO

Somewhere between the Corellian Trade Spine and the Kathol sector, the Star Destroyer *Errant Venture* dropped out of hyperspace, reoriented its massive wedge-shaped frame, and resumed lightspeed. An uninformed observer would have had less than a minute to wonder what a Star Destroyer was doing in such an out-of-the-way part of space and why it was painted red.

Deep in the Destroyer's belly, Anakin Solo hardly noticed the transition, so intent was he on what he was doing. He stood quickly into narrow profile, the point of his lightsaber aiming toward the deck, pommel level with his forehead and pointed at the ceiling. With two quick twists of his wrist, he deflected a pair of stun bolts from the remote whirring around him. He flipped the lightsaber to an identical position behind his back to catch the blast from a second remote, then dropped into a crouch, his luminescent weapon whipping up to high guard. A leaping somersault carried him over the sudden coordinated flurry of shots from the two flying spheres. By the time his feet touched the deck, he was weaving a complex set of parries that sent reddish bolts hissing against the walls.

He was in the rhythm, now, and his blue eyes sparkled like electron arcs as the stinging rays came faster, more often, better timed. After a few minutes of this, sweat was plastering his brown hair to his head and soaking his dark Jedi robes, but none of the painful though harmless attacks had found their mark.

He was warmed up, now.

"Halt," he commanded. Immediately the spheres became stationary and quiescent.

He deactivated his lightsaber and set it aside. From a wall cabinet, Anakin removed another lightsaber, thumbed it on, took a few deep breaths, calmed his racing pulse. It was quiet in the storage compartment he'd converted into his training space. Quiet and spare and off-white. A motley trio of droids regarded him with unblinking eyes. Even the most casual observer could see they had been cobbled together from spare parts, though the central chassis of each was that of a rather common worker drone. They did not look particularly dangerous, until one examined what they held in their hands—wicked-looking staffs, sharp on one end, spoon-shaped on the other. They looked remarkably like snakes, an impression enhanced by the fact that they undulated now and then.

Anakin blew out another breath and nodded at the droids.

"Begin sequence one," he said.

The droids flashed into motion, their spindly frames moving with eye-daunting speed, two flanking him on either side, one driving straight toward him. Anakin backpedaled and parried, dropped, and swept the legs out from under the droid on his right. The other two were attacking, one staff spearing at his neck, the other gone suddenly flexible, flicking around his rising parry toward his back. Anakin stepped forward a centimeter and felt the wind from the vicious whip-over as it came up short of his spine.

That's it, he thought. *I'm learning the range. The smallest movement possible to prevent the attack from landing is the best.*

He dropped the high parry into a riposte. The droid, suddenly too close to him, tried to retreat but stopped instantly, deactivated when Anakin's weapon touched its torso.

The downed droid was back up by then, and Anakin found himself circling, holding them at the very outside of his guard and in his field of vision. That kept them off him, and he could probably do that forever. He wouldn't win the fight that way, though, so he gave them a rhythm to follow and let them try to break it.

One of the staffs suddenly spit a stream of liquid at him. He twisted his body to avoid it, again allowing only a centimeter for the miss. At the same moment, the other droid broke tempo and leapt in deep.

Anakin parried, but the staff wrapped around his wrist. He felt a distinct and painful electric shock. The other droid was an instant behind, leveling a blow at Anakin's skull.

Somewhere a blaster shrieked, and the droid suddenly didn't have a weapon—or the arm that held it.

"Halt!" Anakin shouted, and hurled himself away as the staff instantly released his hand. He came down in a fighting posture.

A dark-haired man with a blaster stood in the doorway. He had a beard liberally tinseled with silver and wore green robes the same shade as his eyes. He held the blaster up in a nonthreatening way, as if surrendering.

"Why did you do that?" Anakin asked, trying to suppress the anger suddenly boiling up. He had worked hard on that droid.

"You're welcome," Corran Horn said, holstering his weapon.

"Those are training droids. They wouldn't have hurt me."

"Oh no? Are those training amphistaffs they're holding? If he'd hit you with it . . ."

"He wouldn't have. They're programmed to arrest their blows the second the staff touches my skin. And yes, they are training amphistaffs. They aren't real."

Corran's eyes widened in surprise. "How did you manage that? Why didn't your lightsaber cut through them?"

"It's not a lightsaber."

Corran's expression was almost worth the damage to the droid.

"It's just a blade-shaped force field, a weak one," Anakin explained. "Wouldn't cut anything. The things my droids have act like amphistaffs and move like them, but they just spit dye and deliver a shock when they hit. They only weigh a kilogram or so."

"I guess I ruined your droid for no good reason, then," Corran said.

Anakin's anger was entirely mastered now. It was something he had been working on. "It's okay. I built it; I can fix it. I've got nothing but time."

"I'm just curious," Corran said, eyeing the droids. "Booster has a couple of duelist elites in storage. Why not use one of them to train with?"

Anakin deactivated the "weapon" and returned it to the cabinet. "Duelist elites don't move like Yuuzhan Vong warriors. The droids I built do."

"I wondered what you've been puttering at for the last few weeks."

Anakin nodded. "I don't want to lose my edge. You saw what happened—the one you shot had me."

"Practice is fine," Corran said. "I just wish you had informed me of what you were doing. Might have saved me a skipped heartbeat and you a droid."

"Right. I forgot," Anakin said.

Corran nodded again, this time with a more thoughtful look in his eye. "You didn't notice me coming. That's not good. You have to learn to extend your sphere of responsibility beyond the immediate battle."

"I know," Anakin replied. "I wasn't using the Force. I'm training to fight without it."

"Because the Yuuzhan Vong can't be sensed in the Force, I assume."

Anakin nodded. "Of course. The Force is a wonderful tool—"

"The Force isn't merely a tool, Anakin," Corran admonished. "It's much more than that."

"I know," Anakin said, a bit peevishly. "But among other things it is a tool, and for fighting the Yuuzhan Vong, it's just not the right tool for the job, no more than a hydrospanner is what you would use to calibrate the input feed of an astromech."

Corran cocked his head skeptically. "I can't precisely dispute that, but it's not because it isn't wrong."

Anakin shrugged. "Try it like this, then. All Jedi training

involves the Force, even combat training. Sensing blows and blaster bolts before they happen, that sort of thing. Shoving our enemies around telekinetically—"

"With some exceptions," Corran dryly reminded him.

"Right. So you should know what I mean. What do you think of Jedi who can't win a fight without resorting to telekinesis? For that matter, you were CorSec long before you were Jedi. You should be able to see that the Force has become as much of a crutch for us as anything. The Yuuzhan Vong prove that."

"Sounding a little like your brother. Are you abandoning the Force?"

Anakin's eyebrows arched up. "Of course not. I'll use it when it works. When I was being hunted by the Yuuzhan Vong on Yavin Four, I discovered ways to use the Force against them. I looked for the holes in the Force around me. I listened to the voices of the jungle and felt the fear of its creatures when the Yuuzhan Vong warriors passed near."

"And you learned to sense the Yuuzhan Vong themselves," Corran pointed out.

"Not with the Force, though. With the lambent I used to rebuild my lightsaber."

"How can you be sure? I've never believed the Yuuzhan Vong don't exist in the Force. They *must*. Everything does. We just don't know how to do it. You attuned yourself to a piece of Vong biotech and now you can sense them. Can you be sure you haven't found where they live in the Force?"

"Maybe I did make some sort of metalinkage, but if I did I think it's more of a translation from one to another. I can't be sure. All I know is, I can use it. But if I lose my lightsaber, or it's destroyed, or the lambent dies—I still want to be able to fight them."

Corran placed a hand on Anakin's shoulder. "Anakin, I understand you've been through a lot. The Yuuzhan Vong have taken much that was precious from you. I'll always be grateful for what you did for my children, and so I'm telling you this as a friend. You need to control your emotions. You can't allow yourself to hate."

Anakin shook his head. "I don't hate the Yuuzhan Vong, Corran. My time with them helped me to understand them. More than ever, I think they must be stopped, but I promise you, I do not hate them. I can fight them without anger."

"I hope what you say is true, but anger is a quick-change artist and a trickster. More often than not, you don't see it for what it is."

"Thanks," Anakin said. "I appreciate the advice."

Corran again looked slightly skeptical. Then he motioned toward the droids. "These droids were a good idea. I'd be happy to help you repair that one."

"That's okay. Like I said, I have plenty of time on my hands."

Corran smiled. "Getting a little deck fever?"

"I'm ready to get back out there, if that's what you mean. But Tahiri still needs me."

"You're a good friend to her, Anakin."

"I haven't been. I'm trying to be."

"Tahiri won't get over her ordeal in a few months. She needs more time. I think she'll understand if you have to go."

Anakin dropped his gaze from Corran's. "I promised her I would stay a while, and that's what I'm going to do. But it's hard, knowing what's going on out there. Knowing my friends and family are fighting while I'm here doing nothing."

"But you aren't doing nothing; you just said it yourself. You're still a part of the defensive effort. Protecting the Jedi students is important. Jumping randomly around the galaxy is probably the safest thing we can do, but there's no telling when the Yuuzhan Vong or one of their sympathizers will pick up our trail. If they do, we'll need everyone we can get."

"I guess so. I'm just so *restless*."

"You are," Corran agreed. "I've noticed you've been kind of itchy. That's why I was looking for you, in fact."

"Really? What for?"

"We need supplies. Obviously, if we're trying to keep our location secret we can't take the only red Star Destroyer in the galaxy into an inhabited system. I was going to take one of the transports out. I thought you might like to go. Hopefully it will be a boring trip, but—"

"Yes," Anakin said. "I'll do it."

"Good. I could use a copilot. I'll meet you in the docking bay tomorrow, say after morning meal?"

"Great. Thanks, Corran."

"No problem. See you then."

THREE

Jacen watched the ship approach as if in a dream. It remained a black presence against the stars—it had no running lights. *It must be in the shadow of the* Millennium Falcon, he thought.

The Force told him there was nothing there at all.

It gradually moved from the umbra into the distant orange light of the nameless star a parsec below them, and now he could see details. Distances were deceiving in space—he couldn't tell how large it was. It was spicular, like two cones with their bases pushed together. Where the cones met, three finned, heartlike structures projected. These Jacen recognized as dovin basals, living creatures that bent space, time, and gravity around themselves. There could be no doubt it was a Yuuzhan Vong ship, for it was made—rather, grown—from the same yorik coral Jacen had seen so many times already. Its surface was roughened by numerous small welts, as if the ship had contracted Bakuran fever bumps.

When he realized the bumps were coralskippers, the Yuuzhan Vong equivalent of starfighters, he suddenly grasped the scale. The thing was the size of a Dreadnaught.

And it was coming for them. It was almost certainly what had yanked them so brutally out of hyperspace.

Jacen snapped out of his fog of confusion and pushed away from the bulkhead. He was in the dorsal gunner's turret. He'd been sitting there in contemplation before the sudden terrifying jolt. His head was bleeding, but not critically, so far as he could tell.

He pulled himself quickly along the rungs of the ladder

into the main cabin. He fought the feeling of falling; it had been a while since he had done any zero-g training.

"Mom! Dad!" His voice rang in the silent ship. A primitive part of him cringed at the sound, warning him that the predator outside would hear him. It couldn't, of course, not through the vacuum, but human instincts were older than space travel.

He got no answer. Frantic now, he pushed himself through the darkness to the cockpit.

He found them there, and for a heart-stopping moment thought they were dead, so still were they in the Force. But both were breathing.

"Dad!" He gently shook his father's shoulder, but got no more than a reflexive response. Still gently, fear overcoming reluctance, he probed a little in the Force, suggesting the older man awake.

Han Solo stirred. "Huh? Whzzat!" Then he jerked fully alert, saw Jacen, and pulled back his fist.

"It's me, Dad!" Jacen said. Next to him, his mother began to stir, too. He couldn't feel anything seriously wrong with either of them. They had both been strapped in their crash couches.

"Jacen?" Han murmured. "What's going on? What happened?"

"I was hoping you knew. As near as I can tell, we've been interdicted by a Yuuzhan Vong ship. It's out there right now. I don't think we have much time."

Han rubbed his eyes and looked at the control panel, where a few feeble lights were still clinging to life. He let out a long, low whistle.

"That's not good," he said.

"Han? Jacen?" Leia Organa Solo sat straighter in the crash couch. "What's happening?"

"The usual," Han replied, flipping switches. A few more indicators came on. "Power system's off-line, artificial gravity off-line, emergency life support on its last legs, big ship full of bad guys outside."

"A really big ship," Jacen added.

"Just like old times." Leia sighed.

"Hey, I told you it would be like a second honeymoon."
Han's voice dropped lower and grew more serious. "You all
right?"

"I'm fine," Leia said. "I'm wondering what made us
black out."

"Probably the same thing that fried the power couplings," Han remarked. Then his eyes widened. "Oh, no."

"I told you it was big," Jacen said, as their lateral drift
brought the Yuuzhan Vong ship into view.

"Do something, Han," Leia said. "Do something *now*."

"I'm doing, I'm doing," he muttered, working at the controls. "But unless someone wants to get out and push . . ."

"Why aren't *they* doing anything?" Leia wondered.

"They probably think we're dead in space," Han replied.
"They may be right."

"Yes, but—" She stopped. Two of the coralskippers had
detached from the larger vessel and were coming toward
the *Falcon*.

Han unbuckled himself. "Take my seat, Jacen. I had a
shielded power core installed, but the couplings have to be
changed."

"I'll do it."

"You don't know the *Falcon* well enough. You two stay
up here. The second I give you power, go, and I mean, *go*."

"We're too close. They'll snatch us with their dovin
basals."

"They'll snatch us for sure if we sit here."

He kicked back through the doorway and was gone,
swallowed by the darkness beyond.

The coralskippers continued to approach, in no apparent
hurry.

"Mom, look," Jacen said, pointing. Against the starfield
were some brighter sparks, drifting in a nebulous lens.

"What is it?"

"Something reflecting the light from the primary. A bunch
of somethings."

"Ships," Leia said. "Other ships they've interdicted."

"Uh-huh. Must be a dozen or more."

"Well." She sighed. "I guess we found out something

useful on this trip. This isn't a safe route to smuggle Jedi through."

A series of curses drifted from somewhere in the back of the ship.

"Han?" Leia shouted.

"Nothing. Hit my head," the answer came back.

Another few moments of rummaging about, and then another, more colorful set of curses.

"It's going to take at least half an hour," Han called.

"We don't have that," Leia whispered. "They'll be boarding us any minute. If they even bother, and don't just cut us to pieces."

"They'll bother," Jacen said. "The Yuuzhan Vong hate to waste good slaves and sacrifices. I guess we'd better get ready to meet them." He unclipped the lightsaber from his belt. Leia unbuckled herself and drew her own weapon.

"You let me deal with this, Mom. You're still favoring that leg."

"Don't worry about me. I was doing this before you were born."

Jacen was about to lodge another protest when he saw the expression on her face. She wouldn't be budged.

As they passed the lounge, a growl that made Jacen's hair stand on end prompted him to ignite the cold green glow of his lightsaber. Two sets of black eyes blinked at the light.

"Lady Vader," one snarled. "We fail you."

"You failed no one, Adarakh," Leia told her Noghri bodyguards. "Something put us all out."

"Your enemies are about, Lady Vader?" the second Noghri, a female—Meewalh—asked.

"They are. Adarakh, you're with me. Meewalh, you help Jacen."

"No," Jacen said. "Mom, you need them more than I do. You know it."

"The first-son speaks right, Lady Vader," Meewalh agreed.

Leia's eyes flashed at the insubordination. "We don't have time to argue about this."

That was confirmed a heartbeat later when something

bumped against the hull, followed by a second, similar impact.

"What's that?" Han called up.

"Just get us some power," Leia called back. "Fine. Both of you, with me. Jacen, watch yourself. None of this not-using-the-Force nonsense."

"I'm over that, Mom."

She kissed Jacen quickly on the cheek. "Watch out for my boy." Then she pushed toward the cargo lifter, where the first impact seemed to have been. The Noghri went silently after her, as nimble in free-fall as on foot.

Jacen shifted the grip on his lightsaber and found a hand-hold to steady his weightless body as he tried to figure out where the second boarder was.

Within seconds, something began gnashing and grinding against the outer bulkheads, enabling him to locate it in the lounge. Moving slowly, he flattened as best he could against what would be the ceiling if the gravity came back on.

Must be grutchins, he thought. Yuuzhan Vong technology was all biologically based. They used modified insectoid creatures to hull ships. There would be fumes from the acid, then, and maybe worse, but there was no time to seek vac suits. If the Yuuzhan Vong were simply going to open the ship to space, they'd all had it. But if the enemy wanted the Solos dead, they would have blasted them while the ship was powered down, since they had, at best, contempt for nonliving tech and no use for the *Falcon* whatsoever. Knowing the Yuuzhan Vong, they were eager for live captives, not freeze-dried corpses.

Jacen calmed his mind and waited.

Not much later, a hole appeared in the wall. As predicted, an acrid, choking stench came through, but not the feared explosive decompression of the cabin. Jacen stayed out of visual range until something poked its head through an opening wide enough for a human to step through.

Jacen flicked on his lightsaber.

Something like a huge beetle was revealed in the viridian light of his blade. Jacen drove his point into its eye before it could even twitch. For what seemed a long moment, the energy blade refused to penetrate beyond the first few centimeters. The creature yanked its head back and forth violently, but Jacen kept the point on until, finally, with a sputter, it pushed in. The beetle spasmed and died.

Jacen came off the ceiling and, avoiding the steaming edge of the hole, hurled himself through the breach.

A flexible coupling had attached itself to the outside of the ship. It was about twenty meters long. Halfway down its length a Yuuzhan Vong warrior pulled himself along by means of a series of knobs protruding from the sides. Jacen kicked against the projections nearest him, accelerating toward the Vong.

His enemy was humanoid, with black hair plaited and knotted behind his head. His forehead sloped sharply down to dark eyes above swollen purplish sacs and an almost flat nose. He wore the characteristic vonduun crab armor and carried an amphistaff coiled around one wrist. A savage grin appeared on his scarred and tattooed face, and he duplicated Jacen's move. The amphistaff straightened, pointing at the young Jedi like a lance.

When they were only about four meters apart, the staff spit something at him. If past experience was a guide, it was almost certainly poison.

Jacen reached for the whirling droplets in the Force, but it felt as if he were reaching through syrup. He stopped it within a few centimeters of his face, at the same time kicking the tube wall obliquely so that he hurled up to the top of it. The warrior passed beneath him, running face-first into the suspended toxin. Grimly, not looking back, Jacen pulled out of the tumble his maneuver had resulted in and propelled himself toward the open hatch beyond. Behind him, the warrior stifled a hoarse cry.

The coralskipper wasn't big, but it was big enough for two. He could see the second warrior, just poking his head out. This time, there was no aerial joust; the Yuuzhan Vong waited for him, feet braced against something behind him, his amphistaff in guard position.

They met in a stir of blows that killed Jacen's momentum and set him bouncing around the coupling, trying to reorient. The Yuuzhan Vong didn't budge, but continued to strike at Jacen in a measured, conservative way. Jacen found he had to fight one-handed and use the other to anchor himself. He kept his lightsaber extended and his movements small. The next time the Yuuzhan Vong struck, Jacen nailed him in the back of the hand. The warrior grunted and released the staff. With a snarl, he launched himself at Jacen.

The sudden attack took the young Jedi by surprise. The warrior managed to get his wrist in a lock, and the two went tumbling back through the tube. Too late, Jacen realized his lightsaber was still on, slicing through the wall of the coupling like tissue.

Needles were suddenly under his skin, trying to push themselves out. Desperate, Jacen brought his elbow up beneath the Yuuzhan Vong's jaw. He felt teeth clack together, and his opponent let go. The slit, now five meters long, yawned into space, and the warrior floated right through. A moment later, the body of the first warrior followed him.

Black spots dancing before his eyes, Jacen managed to grab one of the knobs, but the slit was only a meter away and the pressure of an atmosphere was pushing him toward it. He was going to black out, and he knew it. Grimly, he flicked off his lightsaber and hooked it into his belt, then reached with his other hand and started pulling himself against the wind. His strength was fading fast, however, and even if he made it, it would only be a matter of time before the *Millennium Falcon* was empty of atmosphere.

But he wasn't going to make it. He had failed, not just himself, but his mother and father, as well.

He reached once again in the Force, trying to pull his mass back toward the *Falcon*. He managed the connection, but space had seeped into his head, and darkness with it.

He went out, so far as he could tell, for only a second. Wind was still whistling by, but it had faded to a thin shriek, and in the spots still dancing before his eyes he saw what had saved him. The coupling—alive like all Yuuzhan Vong technology—was sealing itself. As he watched, the last few centimeters of the tear zipped themselves together.

Mom! He could feel the hammering of her pulse behind him, and pain in her not-quite-healed legs.

He propelled himself back into the *Millennium Falcon*, pushing himself madly toward the cargo lift area.

It took him an instant to sort out that that battle was over, too. The Noghri were still dismembering one of the Yuuzhan Vong boarders. The second floated near Leia; his head was drifting a few meters away. Han seemed to have just come in, brandishing a blaster.

"Jacen?"

"Got both of 'em," he acknowledged grimly.

"Great. Leia, you keep watch. Let us know if they send anything else our way. Jacen, you check out those skips and figure out some way we can accelerate without opening ourselves to space."

Right, Jacen thought. The minute the drive went on, the coralskippers would exert their inertia. At some point acceleration would make them massive enough to tear the couplings, no matter how strong they were.

"I'm on it, Dad. And hang on before you engage the drive. I have another idea."

"Always thinking. That's my boy."

FOUR

Nen Yim pushed up through the clear membrane and stroked the pale, feathery coils of the ship's brain, the rikyam, with her shaper's hand. She trembled, her specialized fingers twitching. Once those digits had been the legs of a crustaceanlike creature, bred for no other purpose but to be hands to shapers. Its animal origins were still obvious; her fingers—narrower, slimmer, and stronger than those of the average Yuuzhan Vong—protruded from beneath a dark, flexible carapace that now served as the back of her hand. Two of the "fingers" ended in pincers; another had a retractable blade. All were studded with small, raised sensory nodes that tasted anything they touched. Nen Yim's training as a shaper required that she know by taste all elements and more than four thousand compounds and their variants. She had known the quick, nervous flavor of cobalt with those fingers, savored the pungency of carbon tetrachloride, wondered at the complex and endless variations of amino acids.

And now she trembled, for the scent here was morbid.

"The rikyam is dying," she murmured to the novice at her side. "It is more than half dead."

The novice—a young man named Suung Aruh—twitched the tendrils of his headdress in dismay.

"How can that be?" he asked.

"How can it be?" Nen Yim repeated, anger creeping into her voice. "Look around you, Novice. The luminescent mycogens that once sheathed our halls in light now cling in sickly patches. The capillaries of the maw luur are clotted with dead or mutated recham forteps. The *Baanu Miir*

31

worldship is dying, Initiate. Why should the brain be any different?"

"I'm sorry, Adept," Suung said, his tendrils knotted in genuflection. "Only . . . what is to be done? Will a new rik-yam be grown?"

Nen Yim narrowed her eyes. "Under whom were you trained before my arrival?"

"I—the old master, Tih Qiqah."

"I see. He was the only master shaper here?"

"Yes, Adept."

"And where are his adepts?"

"He trained no adepts in his last year, Adept Nen Yim."

"Nor did he really train any initiates, it seems. What did you do for him?"

"I . . ." His mortification deepened.

"Yes?"

"I told him stories."

"Stories?"

"Crèche-tales, but with adult overtones. He insisted."

"He used you merely to amuse himself? As personal servants?"

"Essentially, Adept."

Nen Yim closed her eyes. "I am assigned to a dying ship. At the mere rank of adept, I am the highest member of my caste, and I haven't even a trained initiate."

"I have heard," Suung said, "that the lack is due to the need for shapers in the battle against the infidels."

"Of course," Nen Yim replied. "Only the senile, inept, and disgraced remain to tend the worldships."

"Yes, Adept," Suung said.

"Aren't you going to ask which I am?" Nen Yim snarled.

The novice hesitated. "I know you were once part of one of the holy programs," he said cautiously.

"Yes. A program that failed. My master failed. I failed. We failed the Yuuzhan Vong. The honor of death was denied me, and I have been sent here to do what I can for our glorious people." *Sent?* she thought in her cloistered mind. *Exiled.*

Suung made no answer, but waited for her to continue.

"Your training begins now, Initiate," Nen Yim said. "For I have need of you. To answer your question, no, we cannot grow a new rikyam for the ship. Or, rather, we could, but it would do the ship no good."

She glanced around. The inner torus of the worldship was sharply curved in floor and ceiling, the color of old bone, illuminated only by the lambents the two shapers carried with them. She looked back up at the rikyam, or what she could see of it. Its numberless coils of neurons grew in the still center of the ship, where neither up nor down existed—unlike the more affluent worldships, the *Baanu Miir* got its gravity from spin, not dovin basals, which had to be fed. Encased in multiple layers of coral-laced shell perforated by osmotic membranes, the brain could be accessed from the inner torus of the ship, where only shapers were allowed. Here, where the ship's spin only imparted a vague rumor of artificial gravity, the membrane could be exposed by stroking a dilating valve in the shell. Only the hand of a shaper could pass through the membrane to the nerve curls within.

"This ship is almost a thousand years old," she told Suung. "The organisms that make it up have come and gone, but the brain has always been here. It has managed the integration of this ship's functions for all of those years, developing outrider ganglia where they were needed, shaping the ship in its own unique way. It is for this reason that our worldships live so well, for so very long. But when the brain sickens, the ship sickens. Things can be done, but ultimately the ship, like all things, must embrace death. Our duty, Novice, is to keep this ship from that desired embrace for as long as possible, until new worldships can be grown or planets settled. In the case of this ship, we must await the former; *Baanu Miir* could never stand the strain of faster-than-light travel. It would take us decades or centuries to reach a habitable world."

"Couldn't the habitants be transferred to a new world on swifter, smaller vessels?" Suung asked.

Nen Yim smiled tightly. "Perhaps when the galaxy has

been cleansed of infidels and the warriors no longer need every vessel available to carry on their war."

"Is there anything to be done now, Adept Nen Yim?" Suung asked. He had a certain eagerness in his voice that amused and even slightly heartened her. It wasn't Suung Aruh's fault he knew nothing.

"Go to the qahsa, Initiate, where the knowledge and history of our people are kept. There you will find the protocols of shaping. Your scent and name will give you access to them. You will memorize the first two hundred and recite them to me tomorrow. You should be able to recall them by name, by indications, by applications. Do you understand?"

His tendrils scarcely managed the genuflection, so disarrayed with excitement had they become. "Yes, Adept. It shall be done."

"Go now and leave me to contemplate this matter."

"Yes, Adept."

A moment later, she was alone in the inner torus. Even so, she looked about furtively before peeling down the front of the living oozhith that clung to her body and served to cover most of it from sight. Beneath the oozhith, clinging to her belly, was a film-flat creature. It retained the vestigial eyes of its fishlike ancestor but otherwise resembled an olive-and-black mottled pouch, which was more or less what it was— a very special sort of container.

She reached back through the osmotic membrane to touch the fractal coils of the rikyam again. With the pincer on her smallest finger, she clipped off four discrete pieces of the brain and placed them in the pouch. The material closed lovingly around the coils, lubricating them with oxygen-rich fluids that would keep them healthy until she reached her laboratory and a more permanent way of keeping the neurons alive.

She took a deep breath, contemplating the enormity of what she was about to do. The shapers were guided and strictured by the protocols, the thousands of techniques and applications given them by the gods in the misty past. To experiment, to try to invent new protocols, was heresy of the first order.

Nen Yim was a heretic. Her master, Mezhan Kwaad, had been as well, before the *Jeedai* child Tahiri took her brilliant head from her neck. Together Nen Yim and she had dared to formulate hypotheses and test them. With her death, Mezhan Kwaad had absorbed most of the blame for both the heresy and the failure. Even so, Nen Yim had been spared only because shapers were already too scarce.

Baanu Miir was dying, as a single glance at its decaying chambers made clear her first day within it. For a brain this ill, no protocol she knew would serve, and as an adept she could not access the mysteries beyond the fifth cortex of the qahsa. She would have to make her own protocol, despite already being tainted with heresy, despite the fact that she was certainly being watched.

Her first duty was not to the calcified shaper codes, but to her people. The gods—if they existed at all—must understand that. If the worldship failed, twelve thousand Yuuzhan Vong would die—not in glorious battle or sacrifice, but smothered in carbon dioxide or frozen by the chill of space. She was not going to let that happen, even if it meant this would be her last shaping and her last act in this life.

She replaced the pouch-creature on her abdomen and rolled the oozhith back over it, feeling the tiny cilia of the garment digging into her pores and resuming their symbiotic relationship with her flesh. Then she left the dying brain and returned through dim and opalescent chambers and corridors to her laboratory suite.

FIVE

"Arrest us?" Mara asked Hamner as the droid set his drink down. Her voice was radium at absolute zero, and Luke shivered. It was the voice of the woman who had once tried to kill him and very nearly succeeded.

"What's the charge?" Luke asked.

"Fey'lya has evidence that you were behind the unsanctioned military action at Yavin Four a few months ago," Hamner said. "That opens you to a variety of charges, I'm afraid, especially since as chief of state he expressly forbade you to engage in any such activity."

"What evidence?" Luke asked.

"The Yuuzhan Vong released a prisoner taken on Yavin Four," Hamner said. "Fey'lya's calling it a 'hopeful sign of goodwill.' The prisoner testified that Jedi were involved with and in fact led an unprovoked attack against the Yuuzhan Vong in a neutral system. He claims to have been a part of that force, which he asserts was led by Talon Karrde. He further maintains that Karrde had frequent communication with you, and that he witnessed those communications."

Mara's eyes had narrowed to slits. "It's a lie. None of Karrde's people would talk. It must be one of the Yuuzhan Vong's Peace Brigade collaborators, coached in what to say."

"But it *is* true, at the bottom of it all?" Hamner said.

Luke nodded tersely. "Yes. After the Yuuzhan Vong warmaster offered to stop with the worlds he had already conquered so long as all of the Jedi were turned over to him, I realized the students at the Jedi academy were in danger. I asked Talon Karrde to evacuate them. When he arrived, the

Peace Brigade was already there, trying to capture the students and turn them over to the Yuuzhan Vong as a peace offering. Karrde wouldn't let them do that. I pleaded with Fey'lya to send New Republic military. He wouldn't. So, yes, I sanctioned his effort and sent what help I could. What do you think I should have done?"

Hamner's long face nodded thoughtfully. "I don't blame you. I only wish you had contacted me."

"You weren't around at the time. I talked to Wedge, but it was out of his hands."

"But their witness is a liar," Mara interjected. "We can prove that."

"And become liars ourselves?" Luke replied. "He's lying about who he is and what he saw, maybe, but most of his accusations are true, if a bit distorted."

Hamner knotted his fingers together. "There's more, anyway. Internal security went back over the records of starship comings and goings in that period. Of course, they already knew Anakin Solo had faked a clearance, but they also discovered you had had a visit from Shada D'ukal, one of Karrde's top people. The transponder ID she used to land on Coruscant was a forgery. Finally, it's clear Jacen and Jaina Solo also left for parts unknown, also circumventing planetary security—in your ship, Mara."

"Again, Kenth, what would you have done?" Mara asked accusingly. "We couldn't leave our students to the Yuuzhan Vong just because the New Republic was too cowardly to act."

"And again, Mara, I'm not arguing with you. I'm just telling you what they have."

"I knew this was going to come out eventually," Luke murmured. "I had thought it might be overlooked."

"The days when Fey'lya might have overlooked Jedi activities are long gone," Kenth said. "It's hard enough for him to hold back the tide of representatives who demand he acquiesce to Tsavong Lah's conditions."

"You aren't saying Fey'lya is on *our* side," Mara said incredulously.

"Mara, whatever else you might think of him, Fey'lya

isn't ready to throw all of the Jedi to the rancors. That's part of the reason he's taking this tack—damage control. By appearing to act against Luke, he can maintain a moderate position regarding more extreme anti-Jedi sentiment."

Luke nodded as if to himself, then directed his gaze at Hamner. "What's your opinion here?"

"Luke, I don't think you'll be brought to trial, or any such thing. The arrest will be a house arrest. You'll be expected to make a general statement to the Jedi to stop any unsanctioned activity. Other than that, you won't suffer any hardship."

"The Jedi are being hunted all over the galaxy. I'm expected to tell them not to fight back?"

"I'm telling you how it is."

Luke locked his hands behind his back. "Kenth, I'm sorry," he said. "I can't do that. I'll try to keep my people out the way of the military, but other than that—well, the Jedi have a mission older than the New Republic."

Something snapped into place in Luke's mind as he said that, solidified a thought as only a spoken word can. He suddenly realized that he meant what he had said with all of his heart and being. What had kept him from admitting it earlier? When had he confused the Jedi ethic with government at large? Why had he been apologizing for so long? Because he feared estrangement from the republic he had helped to build? But they were the ones doing the pushing, not him. Not the Jedi—not even Kyp and the other renegades. Luke might disagree with them in philosophical particulars, but not in the broad strokes—the Jedi were supposed to be helping people, working to bring justice and balance.

"That's why I wanted you to know in time to do something about it if you want to," Hamner replied. He paused, as if considering his next words very carefully. "I don't think Fey'lya imagines you will stand for it, either."

"You mean he thinks we'll run and further implicate ourselves."

"Not exactly. He wants to be able to say you're out of his

reach and no longer his responsibility. To 'pick you out of his fur,' as the Bothans say."

"Oh," Mara said. "He wants us out there, all right, in case he needs us one day, but until then he's perfectly willing to turn his back on us."

"Something like that," Hamner replied. "No move has yet been made to impound your ships."

"He wants me in exile," Luke concluded.

"Yes."

Luke sighed. "I was afraid this time would come. I had hoped it wouldn't. But here we are."

"Yes, here we are," Mara snarled. "Fey'lya had better pray I don't—" Her impassioned diatribe halted in its birth, and a look of profound fear moved across her face. Luke had never seen anything like it on her features before. It was more terrible than he could ever imagine at that moment.

"Ah!" Mara said, in a tiny voice.

"Mara?"

"Something's wrong," she said weakly, her face draining of color. "Something is *really* wrong." She wrapped her arms around her belly and clenched her eyes shut.

Luke sprang from his seat. "Get an MD droid, now," he yelled toward the droid.

In the Force, he felt Mara slipping away.

"Hold on, love," he said. "Please hold on."

SIX

Anakin was busy underneath the supply transport *Lucre*, micro-adjusting the repulsor pads, when a pinkish pair of bare feet appeared. He couldn't see the person the feet belonged to, but he knew who it was immediately.

"Hi, Tahiri," he called.

"Hi yourself," the indignant reply came. Knees squatted down onto the feet, then a pair of hands braced against the floor, and finally green eyes surrounded by a cloud of golden hair appeared. "Come out from under there, Anakin Solo."

"Sure. Just let me finish up."

"Finish up what? You have some reason to be tinkering with this ship?"

Uh-oh. Anakin sighed and pushed himself out from underneath the transport.

"I was going to tell you," he protested.

"I'm sure. When, just before you smoked jets out of here?"

"Tahiri, I'll be back. Corran and I are going for supplies, that's all."

She was staring down into his face now. He could bump her nose with his own by raising up a few centimeters. Her eyes were huge, and not all green, but striated yellow and brown along her iris rims. Had they always been like that?

She punched him in the shoulder, hard. "You could have told me yesterday."

"Ow!" He pushed farther away and sat up. "What was that for?"

"What do you think?" She straightened, too, and the rest of her face came into focus. Her forehead was etched by three nasty vertical scars, like crouching white worms. The

Yuuzhan Vong had tried to make her into one of their own. The scars were the most superficial reminders of the process.

"Look, I know I promised you I wouldn't leave you yet, but this won't take long. I'm getting jumpy."

"So what? Who cares? Didn't it ever occur to you how I might feel?"

"I thought I *had* considered that," Anakin speculated. "Come on, Tahiri. What's really the matter?"

She pursed her lips. In the background, Fiver whirred and bleeped happily at his task of preparing the ship, with a strident note or two aimed at Corran's astromech, Whistler. Across the broad bay, one of Terrik's men cursed as something clanged against the ground. The pain of an insulted thumb wisped by the two Jedi.

"They don't like me here," Tahiri said softly. "They all act like my skin is about to split open and a krayt dragon will step out."

"You're imagining things," Anakin soothed. "Everyone understands you've been through a rough time."

"No. No one understands it at all. Except you. Maybe not even you. They're either afraid of me or repelled."

Anakin tried a sentence or two in his head, didn't like the sound of them, and tried another.

"Have you thought about having those scars removed?" he asked. "Booster's MD droid could do it."

Oops. Anakin realized he should have replayed that one a few times before speaking, too. He saw Tahiri was about to erupt into a full-out verbal assault, and he braced for it.

Wrong again. Her face calmed, and she shook her head. "I paid for them," she said. "I won't give them up."

"Maybe that's what worries people," Anakin said softly.

"Let them worry, then. I don't care."

"But you just—"

"Hush. You don't understand anything after all."

"I don't understand what you're asking me to do. You want me to stay here with you?"

"No, dummy," Tahiri said. "I want you to take me with you."

"Oh." He felt a profound confusion, and suddenly a lot of his father's complaints about women made more sense.

Or less, as the case might be. Tahiri had been his best friend for five years, since she was nine and he was eleven. They had a strong bond in the Force, and were together far more powerful than either was alone. The Jedi Master Ikrit had seen this long ago, and lately had been proven correct. Due to this bond, Anakin and Tahiri could communicate at a level far beyond language.

So why did he spend more than half of his time bewildered in any conversation with her?

"You're sure you're ready for that?" he asked.

"For what? It's just a supply run, right? Minimal danger? Nowhere near Yuuzhan Vong space?"

"Right," Anakin said cautiously. "But there's always danger."

"Especially when you don't trust everyone on your ship."

Anakin's eyebrows dropped. "Okay, now *you're* being dumb. You know I trust you."

"Really? I almost killed you back on Yavin Four, you know."

"I know. And I know that wasn't really you."

"No?" Tahiri's face went curiously blank. "I'm not sure. Sometimes I don't know who I am anymore."

Anakin put his hand on her shoulder. "I do," he said. "You aren't the same as you were before the Yuuzhan Vong captured you. Neither am I. But you're still Tahiri."

"Whatever that means."

"If you want to go with us, I'll talk to Corran. I honestly didn't think you would want to get out so early."

Tahiri shook her head emphatically. "I've spent enough time crying and curled up in a ball. You think you're the only one the walls are closing in on? Whoever I am, I'm not going to figure it out moping around here." Her voice took on a softer, pleading note. "Let me go with you, Anakin."

He mussed her hair, the way he had done a hundred times. It suddenly seemed too familiar, and he felt his face warm. "Okay," he said. "Next time, just ask, though. You don't always have to come after me like I've done something wrong. We don't have to fight *everything* out."

She smiled. "Sorry. You never mean to do anything wrong. But most times it just turns out that way."

SEVEN

R2-D2 tootled and bleeped as he went about the task Jacen had assigned him. The little droid had extended his linkage and repair arms into one of the compact missiles floating near the narrow trash-exhaust tube. In the faint light of the glow stick, the squat, domed cylinder of the little droid looked very much the antique he was.

A clumsy clank sounded behind Jacen as C-3PO struggled with weightlessness.

"Oh dear," C-3PO said excitedly. "I wasn't built for this, you know. Zero gravity confuses my circuits."

"Just hang on to something," Jacen muttered. "When Dad gets the power back on, we'll have gravity again. Just make sure you're on the floor and not the ceiling when that happens."

"Good heavens. Who can tell the difference? I'm going to need a good overhaul when this is all over. This *will* be all over soon, won't it, Master Jacen?"

"One way or the other."

"I almost wish you had left me deactivated."

"Just be thankful you've got good surge overload circuits, or you might have been deactivated permanently." He closed the panel on the final missile. "Well, that will either work or it won't," he said philosophically.

"I don't understand," C-3PO said. "What will work or won't?"

R2-D2 whistled something vaguely condescending and derisive.

"Well, of *course* I shouldn't be expected to understand, you little trash sweeper," C-3PO retorted indignantly. "I'm a protocol droid, not a metal-grubbing screw turner. Oh! No offense to you, Master Jacen."

"None taken. I wish someone a little better at this than I were here—Anakin, for instance. If I've made a mistake, I may well blow us out of the sky."

"Oh, no!"

"Okay, time for your part, Threepio. I need you to cycle this lock manually."

"But, Master Jacen, all of the air will evacuate."

"True. But I won't be here—I'll be on the other side of the outer pressure lock. The vacuum won't hurt you."

"I suppose not. But *why*, Master Jacen?"

"I need you to take each of these missiles to the end of the dump vent and give them a good shove in the direction of that Yuuzhan Vong interdictor."

"Me, handle a concussion missile?"

"If it's any comfort, if it exploded it wouldn't make any difference to you if you were holding it or a meter away, like you are now. There still wouldn't be enough of you left to plate a spoon with."

"But—but—what if I fall out of the ship?"

Jacen smiled thinly. "Don't," he said. "Once all the missiles are away, you and Artoo seal the vent up, cycle the lock again, and get back inside. I'll keep in touch by comm."

"Master Jacen, I am a *protocol* droid!"

"And I would rather be meditating. C'mon, Threepio. You've done more dangerous things than this before."

"Not willingly, Master Jacen!"

Jacen slapped the droid on his metal back. "Show me what you're made of, Threepio."

"I will gladly submit to an internal inspection," C-3PO said.

"You know what I mean. Go."

"Yes, sir." The droid had a noticeable quaver in his voice.

Jacen pushed out, plugged in a portable power source, and cycled the inner lock. It closed under protest, its hydraulics used to a more robust diet of electrons.

He made his way to where his mother was keeping watch from the cockpit.

"All quiet?" he asked.

"For now. Surely they must know something has gone wrong, though."

"Maybe, maybe not. We don't know what their procedures are in situations like this. Yuuzhan Vong warriors are proud—maybe they're giving these first guys every chance to deal with the situation before sending reinforcements. Maybe they're so confident we can't get away they aren't really paying attention. We're about to see how closely they're watching, anyway. I just sent some concussion missiles floating their way. With any luck, they'll think it's flotsam until it's too late." He concentrated briefly. "There. The first is away."

C-3PO was slow. It was a good five minutes before he got the next one out. The third took even longer. Jacen didn't stay to watch. He went down and finished welding auxiliary plating over the holes the Yuuzhan Vong had cut into their ship. It was too thin to have a good chance of holding, but it was all they had at the moment that might do. It would at least give them a few minutes. If worse came to worst—and neither this nor his other plan worked—they could always seal off the cockpit or put on vac suits. Of course, then they had to find a habitable planet or space station, fast.

His father came drifting up from beneath. "Are we ready?" he asked.

"As we'll be," Jacen replied.

"Let's go forward and give it a try, then," Han said. "The Yuuzhan Vong won't wait on us forever."

When they rejoined Leia in the cockpit, however, the enemy ship was still quiet.

Jacen activated the intercom. "How's it going, Threepio?"

"Dreadful, sir. I have two more to go."

"More coralskippers detaching," Leia observed suddenly.

"Negative, Threepio," Jacen said. "Get out of there, now."

"With pleasure, sir."

"Ready, everyone?" Han asked.

"Go," Leia replied.

Han worked his fingers across the instruments, and with a sudden snap, gravity reasserted itself. Jacen's stomach settled back where it was supposed to be, and he felt a wave of dizziness.

"Hang on." Han engaged maneuvering thrusters, and the *Falcon* began spinning like a coin on its side.

Jacen craned for visibility. Below and above, at the extreme edge of his vision, he could make out the coralskippers, still stationary. The living couplings were cinched in the middle, like balloons twisted and tied, and they were still twisting.

"Four times around is going to have to be good enough. Where are your missiles?"

"The first one is ready to go."

"Good thing I had the launchers reinstalled, I guess. Send the detonation signal on three. One, two—"

Jacen held his breath as he keyed the signal on three and blew it out when the distant concussion missile became a small white nova. At the same moment, Han kicked space with the ion drive, and they were *going,* as only the *Millennium Falcon* could go. The attached coralskippers whipped out behind them like braids, and Jacen couldn't see them anymore.

"They're trying to get a lock with their dovin basals," Leia reported.

"Jacen!"

"Yes, sir!" Jacen sent another signal, and the remaining missiles surged to life, burning their propellant cores and hurling their noses at the Yuuzhan Vong ship. Gravitic anomalies appeared and sucked all but one in, but the fourth impacted in a brilliant display.

"They blinked!" Leia whooped. "They missed their lock. Han, get us out of here!"

"What do you think I'm doing?"

The ship suddenly shuddered and yawed.

"What was that? What hit us?" Han demanded, just as it happened again.

"The coralskippers tearing loose," Jacen replied. "And

speaking of coralskippers, there are a couple headed our way. I'm going down to the turbolaser."

"Forget it. If those patches go, I want you up here. We'll outrun the skips."

"They're gaining."

"As soon as we're out of the interdictor's mass shadow, I'm going to lightspeed."

Jacen considered. "They'll catch us before that. I'm going down."

"Jacen—"

He left his father's protest behind him.

C-3PO was just returning to the safe, enclosed ship when the acceleration slapped him against the side of the waste chute. The last missile, which he had been pushing ahead of him back into the ship, suddenly tripled its weight and, as the vector of the force changed, went hurtling out into open space. It banged against C-3PO as it went by, and with a soundless cry of terror he realized he was going to follow it. Clawing desperately, he managed a handhold on the lock mechanism, but his golden legs dangled out into open space. Looking between them, he saw the stars churn around his feet.

"Artoo!" he broadcast frantically.

His digits were slipping.

Well, he thought to himself. *This hasn't turned out to be a good day at all. If only I had stayed on Coruscant with Master Luke.*

EIGHT

Mara had slipped into unconsciousness by the time the island's MD-10 medical droid had been activated. Luke gripped her hand as she lay on the grass near their table. Around them the cool air was fragrant with night perfumes and the gentle music of insects. Kenth Hamner stood by, restless but silent.

Luke summoned Master Yoda's voice. *A Jedi knows not fear.*

It helped, a little, but the fear didn't lurk far under the skin. He couldn't lose Mara, not now. Not ever.

He tried to push that away, as well. There was danger in thoughts like that. And yet the harder he tried, the more difficult it was, and all of his Jedi training seemed suddenly pale before the force of unfamiliar emotions.

Hang in there, Mara. I love you.

He felt her stir. She was in pain, but the Force told him she was still strong. And yet beneath that vitality was the undeniable feeling of *wrongness*. Not like when she had been so terribly ill with her Yuuzhan Vong–created disease, exactly. Could the organism have mutated again? Had her long, hopeful remission ended?

He watched, taut, as the medical droid dispassionately checked her vitals, using sensors to probe into his wife's body.

In the midst of it, her eyes fluttered open again, and he saw his own helpless fear reflected there.

"It's okay," he said. "It'll be okay. What happened?"

"It's the baby," she said. "It's our baby. Luke, I can't—"

"And you won't," he promised firmly. "It's going to be fine."

The MD droid reached a diagnosis a moment later.

"Toxic shock reaction in the placenta," it burred. "Indicates four cc's of cardinex."

"Do it," Luke commanded.

He watched as the hypo delivered the dosage. Within seconds, Mara's breathing calmed and her color began to return.

"What caused it?" Luke demanded of the droid.

"Unknown chemical agent."

"Poison?"

"Negative. Placental reaction unusual. The substance is not otherwise toxic. Substance is complex saline compound, partial analysis . . ." It listed a sequence of chemicals.

"Vergere's tears," Mara said softly. She tried to sit up.

"Just hang on. Stay down for a minute."

"I'm feeling better. Let me up, Skywalker."

"Tears?" Kenth Hamner said, confused.

"The Yuuzhan Vong infected me with some sort of biotic weapon," Mara explained. "It tried pretty hard to kill me. It would have, too, except that that creature with the Yuuzhan Vong assassin—"

"The one who pretended to defect?"

"Elan. Yes. She had a sort of pet or familiar who gave Han a vial of her tears—or at least that's what she said they were. She told him I should take them, and it felt right to me, so I did. My disease went into remission."

Hamner's long face looked thoughtful. "And you think the tears caused what just happened to you?"

"Let's not jump to conclusions," Luke protested.

"I ran out of the tears a few months ago," Mara said. "I've been taking a synthesized version. Luke, it's killing our son."

"You can't know that," Luke said. "The MD droid isn't equipped to do the kind of analysis that would prove that."

"I know," Mara said shakily.

Her certainty felt like ferrocrete. Luke sat down, pushing his fingers back through his hair, trying to think. He nearly jumped at the sound of a distant sonic boom—probably just some hotshot pilot practicing atmospheric maneuvers over the sea.

"I can have you at a medical facility in ten minutes," Hamner told Mara.

"No!" Mara nearly shouted. "Then we'd lose our chance to escape Fey'lya."

"Mara, we don't have a choice," Luke said.

She sat up again. This time Luke didn't try to stop her. "We do," she insisted. "I won't have my child born under house arrest. If I don't take the tears, I should be fine. Isn't that right, Emdee?"

The droid whirred and nodded. "Present danger has passed. Avoidance of the substance will prevent recurrence."

"What if it wasn't the tears at all?" Luke said, exasperation escaping with his words.

"It is," Mara replied. "I know it is."

"Then there was something wrong with the synthetic drug. If we're to synthesize a new one, we need to be here, on Coruscant."

"If we stay, they'll button us in so tight we'll never be able to escape. We'll be at their mercy, and what then? Suppose Fey'lya changes his mind and decides to give us to the Yuuzhan Vong? We'll be trapped, and how am I supposed to fight in this condition? Or worse, with an infant? Luke, it's time. You know it; I know it. So we have do this."

Luke closed his eyes and searched the back of his lids for options. He found none.

"Okay," he said finally. "Kenth, if you could be so kind as to take us to our apartments."

"Absolutely," Hamner said. "I am at your command."

In moments they were airborne. So far as Luke could tell, Mara was fine now. He himself was shaken to the core.

He activated the comm unit and placed two calls—one to Cilghal, the Mon Calamari Jedi healer, the other to Ism Oolos, a Ho'Din physician of great renown. Both agreed to meet him at their apartments. A third call—to the Ithorian Tomla El—revealed the healer was offplanet, working to aid refugees from his destroyed homeworld.

Hamner deposited them on the landing area of their roof.

Cilghal was already there, and the reptilian Ism Oolos arrived shortly thereafter.

Luke and Mara thanked Hamner. The liaison wished them luck and departed.

"You pack, Skywalker," Mara said, once they were inside. "We have to be gone in two hours."

"A thorough examination will take much longer than that," Oolos complained. "Some analyses I must do in my laboratory, to be certain of my results."

"You have to think of your child now," Cilghal agreed softly.

"No one needs to remind me of that," Mara said gruffly. "Get on with it."

Meanwhile, Luke reluctantly began preparation for their flight, but each step he took in that direction felt heavier. Coruscant had the best medical facilities in the galaxy. How could he deny his wife and child that?

He could feel Cilghal, concentrating, reading Mara in the Force, trying to glean information from its generation and interaction in her cells. He caught glimpses of Oolos taking skin and blood samples and sonic readings and feeding the data into his medical datapad.

Mara gave them an hour, then cut them off. Luke stopped what he was doing and came back into the room.

"Conclusions?" Mara asked.

Oolos sighed. "The MD droid was correct. The synthesized tears are having an unforeseen effect on the placenta. The actual attack was triggered by stress, but continuing to take them might well lead to the death of the child."

Cilghal nodded her bulbous head in agreement. "I concur," the Mon Calamarian said.

"Can you resynthesize them?" Luke asked. "Reconfigure the substance so it won't have that effect?"

Oolos clasped his scaled hands together. "We still do not know why the original tears worked," he said, a note of apology in his voice. "We were able to duplicate them without ever really comprehending them."

"Something must be different, though," Luke said, "or this wouldn't be happening."

"Unfortunately," Oolos replied, "I do not believe that to be true. The nature of cell reproduction in a fetus is quite unlike the normal cellular processes in an adult human. The 'tears' caused Mara's cells to mimic that process in some ways, hence her regeneration. The Yuuzhan Vong disease is still in her cells, you understand; her cells have merely been given the power to keep it in check and control whatever damage it causes."

"I still don't understand the problem."

"The problem is, the substance somehow does not recognize true fetal development as a part of the normal functioning of a human body. It thus tries to make adjustments to the developmental process, treating the child almost as it would an illness. In turn, Mara's natural immune system resists and rejects such modifications. Over time, the residue of this conflict has built up enough to cause toxic shock. According to her cellular history, this buildup began with the pregnancy, and only now reached dangerous levels."

"I was taking the real tears in the first months," Mara said.

"Precisely," the healer concurred. "The very qualities that allow the tears to remit your illness are a danger to your fetus."

"But my child is well?"

"I cannot feel that the child has yet suffered any damage from the process," Cilghal answered.

"I believe Jedi Cilghal to be correct," Oolos said.

"But Mara's in her final month," Luke said. "If it took eight months for the toxins to build up—"

"She has reached tolerance saturation," Oolos said. "Her body will flush those chemicals over the course of years, but in the next month she will remain at the danger level. It is unlikely that mere stress will provoke another attack, but a single taste of the tears could bring on a much more violent reaction than that she experienced today."

"Is there any way to flush these poisons artificially?" Mara asked.

"Yes."

"Without risk to my child?"

The Ho'Din scientist lowered the spines on his head. "No. The risk would be measurable."

"Well, let's add this to the 'what I already knew' category," Mara said. "I'll stop taking the tears until our son is born. Then I'll start taking them again."

"We could induce delivery now," Cilghal said.

Mara frowned. "That feels wrong. Cilghal, do you really recommend that?"

"I do," Oolos said.

Cilghal seemed reluctant. "I don't recommend it," she said at last. "Logically, it is the thing to do, and yet when I look down that path, I see deep shadows."

"And if I carry to term, without taking the tears?"

"Shadows there, too, and pain—but also hope."

Mara sat up and turned her gaze to Luke. "We ready to go?" she asked.

"I—Mara—"

"Don't even start. Our baby is healthy, and he'll stay healthy, I promise you that. We'll get through this, no matter where we are. We have to go. Let's go."

"May I accompany you?" Cilghal asked.

"Of course," Mara replied.

"Sadly, I cannot make the same offer," Oolos told them. "My responsibilities to my patients and the New Republic are too great to set aside. I wish I could convince you to remain near, but I surmise I cannot. I wish you only the best, the four of you. I will do what I can to improve the substance, based upon what I know. It would be prudent for you to check with me from time to time."

"Thank you," Luke told the healer. "Thanks for everything."

Jaina rolled her X-wing into the night-shadow of Coruscant, reveling in the feel of the stick in her hand, the shifting crush of acceleration. She felt like shouting out loud, and did. It was good to fly again! This was the best she had felt in a long time.

For months she had been forced out of the cockpit by damaged eyes, and even after they were healed, Rogue

Squadron had shown a marked reluctance to recall her. It had unfolded to her gradually, sickeningly, that given her Jedi status and her involvement in the rescue at Yavin 4, they really didn't want her back. She had gone from being their golden child to their ugly little liability. Only today Colonel Darklighter—the very man who had asked her to join the squadron—had suggested she extend her leave of absence indefinitely.

She didn't care right now. Coruscant was rushing below, a universe of stars turned inside out. She was one with the X-wing. Tomorrow she would hurt. Not today.

She aimed her ship's nose away from the planet and its multitude of satellites, out toward the stars, and wondered where her family was. Anakin was skipping around the galaxy with Booster Terrik, watching over his friend Tahiri. Her twin Jacen was with her mother and father, trying to set up Uncle Luke's "great river"—a series of routes and safe houses designed to help Jedi escape the Yuuzhan Vong and their collaborationist shills. She had stayed behind, assuming Rogue Squadron would recall her any day.

Well, another day, another mistake. She briefly considered chucking it all and heading out, perhaps to find the *Millennium Falcon* and the greater part of her family.

But she had to stick it out. Rogue Squadron was worth fighting for, and eventually they would recall her. How could they afford anyone sitting out now?

Of course, the Yuuzhan Vong had been relatively quiet since Yavin 4—since Duro, as far as the idiot government was concerned. But that couldn't last. Any thought that it could—that the enemy could be appeased by any number of sacrifices and concessions—was wishful thinking of a nearly criminal sort.

Her joy of flying was leaking out of her, swallowed by the sort of mental entropy that seemed to come with growing older. She considered going back, but if she had to sulk out here or down there, she might as well do it out here.

She was still fighting the downward emotional spiral when the comm demanded attention.

It was Aunt Mara, and she sounded more troubled than Jaina felt.

"Jaina, where are you?" Mara asked.

"Just out. What's the matter?"

"We're taking the *Jade Shadow* up. Meet me, will you? It's important." She ticked off a list of coordinates.

"Sure," Jaina replied. "Laying that course now."

"And Jaina—keep your eyes open. Trust no one."

"Mara, what—?"

"We'll discuss it when we rendezvous."

Great, Jaina thought. *What else could be going wrong?* But it could be almost anything, including some possibilities too terrible even to contemplate.

Luke and Mara decided not to risk being seen boarding the *Jade Shadow*. They made their way with an occasional pass of the hand and a suggestion backed by the Force. Some wouldn't remember them at all; others would not be able to recall their faces, though both were well known.

Taking off was a little trickier, but Mara hadn't lost her knack, managing to secure a launch authority using a fake transponder ID and then filing a flight plan to orbit. As Luke watched Coruscant dwindle, he felt, oddly, a strange elation, a kind of freedom he hadn't known he missed. He glanced over at Mara.

"How are you feeling?"

"Fine, now. I contacted Jaina. She'll meet us in orbit." She eased the angle of their climb and glanced at Luke. "This is the right thing to do, you know."

"I'm still not sure."

"It's done, now. Where are we going, by the way?"

"We'll find Booster first," he decided. "I've arranged a way for us to contact him. He'll have some of the medical facilities you need, at least. After that—the Jedi need a haven, a base to operate from. I've already done preliminary searching. That will have to wait, though. Your health is our first priority right now."

She nodded. "I *am* going off the drug."

"And risk your illness coming back, full-blown?"

She pursed her lips. "That's a risk, but right now it looks like the lesser of two." She made a face at her instruments. "By the way," she said, "looks like your first priority has been bumped back. I've got planetary security hailing us and at least four ships on an intercept course."

Luke opened to the hail and activated the visual communications array.

"*Jade Shadow,* this is planetary security." The screen showed a pale gold Bothan male. "You must return to ground immediately. Slave yourselves to us for escort."

Luke smiled tightly. "This is Luke Skywalker of the *Jade Shadow*. We're outward bound and not prepared to turn back."

The Bothan looked extremely uncomfortable. "I have my orders, Master Skywalker. Please help me carry them out with minimum fuss."

"I'm sorry for the inconvenience, Captain, but we aren't returning to ground."

"I'm authorized to use force, Master Skywalker."

"This ship will defend itself," Luke replied reluctantly. "Let us go, Captain."

"I'm sorry. I can't."

Luke shrugged. "Then we really have nothing else to discuss." He switched off the comm.

"Can we outrun them?" he asked Mara.

"It'll be tight." She eyed her instruments again. "Probably not. They must have been on to us almost from the beginning. Two of the ships are coming in from a high orbit."

"Right. Waiting for us. I was more than half expecting that."

"So much for Fey'lya wanting us to escape."

"They have to make an effort," Luke replied. "As efforts go, this isn't a big one."

"No, but maybe sufficient," Mara replied. "We'll at least have to fight them, which won't make us look any better."

Within moments the approaching ships were in sight.

"Military-grade shields," Mara remarked. "Hang on, Skywalker."

A moment later she began to fire.

If we weren't outlaws before, we are now, Luke thought. *How could it have come to this?*

Jaina couldn't believe what she was seeing. The *Jade Shadow* was under fire from four security interceptors. What was going on?

Not that it mattered. She powered up her weapons and dived in, ignoring the hails from the security ships but sending her own signal to the *Shadow*. It was Uncle Luke who answered.

"You two look like you could use a hand," she said. "What did you do to irk the sky cops?"

"Stay out of this, Jaina," Luke told her.

"Yeah, right. That'll happen." She was close enough to fire now, and fire she did, rolling between the trailing interceptor and spearing it with her lasers as she went past. The heavy shield took the shots easily, but she achieved the desired effect; the interceptor had noticed her now. It tried to lock on to her tail, but she was having none of that. Leaning on the stick, she circled tight and planetward. A few lucky shots grazed her shields, but they had a long way to go before they could bring her down. She nosed back up and had her pursuer in her sights again. She held the beak-to-beak collision course long enough to put a few more into its shields, then yawed starboard, missing the oncoming craft by a few meters. She eyed her proton torpedoes speculatively. She could take them out with those, but she still wasn't sure what was going on here, and it was probably a bad idea to kill someone in Coruscant's security force. For all she knew, it might even be a friend of hers. That meant she needed to cripple, not kill.

Both ships turned tight, trying once again to pick up the other's tail. Jaina had the more maneuverable ship and soon found herself flying up the interceptor's exhaust. She stuttered laser fire, following her opponents' attempts to shake her, until finally their shields failed. She cut the drive off as neatly as a gardener pruning a tree, then came around to disable their weapons.

By this time, the *Jade Shadow* only had two pursuers left,

and one of them was in bad shape. She wished she could have seen what tricks Mara had pulled out of her sleeve to achieve that. The *Shadow*'s shields were starting to get a little shaky, but between the two of them, Jaina was certain the remaining interceptors didn't have a chance.

A moment later, a cloud of blips appeared on her long-range sensors. Twelve starfighters, maybe more. And the *Jade Shadow* was flying right into them.

NINE

C-3PO yelped as he lost his handhold, but at the same instant something fastened onto his wrist.

"Artoo! Thank the maker!"

The ship made another violent turn, and C-3PO felt his insides try to escape into space through the soles of his metal feet. R2-D2 lurched forward, but only so far. C-3PO noticed with relief that his companion had secured himself with a cable of some sort.

"Clever Artoo! Don't let go of me!"

Jacen swung around in the laser turret, tracing lines of deadly light through the vacuum, walking them across the nearest coralskipper. Points of absolute darkness swallowed most of the beams before they could strike home, but a fluorescent puff of vaporized coral told him at least one had gotten through. The skip sloughed off starboard, but there were plenty more to take its place. Jacen grimly continued his deadly conversation with them, and they answered with volcanic gobs of plasma.

"Shields are failing," Han's voice crackled over the comm. "Jacen, how's it going down there?"

"Still here, Dad," he replied, swinging his seat to follow a skip so near he could have thrown a rock and hit it.

"We're out of the mass shadow in one minute," Leia said.

Something in the ship shrieked, and the inertial compensators failed. The g's they were pulling tried to smash Jacen into the ceiling. He managed to get his hands up in time to keep his skull from being crushed, but the force of impact stunned him momentarily. The dampeners went back on-line, and artificial gravity dropped him back roughly into his seat.

"That's it for the shields," his father husked.

Groggily, Jacen grabbed the trigger grips as a series of shudders ran through the *Falcon*.

"Go! Now!" Leia cried.

For an instant nothing happened. Then the stars were gone, and Jacen sagged in his couch.

"It was terrible, just terrible," C-3PO went on. "If it weren't for Artoo I would be just space flotsam. Master Jacen, I *told* you I wasn't suited for that sort of thing."

"You did just fine, Threepio. You saved us. Thanks."

"Oh. Well, I suppose . . . you're quite welcome."

"Right. So run some diagnostics on yourself. Relax."

"Do you think we've really escaped them?"

Han stepped into the cabin and answered that. "We left on a pretty messy vector. Even *I'm* not exactly sure where we're headed. We'll drop out soon and get our bearings, but I'm willing to bet we're not being followed. One thing is sure—we'll need repairs."

"The outer bulkheads?" Jacen asked.

"Like you figured. The coupling tore, but I was able to fix it before our patches gave way. Kinda spoils the look, though. It's gonna have to go."

Leia entered and lowered herself onto one of the couches. Jacen noticed she was favoring her right leg more than she had the day before. Her Noghri bodyguards stood silently nearby.

"What did they hit us with?" she asked.

"Something we haven't seen yet," Jacen said. "It may just be a side effect of their interdiction device."

"Or a powerful electromagnetic pulse. It shut our systems down, but didn't really do a lot of damage to them."

"It shut *us* down, too," Leia pointed out.

"Yeah. It did at that," Han allowed.

"So now what?" Leia asked.

"Now? Well, now we know the inner Corellian Run is hotter than novashine."

"For now. Maybe they shift those things around. How many interdictors can they have?"

"Well, I don't know," Han said, shrugging his shoulders. "They *grow* the things, remember?"

"There's that famous Solo charm," Leia remarked. "I wondered where it had gone."

Han opened his mouth to retort, but Jacen stepped in. "That interdictor had been there for a while. Remember the other ships we saw?"

Leia nodded. "True. I'd forgotten that."

"This is nuts," Han opined. "This whole thing. Luke's 'great river.' "

Leia frowned. "Look, we've had some setbacks, but—"

"Setbacks?" Han's brows tried to jump off his head. "Did you just say 'setbacks'?" We had to shoot our way out of the meeting on Ryloth because your 'contacts' turned out to be Peace Brigade—"

"Oh, like your 'good friends' on Bimmisaari? The ones who wanted to decorate their speeder with our heads?"

"As a matter of fact," Han blustered, "things were going just great on Bimmisaari until you . . ."

They continued bickering, and Jacen listened with mixed emotions. On the one hand, it reminded him of old times, at least insofar as he could remember. They had always been like this, right up until the day Chewbacca died. Then— then they almost stopped talking at all. That silence had been one of the worst things Jacen had ever experienced. Now, they sounded like their old selves, but there was something brittle about it sometimes. As if some of the good nature at the base of it had evaporated. As though if the wrong thing got said, something might break.

Still, it was better than the silence.

As Han had guessed, it took a while to get their bearings and calculate a series of jumps that would take them on to their destination, the cluster of black holes known collectively as the Maw. He picked his way carefully through the enormous gravity wells, his old recklessness submerged beneath several layers of responsibility that a younger Han Solo could never have comprehended.

A younger Han Solo had never really believed in death—or rather, had never believed it could touch him. The loss of Chewbacca had changed that forever. Whenever he thought of losing Leia or one of his children, it put liquid nitrogen in his veins.

As he went carefully through the maze of deadly tides, Han was at least confident that there were few beings in the galaxy who could follow him. If an uninformed Yuuzhan Vong ship was tailing them, the invaders were as good as destroyed.

Thus, it was several days before his barely repaired *Falcon* made its final approach to the secret base they had named simply Shelter. It was a patchwork construction, largely put together from the pieces of the infamous Maw installation, which in its own time—the days of the Empire—had been a top-secret weapons facility. The facility itself had been blown to bits by its erstwhile commander, Admiral Daala, but using the wreckage, along with modules imported from Kessel—and with the help of some well-heeled friends—Han and Leia had managed to facilitate the construction of a space station.

As a location, the Maw was just too good to abandon, especially when a safe house was needed.

"Not much to look at," Han muttered, watching the rough cylinder gain resolution and reveal its makeshift nature. The base of it was an asteroid fragment, but living modules, a power core, and a rudimentary defense system rose obviously from its surface.

"But it's something," Leia said, over his shoulder. "It's a start. I never thought you could have pulled together the alliance it would take to build it, but there it is. Good work, Captain Solo." Leia smiled and slipped her hand into Han's.

"I . . . Thanks. But look what happened when I was out here. Anakin was nearly killed on Yavin Four, and we didn't have the slightest idea of what was going on."

"Anakin is safe on the *Errant Venture*, as safe as he can

be anyway. Jaina's on Coruscant. Jacen's with us. I think we've done as well as we can, Han."

"Maybe. Well, let's see what they've done with the place."

Lando Calrissian met them in the functional if unappealing docking bay. Someone had given it a coat of yellow paint, covering the mismatched plating it was built of, which was an improvement over the last time Han had seen it.

"I like what you've done to the *Falcon*," Lando said easily, as they stepped down the landing ramp. "The mottled yellow patches against matte black. Very stylish."

"Yeah, well, I've always had an eye for the trendy," Han replied.

"And the beautiful," Lando remarked, switching his gaze to Leia. "You're more bewitching than ever."

"And you're as glib as always," Leia replied.

Lando smiled his famous smile and bowed slightly at the waist.

"The *Falcon*—" Han began.

Lando waved his hand. "Think of it as done. We may not have much here, but we have what it takes to patch that old hunk of junk one more time, I think."

He scanned over their lived-in clothes and Jacen's bloodstains. "The same goes for the three of you. Visit the 'fresher and my MD droid, please. When you're done, I'd be pleased if you would join me in my stateroom for food and drinks, before we meet with the others who have come."

"The Hutt representative made it safely, then?" Leia asked.

"It was tight at times," Lando said, "but we got him here."

Han cleared his throat. "We can talk about that later," he said. "Jacen, Lando's right. You ought to have that cut looked at. And, Leia—"

"My legs are fine," she assured him.

"Why don't you let the medical droid take a look anyway? It certainly can't hurt."

"There's plenty of time," Lando said. "If you'll just follow me?"

To Han's relief, the MD droid didn't find much on Leia or Jacen to complain about, and so an hour later, freshened and in new clothes, the three of them followed one of Lando's droids to his stateroom. When the door opened, however, Han couldn't repress a grin.

"Why am I not surprised?" he asked.

"Welcome to my humble home away from home," Lando said. "Not up to my usual standards, I'll admit, but it's comfortable enough."

The chamber beyond might have been imported from one of Lando's casinos or luxury barges. The stone of the asteroid had been annealed, etched, and planished to resemble Naboo tile, and the floor was of finest polished Kashyyyk wood. The appointments were all old Coruscant—pre-Empire—comfortable, decadently upholstered in philfiber brocades.

"Have a seat. The droid will bring our drinks."

A shiny new SE-6 domestic sidled up and took their orders.

"Stimcaf," Leia said. "If I have to discuss anything, I want to be at least half awake."

"I have another theory on that," Han said. "I know you, Lando. Surely you have some Corellian whiskey around this dump."

"Only the best, Han, though the best isn't as good as it used to be."

"What is?"

"Besides us?" Lando said. "Not much."

Jacen ordered mineral water.

"Another sober fellow," Lando remarked. "But I think I'll join Han." He leveled his intelligent gaze at Jacen. "And you, young Jedi. How are things with you?"

"Very well, thanks," Jacen said politely.

"You've got a lot of your mother in you. Fortunate choice your genes made." He paused. "I understand you're hot property these days. I think you've even outdone the old man when it comes to the bounty you'd fetch."

"That's not funny, Lando," Han said.

Lando raised his eyebrows mildly. "I didn't say it was. Just making an observation. As you said, you know me."

"Only too well."

Lando made a wounded face, then brightened. "Ah, here are our drinks." He took his glass and raised it. "To the old times, and to better ones."

They drank. Han grimaced. "Boy, you weren't kidding. Whyren's Reserve this ain't."

"There have been better years, I'll grant you that." Lando's voice softened and became more serious. "I'm sorry I didn't make the funeral, Han. Some of my people got trapped near Obroa-skai when the Vong took it. I couldn't leave them hanging."

"I know," Han said, taking another drink. "I heard. That's what he would have wanted you to do."

"And you, Lando," Leia said. "How are things with you and Tendra?"

"Hey, we're making do. Losing Dubrillion wasn't a lot of fun, but I've managed to spread my assets out over the years. I've still got the operation on Kessel, though it's attracted some attention lately."

"Yuuzhan Vong?"

"Nah, just pirates and profiteers. And I've been approached by the Peace Brigade."

That got Han's attention. "Really?"

"I sent them packing. They didn't have the clout to back up their demands, and they knew it."

"Yes, but what did they want?" Leia asked.

Lando chuckled. "The usual. Help hunting down Jedi, though they must have known who they were dealing with. Mostly I think they wanted guards for one of their convoys."

"What sort of convoy?"

"It seems that the Brigade has expanded. They're not just in the business of hunting Jedi anymore—they've taken over the trade routes in Vong-occupied territory."

"They're *supplying* them?"

"And their subject populations. Sure. Somebody has to."

"Of all the vile . . ." Leia couldn't even finish, she was so disgusted.

They shifted to small talk. The whiskey was warming, and Han felt his shoulders relax a little.

"Well," Lando said, when their glasses were dry. "Our allies, such as they are, are waiting. We're probably as fashionably late as we can afford to be."

"Lead the way," Han replied.

Three beings awaited them in a conference room that evinced none of the luxury of Lando's suite—it was clinically spare. The most striking of the trio was a young Hutt, reclining with a bored expression and an impatient twitch in his thickly muscled tail. Next to him sat a human woman in her mid-thirties. Her skin was almost as dark as Lando's, her hair clipped and with severe bangs. She wore a formal business smock, black with a raised white collar. She looked serious, but the female Twi'lek another turn around the circular conference table looked positively grim.

"How thoughtful of you to finally show up," the Hutt remarked.

"Happy to be of service," Han replied, keeping his voice neutral. "And you'd be?"

"Bored," the Hutt replied.

Han frowned and raised his finger, but Lando cut in smoothly. "Han Solo, meet Bana. He's here on behalf of the Hutt resistance."

"And an investor in this . . . place," Bana added. "Despite which I've been ill treated. Kept in closed quarters for the journey. Very inhospitable."

"You understand our desire to keep the location of Shelter a secret," Lando said.

"I understand the insult involved. You imply I might sell the information? My people are fighting for their lives. There is no dealing with the Yuuzhan Vong, neither in goods nor information. They are a mad species, and such sensible things mean nothing to them." He drew his sluglike body straighter.

"No insult was intended," Leia soothed.

The Hutt cocked his head. "You are Princess Leia. You were present when my cousin Randa died."

"I was," Leia agreed. "He died bravely."

"This is Numa Rar," Lando continued, introducing the Twi'lek.

"It is an honor to meet you," the woman intoned, her pale blue head-tails twisting together.

Jacen spoke for the first time since entering the room. "I recognize you," he said to Numa Rar.

"Yes. I was a student of the late Daeshara'cor."

"You may have heard of the resistance on New Plympto, in the Corellian sector," Lando said. "Numa is a leader of that resistance."

He turned to the human woman. "Opeli Mors," he said. "A representative of the Jin'ri trade syndicate."

"Interesting," Han said. "I've never heard of that organization."

"Nor have I," Leia added.

Opeli Mors gave a brief, businesslike smile. "We are a relatively new concern. We formed to meet the needs of refugees soon after the fall of Duro. We welcome the opportunity to expand."

"War profiteers," Leia said.

"No business can operate without an income," Mors said. "Governments have the luxury of taxation. We do not."

"I know your type," Leia replied, her voice climbing several degrees with each word. "Profit is one thing. You people *gouge* until there's nothing left, then abandon your charges when they can no longer pay."

"Not true. We underwrite charity cases with monies we make from those who can afford our services. If we could operate on an entirely altruistic level, we would."

"I'll bet. What were your bosses before the invasion? Racketeers? Pirates?"

A slight line appeared on Mors's forehead. "I came here in good faith."

"Let's all just calm down," Jacen said, reprising the role

of mediator he had performed during the crisis at Duro. "Why don't we just get the preliminaries out of the way?"

"I've all but begged to move this along," Bana said.

"Mom?" Jacen said.

Leia was politic enough to know that her son was right. She nodded, sat, and folded her hands together.

"After the fall of Duro, Tsavong Lah, the Yuuzhan Vong warmaster, promised that if all of the Jedi in the galaxy were turned over to him, he would invade no more of our planets. A lot of people have taken him at his word."

"What concern is this of mine?" Bana asked.

"The Jedi protect even your kind, Hutt," Numa snarled suddenly.

"But if I see clearly where our friend is going with this, it's the Jedi who now need protecting."

"Not this Jedi," the Twi'lek replied. "I do not ask for rescue, only for help in my struggle."

"If you would let me continue?" Leia said mildly.

"Go on, please," Numa said, though she did not seem in the least chastened.

"Yes, we're trying to establish a network to get Jedi off worlds that are hostile to them to places where they can be safe. But Luke Skywalker's plan is much more comprehensive than that. We also want to be able to get Jedi *into* occupied systems—systems like yours, Bana."

"For what purpose?" Opeli Mors asked.

"To help where they are most needed. To connect with underground and intelligence networks. What we are after here is not a Jedi rescue network, merely one that lets Jedi move about in relative safety."

"And these Jedi—they would fight with my people against the Yuuzhan Vong?" Bana asked.

Leia and Jacen exchanged glances. Jacen cleared his throat. "Aggression, as such, is not the Jedi way. We would help, yes."

"Yes? You will run weapons to us? Supplies?"

"The network could be used for that, too," Han said. "As I see it, anyway."

"I should hope so," Bana replied. "The fortunes of our

family are not what they once were. When we spend money, we want a return."

Numa spoke again, dismissing the Hutt with a flick of her lekku. "I have heard, Jacen Solo, that you yourself attacked and humiliated the warmaster. Is this not aggression? Does not Kyp Durron even now take the fight to the enemy?"

"He did it to save my life," Leia said.

Jacen squared up his shoulders. "I don't agree with Kyp's tactics, nor does Master Skywalker."

"Then you would not agree with mine," Numa said. "Perhaps it was a mistake for me to come here."

Jacen studied her for a moment. "Your Master must have warned you of the dark side."

"Fear of the dark side is a luxury the people of New Plympto cannot afford. Will you help us or not?"

Anakin would agree with her, Jacen thought glumly.

"We will do what we can," he told her. "We will bring medical aid and food, help evacuate those who must leave. We will not come in as guerrillas. And avoiding the dark side is not a luxury. It is a necessity."

She did not reply to that, but in the Force Jacen felt her unrepentant.

"Mors?"

The woman stared at the table for a moment, then her gaze found Han's. "Personally, I would like to help," she said. "But my superiors—well. We could supply troops and ships, of course, of the sort experienced at the kind of activity you're planning, but—"

"But we'll have to pay," Leia said.

"Something, yes."

"Look," Han said. "The New Republic isn't in on this. They won't fund it."

"You built this station."

"Out of our own pockets," Lando said. "Even the Hutts contributed."

"Ah, but they stand to gain. Whatever our friend there may say, he knows your Jedi network is one of the slim hopes his people have for survival."

"You're in the same escape pod," Leia snapped. "You

think the Yuuzhan Vong will tolerate your business when they've conquered the entire galaxy?"

Mors shrugged. "Maybe. Maybe not. That's why I *have* been authorized to offer you the loan of one ship, at no charge. We'll consider it an investment."

Han nodded. "Well, that's something." He glanced around the table. "Why don't we see if we can find some *more* common ground?"

Han slouched into the kneading chair in the quarters Lando had provided. Though not as opulent as Lando's, they were more than comfortable.

"This isn't going to work," he muttered.

"Don't be defeatist," Leia said.

"I'm not. I'm being realistic. Somebody has to be, because your brother sure isn't."

"Don't start in on Luke again."

"Look, I'm glad he finally decided to *do* something," Han said, "but he could have chosen something doable. 'Make me a great river, Han, a stream to carry the endangered, the wounded, the weary to safety.' Very poetic. But how do we *pay* for it? Everyone in the room wants to take and take, but they don't want to give."

Leia's expression softened and she stroked her fingers on his cheek. He closed them in his own hand and kissed them.

He started to embrace her, but before he could complete it, she drew back from him a little, though gently.

"We *will* find the money, Han." And her eyes held a fire brighter even than that day on the Death Star when they first met. It burned through him like a blaster bolt. He nodded, and tugged her again, and this time she did not resist.

TEN

Nen Yim contemplated the mass of cells through an external maa'it, at a magnification of several hundred times their actual size, and for the first time in many cycles felt a minute amount of hope. She could not be certain, but she thought there were signs of regeneration; the mass had grown large and infinitesimally more massive. If so, her new protocol seemed to be working. Unfortunately, it would be some time before she could be sure, and though she was short of every resource imaginable, time was the commodity she had in least supply.

She noted the results in her portable memory-qahsa, then moved on to the next batch of trials. Before she could get a good start, however, her door burred softly, indicating a request for admittance to the shaping quarters. She moved to the villip on the wall and stroked it to life.

The face that appeared was the prefect Ona Shai, commander of the worldship. Her eyebrows had been cut into a series of vertical ridges, and one of her ears had been sacrificed to the gods.

"Prefect Shai," Nen Yim said. "What can I do for you?"

"I desire admittance, Adept."

Nen Yim dithered, inwardly. There was no time to hide her work, but then, no one else on the *Baanu Miir* was likely to comprehend what she was doing, much less recognize it as heresy.

"Please enter, Prefect."

A moment later the door burred a different tone, and Nen Yim opened it by exposing her wrist to its chemical sensor.

In person, the prefect was not particularly intimidating. Younger even than Nen Yim, she had been born with a slight stoop to her spine. Another degree of angle, and she would have been sent back to the gods at birth. She was habitually excitable and ill controlled, as was evident now.

"Adept," Ona said.

"Prefect."

For a moment the prefect stood there blankly, as if she had forgotten why she came. She passed a hand across her face, and her eyes wandered. She seemed almost in shock.

"Something has happened," she said at last. "It requires your attention."

"What, Prefect? What has occurred?"

"One-fourth of the population of the *Baanu Miir* is dead," the prefect said.

As Nen Yim stepped through the emergency membrane, she felt the vacuum-hardened ooglith cloaker tighten against her body, maintaining the pressure that kept her blood from boiling away into the airless chamber beyond.

The frozen bodies piled three and four deep on the floor hadn't been wearing cloakers. Nen Yim felt a tightness in her throat that had nothing to do with the hard-shelled variety of gnullith she had inserted there to pass the air from the lungworm coiled on her back.

They had time, she thought. *The air went out slowly, at first. They had time to reach this place, where the ship finally thought to seal itself off. Here they died, beating against a membrane they did not have the authority to permeate.*

"This is no way to die," she heard the prefect murmur over the tiny villips that pressed at their throats and ears.

"Death is always to be embraced," Sakanga, the warrior who completed their triad, reminded her. He was an ancient, almost mummylike man. Like the prefect, he was of the disgraced Domain Shai.

"Of course that is true," Ona said. "Of course."

"What happened here, Shaper?" the warrior asked, turning his attention to Nen Yim. "Meteor impact? Infidel attack?" He paused. "Sabotage?"

"It was not possible to tell," Nen Yim answered. "The rikyam's understanding was hazy. It is why I wished to come here, to seek evidence. The breach is at the end of this arm, that is all I know. Perhaps when I see it, I can say more."

"We should have a master on this ship," the prefect grumbled. "I do not demean you, Adept, but a worldship should have a master shaper on board."

"I quite agree," Nen Yim said. "A master is needed." *A master like my own, Mezhan Kwaad, not one of the mumbling dodderers who pass for them,* she finished silently.

They moved soundlessly through the carnage. Most of the bodies were slaves and Shamed Ones; in death, vacuum had mutilated them as they could not have been in life. Perhaps the gods would accept their final sacrifice, perhaps not. They were, at least, beyond caring.

The capillary platforms that would normally have taken them down the arm were as dead and frozen as the people who had once used them. The three were forced to descend by the bony spine with its intentionally runglike vertebrae. As they descended, their bodies grew gradually heavier with the illusion of gravity created by the ship's spin. Coming back up would be more onerous than descending. She wondered if the decrepit warrior would be able to manage it at all.

The chambers were jeweled with ice crystals, frozen in the act of boiling from and rupturing the soft inner walls. The once-pliant floor was as rigid as the yorik coral on the exterior of the ship, but much more dead.

They continued down, through progressively smaller chambers. They saw fewer dead down here, too, reinforcing Nen Yim's guess. The rupture had ended catastrophically, emptying the arm of air and life in a few tens of heartbeats, but it must have begun small.

Why had the rikyam given no alarm? Why hadn't the seals between each and every layer closed and hardened?

Eventually, they came to stars.

The arm curved toward the end, and "down" followed the anterior edge. Here objects weighed the most; the area had been reserved for the training of warriors originally, but since most able-bodied warriors had moved ahead of the slower worldships to the glory of battle, the tip had been transformed into a crèche, so that the children of the next generation would mature with thicker bones and more powerful muscles.

A futile hope for these children. Those who hadn't been hurled out into space regarded the stars they might have conquered with frozen eyes through a fifty-meter-long tear in the fabric of the hull.

Nen Yim shivered. The stars were decidedly *down*. If she were to fall, the spin of the ship would sling her irrevocably into trackless parsecs of nothing.

And yet it was glorious. As she watched, the disk of the galaxy spun into view, too enormous for even such a large gash to fully frame. The Core blazed, a white mass tinged blue, spreading into arms that gradually faded toward cooler stars. Technically, the *Baanu Miir* was already within the boundaries of that great lens, but even the nearest world was unreachably far from the *Baanu Miir*.

That became even more apparent as she examined the rupture. The edges of it were curled outward, revealing the tripartite nature of the hull. The outer shell was yorik coral, rigid metal-bearing nacelles wrapped around the hardy, energetic organisms that created and tended them. Below that were the sheared and frozen capillaries that carried nutrients and oxygen out to the arms and pumped waste products back for the maw luur to cycle and recycle, supplemented by the hydrogen atoms that the dovin basals pulled from surrounding space. There also were the muscles and tendons that could flex the great arm, contract it if need be, and here something had failed. When the rift occurred, the medial hull should have drawn together and been sealed by its own freezing. The outer hull would have replicated and closed the gap, and over time the dead, frozen cells should have been replaced by vibrant new ones. The soft, pliable inner hull would have healed as well, eventually leaving nothing more than a faint scar to remind of the disaster.

"What happened?" the warrior asked. "I don't understand this."

Nen Yim pointed to the rent mass of striated muscle.

"It tore itself," she said.

"What do you mean, it tore *itself*?" the prefect asked. "How can that be?"

"The muscles spasmed, as the muscles of your leg might after much exertion. They contracted and split the hull, then kept contracting, tearing it wider."

"That's impossible," the warrior grunted.

"No, only undesirable," Nen Yim replied. "The rikyam is supposed to monitor such fluctuations and moderate them."

"Then why didn't it?"

"My deduction? Because the rikyam's senses in this arm are dead. It is unaware that anything here exists. Very likely the impulse that ripped the hull was one of the few random impulses to enter here from the brain in many cycles."

"You're saying the rikyam itself did this?" Ona asked.

"Only indirectly. What you behold is the result of a ship-brain so far gone in senility that it is losing control of its motor functions."

"Then there is no hope," the prefect murmured.

The warrior glanced at the prefect in irritation. "What is this babble of hope? The Yuuzhan Vong were born to conquer and die. This is an obstacle, nothing more."

"Can you heal it?" Ona Shai asked Nen Yim.

"We can seal the rupture. The damage is crippling; the entire inner hull is dead. The medial hull will take many cycles to regenerate, assuming the maw luur still nourishes it. We can perhaps grow a ganglion to control the functions of this arm, but it will remain disconnected from the brain. Furthermore, it is probable that the rikyam is losing control of the other arms as well, if it hasn't already."

"You're saying we must abandon *Baanu Miir*." The prefect's voice was flat.

"Unless the rikyam can be regenerated. I am giving this all of my attention."

"See that you do. Meanwhile, a new worldship is being grown. I will petition that our people be transferred there. Yet many of the ships are failing; our chances are slim."

"Whatever our fate, we will meet it as befits the children of Yun-Yuuzhan." Sakanga gestured at the rim of the galaxy slipping from view. "Already we have warriors poised near that bright center. All of those worlds beneath us will be ours. Our sacrifices here will not be forgotten. It is not our place to complain."

"No," Nen Yim agreed. "But we will do what we must to ensure *Baanu Miir* provides another generation for that conquest. *I* will do what I must." *Though it will only earn me dishonor and death, I will do what I must.*

ELEVEN

Luke watched the blockade grow larger.

"Oh, boy," Mara said.

"No," Luke murmured, placing his hand on her shoulder. "Don't you see? They're no danger to us."

Jaina's voice crackled over the comm. "That's Rogue Squadron! I can't *believe* they would—"

She was interrupted by a hail that came simultaneously to the *Jade Shadow*.

Gavin Darklighter's image appeared on the *Shadow*'s display.

"*Jade Shadow*—it looks like you could use some help."

"This is unwise, Gavin," Luke responded carefully. "Those are Coruscant security forces pursuing us."

"I've explained their mistake to them," Gavin replied. "They won't trouble you again."

"They'll just send for more ships. This could really develop into a situation."

"Maybe the sort of situation the New Republic needs," Gavin replied. "First Corran, now you? Enough is enough. Fey'lya is selling us off to the Yuuzhan Vong a piece at a time."

"No, he's not. I have my disagreements with him, obviously, but he's trying to save the New Republic, in his own way. A civil war can only make us weaker."

"Not if we make it quick and painless. Not if we have real leadership when it's over, rather than the fractured, squabbling crowd that's got us sitting on our thumbs."

"You're referring to democracy," Luke replied. "Something we all fought very hard for. We can't throw it away simply because it becomes inconvenient. Gavin, we aren't having this conversation."

"Okay. I just wanted you to know you have support."

"And I appreciate it. But now is the time for you to flame out of this situation. If we go right now, we'll get a clear jump. Then you start talking your way out of this mess."

"You're sure you don't want an escort?"

"Positive."

Gavin nodded. "Understood. Take care. Mara, you too."

His face vanished from the screen, and Luke suddenly felt his fingers trembling.

"Luke?" Mara said, concern in her voice.

"That was too close," he said. "Too close. I won't be the excuse for a coup. Am I doing the right thing?"

"Absolutely. Let them arrest you, and you think this resistance won't come back up?"

"Did you know the squadron would do this?"

"I'd guessed it."

"And you think if we give up . . ."

"An attempted coup within a week, my guess. At the very least an extremely volatile situation. Skywalker, you were seeing clearly earlier. We have to go. For the New Republic's sake, for the Jedi's sake—and not least by a long shot, for the sake of ourselves and our son."

Jaina answered the private hail from Gavin Darklighter, trying to keep composed.

"Yes, Colonel," she said. "How may I help you?"

"Watch after Master Skywalker, Jaina. He needs you."

"I'll do my best, sir. Is that all?"

"No." Gavin's voice crackled. "I made a mistake not putting you back on duty once your vision was recovered. I let you down, and I'm sorry for that. I'd like you to consider yourself still a part of the Squadron."

"I appreciate that, Rogue Leader," she said quietly. "You understand that right now—"

"As I said. Master Skywalker needs you now. You're still on leave, as far as I'm concerned. Go, and may the Force be with you."

*   *   *

"Jaina, I need you to do something," Luke said. Coruscant was light-years behind them. There was room for an X-wing on the *Shadow,* but that space was already occupied by Luke's starfighter. Thus, they chatted over the comm. Mara and Luke had filled her in on the details of their flight from Coruscant, and Jaina in turn had explained her continued detachment from Rogue Squadron.

"Yes, Uncle Luke?"

"I need you to find Kyp Durron for me. I need to talk to him."

"He didn't have much good to say at the last meeting. Why should things be any different now?"

"Because things *are* different now," Luke replied. "Now I may have some things to say he might want to hear."

"Unless you're going to join him in guerrilla warfare against the Yuuzhan Vong, I doubt that," she replied.

"Be that as it may. It's imperative that the Jedi start drawing ourselves back together."

"If you ask me to find him, I'll find him," Jaina said. "I found Booster Terrik, didn't I?"

"This will be a lot easier than that, I should think," Luke replied. "I know exactly where Kyp is."

"How?"

"Kyp worries me. I took the liberty of placing a tracer on his ship."

"What? If the Yuuzhan Vong pick that up—"

"I didn't endanger Kyp. It's something new one of Karrde's people came up with to help us find each other without leaking our positions to the Yuuzhan Vong or their collaborators. Booster has one, too, so we'll be able to find the *Errant Venture* with relative ease. It's a fixed-signature signal, passed through relays and the HoloNet, and gives an off-read within a range from ten to fifty light-years. No one without the encryption key can use it to track him, in other words. At short range it sounds like engine noise, and if Kyp cuts his power to hide from sensors, it'll go off, too."

"Wow. Have I been fitted with one of those?"

"No, but the *Shadow* has, and I'll give you that encryption, too, along with Booster's."

"Sounds good. Where's Kyp now?"

"That's the disturbing thing. He's near Sernpidal."

A shiver feathered along Jaina's neck.

Sernpidal. Where Chewie had died. Sernpidal was as deep in Yuuzhan Vong territory as one could go.

This wouldn't be another little fetching mission. This could get very nasty indeed.

"That's a long way," she said. "I hope you have some extra juice over there for me."

"Plenty. We'll hook you up, and I'll transfer some supplies as well."

He grimaced, and she could tell that sending her off like this wasn't something he did without reservations.

"Thanks, Jaina," he said. "And may the Force be with you."

PART TWO

PASSAGE

PART TWO

DAMAGE

TWELVE

"Oh!" Tahiri exclaimed, wrinkling her nose. "It *stinks*."

"Yep," Corran agreed. "Welcome to Eriadu."

Anakin agreed, as well, albeit silently. But it was a complex stink. If he imagined this stuff Eriaduans sucked in every day as a painting, an oily, bitter, hydrocarbon stench would be the canvas. Sulfury burnt yellow swirled over it, interspersed with starbursts of white ozone spangles and green chloride stars, all under a gray wash of something vaguely organic and ammoniac.

A light rain was falling. Anakin hoped it wouldn't burn his skin.

"Is Coruscant like this?" Tahiri asked. She had already forgotten the smell and was tracing with eager eyes the clunky but sky-reaching industrial buildings on all sides of the spaceport. Low leaden clouds dragged over the tallest structures, though the canopy opened in places to a more distant, pastel yellow sky.

"Not really," Anakin said. "For one thing, the buildings on Coruscant aren't this ugly."

"It's not ugly," Tahiri said. She sounded defensive. "It's *different*. I've never been on a world with this much . . . stuff."

"Well, Coruscant's got more 'stuff,' and now that I think about it, the lower levels make this look like a cloud city. But at least the air is clean. They don't muck it up like this."

"You mean this isn't natural, this smell?" Tahiri asked.

"Nope," Corran said. "They make things cheap and dirty here. The perfume you've noticed is one of the by-products. If they don't watch it, Eriadu will become another

Duro. Well, what Duro was before the Yuuzhan Vong got hold of it, anyway."

"I don't think you ought to go barefoot here, Tahiri," Anakin remarked.

Tahiri looked down at the grimy duracrete landing field and grimaced. "Maybe you're right."

Off to their right, a bulk freighter cut its underjets and settled on repulsorlifts.

"Okay," Corran said. "I'm going to arrange for the supplies we need. You two—"

"Stay and guard the ship, I bet," Anakin muttered.

"Right."

Tahiri's brow ruffled. "You mean I came all this way and don't even get to see the place?"

"No," Corran said. "When I get back, we'll go into town and find someplace to eat. We'll do a little exploring. But I don't want to stay long; there's no reason for anyone to double-check our transponder code, but if they do, we could run into a little trouble."

"Well . . . okay," Tahiri assented. She sat on the landing ramp, legs folded underneath her. Together she and Anakin watched Corran flag a ground transport and enter it. A few moments later, the blocky vehicle vanished from sight.

"Do you think people from here think clean worlds smell weird?" Tahiri asked.

"Probably. What did you think of Yavin Four, after all those years on Tatooine?"

"I thought it smelled weird," she concluded, after a bit of thought. "But in a good way. Mostly in a good way. I mean, part of it smelled like a kitchen midden or a 'fresher sump. But the blueleaf, and the flowers . . ." She trailed off, and her expression changed. "What do you think the Yuuzhan Vong did to Yavin Four after we left? Do you think they changed it, you know, like they did some of the other planets they captured?"

"I don't know," Anakin said. "I don't want to think about it." It had been hard enough to see the Great Temple where so much of his childhood had been spent destroyed. To imagine that the verdant jungle and all of its creatures were also gone was more than he was willing to put himself through without proof.

Tahiri's face stayed long.

"What?" Anakin asked, when she didn't say anything for a while.

"I lied a minute ago."

"Really? About what?"

She nodded at the cityscape. "I said it wasn't ugly. But part of me thinks it is."

"Well, *I* don't think it's all that attractive," Anakin replied.

"No," Tahiri said, her voice suddenly husky. "It's not like that. It's just that part of me sees this and thinks *abomination*."

"Oh."

The Yuuzhan Vong had done more to Tahiri than cut her face. They had implanted memories in her—of their language, of a childhood in a crèche, of growing up on a worldship.

"If you hadn't rescued me, Anakin, I would be one of them now. I wouldn't remember any other life."

"Part of you would have always known," Anakin disagreed. "There's something in you, Tahiri, that no one could ever change."

She shot him a startled frown. "You keep saying things like that. What do you mean? Is it good or bad? You mean I'm too stubborn, or what?"

"I mean you're too Tahiri," he said.

"Oh." She attempted a smile and half succeeded. "I guess I'll take that as a compliment, since you never give me any obvious ones."

Anakin felt his face warm. He and Tahiri had been best friends for a long time. Now that she was fourteen and he was sixteen, things were getting very confusing. It was like her eyes had changed colors, but they hadn't. They were just more interesting somehow.

She *had* cut her hair, right before they left for Eriadu— that had been a shock. She now wore it in a kind of bob, with wispy little bangs that tickled at her eyebrows.

She noticed his regard. "What? You don't like my hair?"

"It's fine. It's a nice cut. About the same length as my mom's is now."

"Anakin Solo—" Something inside her cut her sentence off short.

"Did you feel that?" she asked in a hushed voice.

And at the moment, he did. Something in the Force. Fear, panic, resolution, resignation, all bound up together.

"It's a Jedi," he murmured.

"A Jedi in trouble. Bad trouble." She uncoiled like a released spring. "Where are those shoes?"

"Tahiri, no. I'll go. Someone has to stay with the ship."

"You do it then. I'm going." She stood up and went into the ship. Anakin followed. She found a pair of walking slippers in her locker and put them on.

"Just wait a second. Let me figure this out."

"I don't need you to figure anything out for me. One of us is in trouble. I'm going to help."

She was already on her way out and down the landing ramp.

Repeating some of his father's more inventive expletives, Anakin hurriedly sealed the ship and ran after her.

He caught up with her at the customs-and-immigration line. She breezed past everyone else, but was stopped at the force gate, where a gray-haired official frowned down at her.

"You have to go to the back of the line."

"No, I don't," Tahiri said, passing her hand impatiently.

"You don't," the woman agreed. "But I need to see your identification."

"You don't care about that," Tahiri insisted.

"Never mind; don't bother," the official replied. "What's the purpose of your visit to Eriadu?"

"Nothing that would interest you. I have to get through, now!"

The woman shrugged. "Okay. Go on through." She dropped the force barrier, and Tahiri dashed past.

"Next."

"I'm with her," Anakin informed her. "You need to let me through, right now," he added.

"You need to be with her," the official said, dropping the force gate again, long enough for Anakin to get through.

Behind him, he heard the next person in line say, "Why don't you just let me through, as well?"

"Why would I do that?" the official wondered caustically.

Naturally, he'd lost sight of Tahiri, but he knew where she was going. The Jedi they were both feeling was in more distress than ever.

Anakin pushed his way through the rain-slickered portround crowd, through vendors and street performers, past long rows of cantinas and tapcafs and souvenir shops full of mostly fake lacy shellwork and grossly caricatured statuettes of Grand Moff Tarkin.

Three streets in, the crowd seemed to dissipate, and the grubby lanes were almost empty, except for the occasional six-legged rodent. Here the scent of hot metal was overpowering, though the streets were relatively cold and the rain had increased. And ahead of him somewhere, a Jedi's feet were slowing.

Anakin turned into a long cul-de-sac formed on the left by a chrome-facade skyscraper and on the right by the ribbed-steel wall of a ten-story-high heat sink, steaming in the rain. The end of the alley was the back of another building faced in blackened duraplast. A crowd of vagabonds was gathered, watching a murder about to happen.

The victim was a Jedi, a Rodian. He stood against the heat sink, trying to keep his lightsaber up. Five beings faced him—two with blasters, three with stun batons. All had just turned to face Tahiri, who was about six meters from them, arriving at a dead run, her lightsaber swirling bright patterns over her head.

Anakin saw all of this from a distance of fifty meters or so. He tried to coax his feet to lightspeed.

Taking advantage of Tahiri's distraction, the Rodian lurched forward. One of the men with a blaster shot him, and the descending screech of the bolt reverberated in the alley.

Tahiri's blade sheared through a stun baton, nearly taking the hand of the thickset woman wielding it. Anakin winced; Kam had been working with Tahiri on her lightsaber technique, and she was a quick learner, but still a novice.

Novice or not, the thugs with the stun batons backpedaled, drawing blasters instead of taking up the fight hand to hand. Tahiri pressed on, catching one of them and snipping the end of his weapon off. The next man back fired at her and missed. They started to encircle her.

Finally, Anakin arrived. He recognized the Rodian Jedi as Kelbis Nu. The man who had shot the Rodian saw him coming, took careful aim, and fired twice. Two bolts winged into the alley walls, courtesy of Anakin's lightsaber. He was running past the man, deftly slicing the blaster in half as he went, when he felt a gun pointing at him. He dropped and rolled as the bolt screamed over his head.

A person screamed, too—the man who had shot Kelbis Nu. The blast meant for Anakin had struck him high in the chest, and he fell, legs kicking.

Anakin came back to his feet and found Tahiri facing two men still armed with blasters and two unarmed. They looked uncertain.

It was only then that Anakin realized, by their patches and uniforms, that they were Peace Brigade.

The thugs started backing out of the alley in a small knot, blasters pointed defensively. Anakin stood about a meter to Tahiri's right and a little in front of her.

"Let's take 'em," she said. Her voice had a furious, cold quality to it that Anakin had heard twice; once when she was under the heaviest influence of her Yuuzhan Vong conditioning; once in a vision he'd had of her as a dark Jedi, her face mutilated by the scars and tattoos of a Yuuzhan Vong warmaster.

"No," Anakin said. "Let them go."

His generosity didn't stop the Peace Brigaders from taking a parting shot as they ducked around the corner.

"Jedi brats!" one of the men shouted. "Your days are numbered!"

When he was sure they weren't just hiding around the corner, waiting for his guard to drop, Anakin turned to survey the damage.

The Peace Brigader had stopped moving. Kelbis Nu was still alive—barely. His glassy eyes were looking beyond Anakin, but he reached up a hand.

"Ya . . . ," he said weakly.

"Tahiri, use your wrist comm. Try to find the local emergency channel." He took Nu's hand and pulsed strength from the Force into him. "Hold on for me," he said. "Help will be here soon."

"Ya—ya—ya . . . ," the Rodian gasped.

"Don't try to talk," Anakin told him. "Waste of strength."

Suddenly Kelbis Nu went still, his trembling ceased, and for the first time he seemed to actually see Anakin.

"*Yag'Dhul,*" he whispered, and behind that whisper was a stormwind of danger.

That was all. The Jedi's life left him with his last breath.

Tahiri was shouting at someone over her wrist comm.

"Never mind, Tahiri," Anakin said. "He's gone." Tears started in his eyes, but he battled them down.

"He can't be," Tahiri said. "I was going to save him."

"I'm sorry," Anakin said. "We got here too late."

Tahiri's shoulders began to twitch, and she made a sound like hiccuping as she fought to control her tears. Anakin watched her, wishing he could help, that he could make the grief go away, but there was nothing he could do. People died. You got used to it.

It still hurt.

"He said something at the end," Anakin told her, hoping to distract her.

"What?"

"The name of a planet, Yag'Dhul. It's not far from here, right where the Corellian Trade Spine and the Rimma Trade Route meet. And I felt . . . danger. Like he was trying to tell me something bad is happening there." He glanced down at the bodies. "C'mon. We'd better go."

"We have to do something," Tahiri said. "We can't just let those guys get away with it."

"We can't hunt them," Anakin said.

"Why not?"

"Because we're Jedi, not assassins."

"We could at least tell security or whoever enforces the law around here."

"We're supposed to be here anonymously, remember? If we draw attention to ourselves, we endanger the mission."

"Some mission. Getting supplies. This is more important. Anyway, we've already drawn attention to ourselves." She nodded at the crowd of vagrants drifting toward them, the curiosity of two dead bodies overcoming their fear of two live Jedi.

And as if to highlight her point, a trio of groundcars arrived at the end of the alley and disgorged armed, uniformed people.

"I guess we'll be talking to security after all." Anakin clipped his lightsaber to his belt and held up his hands to show they were empty.

The officers approached warily, led by a lanky, craggy-faced man with the fading remnants of a black eye. He looked down at the two bodies and back up at them. Then his eyes focused on their lightsabers—Tahiri still had hers in her hand.

He raised his gun. "Place your weapons on the ground," he said.

"We didn't do this," Tahiri exploded. "We were trying to help."

"Put it down, now, girlie."

"Girlie?"

"Do as he says, Tahiri," Anakin said, carefully detaching his weapon and placing it near his feet.

"Why?"

"Do it."

"It's good advice, kid," the officer said.

Radiating anger, Tahiri placed her lightsaber on the duracrete.

"Good. As officers of the judicials, it is now my duty to inform you that we are detaining you for questioning and possible prosecution."

"What? You're arresting us?" Tahiri said.

"Until we sort this out, yes."

"Ask the crowd. They saw what happened."

"We will; don't worry. There will be a thorough investigation. Make this easy on yourselves."

But words are only the shadows of thoughts, and behind the officer's words, Anakin felt something that suggested that this was going to be anything but easy.

THIRTEEN

By the time Jaina reached the vicinity of the Sernpidal system, her X-wing felt like a suit of clothes she'd been wearing for *way* too long.

In fact, her clothes felt that way, too, but more so.

Jedi meditation techniques and isometrics made the long hyperspace jumps bearable, but nothing could hide the fact that there was no room on an X-wing for a shower. Or room to stand up, to walk, to *run*.

That's not likely going to happen anytime soon, she chided herself. *So concentrate!*

She was near her goal now. Somewhere down there—or so the tracer told her—was Kyp Durron. Or his X-wing, at least.

Or merely the tracer beacon, if Kyp was more clever than Uncle Luke imagined. Jaina started sweeping with long-range sensors.

Kyp wasn't at Sernpidal anymore, but a system several very strange jumps away. The star at the bottom of the gravity pit was old, a white dwarf that at this distance was barely brighter than its much more distant, hotter cousins. It was wreathed with a lazy torus of nebulas ejected when the star collapsed into its present pale form. Jaina had appeared in the inner fringe of the gas cloud.

She punched up the stellar survey and found a brief entry more than two hundred years old. The star had a number but not a name. Six planets. The nearest to the sun was a lifeless rock; the next three were sheathed in frozen carbon dioxide and water ice. On the outer planets, the ice got more exotic: methane, ammonia, chlorine in various compounds. The largest planet, a gas giant, had picked up its own nebula from the outbound gases expelled from the parent star.

No known intelligent life in the system, no known life at all. No resources that couldn't be found more easily elsewhere, and no reason to come back.

But Kyp Durron had come here.

She followed the beacon in, dropping from above the plane of the elliptic. It took her to the fourth planet, a rock half the size of Coruscant that made Hoth seem like a hothouse. She tried not to fidget.

She hadn't expected to come in unnoticed, and she didn't. As she was making orbit a pair of X-wings rose up to meet her. One had the beacon in it.

A few moments later, she answered what turned out to be Kyp's hail.

"Amazing," he said. "Simply amazing. Jaina Solo, you continue to find ways to surprise me."

"Hello, Kyp."

"I'd ask you what could have possibly brought you to this place, but I almost don't want to know. If the Force guided you, it's almost too frightening."

"How so?"

"Because I was just about to come looking for you and Rogue Squadron," Kyp answered, sounding sardonic.

"Really."

"Yep. I've found something, Jaina—something I can't handle with my Dozen. Something that could strike a death blow to the New Republic if we don't deal with it now, while we can."

"What are you talking about?" Jaina asked.

"I'd rather tell you in person. Follow me in—we don't have much down there, but it's better than the cockpit of an X-wing."

Kyp and his followers had melted tunnels and caves through the water ice and sealed it, then sifted an oxygen-nitrogen mix from higher up, where the planet's atmosphere had condensed when its primary went cold.

"We keep it right at freezing in here," Kyp explained, "so our humble home doesn't melt." He handed her a parka. "You'll want that."

"To tell you the truth," Jaina said, "the cold feels good. Almost as good as it feels to stand up." Her legs were having a little trouble finding their stride in the lower gravity.

"Well, like I said, it's not much, but we like it," Kyp said.

"Kyp, what are you doing all the way out here? This whole sector must be crawling with Yuuzhan Vong."

"Oh, they aren't far, though you'd be surprised by their numbers, I think—but they aren't *here*. No worlds to colonize, no slaves to be had, no machines to be destroyed."

"Except you, your people, and your ships."

"Good point. But there are a lot of these played-out star systems near the Rim. This one isn't even particularly rich in ore because the star died with a whimper—no supernova to spew heavy metals all over the place. I don't see them looking here when all of their efforts are focused on the Core."

"You think they'll push toward the Core?"

Kyp rolled his eyes. "You're smarter than that, Jaina. The Yuuzhan Vong are taking a breath, that's all, hoping their collaborators will do some of the work for them. But they're building up everywhere. And what I've found out here—"

"Yes, you mentioned that."

"First things first, Jaina. Do you mind telling my why *you're* here? And, in all seriousness, give me a little hint as to how?"

"Master Skywalker sent me to talk to you."

"Really? He has something new to say?"

"He and Mara fled Coruscant after Borsk Fey'lya ordered their arrest."

Kyp blinked, and his brow creased.

"Come in here and sit down," he said. He ushered her into what was obviously his war room—a portable sensor sweep, a tactical display, and star charts were its furnishings. He pulled up a collapsible chair for Jaina and one for himself.

"That was uncommonly stupid," he murmured. "Even for Fey'lya. Do you think our chief of state is working with the Peace Brigade?"

"Master Skywalker doesn't think so. Neither do I."

"Huh," Kyp said dubiously. "So what is Master Skywalker doing now?"

"Aunt Mara's pregnant, you know. It's not long before her time comes. Uncle Luke's hiding out with Booster Terrik. He intends to find a planet to build a Jedi base on."

Kyp's eyes narrowed. "A base for what?"

"To operate from. A place where endangered Jedi can go, a place for them to strike from."

"Jaina," Kyp said, "choose your words carefully. What do you mean by 'strike'? Don't put words in the Master's mouth just because you think I want to hear them."

Jaina looked down at the floor. "No," she said, "he's still not advocating what you're doing. He's trying to build a network to pass people and information in and out of Yuuzhan Vong space. A system of places like this, and ships—"

"But no direct action. No bringing the fight home to the Yuuzhan Vong."

"Not exactly—not the way you mean. But, Kyp, he is doing something, and he needs your help."

Kyp shook his head. "I think he sent you out here to find out what I'm doing."

"Partly. But he also sent me to bring you back into the fold."

Kyp rubbed his jaw thoughtfully for a moment. "I don't object to what Master Skywalker is doing. I have my bolt-holes and contacts, but they're limited, scattered, one day at a time. I don't have the resources or the leisure to build and maintain a stable network. If Luke does, that's great. I wish he would take a more active hand, but this is more than I was starting to think he would do. He's right; I can be of help to him, in certain sectors. And I'll do it—I'll meet with him. But Jaina, I need something from you in return." He frowned. "Though this arrest business changes things." He mulled that over a bit and shrugged. "I'll lay it out for you anyway. I'm not on good terms with any of the military leaders. I need someone who is. Is that still you?"

Jaina thought back to her last encounter with Rogue Squadron. And Wedge Antilles, so far as she knew, was still on the side of the Jedi.

"They might listen to me," she allowed.

"Or your mother."

"What do you need, Kyp?" Jaina asked wearily.

He looked at her as if for the first time. "It can wait a few hours," he said. "Why don't you get cleaned up? We sank an old cargo tank to use as a warm room. There's a hot tub of water calling your name."

"That sounds really, really good," Jaina said. "That's not a proposition I'm prepared to refuse, anyway."

The rogue Jedi's eyes twinkled mischievously. "When you're done, we'll discuss what other propositions you might find interesting."

That did something tickly to Jaina's stomach. She tried to ignore it.

Clean and in a change of clothes, Jaina spent half an hour limbering up, enjoying the luxury of motion. Then she rejoined Kyp in the tactical room. A few more of his Dozen—plus however many now—were in evidence. They nodded at her when she entered.

"That better?" Kyp asked.

"A lot better," Jaina told him. "Solar diameters better. Parsecs better. So. What's up?"

"I like that," Kyp said. "You get to the point." He gestured for her to take a seat.

"Like I said earlier," he began, as she settled into the reinforced flimsiplast chair, "we've been mostly taking things day by day. Harassing Yuuzhan Vong convoys, providing aid to resistance movements, keeping our receivers tuned. The problem was, nothing we could ever do was enough. We were no more than ore mites, irritating the Vong. The other thing I realized was how little we really know about them. How many are there? Where do they come from? Are they *still* coming? So a few months ago I decided to spend some time on an extended recon. We began at the Rim, where they first entered, then visited Belkadan and Helska. It wasn't easy, but it wasn't as hard as I expected, either. I found a few answers. I found a lot more questions. But Sernpidal—Gavin Darklighter took Rogue Squadron to Sernpidal. After."

Jaina stiffened.

"Right," Kyp said. "You were with him, weren't you? What you saw was confidential, not something for crazy Kyp Durron to know. But when people see strange things, Jaina, they talk." He leaned forward on his elbows. "I've been known to accuse the New Republic and the Jedi of being slow to act, of having their priorities confused. Sometimes I've been right; maybe other times I've misstated the case. This time . . ."

He tapped on a holo display, and the Sernpidal system appeared. An adjustment, and a small section of it came into tight focus—a crescent of debris.

"The remains of Sernpidal."

Jaina suddenly felt her throat closing and tears welling behind her eyes. She'd thought she had a handle on this, on Chewbacca's death, but seeing the wreck of an entire planet, knowing somewhere in that jumble of rocks were the molecules that had once knit together into a person who had lived and loved, had held her when she was young—it stung. In some ways, Chewie had been a bigger part of her life than her own mother.

Kyp felt her grief and gave her the space of a few moments to adjust. Then he pointed to the holo.

"They did it to make ships," he said softly. "They grow the ships as they grow all of their tools. They feed the young ones on broken planets." He looked significantly at Jaina. "You knew this, right?"

She nodded.

"Right. Coralskippers, bigger ships, all of the things we've seen already. But then there's this."

He magnified yet again.

As they looked at the image, Kyp continued. "Gavin Darklighter saw the Yuuzhan Vong growing a ship the size of the Death Star. Why didn't anyone think that was a serious thing?"

The . . . thing . . . portrayed in the holograph was clearly a Yuuzhan Vong ship. It had the same organic look to it, and in color and alternating textures rough and smooth was much like the larger ships Jaina had already seen. But in form it was quite different.

It spidered across the sky, a huge, multilegged monster with each leg—or arm, or whatever—curving in the same direction, so the whole thing looked like a mad sculptor's attempt to portray a galaxy. It was beautiful and terrible, and it made her mouth dry to look at it.

"It didn't look like that before," Jaina said. "It was just an ovoid."

"What you and Gavin saw was hardly more than a seed," Kyp said. "That thing could swallow Death Stars for lunch. And no one has done *anything*."

"We've had our hands sort of full," she replied, aware that her voice was hushed. "How did you get this? Surely after Rogue Squadron's recon, the Yuuzhan Vong buttoned up the system."

"Oh, indeed they did," Kyp replied. "And for anyone besides someone trained as a pilot *and* a Jedi, I would say it was nearly impossible. But I'm the guy who guided your father through the Maw, using nothing but the most rudimentary command of the Force, and I've come a long way since then. Fluctuations in gravity are always squirreling little hyperspace entry points in and out of existence, spalled off larger ones. The Sernpidal system has been unstable since they destroyed the planet, which is how Darklighter got in. The Yuuzhan Vong have mostly corrected their earlier mistakes, but they can't cover all of them, especially those near the primary—and also when they're creating their own gravitic anomalies."

"Maybe because they think no one would be stupid enough to jump that close to a star?"

"Stupid or not, it worked. Despite that they very nearly

interdicted me. I lost a wingmate and made a jump out that nearly shredded me near a neutron star." He grinned again. "But it was worth it. I got a good, close look."

"You know what it is?"

"Yes. The whole thing isn't on-line yet, but they were putting some of its systems through trials while we were there."

"So what is it?"

"A gravitic weapon."

"Like a dovin basal?"

Kyp laughed. "Dovin basals, the big ones, can pull down a moon. They can generate anomalies that resemble quantum black holes. This thing could collapse a star."

"How do you know that's what it is? Why haven't we seen something like this before?"

"It's taken them a long time to grow it, Jaina. They couldn't grow one out there in the void between the galaxies, could they? And maybe not just any planet will do—maybe there was something special about Sernpidal. But remember, this was one of the first things they did when they began the invasion of our galaxy."

"There is some evidence they've been out on the Rim for at least fifty years," Jaina pointed out.

"I've seen a little evidence of that, too. But they weren't ready to invade, then. Blowing up a planet might have attracted someone's attention." He held up his hands. "I don't know. I only know one thing—that thing has to be stopped, now, before it's operational."

"I still don't understand how you can know what it is," Jaina said. "You've never been shy about jumping to conclusions."

Kyp tapped the holo console again. The view zoomed out.

"This is time lapse," he said softly. "Remember that Sernpidal was a hundred and fifteen thousand kilometers from its primary, which is still the approximate position of this weapon."

Jaina watched, at first not understanding what she was seeing. From the primary's corona, a small flare erupted, something she had seen happen on numerous occasions around numerous stars.

But the flare kept going, first a full solar diameter, then two. And as it grew longer, it gathered strength rather than diminishing, became a ribbon of superheated hydrogen and helium, dimming and cooling as it went but still clearly visible. In the artificial quickness of time lapse, it was only moments before the streamer reached the gigantic Yuuzhan Vong construction.

"Emperor's black bones," Jaina breathed.

"You see?" Kyp said. "Extrapolate. Only about an eighth of its systems seem to be 'alive,' yet it can generate a gravity well powerful enough and focused enough to pull enormous quantities of solar atmosphere over a hundred thousand kilometers. The dovin basal on Sernpidal pales to absolute insignificance next to that. Think of the size of the singularities it can create—big enough to swallow a ship? A *planet*? If we let them take that thing out, *nothing* can stop them."

Speechless, Jaina could only nod in horrified agreement.

FOURTEEN

"Oh, my goodness," C-3PO bleated as the *Falcon* dropped out of hyperspace with a sort of flat thud that sent them all a centimeter into the air. "It's another one of those terrible Yuuzhan Vong interdictors!"

"Relax, Threepio," Han said, his voice so dry he sounded almost bored. "The inertial dampeners are just being a little cranky, that's all. Lando's so-called technicians were a little less than thorough."

"More likely they didn't understand the extent to which this ship is put together with chewstim and wishful thinking," Leia joked. "No one else has *ever* been able to repair this thing except—"

She broke off, and Han knew why. The unfinished thought, *except you and Chewbacca*, was true. He and Chewie had made the *Falcon* galaxy-famous for doing the impossible, but it had almost always involved the Wookiee and him improvising circuits even as their shields were failing.

"You can say it," he told her.

"Look, Han," Leia said softly. "He can never be replaced—"

"No," he replied, more sharply than intended. "Not with Droma, not with you." His voice softened. "But he could never have replaced you, either, Leia. Let's leave it at that, huh? I like my new copilot just fine."

"Thank you. That means a lot to me."

"I mean, she's a little mouthy for my taste, and kinda snooty, but at least she's easy enough on the eyes—even with the new hairdo."

Leia's tender expression was metamorphosing into something less benign when the mass detector bleeped and C-3PO cried, "I told you! I absolutely told you!"

"Threepio," Han snapped, "have you ever been fired from a concussion missile tube?"

"No, sir. Of course, I *did* nearly fall out of the garbage-ejection tube a short time ago, which I must admit was terrifying, simply *terrifying*. I—"

"Threepio!" Han shouted.

C-3PO cocked his head and put one golden finger to the slit that implied his mouth. "Perhaps I should go see what Artoo is doing."

"Yes, do that."

Meanwhile, Leia had been analyzing whatever it was that had come out of hyperspace right behind them.

"It's a freighter," she said.

"A freighter? Here?" They were in occupied space, not far from Tynna.

Leia brought up the profile, revealing a blocky drive married to a long series of detachable storage pods headed up by a narrow habitation compartment. "Kuat Drive Yards *Marl*-class heavy freighter," Leia confirmed.

"Out *here*?" Han repeated incredulously. "She'll be easy pickings for the first Yuuzhan Vong ship she runs into. And where could she be going? Hutt space?"

"Maybe it's a relief vessel," Leia said. "Or a smuggler running weapons to the Hutts."

"That thing's got no legs," Han said. "Any smuggler worth his spice would know better."

"Well, there it is," Leia said.

"I can see that." He set his lips. "I just had an unpleasant thought."

Leia nodded grimly. "I just had the same thought."

"Yeah. Have they seen us yet?"

"I doubt it."

"Let's keep it that way. Run silent and let them pass. We'll see for sure where they're going."

"Why don't we just ask them?"

Han gave her a brief open-mouthed stare. "Boy, do you

have a lot to learn. Let me handle this, willya? I know what I'm doing."

"Right. I've heard that a time or two. I've usually had cause to regret it."

"At least you always *lived* to regret it, sweetheart."

When the *Falcon* powered down, Jacen was deep in meditation. He'd spent hours coaxing his wants, needs, and expectations into corners of his mind far from the conscious, surrendering himself into the silent flow of the Force.

He tuned out the sensations of the Force around him: his mother, the lesser voices of his father and the Noghri, the faint impressions of the droids and the ship itself. He wasn't searching for anything at all, merely trying to become a part of the living Force, detached from the particulars of it. Just to feel it ebbing and flowing through him, not even seeking understanding, for in seeking one often missed what was sought, or came to an understanding tainted by desire.

Desire, like fear and anger, had to be released.

For a brief moment he almost found that center he was searching for, the universe spreading out in its entirety, and in that instant he saw again a vision of the galaxy tipping, of a fundamental imbalance waiting to happen.

There, memory and desire betrayed him. He saw himself facing Warmaster Tsavong Lah, his mother bleeding at his feet. He saw his brother, Anakin, confident and cocky after his escape from Yavin 4. He saw himself, only days before, slaying the two living coralskippers and their pilots.

The death of one diminishes us all. Surely that had to be the case with the Yuuzhan Vong as well, though they didn't appear in the Force.

Which was impossible, if the Force was what the old Jedi Masters said it was.

He actually wished Anakin were here, so they could have one of their arguments. Anakin now held that what they knew as the Force was only a manifestation of something greater, more overarching, something Jedi could only glimpse. To Jacen that felt utterly wrong, and yet it was hard to dispute that it fit the facts as they stood now.

Anakin also thought of the Force as little more than an energy source, something with which the Jedi worked their wills. That also felt wrong, and yet Jacen now seriously questioned the opposing view, that the Force had a will of its own, and that the proper role of the Jedi was to understand that will and work through it.

Neither extreme felt right in Jacen's gut, and yet he had no answer of his own. He had abandoned his vow not to use the Force, but it had given him no more certainty about when or how it *ought* to be used, or what a Jedi *ought* to do. Again, Anakin's certainty was both enviable and worrisome. Anakin was determined to oppose evil, and just as determined that he could know what evil was, even without the Force to enlighten him.

Maybe Anakin was right. Jacen knew that he couldn't just stand by and do nothing. He had been given gifts and learned to use them, and it was incumbent on him that he find the proper way to do so. But how was he to judge? *Who* was he to judge?

Maybe he had been wrong to strike out on his own, to leave the apprenticeship of Master Skywalker. But somehow, he knew, Uncle Luke's path could not be his, no more than Anakin's could be.

As it was, he took each situation as he found it. He'd hated killing the Yuuzhan Vong, but the situation hadn't suggested or allowed for any alternative other than the death or capture of his family. It may have been a bad choice, but at the time it was the only one he was capable of making.

He tried to untangle himself from this internal dialogue, but the more he tried, the more frustrated he became, and he was on the verge of admitting failure anyway when something changed around him.

He came back, bringing the near world into focus, and found everything off but emergency lights.

"Dear me!" C-3PO moaned. "I knew it!"

"Threepio?"

"Master Jacen! You're conscious!"

"What's going on, Threepio? How long have we been powered down?"

"Ever since that mass came out of hyperspace," C-3PO said. "I wanted to help, but Captain Solo was quite unpleasant."

"I'm sure it's not you he was mad at, Threepio," Jacen assured the droid. "I'll go see what's going on."

"Look there," his father was saying as Jacen entered the cockpit.

"I see," Leia breathed. "Yuuzhan Vong."

Jacen studied the long-range scanner readouts. "They're attacking that freighter?" he asked.

"No," Han said. "They ain't attacking it, kid. They're escorting it."

"Escorting? Where are we?"

"One jump from the Cha Raaba system," Han replied.

"Cha Raaba? That's where Ylesia is, right?"

"Kid gets a gold epaulet," Han murmured.

"And Ylesia is where the Peace Brigade is headquartered," Leia added. "So that ship—"

"Supplies for the Brigade and the Vong," Han concluded. "Couldn't have figured it better myself. Looks like Lando was right, only if the Peace Brigade is moving stuff inside Yuuzhan Vong space, someone must be moving it to them from *outside*."

"Well, we have to stop them!" Leia said.

"What?" Jacen asked. "Why? They haven't attacked us. They don't even see us."

"True enough," Han said. "Gives us a nice advantage."

"But—I thought this mission was about setting up networks for refugees and intelligence. No one said anything about taking the fight to the enemy."

"Hey, Jacen," Han said, "it's not as if we're going out of our way to harass collaborationist shipping, though why the thought of doing so should upset you I can't imagine. But there they are, and here *we* are—"

"Can we just disable them?" Jacen asked.

"Jacen," Han said, turning to face him, his eyebrows lifting. "Jacen, in case you didn't notice, there's a *war* on. Now, I know you've gotten all mystical on me lately, and I'm trying to be understanding, but if you expect the rest of us to go along with your philosophy of the day, think again. You stick with the Force and let me deal with this. Anyway, for all you know that freighter could be full of slaves and sacrifices. You really want to leave them to the mercy of the Vong?"

"I don't feel anything like that in the Force," Jacen said firmly.

"Jacen," Leia chimed in. "You know I respect what you're trying to do, but you have to understand something—"

"I understand," Jacen interrupted. "I understand that you told me this mission was about something I could get on board with, and now in the middle of the flight you're changing the coordinates. I'm not trying to tell you what to believe. But when you brought *me* along on this trip—"

"When I *brought* you along on this trip," Han roared, "I never said you could be *captain,* and I didn't tell you this is a democracy. Jacen, I love you. But sit down, shut up, and do as you're told."

Jacen was so stunned by his father's anger that it did not, at that moment, even occur to him to continue the argument.

"Great," Han said. "So here's what we're going to do. We're going to take out that Yuuzhan Vong escort, and then we're going to make the freighter an offer."

"Offer?" Leia said.

"Yep. We'll offer not to blow her open if she surrenders quietly." He checked his panel. "Power in five minutes. Jacen, get down to the turbolaser."

Jacen hesitated, a painful, sickening knot growing in his gut. "Okay."

"And I want you to use it if needed."

"I will. Sir." And with that he stalked out of the cockpit.

FIFTEEN

The villip squirmed, stretching itself to its limits in an attempt to portray the fine mass of tendrils that composed the living headdress of Master Tjulan Kwaad. It did not entirely succeed, but did so sufficiently well that Nen Yim was able to tell that the senior master of her domain was agitated.

"Why disturb me over such a question?" Tjulan Kwaad asked. "You have access to the Qang qahsa, do you not?"

"I do indeed, Master Kwaad," Nen Yim replied. "However, the qahsa does not grant a mere adept entry to protocols beyond the fifth cortex."

"Nor should it. Adepts are not ready for such secrets. Especially adepts such as yourself. You and your deceased master disgraced our domain."

"That is true," Nen Yim said carefully. "However, Warmaster Tsavong Lah chose to pardon me and . . . reward me with a chance to further serve the glorious Yun-Yuuzhan. I should think my domain would do as much."

"Do not presume what your domain would do," Tjulan Kwaad replied testily. "Even the Yim crèche would not do as much. The warmaster is a warrior, covered in glory and more than ample as a warrior. But he is not a shaper, and he docs not know how dangerous your heresies are."

"Those were the heresies of my master, not mine," Nen Yim lied.

"Yet you did not report her."

Yun-Harla aid me, Nen Yim prayed. The mistress of trickery loved lies as much as Yun-Yammka loved battle. "How could discipline be maintained if every adept felt free to question her master?"

"You could have reported her to *me*," Tjulan Kwaad roared. "You owe fealty to me as lord of your domain. Mezhan Kwaad was as much my subordinate as you. That you neglected that relationship will never be forgotten!"

"My judgment failed, Master. That does not change the fact that this ship is dying, and I need your help."

"Each of us begins to die the instant we are born. Our ships are no different. That is existence, Adept." He spoke her title as if it hurt his mouth to do so.

Undeterred by his ire, Nen Yim pressed on. "Master, is it not true that the Yuuzhan Vong need every breath of every one of us to complete the task of conquering the infidels?"

The master laughed harshly and without a trace of real humor. "Look around at the misfits on your ship, and you will know the answer. Were they worthy, they would be at the point of our talons."

"An arm must drive the talons," Nen Yim replied. "A heart must pump the blood to nourish the muscles that propel the arm."

"Phahg. A metaphor is a preening lie."

"Yes, Master." Her experiments had yielded mostly frustration. She had been able—without resort to ancient protocols—to coax neurons into reproduction and shape ganglia that could perform many of the operations of the brain. She could probably, given time, shape an entirely new brain, but as she'd explained to her initiate, Suung, that would not solve the problem. She needed to regenerate the old brain, complete with its memories and eccentricities. Anything else she did only delayed the inevitable. Further, any master who examined her work would know instantly that she had been practicing heresy, and then her efforts to save the worldship would end quite decisively. She had hoped that the knowledge in the vast Qang qahsa library rikyams of the shapers would yield a helpful protocol at some cortex beyond her access, but if a master of her own domain would not help her, no one would.

"I thank you for your time, Master Tjulan Kwaad."

"Do not disturb me again." The villip smoothed back into its normal shape.

She sat for a time, tendrils bunched in despair, until her novice entered.

"How may I serve you today, Adept?" Suung Aruh asked.

Nen Yim did not spare him a glance. "The freezing of the arm has further diseased the maw luur. Take the other students and floss the recham forteps with saline jetters."

"It will be done," Suung replied. He turned to leave, but then hesitated. "Adept?" he said.

"What is it?"

"I believe you can save the *Baanu Miir*. I believe the gods are with you. And I thank you for tending to my education. I did not know how ignorant I was. Now I have some measure of it."

Nen Yim's sight clouded, the protective membrane over her eyes reacting to sudden intense emotion as it did to light irritation. She wondered briefly if anyone knew why such dissimilar things should provoke the same reflex. If it *was* known, she had never heard it. Perhaps that knowledge, too, was beyond the fifth cortex.

"The gods will save us or they will not, Initiate," she replied at last. "It is not to me you should direct your confidence."

"Yes, Adept," he said, in a subdued voice.

She regarded him. "Your progress has been quite satisfactory, Suung Aruh. In the hands of a master you could be shaped into a most useful adept."

"Thank you, Adept," Suung replied, trying to hide a look of surprised gratification. "I go now to my task."

As he left, she noticed the villip pulsing for attention. Wondering what new sarcoma was gnawing at the fabric of her life, she rose and stroked it.

It was Master Tjulan Kwaad again.

"Master," she acknowledged.

"I have reconsidered, Adept. I am unswayed by your arguments, but I feel it foolish to leave you unsupervised lest you bring more shame to us all. I have dispatched a master to govern you. He will arrive within two days. Obey him well."

The villip cleared before she could answer. She stood staring at it as a beast stares at the wound that is killing it.

It hadn't occurred to her that Tjulan Kwaad would *send* a master, only that he might find the protocol and transmit it to her. A master, here, would see what she had done, and know.

Perhaps the new master would save *Baanu Miir,* and that was good. But Adept Nen Yim would soon embrace death.

SIXTEEN

The interrogation chamber was a bleak, washed-out yellow room on the third floor of a building painted entirely in the same color. A sickly sweet scent like burned sugar and hair blended with ammonia seemed to ooze from the flaking duraplast, and the sickly light of ancient argon arc fixtures blanched any real color that entered the building.

Brought in in stun cuffs, Anakin and Tahiri had been hauled through a lower floor seething with judicials, prisoners, and clerks to this nearly abandoned area of the building. There the two Jedi had been separated and placed in different rooms. He could still feel Tahiri's presence, of course, and not far away, which was comforting.

"We have witnesses now who substantiate the charge of murder," the judicial with the bruised eye—Lieutenant Themion, as it turned out—informed him.

"Right. They killed the Rodian," Anakin said.

"I'm talking now about the man *you* killed."

"We didn't kill anyone," Anakin protested. "We saw someone in trouble—"

"A Jedi, like yourself."

"Yes. We were trying to help him when the Peace Brigaders starting blasting at us."

"The way I hear it, *you* attacked them."

"My friend drew her weapon, yes," Anakin replied. "They were murdering the Rodian."

"Then you charged them, fought, and shot one with a blaster."

"No!" Anakin said. "How many times do I have to tell

you this? One of them shot at me, missed, and hit the other guy. I didn't kill anyone, and neither did my friend."

"We have witnesses who saw it differently."

"You mean the other Peace Brigaders, don't you?"

"And some of the vagrants in the crowd."

That took Anakin aback. "Why . . . why would any of them say that?" he wondered.

"Maybe because it's true," Themion suggested.

"No, it's not true. They're lying, too. Maybe the Peace Brigade forced them to." *Or maybe you did, Lieutenant Themion.*

"Let's back up," Themion said. "You saw the Rodian struggling with the Peace Brigaders. Rodians are a vile, murderous lot. Did it ever occur to you that maybe he had *done* something? That the officers of the Peace Brigade were just doing their duty?"

"The Peace Brigade is a collaborationist organization," Anakin said hotly. "They sell us out to the Yuuzhan Vong."

"The Peace Brigade is a *registered* organization," Themion informed him. "They are licensed to make arrests, and to deal with those who resist arrest." He scratched his chin. "They are certainly entitled to defend themselves against offworld, troublemaking Jedi," he added.

Uh-oh, Anakin thought. So his suspicion had been correct. The police and the Peace Brigade were in this together.

"Am I entitled to an advocate?" Anakin asked.

"One has been assigned you."

"When can we meet?"

"Not until your trial, of course."

"You mean my sentencing."

The officer smiled. "It might go easier on you if you tell us the rest. Who sent you. Which ship is yours. Your name."

"I want to see the ambassador from Coruscant."

"Yeah? I'm afraid I don't have that comm ID handy. If you want to call someone on your ship, and have *them* contact the ambassador, that's fine."

Right. Then they'll get Corran, too.

"No, thanks," Anakin said.

The officer stepped forward quickly and slapped him so hard his head rang.

Tahiri, wherever she was, felt it. She responded in the Force in one of those rare, clear-as-transparisteel moments. *Anakin!* And pain, and fear, and anger.

"Tahiri!" Anakin shouted. "No!"

"Your friend has already confessed," Themion said. "She was stubborn, too." He hit Anakin again. This time Anakin faded a little from the blow to reduce the impact, but it still hurt.

Somewhere near, a storm was gathering.

"Don't hit me again," Anakin said sternly.

Themion misunderstood. "Aw, does that hurt, little Jedi? Try this." He pulled a stun baton from his belt.

"Really," Anakin said.

Themion raised the weapon. At the same moment, the door wrenched open with a squeal of metal. Tahiri stood there, a blaster in one hand.

"*Do-ro'ik vong pratte!*" she shouted.

Themion, open-mouthed, turned to face her and she hit him with a Force blast that threw him three meters. He would have gone much farther, but the jaundiced wall stopped him with prejudice, and he collapsed, groaning.

"I warned you," Anakin said.

Tahiri rushed to his side. "Are you all right?" she asked. "I felt them hitting you."

"I'm fine," Anakin said, rising from the chair. Unknown to the officer, he'd already unlocked his stun cuffs using the Force; now he shucked them from his wrists.

"You're not fine," Tahiri said, touching the side of his head. He winced. "You see?" she said. She turned back toward Themion, who was trying to rise. "You smelly Jawa, I'm going to—"

"You're going to put the stun cuffs on him and that's *all,*" Anakin said.

"He deserves worse. He's a liar and a coward who beats helpless people." Her eyes narrowed.

"Stay out of my mind, you stinking Jedi," Themion snarled.

"Give me the blaster, Tahiri."

She handed it to Anakin without looking.

"Now," Anakin said. "You let her put these cuffs on you, or I'll let her do whatever she wants."

Themion let her. Then Anakin leaned around the doorway. A blaster bolt greeted him—down the hall, another judicial was rushing forward.

The shot missed, and he ducked the next one. He felt another surge in the Force, and the judicial went flying into the corridor wall. The impact knocked his senses out of him.

"I think we'd better leave," Tahiri said, from behind him.

"I think you're right," Anakin replied. He knelt and took the guard's blaster and dialed it down to the lowest setting. He took the stun baton, too.

"After we find our lightsabers," Tahiri said.

"*If* we can find them," Anakin cautioned. "They took mine somewhere downstairs. Or at least I think so."

They reached the turbolift with a minimum of effort.

"Be ready when we reach the bottom floor," Anakin said. "They're sure to be ready for us. One of these guys must have called down by now."

Tahiri nodded, an unsettling smile on her face.

"Tahiri?"

"Yes."

"Beware of anger."

"I'm not angry," she said. "Just ready."

Anakin eyed her dubiously, but they didn't have time to go over it now. "Stand against the sides of the lift. They may shoot before it even opens."

She did as he suggested. A moment later, the doors sighed open.

No sizzling bolts of energy greeted them. Instead they were met by laughter and shouts of encouragement. Puzzled, Anakin peeked around the lift door.

Two judicials stood in a ring formed by their comrades. They were swinging clumsily at one another with lightsabers. One was Anakin's, the other Tahiri's.

"Use the Force!" someone hooted, as the man wielding Anakin's violet blade accidentally sliced a desk in half.

It took only a minor suggestion that they weren't there for Anakin and Tahiri to walk out of the lift and around the edge of the excited crowd. Apparently, either no one upstairs *had* called down or—more likely—no one here had bothered to answer the call. In any event, everyone in the building seemed completely engrossed in the "duel."

"Keep cool, Tahiri," Anakin said as they drew near the door to the outside. "I have an idea."

The fellow holding Anakin's lightsaber made a clumsy jab at the other judicial, who replied with an equally inept circular parry. Anakin took that opportunity to use the Force to wrench his weapon from the officer's hands—it looked as if the parry had disarmed him. The lightsaber flew high in the air, sending everyone in its possible trajectory scurrying away. It struck the argon arc fixture in the ceiling, then continued on to strike the power grid node on the other side of the room. The room plunged into darkness, save for the two lightsabers, both of which suddenly vanished.

On the street, Tahiri burst into laughter.

"Don't laugh," Anakin said. "Run!"

"I'm just thinking we probably saved their lives," Tahiri replied. "The way they were going, they would have lost at least a hand or two. If—" She stopped as Anakin abruptly halted.

"What?" Tahiri asked.

"Maybe running is the second-best idea," Anakin said, pointing at the police airspeeder parked in front of the station.

The two jumped into the rusty orange vehicle. It had an old-fashioned computer input, and it took Anakin only a few seconds to slice into the security system. Just as a mob of officers burst onto the street, he bypassed the code and started the speeder. He throttled it up to full as he turned the corner and climbed, ignoring the craft's artificially frantic warning that he was not in an authorized traffic lane.

A few blaster bolts seared by, along with a number of obscenities. Then the judicial ward was behind them.

*   *   *

By the time they reached the spaceport, Anakin and
Tahiri had picked up a respectable tail and were starting to
dodge long-range fire. For that reason, when Anakin saw
the *Lucre*'s cargo port open, he drove the nimble craft directly into it, nearly clipping a very surprised Corran Horn
while doing so.

"Sithspit!" the older Jedi shouted. "What do you think—"

"Close the landing ramp, Corran! Close it now!"

"What? What have you—"

Several bolts fizzling against the bulkhead cut Corran
short. On reflex he slapped the close mechanism, carefully
not showing himself through the port.

"I take it we need to fly?" Corran said as Anakin and
Tahiri dismounted the speeder. *What have you done now,
Anakin?*

"Might not be a bad idea," Anakin replied. He was
trying not to sound cocky, and failing.

"I'll be very interested to hear why," Corran snapped.

"Fly now," Anakin said, heading for the cockpit. "I'll explain later."

"Explain *while*," Corran said as they settled behind the
controls.

"Right," Anakin said as the engines begin to whine to
life. "It started when we felt a Jedi in trouble . . ."

"You're right; it can wait," Corran decided. Hearing the
story was probably only going to make him angrier, a distraction he didn't need right now. "And *I'm* flying. You calculate a series of jumps, at least three, and close together."

"To where?"

"Anywhere. No, strike that. Not back toward the *Errant
Venture*. Coreward. We'll find the *Venture* later."

"Okay," Anakin said. "Working on solutions now."

"And hang on. Tahiri, you strapped in?"

"Yes, sir."

Corran rose on repulsors and kicked the engines violently
into light. The *Lucre* sliced through the murky clouds, where
Corran steepened their angle, watching his sensor readouts,

wondering how long it would take the Eriaduans to scramble their fighters, trying desperately to remember what he knew of their planetary defense from his days in CorSec.

Soon enough, both questions were answered: not long and not nearly enough, respectively. As several heavily armed interceptors closed from several sides, he cleared his throat.

"Any time now, Anakin."

"Hang on," Anakin replied. "I have three jumps. I'm rechecking the last bit."

"No time. Lay it in and let's go."

The transport's shields trembled beneath a terrific blow. The port opaqued.

"Wow!" Anakin said. "What—?"

"That was no interceptor," Corran said grimly. "That was a planetary defense laser. Are we laid in?"

"Sort of . . ."

"Great." Corran broke atmosphere, engaged the hyperdrive, and the stars sleeted out of existence.

The first jump took them no more than half a light-year, and Corran had time to see that one of the interceptors had correctly guessed their vector before they jumped again, seconds later. The second jump was longer, followed immediately by a third. It was hard to tell, but it looked as if they lost their tail on that one.

"How long is this jump, Anakin?"

"A few hours."

"Great. Then why don't you explain to me, in great detail, why you were joyriding on a judicial speeder. And do *not* leave out the part that explains why people were shooting at *me,* and why you two disobeyed my direct order."

"I understand why you did it," Corran said when the two had finished relating their story. "But you shouldn't have."

"Why?" Tahiri demanded. "Wouldn't you have done the same?"

Corran hesitated fractionally. "No. I felt Kelbis Nu, too, but so dimly I couldn't figure out where he was. But even if I'd known, I have both of you to think of. As you should have been thinking of me. Anakin, you've always been impulsive—"

"This was my fault," Tahiri interrupted.

"Yes. Emphatically, *yes*. But Anakin set the example. Didn't either of you learn anything on Yavin Four?"

"Yes," Tahiri said. "I learned that the Jedi can count on no one but ourselves."

"Really? Your dad is no Jedi, Talon Karrde is no Jedi, nor were the people under his command who died trying to rescue you."

"Well, no one was going to rescue Kelbis," Anakin pointed out.

"Including you."

"But we might have. We had to try."

Corran looked at them both tiredly.

"This isn't over," he said. "When we get back to the *Errant Venture,* we're going to have this talk again, with Kam and Tionne and anyone else I think of who might be able to get a word past this youthful, idiotic self-confidence of yours. But for the moment—you say Kelbis said something about Yag'Dhul?"

"His last word," Anakin said. "It took a lot out of him to say even that. He really wanted me to know something. I think Yag'Dhul may be in danger."

Corran's eyes narrowed, reflecting a sudden, plunging-stomach suspicion. "Anakin, *where* is this jump taking us?"

"You said Coreward," Anakin replied innocently.

"Tell me we aren't going to pop out in the Yag'Dhul system."

"We aren't going to pop out in the Yag'Dhul system," Anakin told him.

"Good," Corran said, relieved.

"We're going to come out really near it, though," Anakin added.

"Why you—" Corran held back a series of specifically Corellian words he that *really* wanted to use. But Tahiri was only fourteen. Would he make it through Valin's and Jysella's teenage years without turning to the dark side?

Probably not. "How close?" he said, trying to sound not quite as irritated as he was.

"One jump. I thought you'd at least like to check it out."

"Anakin! Supplies! We were just supposed to get supplies, not mount a search-and-rescue–recon mission!" He buried his face in his hands. "Now I understand those pitying looks Solusar was giving me before we left."

Corran wished Mirax were here. She knew how to deal with this kind of thing. "How long before realspace?"

"Another five minutes."

"Terrific. Now listen to me very carefully. I am the captain of this vessel. From now on you don't even visit the 'fresher without my say-so, either of you. You will follow my orders. That means, by the way, that you do not imagine or guess at my orders, but actually wait until you hear them."

"I *was* following orders," Anakin protested. "You said to jump Coreward."

"Don't insult us both, Anakin. You're better than that."

"Yes, Captain."

"Good." Corran settled himself before the controls and awaited the reversion to sublight speeds.

They reentered realspace with a pockmarked asteroid nearly filling their field of vision. Corran swore and decelerated, cutting hard toward the nearest horizon of the rock. A jagged crater edge loomed, and he knew they weren't going to make the angle. Desperately he switched on the repulsorlift.

The *Lucre* squealed a metallic protest as the field bounced them none too gently away from the asteroid. Corran let out his breath and killed their motion relative to the planetoid until he could get his bearings.

A good thing, too, because in the surrounding space he made out hundreds of asteroids, densely packed. It would take a good deal of care to fly out of it unscathed.

"You could have warned me about the asteroid field," Corran told Anakin.

"I would have if there had been one," Anakin said in a strange voice.

"It wasn't on the charts?"

"It's still not," Anakin said. "Look at the sensor readings."

Corran did, and swore again as everything snapped into focus. Aside from the cratered stone he'd nearly hit coming out of hyperspace, the rest of the objects near enough to see had the organic but all-too-familiar lines of ships grown from yorik coral.

"This is a Yuuzhan Vong fleet," Anakin said.

SEVENTEEN

"I've located the *Errant Venture*," Luke said. "Not far from Clak'dor. We'll be there in a day or so."

Mara nodded. "Good," she said shortly.

"How are you feeling?"

Mara shot him a dirty look. "Skywalker, why do you ask questions you know the answer to? I feel overweight. My ankles feel as if I have stun cuffs permanently fastened to them. I'm always nauseated. Nobody told me I would get nauseated again. I thought that part was over early on."

"So did I," Luke replied. He pressed his lips together. He sensed more than mere irritation behind Mara's words. There was a kind of defensiveness about her outburst. "Is there something you want to tell me?" he asked gently.

"If I *wanted* to tell you, I would, wouldn't I?"

"Not if you thought it might upset me," Luke said.

"You've got me. I hate that shirt. In fact, I think you're a crummy dresser, period."

"You bought me this shirt," Luke reminded her. "Mara, are you sick again? Have you come out of remission?"

Mara studied her fingernails. "Cilghal's keeping tabs on that," she said, still with that underlying air of defiance.

"And?"

Mara's face pinched tight. "The disease isn't present in our child."

"Is it active in you again?" Luke demanded.

Mara watched the starfield for several long minutes. "Maybe," she admitted. "Maybe."

* * *

As predicted, they found the *Errant Venture* about one standard day later. The Star Destroyer opened a berth for them, and he navigated the *Jade Shadow* in without incident.

A small crowd awaited Luke, Mara, and Cilghal. Booster Terrik, captain and owner of the *Errant Venture,* stood in front, a great gundark of a human with an impressive, well-tended beard and curling mustachios. Just behind him and to the side were three more humans, two in Jedi robes. Luke recognized Kam Solusar by his sure stance, haunted features, and receding blond hair. His wife, Tionne, was as unmistakable; her hair was a silver river cascading down her shoulders. The third human was another woman, clad in a dun jumpsuit, her black-glass hair cut in a bob: Mirax Terrik Horn, Booster's daughter and sometimes business partner. She was married to Corran Horn, who was conspicuous by his absence.

Behind them were some thirty-odd youngsters of at least seven species. This was what remained of the academy on Yavin 4, the praxeum that had trained almost a hundred Jedi. Now Yavin 4 was occupied by the Yuuzhan Vong, the temple that had housed his students destroyed. With half the galaxy hunting for Jedi gifts to present to the Yuuzhan Vong warmaster, the only safe place for the moment was no place. For months, Booster had been jumping randomly about the galaxy to keep the students hidden.

Two others were missing as well, Luke noticed. Anakin Solo and Tahiri Veila. Knowing Anakin, that was a bad sign. Luke made a mental note to ask after him as soon as the pleasantries were over.

"Look there," Booster growled, as Luke and Mara descended the landing ramp. "There's the man who made the once mighty and terribly feared Booster Terrik into a glorified baby-sitter. I ought to space you right now, Jedi."

"I can't tell you how grateful I am," Luke said. Though he knew Booster meant well, he didn't have the energy or inclination for banter at the moment.

"You ought to be. Jedi brats." He mussed the hair of a young boy with brown hair, then the girl next to him. "With some notable exceptions, of course," he amended.

"You're funny, Grandpa," the boy said. Then he turned his brown eyes toward the *Jade Shadow* and Luke and Mara. "Hello, Masters."

"Hello, Valin," Luke replied. "I hope you've been staying out of trouble and concentrating on your lessons."

"I have, Master Skywalker. I promise."

"And the rest of you?" Luke directed his gaze over the assembled students.

In return he got a chorus of assents and barely bridled enthusiasm.

"Well, that's good, then. Kam, Tionne, Mirax. Good to see you."

There was a round of clasping and hugs, and then a moment of awkward silence.

"I guess we need to talk," Luke said at last. "I need to fill you all in on a few things."

"That's all very well," Mirax said, "but Mara looks tired."

"I'm okay," Mara disagreed.

Mirax shook her head. "I've had two kids. I know that look. Let me take you someplace where you can freshen up, and let the rest of them have their conference. Luke doesn't need you for that, does he?"

"I guess not." She shot Luke a look, and he knew what it meant. *My health concerns are private. You will not speak of them.*

He nodded to let her know he understood.

Out loud, what he said was, "If you're tired, go with Mirax. If I leave something out, you can fill them in later."

Mara smiled wanly. "Put on a little weight and everyone treats you like an invalid."

"You'll see how long *that* lasts after the big event," Mirax said. "When Baby Skywalker has a little accident, everyone will magically think you're plenty strong and capable."

"Boy. And I thought this was the best part."

"Yep," Mirax said. "That's exactly what I'm telling you. Come along now. I've got a comfy couch with your name on it."

"I'll come with you, too, if you don't mind," Cilghal said.

"Of course," Mirax replied. "The more the merrier."

They sat around Booster's circular conference table, absorbing the news.

"Do you really think you would have been arrested?" Kam asked, folding the fingers of both hands together into one very large fist.

"I honestly don't know," Luke replied. "Hamner thinks the whole thing was a ploy engineered to get me away from Coruscant. He may be right. Borsk Fey'lya has never been one of our strongest supporters, but I can't see him thinking that arresting me would solve any of his problems. In fact, I think we narrowly escaped an insurrection *because* he ordered my arrest."

"Last I heard," Booster said, "the senate was divided over the Jedi question. Maybe it's tipped, and Fey'lya was just being the politician he is."

"Maybe," Luke agreed. "In a way, it doesn't matter. What does matter is what we do now."

"And that is?"

"Right now, Han, Leia, Jacen, and a number of other allies are out there creating a network to help Jedi or whoever else needs to escape from danger zones—to get us in and out of Yuuzhan Vong and Vong-sympathetic space as safely as possible. I have no doubt that in time, that network will be in place. But when that day comes, we need a terminus—a planet that only we know about, that only we can find. We can't just keep hopping around the galaxy—we have to have a home base to plan and act from. If Han and Leia are creating a great river, we need a sea for it to flow into."

"Well, that sounds good to me," Terrik said. "I certainly don't want *all* of you robe-wearing freeloaders on my ship. You have someplace in mind?"

"Frankly, no. I was hoping for some suggestions."

"The Maw installation," Kam said.

"We're already using that," Luke said, "but the Maw is pretty well known. Almost impossible to navigate in, but well known. Any number of collaborators could at least point the Yuuzhan Vong there, and we still don't know the limits of their technology. We're risking a base there, a safe house, but I won't place the future hope of the Jedi in that exposed a position."

"If there were another cluster of black holes like the Maw . . . ," Tionne began.

"Well, there is," Booster said. "Or at least a place like it. Worse, actually."

"Where?"

"Think. What makes the Maw such a nightmare? All those mass shadows, butted up against each other. Gravity bending space and time so much that almost no hyperspace route is a safe one. There's another place like that."

Kam nodded. "The Deep Core," he said. "Terrik, you're crazy."

"You're the one who suggested the Maw," Booster pointed out.

"Yes, but we know how to get in and out of the Maw."

"Somebody *found* the way," Booster said.

"Right. Somebody crazy."

"Kyp found it, too," Luke said. "Using the Force. If Kyp could do it at the Maw, we can do it in the Core. It just won't be easy."

"A world of our own," Tionne lilted. "A Jedi world, safe for the children. It's a worthy goal."

"Worth a song or two, wouldn't you say?" Booster asked.

Tionne, well known for her ballads, nodded and enigmatically smiled.

Not so enigmatic to Kam. His eyes went very wide. "Us?" he said.

His wife continued smiling. "The students will have Luke, at least until Mara gives birth, and I suspect for a bit after. And they will have Corran when he returns. We have been too long sedentary, Kam. *You* have. This will be good for us."

Booster bellowed laughter. "I suspect we've found your madman, Solusar."

Kam set his shoulders uncomfortably. "Yes, perhaps you have," he acknowledged.

"Speaking of Corran," Luke said, after smaller versions of Booster's laughter had wandered around the table, "where is he? I didn't see Anakin either."

"Boy was getting deck fever," Booster said. "He went with Corran for supplies."

"They took Tahiri with them?"

"I don't know about that," Booster said.

"He did," Kam said.

Booster's eyes narrowed in anger. "Without asking my permission? Who's captain here, anyway? When that Cor-Sec whelp my daughter married gets back, I'm going to teach him who is, that's for sure."

"I'm sure Corran knew what he was doing," Luke said.

"Oh, I wouldn't go that far," Kam averred. "He took Anakin and Tahiri, together? No, I doubt he has any idea whatsoever what he's doing."

EIGHTEEN

The *Lucre* was a Codru-Ji sword dancer gone mad, gyring, whirling across a stage of plasma bursts and coralskippers flying as thick as swarming insects.

"Twenty kilometers down, another thousand to go before clearing the fleet," Corran said coldly.

Anakin didn't answer as the *Lucre* dropped into a sudden, hard-out sprint, a bid to close that impossible gap.

It wasn't going to happen. Coralskippers contracted around the ship in a sphere, and the shields flared with the effort of absorbing the energy of the constant plasma bombardment. All too soon, the shields failed, and the next round of hits were to the drive.

"So long," Corran said. Then the *Lucre* was an expanding fury of superheated helium and metal fragments.

"Wow," Tahiri breathed. Her voice sounded tinny in the helmet of Anakin's vac suit. "That didn't take long."

"No," Anakin said. It had only been minutes since they set the ship off on its preprogrammed suicide course and launched themselves from the hatch under cover of a barrage of laser and missile fire. In the five minutes it had taken them to reach the asteroid's surface, the *Lucre*'s brief solo career had begun and ended.

"No gawking," Corran said. "There's a fissure over there. Let's move toward that. They might get the bright idea to search here at any moment."

Tahiri took a step in the desired direction and was suddenly floating away from the surface. She yelped, flailing her arms.

Corran caught her foot, and her momentum pulled him

off his feet. Anakin grabbed them both with the Force and brought them back to the asteroid's surface.

"Don't walk," Corran advised. "The gravity here is negligible, just enough to give your inner ear a sense of up and down. Don't let it fool you—the escape velocity of this rock is about five kilometers an hour, if that. Pull yourselves along." He maneuvered himself so his body was parallel to the surface and began doing just that, grasping at the uneven stone. Tahiri and Anakin followed his example, as silly as it felt. Anakin glanced often at the space around them, but none of the Yuuzhan Vong ships seemed to be moving in their direction.

They reached the fissure, a cleft that dropped slantwise into the asteroid for about twenty meters. Because of the angle, at the bottom of it they could see only a narrow slice of starscape. That was good, because it meant only a small slice of the starscape could see *them*.

"Now what? Anakin asked.

"Now we wait." Corran carefully shrugged off the metal case he'd worn like a backpack. "With the survival kit, we can hold out for maybe three days. Hopefully the fleet will move out before then, and we can activate the emergency beacon. Given considerably more luck, a ship will happen by and pick us up."

"That's a lot of luck," Anakin remarked.

"Well, if nothing else, maybe this will teach you that luck isn't the bottomless well you seem to think it is," Corran said.

"We might have tried to run for it," Anakin said peevishly.

"You saw what happened."

"I can fly better than a computer."

"Not that much better," Corran said.

"But now we're stuck here. This fleet must be the danger Kelbis Nu was trying to warn us about. If we wait for it to leave, it'll be too late to warn Yag'Dhul."

"Well, you have a blaster and a lightsaber," Corran said dryly. "Given your opinion of yourself, you might as well take on the fleet with those."

Anakin felt Corran's sarcasm like a physical blow, and it stung. "I'm sorry," he said. "I thought I was doing the right thing."

"No doubt," Corran replied.

"Captain Horn," Tahiri said suddenly, "if it weren't for Anakin trying to do the right thing, your kids would be Yuuzhan Vong captives right now. In fact, along with me and the rest of the candidates, they would basically *be* Yuuzhan Vong. He got us out of that; he'll get us out of this."

Corran was silent for a moment. "You know I'm grateful for what you did on Yavin Four, Anakin. Tahiri's right. But I'm afraid you learned the wrong lesson there, and Tahiri along with you. You can't stroll up to *every* reactor going supercritical and walk away again. You aren't immortal, and you aren't invincible. So far your quick thinking and strength in the Force have just barely managed to counterbalance your recklessness. But one day, the fraction is going to tip on the other side of the line. Maybe it already has. If you don't come to terms with that, you're going to get a nasty surprise."

Anakin thought of Chewie, of Daeshara'cor, of Vua Rapuung, the Yuuzhan Vong who had saved his life. All dead now. "Everyone gets a nasty surprise someday," he said. "I'd rather get it standing up than lying down."

"Getting killed isn't the only danger, Anakin. You rely heavily on the Force. It informs your every action. Just now you pulled Tahiri and me back to the surface of the asteroid with it, when you might have done so with your hand."

"And I might have drifted off with you. It was easier, more certain."

"And you made that decision reflexively, without thinking. In emergency situations, in battle, you make a lot of decisions like that. If you make the wrong one—"

"I'll go to the dark side," Anakin said. "So I keep hearing."

"Being cavalier about it won't help."

"Captain Horn, I've thought about the dark side for most of my life. My mother named me after the man who became Darth Vader. The Emperor touched me through her womb.

Every night I had nightmares that ended with me in my grandfather's armor. With all due respect, I think I've probably thought a lot more about the dark side than anyone I know."

"Probably. Inoculation doesn't make you immune."

"It does in medicine," Anakin said.

"I'm guilty of a bad analogy then. I do *not* stand corrected on the point."

"This is going to be a fun three days," Tahiri said.

A standard day passed, though of course they only knew that by their chronometers. The asteroid wheeled slowly, about once every four hours. Anakin spent much of his time watching the fleet through the narrow window the fissure left them, trying to estimate how many ships there were. With electrobinoculars, he managed to reckon at least four capital ship analogs and as many as thirty smaller warcraft. That wasn't counting coralskippers, of which about one-third were at any given time flying patrol. The rest remained docked to their larger brethren.

Anakin drew his lightsaber and closed his eyes, concentrating, trying to feel the Yuuzhan Vong ships through the blade's lambent heart. They were there, a faint presence, with none of the clarity offered by the Force. On the other hand, the Force offered nothing at all where the Yuuzhan Vong were concerned.

"You *can* feel them," Corran's voice burred.

Anakin turned. Corran was pulling himself gingerly along the fissure wall.

"Yeah. A little."

"I wonder if we can get our hands on a few more of—what did you call them?"

"Lambents."

On Yavin 4, the crystal in Anakin's lightsaber had been destroyed by a close brush with the singularity of a dovin basal. Pretending to be a slave, working the fields that grew various sorts of Yuuzhan Vong greenware, he'd been assigned to work a field of lambents. The plants produced small living crystals that the Yuuzhan Vong used for hand torches and valence inputs. The crystals were controlled via a telepathic bond formed when the crystals were harvested. Anakin had bonded with a lambent and used it to rebuild his lightsaber, with the unexpected result that he could now occasionally sense the Yuuzhan Vong and their living servants. It had given him the edge he needed to survive Yavin 4 and rescue Tahiri.

"Right, lambents. If we could build more lightsabers like yours, it could be a big help to us."

"I don't know. Uncle Luke examined mine. He couldn't get the lambent to react to him at all when he turned the lightsaber on."

"Because it's bonded to you?"

"I don't think so," Anakin replied. "The Yuuzhan Vong use lambents attuned to other Vong. You'd think my lambent would react to other humans, since I attuned it. Anyway, to get more, we'd have to stage a raid on some Yuuzhan Vong ag planet. That would probably be too aggressive, for Jedi." He fought and failed to keep an ironic tone from the statement.

Corran had reached him now. The mirrored faceplate of the vac suit still gave back only stars, but he could feel the older man's serious expression.

"Anakin, switch to a private channel."

"Hey!" Tahiri broadcast, from somewhere.

"I need to talk to Anakin alone," Corran said. "It won't take long."

"Better not. It's spooky enough out here without you guys getting all secretive on me."

They changed frequencies. "Look, Anakin," Corran began. "I was a little hard on you back there. But I want you to understand that it's not just about you. You may not know it, but all of the younger Jedi and a lot of the older ones look up to you. The buzz is you're the next Luke Skywalker, at the very least."

"I don't encourage those rumors," Anakin said. "I don't like them."

"I believe that. It's also irrelevant. They're starting to

emulate you. Tahiri, back on Eriadu and on Yavin Four—classic Anakin. On Yavin Four, Sannah and my son, Valin, were trying to be like you when they pulled their foolish stunt. All the candidates want to be like you, but the fact is, most of them *can't*. They don't have the raw strength or the talent to pull themselves out of the kind of scrapes you get into. Part of being a Jedi is setting an example."

"I know that," Anakin said.

"And believe it or not, you can still learn a thing or two from your elders."

"I know that, too, Corran. I'm sorry if I've been disrespectful." He paused. "And I'm sorry I led Valin into danger. I didn't mean to. It never occurred to me that he would follow me."

"But he did," Corran said gently. "He's lucky you were there to get him out of it. As Tahiri was lucky on Eriadu."

"Yeah. Corran?"

"Yes?"

Anakin deliberated a moment before continuing. "About Tahiri."

"You're worried about her."

"Yes."

"Want to explain why?"

Anakin almost did, but then he shook his head. "I want to think about it some more. And I want to talk to her."

Corran chuckled softly. "Well, we've got nothing but time. I'm sure you'll find an opportunity soon enough. Just give me the sign if you want me to switch channels."

"Thanks. And Corran?"

"Yes?"

"I do respect you. But you flew with Rogue Squadron. Weren't you ever the least bit reckless?"

Corran's mirrored face stared back at him. "Yes," he said. "And one day, hopefully, you'll be able to understand something about what it cost me."

It didn't take long for Tahiri to come over, curious as to what he and Corran had been discussing.

"Why are they just sitting there?" she asked, waving a gloved hand at the visible stripe of stars and ships above them.

"Any number of reasons," Anakin replied. "They may be waiting for more ships, or for some sign from their gods."

"Yeah." She stepped forward a little too hard and bounced up. She steadied herself against the slanting stone. "Are we going to make it through this?" she asked.

"Yes," Anakin said, without hesitation.

"I thought so." She nevertheless sounded a little scared.

"Come here," he said.

She moved until they could touch.

"Switch off your comm and touch your helmet to mine." It's not that he didn't trust Corran not to listen, but after all, the man had been in espionage most of his life.

Tahiri did as he said, and their helmets met with a soft thunk. He couldn't see her face, but he could imagine it there, centimeters from his own. He could almost see her eyes.

"What's the big secret?" she asked. Coming through two layers of alloy, her voice sounded distant and metallic.

"Are you okay?" he asked.

"Sure."

"Do we need to talk about what happened back on Eriadu?"

She didn't answer.

Anakin hesitantly pushed on. "That was a Yuuzhan Vong battle cry. When you broke in to rescue me."

"I know. It just sort of . . . came out. Anakin, all of the words they put in me are still there. The other stuff faded, or most of it. But their language—I still hear it. Sometimes I think in it."

"It, um, worries me."

"It shouldn't. I'm okay."

He wound up his courage a little tighter. "I should have told you this a while back," he said. "I waited because you already had enough to worry about, after we got off Yavin Four."

"What?"

"I had a vision about you. At least I think it was a vision."

"Go on."

"You were grown up. You were, umm, scarred up and tattooed like Tsavong Lah. You were Jedi, but dark. I could feel the darkness radiating from you."

"Oh."

"It worried me."

"And you didn't tell me this? You didn't think I should know?"

"When you killed the shaper, I saw the look in your eyes. The look *she* had."

"By she you mean me, of course. The she I might have been if you hadn't rescued me."

"Something like that."

"You don't think . . . you don't *still* think that could happen to me? That I could end up like the me in your vision? How could I? You saved me from them, stopped them before they finished."

"I thought so. Think so. But when you came through that door speaking Yuuzhan Vong—"

"It's nothing," Tahiri insisted. "It's just words. And I would never hurt you."

That rang strange. "Who said anything about you hurting me?" Anakin asked.

"I just assumed, in your vision, I was threatening you."

"No," he said, a little suspicious but not willing to push it. Had she had a vision, too? She somehow didn't sound surprised at his. "No," he continued, "it was like I was looking through someone else's eyes, not my own. I don't think I was there. But whoever was—you said something about them being the last. Just before you killed them."

"Anakin, I'll never join the Yuuzhan Vong. Believe it." Even through two helmets, her voice rang with utter conviction.

"Okay," he said. "I just wanted to tell you. I thought you ought to know."

"Thanks. Thanks for not keeping me in the dark."

"You're welcome."

Their helmets were still touching, and she didn't say anything else. He was glad he couldn't see her face, because he would have had to look away.

And yet he *wished* he could see it.

Her gloved hand came up slowly. He took it and felt something almost like an electric jolt. They stood that way for a long time, until Anakin felt suddenly very . . . awkward.

He was about to let go when the asteroid suddenly began to vibrate, a faint tactile buzz coming from everywhere. At the same time, Anakin felt weight, dragging him not toward the surface of the asteroid, but against the wall of the fissure.

"What?" He suddenly thought to switch his comm back on.

". . . under acceleration!" Corran was shouting.

It took only an instant for the implications of that to sink in. Then Anakin flicked on his lightsaber. The blade limned the stone around them in purple light.

Anakin sliced through the stone, five strokes that set a chunk of nickel-steel floating to butt against the new "down" of the fissure wall.

The stone went down only about twenty centimeters. Below that was yorik coral.

"This is a ship, too!" Corran shouted.

To prove him correct, the g forces continued to mount.

NINETEEN

Jaina was awakened by a blaring horn and the arrhythmic thumping of running feet. She sat up, trying to remember where she was.

The walls, ceiling, and floor were of blue-black ice. She'd been sleeping in her flight suit inside a thermoskin. Right, she had it now. Kyp's hideout.

The other two people sleeping in the chamber—a human female named Yara and a disheveled Bothan whose name she had forgotten—were clambering to their feet. Jaina shrugged on her parka and followed them into the corridor and down to the command center.

Kyp was there, calmly giving orders. He saw Jaina and smiled, and she felt that funny little twist in her stomach again.

"Good morning," Kyp said. "Sleep well?"

"Not bad, considering my bed was a block of ice," she replied. "What's going on?"

"Yuuzhan Vong recon just popped into the system. Not much of an outfit, but I don't want them to find us here. If we hurry, we can jet out the back way before they're any the wiser." He locked his gaze on her. "That means I'm going to have to ask for your decision—now. If you won't take this to someone in the military, I'll have to do it alone. I'll never convince them, but I have to try."

His sincerity and urgency burned fiercely in the Force. Jaina remembered the column of sunfire, creeping toward the Yuuzhan Vong weapon. It wasn't as if Kyp didn't have proof. She at least owed his evidence a hearing, didn't she?

"I'll go to Rogue Squadron with it," she said. "It's the

only place I know where I might still be welcome, and Colonel Darklighter will know what to do. But I'll need your data."

"Packed up and ready to go. And I'm going with you, just to make sure you get there."

"That might not be a good idea. If Uncle Luke isn't safe on Coruscant, I can't imagine you would be."

"Or you, for that matter," Kyp added. "After all, you were last seen fleeing with them. I was hoping you could arrange a rendezvous someplace else."

Jaina hesitated. "We could try that—I could send a message to Colonel Darklighter. But what if the Yuuzhan Vong or the Peace Brigade traces the communication?"

"You're a smart young woman. I'm sure you can think of someplace you and Darklighter know that you can refer to obliquely."

"Sure, probably."

Kyp's grin expanded again. "Good." He jerked his head in the direction of the bay. "I took the liberty of refueling your X-wing and giving it the once-over. I'm afraid there's no time for you to give it a personal inspection. We've gotta haul jets."

"Okay," Jaina said, "but if I flame out from a cracked nacelle, I'm holding you responsible."

"Don't worry. I prefer my friends uncooked. Especially my more attractive ones."

"Boy, you've been practicing that flattery stuff, haven't you?" Jaina shot back. "I've already agreed to help you. No need to pour frill syrup on honeycrust."

"I wasn't," he replied, smiling that annoying smile again.

They reached the X-wings in silence, where Kyp's people were already arrayed. There were more than a dozen and one, now, and she recognized few of them. They all had a certain raggedness to them, a look of almost never sleeping. They had eyes as hard and glinting as Corusca gems, and they looked at Kyp as if he were some Master of old.

"All right," Kyp told them. "We want to fly quiet this time. Most of you know we seeded a moon of the sixth planet with a signal emitter. They'll go there first and find nothing but a wayward probe. Keeping the planet between us and them will allow us a sunward course. By the time we need to change our vector, the solar radiation ought to cloak us from their long-range sensors. Then we put the sun behind us and make the jump. Any questions?"

There were none, only a swelling sense of pride and confidence. Jaina tried to shrug it off—these weren't *her* feelings, after all. But it was infectious.

"Great," Kyp said. "As soon as we're out, I'll trigger the thermal charges. They won't find a thing, and we can always dig in here again."

They cleared the planet without incident, keeping comm silence until they were well around the primary. There, Kyp peeled off from his wing and came alongside Jaina. He signaled for her to switch to a private channel.

"Ready?" he asked, when she'd made the switch.

"I didn't think we had reached the node."

"The Dozen are headed to another hiding hole. We're heading Coreward. We split up here."

Jaina nodded. "Just give me the jump, so I can lay it in."

"Coming," Kyp said.

They made the jump, and then another. After that they had a long realspace jaunt through another uninhabited system.

"Jaina?"

"Still here," she said. Kyp was only about ten meters away. He had his cockpit light on, so she could see his face through the transparisteel.

"Why did Luke send you? Really?"

"I didn't lie to you. He's trying to pull the Jedi back together." She paused. "He also wanted to know what you were up to."

"That's very paternal of him," Kyp remarked. "Almost as paternal as planting a tracer in my ship last time I was on Coruscant."

"You found—" She suddenly recognized that Kyp had been nudging her very subtly in the Force.

"Don't ever do that," she snapped.

"I do what I must," Kyp replied. "I guessed there was a tracer. I couldn't find it. Must be something new. I had to trick you into confirming it, though, and I respected your intelligence enough to believe you wouldn't fall for such a simple ruse without a nudge. I do apologize, but then, you did come to spy on me."

"If you think that, you don't know much about me," Jaina replied. She glared across the empty space at him.

"Perhaps that's true. But you didn't willingly tell me about the tracer."

"That's not my secret to give out."

"Neither are mine. Do you understand?"

Jaina thought about that a moment, then nodded. "Understood."

"Okay."

"No, not okay. I'm still not happy with you, Kyp. I don't think I like who you've become."

"I've become what I need to be. What your uncle Luke was in the war against the Empire."

"Boy, you must love your mirror."

"No. I'm not saying I like what I've become either, Jaina. Your uncle Luke eventually went to the dark side—"

"Hey," Jaina snapped. "At least he fought it. You spent what, a *week* training to be a Jedi before the dark side seduced you?"

Kyp laughed easily. "Something like that."

"And you blew up a planet, right? If it hadn't been for Master Skywalker speaking for you, you'd be in prison to this day, if not dead. And my father—"

"I know what I owe Han," Kyp said. "I won't forget it. I haven't even begun paying off that debt."

"Or the one to Uncle Luke. But that doesn't stop you from bad-mouthing him all over the galaxy, does it? It doesn't stop you from undermining him as a leader."

"Any time Luke is ready to be a leader again, I'm ready to follow him," Kyp said.

"Riiight. Just so long as he tells you to do things you already want to and doesn't tell you to do anything you don't want to."

"You've just described what a real leader does."

"Yeah? And that's what you are, aren't you? A leader. I see the way your squadron looks at you. You like it too much. I doubt very much you would give that up, whatever course of action Master Skywalker might lead us on."

"Jaina," Kyp said, after a moment, "I won't say you don't have a few good points there. Maybe I am addicted to this now. That doesn't mean it shouldn't be done. Every day, thousands of living, breathing beings are sacrificed to the Yuuzhan Vong gods. There's a pit on Dantooine. I've seen it. It's almost two kilometers across and full of bones. And the slaves, what they make the slaves do . . ."

He stopped, and she felt waves of anger, pity, and grief lap over her. "The Vong obliterate whole worlds, and yes, I know I did that once, but I'm not crazy enough to think it was *right*. The Vong think it's a holy obligation. Maybe Master Skywalker is right to urge a passive role. Maybe that's what the Force really asks of us. But I don't believe it. Luke Skywalker risked everything in *his* war, the war against the Empire. Everything, including the peril of turning to the dark side as his father did. That was his war, Jaina. *That* was his war. This one is ours. Luke wants to protect us from ourselves. I say we're all grown up. The old Jedi order died with the Old Republic. Then there was Luke, and only Luke, and a lot of fumbling to re-create the Jedi from what little he knew of them. He did the best he could, and he made mistakes. I was one of them. His generation of Jedi was put together like a rickety space scow, but from it something new has emerged. It's not the old Jedi order, nor should it be."

His eyes burned across the space between them like quasars. "We, Jaina, are the new Jedi order. And this is *our* war."

TWENTY

The *Millennium Falcon* was purring, and the controls felt just right in Han's hands. Better than they had felt in a very long time, as a matter of fact. Oh, the coralskippers tried their best. They swooped in close, firing their molten projectiles and skittering away from return fire like a school of particularly ugly fish. The larger craft—about the size of the *Falcon* itself—kept a steady fire of its own weapons, releasing whole flights of grutchins. But today was not a lucky day for the Yuuzhan Vong, at least not so far.

Han whooped and turned tight, scraping so close to the transport analog that one of the pursuing coralskippers, already singed by laser fire, smacked right into it.

In his peripheral vision, he saw another skip flame out, drilled by turbolasers.

"Kid can shoot," Han told his copilot.

"He's your son," Leia said. Her voice surprised him. For a nanosecond he'd forgotten it was her there, expecting to find Chewie instead.

And the odd thing? He didn't feel the gullet-sucking sorrow he usually did. A little wistful, maybe, a little melancholy. A little happiness, too, to have his wife beside him. He'd nearly wrecked that, hadn't he?

He blinked as a volley of Yuuzhan Vong ordnance found his shields when they shouldn't have.

"Like I said, *Han*—" Leia sputtered.

He'd built some distance from the largest Yuuzhan Vong vessel. Now he turned and built g's toward it. "Concussion missiles when I tell you."

"Han?"

The Yuuzhan Vong ship loomed closer and closer, and Han grinned out of the side of his mouth.

"Yeah, sweetheart?"

"You've noticed we're going to hit that thing?"

Han held course.

Leia nearly shrieked because the alternating smooth and striated pattern of yorik coral filled nearly the entire viewport. At the last instant Han nosed up slightly to miss by a few tens of centimeters.

"Missiles, now!" Han said.

The missiles detonated just behind them, a full spread. The Yuuzhan Vong ship broke in half.

"Noticed I'm going to hit *what* thing?" Han asked innocently.

"Have you lost it?" Leia exclaimed. "What do you think, that you're twenty again?"

"It ain't the years—"

She smiled, leaned over, and kissed him. "As I've said before, you have your moments. I always knew you were a scoundrel at heart."

"Me?" The exaggerated innocence that had once come so naturally felt suddenly right again.

The rest of the Yuuzhan Vong ships went out like Hapan paper lamps caught in a high wind, and Jacen shot them into star food. Without the yammosk on the larger ship to coordinate them, the skips were less than dexterous.

"Speaking of scoundrels," Han said, tapping on the comm unit.

"Hailing the freighter *Tinmolok*."

The hail was answered immediately. "Yes, yes. Do not shoot! We are unarmed! We are Etti! We are not Yuuzhan Vong!"

"So you say," Han said easily. "I can see that you're taking cargo into occupied space."

"Relief only! Food for the native populace!"

"Oh, really? Well, now, that I've got to see. I'm coming alongside."

"No, no, I . . ."

"No problem. Just glad to be able to help."

"Please, Captain, may I ask who you are?"

Han leaned back and clasped the back of his head in his hands. "You, sir, are speaking to the proud captain of the, ah—" He glanced at Leia. "—*Princess of Blood*. Prepare to be boarded."

Leia rolled her eyes.

"This is piracy," the Etti captain—one Swori Mdimu—grumbled as Han and Jacen took possession of the crew's sidearms.

"That's good," Han told him. "I thought I was going to have to write it down for you, so you'd know what happened. Though for the record, it's actually privateering. See, *pirates* steal from anyone. They're greedy, and they just don't care who they hijack. Privateers, on the other hand, only attack ships allied with a certain fleet. In this case, I'm choosing for my targets any lowlife gutless and stupid enough to supply the Yuuzhan Vong or the Peace Brigade, or any other collaborationist scum, with anything whatever."

"I told you—"

"Look," Han said. "In about five minutes, I'm going to see your cargo. If it's just a bunch of food that the Yuuzhan Vong are buying for their captives out of the goodness of their sweet, tattooed hearts, I'll let you go, with apologies. But if I find you're carrying weapons and ordnance, or any other sort of war matériel, I'm going to smack you around. And if you have *captives* . . . Well, you have an imagination. Use it."

"No!" the captain said. "No captives. It's as you said. Weapons for the Peace Brigade. Not my idea! I have an employer. I need this job. Please don't kill me and my crew."

"Quit your whining. I'm not killing anybody, this time. I'm setting you adrift in one of your shuttles."

"Thank you. Thank you!"

"Here's how you thank me," Han said. "You tell anyone who'll listen that we're out here. Any ship delivering to a Yuuzhan Vong–occupied system is *mine*. And next time, I may not take prisoners. You get me?"

"I get you," Swori Mdimu said.

"Great. My, ah, *buddy* here is going to put you all in stun cuffs now. I'm going to have a look at your cargo. If there are any surprises waiting for me, better tell me now."

"There—there are two Yuuzhan Vong guards. They will be alerted."

"No kidding?" Han said. "Okay, so we're cuffing you *and* locking you up. Then the two of us will take care of these guards."

"Two of you?" the Etti said incredulously. "Against Yuuzhan Vong?"

"Hey, don't worry. You want us to lose, right? But if we don't, I'll be back, and we need to have a little talk about who exactly your employer is."

Once the prisoners were secure, Han started off down a corridor.

"Da—ah, Captain?" Jacen said. "Cargo hold's the other way."

"That's right," Han told him.

"What're you . . . ?"

"Just stay here. If the Yuuzhan Vong come up, give a yell. I'll be on the bridge."

Han returned from the bridge a little later, and the two of them went to the cargo access axis. At the first set of locks, they found two Yuuzhan Vong guards, collapsed near the door. Their faces were masses of purple—not from their own scarification, but from the capillaries that had burst beneath their skin.

"You killed them," Jacen said dully, hardly believing it. "You sealed off the compartment and let the air out."

Han glanced at his son. "Right on all but one count. They aren't dead."

Jacen frowned and knelt to search for some sign of life, since with the Yuuzhan Vong the Force could not help him. One of the two stirred at his touch, and he jumped back.

"See?" Han said, a sure note of satisfaction tinting his voice. "I just dropped the pressure until *they* did. There are surveillance cams in here."

"Oh."

"Better cuff 'em, unless you want to fight 'em. I thought things would go smoother this way."

"Dad, what if there had been captives in here?"

"Then I would have *seen* them on the surveillance. Jacen, give the old man some credit."

"Permission to speak freely, Captain."

Han sighed. "Go ahead, son."

"Dad, I don't like this. Maybe you think being a pirate is okay, but—"

"Privateer," Han corrected.

"You really think there's a moral difference?"

"If there's ever a moral difference in being on one side instead of the other in a war, yes. Doesn't your all-knowing Force tell you that?"

"I don't know what the Force wants. That's exactly the problem."

"Yeah?" Han said sarcastically. "You knew what to do when you found your mother with her legs half cut off. Fortunately. Or do you think it was wrong to save her life?"

Jacen reddened. "That's not fair."

"Fair?" Han threw his hands up. "Kids these days. Fair."

"Dad, I know the Yuuzhan Vong are a darkness that must be fought. But aggression—that's not my way. Setting up Uncle Luke's great river, that I know I can do. This . . ."

"And you thought we were going to be able to carry out Luke's grand scheme without ever getting our hands dirty? You heard them back at the Maw—we need ships, we need supplies and weapons, we need *money*." Han tapped up the ship's manifest on the captain's datapad and whistled. "And now we have all three. Three E-wings, right out of dry dock. Lommite, about two hundred kilos. Enough rations to feed a small army." He glanced back up at Jacen. "Not to mention that the Peace Brigade doesn't get any of this stuff. C'mere. I want to see something."

They made their way through the crated supplies until they came to those the manifest designated as weapons. Han worked the seal on one until it popped open.

"Well, how do you like that?" Han remarked.

"Emperor's bones," Jacen breathed.

The crate contained not blasters, stun batons, or grenades, but Yuuzhan Vong amphistaffs.

"Looks like our Brigade buddies are making the transition away from the evils of technology," Han said. "Wonder if they've started scarring themselves yet?" He looked significantly at Jacen. "You still don't think this was worthwhile?"

Jacen stared at the hibernating weapon-beasts.

"It's done, now," he allowed.

Han shook his head. "I don't think so. I want to find out who is sending this stuff. Those amphistaffs were grown somewhere. Where? Duro? Obroa-skai?"

"You told the captain of this ship you would continue hijacking ships bound for Yuuzhan Vong space. Was that the truth?"

"It was. I've been trying to explain why."

"It's a bad idea."

"Well, maybe. But like I told you earlier, I'm the captain."

"It's not that simple for me."

"No? Then here's something real simple. We're taking this freighter and its cargo back to the Maw. When we're done, you're free to take one of these E-wings to Luke and sit the rest of the war out meditating or whatnot. Become a nurse or something. I don't care. But if you're going to keep this up, I don't want you on my ship, son or not."

Jacen didn't answer, but his face went all stony. It was times like this that Han occasionally wished he had just a little of that Force ability to feel what others felt, because Jacen was a blank slate to him more often than not.

As his son vanished around the corner, Han realized exactly what he had said, and memory suddenly jolted through him with the force of vision. He saw himself with Leia in the cockpit of the *Falcon* the day they'd met, right after escaping the Death Star. "I ain't in this for your revolution," he'd told her. Not much later he'd told Luke much the same thing, dodging out of the fight against the Death Star for what seemed all of the right reasons, not the least of which that it was hopeless. *That* Han Solo had had a pretty weak grip on the idea of a worthy cause.

Somehow, things had gotten turned around. Not front to back, but in a weirder way. Ultimately it was because he just didn't understand the kid, and the kid hadn't a clue about Han.

Anakin he could understand. He used the Force in exactly the way Han would, if he had the ability. Jacen had always been more like Leia, and in the last year or so the resemblance had only grown stronger.

But here, suddenly, in the least flattering way he could imagine, the Solo genes were finally showing.

"Don't go, son," Han murmured, but there was no one to hear him but the sleeping weapons.

TWENTY-ONE

Corran flicked on his lightsaber and began helping Anakin cut into the ridge on the Yuuzhan Vong ship. Tahiri got the idea and joined them. Together, they sawed a hole deep into the ridge before Anakin's knees began to buckle from his rapidly increasing mass.

Suddenly a chunk of the ship broke free and fell inward, pushed by the same acceleration that was about to kill the three Jedi. Atmosphere blew out, curtains of ice crystals sparkling in the starlight as Corran leapt through the gap, pulling Tahiri with him. Anakin followed.

Normal weight returned instantly as they entered the ship, probably due to the same gravity-bending dovin basals that drove the craft.

Anakin looked around him to see where they were.

In the mingled glow of their lightsabers, Anakin made out a dark grotto, walls haphazardly patched with luminescence. Even as he watched, however, the light faded as the bitter cold and vacuum that slunk in with the Jedi killed whatever plant or creature manufactured it. The chamber's function was difficult to determine. The roof was very low, no more than a meter and a half, and it rambled on for a considerable distance. Black columns or tubes ran from floor to ceiling every two meters or so. The columns bulged in the middle, and Anakin thought they were pulsing faintly.

Corran gestured for the two younger Jedi to touch helmets with him.

"Someone will show up to check the hull breach soon," he told them. "We need to be ready."

"I'm ready," Tahiri said. "Really ready. This is a lot better than sitting on some old rock, waiting for them to find us."

Anakin sensed a bit of annoyance from the older Jedi as Corran went on with his analysis. "I'm guessing this section, whatever it is, is sealed off, else there would still be air whistling through. We need to find the lock."

"Too late for that," Anakin said as his lambent lisped a faint warning. "We've already got company coming. Close."

"How can you tell?"

"I feel them."

Corran nodded. "May the Force be with you," he told them. Then he moved off to crouch near one of the pillars.

Light appeared toward the far end of the chamber: six lambents like the one in Anakin's sword. In their light he saw six shadowed bipeds stepping through a typical Yuuzhan Vong dilating lock. He took deep breaths, relaxing his muscles one by one, preparing for the fight.

Closer, he saw they wore rust-colored formfitting suits—creatures really, of course, probably some vacuum-hardy variant of the ooglith cloaker. Their faces were visible, however, through transparent masks. To Anakin's surprise, only two of them revealed the facial scars of warriors. Two others had the more delicate tattoos he had come to associate with shapers. Indeed, their cloakers bulged conspicuously around their heads, doubtless due to the tendril-bearing creatures they wore as headdresses. The remaining pair had the look of workers or perhaps slaves.

The two warriors set themselves in guard stances while the shapers examined the hole.

Anakin felt rather than saw Corran creep forward, not toward the group of Yuuzhan Vong, but toward the door they had entered through.

Moving carefully but as quickly as he could, Anakin followed, tapping Tahiri on the shoulder to get her attention.

Come on, he suggested in the Force, hoping she got the sense of it.

She did. The three crept through the darkness behind the repair party. In the vacuum, their feet made no sound at all.

They had almost reached the lock when Anakin felt the tingle of approach behind him. He turned in time to see a warrior loom up silently, amphistaff arcing toward Anakin's head.

Anakin leapt back at the last instant, nearly letting the weapon graze him. He flicked his lightsaber on, and it blazed to life. The warrior's eyes went wide with surprise.

He didn't know what he was facing, Anakin guessed.

Whatever his feelings, the warrior didn't hesitate long. He renewed his attack, spearing with the sharp end of the weapon. When Anakin caught the attack in a circular parry and pressed to bind, the staff suddenly went limp, escaping his net of light. It came flicking in an arc toward his face, now semirigid.

Anakin launched himself forward and under the attack. As he passed by the warrior's right side, he lifted his weapon parallel to the floor in a cut across his opponent's face. The energy blade sliced through the mask, and the warrior fell back, flailing, air and blood mingling and freezing in a mass around the cut.

The other warrior was battling Corran, while Tahiri tried to work the lock.

Corran's dual-phase weapon moved in tightly controlled arcs, always where it needed to be. That fight was nearing its end, too. Corran had stripped a long patch of cloaker from his enemy's arm. It was already healing, but vacuum and frostbite had done their damage; the arm hung uselessly. Corran parried a flurry of increasingly wilder and more desperate attacks. Taking the last in a parry that pushed his opponent's staff high above their heads, he then turned his point down and drove it into the warrior's exposed armpit. The blade sank deep, but the warrior still brought his weapon down, cracking solidly against Corran's head. Both men fell away, Corran with his hands to his helmet, the Yuuzhan Vong writhing in death throes.

Anakin spun to face their remaining enemies, but none was moving toward them. *Not warriors,* he thought. *But still dangerous,* he amended, remembering the deadly tools on the shaper Mezhan Kwaad's hands. Still, he ought to feel them approaching, if they tried.

Anakin knelt by Corran. The amphistaff had dented the helmet of the vac suit, but worse, a crack had formed between the metal and the transparisteel—he could tell by the rime of frost forming on it. Corran was already struggling for consciousness.

Tahiri was still working at the lock. Anakin pressed his gloved hand over the crack, wishing he had a patch, but those were in the emergency pack, on the other side of the room past the Yuuzhan Vong. By the time he went there and got back—assuming he didn't have to stop and fight— Corran would be dead.

He increased the feed of Corran's oxygen in hopes of keeping the pressure high enough to prevent his blood boiling.

Pale light fell across them, and he looked up to see that Tahiri had finally cycled the lock. He dragged Corran through, and within seconds the smaller chamber beyond was pressurized. They passed through the inner lock more easily and into another corridor, this one still illuminated by the phosphorescent fungi.

Anakin quickly worked Corran's helmet off. The older man was red-faced and had a nasty bump on his head, but otherwise seemed to be in pretty good shape. Within a minute he was standing, albeit shakily.

"Thanks, Anakin, Tahiri. I owe you both." His head jerked this way and that. "We need to keep moving," he said. "A ship this size could have a hundred warriors on it."

"I've never been so glad to be wrong," Corran admitted later. In under an hour they had defeated the remaining five warriors on the ship and rounded up and incarcerated the rest of the less military Yuuzhan Vong. Now the three Jedi sat in the control room, or what passed for it.

The ship—if by ship one meant the available living space—was actually quite small. The bulk of the vessel was the concealing stone of the asteroid and vast caverns of greenware that none of them could even guess the function of.

"We were lucky," Corran said. "If we'd been most places on the surface, we would have had to cut through fifty meters of rock. As it was, we were on the cooling fin—at least that's my guess as to what it was."

"This must be some sort of scout ship," Anakin guessed.

"Or a surveillance craft," Corran said. "At the moment, that's not the most important question. We need to know three things, fast." He ticked them off on his fingers. "One: does the rest of the fleet know we've captured it? Two: where is it going? Three: can we fly it?"

"Tahiri?" Anakin said.

Tahiri had settled into the chair facing what Anakin knew from experience to be a bank of indicators—embedded lumens, several villips, patches of varying texture and color that were probably manual controls. The real key to flying the craft rested in the loose cap Tahiri held in her lap. Called a cognition hood, it established a telepathic link between pilot and ship.

"I can fly it," she said softly.

Corran grimaced. "Why not let me try it? We still don't know what hidden dangers using that thing might have."

"I've flown one before," Tahiri said, "On Yavin Four."

"It has to be her," Anakin said. "She speaks and thinks in the language, for one thing. Since the scientists have my tizowyrm, she's the only one of us who can. And . . ." He trailed off.

"They changed my brain," Tahiri said bluntly. "I can fly it. You can't, Captain Horn."

Corran sighed. "I don't like it, but you might as well give it a try. At this point I have to admit you two have a lot more practical knowledge than I do when it comes to Yuuzhan Vong technology."

Tahiri nodded and placed the cap over her short golden hair. It writhed and contracted to fit. Her eyes clouded, and sweat started on her brow. Her breath chopped raggedly.

"Take it off," Corran said.

"No, wait," Tahiri said. "It was just a little different that time. I can handle it. I'm adjusting." Her brow furrowed in concentration. "The ship's name is *Stalking Moon*. A hyper-drive jump has been laid in. It's coming up in about five minutes."

Two organisms suddenly waggled to life, and between them appeared a hologram, showing something that might have been a map, complete with unfamiliar icons. One, shaped like a three-pointed star, was highlighted in red and moving rapidly. A few of the others were moving as well.

"That's the fleet," she said. "The fast-moving thing is us." Her head turned toward them, though her eyes were hidden by the hood. "I don't think anyone is following us."

"Can you tell where the jump is taking us?"

Tahiri shook her head. "There's a designation. It trans-lates to something like 'next prey to feel our talons and glory.' "

"Yag'Dhul?" Anakin speculated.

"We'll see soon enough," Corran replied. "If so, this ship may have been sent ahead to make tactical maps or some-thing. We may be the first of the fleet to arrive. Anakin, you may get your chance to warn Yag'Dhul."

"True," Anakin said. "If the—who lives at Yag'Dhul, anyway?"

"The Givin," Corran said.

"The Givin don't blow us out of the sky. We are, after all, in a Yuuzhan Vong ship."

"Well, there is that," Corran said. "But we have a better chance there than staying here. If Yag'Dhul is where we're going. We're headed back to a Yuuzhan Vong base, for all we know."

"You want me to try and stop the jump?" Tahiri asked.

Anakin watched Corran consider that. Then the older Jedi shook his head in the negative.

"No," he said. "We're in this deep. Might as well see what the bottom looks like."

TWENTY-TWO

It was hard to read a Mon Calamarian. With their bulging, fishlike eyes and wide lips, they looked, to the untrained human eye, perpetually surprised or amused. They lacked the same complex facial muscles that humans had evolved for nonverbal communication, their species being possessed of another set of semiotic tools for that purpose.

Nonetheless, Mara somehow saw the horror on Cilghal's face when the healer entered the medical chamber Booster had allowed her to set up.

"Oh, no," Cilghal murmured. Her partially webbed digits fluttered in agitation. "Please, Mara, recline." She indicated an adjustable medical bed.

"No problem," Mara said. Her knees had gone flimsy on the short walk over from her quarters. Her mental image of herself had morphed into a huge bloated thing balanced on ridiculous, straw-thin legs.

What she saw in Cilghal's clinical mirror fit no image of herself at all, past or present. Her eyes were sunken into gray pits, their emerald color faded to a sickly yellow. Her cheeks were hollow, as if she hadn't eaten in days. Her skin was so pale the vessels stood out like topographic maps of a river delta on Dagobah.

What a beauty, Mara thought. *I could dance in Jabba's palace again, if I could dance. Of course, I'd attract a different type of admirer than I did last time . . .*

Wait'll Luke sees this. He's going to have a meltdown. Unwilling to run the risk that some slicer could trace a HoloNet communication back to the *Errant Venture,* Luke had taken his X-wing out to contact several eminent physicians and transmit Mara's latest test results. He'd been gone three days.

"I need to know what it means, Cilghal."

"How do you feel?"

"Hot, cold. Nauseated. As if nanoprobes are trying to carve my eyes out from behind with microscopic vibroblades."

The healer nodded and placed her webbed hands so gently on Mara's abdomen that it might have been sheets of flimsiplast that floated there.

"Three days ago, when you went into meditation, how did you feel?" Cilghal asked.

"Sick. I already knew it was coming back. I thought if I was alone, in total concentration and without distraction, I might be able to control it like I did before."

"This is not like before," Cilghal said. "Not at all. The rate of molecular mutation has increased fivefold. It's much worse than before you began taking the tears. It might be because so many of your body's resources are tied up in the pregnancy; it might be because the serum weakened your ability to fight without it." She closed her eyes, and Mara felt the Force in motion, within and about her. "It's like dark ink, staining your cells. Spreading."

"The baby," Mara demanded. "Tell me about my son."

"The Force burns bright in him. The darkness hasn't reached there. Something keeps it at bay."

"Yes!" Mara whispered, clenching her fists.

Cilghal's eyes wobbled together so her gaze met Mara's. "It's you, isn't it?" the healer said. "You're putting everything into keeping the disease from entering your womb."

"I can't let it," Mara said. "I can't."

"Mara," the healer said, "you are declining at a terrifying rate."

"I only have to last until the birth," Mara pointed out. "Then I can start taking the tears again."

"At this rate, I'm not sure you will survive the birth," Cilghal told her. "Even if we induce it, or do it surgically. You're already that weak."

"I don't *lose*," Mara told her ferociously. "I'll be strong enough when the time comes. It can't be much longer, can it?"

"You aren't listening to me," Cilghal said. "You could die."

"I *am* listening to you," Mara replied. "It's just that what you're telling me doesn't change anything. I'm going to have this baby, and he's going to be healthy. I'm not going back on the serum. I've come through tougher things than this, Cilghal."

"Then let me help you. Let me lend you some of my strength."

Mara hesitated. "I'll report every day for monitoring and whatever healing you can accomplish. Is there anything else I can do?"

"More than once a day," Cilghal said. "I can strengthen the power of your body to fight. I can cleanse it of some toxins. I can fight the symptoms. But the disease itself . . . there's nothing. No, I can think of nothing else to do." Despair and failure seemed to drift from the healer.

"I need your help, Cilghal," Mara said. "Don't give up on me yet."

"I would never, Mara."

"Good. I need to eat, but I'm not hungry, and I can't keep anything down. I'm sure you can help me with that, right?"

"That I can help with," Cilghal replied.

"It's one thing at a time, old friend," Mara said. "Every parsec begins with a centimeter."

Cilghal nodded and went off to gather some things from storage. Mara lay back, suddenly dizzy, wishing she felt half of the confidence she espoused.

TWENTY-THREE

Master Kae Kwaad was as lean as one of Nen Yim's shaping fingers. He walked with an odd limp and a strange twist to his shoulders. His headdress was a ropy, unkempt mess. He wore a masquer to conceal his real face, a fashion among the Praetorite Vong but not common among shapers of any domain for decades. The masquer portrayed young, clear features, with scarlet-tinted yellow eyes. His real age was difficult to determine, though his skin had the smoothness of relative youth.

"Ah, my adept," Kae said as Nen Yim made the genuflection of greeting. "My willing adept."

Nen Yim tried to keep her expression neutral, but she heard something in his voice that suggested a leer behind his masquer. And the way his eyes traveled over her—what sort of master was this? Masters were above the carnal, beyond it.

No, she remembered. That was what was taught, but her old master Mezhan Kwaad's downfall had had much to do with her forbidden affair with a warrior. Masters were *supposed* to be lustless. Supposing it did not make it so.

The master brought up the seven shaping fingers of his left hand and touched them to her chin. To her distraction, the fingers seemed cramped, or paralyzed. "Yes," he murmured. "A very talented adept, I'm told." He noticed her regarding his hand. "Ah," he mused. "My hands are quite dead, you see. They died some years ago. I do not know why, and the other masters did not deign to replace them."

"That is unfortunate, Master."

He chucked her under the chin. "But you will be my hands, my dear—what was your name?"

"Nen Yim, Master."

He nodded sagely. "Yim. Yim Yim Yim." He clubbed his twisted, dead hands together. His eyes were open but seemed to see nothing. "Yim," he concluded.

Yun-Yuuzhan, what part of you was he? she wondered, quills of disgust pricking up her spine.

"I do not like that name," Kae Kwaad said in a sudden, angry burst. "It offends me."

"It is my name, Master."

"No." Wiry muscles quivered in his arms, as if he were on the verge of attacking her. "No," he repeated more calmly. "Tsup shall be your name. Nen Tsup."

Nen Yim stiffened further. Tsup was the name of no crèche or domain she had ever heard of. It was, however, an antique word for the sorts of slave who tended their masters in unseemly ways. The word itself was so obscene it was rarely used anymore.

"Come, then," the master said, with an air of detachment. "Acquaint me with my demesne."

"Yes, Master Kae Kwaad."

Feeling ill, Nen Yim led him through the moldering halls of the worldship to the shapers' quarters, through a tremoring hall that had begun to have periodic spasms, past her own quarters to the master's apartments, which had stood empty since before her coming to *Baanu Miir*. Five slaves staggered behind them, nearly buckling beneath the weight of enormous transport envelopers.

When the opening dilated, the master stood, staring into space.

"Where am I?" he asked, after a time.

"Your quarters, Master."

"Quarters? What, by the gods, are you talking about? Where *am* I?"

"On the *Baanu Miir*, Master Kae Kwaad."

"Well, where is *it*?" he screeched. "The coordinates. The exact location. Must I repeat myself?"

Nen Yim found herself twisting her fingers together, like a terrified crècheling. She stopped it immediately. "I do not know, Master. I can discover it."

"Do so!" His eyes narrowed. "Who *are* you?"

"Your adept, Nen Yim."

A crafty look came over his face. "I do not like that name. Use the one I gave you."

"Nen Tsup," she said softly.

He blinked, slowly, then snorted. "What a vulgar little thing you are." He sneered. "Hurry. Find out where we are. And then we shall shape something, yes? It will amuse us."

"Master, I wish to speak to you about the ship's rikyam, when you have the time."

"Time? What is that? It is nothing. The brain will die. You do not confuse me with your talk, Adept. No, you do not confuse or amuse or titillate me, though you think it. Yun-Harla herself could not have me! Flattering yourself. Trying to trick me. Get out of my sight."

When she was alone, Nen Yim sank down into a crouch and softly beat the heels of her hands against her head.

He is mad, she thought. *Mad and crippled. Tjulan Kwaad sent him to taunt me, nothing more.*

Beneath her feet, she noticed, a patch of the inner hull was rotting.

A day passed without her seeing him, but when Nen Yim entered her laboratory, there was the twisted, demented Kae Kwaad. He'd somehow unsealed the dermal shelf where her experiments were hidden and was stroking her personal qahsa with the carapace of his right hand. She hadn't tried particularly hard to hide anything, reasoning that doing so was wasted effort. Her modifications to the ship were ample evidence of her heresy. Hiding the experiments would only delay the inevitable.

"I like this," Kae Kwaad said, waving at her tissue samples. "I like the colors." He smiled vaguely and pointed his useless digits to his eyes. "They trickle in here, don't they? After that they don't get out. They just talk and whistle, wriggle and curl." He scratched one dead hand absently against the other.

"Tell me what you're doing, Adept," he said.

"Master, I'm only doing my best to heal the ship. If I have

strained protocol, it was only because I thought it best for the Yuuzhan Vong."

"*Strained* it? Strained it?" He laughed, an unpleasant scratching sound. Then, as abruptly, he folded down onto one of the slowly shifting benches and placed his head between his hands.

"I requested a master because I do not have access to protocol records above the fifth cortex," Nen Yim went on. "I had no answer to the rikyam's dilemma, so I sought one."

"And now you have a master." Kae Kwaad chortled. "And now we shall shape."

"Perhaps Master Kae Kwaad would like to review the damage to the spiral arm."

"Perhaps the master would have his adept listen instead of speak. Today we are shaping. Recall the protocol of Hon Akua."

Nen Yim stared at him. "We are to form a grutchin? But the fleet is replete with grutchins."

"Inferior grutchins. Your generation! In your haste to make them stronger, faster, tougher, you have forgotten the most important aspect of shaping! The essence!"

"What is that, Master?"

"*Form.* Have you ever seen a perfect grutchin, Adept?"

"I . . . do not know, Master."

"You haven't! You have *not*! In the mind of Yun-Yuuzhan is a perfect grutchin. It has never been seen by Yuuzhan Vong except in the protocols—never in living form. You and I, Adept, will incarnate the grutchin in the mind of Yun-Yuuzhan. It shall be perfect in form and proportion, precise in hue. When we are done, Yun-Yuuzhan will know us for true shapers, who create in his image."

"But the rikyam—"

"The rikyam? How can you even think of such a mundane matter when we are to embark upon *this*? Once we have created the perfect grutchin, do you really expect Yun-Yuuzhan—or those simpletons Yun-Harla or Yun-Ne'Shel—will deny us anything? Now we must work!"

It was soon after this that Nen Yim began to seriously consider the murder of Master Kae Kwaad.

PART THREE

DESCENT

TWENTY-FOUR

Leia found Jacen where he had been for the last several days—tinkering with one of the captured E-wings. Since they had taken the freighter, he had hardly said a word to anyone, and on their return to the Maw he had thrown himself into the project of fitting the fighter with augmented shields and readying her for extended flight. Han had been almost as sullen. Her husband was tough, but there was only so much loss that even Han Solo could take. It had been good to see something of his old cocky, arrogant self reemerge, though she wasn't going to admit that to him aloud.

But Han's good humor had been short-lived. His fight with Jacen and the following silence had managed to leak most of the fuel from his engines.

Jacen glanced down at her from near the astromech housing, but didn't say anything.

"Jacen," Leia said, "could I talk to you, please? Or do you intend never to speak to me again?"

Jacen gazed down again. "What's there to talk about? I think you and Dad have presented your point of view from pretty much every angle there is, and I think you know mine."

"It must be nice to be so sure about everything," Leia told him.

Jacen uttered a short, guttural laugh. "Yeah," he replied, "must be."

That had a raw sound to it that bothered Leia. How could someone so young sound so cynical? Especially Jacen, whose ideals had always been lofty ones. Of course, she knew better than anyone that most cynics were crash-burned idcalists. Was Jacen that hurt?

It made what she had come to say all the harder, but she had to say it.

"Anyway," she said, taking the plunge, "you're wrong. There *is* another angle to look at this from."

"And what would that be?" Jacen asked. She didn't know whether he sounded more like Han or herself in that moment of caustic sarcasm, and she wasn't sure which would make her angrier.

"Jacen, would you knock off the rebellious teen act for just a minute? And maybe consider for just a second that the entire galaxy doesn't spin around you and your moral decisions?"

Jacen continued to stare stonily at her, but he lifted his shoulders lightly, as if accepting yet another onerous burden. "I can try that," he said. "What have I missed?"

"You've missed that your father needs you, that's what. That I need you."

"That's not fair," Jacen said. "I don't want to be a pirate, so you'll try emotional blackmail?"

"Is that what you call it? Jacen, maybe we weren't the best of parents. Maybe we weren't around as much as we could have been, and maybe this is your way of paying us back. But if your only interpretation of 'your father needs you' is that I'm trying to manipulate you, then I've been a far worse mother than I ever dreamed. If that's all you see, by all means, go. I wouldn't want you on those terms."

"Mom, I—" His voice went strange, and with a sudden start she saw he had tears in his eyes.

"Oh, Jacen—" she began.

"No, Mom, it's all right." He clambered down from the craft and wiped at his eyes. "I deserved that."

"I didn't come here to hurt you. I'm not even sure I came here to persuade you to stay with us. I just wanted to try to explain why your father is acting the way he is. Jacen, your dad is always proud of you even when he doesn't understand you, which is most of the time. He's always tried to be supportive of your decision to become a Jedi Knight, even though the farther you step into that world the farther you go from him. You're more a part of Luke's universe than you are of his, and his biggest fear is that you're ashamed of him, or somehow think him less because of what he is, because he can never be or even fully understand what you're becoming. Deep down he knows he's losing you a little more each day, and that soon enough you'll be strangers. This little spat of yours has only served to confirm that for him."

"He told you all of this?"

"Of course not. Han doesn't talk about things like that. But I know him, Jacen."

"You're right, then."

Leia frowned, a little confused by this sudden turnabout. "About what?"

"You're right—I hadn't quite seen things from that vector. Thanks. Thanks for telling me."

She reached to embrace him, and to her relief, he folded willingly into her arms.

"How could he ever think I was ashamed of him?" Jacen whispered.

They parted, and Jacen looked at her through tear-sparkled eyes. "This is one of the hardest things I've ever had to do," he said.

Leia's heart felt like neutronium. "You're still going?" she asked.

He shook his head. "I decided to stay with you guys two days ago."

"What?"

"Dad was right. Or part of what he said was right. I made a commitment when I came out here with you. I'm holding to that commitment. And with me along, we're more likely to be able to hijack these ships without hurting anyone. I'll be able to tell if there are captives on board. Turning my back on this whole thing feels worse than being a part of it. I still don't like it, but I'll do it. I won't fight Dad anymore."

"Then why have you been working on the E-wing?"

Jacen shrugged. "It was something to do other than sit

around waiting to get into another fight. Somebody can use it. That's why we took it, right?"

"Right," Leia assented.

"So when do we head back out?"

"Soon. The captain of the freighter gave up some interesting information. They came via Wayland, which is where they picked up the weapons, but most of the cargo originated on Kuat."

"Kuat?"

"Yes," Leia said. "Of course, we don't know exactly who sent the supplies—the company name they gave was a shell, and we haven't worked back to who's really the source of the funds, but we will."

"Jaina thought there was something rotten about the senator from Kuat, Viqi Shesh, when they met back on Duro. You don't think . . . ?"

"I don't trust Viqi Shesh as far as an Ewok could throw her," Leia said. "But it's still too early to make accusations." She paused. "By the way, there's something else you should know—there's news from Coruscant. Chief Fey'lya ordered Luke's arrest."

"You're kidding. He really made good on that threat?"

"Maybe, or maybe it was just a more elaborate bluff. Luke and Mara didn't take any chances, though. They left before the arrest could be made and joined up with Booster." Her voice softened. "So you see, there are other things you *could* be doing."

"Now you're trying to change my mind again?"

"No," Leia said firmly.

"Fine," Jacen answered. "What else did you learn from the captain?"

"That there will be another ship along in a few days—a freighter full of captives."

Jacen tried on a little smile. "Well, I'd better finish up with this E-wing today, then, if the *Princess of Blood* is going to be there to meet it."

"Don't *you* start that nonsense, too. Just because you're going with us doesn't mean you have to indulge every stupid thing your father comes up with, you know," Leia said.

"No, you're right to the core, Mom. We Solo men have to stick together. And I kinda like the name. I've been thinking about something to paint on the side—"

"This conversation is now over," Leia said, as seriously as she could. But she felt she could breathe freely again for the first time in several days, as if her lungs were suddenly twice the size they had been.

"Let me tell Dad, huh?" Jacen said.

"You've got it." With a lighter step, she went to make her own preparations.

TWENTY-FIVE

The reversion to realspace was different in the Yuuzhan Vong ship, somehow. Slower, maybe. Anakin made a mental note to try to discover whether that was merely perceptual or real. If the latter, were the alien ships more vulnerable during reversion? It would be worth knowing.

"Well?" Corran said, studying the changed star chart. "Where are we? Are we surrounded again?"

Beneath the hood, Tahiri turned her head this way and that, as if looking for something.

"Nothing that I see," she said. "There are plenty of ships in the system—most of them around that planet with three moons—but none of them look like Yuuzhan Vong yorik coral. And none of them seems to be paying attention to us."

"Interesting," Corran mused. "Three moons, eh? Is there a space station near that planet?"

"That could be what that is," Tahiri said.

"From your description, this likely *is* the Yag'Dhul system. The Givin have pretty good detection equipment. I wonder if this ship somehow dampens the hyperwave shock during reversion? Or if it's fully cloaked?"

"I'll ask the ship if you want," Tahiri said.

"Do that."

After a brief pause, Tahiri shook her head. "It doesn't know, or I'm not asking the right question. But it doesn't detect any probes locked on us."

"Maybe that's why the slower reversion," Anakin speculated.

"You noticed that too, huh?" Corran said. He rubbed his hands together. "Well, at least we didn't jump straight from a supernova into a neutron star. Though I suspect we don't have a lot of time here. Tahiri, any sense of what this ship was supposed to do once here?"

This time Tahiri nodded in the affirmative. "Yes. We're supposed to scent the readiness of the enemy."

"So it *is* a scout ship," Anakin said.

"Which means the main fleet will be expecting intelligence from us," Corran concluded. "The question is, how long will they wait before deciding something has gone wrong? Tahiri, can you fake a message? Stall them a little?"

Tahiri shook her head. "No. I'd have to use a villip, which means they would see my face."

Anakin watched Corran ponder that unhappily for a few seconds. "There are always the prisoners," he told the older Jedi.

"I realize that," Corran said, "though I doubt we can hope for their cooperation. It's worth a try, though. Meantime, we have to make contact with Yag'Dhul. Any ideas there?"

"The warmaster had a villip modified to broadcast on our frequencies," Anakin said.

"True. Can you do that?"

"No," Anakin confessed.

"Tahiri?"

"The ship doesn't know how to, and neither do I. We can fire a remote villip at a ship if it gets near enough."

Corran barked a phrase of laughter. "Which would certainly be interpreted as an attack. That's a last-ditch option. Anything else?"

"Sure," Anakin said. "I can modify the emergency beacon in the survival pack and run it through one of our wrist comm units."

"Do it, then," Corran told him. "Meanwhile, I'll interrogate prisoners while Tahiri keeps an eye on surrounding space and an ear up for queries from the fleet. Anakin, be back here in half an hour."

Corran surveyed the prisoners. The prison was makeshift—there probably was a real one someplace, but Corran hadn't wanted to waste the time looking for it. Using medical tape from the survival pack, Corran had fastened the living captives to the walls of the corridor leading to the helm, where he could keep an eye on them.

He studied the shapers first. They both had headdresses that looked like squirming masses of snakes. One had a hand that resembled some sort of sea creature, except that the fingers had tool attachments: pincers, a knife, and so on. Tahiri had insisted that the shapers needed to be strip-searched, and Corran had agreed to a hasty one. The search had produced several dubious organisms that had been placed in another chamber some distance away.

The remaining survivors Anakin and Tahiri had identified as members of the Shamed caste—workers who maintained the more unpleasant functions of the ship.

He didn't see anything in any of their eyes he thought he could work with—no fear or uncertainty, just a nearly uniform and haughty anger. Still, with a species you didn't know, it was hard to tell what facial expressions meant.

"Do any of you speak Basic?" he asked.

One of the shapers lifted his head, his orange-limned eyes fierce. "I speak your infidel tongue. It tastes like the waste excretions of an ill vhlor on my tongue, but I can speak it. Please, ask me something so I may deny it to you."

Not too promising. "We infidels don't normally sample the waste excretions of ill animals, so I don't fully understand the reference," Corran said. "I suppose that such delicacies are reserved for the Chosen."

"It's not possible for you to mock me," the shaper said softly.

"Sure it is. You may be dense enough not to recognize it, but I can certainly mock you."

"What do you want with me, infidel?"

"What's your name?"

"I am Kotaa of the glorious Domain Zun-qin," he replied.

"Who was designated to make contact with the fleet once this ship was in the Yag'Dhul system, Kotaa Zun-qin? What was he supposed to say?"

"He will say nothing. You killed him. The warriors are in

charge of this mission, of course. And do not think I will aid you in any scheme to defraud my people, *Jeedai*. Our fleet is poised to strike, as you must know, and strike it will."

Corran's eyes narrowed—not at Kotaa's words, but at something he had caught from the corner of his eye when the shaper had said the word *Jeedai*.

"I don't suppose you want to tell me when they will strike if they don't hear from us?"

"I would be happy to vivisect you," the shaper offered. "So that your death might offer the Yuuzhan Vong knowledge and thus have meaning. I am inclined to do you no other favor."

"I'll keep that in mind," Corran said. "I don't get an offer like that every day. Every other day, maybe . . ." He turned away from the shaper and looked more closely at the others. "Anyone else care to insult me?"

"I alone am able to mutter in your tuneless language," Kotaa Zun-qin said.

"That's fine," Corran said. "I have a translator." He approached one of the Shamed Ones. This was a smallish female, her only identifying marks a trio of poorly healed puckered burns on each cheek. He cut her free of the med tape binding her to the bulkhead. The shaper yammered something at the Shamed One in Yuuzhan Vong, and she answered tersely.

Corran pulled his blaster and motioned for the Shamed One to go ahead of him. Together they went up the corridor and into the control room.

"What's going on, Tahiri?" Corran asked.

"Not much. We're still not noticed, so far as I can tell, and no more Yuuzhan Vong ships have jumped."

"No news is good news. Can you talk to one of the Vong for me?"

"Yuuzhan Vong," Tahiri corrected.

"Whatever. Can you translate?"

"Sure," she said cheerfully, removing the control mask from her head.

When the Shamed One saw Tahiri's scars, her eyes widened, and she gabbled something in her own language.

"What did she say?" Corran asked. He really hated having to rely on secondhand information. He hated having *no* information even more.

"She noticed my scars," Tahiri explained. "She asked if I am the Jedi-who-was-shaped."

"She's heard of you?"

"I guess so."

Very, very interesting, Corran thought. Unless this one was actually at Yavin—and what would the odds of that be?—word was getting around, even among the Shamed Ones. Maybe especially among the Shamed Ones.

"Ask her name," Corran instructed.

"It's Taan," Tahiri said after consulting with the Yuuzhan Vong.

"Tell Taan I saw her make a strange face when the shaper called me a Jedi," Corran said. "Ask her what that meant."

Tahiri conversed with the Shamed One briefly, then turned her green eyes up to Corran.

"She wants to know if it's true what they say about the Jedi."

"What do they say?"

"That the Jedi are the salvation of the Shamed Ones."

Corran considered that. "She thinks of you as something special, doesn't she?"

Tahiri's cheeks pinkened. "Apparently the story of what happened on Yavin Four is a popular one among the Shamed Ones. Or a version of the story, anyway."

"Really. Can you get the short version from her? And be sure not to correct her if her story conflicts with the facts."

Looking a bit puzzled, Tahiri asked the question and received a lengthy answer. She translated it for Corran verbatim, in pieces.

"The Jedi have powers that no Yuuzhan Vong has. We know the warriors, the shapers, and the intendants are jealous of these powers. Some even fear them. At first we feared the Jedi, too, for they were infidels and dangerous foes. But on Yavin Four, two Jedi came. They came to redeem Vua Rapuung, once a mighty warrior who was marked with Shame by the shaper Mezhan Kwaad. One of the Jedi had been captured by this same shaper, and another became the comrade of Vua Rapuung. Together, side by side, the Shamed One and the Jedi defeated the shaper and redeemed Vua Rapuung. He died as no other warrior has died, saluting an infidel. The gods not only permitted this, they must have aided it. Now many say that perhaps the high castes do not know the will of the gods as well as they say, or perhaps they are hiding our redemption from us. Perhaps Shamed Ones are not shamed because it was ordained. Perhaps the Shamed Ones are not shamed because the gods hate them. Perhaps instead, our status is imposed on us by the high castes so they will have hands to do the least and most onerous of tasks, so they may live lives of glory and not debase themselves with the mundane. Perhaps the Jedi are our salvation. The legend of Vua Rapuung and the Jedi suggests it, and is often told."

"Wow," Corran said, when the recitation was done. "Are you sure you got all of that right?"

"Pretty sure," Tahiri said. "I might have used a different word here and there, but it still comes out to the same thing."

"Ask her if *she* believes this."

Again, his query was translated and asked.

"She wasn't sure. Now that she sees our might, she thinks it may be so."

"Ask her if she is willing to work with us, as Vua Rapuung did."

More unintelligible chatter; then Tahiri grinned. "She says she will help us, if there is anything someone as humble as she can do."

"There is something we can try, at least," Corran said. "It may not work, but it should be better than nothing."

Anakin returned to the helm, lugging the communication device he had patched together from the beacon and his comlink. He found Corran and Tahiri with a Yuuzhan Vong of the Shamed caste. The Shamed One was talking to a villip. The villip had modeled itself to the massively scarred visage of a warrior.

"What—" he began, but Corran cut him off with a severe look and a finger held to his lip. Anakin took the hint—the villip might pick up his extraneous sound and transmit it, as well. He chewed his lips restlessly. The face on the villip scowled and barked, hissed, and finally, more calmly, seemed to give a series of instructions. Then the villip relaxed into its normal, neutral form.

Corran glanced at Tahiri. "Well?" he demanded.

"I think it went pretty well," she said.

"*What* went pretty well?" Anakin asked.

"Our friend here just spun off quite a tale," Corran told him, nodding at the Yuuzhan Vong. "She told the commander of the fleet that when they came out of hyperspace, something went wrong. She didn't know what, because she is merely a Shamed One. She was tending the grutchin larvae, located near the primary dovin basal, and felt a weird jolt. When she didn't receive any orders for a time, she went to see what was needed of her and found the whole crew dead, in fact, hardly recognizable, pasted all over the bulkheads."

Anakin pursed his lips and then chopped his head forward. "I like it," he said. "That leaves a couple of possibilities for the commander to think about. Either she's lying, and there's been a revolt on board the ship, or she's telling the truth. If she's telling the truth, they'll know that what she described was the result of a complete failure of the dovin basal's ability to negate inertia—except right at the base of the basal. After that, they have to decide if the *Stalking Moon* ran into something natural—I dunno, a quantum black hole that made the basal recoil, something like that— or some superweapon the Givin have in place to wreck unwanted ships."

Corran nodded. "Glad you approve," he said sarcastically. But beneath his tone Anakin sensed a cool admiration that made him feel suddenly self-conscious.

"You ever consider a career in covert security?" the older Jedi asked. "Anyway, yes, that's basically what I was thinking. Even if they think option one is the case—"

"Revolt?" Tahiri said doubtfully. "I don't think so. Even

if they could conceive of Shamed Ones killing warriors and
shapers, they wouldn't *want* to admit it. Do you know what
would happen to the commander who let something like
that happen on his watch?"

"As I was saying," Corran went on, a little testily, "even
if they consider one, they have to consider the others before
they bring a whole fleet here or even a second ship. They're
trying to explain to Taan how to relay the telemetry of the
sensing nodules, and she's pretending to cooperate. So. Let's
hope they're for real and we have a bit of time. Anakin, you
were successful?"

"Yes. The signal isn't that strong, so it may take a few
moments to tune."

"Get started, then."

Anakin nodded and set to work. "Why Yag'Dhul, do you
think?" he asked Corran, as he fiddled with the gain, fo-
cusing on the distant hum of hyperwave noise from farther
insystem. "I mean, if they want Coruscant, they already
have Duro to stage from."

"They're closing their back door. Yag'Dhul sits on the in-
tersection of the Rimma Trade Route and the Corellian
Trade Spine. It also gives them a clean shot at Thyferra."

"Oh!" Tahiri said. "Bacta!"

"Right. If they control bacta production, they control the
health of everyone in the galaxy. Or maybe it's a ruse—the
New Republic puts a lot of ships and matériel at Thyferra,
and the Yuuzhan Vong try to take Fondor again or push on
to a less-defended Coruscant from Duro. Either way,
holding Yag'Dhul gives them a lot more options."

Anakin had a steady feedback response. "All right," he
said. "We're ready."

"Hail the planetary defense force," Corran said. He
closed his eyes, concentrating. "Try . . ." He reeled off a
quadratic equation, then smiled wearily. "It might not be
right, but it ought to get their attention."

"Hailing, Captain," Anakin said.

Five minutes later, there was still no response. Anakin
modulated the wave form, sharpened the gain, and repeated.

"It ought to be working," Anakin muttered. "Unless they're deaf."

"Or unless their attention is focused elsewhere," Corran mused.

"What do you mean?" Anakin asked. "Why wouldn't they be watching their borders?"

"You don't see any ships or even probes in this region, do you? The Yuuzhan Vong have softened up other worlds with internal conflict and other methods of espionage. They may already have agents here."

"Or maybe they've already poisoned Yag'Dhul, like they did Belkadan."

"Too slow. Word would get out," Corran said.

"Unless they use something we haven't seen yet," Tahiri pointed out. "That's what shapers do, you know, come up with new things."

Corran nodded. "They do seem to keep condensing weapons out of nebular gas," he allowed. "But—"

Their speculation was cut off by a whine and sputter from Anakin's rewired comm unit. Behind a sleet of gravitic interference, the naturally armored figure of a Givin glowered at them with empty eyes. More than anything his— her?—face resembled a large human skull that had been melted, allowed to sag, and re-form.

"Yag'Dhul primary bastion to unidentified ship," the Givin said. "You have used an outdated and illegal hail code. However, your ship conforms to the configuration of a Yuuzhan Vong reconnaissance vessel." Then the mouth slit clattered something unidentifiable.

To Anakin, anyway. Tahiri gave a little gasp of horror.

"What did he say?" Corran demanded.

Tahiri turned her aventurine gaze on the other two Jedi. "It's Yuuzhan Vong. He said, 'Welcome. We've been expecting you.' "

TWENTY-SIX

Wedge Antilles pinched his face in a scowl. Unlike some other things about him, time had only made his glare more impressive. Jaina felt it brush her and shivered, though she knew she wasn't its intended target. That would be Kyp, seated between her and Gavin at the roughly finished wooden table.

"General Antilles—" she began, but then the full weight of his anger *did* fall on her, stopping her cold.

"You should have told us he would be here, Lieutenant Solo," Wedge said, his voice as soft and tense as the wire on Tionne's lute. "It was less than honest, and far less than I expect of you."

Beyond the rustic stone walls of the hilltop garden and its topiary canopy, the sun jeweled the Silver Sea with noontime light, and the fields that rolled up to the shore breathed of bristing blooms and balmgrass. A herd of stumpy, gracile-necked fecklen whirred and boomed their displeasure at a family of hopping squalls. The sky was blue, with no hint of vapor. After the cramped quarters of an X-wing, a ranch on Chandrila was the best meeting place Jaina could have imagined. More practically, it was also a place where it was easy to see one's enemy coming and speak freely, with only minimal fear that unwanted ears might hear. That was especially true because the estate was owned by a trusted relative of Gavin Darklighter's wife, Sera.

But that lovely world all but vanished for Jaina, replaced by Wedge's eyes, those verdant polished spheres that had seen so much combat and tragedy, that had looked kindly on her as a child. Wedge, who had fought alongside her father and mother and her uncle Luke from the very beginning. To have him glare at her like this was . . . very difficult.

She felt a sudden, comforting presence, and for a minute accepted it, grasped for it even. She needed every reassurance she could get. Then she recognized it as Kyp's touch. That was the last thing in the universe she needed right now, comforting or not.

Get back, Kyp.

She swallowed and addressed Wedge again. "General, I apologize, but I didn't think you would meet with me if you knew Kyp was involved. Neither did Colonel Darklighter."

Antilles now turned his ire toward Gavin. "You were in on this too, Gavin?"

"She could have hidden Durron's connection from both of us, Wedge, simply by not bringing him along when she met with me. She didn't. She was up front with me. I advised her to do things this way because I know you and—more to the point—I thought there was every possibility that my call to you was monitored. There are plenty of people who would love to make a present of Kyp Durron to the Yuuzhan Vong. You want to blame someone, blame me."

General Antilles chewed at that, didn't seem to like it, and swallowed it anyway. He glanced back up at Kyp. "Durron, I don't like you," he said. "The very best thing you are is a murderer. The very worst—"

"Wait a moment, General," Kyp interrupted. "You know what I was going through back then. Han Solo and Master Skywalker forgave me and brought me back into the fold. I had hoped that you could, too."

"You don't deserve their forgiveness," Wedge shot back. "Look how you've repaid them. Luke you denounce and deride, and as for Han, you've roped his daughter into a politically precarious position, if not something far worse."

"General," Kyp said quietly, "I'm sorry about Qwi Xux. I've told you that before. At the time I thought what I did was for the best. She had information in her head that could have brought the New Republic to its knees."

"You leave her out of this," Antilles warned. "You don't

even so much as speak her name, or I'll blast you where you stand."

"General," Jaina said desperately, "please. Whatever you may think of Kyp, he's discovered something important. Something that threatens us all."

"Fine," Antilles said, sitting back and brusquely waving his hand. "You have evidence of this danger? Let me see it. The sooner this is over with, the sooner I can find some clean air to breathe."

The four of them watched in silence as Kyp replayed the holo Jaina had seen last beneath the frozen surface of an unnamed world. When it was over, the silence continued for some time. It was Wedge who broke it.

"Emperor's black bones," he muttered.

"That was my reaction," Gavin replied. "Now you understand why I thought you should see this."

"Yes. I suppose I do." Wedge straightened and knitted his hands together. He looked at Jaina. "You've seen this for yourself?"

"No," Jaina admitted. "I've seen this same holo. But it's pretty clear what it is."

Wedge rubbed his forehead. "No," he said, "it's not unambiguous. It could be a fueling device, for instance."

Kyp cleared his throat. "General Antilles, may I speak?"

"Go ahead," Wedge said, grimacing.

"It may be a fueling device, of course. That doesn't mean it isn't a weapon. If that ship can manipulate gravity at that scale, only fools wouldn't understand its military implications. Whatever you might say about the Yuuzhan Vong, they aren't fools."

"No," Wedge said. "No, they aren't. But until we see it used militarily—"

"It would be too late then, General," Kyp burst out, leaping to his feet.

"Shut up and sit down," Wedge snapped. "Let me finish what I was saying."

Kyp's lips remained pressed tight, and for an instant Jaina caught a glimpse of something she didn't understand. It passed quickly.

Kyp sat down.

"You're done, Durron? Good. What I was saying was, until we have real evidence that this is a military weapon, we can't go to the senate with this. Maybe not even then."

"Why?" Jaina asked.

"Because they won't do anything," Wedge replied. "At least not right away. And senate security is leakier than a gas siever. The Yuuzhan Vong would know within hours that we're aware of their superweapon. Hours after that, their officials would assure Borsk Fey'lya that it's either harmless, or something meant only to be used in their own defense. They'll reiterate that they have no designs on the rest of our systems so long as we comply with their demands."

"You mean like turning anyone with Jedi training over to them," Jaina interjected.

"Right. Which brings up my final point in this round." He looked straight at Kyp. "When they consider the source, a lot of senators would rather trust the Yuuzhan Vong than Kyp Durron."

Kyp bore that silently. Jaina couldn't.

"Your pardon, General, but that's absolutely insane. Kyp's been out there fighting while the senate has dithered, caved to Yuuzhan Vong demands, and ordered the arrest of Master Skywalker. If anyone isn't to be trusted, it's Fey'lya and the senate."

She braced for another salvo from Wedge, but he smiled gently instead. "Solo, that's what I just said."

"It is?"

"More or less. Understand this, though—I know you don't care for Chief Fey'lya. I don't either. But he isn't a traitor and he's not stupid. He doesn't think the Yuuzhan Vong will keep their word any more than you or I do. But he *is* a politician, and he thinks he can play that game better than they can. Everything he's doing is aimed at buying time, and he's right. Time is what we need, to understand Yuuzhan Vong technology, to digest their tactics, to strengthen our own forces. Fey'lya will never order a strike while the

Yuuzhan Vong are quiescent. He'll maintain the illusion of truce as long as he can."

"So you're saying there will be no military mission to take this thing out?" Gavin said, outraged.

"No official mission, no," Wedge replied.

"Then what *are* we going to do?" Jaina asked.

"Whatever we do," Wedge said, "there will be repercussions. Anyone involved in this could easily end up in the same escape pod as Luke."

"Wouldn't that be a shame," Gavin drawled. "Rogue Squadron has resigned from the New Republic before. We can do it again."

"Rogue Squadron can't handle that," Wedge said, waving at the frozen holo of the ship and its trail of starfire. "Can it, Durron?"

Kyp nodded reluctantly. "The Yuuzhan Vong have the Sernpidal system locked up tight. It will take real muscle to get in there. But if we take out that thing, we also take out their major shipyard. You want to buy time, General? That could buy you quite a lot."

"I see that, Durron. But I'm just a retired adviser to Rogue Squadron. I don't have the power to send a fleet."

"General, with all respect," Jaina said, "you may not have the official power, but you have the influence."

Wedge folded his arms and regarded her for a long moment. "Solo, do you believe this? Do you believe what Durron has shown us?"

Jaina felt the weight of that question pressing her toward the planet's core. *This is why Kyp wanted me here,* she reflected. *They trust me.*

"Yes," she said. "I believe him."

The general hesitated another few seconds, then held up his hands in surrender. "Gavin, I don't have to ask where you stand on this."

"No, sir, General. I saw that thing when they were growing it, when there was plenty of time to destroy it. I had to sit around while my information was all but ignored, and now we have something to deal with that we may not be able to stop at all. But Rogue Squadron will give it its best shot."

"Volunteers only," Wedge warned.

"Of course. As if that will make a difference."

Wedge grinned wryly. "I understand, but the point has to be made. As I said, I want everyone to understand the political as well as the mortal danger inherent in this."

"Understood."

"Very well. I'm going to contact Admiral Kre'fey. I think he will be extremely interested in this situation. If that falls through, well, we'll go from there." He turned to Kyp. "I want you to understand something, Durron. You will not be in control of this mission, nor will you be at liberty to command your gang of pilots unsupervised. We'll need every ship we can get, but not if that means the chance of an unpleasant surprise from a bunch of undisciplined hotshots."

"If my pilots were undisciplined, General, they would not be alive," Kyp replied. "But if you're making my participation dependent on following orders, that's fine with me—so long as I'm involved in the decision-making process. They are my pilots—I owe them a voice."

"A voice you'll get," Wedge replied, his own speech strained. "But for the duration of this mission, you will submit to authority."

Kyp nodded fractionally. "As you say, General."

Antilles rose, nodding at Gavin and Jaina. "Colonel, Lieutenant. I'll speak to you later."

That's the problem with trying to hide from a Jedi, Jaina thought. Through the spirate leaves of the tintolive trees grappling with the hillside, she could see Kyp, dressed in Jedi robes, walking up the flagstone steps to the small pavilion she had found in her search for solitude. The afternoon had brought puffs of cloud with it to wander shadows across the plain below. A lone, distant peak was crowned with darkness and lightning, a reminder that not all water vapor was so peaceful. Behind her, the centuries-old villa rambled across the ridgetop, a maze of gardens, orchards, and cool stone halls. Her mother had once described a family estate on Alderaan. Jaina imagined it had been much like this.

"Hello, Kyp." She sighed as he came around an immaculately groomed stand of some sort of feather-leafed tree with bark scored into diamond patterns.

"You're avoiding me," he said.

"You noticed."

"Mind telling me why?"

"Because I know you're going to ask me to fly with you, and I can't." *And because you're hiding something from me.* But she didn't want to give that last up to him just yet.

Kyp leaned his shoulder against the nearest tree. "Why not?" he wondered. "Not that I was going to ask." His voice was gentle, jovial, and he grinned suddenly at something he must have seen on her face.

"What's got you so amused?" Jaina asked.

"You looked . . . surprised. It's fetching."

"I fetch nothing," she snapped. "It's just *you*. You're all over the grid. One minute you're as touchy and surly as a feral bantha, the next you're the meditative Jedi Master, the dear friend, the sensitive fellow. Who are you, Kyp?"

"Who are you, Jaina?"

"Oh, no. Don't start that with me."

"The questions you ask condition the answers you get," he said with a small shrug.

"Okay, okay. So you didn't come to ask me to fly with you."

"No, you were right about that," Kyp admitted, absently scratching his left ear. "I intended to ask."

"So you've asked and I can't. For a lot of reasons. Not the least of which is that I'm still a member of Rogue Squadron, and they'll be in the same battle."

"As you say, asked and answered. But I have a more important request."

"Get to it, then."

Kyp straightened and clasped his hands loosely together. His features took on an unusual gravity. Behind him, in the middle distance, a flock of avians with quicksilver wings rose toward the sky. A moment later, when the mutter of thunder that had startled the flock reached her ears, Kyp was still hesitating.

"I'd like you to be my apprentice."

"You're kidding."

"Not in the slightest. You've interrupted your Jedi training. I think you should take it up again. I think you will bring something very special to the order."

"Yeah? And why wouldn't I go back to Aunt Mara, then?"

"Because she's unavailable. Besides, you don't agree with her. You have much more in common with me."

"In a Sarlacc's belly."

"Whatever. But you know it's true." He paused. "You're trying too hard, and maybe it was too early for me to ask. I like you, Jaina, and I value what you are and what you could be. Keep it in mind. I'll leave you to the peace you sought." He turned to go.

He was almost out of sight when she leaned forward and called out to him.

"Wait."

He turned slowly.

"I . . . uh, I'll think about it. Probably not for long, but yeah, I'll think about it."

"Good," he replied. "That makes me happy."

"Yeah, well, don't get too happy," she said.

She didn't watch him go. Instead she turned her face out to the vista.

I'm blushing! She berated herself. *How ridiculous.*

But she didn't feel *merely* ridiculous. She felt . . .

No. Forget it.

So she turned her thoughts outward, to space above, to her brothers and her parents, wondering how they were, what they were doing, hoping they were well.

And to the coming battle.

TWENTY-SEVEN

"Chalk up another one for the *Princess of Blood*," Han said, lifting a mug of something the bartender had called Corellian ale—and which was certainly anything but. "That's what? Our fifth cargo?"

"Losing count already, Dad?" Jacen asked, sipping his own dubious concoction.

Around them, the cantina was color and sound, motion and emotion. Even without consciously using the Force, Jacen felt mired in swirling drunkenness, avarice, secret sorrows, and public appetites.

Harsh Tatooine light lanced into the cantina through two windows facing out into the street. Above, various species mingled on a second-story balcony that circumscribed the round central room. In the center of the dusty floor of yellowish tiles, a Dressellian slung drinks from within a circular, red-topped counter.

Near Han and Jacen, ten bovine Gran clad in matching umber jumpsuits clustered together around a table too small for them. They whispered in their sonorous tongue, casting occasional three-eyed glances at two rodentlike Chadra-Fan squinting across another table at a Dug and arguing in loud tones over a hand of sabacc.

"You aren't going all meditative Jedi on me again, are you?" his father asked, with that little quirk in his mouth.

"No," Jacen answered solemnly. "I'm all pirate. I pillage; therefore I am."

"That's the spirit." Han cocked an eyebrow quizzically. "Really? No lectures for the old man?"

"None at all. It's not like we're keeping what we take. It's being put to good use."

Han sighed. Jacen thought it sounded a little mournful. "Yeah," he said. "That's true. Look, son, I've been thinking—after this war is over, we're going to have bills to pay. The senate has had most of my assets seized, and who knows if we'll ever see them again." He put his elbows on the table and steepled his fingers. "So—"

"Dad! No!" Jacen said. "If we're aiding the resistance, that's one thing. But if we keep more than operating expenses, we really *are* pirates."

"Right, sure, but just a *little* off the top wouldn't make much of a difference, would it? In the long run?"

Jacen stared, horrified at his father's sincere gaze—until the elder Solo winked, and he got it.

"You were having me on."

"Just checking, kid. Making sure you really were still my son Jacen."

"I am that—whoever he is, that's me."

Han looked down at the table. "Yeah. And . . . uh, whoever he is, I'm, uh, very proud of him."

"Thanks, Dad," Jacen said. He wanted, suddenly, to give his father a hug, but the newest cantina at Mos Eisley spaceport probably wasn't the best place to do that.

"Anyway," Han said. His gaze shifted about uncomfortably, then needled out someplace past Jacen. "There we go," he said. "The rest of our dinner party."

Jacen didn't turn. One thing he'd learned around his father—if there were only two of you in a place like this, it was best if you weren't both looking in the same direction.

"Well, well," a profound bass boomed behind them. "Han Solo. And if I make my guess, one of his spawn."

"Hello, Shalo. How are things?"

"I don't believe it. The great Han Solo actually knows my name. I told you I was sending Terya."

"I have a good memory," Han replied. "And Terya is a Rodian." He glanced around the cantina. "Looking good. How's business?"

Shalo finally moved into Jacen's field of vision. He was

human and surprisingly small to have such a deep voice. Bald, craggy-nosed, about his dad's age.

"Not bad," Shalo said. "The Yuuzhan Vong snubbed their flat noses at Tatooine, so we're the center of commerce out here on the Rim, these days."

"Uh-huh. That's pretty convenient for you, I guess. I hear you're giving even Chalmun's some competition."

"Yeah, well, times change. Business changes. My drinks are cheaper."

Han jerked a thumb toward the man. "Last time I saw Shalo here he was a petty thug at the bottom of Durga the Hutt's food chain."

"That was a long time ago."

"Sure. And after that you worked for Hirth, out of Abregado-rae. That went sour, too, didn't it? Then you got involved with the Hutts again, and they sent you here to manage one of their operations. Come to think of it, I guess the occupation of Nal Hutta is the best thing that ever happened to you, huh, Shalo? Now the operation's all yours."

"It ain't been bad. Solo, you got a point? I'm a busy man. I've heard you're back in business, so to speak. You have something you want moved?"

"Not exactly, Shalo. I need a little information."

"So long as you're willing to pay for it."

"Sure," Han said. "Like you said, I'm back in business now." He passed a hundred credits across the table toward Shalo. "Gesture of good faith," he said.

"Okay. What do you want to know?"

"There's a certain shipping concern. I think you know the one I mean—has certain *occupational* interests?"

"I can't say I know what you're talking about. There are lots of shipping firms."

Han leaned forward a little. "But this one ah, c'mon, Shalo. Who do you sell all your slaves to?"

"Slaves? I'm not in that business, Solo."

"You disappoint me, Shalo."

Shalo smiled and shook his head. "No, you disappoint *me*, Solo. I guess everyone gets old. Now your son pays the price."

Han looked at Jacen in mock surprise. "You're picking up the tab, son?"

"My boss doesn't pay me that well," Jacen replied.

Han looked at Shalo. "I guess now we don't know what *you* mean, Shalo."

"I mean there's no bounty in the galaxy higher than the one on your boy, here, and I'm collecting it." He raised his hand and dropped it.

Nothing happened. Puzzled, he repeated the signal frantically.

A bright green shaft of light suddenly appeared, jutting out of the tabletop. It terminated a centimeter from Shalo's throat.

"Urk," Shalo said.

"Please don't move," Jacen requested sincerely.

"You get 'em all, Karrde?" Han called into the silence that now ruled the cantina. He kept his eyes focused on Shalo.

"Shada has it under control," a cultured voice came back. "We'll be right there. I'd like to make sure all of my people are in position."

Jacen couldn't glance around, but he felt a number of newcomers enter the cantina.

"Take your time," Han called back. "I was just having a chat with my old buddy Shalo."

"You're crazy, Solo," Shalo said.

"Now, is that polite? Listen, Shalo. I can wipe out you and your whole petty operation if I want—or you can cooperate. I . . ." Han smiled and shook a finger. "You know—I *did* know about your employees with the blaster rifles. So did my colleagues. One of them—do you know Shada D'ukal? She can be very disarming."

"D'ukal is here?"

"I love the way you say my name," a woman's voice said from just behind Jacen. She stepped into view.

Shada D'ukal was a strikingly handsome woman in perhaps her late forties with long black hair streaked liberally with pure white. The man next to her was a good match to her with his silver-streaked hair and impeccable goatee.

"Captain Karrde," Han said, standing. "I'm so glad you could make it. Shada, good to see you again. You've both met my son Jacen."

Karrde stroked his goatee and studied the offered seat with mock suspicion. "Oh, well," he said at last. "If I can't trust a scoundrel and a pirate, who can I trust?"

"Hey, I trusted you."

"A good thing, too," Shada said. "Two of the sharpers were assassin droids."

"Shalo, I'm impressed."

The two newcomers sat down. "Hello, Jacen," Shada said. "I'm a little surprised to see you here."

"You're not the only one," Jacen replied.

"It's the Solo blood," Han opined. "It comes with the looks. So how's things with you two?"

"Things are going well enough on our end," Karrde said. "I think I can meet whatever needs you have. But first, I have a little present for you."

"Hey?" Shalo said. "Could you please have your Jedi get that thing away from my throat?"

Han raised both brows skyward. "Oh, you mean *this* Jedi? My eldest son? The one you were going to turn in for the biggest bounty in the galaxy?"

"I wouldn't have actually *done* it," Shalo explained. "I was going to try to extort protection from you, that's all."

"Yeah, right. You're slime, Shalo. You give the Hutts a good name. And now you're going to give *me* something."

"Wh-what?"

"What I *asked* for, you vac-head."

"Oh. The shipping company."

Han nodded. "That's right, the shipping company."

"Berths fifteen through eighteen. It's all I can tell you."

Han leveled a finger. "Shalo . . ."

"Hey, it's not like they have a name and a logo. They just come and pick 'em up."

"The slaves?" Jacen asked. "What do you suppose happens to them?"

"I don't know. I don't ask questions."

"You know where they go," Jacen accused.

"I deny that."

Jacen caught something then, in the Force.

"Hey, Dad?"

"In a minute, son." Han jerked his chin toward Shalo. "Let him deny it," he said. "It doesn't matter. We'll check out your story, Shalo, and if it turns out you're lying to us—"

"Yeah, yeah, you'll be back, I know."

"No. Oh, no. You're going *with* us. But for right now, I'm going to turn you over to this nice lady here, okay? I need to talk to my other friends."

Shalo turned to see the "nice" lady and blanched when his eyes fell on a towering, white-furred, heavily fanged humanoid. The beast hissed and spat something that might have been a language.

"No, H'sishi," Karrde said gently, apparently answering. "You can't eat him. Yet."

Shalo's face was nearly as white as the Togorian's fur as she led him off.

"Now," Han said, "what's my surprise?"

Karrde smiled. "I had my slicer look into those ships you've been hitting, the ones coming out of Kuat. It took some doing, even for him. The funds for the ships were washed so many times they ought to be random molecules by now. But in the end, it looks like the allocation can be traced back to the office of Kuat Photonics."

"Kuat Photonics?" Jacen asked.

"A privately held corporation." Karrde handed Han a data card. "A list of the owners."

"Would Viqi Shesh be on that list?" Jacen asked.

Karrde studied him. "You expect her to be?"

"We had some trouble with her at Duro," Jacen said. "It was just a feeling."

"Sorry to disappoint you," Karrde said. "Not under that name."

"Maybe you could check the names?" Jacen asked. "See if they're legitimate?"

Karrde laughed sardonically and looked at Han. "Is that the Solo sense of humor, or is he serious?"

"I take that to mean no," Jacen said dryly.

"What he means is," Han explained, "it would take a long time—a *very* long time—and probably get us nowhere. Meanwhile, we'd be there instead of here, where we can actually stop the ships. If Shesh is behind this, we'll hurt her more out here than on Coruscant."

"The old man has it right," Karrde said. "The tracks my slicer found are faint to begin with. They could be easily erased."

"But we might find proof," Jacen argued. "Real proof."

"Maybe," Han said. "Maybe at berths fifteen through eighteen."

"Are we going to hit them?" Shada asked.

"Hit them? No. They'll be easier pickings in space."

"Shouldn't we at least check them out?" Jacen said.

Shada nodded. "I'll have look."

Jacen straightened. "Mind if I tag along?"

"I do," Han said. "Or didn't you get that part about the bounty on your head?"

"Jealous, Solo?" Karrde asked Han.

"How's that?"

"Well, your son is pulling down easily three times what you were ever worth."

"Inflation. In Imperial credits it works out about the same. And don't distract me—Jacen goes back to the *Falcon*."

"Oh, no. You aren't my captain on the ground, Dad."

"Where did you pick up *that* nonsense?" Han growled.

"You wanted me to help with this business—I'm helping. If Shada will have me, I'm going with her."

"A lady never minds the escort of a handsome gentleman. Especially one with Jedi powers."

Han threw up his hands. "Fine. I give up. But you can make that two handsome escorts, because I'm not letting my son out of my sight. I know this slagheap too well."

Karrde's eyes narrowed, suddenly, and he drew his blaster. "This is, for the moment, an academic conversation, my friends."

"Why?" Jacen asked.

His answer came as blasterfire.

TWENTY-EIGHT

Nom Anor, alone in his sleeping chamber, prodded the gablith masquer that gave him the appearance of a Givin, and it peeled off. A little more reluctantly, he coaxed the communication gnullith-villip hybrid from his throat. The sleeping quarters were always pressurized, no matter what, so he ought to be safe. Even Givin could not stand exposure to hard vacuum indefinitely.

Posing as a Givin had more unique challenges than any role he had assumed before, their language not the least. When speaking to one another, they expressed themselves in phrases that more resembled calculus than grammar, though of course the two had much in common. Even with the tizowyrm to translate for him, Nom Anor still often tripped on the language. For that reason alone, many of the Givin knew who and what he really was—it was only with the help of his local agents that he managed to remain disguised to the rest.

This he disliked. Long experience had taught him that Nom Anor could count only on Nom Anor. And if he were discovered by the wrong people . . .

He put the gnullith-villip back on. Why take chances?

Noting the time on the ridiculously complex Givin chronometer, he withdrew the box that housed his villip and prepared to stroke it to life. He found it already pulsing for attention, and in a few moments he regarded a facsimile of Commander Qurang Lah's face.

"The *Stalking Moon* is in this system?" Nom Anor asked the warrior.

Qurang Lah's features twisted into a glare.

"Your perfect plan develops clots of blood," he growled.

"You mean the Rodian Jedi?" Nom Anor asked. "Our agents on Eriadu have dealt with him."

"Yes? And the infidel ship that jumped into the midst of my fleet?"

Nom Anor didn't blink. He couldn't. It had rapidly become clear, working with Qurang Lah, that the warrior harbored a deep resentment toward him. This was not unexpected, but it was not trivial, either. Nom Anor had no warriors loyal to him; he had to rely on Qurang Lah to place his fleet and troops when the time came. There would come a moment when Nom Anor was truly vulnerable, and at that moment, Qurang Lah might hold the key to his survival.

That, to Nom Anor's mind, was the only flaw in his plan, whatever trouble Qurang Lah thought he foresaw.

"Your fleet is on a major shipping route," the executor said. "The possibility of a chance meeting with an infidel ship was known to us. I'm certain you destroyed it."

"Almost instantly. But now we have lost contact with the *Stalking Moon*."

That was an unpleasant surprise. "Perhaps they've merely experienced disorientation after leaving hyperspace. The cloaking shadow it wears is prone to complications."

"And perhaps your 'allies' were waiting for her and *destroyed* her as she reverted."

"That's not possible," Nom Anor said. Or was it? The Givin were stranger even than the humans, much harder to read. Had he miscalculated so badly?

No. This was a minor setback, nothing more. The plan was good.

"We have some hours, yet," Nom Anor assured the warleader. "I shall discover what troubles, if any, the *Stalking Moon* is having and report promptly back to you."

"See you do," Qurang Lah snapped.

Nom Anor's expression soured as the villip calmed. If something had happened to the advance ship, could he still convince his Givin allies to perform their act of sabotage?

Of course he could.

But he smelled Jedi in this somewhere, beyond the lone Rodian who had identified Nom Anor as Yuuzhan Vong when visiting Yag'Dhul Station. It had been easy enough to have him tracked and murdered, and his Peace Brigade contacts on Eriadu assured him that the Rodian had never had a chance to communicate to anyone else.

But then the Peace Brigade had been known to lie before, when they thought it made for better groveling, and the Jedi had the power to send thought without words.

Nom Anor sat and composed his ideas carefully. If there were Jedi here, what would they do?

He had to be ready for them when they came. He *would* be. And perhaps, added to the conquest of Yag'Dhul, Givin slaves, and the threat to the source of bacta in the nearby Thyferra system, he would have another jewel or two to hand Tsavong Lah.

TWENTY-NINE

Luke gripped Mara's hand and tried to keep his tears at bay, tried to make his mind still, free of pain, fear, and grief.

"Cut it out, Luke," Mara said. "You're giving me the creeps." Her voice was a dry croak, barely louder than the stridulations of larval tlikist.

Luke took a shuddering breath and tried to smile. "Sorry," he said. "Not one of my better days."

"It's got to be better than mine," Mara said.

Her hand in his felt papery and hot. He gripped it harder, feeling the disease beneath. It was in furious motion, mutating at rates that medical science had once considered impossible. The only still point in her body was that place where their child floated. Somehow, even now, when her skin had gone blotchy and her hair was falling out, when the chain reaction that was fast approaching meltdown raged in her flesh, she still kept their child safe.

"Maybe—maybe it's time to let Cilghal induce labor," he said.

"No." Mara's voice cracked on the word, but it was the loudest noise she had made in days. Her eyelids dropped over her pale orbs. "I told you," she whispered. "I can feel it's wrong. If I do that, we'll both die."

"How can you know that?"

"How can you ask? I *know*. The Force."

"But this is killing you, Mara," he said. The words sounded as if someone else were saying them, like an unknown language.

"No. Really? I would never . . . have . . . guessed."

He felt her fluttering toward unconsciousness again.

"Mara?"

"Still . . . here."

Luke glanced at the sleeping form of Cilghal on a nearby cot. The healer worked night and day, using the Force to slow the progress of the disease. The results were hardly noticeable. Only Mara had ever been able to control it, but her terrific will was too focused now.

"Mara," he said softly. "Mara, you have to let me in."

"I can manage, Luke."

"Mara, my love . . . no games this time. You want to do this your way, and I respect that. Now you have to respect me. That's my child, too—and you, you're the best part of my world. Let me help."

"Selfish," Mara said.

"Yes, maybe," Luke admitted.

"Meant me," Mara corrected. "Help our child."

Luke reached into her, then, into the maelstrom. He felt how truly feeble her life was. Her pain racked his body; her dark fevers gnawed at the fringes of his brain. It was overwhelming, and the most profound sensation of hopelessness he had ever felt shuddered through him.

No. I'm not here to take her pain. I'm here to add my strength. He knew it, but it felt beyond his control. There was too much, coming too fast. He pushed at it, forcing it away, trying to flow a river of vigor into her, but she wasn't there to receive it, to use it as only her body knew how. He was at the mercy of her disease as much as she was.

He heard a noise and realized he had cried out.

Calm. I am calm. I bring calm with me, and tranquility. I am tranquility.

But the sickness laughed at him. Starbursts of images and sensation exploded everywhere. He saw Palpatine's leering face, saw his own, younger features through a veneer of hatred. He was a child on the street, cold and lonely.

All negative feelings, all fears and hates and greeds. Only the worst of Mara was here, where the disease had its way.

He fought the despair, but it pooled in his feet and slowly, slowly filled him up, sap climbing inside a tree.

He knew in that moment he could never save her. Mara was lost to him, forever.

THIRTY

"Oh, Sithspawn," Corran swore.

"The Givin are in league with the Yuuzhan Vong?" Anakin said doubtfully. "The Givin build *ships*. The Yuuzhan Vong *hate* technology."

"Yeah, but their real estate isn't all that promising," Corran said. "Maybe they figure that if they cooperate, the Yuuzhan Vong won't bother 'em much."

"I don't understand," Tahiri said.

"Yag'Dhul has three moons," Corran explained. "The tidal forces are so strong that at times and places the atmosphere itself gets rolled back, exposing the surface to space. The Givin actually evolved to survive in vacuum for short periods of time. What would the Yuuzhan Vong want with a planet like that? The location, yes, because it's strategic for purposes of their conquest. But they probably wouldn't settle the planet."

"I think they're waiting for a reply," Anakin noticed, gesturing at the tiny image of the Givin.

"Tahiri, tell them in Yuuzhan Vong we're having some minor difficulties, and we'll be back in touch in a moment."

"Sure." She said something into the comm unit. Then she looked back up. "They want to know why we aren't using the villip. They have theirs with them."

"Brother. This gets worse and worse." Corran stared at the row of villips. One was pulsing slightly. Was that it?

"Tell them it's none of their business," he said. "Make it sound like we're mad about something. No—wait. Tell them—tell them the sound of them speaking the Yuuzhan Vong language so poorly is insulting to us. Tell them we'll spcak the infidel language, Basic, and that the commander is about to speak to them."

Tahiri did so, after which Corran took up the comm unit. Keeping the visual off, he tried to remember the cadence of Shedao Shai's accented Basic, back when he had dueled with the man.

Here goes nothing. He started to open his mouth, then quickly changed his mind. "Tahiri, Anakin—give me a name. A credible name."

"Hul," Anakin said. "It's a warrior's name."

Corran nodded, flicked the comm back on. "This is Commander Hul Lah," he snarled. "Is everything prepared?"

"All is in readiness, Commander," the Givin answered. "The defense grid will fail in 15.08357462 standard hours. You may bring your fleet from hyperspace then."

Corran blinked. Something about that . . .

"There is no suspicion, then?" he asked.

"None. The Body Calculus is completely unaware of our vector with you. The failure of the defense grid and long-range communications will seem accidental. Only when you take possession of our system will the truth be known. We have hidden our factors carefully."

"Commendable. We will verify this, of course, but you may rest assured that if you are telling the truth, the glorious Yuuzhan Vong will honor our agreement with you."

"Thank you, Commander."

"Hul Lah, out."

Corran pursed his lips thoughtfully. "Those guys aren't the government," he said. "Or at least, not all of it. It's just some faction."

"Let's contact the real government, then," Anakin suggested. "Let 'em know what's going on before their defense grid fails."

"That's a problem," Corran said. "We don't know anything about who we just dealt with. It might be the local chapter of the Peace Brigade, or it might be a faction in the Body Calculus. Either way, the odds of contacting the wrong people are way too high."

"Maybe we should just get out of here and alert the New Republic military, then," Anakin suggested.

"It's an idea, but it will lose us Yag'Dhul. There's no way to get a fleet here in fifteen hours. If the Givin had their own fleet scrambled, there might be a chance of holding the Yuuzhan Vong off long enough for a New Republic force to arrive, assuming the Senatorial Oversight Committee releases them to do so. No, we've got to get the attention of the right people, before the defense grid goes down."

"Umm," Anakin mused.

"What? Out with it."

"Well, I have an idea, but you aren't going to like it."

"I'll take anything I can get right now. Talk."

"We attack Yag'Dhul before the grid goes down. Whoever comes out to stop us, that's who we want to talk to."

"I don't like it," Corran said.

"I didn't think you would."

"I don't like it, but it will work. Anakin, calculate a jump that will put us as close as safely possible to Yag'Dhul—or better, the space station. Tahiri, can you figure out how to lay it in?"

"Sure. All I have to do is see it in my mind."

"Let's get cracking, then. I want to do this before common sense sets in."

They reverted two hundred kilometers from the orbit of Yag'Dhul's farthest moon, a short distance from the military station that Booster Terrik had once commanded. Corran had fond memories of the place, because it reminded him of his early days with Mirax. It felt strange to be attacking it.

The station, which had been Rogue Squadron's base during the Bacta War, was now part of an expanding Givin military-industrial complex. Unhappy with having their system being used as a battleground by foreign forces, they had demanded and been ceded the station a few years after the truce with the Imperial Remnant. It now protected their shipyard.

"I'll bet they'll notice us," Anakin remarked, watching

through a transparency that Tahiri had opened up to give them a view of surrounding space. "Hyperwave dampeners or not, rocks this size don't just appear out of nowhere."

"Unless the grid is already down," Corran replied.

"Oh, I don't think it is," Tahiri said. "Or at least, that would be a big coincidence. Twenty somethings are on their way."

"Twenty what?" Corran asked. "Starfighters, corvettes, capital ships?"

"I don't know," Tahiri replied. "I don't know a lot about ships."

"Well, how big are they?"

Tahiri didn't answer for a few moments. "I'm not sure how to read that," she said. "They're sort of clusters of spindly rods. Three engines each. Real fast."

"Starfighters? How far away?"

"Fifteen phons and closing."

"What's a phon?" Anakin asked.

"I don't have any idea," Tahiri replied. "They just implanted the language, not conversion charts."

"Bring her around, thirty degrees starboard," Corran said.

"Starboard?"

"To your right! Your right hand!"

"Don't get touchy, Captain Horn," Tahiri said. "I'm doing my best, but I'm not a pilot! And I can't tell if I've turned fifteen degrees or not."

A dull thud echoed through the ship. Tahiri gasped.

"What was that?"

"That hurt!" Tahiri said. "Something just blew up part of us."

"Are they hailing?"

"I—" She broke off again as several more impacts rocked the ship. The last one was very loud.

"That broke the skin," Tahiri said. "We're losing air. I'm going to shoot back."

"Don't shoot back," Corran said. "Do you hear me, Tahiri? Do not shoot back."

"The ship wants to," she wailed. "It's hurt."

"Don't let it."

"They're hailing," Anakin said. "Standard frequency."

"Answer, then, fast. Tahiri—turn away from those ships and run as fast as you can."

"They're a lot faster."

"Well, use the dovin basal to absorb their shots, if you can figure out how to do that."

"The ship is doing it already," she replied. "It's just not very good at it."

"Not a warship," Corran muttered. "Anakin?"

"Something's wrong with the transponder," Anakin said.

"Well, fix it!"

"I'm trying."

"Tahiri, can you take evasive action?"

"I'm evading as much as I can. But this is a really big ship, and they're really fast."

Another staggered series of blasts ripped along the side of the *Stalking Moon*, and now Corran could see their antagonists, flitting about in admirably swift craft. He didn't recognize the design, but the Givin were known for quality if not quantity in shipbuilding. A good quarter of the racing yachts in the galaxy were built in the Yag'Dhul system.

Corran glanced at Anakin. The boy—no, the young man—was working calmly at the cobbled-together communications device, one lock of hair falling in his face. He didn't look like someone who feared death in the slightest. Probably he didn't. Taan, the Shamed One, was as impassive and quiet as she had been since her conversation with the distant Yuuzhan Vong commander.

The ship jerked and shuddered, and somewhere near, Corran heard the sound of air screaming out into vacuum. A smell like vaporized rancor swirled into the chamber.

"We're dying," Tahiri said dully. "Let me shoot back. Please."

"No."

"Got it!" Anakin said.

"Give me that!" Corran grunted. "Make sure the visual is on, this time."

The Givin who appeared on the tiny screen didn't waste

any time with polite mathematical greetings. "Yuuzhan Vong ship, this is Dodecian Illiet. You will stand down and surrender or be destroyed."

"Dodecian Illiet," Corran replied, "this is the captain of the Yuuzhan Vong vessel *Stalking Moon*. We surrender."

The Givin didn't blink—he couldn't—nor could his exoskeletal face register any other emotion Corran recognized. But he still gave the impression of vast surprise.

"You are not Yuuzhan Vong," the Givin said.

"It's a long story," Corran replied. "We did not intend to attack you, only to get your attention."

The Givin paused, listening to someone off-screen, then turned his empty eyes back to Corran.

"Our attention you have, Corran Horn. Prepare to be boarded."

THIRTY-ONE

"Shalo was smarter than I thought," Han snarled as he drew his blaster. "He had backup for his backup."

Jacen tried to pick apart the action. Karrde had placed people strategically within the cantina—both in the balcony and on the floor—to disarm Shalo's men, and then set up a cordon outside. That outer ring of protection was now under attack by a third group. A very numerous third group. Karrde's people outside were already down or had retreated within the building.

"Help me with this table," Han said.

Jacen grabbed one edge and helped his father drag it to one of the windows. Several bolts seared by their heads as they barricaded the opening, bringing with them plumes of ubiquitous Tatooine dust.

"This planet always was bad luck," the elder Solo grumbled. He lifted his blaster and fired a couple of shots over the edge of the table without looking.

"Good thing you have the situation completely in control," Jacen remarked.

"Hey, no plan is perfect. Did you get a look at who they were?"

"Peace Brigade, I'm pretty sure."

"I'm getting tired of those guys. Shalo set us up."

"Imagine that, one of your old buddies setting you up."

"Well, there's been worse," Han said. "You ready?"

"Ready for what?"

"I give it about six seconds before they start lobbing grenades in here. We do *not* want to stay here. On three?"

"Three it is."

"Karrde?" Han sang out.

"Busy," Karrde replied, firing through the doorway.

"Give us some cover."

"You got it."

"One, two—hey!"

On two Jacen ignited his lightsaber and bounded to his feet. He was immediately forced to deflect three blaster bolts in quick succession. His father popped up behind him, nailing one of his assailants with the first shot.

"That building across the street," Han said. "Go!"

Fire rained down from the rooftops as they raced across the sunburned ground. Jacen deflected the more accurate shots while his father blazed away. Jacen slashed open the closed door of the trinket shop directly across the street, and the two men ducked in. A veritable barrage shredded the door frame behind them.

"They can throw grenades in here, too, you know," Jacen remarked.

"Sure, but now we have 'em in a crossfire."

"My door!" shrieked the Toydarian merchant behind them.

"Sorry about that," Jacen told the merchant.

"Sorry? Sorry won't—eep!"

A concussion grenade bounced through the door, and the Toydarian flitted for cover.

"See?" Jacen said. He gave the bomb a telekinetic swat that sent it back out the door.

His father seemed to have predicted the trend. What was left of one of the cantina windows blew out with a billow of flame.

"Karrde!" Han shouted, firing wildly at anything moving on the street.

Han was interrupted by the Gamorrean who came blazing around the edge of the door. The being's close-range fire missed, but the butt of his weapon didn't when he dealt the Corellian an uppercut that lifted him off his feet. His father's body knocked Jacen off-balance, and before he could recover, the Gamorrean, squealing and snorking, wrapped his thick limbs around Jacen's body and slammed him into the nearest wall. The Jedi's lightsaber went flying.

Stunned, Jacen boxed his attacker's ears, but if there was any effect, he didn't notice it. He tried to focus on retrieving his lightsaber, but in all of the confusion he couldn't be sure where it was.

He felt the Gamorrean, though, felt his heart hammering in his chest. He could easily reach out in the Force and . . .

No. He would die first.

And that was coming up fast, because he couldn't breathe. He beat feebly at his attacker's head as outside the twin suns seemed to be going out.

Then he was falling, slumping against the wall and covered with ceramic statuettes of Sand People and Jawas falling from the shelves above. The Gamorrean had turned back to Han, who had just clobbered it over the head with some sort of larger stone statue. His father's eyes were widening in surprise at the fact that the Gamorrean hadn't collapsed, but only gotten madder.

"You're a thickheaded son-of—" he began, but then had to duck a powerful right.

"Look," Han said, dancing back from the Gamorrean, "you don't know who you're dealing with. If you just go ahead and surrender, I'll go easy on you." He looked suddenly past his enraged opponent to Jacen.

"That's right, Jacen. Use your lightsaber!"

Jacen was still trying to find his feet, much less his lightsaber. *What's he talking about?*

The Gamorrean turned, though, and Han hit him over the head again, holding the statue in both hands. This time it broke. The Gamorrean, looking puzzled, collapsed.

"You okay, son?" Han asked.

"Yeah. A little woozy."

Han hefted the half of the statue that remained in his hands, then proffered it to Jacen. "Here, a little souvenir."

Jacen turned it over in his hands and uttered a small laugh. Very small, because it hurt his stressed—perhaps cracked—ribs.

Han, meanwhile, was rooting for his blaster, one eye on the door.

"I should have known that old smuggler wouldn't sit still to be blown up," Han muttered.

Looking past his father, through the dust and smoke, Jacen could make out a pair of figures on the rooftop—Karrde and Shada. They had just finished the snipers there and were now using the high ground to clear the streets. The job was almost done.

About fifteen minutes later, Jacen and Han met outside with Karrde and his people. By some minor miracle, none of them had been killed, though several would be in bacta tanks for a while.

"I'd say Tatooine isn't going to be one of your safe houses," Karrde remarked. "I also suggest we get off this ball of rock before the Brigade convinces the spaceport to impound our ships, if they haven't already."

"I wouldn't worry too much about that," Han said. "The Darklighter family still has some clout, and we're at their dock. Still, it would probably be best to get out of here." He shook his head in disgust. "What a waste of time this was. Now that they know we're here, we'll never find out anything about their operation."

"Oh, I wouldn't say that," Jacen said.

"What do you mean?"

"We've still got Shalo, right?"

"Unless H'sishi was ambushed on the way back to my ship."

"I got something from him, something he was hiding. I tried to tell you."

"What?"

"I'm not sure. But he was expecting something. Something big."

Shalo was a good deal more subdued during his second interview, and much more cooperative.

"A convoy is stopping off here," he admitted. "Day after tomorrow. On its way to Ylesia."

"What's the cargo?"

"Oh, you know, cargo."

"No, I don't know," Han said. "Please, enlighten me."

"Spice, weapons, maybe a few, uh . . . a few slaves."

"Sacrifices for the Yuuzhan Vong, you mean. You're quite a piece of work, Shalo."

"I'm a businessman, Solo."

"Sure. Tell you what, once we're done with this convoy, we'll drop you off someplace where you can get nice and cozy with your new business partners. Nal Hutta, maybe."

Tsavong Lah regarded the strange creature before him. It looked like some shaper's fevered joke, with its short, ruffled feathers, spindly limbs, and cochlear antennae. It blinked luminous, slanted eyes at him and stretched its ridiculously wide mouth to speak.

"Greetings, Warmaster," it said.

The warmaster considered her for another moment before deigning to answer.

"The deception-sect priests and the haar vhinic tell me you have yielded much useful information concerning the infidels. You seem to have been most observant during your captivity."

"I would do more," Vergere said boldly.

"So I am also told. You have information regarding the ship that has been harassing our infidel lackeys." As he spoke, a pair of villips projected an image of a matte-black ship, lens-shaped, with odd projections.

"I know the ship," Vergere replied.

"And why would you speak this only to me?" the warmaster rumbled.

"Because," Vergere said, "I think the identity of this ship would be of particular interest to you, and because I believe you would prefer to have this information discreetly."

"You presume much about me, familiar-of-a-dead-priestess."

"If I presume incorrectly, I am prepared to embrace punishment."

Tsavong Lah gave her an abbreviated nod of approval.

"Waste no more of my time," he said. "Say what you came to say."

"I know the ship because it is the one from which I escaped," Vergere told him. "It is the *Millennium Falcon,* and its captain is named Han Solo."

"Solo?" Tsavong Lah felt a surge of rage at the name, and his vua'sa foot-claws clacked restlessly against the deck.

"Solo," the creature said. "Father of Anakin Solo, who caused the late distress at Yavin Four, or so I'm told. Father of *Jacen* Solo."

Tsavong Lah reared to his full height. "You were correct, familiar. This *is* of interest."

"Find the *Millennium Falcon,* Warmaster, and you will find Jacen Solo. I believe he is aboard her. If he is not, once you have his father, he will not be long in arriving. It is the way these infidels think."

"Indeed," the warmaster replied, a vast satisfaction rising in his blood. "And the *Jeedai* are most particularly weak in that respect."

THIRTY-TWO

Admiral Traest Kre'fey seated himself in the tactical chamber room of his flagship, the *Ralroost*. His violet eyes were sternly set, but Jaina nevertheless felt a brief but tangible impulse to stroke his fur, which was whiter than the wastes of Hoth. Contrasted with his black flight suit, it positively shone.

It was a feeling that evaporated immediately when the dignified Bothan began to speak.

"I've reviewed all of the information presented me," he said. "General Antilles, is there anything missing? Any other little surprises?"

"No, Admiral," Wedge replied. He glanced aside at Kyp. "Not that I know of."

"Well," the admiral mused. "Who would have guessed that the Yuuzhan Vong were another pack of superweapon aficionados. I thought we were done with that when we were done with the Empire."

"Apparently not," Gavin Darklighter said dryly. "I share General Antilles's distrust of Kyp Durron, but—"

"*This* I'm getting tired of." Kyp grunted and stood. "If you will excuse me, I'll go destroy it myself—with my lightsaber if I have to. This isn't worth the bother."

"Oh, Kyp, sit down and let Colonel Darklighter finish," Jaina snapped.

"Yes, why don't you do that?" Admiral Kre'fey said dryly. "And in the meantime, why don't you credit me with the brains to sort things out for myself, without the benefit of your posturing? Believe it or not, Master Durron, I can sympathize with you to a certain extent. Like yourself, I've found it more productive to fight the Yuuzhan Vong in my own way, without bureaucratic shackles. It has made me quite as unpopular as you are."

Kyp dropped his head fractionally. "Your pardon, Admiral. I'm an admirer of yours; I'll make no secret of that. If I could have found you, I would have proposed alliance long ago. But about one thing you are mistaken. While the New Republic may have little use for either of us, you are still better liked in most quarters, as present company demonstrates."

"Well, son," the admiral said, "I suspect that in great measure that is a burrow you've buried yourself in. Don't expect anyone else to dig you out."

Kyp merely nodded and returned to his seat.

"Admiral," Gavin said, "may I continue?"

"Please."

"I was saying that Durron and his Dozen-or-so went to what must have been desperate lengths to get this information. You remember, Admiral—we were there *before* the Yuuzhan Vong buttoned down the system as tightly as they could. What he got out of that is the clearest proof we're going to get that the Yuuzhan Vong are priming something very dangerous indeed. It's my opinion that we ought to do something about it."

"General Antilles?"

Wedge clicked his tongue. "I agree," he said.

"As do I," the Bothan concurred. "You see, Master Durron, what another moment of silence would have cost you? Nothing at all."

"I understand, Admiral. My apologies."

"Very well. I've been looking for a good target to take out, and this will do nicely. The nice thing about superweapons is that they are usually big, and this one seems no exception. I should think we will be able to hit it."

"Hitting it will be the very least of our worries," Gavin said. "From what Kyp said, the Yuuzhan Vong have pretty much mapped all the safe hyperspace jumps near the weapon and have them effectively blockaded. Since Sernpidal is also one of their major shipyards, and since the Yuuzhan Vong haven't started any new offensives lately, we can expect a pretty warm reception."

"I'm sure that's so, Colonel Darklighter. However, I have information that perhaps you do not. Sernpidal is one of the several parts of occupied territory that has been of interest to me in the past months. I've watched it—from somewhat a greater distance and with a good deal more caution than Master Durron, but I have watched traffic to and from it. In the last week, a large number of ships have departed Sernpidal. I was unable to determine where they were bound."

"A new push?"

"Possibly they are merely reinforcing their borders with new ships," Kre'fey said. "Or perhaps they are preparing the way for this superweapon of theirs. I should hasten to point out that nothing nearly the size of the weapon has been observed leaving, so it is presumably still there."

"But maybe not for long, if the Yuuzhan Vong are about to renew their Coreward advance," Wedge mused. "Maybe the whole peace-for-Jedi deal was an even greater ruse than we suspected—not just to get rid of the Jedi, but to give them the time to finish growing that thing."

"We're agreed, then, the sooner we act the better," Kre'fey said.

"Sure," Gavin said. "But getting *in*—"

"I have an idea about that," the Bothan said. "If I may."

"Of course, Admiral."

"When Colonel Darklighter and I last entered the Sernpidal system, we were able to evade the Yuuzhan Vong defenses because when Sernpidal was destroyed, the redistribution of the planet's mass opened up new hyperspace entry and exit points in the resulting asteroid field. The Yuuzhan Vong couldn't risk jumping into the asteroids after us because they hadn't calculated the positions of those points. By now, they must have accounted for all such locations. Master Durron, what enabled you to enter the system after those shifts were accounted for by the Yuuzhan Vong?"

"The Force, Admiral, is a powerful ally. I've had some experience with using the Force to read gravitic fields. We awaited our opportunity, and we got it when they tested their weapon. The size of the gravitic anomaly shifted the gravitic profile of the asteroid belt enough for us to risk a jump."

"And we may now assume they have countered that possibility."

"It seems likely."

"What I propose, then, is this. I know where I can procure an old *Immobilizer*-class Interdictor. She's not much to look at. She was hulled in battle and left adrift, where she was largely gutted by scavengers. Two of her mass-shadow generators are intact, however. I'd begun restoring her, but it's a dauntingly expensive task. She's got no life support, half her armor is gone, and she lacks engines. However, I could fit her with a hyperdrive and shields quite easily. We could then tow her where we need her."

"Oh, I like this," Wedge said, rubbing his hands together. "It's crazy—begging the Admiral's pardon—but—"

"You're going too fast for me, Admiral, General," Jaina said.

"We jump the Interdictor into one of the blockaded coordinates," Kre'fey explained. "No crew, with rudimentary automation. The instant it arrives, its shields go up and the gravity wells go on."

"And it lasts about half a minute, if that," Jaina replied.

"Which is plenty," Wedge explained. "The gravitic fluctuation will shift things enough to move the safe entry point. We should be able to calculate where to. Two seconds after we send the Interdictor, we start piling starfighters through. Hopefully the difference in location will be great enough that we'll miss whatever nasty surprise they have waiting for the next ship to attempt a deep-space jump."

"Exactly, General," Kre'fey said.

"That'll work," Gavin said. "At least, I think it will."

"It will get us in where they aren't expecting us," Wedge said. "More, we can't ask for."

"It will be enough," Kyp said excitedly. "It will do." The rogue Jedi stood. "I am prepared to place my people under your command, Admiral, for the duration of this mission. I'm sure you'll put us to good use."

"I'm sure I will, Master Durron. We should begin coordinating now. In two days' time, the Yuuzhan Vong will discover that someone in this galaxy still has teeth. Strong, sharp ones. Let's reconvene in three hours' time to discuss the specifics. For now we're adjourned."

THIRTY-THREE

"I really wasn't designed for this," C-3PO said, for something to the power of a hundredth time. "The waiting is really the worst of all."

Han checked the console, saw nothing again, laced his hands behind his head, and leaned back. "That so, Goldenrod," he said. "Personally, I think it would be worse to have our hull blown open by proton torpedoes."

"Well, yes," C-3PO admitted, "that might be—"

"Or lose power and life support and drift forever in the cold dark of space."

"Oh, how horribly vivid. That certainly doesn't appeal—"

"Or worse yet, what if we're captured? They'll give us to the Yuuzhan Vong for sacrifice. Just think what the Vong would do to *you*, Threepio. They wouldn't do it fast, not given how much they hate droids. They'd do it slow, keep you aware for every second of the terrible—"

"Captain Solo?" C-3PO interrupted plaintively.

"Yeah, Threepio?"

"I've reconsidered. Waiting isn't so bad after all. Why, for all I care, we can wait forever."

"Don't let him get to you," Leia said from the copilot's chair, her eyes closed. "Everything will be fine."

"Oh, thank you, Princess," C-3PO said. "It *is* nice to be reassured, from time to time."

"You're welcome, Threepio. It's the least I can do, considering we'll probably be vaporized in this next exchange. I'd rather you went comfortably."

"Vaporized?" C-3PO gasped. "I—I believe I'll see if

Master Jacen needs some help with—with whatever he's doing."

"You do that, Goldenrod," Han replied. C-3PO clanked off, making worried noises.

"That was mean, Princess," Han remarked. "I like this side of you."

"I was trying to sleep."

"Well, *I* can be quiet."

"No, that's okay. I'm awake, now. What's going on?"

"Not much. Karrde showed up a while back, with four ships. Should be more than enough, given the size of the convoy Shalo described."

"When do we expect them?"

"Any time now. An hour from now or ten."

She nodded and sat up sleepily. "You got my son a little banged up down on Tatooine," she accused.

"Well, he's not the first and he won't be the last to take a bruise or two on that forsaken planet." His cocky tone relented a little. "I didn't think I was putting him in real danger."

"No, I understand," Leia said softly. "Being a mother creeps up on me sometimes. It's a shame it didn't creep up on me more often when they were little."

Han took her hand. "We didn't have the luxury to be perfect parents," he told her. "Whatever that is. The thing is— they turned out okay."

"I know. That isn't the issue. Han, they won't ever be little again. It's over. Even Anakin is almost grown, and I missed so much of it. And Jaina—"

"There's nothing wrong with Jaina she won't outgrow."

Leia shook her head. "I don't know. She can be so bitter sometimes, and I really can't blame her. For all of her toughness, she's also fragile." She patted him on the shoulder. "Like someone else I know."

"Ah, carbon sluff," Han said. "I ain't breakable. You ought to know that by now."

"We're all breakable, Han."

"Huh."

"But I digress. I don't think it was a bad thing to take Jacen down there. You two seem . . . better for it."

Han shrugged. "What you said—about missing so much time when they were little. Maybe I, uh . . . feel a little of that. Maybe I sort of like having him around, working with him. When he's not going all moral on me, at least." He patted her on the shoulder. "Like someone else I know."

Leia shot him a fond smile disguised as a sarcastic smirk. She quickly let it relax. "Have you told *him* that, Han?"

"Nah. It might go to his head. I figure with that Force stuff he sort of knows anyway."

"You above all people should know that sometimes those most sensitive to the Force can be the most clueless about people."

"Well, you have a good point there," Han replied. "Sometimes I think—"

Suddenly ships began reverting to sublight.

"Heavy freighters," Han said, sitting up. "There's our convoy. Get ready, *Princess of Blood*."

"You've always known how to flatter a girl, Han."

"That escort," Han muttered after a little more study. "Two capital ships. I don't like it."

"You don't think a heavy escort makes sense?" Leia asked. "They know we've been intercepting their shipping. They don't know about Karrde. Two capital ships and the starfighters they can carry would be plenty to deal with the *Falcon*."

Han shot her a hurt look.

"Hey, I'm just being realistic," Leia said.

"So am I. You're right. Two capital ships seems like overkill."

"Let's back off, then," Leia said. "There'll be other convoys."

"The freighters. Scan them."

"Ouch," Leia said. "Nasty thought."

"Yeah. I have lots of those."

"Well, they look clean. I don't think they're hiding a fleet.

There is an odd radiation signature from that last cargo pod. Looks incidental, though."

"What's going on up there?" Jacen called from the laser turret.

"Your father is having second thoughts," Leia called back down.

"Huh? I'm just being a little cautious," Han said.

Leia frowned. "Seriously, Han. If you have misgivings, let's get out of here."

Han sighed. "I just don't like it. Maybe I'm getting old." He leaned forward and tapped on the comm unit. He and Karrde had a limited-range tight-beam system set up that was unlikely to attract attention.

Karrde appeared a few seconds later.

"Doesn't smell good, does it?" Karrde said.

"You read my mind. It's like they're trying *too* hard to look well prepared. If that makes any sense."

"It doesn't, but I know what you mean. Maybe we should let this one pass."

"Han—" Leia interrupted.

"Just a minute," he said. "Okay, Karrde, maybe—"

"*Han!*"

"Hello!" Karrde said. "Well, at least we haven't completely lost it. Yet."

"Huh?" Han stared where Leia's finger was pointed. A Yuuzhan Vong frigate had just dropped out of hyperspace, along with an interdictor like the one they had run into earlier. As he watched, coralskippers were already detaching.

"Well," Han remarked. "Things get more interesting all the time, don't they?"

THIRTY-FOUR

"Looks like it was built for children," Tahiri commented as the three humans were escorted through Yag'Dhul Station.

"Rebels built it during the war with the Empire," Corran informed her. "I've heard it said that they made it small to give stormtroopers a hard time if they ever invaded."

"What's all that on the walls?" Every square centimeter seemed to be covered with fractal patterns and notation in some sort of script. Now and then something seemed vaguely familiar, more often not.

"Givin decorative motifs, I'd guess. Rogue Squadron sure didn't paint this stuff."

"Looks mathematical," Anakin said.

The four Givin guards, who might have cleared things up, either didn't speak Basic or had no desire to talk. Soon enough, however, they were gently pressed into the largest room Anakin had seen thus far. It still wasn't very big, but tactical stations and a bank of holoprojectors with various views of the surrounding space made it somehow comforting after the Yuuzhan Vong ship. This was tech he was familiar with.

The Givin waiting for them was not as comforting. His exoskeleton had been painted with many of the same symbols Anakin had seen on the walls. Anakin guessed him to be the same one who had demanded their surrender.

"Dodecian Illiet, I presume," Corran said.

The Givin rose. He spoke in oddly clattering Basic. It sounded somehow more mechanical than it had over the comm.

"I am he," he replied.

"Have I had the pleasure? You seem to know my name."

"We made it our business to know who was in our space. You were among those waging war against Ysanne Isard from here."

"We had the permission of your government when we were here."

"Another spring tide cubed, another government," the Givin replied. "I did not recognize you myself—soft-bodied creatures are difficult for us to distinguish between, except at the rudest scale. Our computer system compared voice and facial records and estimated your identity at a 98.2 percent probability. I confess, I was uncomfortable with such a high margin of error, but when I addressed you your reaction seemed to confirm the probability. Are you indeed he?"

"I am Corran Horn, yes," Corran replied. "Any grievance you have against Rogue Squadron is mine. It does not adhere to these two."

"The only grievance against you is entering our system and apparently beginning an attack run on our station. That, however, is a rather severe charge."

"I apologize again," Corran said. "I hope it was noted that we did not fire on you, even when fired upon."

"It is so noted and numerated. I shall be happy to hear you balance the equation before us."

Anakin couldn't feel a trace of deception in the dodecian, and he was trying. That seemed a good sign, at least.

"I think these are the right guys, Corran."

Corran shot him a cautioning glance, but addressed his next sentence to the Givin.

"We've come to warn you, Dodecian Illiet, that a Yuuzhan Vong fleet is preparing an invasion of this system. The ship we were piloting was a scout ship we captured. It was designed to come here unnoticed and contact some faction of your own people. This faction has apparently arranged for your defensive grid to collapse shortly, to facilitate the invasion."

The Givin absorbed this silently, though Anakin got the impression he was also listening to someone else, commenting on what Corran was saying.

"Explain in detail," the Givin finally said.

"There's not much time—"

"You leave us with too many unknown factors. More detail."

Corran laid it all out, starting from their jump into the Yuuzhan Vong fleet, ending with their surrender. The Givin asked few questions, seeming content mostly to listen. When Corran was finished, the dodecian rapped his fingers against the table. They sounded almost as if they were made of ceramic.

"You are Jedi," he said at last. "The Yuuzhan Vong seek you."

"Yes."

"Perhaps you tell me this only to save yourselves."

"If you don't believe me, double-check your defensive grid."

"It is being done," the Givin replied.

"You'll have proof enough when the Yuuzhan Vong show up," Tahiri blurted.

"True," the Givin said, apparently not caring which of the humans it was speaking to. "But even so, what use have they for our system?"

"We think they wish to stage a strike at Thyferra, and perhaps then the Core."

"Ah. So they have the same use for our system that you did, Corran Horn."

"Umm . . . yes."

"And perhaps as little impact on our way of life."

"You think so? And yet these Givin I first spoke to were collaborating with the Yuuzhan Vong for some reason."

"Yes, that is of concern," the dodecian said. "Our politics are . . . complex, and needn't concern you. However, though such collusion with the Yuuzhan Vong might have been designed to upset the Coalition of Factors, there is still no reason to suspect that the Yuuzhan Vong actually pose a threat to our species."

"But," Anakin said, "they pose a threat to this station, and to your shipyards. The Yuuzhan Vong hate all technology."

"Then perhaps we will hide the ships until they have gone."

"Consider," Corran said. "Since I was last here you've taken pains to integrate with the economy of the New Republic. You crewed this station, as I understand it, so your system would no longer be a battleground for foreign powers. You expanded your shipbuilding capabilities. Will you risk sacrificing that?"

"We certainly risk it if we engage the Yuuzhan Vong in combat. From what we understand, they can be quite formidable."

Tahiri abruptly interrupted. "If you don't fight them, you'll be slaves," she said. Her voice had gone low and weird, as it had when she thought she was a Yuuzhan Vong, back on Yavin 4.

"There is no reason to suspect that."

Tahiri laughed. "I was a Yuuzhan Vong captive. I've seen what they do. Don't you get it? Right, they may be staging a strike on Thyferra from here. They may have ten reasons for being here. But I can tell you what one of them is."

"Explain," the Givin said.

"You. Your species. The Yuuzhan Vong make every tool they use from living things. They believe life was given to them by the gods to shape. You think they aren't interested in ready-made sentient beings who can survive in vacuum? The things they could make with you! They'll blow up this station and blast your ships and cities into ions. Then they'll take you and give you to their shapers. That will be the end of your complicated politics, Dodecian."

"Emperor's bones, she's right," Anakin said.

The Givin was silent for a half minute. "You really think this is true?" he asked at last.

"If you let them in without a fight, you've got no chance," Tahiri assured him.

The Givin paused again, and again Anakin got the impression he was listening to some far-off voice.

"It is confirmed," the dodecian said. "The defensive grid has been sabotaged. Fortunately, it can be remedied."

"Does that mean you'll fight?" Corran asked.

"I do not know. That decision does not lie with me. But we have taken into account all you said."

"Let me contact Coruscant," Corran said. "I can try to get more ships here, though I can't promise anything."

"I will enter that request," the Givin said.

"Another thing. What have you done with the Yuuzhan Vong we took captive?"

"They are being questioned, to verify or dispute your story."

"But Taan—" Tahiri began.

"Will be fine," Corran said, cutting her off.

"The prisoner will not be harmed," the dodecian confirmed. "Now. If you will accompany my aide, you will be provided with quarters and repast fit for your species."

"Are we prisoners?"

"I would prefer you did not think of yourselves as such. You have been allowed to retain your Jedi weapons. But I would also prefer you remain confined to the quarters we assign you. The station is delicate. Were there to be violence of any sort, it could well suffer explosive decompression."

"I understand," Corran said stiffly.

Anakin did, too. It was a polite threat. Try to escape—suck vacuum. That was an equation it didn't take a Givin to understand.

"That is well," the dodecian replied.

Anakin caught something, then, from the dodecian, something so tangible it almost formed words. If it were put into words, it would go something like, *We have Jedi to bargain with. That also is a factor.*

THIRTY-FIVE

Though his mind and mood sped through an astonishing array of transmogrifications, the perfect-grutchin idea somehow remained fixed firmly in the faltering brain of Master Kae Kwaad. Nen Yim and all of her apprentices were pulled even from standard maintenance and set to the task of weeding through grutchin germ plasm in search of "perfect" structures, incubating larvae and discarding those that displayed any slight deviation of form or color that Kae Kwaad detected. During this time, the master became ever more offensive, at one point demanding that Nen Yim work in a state of complete undress. At another, he forced Suung to get down on hands and knees and act as his stool, a task fit only for a slave.

Nen Yim considered the inventory of toxins that one might accidentally ingest or accidents that might befall one in the business of shaping. Her plans began to form themselves.

Ona Shai gripped her hands into fists behind her back and shot Nen Yim a deep glare.

"The capillaries of the maw luur are belching half-digested wastes in the Toohi sector," the prefect complained. "Many Shamed Ones have sickened from the fumes and cannot perform their tasks to full efficiency. A few have died."

"That is regrettable," Nen Yim replied. "However, I am uncertain why you discuss it with me."

"Because your master will not admit me or speak to me via villip," the prefect snarled.

"I am his adept. I can do nothing without his leave."

"When you were the head shaper, things got done," Ona Shai said. "Since this master has arrived, conditions have only gotten worse."

"If I agreed with that, I wouldn't be at liberty to say so," Nen Yim told her.

"I don't ask you to gossip with me as if we were a pair of slaves," the prefect snapped. "I'm asking you to intercede, to place my words in the master's ear. To release *you*, at least—or even Suung Aruh—to tend to this problem with the maw luur."

"I will certainly mention your concern."

Ona Shai nodded tersely and turned her back on Nen Yim. She could see the ridged muscles of the prefect's back, as tight as the tendon-rigging of a landing sail. She also noticed that she had recently sacrificed three fingers to the gods.

"This ship must last another year, at least, Adept. If it does, some of our habitants may survive to be offloaded onto a new worldship."

"I will speak to the master," Nen Yim replied. "I can do no more."

Ona Shai dropped her head. "Disgraced we may be, Nen Yim," she murmured. "But the gods cannot intend for us to die out here, so near the glory of conquest, able to see our new worlds but not to ever touch them. Death is nothing, but the ignominy . . ."

"I shall speak to him," Nen Yim repeated.

Her path back to the shapers' quarters was a crowded one. The Toohi sector was not the only dispossessed part of the ship; the Phuur arm had become unlivably cold toward the tip. With nowhere else to go, Shamed Ones and slave refugees crowded the halls. Their rustle of conversation quieted where she passed, but behind her it began again, with an angrier note to it. Once or twice, she was certain she heard the word *Jeedai*, and felt a quiver run along her spine.

Tsavong Lah had killed nearly every slave and Shamed One who had been at Yavin 4, yet still somehow the legend of the *Jeedai* had spread even here.

Was this yet another thing she would take the blame for?

She found Kae Kwaad where she often did, clucking over the grutchin larvae, his useless hands drawn up onto his knees. He did not even glance at Nen Yim as she entered.

"I've spoken to the prefect," she said. "Ona Shai urges that we turn at least some attention to the functioning of the ship. Toohi sector is now experiencing noxious fumes."

"That's interesting," Kae Kwaad said thoughtfully. He pointed at one of the larvae, indistinguishable from the rest. "This one will have to be destroyed. Its color is off."

"Indeed," Nen Yim said.

"See to it," Kae Kwaad said. "I must rest now."

"You should speak to the prefect," Nen Yim pressed.

"What would a master shaper have to say to the likes of her?" Kwaad sneered. "You have spoken to her. It is enough."

Nen Yim watched him go, then despondently turned her attention to the larva. She was carrying it toward the orifice, to feed it to the maw luur, when she suddenly understood that she was no longer considering the death of Kae Kwaad, but was committed to it. Not only that, but she had chosen the method of his death.

Grutchins were used to breach the hulls of infidel ships and contained an acid powerful enough to eat through metal alloys. A single bite from one would be sufficient to end the life of her miserable master.

So instead of destroying the pupa, she worked her own shaping on it. She removed neurons from the tiny brain of the grutchin, and with the protocol of Qah imprinted a simple series of reflexes keyed to the scent signature of Kae Kwaad, which she obtained from skin cells shed in his quarters. As a failsafe, she made the triggering of the reflexes dependent on a word she herself would utter.

When the grutchins had matured, she would speak the name Mezhan, and Kae Kwaad would die, her new master slain symbolically by her old.

When she was finished, Nen Yim slept, and for the first time since Kae Kwaad had come aboard the *Baanu Miir,* her sleep was peaceful and dreamless.

*   *   *

A ket later, the pupae began to molt.

When he saw the small but adult beasts, Kae Kwaad began to shriek incoherently and sank into what appeared to be a deep depression. Calmly, Nen Yim bore his ranting and whims, waiting until the end of the day, when the initiates had been dismissed.

"I want all of the initiates killed," Kae Kwaad said quietly. "They are plotting against me."

"I am sure they are not," Nen Yim told him. "They have worked diligently. It is only their training that is at fault, and I am to blame for that."

Why was she trying to reason with him, even now? She eyed the grutchins, an arm's length away. She and Kae Kwaad were alone now. She need only speak the word.

She had taken the breath for it when he spoke again.

"No, Nen Tsup, seductive Nen Tsup, perhaps I am to blame. It is my hands, you see. They are not as steady as once they were." She noticed that he spoke with a sort of glacial slowness, and his eyes had a peculiar look to them. "My thoughts are drops of blood," he whispered. "Pooling at my feet. My every thought is a sacrifice."

Nen Yim hesitated. It was as if, far in the distance, she saw a door dilate open, with strange light beyond. She kept the word in her throat and moved nearer, near enough that their bodies were touching. His glazed eyes met hers, and she endured as he caressed her with those stunted hands.

How is it you were not sacrificed to the gods, Kae Kwaad? she wondered. *How is it you live to shame your domain and species?*

For an instant his eyes changed, sparked, as if he knew what she was thinking, as if they were in on the same joke and only pretending to act their roles.

It was gone very quickly.

"Master," she asked, "why is it you do not replace your hands?"

He looked down at them. "My hands. Yes, they should be replaced. But it is denied me. Only another master can access that protocol, and none will do it. They are all against me, you know."

"I know," she whispered, leaning her mouth near his ear. "And yet," she said, lowering her voice even farther, "you *are* a master. You could do it yourself."

"I haven't the hands to make hands."

"But *I* do, Master Kae Kwaad. I do."

"And you would have to learn the protocol," Kae Kwaad replied. "And you are forbidden it."

Now her lips were touching his ear. "I might do much that is forbidden, Master," she said.

He turned to look at her. She saw nothing behind his eyes, now, and it suddenly occurred to her that he might be worse than mad; he might be using one of the ancient, forbidden toxins that induced stupor. Such a self-indulgence . . . *would be exactly like this being,* she finished.

He hit her, then, a backhand that shattered one of her teeth and sent her spinning to the ground with the taste of blood in her mouth. She lay there, expecting him to follow the attack, ready to speak the word. This was her last chance; if she hesitated longer, he would have the grutchins destroyed because he thought them somehow imperfect.

He kept looking at her with that same vague expression, as if he had never moved his hand, never touched her.

"Fetch the Qang qahsa villip," he said quietly. "I shall give you access. You shall shape me new hands. The perfect grutchin will not escape us."

A trembling, diminutive triumph quivered in Nen Yim's breast. She nurtured it with caution. Much could still go wrong, but she had found a chance, at least, to save the worldship. Though she wished she could bathe her body in acid to erase Kae Kwaad's touch, he had agreed to give her the thing she needed most.

As she went to find the villip, she promised herself that whatever else happened, whether she saved the ship or failed, whether she was executed for heresy or not, this wretched, pathetic thing whose touch had polluted her would die before she did.

PART FOUR

REBIRTH

THIRTY-SIX

Realspace greeted Jaina with an actinic flare and a shock wave that bucked her X-wing violently. She flinched instinctively, closing her eyes against the glare, the memory of impaired sight still imprinted on her nervous system.

Have some sense, girl, she thought, forcing them back open. *You're in enemy territory!*

And about to smack into an asteroid, the same one the coralskipper Gavin Darklighter had just drilled had exploded against. She yawed hard to port to avoid an identical fate.

"Heads up, Sticks," Gavin's voice crackled in her ear. "Rogues, form up. We've got plenty of company on the way."

"As ordered, Lead," Jaina said, weaving her way through the irregular bits of shattered planet that stretched as far as her sensors could make out.

Starboard and above her horizon, the yellow star at the heart of the system was half eclipsed by the outstretched arms of the distant gravitic weapon. Nearer and dead ahead was the more immediate target of Rogue Squadron—the cordon where Kre'fey's stripped-down Interdictor had sacrificed itself. Its shields had already collapsed, and its massshadow generators were random ions; but an expanding cloud of superheated gas marked clearly where it had been. Wedge had added one thing to the Bothan admiral's already good idea—he'd rigged the reactor to go supercritical when the shields reached 12 percent.

There was no knowing how many Yuuzhan Vong ships it had taken with it. However many it had, there were plenty left coming through the drifting planetary shards, and they were the business of Rogue Squadron. Calculations had shown that the temporary shift in gravitic stresses in the system would give them a very small window of opportunity—not big enough to risk Kre'fey's larger ships on, but plenty big enough to sneak the Rogues and Kyp's Dozen through. The Dozen were headed straight for the weapon to scout out whatever forces were guarding the thing. The Rogues' job was to clean out the Yuuzhan Vong nested around the stable hyperspace entry, which was the only way in for the *Ralroost*—and for the Yuuzhan Vong forces at the perimeter of the system. The Rogues had to gain control of it.

"I make something big at the target coordinates," Gavin informed them. "Might be a ship; might be a battle station. Designate Wampa. One-flight, we'll take that. Two and Three, keep those skips off us."

Jaina double-clicked to acknowledge, and peeled off with Three-flight, lining up off Twelve's port wing. She felt a brief sadness, remembering that she had once flown wing for Anni Capstan, back when she first joined the squadron. Anni had died at the Battle of Ithor. Twelve was a stranger, a Duros named Lensi. Jaina had met him in the final briefing.

"Turn two hundred thirty-one to twenty-three," Alinn Varth, leader of Jaina's flight, ordered. "We'll take that bunch."

Jaina acknowledged and did as ordered, seeing as she did so a flight of eight skips in pyramid formation, coming in fast. The space around was relatively clear of asteroids now, reflecting the low mass-density that made the area safe for jumping into and out of. Jaina felt exposed.

"Only two to one," Lensi said. "Not bad."

"Don't get cocky, Twelve," Varth snapped. "This is just the first course."

"As ordered," Twelve responded. Then he rolled, firing splinter shots at extreme range. Jaina stayed with him, but held her fire until they were closer in. The skips began firing all at once; Jaina jinked the stick and cut a hard corkscrew turn. The plasma globs went by without even singing. Now behind the skip that had fired at her, she got a targeting lock on it and began spraying it with underpowered shots. The skip produced a void and began absorbing them, but in doing so lost some of its mobility and taxed its power. When the shots started getting through, Jaina switched to a full-power quad burst.

To her surprise, the anomaly gobbled that, too.

Sithspawn. "Watch it, Twelve," Jaina said. "They're on to the bait and switch. They're letting the splinter shots in early."

"Acknowledged. Let me dust that off your tail, Eleven."

A quick glance showed Jaina she had indeed picked up an admirer. She yanked her stick back, hard, but the skip followed. Her shield took a hit.

Twelve dropped in behind the skip while Jaina put her X-wing through a series of convoluted maneuvers. The skip hung right in there.

"Grounded for too long," she muttered.

Then the tagalong flared and tumbled, trailing plasma.

"Thanks, Twelve," she said.

"Not a problem."

Jaina dropped and rolled down to target another coralskipper. Like the previous one, this one started letting the splinters through early.

"We can learn, too," she said under her breath. She kept up the spray, fired quad lasers, then fired again on full power. Three glowing holes appeared in the skip. It continued along its vector, no longer firing. Jaina wasted no more time on it, but found Twelve and dropped back to his port.

"Let's get that stray," Twelve said.

"Negative, Twelve," Nine's voice crackled. "Re-form. We can't get them all, and we can't afford to let them separate us for any length of time."

"As ordered," Twelve acknowledged.

Four more skips were coming in. *If we don't get this door open soon,* Jaina thought, *we'll never get it open at all.*

A sudden harsh crackle quivered Jaina's eardrums. Then

Gavin's voice. "I've lost Three," he said. "Deuce, take my back. I'm going in."

Jaina gritted her teeth, wishing she could see what was going on at Wampa, but she had her own problems. Three skips came up on her port. She hated to do it, but after a little splinter fire she switched to proton torpedoes. A void appeared to catch the deadly missile, and as programmed the warhead detonated before it could be sucked in. The bonus was that the explosion was near enough to take out all three Yuuzhan Vong fighters.

That's right, boys. Keep coming like that.

Then it occurred to her they were probably encouraging her to waste the torps. After all, they were never going to take out that monster down in the shipwomb with lasers.

But of course, they couldn't take it out at all if they died here. One thing at a time.

The *Falcon* bounced on the expanding plume of vaporized coral her lasers had just coaxed out of the interdictor. Han's view of the massive ship broadened, and also allowed the fifteen or so coralskippers on his tail a shot at the *Falcon* without danger of hitting their mother ship. Cursing, Han dived low again and quickly encountered the major problem with that, one he had never encountered while using similar tactics against Imperial Star Destroyers.

The Yuuzhan Vong ship opened a void. If Han's reflexes had been a single twitch slower, they would have smacked right into it, and he didn't want to find out what that would do. He hit the repulsors and bounced again, intentionally this time, hurling the *Millennium Falcon* into a tight arc that quickly became a circle. The skips followed—in time for half of them to run into a new explosion, this one from a concussion missile.

"That's better," he grunted.

"We're doomed," C-3PO noted.

"Lock it down. We've seen a lot worse than this."

"Might I point out—"

"No."

The quad lasers were pounding steadily, Jacen and Leia doing their part. A gratifying number of skips had already succumbed to his family's efforts, but they weren't the problem. The big ships were the problem, especially the Interdictor.

Only the *Falcon* had a shot at it. Karrde's ships were fighting for their lives against the two Peace Brigade vessels and the Yuuzhan Vong frigate analog.

"Han Solo," he muttered, "suckered into the most obvious pirate trap imaginable. I'll never live it down."

"I'll add that to the list of other things you'll never live down," his wife's voice said over the open intercom.

"Yeah, well, you'd better hope I *do* live this one down, sweetheart."

"Dad?" Jacen said. "Did I ever mention this whole pirate thing was a bad idea?"

"Why no, son, you—Wow!"

His exclamation was comment on the jet of plasma the interdictor had just released. Its diameter was greater than that of the *Falcon,* spearing up like a solar flare. He avoided it by a turn so sharp that even with the inertial compensators at 98 percent, the g's sent blood rushing from his head.

Behind him, he heard a loud clattering sound as C-3PO smacked into a bulkhead. Again.

"Okay," Han muttered. "Time for a change in strategy. Threepio, quit fooling around and haul yourself up here. I need you."

The golden droid's head peeped around the corner. "You need *me*? I would be happy to be of service, Captain Solo, but I don't see how a protocol droid could be of help. Unless you want me to transmit our surrender, which I must say seems like a bad idea, even when you consider the alternative."

"That's not it," Han said, weaving through a cloud of fresh skips. "Earlier, we noticed an odd radiation signature from one of those cargo pods. Figure out what it is."

"Sir, I really don't see—"

"It's that or you start working on your surrender speech."

C-3PO moved to the sensor readout. "I'm quite sure I don't know what I'm doing. Nevertheless, I hasten to be of service. Oh, why didn't I stay with Master Luke?"

THIRTY-SEVEN

"This is driving me crazy," Tahiri fussed. "Not knowing. For all we can tell, the Yuuzhan Vong have already taken over the entire system."

"I think there are a few hundred Jedi proverbs about patience," Corran said. "Though they all elude me just this moment. Try to follow Anakin's example." He paused. "I can't believe I just said that."

Anakin hardly paid attention to his companions. He was mostly beyond the plain, boxy room they were "guests" in, riding the Force out through the reaches of the Yag'Dhul system. He brushed the intricate, mathematical beauty of the tides of the planet and its three moons, felt the straining of Yag'Dhul's atmosphere toward space. He heard the whispering of millions of Givin minds in the corridors of their hermetically sealed cities. He touched a billion shards of stone and ice that had never cohered into planets, biding their time until the sun finally caught them in its fiery noose.

And he felt *them*, the Yuuzhan Vong. Not in the Force exactly, but through the telepathic lambent incorporated in his lightsaber. The feeling was akin to a faint, staticky comm signal—but it was unmistakable.

"They're here," he said.

"Who?" Corran asked.

"The Yuuzhan Vong. They're in the system. I can't tell anything else, nothing about how many or how—" He choked off as something new, strong, and terrible struck him in the Force. He gasped, and tears welled in his eyes, spilling down his cheeks.

"What?" Tahiri said. "What's wrong?"

"Mara," Anakin managed. "Don't you feel it? Aunt Mara is dying. And Uncle Luke . . ." He sprang up from his cross-legged position. "We have to get out of here. Now." He drew his lightsaber.

"Anakin, we can't," Corran said. "The dodecian wasn't kidding when he threatened to decompress the station. The Givin can survive in vacuum, remember?"

"We have to do something," Anakin said hotly.

"Anakin, dying on Yag'Dhul Station won't help Mara. We have to keep our heads."

"I won't just sit here and wait for them to come for us. We can't leave it up to the Givin to decide whether we live or die."

"I say we escape," Tahiri said. "All we need is another ship."

"As long as you're wishing for the unlikely," Corran said, "why not at least wish for vac suits first. That way we would at least stand a chance of reaching the imaginary ship we're going to steal."

"You used this place as a base once," Anakin reminded him. "Don't you know where they would keep vac suits?"

"Well, I've considered that, of course, but I don't see any reason the Givin would still have those around. Or that they would be in the same place they were twenty years ago."

"We could use the Force, make one of the guards take us to them," Tahiri said.

"Absolutely not," Corran said with a frown. "You're not going to the dark side on my watch. Do it on Luke's."

"What, then?" Anakin asked.

"Consider also that the odds this room is being monitored are extraordinarily high," Corran said.

"Since when did a Corellian ever care about odds?" Anakin muttered.

"Fine. No odds. They *are* listening to us. Count on it."

Anakin knotted his fingers in frustration. "Then I hope they hear me when I point out how ridiculous this is. We came here to warn them, and this is how they repay us?"

"Anakin, look at it from their point of view. We came

here in a Yuuzhan Vong vessel and acted as if we were going to attack their station. Now we claim a huge fleet is on the way to conquer their planet, and further we accuse them of having at least one faction collaborating with the Yuuzhan Vong. It would be hard for me to swallow."

"Well, they have their proof by now."

"There is that," Corran admitted. "You can't tell how close the Yuuzhan Vong are?"

Anakin shook his head. "No. It's not like that."

As if on cue, a deep tremor ran through the station.

"But if I had to guess," Anakin went on, "I would say they were really, really close."

"Right," Corran said. "We have to get out of here."

"Haven't we just been saying that?" Tahiri complained.

"The difference is, now *I'm* saying it," Corran replied. Unhitching his lightsaber, he went to the door.

It wasn't locked, and there were no guards outside.

"Interesting," Corran said, as the station trembled again.

Struck by a sudden suspicion, Anakin reached out in the Force once more, this time narrowing his focus to the station itself. To his relief, his suspicions were not confirmed. The Givin hadn't abandoned the station and them with it.

In fact, at that moment, two Givin carrying blaster rifles entered through the hatch at the end of the hallway.

"Jedi," one said, in clipped Basic. "You will come with us."

"We can take them," Anakin said, very low.

"Probably," Corran acknowledged. "But we aren't going to. Not yet, anyway." He smiled at the Givin. "Lead on," he said.

They passed several more Givin in the hallways, all in a rush, none seeming inclined to notice them. When they reached the command center they found it in a flurry of activity and eerily silent. The viewscreen depicted several large Yuuzhan Vong ships firing globs of plasma.

Dodecian Illiet glanced up at them as they entered.

"It would appear you were correct," he said tightly. "Congratulations."

"It would have been nice to hear that a few hours ago," Corran said.

"No doubt. You three will want vacuum suits. When the Yuuzhan Vong board, we will empty the station of air."

"Aren't you fighting back?"

"We are, but this station has limited firepower. Our shields will not hold much longer, and our fleet is assembling to protect Yag'Dhul. We can expect no help from them. The Yuuzhan Vong force is indeed quite formidable. I expect we have very little chance of victory."

"Don't be so hopelessly optimistic," Corran said.

"Perhaps I misphrased, somehow," the Givin said. "I did not mean to imply optimism on my part."

"I was being sarcastic," Corran said. "Never mind. Where are the vac suits?"

The dodecian gestured at another Givin. "In the old storage lockers at what you may remember as designated ring one-C of the docking area. My subordinate will take you to them in case your memory fails. I regret your position in all of this. I regret further that an attempt was made to bargain with your lives."

"They didn't bite?"

"On the contrary," Illiet said. "I reached a settlement with them. They promised to spare our station if you were turned over to them."

"Then why . . . ?"

"I did not believe their promise," the dodecian said. "Go. There is a small ship at docking port twelve, berth thirteen, if it has not already been destroyed. I grant you use of it. The rest of our vessels were used to evacuate unnecessary personnel before the attack commenced."

"Thank you," Corran said.

"Thank you for your efforts on our behalf," the Givin replied. He looked back at the tactical readouts. "You should hurry." He didn't look back up.

THIRTY-EIGHT

Nen Yim bathed in a sea of knowledge. Protocols glistened and swirled in the depths, revealing the foundations and endless permutations of life in intimate and splendid detail. Beneath the cognition hood her expression was one of awe and wonder, and for the moment she was the eager, maze-eyed young woman she had been only a few cycles before, loving and in love with the art of shaping, with knowledge itself.

She had long since passed the fifth cortex into the realm of the masters. Here were the living designs for the dovin basals, the thought-seeds of yorik coral, and yes, the protocols governing the creation of master hands. These she passed, navigating the shoals and depths with her questions, steering with her determination.

She found the germ of the worldships and swam through its thick skin. Parts she had seen before, of course—the outline of the recham forteps, the pattern of the osmotic membranes of the endocrine cloisters—but these were only components. She had never seen the profound logic of the vessels laid out holistically. Her grasp of the organic relationships between organs had been based mostly on deduction, and she found it instructive to observe where she had been right and where wrong.

At the center of it, at the outer limits of the seventh and final cortex, she found, at last, the brain. Its making uncoiled for her. She opened herself in turn and absorbed the information, let it fill the places her vaa-tumor had burned a place for. Strands of amino acid sequences flowed by like twisting rivers, pooling in her enhanced memory. Neurons divided, splitting and scrolling into million-branched ganglia that further folded into cortical coils. Subsystems nomic and autonomic explained themselves as the developmental process continued, finally settling into stability, maintenance, reorganization, stasis.

And in the end, when it had all come and gone, when her own brain strained at the rush of knowing, she understood at last.

The ship was doomed. The rikyam would die, and there was no protocol to stop it. Wonder dimmed in her, and the vast living library around her suddenly stood revealed to her not so much as a storehouse, but as a prison. Or a mausoleum, for though it created the impression of being alive, everything in the great Qang qahsa was desiccated, sterile, unchanging. There was nothing new here. If the protocols truly came from the gods, the gods had not seen fit to add anything to the sum of Yuuzhan Vong knowledge in a thousand years.

But that was impossible. Since the invasion of the infidel galaxy, new protocols had been handed down from the gods to Supreme Overlord Shimrra and thence to the shapers. The gods had been generous, especially in doling out weapons. Where had that knowledge gone?

That thought stirred something in the Qang qahsa, as if it had been waiting for someone to think it. The seventh cortex faded from her consciousness, leaving her adrift in peace and dark, more confused than ever.

There is nothing beyond the seventh cortex, she thought. I have moved to a place the gods have not yet filled.

If there were gods. Mezhan Kwaad had denied them. Perhaps . . .

But even as she renewed her doubt, something changed in the void. Like a light in the distance, or a tunnel opening.

And then she beheld something that could not be there.

An eighth cortex.

With renewed hope she moved toward it.

The membrane resisted her, filling her with pain that etched along her every nerve ending.

This place is forbidden, even to masters, the qahsa told

her. It was the first time it had spoken to her in something resembling language, the first time she felt its ancient sentience notice her. She recoiled. *Who may come here if not master shapers?*

Return, the voice said.

I cannot, she answered. Breathing hard, Nen Yim ignored the voice of the qahsa and pushed forward with her mind, accepting the pain, making it a part of herself. The agony grew, burning away her thought, but she held to her purpose, made it an animal thing that pain only fed and could never quiet.

Her heart beat unevenly, and her breath chopped. She tasted blood. Beyond the cognition hood, she was distantly aware that her body was arching in tendon-ripping spasms.

Open! she shrieked. *Open to me, Nen Yim! Open or kill me!*

And suddenly, like waters parting before swimming hands, the eighth cortex opened.

She looked within, and all hope vanished. She collapsed into her grief and was lost.

Light filtering through her open eyes woke her. A sour smell cloyed in her nostrils, and she realized that it was her own congealed blood. She tried to move and found her body almost paralyzed with pain.

Standing over her, grinning, was Kae Kwaad.

"What did you see, little Nen Tsup?" he asked gently. "Did you see it all? Are you satisfied, now?"

"You knew," she said.

"Of course I knew."

She looked groggily around. They were in the shaper laboratory.

"Mezhan," she said.

Nothing happened, except that Kae Kwaad grinned more broadly. "I suspect that word was supposed to trigger something. The grutchin you altered, perhaps? I took the precaution of destroying it."

Something about Master Kwaad's speech seemed very different. Wrong.

"Clean yourself up, Adept," the master said softly. "We have a journey before us, you and I."

"Where?" she managed to ask, through lips her own teeth must have gnashed and torn.

"Why to see *him*, of course. Supreme Overlord Shimrra. He is waiting for you."

THIRTY-NINE

"Eleven, you've got two on your tail."

"Thanks, Ten," Jaina answered, "but tell me something I don't already know." She jiggled the etheric rudder, watching the trails of superhot gases whip soundlessly past. Off to starboard, she caught a glimpse of the battle at Wampa, but the flashing lasers and long plumes of incandescence didn't tell her anything except that *someone* was still trying to cook the rock.

She took a hit. The starfield tumbled crazily, and her cockpit was suddenly hotter than the midday double suns on Tatooine. Sparks crackled across her console, and every hair on her body stood at attention.

My engines are gone, she thought. *I'm dead.*

Interestingly, the thought did nothing to frighten her. Her only regret was that she wouldn't get to see the big show at the end.

"Captain Solo, the Yuuzhan Vong ship is hailing us," C-3PO shouted excitedly. "They must have a modified villip on board."

"You tell them I'm a little too busy shooting down their ships to answer them," Han replied, flipping the *Millennium Falcon* ninety degrees to squeeze thinwise through a tightly formed wedge of skips.

"They seem quite eager to communicate," C-3PO persisted.

"Well, tell them we'll call back." He'd been forced away from the interdictor by seemingly endless swarms of coralskippers. Now the monstrous ship was following them, trying to establish the dovin basal equivalent of a tractor lock. In desperation, Han drove for the freighters, figuring he could at least use them as shields.

He hadn't had time to check on Karrde lately, though the barked commands over the open channel told him the information broker was still alive, at least.

He made the largest of the freighters, dodging its insignificant defensive lasers with ease, and once there looped around to face his pursuit, a determined snarl on his face.

He blinked. There was nothing there. Not a single coralskipper had followed him.

"Sir," C-3PO said, "the commander of the Yuuzhan Vong warship *Sunulok* has called his ships back. If we do not answer his hail, he will commence hostilities in sixty seconds."

Han checked his sensor display. The coralskippers had retreated to the vicinity of the interdictor, which was now at a stop relative to the *Falcon*. He estimated he was outside of the *Sunulok*'s tractor range—barely.

He eased back half a klick, to see what would happen. The ships didn't budge, though he noticed Karrde hadn't had any such reprieve. Off to his port, that battle raged on. It looked like Karrde was losing.

"Better let me talk to 'em, Threepio," Han said. "I don't think letting them speak to a droid is going to make them any happier."

"Indubitably, sir."

Keeping a careful eye on both the viewport and sensor displays, Han keyed on the comm.

"*Sunulok*, this is *Princess of Blood*. You ready to surrender, yet?"

The Yuuzhan Vong were not.

"This is Warmaster Tsavong Lah. You waste my time with nonsense," the warmaster grated.

"Hey, you called me. What do you want?"

"You deny me visual, skulking coward," he said. "But it avails you nothing. You are Han Solo, and your vessel is the *Millennium Falcon*."

Well, I wonder who he bought that information from?

Han thought. *So much for the anonymity of piracy.* "You're callin' *me* a coward?" Han exploded. "You're the scum who had his underlings cut my wife."

"She was not worthy to fight me. Neither was your *Jeedai* son."

"Listen, scars-for-brains, I couldn't care less how you explain your weak knees and yellow belly. We had a good fight going here. You want to finish it, or you want to call it quits? Either way is fine by me."

"Jacen Solo is with you. I want him. Alive. When I have him, you're free to go."

"Oh, sure. I'll just put him in an escape pod and send him over."

"Dad?" Jacen's voice came up from the intrasystem channel. "Dad, maybe it's not a bad idea. If I can get him to duel me . . ."

Han ignored Jacen and turned to C-3PO. "You got a read on that radiation signature yet?"

"Yes, sir, but I'm afraid it's not very helpful. It's very low grade—the cargo pod contains liquid hydrogen enriched with tritium."

"Cheap reactor fuel," Han grumbled. "Industrial waste. I was hoping for a cargo of ion mines, or something."

"I'm sorry, sir," C-3PO said.

"Infidel," Tsavong Lah roared. "There is no sign you are preparing an escape pod."

Han's jaw dropped. "This guy doesn't have any sense of humor at all. He really thinks . . ."

Well, let him think it, then. He opened the channel for a reply. "Just give me a sec, will you? He is my son, after all."

"You have two minutes."

Han chewed his lip, thinking furiously.

Leia called up from below. "Han, couldn't you put a concussion missile in the escape pod?"

"Nah, they'll catch that," he said. "Waste of a missile we'll probably need."

"It's got to be me, Dad," Jacen said. "I'm going back there."

"Oh, no you're not." Han swung on C-3PO. "Jettison

both escape pods. Now. *Right* now. Aim them both at the Vong ship."

"Sir, I'm not sure which—"

"There," Han said, pointing. He cut the engines back in and began creeping back toward the freighter and the Yuuzhan Vong ship it nearly eclipsed. Two escape pods suddenly went tumbling across his field of vision.

"Hopefully, it'll take 'em a few seconds to figure out there's no one on board," Han said. He fired his forward lasers. "Goldenrod, take a deep breath. If this doesn't work . . ."

"But, sir, I don't *breathe,* of course I—oh, no!"

Anakin, Tahiri, and Corran followed the Givin through the cramped corridors of the Yag'Dhul space station, their footing upset by ever-more-violent explosions.

"Do you have any idea where we're going?" Anakin asked Corran.

"The basic layout hasn't changed that much," Corran said. "We're headed down toward the berths."

"Yes. Going to the berths," the Givin said helpfully.

They reached an axis a few moments later and piled into the turbolift, which, at the Givin's command, whirred them down toward the anterior berths. Power flickered, and the lift jarred to a halt, only to start again a moment later when the lights came back on, albeit dimmed.

"I'll be sorry to see this place go," Corran murmured.

Anakin caught a thread of wistfulness in that, something like he got from his father now and then. Almost . . . almost as if Corran wished he were younger again.

Which was ridiculous. The older you got, the more people took you seriously. Anakin was very much sick of being treated like a kid, especially by people who knew less than him.

Mara . . . Mara had treated him more like an adult. And Mara was dying, and there was nothing he could do. He almost wished the turbolift would open to a bunch of Yuuzhan Vong, so he'd at least have someone to . . .

That's not a wish, he realized. *That's the lambent.*

"Guys," he said quietly, "you'd better activate your lightsabers."

At least Corran didn't ask questions, this time. He just did it.

The door whisked open, and there they were. Six Yuuzhan Vong with amphistaffs.

"Me first," Corran said, leaping out, lightsaber blazing. Tahiri was a blur, and Anakin right behind her when he realized he only counted five Yuuzhan Vong warriors outside.

But the lambent said six.

He spun—almost in time. The Givin struck him across the bridge of the nose with a tightly balled fist, propelling him from the turbolift into the enemy-filled room beyond. His body struck Corran in the back of the knees. Surprised, the ex-CorSec Jedi still managed a shoulder roll, though Anakin caught a bright glimpse of pain from him as an amphistaff struck a glancing blow. Head ringing, Anakin brought his radiant weapon up in a high parry he knew he had to make, felt the sharp thwack of a staff across it. Still aware of the danger at his back, he then threw himself to the side. He rolled up to see Tahiri doing a high, Force-aided flip to land in a protective stance beside Corran. Anakin rose and threw the most powerful telekinetic blast he could at the group of Yuuzhan Vong.

If they had been any other species, it would have pasted them to the wall. Instead, two fell and the other three staggered as if in a high wind. Tahiri, unable to affect them at all, found another solution; a stack of cylinders in the corner suddenly flew into the already off-balance warriors, sending the rest of them down. Only the Givin, who had stepped back from the action, kept his feet, and he was laughing, a harsh, very un-Givinlike laugh.

From side corridors, eight more Yuuzhan Vong filed into the far side of the room from where the Jedi now stood against a bulkhead, lightsabers bristling out like quills.

The Givin reached up, touched the side of his nose, and something oozed off, revealing the Yuuzhan Vong beneath.

"A good effort, for infidels," he said, taking an amphistaff proffered by one of the newcomers. He looked squarely at

Anakin. "Not the Solo the warmaster wishes most, though after Yavin Four your worth has risen immeasurably."

"I don't know you," Anakin said.

"No. But your mother and I have met. I am Nom Anor, and you may consider yourself my captive."

"We'd rather not jump to that conclusion, if you don't mind," Corran said.

"The odds are against you."

"You must not know much about Corellians," Corran said.

"Don't be tiresome. You three have earned respect. If you were not infidels, I might even call you warriors."

"I can't say the same for you," Corran said. "What about it, Nom Anor? Me and you, man to man."

"Duel you as you dueled Shedao Shai? And if I win, the rest of you would surrender?"

"No. But you could prove you aren't afraid to face me."

"Sadly, my duty to my people forces me to decline your offer," Nom Anor said.

Tahiri suddenly began shouting in Yuuzhan Vong. The warriors looked at her, first puzzled, then angry. One turned and spat something at Nom Anor.

"What did you say?" Anakin asked.

"The warriors with him don't speak Basic, and they don't have tizowyrms. They didn't realize that Nom Anor was turning down a challenge. I told them you were the slayer of Shedao Shai."

"Good going, Tahiri. Now what?" Corran asked.

"The head warrior of this bunch—Shok Choka—wants to take up the challenge."

"Tell him I accept," Corran said.

"No," Anakin said. "Tell him *I* accept. Tell him I slew many warriors on Yavin Four. Tell him I fought with Vua Rapuung. Tell him I demand my right to combat, or I will carry their names as cowards to the gods."

Nom Anor was shouting himself hoarse in Yuuzhan Vong, but the warriors seemed to have almost forgotten he existed. It would have been funny if the situation hadn't been so deadly.

As Tahiri translated, Anakin stepped out, lightsaber blazing. The other warriors fell back, forming a ring. Shok Choka stepped into it.

FORTY

When Jaina's engines came back on-line and she realized she wasn't going to die—at least not right away—she was, naturally, grateful. When, an instant later, Two and Ten dusted the skips off her tail, she was ecstatic. She proved this by frying the two skips hanging tight on Nine.

But the best part was watching Wampa blow. It came apart in eight symmetrical plates billowing outward on a ball of fire. The wave of charged particles blew over her at lightspeed, nearly—but not quite—generating enough static to drown out Gavin's fierce cry of exultation.

After that, the Rogues cleaned up the remaining skips—without their war coordinator, apparently on Wampa, they weren't that much trouble. What was left of Rogue Squadron re-formed.

They'd lost Three and Four, and Eight was hobbling along on one damaged engine.

"Dozen, how's it going down there?" Gavin asked.

Kyp's voice came through a steady throb of gravitic distortion.

". . . lost five starfighters. Can . . . hurry, or you'll miss the party."

"Hang in there, Dozen, we're on our way."

And then, another beautiful sight. The *Ralroost*, reverting to realspace in all her glory, followed by two corvettes and a heavy cruiser.

"Kre'fey here," the admiral's voice boomed. "Congratulation, Rogues. Excellent work. If you don't mind, we'll clear a path to target prime now."

"Admiral," Gavin replied. "We don't mind at all."

Trailing the *Ralroost,* Jaina turned her nose sunward and dived.

"We're going to hit!" C-3PO squealed.

"That's the general idea, Professor," Han said. The *Falcon* bumped into the side of the freighter module—two quick shots from the forward laser had cut it adrift. Now he engaged the *Millennium Falcon*'s main engines and cranked them to full. The cargo pod lurched into motion, aimed straight at the Yuuzhan Vong Interdictor. The *Falcon* rattled like a metal bearing in a vorth cage, but Han held her nose steady.

"What in blazes is going on up there?" Leia shouted over her the intercom.

"Just keep a lookout for skips. We'll be seeing them pretty quickly."

He was right—it didn't take the *Sunulok* long to figure out he was up to something. Coralskippers came howling in, blazing away at both the cargo pod and the *Falcon*. The trembling of the *Falcon* took on a different tone, now, as plasma bursts ate her shields. But the deciding factor for Han was the sudden bloom along the outbound rim of the freighter module. He turned the *Falcon*'s nose up and *flew*.

"I hope you know what you're doing," Leia said.

"Relax, sweetheart," Han said, though he felt anything but relaxed. His hands had a death grip on the controls as he tried to coax more speed from his great bird.

Then something stopped them, hard. The interdictor had finally gotten its lock. Han blanched and tried the repulsorlifts, glad he hadn't told C-3PO what he was doing so the droid could quote him the odds.

He was stuck. He could only watch now.

The tanker module was still hurtling toward the *Sunulok* too fast for the huge vessel to dodge without a hyperspace jump, but it was coming apart under the steady fire of the smaller ships. Han watched as its liquid contents continued, undeterred, spreading in a bizarre funnel-profile wave toward the Yuuzhan Vong ship.

"I don't understand, sir," said C-3PO, in a hopeless and

subdued voice. "What could liquid hydrogen possibly do against—"

"Watch and learn, Threepio," Han said. Then, under his breath, "At least I hope." He fired three of his six remaining concussion missiles. "Leia, Jacen. Target the Interdictor, full power. Give her everything you've got."

"But the hydrogen won't burn without oxygen," C-3PO said.

"Sure won't," Han replied.

The lasers lanced out just ahead of the missiles. At about the same moment, the *Falcon*'s shields went down and the skips started taking her apart.

And then everything broke loose.

Shok Choka was big, even for a Yuuzhan Vong warrior. Each ear had three large chevrons cut from it, and a mounded scar ran from his chin, sliced through his lips, and continued along the ridge of his skull. He held his amphistaff behind his back, the hand grasping it a little lower than his waist. He locked his amber gaze on Anakin's ice-blue eyes. His knees were bent, and though he was perfectly still, he somehow projected corybantic motion.

Anakin cut his lightsaber off and held it loosely at his side. He began to circle the warrior slowly in a relaxed, almost contemptuous manner. Calm flowed through him. Shok Choka followed him with his predator gaze.

Anakin stopped, smiled faintly, then stepped into the warrior's range.

The Yuuzhan Vong moved almost faster than vision could process, the rigid amphistaff chopping down. Anakin's saber burred on, and he raised it in a wide, high block. Choka, anticipating that, arrested the slash and instead lunged in to spear Anakin in the throat. Anakin retreated, dropped his parry, again low and wide, as if he were defending for two people instead of one. That placed Choka's weapon so far out of line he couldn't make the third parry, but instead had to flip back toward Anakin and Tahiri. His still-live blade, slashing wildly, scored a meter-long cut through the bulkhead that only just missed Corran.

Stamping and howling, Shok Choka came on. Anakin blocked a powerful blow that carried his blade into the bulkhead for a second time in a long, elliptical slash. He ducked a vicious jab that spanged into the wall and rolled forward, past Shok Choka's stamping feet and back out into the center of the room. Even as he stood, the warrior was renewing his attack.

Now, suddenly, Anakin tightened his defense, so that rather than pushing the Yuuzhan Vong's blows as far away from him as he could, they were missing him by centimeters. Still smiling, he fell into the counterrhythm of the dance, the amphistaff whipping and whirling, spearing and slashing.

The warrior suddenly dropped and swept Anakin's feet from under him, something the young Jedi hadn't seen coming at all. He thudded to the floor awkwardly and threw his blade up to catch the inevitable downward blow, but the staff whipped around and cut his shoulder, the deadly poisonous head slapping against the floor centimeters from his arm. Anakin caught the amphistaff with his left hand and with his right, lifting from a prostrate position, drove his weapon through the knee joint of Shok Choka's armor. The warrior grunted and aimed a powerful punch with his left fist toward Anakin's head, but Anakin wasn't there. Releasing the amphistaff, ignoring the cut in his hand grabbing it had caused, he bounded up and was suddenly standing above the warrior, who had overcommitted to the punch. In the split second while Shok Choka decided whether to tumble forward or attempt to regain his balance, Anakin cut his head off.

Before the body could hit the floor, Anakin bounded toward his friends. Corran had already seen the plan, and with a single swipe of his own blade finished cutting the bulge-sided triangle Anakin had begun in the bulkhead with his "wild" parries. The other Yuuzhan Vong, stunned by the death of their war captain, hesitated an instant too long. One got a parting shot at Anakin, the last of the three to duck through the small opening. Several somethings cracked against the metal bulkhead—thud bugs, probably.

Then he was through, turning a corner in the corridor behind Tahiri, and they were all running as fast as they could manage. They passed through a pneumatic bulkhead. Anakin slashed the controls as it sighed closed. He caught a glimpse of a Yuuzhan Vong face turning the corner, and a second later heard a thud on the other side of the door, then several more. Glancing back over his shoulder as he continued to run, he didn't see it open.

"You did that on purpose!" Corran accused. "I thought at first you were just fighting sloppy."

"We need to find berth thirteen!" Anakin gasped.

"On it," Corran shouted back. "This way."

"How far do we have to go? Because—" Tahiri began to ask.

"Just keep running," Anakin urged.

"—because my ears are popping," she finished.

Anakin realized that his were, too, and that he was a lot more winded than he ought to be.

"Sithspawn," Corran said. "The Givin have opened the station to space. We'll never make it to berth thirteen." He stopped, looked around. "Wait a minute," he said. "Follow me."

He led them down a side corridor, where he paused.

"They've changed the designations," he muttered, "but I think this is it." He keyed a door open.

"We *might* make it to the ship," Anakin shouted, following him into the room beyond. It was wall-to-wall storage lockers.

Corran sounded as if he were across a space twice as large when he replied. "No way. We're not even to the docking ring." As he spoke, he began cutting though the locks on the lockers with his lightsaber.

"Check the unlocked ones, you two," Corran ordered. "We're looking for vac suits. This is the sector Illiet told us to go to."

Anakin did, feeling the air grow thinner and colder as he did so. Most were empty. "But what if Illiet was in with Nom Anor?"

"I doubt it. If he was, why such an unwieldy trap? Nom

Anor must have contacted the other Yuuzhan Vong to meet him, to get him off the station. Hah!" He yanked a large vac suit from one of the lockers. "Look at this thing," he said. "It must be twenty years old."

The next locker turned up an airpack, but no suit. Neither did the next few, and Tahiri was starting to giggle with hypoxia. Anakin felt symptoms himself.

"Okay, that's it," Corran said. "You two. Get in there." He pointed to one of the large lockers.

"Why?" Anakin asked.

"Just do as I say. This one time, please, without questions, just do what I tell you to."

It seemed funny that Corran was shouting at him again. Part of Anakin knew that was a bad sign.

He grabbed Tahiri's hand and pulled her into the locker. Corran shoved the airpack in behind them.

"Minimum feed to keep you alive. Remember the locker is probably leaky." He swayed on his feet, seeming to nearly collapse. "I'll be back. There's another set of lockers down the hall."

He slammed the locker door, and they were in total darkness. Anakin felt around for the feed valve, and soon a small hiss escaped the airpack. He turned it up until his dizziness subsided.

"What if he doesn't have enough strength to get the suit on?" Tahiri said. "What if it's leaky?"

"Don't think about it," Anakin said. "We can only wait now."

"The walls are getting cold," she said.

They'll get a lot colder before it's over, Anakin thought. *Unless the Yuuzhan Vong light the station up and blow it to atoms. Either way it won't be long before we don't care anymore.* Maybe Corran was right. Maybe his luck had finally run out.

"Don't worry, Tahiri," Anakin said, contrary to what he was thinking. "Corran's been out of more scrapes than the two of us put together. He'll be back."

FORTY-ONE

The space around the *Sunulok* birthed stars. That's what it looked like, anyway, and in astrophysical fact that was more or less what was happening.

The cloud of boiling liquid hydrogen had enveloped most of the Interdictor, and wherever a laser beam or concussion missile pierced that gauzy haze an unbearably bright pinprick of light erupted, then quickly blossomed larger before suddenly going out.

"Keep firing, you two," Han told his wife and son, adding the forward guns to the mix.

"I see it, but I don't believe it," Jacen said. A constellation of the expanding and deflating suns burned around the *Sunulok,* now, so brightly they almost couldn't see it, and Han laughed aloud, though the coralskippers were still pounding the *Falcon*. The dovin basals' grip on the *Falcon* suddenly relaxed, and the laser beams were lancing through the hydrogen cloud to burn clots off the Yuuzhan Vong ship itself. Targeting the cluster of dovin basals, Han launched his last spread of concussion missiles and then threw the *Falcon* back into drive.

He punched up Karrde's comm channel. "Hey," he said, "the interdictor is out of commission, but I can't say for how long. If I were you I'd go to lightspeed."

"That's the most beautiful thing I've heard in a long time," Karrde replied. "I'm gone."

"Keep those skips back until we hit hyperspace," Han told Leia and Jacen.

"Can do," Jacen called back up.

Behind them, Han was gratified to see plasma boiling

from the *Sunulok*. A few minutes later, they'd left the Interdictor—and the rest of their enemies—light-years behind.

Jaina saw Ten shredded against an asteroid, and pressed her lips tight in anger. She hadn't known the Twi'lek in the pilot's seat, but he'd been part of her flight, and he'd saved her life at least twice in this fight.

What's worse, Alinn Varth, Three-flight leader, had been dropping in to take out the coralskipper on Ten's tail, and ended up flying straight through the burning debris as it skipped off the intervening rock. Jaina watched in horror as her leader's X-wing vanished, haloed in inferno.

But Varth came out the other side, banking, three skips on her tail. Jaina dropped down like a bird of prey, spraying the lead skip, then launching one of her remaining three proton torps. The resulting explosion cracked two of the fighters and sent the third spinning aimlessly.

"Thanks, Twelve," Varth gasped.

"You okay, Nine?"

"Negative. I've lost guns and short-range sensors."

Gavin heard. "Fall back, Nine."

"Colonel—"

"Fall back. That's an order."

"Yes, sir," Varth said. "As ordered, sir."

"It's just us," Lensi said, for once not sounding brash.

"It'll be just me, if you don't watch it," Jaina replied. "You've got two coming down."

"Got 'em. Thanks, Sticks."

The weapon was *huge* now that they were closing on it. *Maybe it's not fully alive yet,* she hoped.

Kre'fey had been as good as his word; the *Ralroost* and her companions had cut through the defense perimeter around the weapon that had so successfully kept Kyp's squadron at bay, leaving the faintly glowing hulks of two Yuuzhan Vong capital ship analogs to mark the way in. Now they were setting up for the run on the gravitic weapon, and roles had reversed. This wasn't the fabled Death Star; if the Yuuzhan Vong ship had a weak point, it was unknown to the motley forces attacking it. In Kyp's holo, the huge iris in the center of the thing had seemed to project the gravity field, so that was number one priority, and when taking out something you didn't understand, honking gobs of firepower was always the safest bet. The *Ralroost* had the guns—it was up to the starfighters to see she had a chance to use them.

There were two more large ships in the system; One had moved between Kre'fey's flotilla and the weapon; the other was hanging back, presumably to control the ample swarms of coralskippers that were still massing against them.

"Seven," she heard Gavin say, "break off and take lead with Eleven and Twelve."

"Mind if I cut in?" a new voice asked.

"Wedge?" Gavin said. "You're sure you want to do this, what with your arthritis and all? How'd you slip your nurse?"

"Told her I was going to take a steam bath," the aging general quipped. "What've you got for me?"

"Good to have you, General. Gives us two full flights. Take Seven, Eleven, and Twelve. Guys, you are now designated Two-flight."

"I copy, One Leader," Jaina said. She could hardly believe it. She was flying with Wedge Antilles!

"Good enough," Wedge said. "Tighten up, Two-flight. Looks like we have some business up ahead."

The next wave of skips hit them and hit them hard, fighting with a sort of desperation that Jaina hadn't yet seen in the Yuuzhan Vong. They came in clusters, three flying as shields for a fourth. Jaina needled them at long range with her lasers, determined not to waste another proton torpedo if she didn't have to.

"I don't like this," Wedge said. "They aren't maneuvering. They're just coming head-on."

"Makes them easy pickings," Lensi said. From the corner of her eye, Jaina saw one of his targets flare out.

"Too easy, Twelve," Wedge said.

One of Jaina's targets tumbled out of formation, its cockpit a fused mass of coral.

"Two-flight, break!" Wedge suddenly shouted. Even as he did so, the cover skips broke, and their undamaged charges accelerated through the gap. They weren't firing weapons, and they weren't throwing out voids.

Jaina jerked her stick up, and the skip rose to meet her.

"I'm going to hit!" Seven screamed, before his channel went dead.

The voids slowed the skips down. When they weren't using them, they were incredibly maneuverable. Jaina's climb was as tight as she could get it, but the skip was matching her, still coming on, still at the bottom of her field of vision, clearly determined to ram her. Meanwhile, the remaining two skips that had flown shield for it were trying to pick up her tail. She had nowhere to go, and if she brought her weapons in line to fire, she'd meet her enemy head-on, as Seven had just presumably done.

Suddenly a quad burst of lasers from above her imaginary horizon cut the skip in half. Jaina didn't have time to see who her rescuer was. She jammed the stick down and starboard, skimming by the wreckage of the coralskipper and shaking the two behind her.

Except the two behind her were already gone.

"You're clean, Jaina," Kyp's voice informed her. "General Antilles, permission to fly what's left of my Dozen with you."

"Granted, Durron. I'll take what I can get, now."

The *Ralroost* and its escorts had taken a lot of hits in the first wave of suicides, but once the tactic was understood, the remaining starfighters fanned out and picked off the determined skips far in advance. The Yuuzhan Vong that made it through their runs intact ended up behind them, where collision was much less effective. They still had their weapons, of course, and it made Jaina more than a little nervous to have so many live enemies at her back, but target prime was just ahead, and she had a job to do.

The *Ralroost* opened up on the galaxy-shaped ship. Red streamers of plasma lanced out from the curved tips of the Yuuzhan Vong weapon, but the destroyer's shields handled the fire easily.

"I don't get it," Jaina said. "Why use conventional weapons? Why aren't they using the gravity weapon?"

"It's our lucky day," Kyp said. "It must be off-line."

Multiple proton concussions blossomed at the axis of the Yuuzhan Vong weapon, rendering it a dull-red glowing mass.

"Jaina, behind you!"

Kyp's warning came too late. Twin bursts of plasma sheared through her shields and into her ion engines. A quick babble from her astromech told her that if she didn't shut down in fifteen seconds, the whole mess was going supercritical. She'd lost a stabilizer, too, and the ship was spinning crazily.

And she still had a tail. Kyp got one of them, but the other just kept coming.

This is it.

The Yuuzhan Vong superweapon filled most of her gyrating vision, now. Grimly, she did her best to aim for it, then shut down. Maybe she could skip off it with repulsors. If not, at least she would put another ding in the thing.

But then something in the huge craft made a very big bang, and all she saw was inferno.

"Corran's been gone a long time," Tahiri whispered.

"Not so long," Anakin replied. "Only about five minutes."

"Seems longer." He felt her shiver, probably from the biting cold. In fact, the only part of Anakin that wasn't freezing was the strip along his side where he was pressed against the younger Jedi.

"There has to be something we can do," she said. "If we can yank Massassi trees out of the ground with the Force, surely we can—"

"What? Pull a bunch of oxygen molecules up here from Yag'Dhul, seal up the station, and repressurize it?"

"Hey, at least I'm trying to think of *something*."

"So am I," Anakin said, his voice rising a little. "If you have an idea, let's hear it."

"You know very well I don't have an idea," Tahiri snapped back. "You'd feel it if I did."

"Tahiri—"

"Oh, just shut up."

Anakin suddenly understood. Tahiri was frightened, as frightened as he had ever known her to be.

"I'm scared, too, Tahiri."

"No, you're not. You're never scared. Even when you *are*, you aren't by normal standards."

"I was scared when I thought I'd lost you on Yavin Four."

She was silent, and Anakin lost his read on her, but he suddenly felt her shoulders quivering and knew she was crying.

Reluctantly, he reached his arm around her.

"I'm sorry," she sobbed. "I got you into this. Corran's right—I keep thinking I can be like you, and I'm not. You always win, and I always screw up. If it weren't for me, you'd be back on the *Errant Venture* right now."

"But I'd rather be here with you," he said.

He couldn't see her face turn toward him or see the widening emeralds of her eyes, but he knew they were there.

"Don't say things like that," she murmured. "I know you think I'm still a little kid. I—"

She stopped, very suddenly, when he found her face with his fingers. Her cheek was smooth and cold. He found a stray lock of hair across her eyebrow and traced lightly over the raised scars on her forehead.

Anakin rarely did things he didn't know he was going to do. But it had never occurred to him that he was going to kiss Tahiri until his lips were already touching hers. They were cold, and she pulled back.

"Oh," she said.

"Oh?"

"*That* was a surprise."

"Sorry."

"No—c'mere." She took his face in both hands and pressed her lips against his. It wasn't a big kiss, but it was sweet and warm, and it jolted through him like ten g forces.

"Your timing is perfect," she breathed. "Wait until we're doomed to give me my first kiss."

"Mine, too," he said, his face warming despite the cold. "Umm . . ."

"How was it?" Tahiri said, answering his unverbalized question. "Kind of weird." She kissed him again. "Nice."

She took his hand and put her cheek against his. "If we survive, we'll have to figure this out, you know," she said.

"Yeah."

"I mean, I'm not the kind of girl who'll kiss just anyone on a first-time-to-be-stuck-in-a-locker-on-an-airless-space-station."

"Might be simpler if we don't make it," Anakin remarked.

"Yeah. Are you sorry?"

"No. No, not even a little."

"Good."

"So let's survive," Anakin said, "so we get a chance to figure this out, okay? Do you think you can manage a hibernation trance? Our air will last a lot longer that way."

"I'm not sure. I've never done it."

"I'll help. Just clear your mind—"

"Maybe you don't know very much about girls. You just *kissed* me, and now you want me to clear my mind? It's like there's a tribe of Ewoks dancing in there."

He squeezed her hand. "C'mon. Try."

Something clanked outside.

"Did you hear that?" Tahiri whispered.

"Yeah. But how? There shouldn't be any air to carry the sound." He reached for his lightsaber.

Something started working at the locker door. It swung open, and Corran was crouched there, an expression of extreme concern on his face. He still had a vac suit on, but without the helmet.

"You're okay," he breathed.

"We're okay," Anakin acknowledged. "Where did the air come from?" He started crawling out of the cramped space.

"I remembered there was a modular backup system. I was afraid the Givin had taken it out, but they haven't. I sealed up the room and pumped air in. It probably won't last long, so get into those, quick." He gestured toward a pair of smaller vac suits.

As they were scrambling into them, Corran shot Anakin a peculiar look.

"What?" Anakin said.

"Should I have left you two unchaperoned?"

Vaping Moffs! Does it show? Anakin wondered.

Just once, he wished most of the people he knew weren't Jedi.

"You fools," Nom Anor hissed at the three warriors. "First you let them slip from your claws, now you cannot find them again? You are a disgrace to the Yuuzhan Vong."

He stood next to where the ship the warriors had come on was connected to the infidel space station by an oqa membrane, speaking through the gnullith-villip hybrid in his throat. He disliked having to command through the thing, for it distorted his voice somewhat, lessening its effectiveness.

The new leader of the warriors, Qau Lah, threw a withering glare his way. "The infidels opened their station to space. We were forced to obtain ooglith cloakers, as you know, since you wear one yourself. We *will* find them." He lifted his chin and bared his teeth. "Besides, it is the Yuuzhan Vong who does not accept challenge from a worthy opponent who disgraces his people."

Nom Anor narrowed his eyes, then chopped his hand in a gesture of command. "Go. Find them."

As they turned, he lifted the infidel blaster he had secreted in his sash. It made him feel vaguely sick to handle it, but he had learned to do all sorts of distasteful things lately.

He shot Qau Lah in the back of the head from a meter away, then the warrior next to him. The third managed to raise his amphistaff before the blaster burned a hole through his face.

That was three. Cursing to himself, Nom Anor started off to find the rest of the warriors who had seen him with the Jedi, to make certain none of them would carry report of what they had seen back to Qurang Lah.

FORTY-TWO

"What happened back there, exactly?" Leia asked.

"Hand me that," Han said, gesturing toward his tools.

The *Falcon* had made five quick jumps with no sign of pursuit. Now they were headed for the Maw, but Han wasn't waiting for the facilities there to begin his repairs. The second he thought they were safe, he'd begun tending to his baby.

Leia handed him the demagnetizer.

"Not that," Han said. *"That."* He pointed just as vaguely. "The thingie."

"*Which* thingie?"

"The hydrospanner."

She handed it to him, rolling her eyes. "I'm not gonna sprout fur, you know," she said. "I'm not going that far."

"I don't know," Han replied dubiously. "I knew this woman once, real pretty. Hit fifty and grew a mustache."

"*Han*. The *Sunulok*?"

"Ask your son. He's the one with the education."

Jacen turned from his own work on the power core. "I'm pretty sure I get it," he said.

His mother looked up at him. "Do tell."

"The cargo tanker was full of liquid hydrogen, right?"

"That far I got."

"Dad dumped it all over the *Sunulok*, and we fired into it. That didn't do anything, except the *Sunulok* produced voids to swallow our shots. They started swallowing hydrogen as well."

"And choked on it? What?"

"The voids are like quantum black holes. You reach

266

the event horizon—which in this case is more or less microscopic—and gravity becomes nearly infinite. Which means acceleration does, too. When a concussion missile hits one, for instance, the matter in it is instantly compressed into neutrons and then, *blip,* singularity. Just like a black hole. And like black holes, if you dump in too much matter at once, it has to queue up to get in. It starts compressing *outside* the event horizon, so on the way in it undergoes fusion."

"And the black holes swallow most of the energy," Leia said.

"Exactly. The light we saw was only a fraction of the energy being produced, the part that escaped. Most of it went into the singularity. We know from experience that disappearing energy taxes the dovin basals, right? In a few seconds the *Sunulok*'s voids swallowed dozens of hydrogen fusion explosions. It shut them down."

"Looks like *all* of your education wasn't a waste," Han remarked.

"Wow," Leia said. "That could be a good countermeasure against those voids."

"Not really," Han said. "It would only work if the hydrogen density was like it was—it was still semiliquid. In another few seconds, it would have dispersed enough that it wouldn't have done anything. If the *Sunulok* had been moving, they would have whipped through it in a second. No, we had the perfect setup, and since I'm pretty sure the *Sunulok* survived, the Vong probably won't let that happen again. Nice thought, though."

Jacen was about to add something else when the Force blindsided him with agony. He must have cried out, because both of his parents looked at him at once.

"What is it, Jacen?" Leia asked.

"It's Aunt Mara," he replied shakily. "Something bad is happening to Aunt Mara."

Aunt Mara! Jaina felt the pain and despair hit her like the heavy end of a hammer. She shook her head, not sure where she was. Had she blacked out?

Stars tumbled by, and her astromech chirped frantically.

Oh, right. She'd been flying into the Yuuzhan Vong super-weapon, when it exploded.

Aunt Mara! The spike in the Force was fading, but the impression remained of Mara unraveling like a rotten phil-fiber.

Jaina balled her fists in frustration. Mara was hundreds of parsecs away, and here she was in a dead ship.

I can't help her now, Jaina thought. *Got to help myself first.*

She and her astromech managed to kill the tumble, but they were still without engines. Far behind her she could make out the wink of laserfire through a cloud of gas that must be the debris of the Yuuzhan Vong weapon.

We did it!

She was drifting sunward, but was outside of the asteroid field and in no obvious or immediate danger. At least she didn't think so until she noticed, ahead of her, a heart-shaped chunk of yorik coral. A *big* hunk.

After a few missed beats of her own heart, however, she saw it wasn't under power. In fact, what it looked like more than anything was a dovin basal. Alone, unattached to a ship.

"You think it's flotsam?" she asked the droid.

It whistled a noncommittal reply. It was too busy to care about space junk.

Curious, Jaina adjusted her sensors, and noticed something else strange. The dovin basal had a twin, about a hundred klicks away, in the same orbit. Inward, toward the primary, another pair—and another, and another. It was a sort of corridor of dovin basals stretching from the Yuuzhan Vong superweapon almost to the star in the center of the Sernpidal system.

"Oh, no," she said. "No, Kyp, you didn't. Not even you would . . ."

No, of course he would. And he had made her part of it. And she had brought in Rogue Squadron.

She wanted to throw up. If she hadn't been in a sealed cockpit with limited room to do so, she probably would have.

The astromech informed her that it had managed to rig a new antenna. Jaina opened a channel.

"Rogue Leader, you out there?"

Static, and then Gavin Darklighter's voice. "Jaina? Jaina, thank goodness you're alive."

"Copy, Rogue Leader. Can you send somebody to pick me up?"

"Absolutely. We're finished here."

"Colonel Darklighter, you might want to come yourself. There's something here I think you should see."

FORTY-THREE

Luke.

Luke awoke to his name and found Mara's hand on his arm. Her eyes were clear, and her lips were quivering as if she were trying to speak.

"Mara," he murmured. "Mara." He had more to say, but he couldn't get it out. *I love you. Don't die.*

Her head inclined, very slightly. He took her hand and felt the pulse there, stronger than it had been in days, but irregular.

Now. We have to do it now.

"Do what? Mara, I don't understand."

Now. Her eyes closed again, and her pulse dropped away.

"No! Mara!"

When Darth Vader had suddenly realized that he had a daughter as well as a son, Luke had felt a desperation that was the palest reflection of this. He'd hurled himself at the black-armored figure that was his father, battering him with his lightsaber until he cut Vader's arm off. In doing so Luke had taken a decisive step toward the dark side.

Now, though his body did not move, he hurled himself at Mara's disease with the same blind, desperate fury, battering against it with the Force, trying to shatter the slippery, mutable compounds of which it was made. The electrifying strength of anguish drove him on, and the fact that he was trying to do the impossible meant nothing. He clenched his fists until the veins stood out on his arms, attacking something he couldn't see.

That wasn't there to see.

No. Luke, no. Not this way.

Luke fell away, trembling. "How then?" he shouted, maybe at Mara, maybe at the universe itself.

"Luke!" Cilghal was standing in the doorway. "I felt—"

"She wants me to do something, Cilghal," Luke snarled. "She diverted some of her energy to wake me, and a little more to stop me from . . . What does she know, Cilghal?"

"I don't know, Luke," Cilghal said. "But you've been telling your students attack is not the answer. Trust yourself— you're right. You need to calm yourself."

A retort got hung just inside of his throat. How could Cilghal possibly understand?

But she was right, of course. It was easy to remain calm when nothing upsetting was happening.

"I know," he admitted, his breathing evening out. "But I *know* I have to do something. Now, or she'll die."

"Let me try," Cilghal said. "Maybe I can understand what she wants."

"No. It has to be me. I know that."

He calmed himself further, sloughing off his darkening emotions, cleansing himself with deep, slow breaths. Only when he felt truly centered did he reach out toward Mara again, probing her gently through the Force rather than attacking her disease.

Attack is not the answer.

But she was so far gone. There was nothing to defend, except . . .

And suddenly, he thought he understood. One part of Mara was well—better than well, free of all disease. *That's* where he needed to be, not waging warfare, but strengthening, defending from the one fortress that still stood.

He reached out again, this time as lightly as one of Mara's caresses, into the place where their child rested, and there he found his wife, wrapped around the baby like a durasteel wall.

"Let me in, Mara," he said aloud. "You have to let me in." He laid his hand on her arm, squeezing gently. "Let me in."

Skywalker?

"It's me. I think I understand, now. I'll do what I can. But you have to let me in."

The wall wavered, but held. Had he guessed wrong? Had she herself already forgotten, her memory erased by the pain?

"I love you, Mara. Please."

He trembled, still touching her arm. He couldn't force her. He wouldn't if he could.

Come on, Luke.

The gate opened, and he felt another pulse, another life. He reached for his son.

The child stirred, as if recognizing his father's touch. He reached back, and Luke felt little tickling thoughts, like waking laughter and amazement. It was a voice both familiar and infinitely strange. It was a voice becoming real.

"I love you. I love you both," he breathed. "Take my strength."

He and Mara joined like fingers twining, and like a tiny third hand, the unborn child linked with them as well. A human child. His child. Mara's child.

The mutual grip grew stronger, but it wasn't the desperate strength of combat or the raging power of a storm. It was a calm, enduring, and at the same time fallible, mortal embrace—the embrace of family long separated.

They mingled, each with the other, until Luke felt his identity blur, and he began to dream.

He saw a young boy with hair of pale red-gold, tracing lines in the sand. He saw an older boy, kneeling by a river course, rubbing a smooth, round stone between his fingers and smiling. The same boy, perhaps ten years old, wrestling with a young Wookiee.

He saw himself, holding the boy, watching glowing lines of traffic move through the sky of some strange world—like Coruscant, but not Coruscant.

He did not see Mara, though he looked, and that brought a new note of discord to his thoughts.

Always in motion is the future, Yoda had once told him. Still, he reached farther, searching for Mara, farther along that uncertain, shifting path. The boy grew older; he was at the helm of a starship of strange design . . .

All futures exist in the Force, a familiar, impossible voice suddenly said. *You do not choose the future so much as it chooses you. Do not look for answers there.*

"Ben?" Luke croaked, stunned. It couldn't be Ben, of course. That time was long gone, and his old Master was truly one with the Force, unreachable, and yet . . .

But it didn't matter whether it was Ben, the Force, or a part of Luke himself that had just spoken. It only mattered that he had glimpsed what might be, and only the tiniest part of that, but it was only what *might* be. He couldn't let it concern him—now was not the time for searching or speculation, for both were active manifestations of doubt, and he could afford no doubt right now. Doubt was more deadly than the Yuuzhan Vong disease. It was the only real limitation a Jedi had.

He let the images slide away, and felt again only the moment, three hearts beating, three minds becoming one.

Hi there, Luke. Glad to have you back, Mara seemed to say. And then they were expanding, extending outward in every direction, like a galaxy being born. Like anything being born. Like life itself.

FORTY-FOUR

"Wow," Anakin said, when he saw the ship waiting for them in berth thirteen. They'd squeaked by two groups of ooglith-cloaked Yuuzhan Vong prowling the halls, apparently still searching for them, and had expected a fight when they reached the ship—if the ship was even still there. It was, and the Yuuzhan Vong weren't.

"Maybe Nom Anor and his bunch got caught when the air went out," Corran speculated.

"Wow," Anakin repeated.

"Don't gawk," Corran said. "We don't have time for it. It may take us some time to figure out how to work this thing. There is still a fleet out there, remember?"

"Right," Anakin said. "Sorry."

But it was hard not to be impressed. The Givin ship was simple, elegant, nearly all engine, about the size of a light transport. A bundle of spindly cylinders protruding from a relatively enormous engine torus made up the core of the ion drive, though three more extended on booms from the side of the main assembly. These last weren't fixed, either, but could be maneuvered in a complete sphere. Forward of that was the hyperdrive assembly, and almost as an afterthought, it seemed, a crew section and cockpit that was nearly all transparisteel.

On board they found that only the sleeping compartment could be pressurized. The life support unit was thus commensurately underpowered, so they remained in their suits. The controls were a complete mystery until Corran pointed out they were laid out mathematically according to Ju

Simma's theorem. Once that was understood, the ship was weird to operate, but not particularly difficult.

Corran took the controls and unlocked the docking bolts.

"Here we go," he said. "The pitiful laser this thing has won't be of much use in a fight, so we're just going to run, unless anyone else has a better suggestion."

"But the station—" Tahiri began.

"Is doomed. And the best hope for the Givin is reinforcements from Coruscant."

"I was thinking about Taan."

"I'm sorry," Corran said. "But the Yuuzhan Vong will probably retrieve her. If she's lucky . . . Anyway, we're out of this, just as soon as I can get us out. Let's see, where would the inertial compensator be?"

Anakin pointed to a logarithmically scaled input. "I'm guessing that's it."

"We'll see. Strap in and hang on. I hope this thing has the legs it advertises."

It did. Anakin could barely restrain a whoop when they blew out of the dock. If he had been flying, he wouldn't have been able to keep it in.

"An A-wing couldn't touch this thing," he said.

"It's not all about speed," Corran said.

"If you're running, it is," Anakin replied reasonably, as they streaked past a patrol of coralskippers. They turned late, like a herd of startled banthas, and began pursuit. Within a minute the skips must have been under top acceleration, but they looked almost as if they were standing still.

As Anakin studied the sensor readouts from the copilot's station and began calculating a series of jumps, he began to feel less cheery.

"We've got some ahead of us, closing. Heavy cruiser analogs, two of them."

"We'll see how well the Givin build shields, then," Corran replied.

Minutes later, Corran was juking and jinking through

heavy fire. The shields held admirably well, but as pre-dicted, the laser was useless. Corran cut the ship onto a course perpendicular to Yag'Dhul's ecliptic plane, fighting for enough distance from the planet and its three massive moons for a safe jump, but they ran into trouble there, too, in the form of more Yuuzhan Vong ships.

"Thick as gluttonbugs," Corran remarked.

"I can lay in a short jump," Anakin said.

"In an unfamiliar ship? Very dangerous."

"What choice do we have?" Anakin replied.

In response, Corran turned back toward Yag'Dhul, diving toward the thick of the fighting, where the delicate-looking Givin ships were taking on twice their number of Yuuzhan Vong vessels. To Anakin, it didn't look like a very good place to be. "We should jump," Anakin repeated.

"Anakin, I was flying when you were nothing more than a fight brewing between Han and Leia. Before that, even. Give me credit for knowing a thing or two."

"Yes, sir."

"Program the jump, just in case. But we're not going to try it unless we run out of options."

They whipped through the Yuuzhan Vong perimeter, shaving as near the big ships as Corran dared—which was pretty near—and dancing evasively through skips. Anakin took potshots with the laser, and though he never managed to get through the void defenses the ships generated, it still felt better than doing nothing.

"We're going to make it," Corran said. "The ships up front are too busy to—" He broke off as every single Yuu-zhan Vong ship ahead of them suddenly turned and began accelerating in their direction.

"Sithspawn!" Corran sputtered, pulling up hard to avoid a coralskipper that appeared intent on taking them out with its own mass.

It dodged by them, not even bothering to fire. In utter confusion, Anakin watched the rest of the Yuuzhan Vong fleet race past them, out toward interstellar space.

"The ones farther out are jumping," he reported, study-ing the sensor readouts. "They're running. I don't get it.

What could the Givin have done to light their jets like that?"

"It's not the Givin," Corran replied, his voice edged with astonished relief. "It's something else."

"Recalled?" Nom Anor spat, staring incredulously down at the villip and its portrait of Qurang Lah. "But we are near victory! Their defenses crumble."

"Meanwhile, an infidel fleet desecrates and obliterates our primary shipwomb."

"Impossible," Nom Anor said. "Their ridiculous senate could not possibly have approved of such a strike without my knowing. Even if the military launched such a campaign without senate approval, my sources would have informed me."

The commander snarled a sort of smile. "It would appear, Executor, that Yun-Harla has abandoned you. Opinion is that you are perhaps not as clever and useful as you make yourself out to be. You have been outmaneuvered by the infidels. They set a trap, and you led us into it for them."

"Absurd. If there is an attack on the shipwomb, it is unrelated to this mission."

"Not unrelated at all, since you had us commit our reserves for this battle. Had they remained at the shipwomb, they would have been sufficient to repel the infidels. As it is, we have only a narrow chance of reaching the battle in time to salvage anything."

"Then let us remain here. We have now demonstrated to the infidels that we intend to continue our conquest of their galaxy—unless we finish here, we will have nothing to show for that tactical loss."

Qurang Lah showed his sharpened teeth. "The loss is yours, Executor," he said. "You may be sure that the warmaster will hear a most complete version of how you've bungled this entire business." His eyes narrowed. "Let me speak to Shok Choka."

Nom Anor kept his face impassive. "He was slain by the *Jeedai*. All of your men were."

The commander's face pulled into an incredulous frown. "All of them? And yet you made it safely back to your ship?"

"I was separated from your warriors and the *Jeedai* when the Givin emptied their station of atmosphere."

Qurang Lah held his stare for another moment. "Yes," he said softly. "The warmaster will hear much from me."

Before Nom Anor could begin another rebuttal, the villip cleared, leaving him to pace the decks of his ship in frustration.

Not to mention trepidation.

FORTY-FIVE

Jaina climbed out of her X-wing wearily, feeling far older than her eighteen years. She wanted to get in bed, turn the lights out, and stay there.

She wanted Jacen, and Anakin, and her mother and father. She wanted to hear C-3PO going on inanely, and she wanted to see Aunt Mara, to find out what was wrong with her.

What she got instead was Kyp Durron, climbing out of his starfighter, a grin smearing across his face as he walked toward her.

In a way, he would do.

She watched him come, with that stupid smile, until he was close enough. Then she slapped him, hard.

His smile faded, but otherwise he didn't react.

"You *knew*," she said. "You knew, and you lied, and you made *me* a part of it."

The other pilots, in the middle of postbattle jubilation, were starting to stare.

"What are you talking about?" Lensi asked. Jaina had seen the Duros coming from the corner of her vision.

"Tell him, Kyp. Tell him what his friends died for. Tell them that thing we just paid so dearly to blow up wasn't a superweapon. That it wasn't a weapon at all."

Kyp straightened and folded his arms. "Everything the Vong possess is a weapon," he said.

"B-but the footage we saw in briefing," Lensi stammered. "I *saw* what it did. It pulled fire out of Sernpidal's sun."

"No," Jaina said. "That's what it looked like, but that's not what happened. The Yuuzhan Vong set up a relay system of hundreds of dovin basals, hung in a long corridor all the way to the sun. It was just a big, unwieldy linear accelerator, a way to get hydrogen and helium to use in their shipbuilding, or something. But a giant gravitic weapon? No. Kyp made that up, to get us here."

While talking to Lensi, she hadn't taken her gaze off Kyp's face. Nor did she now.

"What was it, Kyp? What did we just blow up? Or do you even know?"

"I know," Kyp said. "It was a worldship, a new one. If it's any comfort, it wasn't finished, and there probably weren't many Vong aboard."

"Then why did you want it blown up? Why did you lie?" Lensi asked.

Kyp's face hardened. "The Yuuzhan Vong have destroyed, conquered, and raped our planets. They enslave civilian populations, and they sacrifice our citizens by the thousands. But until today, the only Vong we've hurt are those who come against us—the warriors. I wanted to hit them where they live, to let them know their civilians aren't sacrosanct if ours aren't."

"Then why an *empty* worldship?" Jaina asked. "Why not just pick a full one and blow it up, Kyp? You can't tell me *you* would be squeamish about that."

"You're wrong about that, Jaina, and I think you know it," Kyp said. "But sure, from what I've managed to find out we could have probably blasted one of their older ships. But that wouldn't have really hurt them. This does. Their worldships are dying, and a lot of them aren't in good enough shape to make it anywhere they can let people off. This one would have been hyperdrive capable, and it could have housed the populations of many of their smaller worldships. Now they have to choose between letting their children die in space or expending military resources to move them to conquered planets. Either way, it only helps us fight them—and it sends a message."

"Yeah, right," Jaina snapped. "It sends the message that we're not any better than they are."

"*We* were here first. It's *our* galaxy. If they had come peacefully, we would have given them the space they needed." He lifted his chin and raised his voice to address everyone in the room. "You should all be proud of what you did today. You fought against terrible odds and you won. You struck a blow against the Vong, and a good one. This was for Sernpidal, for Ithor, for Duro, for Dubrillion, for Garqi—for every planet the Vong have despoiled."

To Jaina's utter astonishment, he got cheers. Not from everyone—she saw Gavin and Wedge across the room, their faces tight and angry. But *nearly* everyone.

"Ask them, Jaina. You don't really have a homeworld. You were raised all over the galaxy. Most of these people know what it's like to have had a home, and too many of them know what it's like to lose one, thanks to the Yuuzhan Vong. You think they mind evening the score a little?"

"I think you owed us the truth. Maybe we would have decided to help you if you had been straight with us."

"And maybe you wouldn't have. As long as you thought it was a superweapon, you were ready to go. But we've set them back here more than the destruction of any weapon. By the time they grow another one—"

"—their children start dying. Right. I get that. Bravo, Kyp. Well done. Except you used *me*. You made *me* tell your lie, and now the blood of every Yuuzhan Vong child who suffocates in space is on *my* hands, too."

"There's more to this universe than Jaina Solo, believe it or not," Kyp said, very quietly. "I'm sorry you feel used, and I wish I hadn't had to lie to you. But I did have to. You wouldn't have helped me otherwise."

"And I'll never help you again," Jaina said. "You can count on it. If you were dying of thirst on Tatooine, I wouldn't even spit on you." And with that she left, found the stateroom she had been assigned, turned out the lights, and wept.

The next day, with Gavin Darklighter's permission, she left to find the *Errant Venture*.

FORTY-SIX

"It's a weird thing," Corran said, as the *Errant Venture* grew larger through the transparisteel lozenge of the Givin ship.

"What's that?" Anakin asked.

"Being happy to see my father-in-law's ship."

"Ah." Anakin tried to smile, but he couldn't. He'd been searching for Aunt Mara in the Force. The results were ambiguous—at times he thought he had her, but at other times it didn't seem like her at all. The feeling that she was dying had scarred his mind, and deep in his gut he feared she was already dead and his occasional sense of contact was merely a residual imprint of her living self.

He turned to go back and wake Tahiri and found her standing only a meter or so away. She gave him a brief smile.

"Uh . . . hi," he said.

"Hi," Tahiri replied. Her eyes refused to settle on his for long, but he could feel her uncertainty matching his own. "Looks like we're almost there," she pointed out unnecessarily.

"Yeah." Why did his fingers feel like hammers and his legs like spongy pillars? This was *Tahiri*.

"And we can finally get out of these things for good," Tahiri went on. "I never want to wear a vac suit again as long as I live."

"Right. Me either." The suits had made a recurrence of what had happened in the locker on Yag'Dhul Station impossible. What would happen when they were in shirtsleeves again?

It was a nearly terrifying thought.

"You think Mara's okay?"

Anakin shook his head. "No."

"She will be. She has to be."

"Yeah." A long, awkward silence followed as they drew near the *Errant Venture*. Corran was busily trying to prove they were who he said they were—despite the fact that they weren't in the same ship they'd left in—so he could get clearance to enter the docking bay.

"Hey, Anakin?" Tahiri asked.

"Yeah?"

"What's going on? You've hardly said two words to me since we left Yag'Dhul."

"We were kind of busy, and I . . . I'm worried about Aunt Mara."

"Uh-huh. Look, have you changed your mind?"

"About what?"

"About . . . you know. Are you sorry now? I mean, we were about to die and everything. It's perfectly understandable, because we've been best friends for so long, but maybe now you're thinking I'm too young, and remembering all the trouble I've gotten you into, and, well, maybe we ought to just forget . . ." Her green eyes did meet his then, with a sort of ionic jolt.

"Tahiri . . ."

"Right. I get it. No harm done."

"Tahiri, I haven't changed my mind. I'm not sorry at all. I don't know exactly what it all means, and we *are* young, both of us. But I don't regret kissing you. And, um . . . it wasn't just because I thought we were dying."

"Yeah?"

"Yeah."

"Well, okay then."

He was trying to decide what to say next without totally messing up the situation, when a staggering pain suddenly jolted through him.

"Aunt Mara!" he gasped. "Aunt Mara!" Another blinding wave of agony made his knees buckle.

*　　*　　*

The instant they were docked, Anakin bolted from the ship, pushing past the Jedi students who had come out to greet them, running as fast as he could toward the medical lab. In the turbolift, the worst agony yet ripped through him so powerfully that he was forced to block himself off from it before he fainted.

Outside the medical facility he found Mirax, Booster, Valin, Jysella, and half a dozen other people jittering around. When Anakin burst onto the scene, all eyes turned toward him.

"Aunt Mara!" he gasped. "What's wrong with Aunt Mara?"

Mirax embraced him. "Mara is fine," she said. "Where in space have *you* been? Is Corran with you?"

Anakin brushed off the question. "But the pain . . ." he began.

"It's normal," Mirax replied. "Corran?"

"Corran's fine," Anakin said. "He'll be right here. Mirax, I felt her dying."

"She was. Now she's not. Somehow, in the Force, she and Luke . . . We don't know how. But the Yuuzhan Vong disease is gone. Completely."

"Then the pain—"

"Natural. Hideous, overwhelming, but natural. Believe me, I've experienced it twice."

"You mean . . . ?"

A few moments later the door sighed open. Cilghal stood there, looking very, very tired.

"You can come in now," she said. "A few at a time, please."

Anakin and Mirax went in first.

Mara still looked sick. Her face was sallow, and sweat sheened her brow. But she was smiling, her jade eyes filled with an unfamiliar sort of happiness. Luke knelt at the bedside, holding her hand.

"Luke, Mara," Mirax said. "Look who I've brought."

"Anakin!" Luke said. "You're okay! Are Corran and Tahiri with you?"

"Yeah," Anakin said absently, his attention fixed on the small bundle in the crook of Mara's arm. He stepped closer.

Small dark eyes glanced vaguely in his direction, passing over him as if he didn't exist.

"Wow," he breathed.

"Hello, Anakin," Mara said weakly. "I knew you'd be here."

"I thought you were . . . Can I come closer?"

"Sure."

Anakin stared down at the newborn. "Are they all that ugly?" he blurted.

"You'll want to rephrase that," Mara said, "after what I just went through. Think in the general direction of antonyms."

"I mean, he's—"

"His name is Ben," Luke said.

"He's beautiful. In the Force, and . . . But he's all sort of squinched and wrinkly."

"Just like you were," Mara said.

"And you're really okay?"

"I've never, ever been better," Mara told him. "Everything is perfect." She looked down at her child. "Perfect." As weary as it was, her smile had enough wattage to light all of Coruscant.

FORTY-SEVEN

Nen Yim walked with bowed head through the labyrinthine corridors of the great ship. Sculpted pylons of ancient but living bone raised the vast ceilings, and choirs of rainbow qaana hummed hymns to the gods through their chitinous mandibles. Rare paaloc incense—forbidden to all but the highest of the high—remembered the ancient homeworld of the Yuuzhan Vong to the hindmost recesses of her brain.

Kae Kwaad slunk beside her, strangely subdued.

In the center of the vast chamber, they came to a raised dais of pulsing, fibrous hau polyps, and atop it, shrouded in darkness and translucent lamina, reclined an enormous figure. Only his eyes were clearly visible, glowing maa'it implants that shifted through the colors of the spectrum. Other than that was only an irregular shadow that sent shivers of worship aching through her body. For a terrible moment she believed she had been brought into the very presence of Yun-Yuuzhan himself.

Kae Kwaad prostrated himself. "I have brought her, Dread Shimrra."

The eyes burned into her, but it was long, tremulous heartbeats before the figure spoke.

"Would you look upon me, Adept?" he said, his whispered voice surely as majestic and terrible as that of the god he resembled. "Would you look upon me and die?"

Nen Yim supplicated. "I would if you wish it, Dread Lord."

"You are a heretic, Nen Yim. Bred of heretics."

"I have done what I thought I must for the Yuuzhan Vong. I am prepared to die for my transgressions."

Shimrra made a noise, then—a rustling, vaporous noise that she only gradually recognized as laughter.

"You have seen the eighth cortex."

"I have gazed within it, Lord."

"And what did you see there? Speak."

"I saw . . . the end. The end of the protocols. The end of the secrets. Besides those few marvels the gods have gifted us with since our arrival at the infidel galaxy, the store of our knowledge is nearly exhausted."

"So it is," Shimrra acknowledged. "You alone of all shapers know this." Something that was not a natural hand gestured at Kae Kwaad from the shadows. "Onimi. Reveal yourself."

"Yes, Dread Lord." Kae Kwaad—no, *Onimi*—capered, then. With a twist, the dead shaper hands dropped from his wrists, revealing ordinary Yuuzhan Vong digits. He stripped off the masquer that hid his face, and bile rose in Nen Yim's throat at what she saw there.

The man she had thought a master shaper was deformed. Not scarred or modified as sacrifice to the gods, but misshapen as one born cursed by them. One eye lolled lower on his face than the other, and part of his skull was oddly distended. His mouth was a twisted slash. His long, lean limbs twitched with a sort of mad delight.

"Onimi is my jester," Shimrra murmured. "He amuses me. Sometimes he is useful. I sent him to watch you and fetch you."

"You see, my sweet Nen Tsup?" Onimi crowed. "You see?"

But Nen Yim did *not* see. She did not see at all.

"Silence, Onimi. Prostrate yourself and be silent."

The jester flattened himself against the coral deck and whimpered like a fearful beast.

"Yun-Yuuzhan shaped the universe from his own body," Shimrra intoned, his voice now modulated like a sacred chant. "In the days following his great shaping, he was weak, and in that time Yun-Harla tricked him into giving her some of those secrets. These she passed to her hand-maiden, Yun-Ne'Shel, and thence to me. I am the gateway of that knowledge. But Yun-Yuuzhan never gave up all of his secrets. Many he still holds for us, free of Yun-Harla's deceptions. They await us. I have seen it in a vision."

"I still do not understand, Dread Lord. The eighth cortex—"

"Silence!" The voice raised suddenly to a mind-numbing rumble, and Nen Yim found herself as prostrate as Onimi. She prepared herself for death.

But surprisingly, when he resumed, Shimrra's voice was again mild. "In my vision, Nen Yim, you were raised to the rank of master. In my vision, you quested for the knowledge that Yun-Yuuzhan holds out. He offers it, but he demands sacrifice and labor to obtain it. He requires that you pursue your heresy."

Nen Yim, afraid to speak, lay quiet, slowly understanding that she was not to die after all.

"The other shapers are the dupes of Yun-Harla," Shimrra went on. "They shall not know of this. You will labor here, with me. You will have the resources and assistants my household provides. Together with me, you will bring the deepest secrets of shaping forth from the waking mind of Yun-Yuuzhan, and before that unleashed knowledge, the infidels will fall." He paused. "Now, you may speak."

Nen Yim composed herself. "Dread Lord, the inhabitants of the worldship *Baanu Miir*—"

"They are nothing. They are dead. They might have been spared but for the infidels, who desecrated our shipwomb and destroyed the new worldship there. It is nothing. They were the old. The shapers are the old. You are on the new path, the most sacred of all, Master Nen Yim. Forget what has gone before."

They are nothing. The infidels had killed them, everyone on *Baanu Miir,* on every worldship too old and worn to achieve faster than lightspeed. In her heart, at that moment, Nen Yim felt a hard rage and made a solemn vow. Up until now, the infidels had been an interesting problem to her, almost an abstraction. Now they were her enemies in the deepest sense. Now she would work to bring about their annihilation.

And behind that quiet rage, quickly overwhelming it, overwhelming even the godlike presence of Shimrra, rose a strange, dark glee.

Now my shaping truly begins, she thought. *And the universe shall tremble at what I create.*

EPILOGUE

Luke warily regarded the holographic image of Borsk Fey'lya, chief of the New Republic.

"So you're saying I'm free to return to Coruscant?" the Jedi Master asked the cream-colored Bothan's diminutive image.

"If you wish," Fey'lya replied. "I want you to understand that the original order for your arrest came from the senate, not from me. It took some time, but I have exerted the pressure necessary to have it rescinded."

"I appreciate that, Chief. But I seem to remember that it was *you* who threatened me with arrest a few months ago. How can I be certain that this isn't just a trick to lure me back?"

"In point of fact," Fey'lya said, "I hope you *don't* come back."

"Why is that?"

"Don't take me for a fool, Master Skywalker. I am aware of at least some of your activities. It is perhaps possible that some of them are . . . useful. However, there are still elements in the senate—powerful elements—who cite you and your Jedi as the cause behind the Yuuzhan Vong breaking their truce. Now, you and I know—whatever I may have said before of political necessity—that the truce was broken because the Yuuzhan Vong very simply want every world in our galaxy. But, though I've made the arrest go away, I still am not in a position to actually sanction your rogue ies."

"er words, you want deniability."

"niability, Master Skywalker. I want to keep it

that way, for the time being." He paused. "In time, things may change."

"I think I understand you, Chief," Luke said. *In time we Jedi may be your only hope.*

"Good. In that case, I'll bid you good day—or night, whichever it is, wherever you are. And, Master Skywalker?"

"Yes, Chief Fey'lya?"

"I hope things go well with the birth of your child."

"As a matter of fact, I now have a son," Luke said.

"My deepest congratulations to you and your wife," Fey'lya said.

"Thank you," Luke replied. "May the Force be with you."

The Bothan nodded gravely, and his image wavered out.

"How could you be so calm with that preening Hutt-drool?" Mara asked. She was half reclining on the bed, Ben sleeping—finally!—in her arms.

Luke shrugged. "It would have been the easy path to show him anger. After all, his actions nearly cost me everything." He sat on the bed next to her, and she nestled under his arm. He looked down at his son.

"But we're okay. He's not worth the pain of anger. Besides, if we can mend skyhooks instead of crashing them, we should."

"You're such a softy, Skywalker," she said, but nestled deeper into his arms, so he could reach all the way around her.

"You had another communication while I was in the 'fresher," she said.

"I was just getting to that. It was Kam. He and Tionne think they've found the planet we're looking for. And they send their congratulations."

"So they're headed back here?"

"Yep."

"Wow. And the *Falcon* showed up yesterday. When Jaina gets here, it'll be a real reunion."

"Yeah." Luke touched the tiny, perfect digits of Ben's hand. "And guess who'll be the center of attention? That's you, fellah." He cocked his head. "He looks like you today."

"He looks healthy," Mara said softly. "After that, he could look like a Dug for all I care."

"You did it, Mara," he whispered, kissing her cheek.

"*We* did it, Luke."

"Now I only want to know one thing," Luke said.

"That being?"

"How long before we get to sleep through the night again?"

Mara snorted and patted his hand fondly. "If this one is anything like the Solo kids, I'd say at least another twenty years."

Something in Ben's gray eyes seemed to agree.

Chapter One

1834

Slow Woman forced herself to keep going, in spite of the pain. She was a Comanche woman without a husband, taken in by her dead husband's brother, who might just as easily cast her out if she would cause too much fuss and show weakness. Although this was her first baby and she was afraid of the unknown, she knew she must be brave, and she struggled on, taking moments to stop and grip her swollen belly when another contraction came.

How she missed Many Horses, in whom she had taken such pleasure after becoming his wife. Many Horses would have been proud and boastful about the life she carried . . . if, indeed, it was his seed that had planted that life.

She sat down to pull up the ankle flaps of her fringed moccasins in order to guard her ankles against the harsh plant life of the western plains of Texas. The tribe with which she traveled was headed into the mountain ranges to hunt, after which they would again descend into Mexico to raid and loot their ancient Spanish enemies.

Now there was another enemy who was making much trouble for the Comanche. They were the white American settlers in Texas, who now called Comanche country their own. It was white men who had killed her husband when they had caught her and Many Horses mating by a river—

7

white men who had raped her, each taking his own turn. Her humiliation and grief were great, and she knew that the life in her belly could very well carry white blood.

The rest of the tribe walked or rode past Slow Woman as with great effort she again got to her feet. She coughed on the alkaline dust that was stirred, then bent over in another gripping pain. Instinct told her the baby would come quickly now. She waited for the rest of her people to pass by, then grasped hold of her horse and staggered to a tumbled pile of large boulders. In the middle of the rocks was a hollow space, where the shadow of one overhanging rock provided some relief from the hot sun. It seemed as good a place as any to give birth.

Her horse bent its head to nibble at a drying bunch of buffalo grass, and Slow Woman managed to raise up and pull a blanket from its back. She threw it down and squatted over it, pulling her tunic to her waist. Soon she was in too much agony to worry over whether the horse would run off. She wondered if her sister-in-law's nagging warnings that she was too young to have a healthy baby could be true.

The thought frightened her, but she reminded herself that very often fourteen-year-old Comanche women had no problems with having babies. Some bore children at even younger ages. She refused to think about the greater majority who had died, or who had weak babies that were killed.

As was the custom, this was a task a Comanche woman had to do alone. She would simply have to follow and catch up with the others as soon as the baby was born. Perhaps her brother-in-law and sister-in-law would drop back and wait for her, but in these days of being hunted like rabbits by white men, it was dangerous to fall away from the others, as she and Many Horses had learned the hard way.

Her thoughts swam with a mixture of the beauty of lying with Many Horses, and the ugliness of her attack by the white men. Which seed had produced this baby? Should she keep it and nurse it, or should she kill it? How

8

could she be sure at birth if the child had white blood, for all newborns were red and wrinkled, the color of their eyes hardly discernible.

She dearly wanted this little baby, and she began to pray to the spirits as she grunted and cried out, "Let my child be a son!" If it was a boy, even though it was a half-breed, she might be allowed to keep it. Sons were vital as protectors and providers. Yes, she decided, she would make her people let her keep this baby, for there was always the chance that this was the child of Many Horses.

Through agonizing pain that tore at her insides, she was vaguely aware that the sun's position in the sky had changed from mid-morning to mid-afternoon. Now the rock hardly shielded her, its shadow cast in a different direction. The sun glared down on her without mercy as she remained squatted in tearful childbirth, until with one agonizing push a squirming bit of life fell onto the blanket. Quickly she took a knife from a belt at her side and cut the cord that had been the child's lifeline while it grew inside of her. She cleaned membrane away from the baby's face, turning it over and patting its back as she had seen other women do with new babies to help them begin breathing.

To her great joy she realized the child was a boy. As it began to squawk its pitiful first cry, another pain hit Slow Woman, surprising her with its intensity. Surely once a baby was born there should not be this same pain. Her insides seemed to be contracting again, and to her amazement and horror she realized another baby was coming.

Twins! It seemed incredible and cruel. Twins were a bad omen. The Comanche never allowed twins to live. For two bodies to share the same spirit meant neither could be strong. She wept as the second child was born, another boy. Through tears she cut its cord also and got it breathing. Minutes later she pushed and worked to rid herself of the afterbirth, while both babies lay squalling, their little limbs flailing, their bodies still covered with blood and membrane.

9

Slow Woman wiped away her tears and rose, going to her horse to get a canteen. She was proud of having her own horse. It had belonged to Many Horses, who had been a proud warrior and had earned his name by stealing many horses from Mexicans and enemy Indians and the white man. Slow Woman had given all but one of the horses to her brother-in-law in payment for taking her in.

She wet a soft piece of deer hide and washed herself, then wrapped a piece of flannel from a white man's shirt around herself to catch the bleeding. She wet another piece of flannel from her canteen and knelt to wash the babies.

She stared at the crying infants, awed at how they seemed exactly alike. Their little fists were clenched as they bleated in angry hunger, sounding almost like little sheep. Her throat tightened at the thought of how the Comanche men would destroy this life she had just expelled if they saw she had twins. Her eyes misted as she gently washed them. Did they belong to Many Horses? Her heart still ached for her husband, and she had so looked forward to holding a child of his blood to her breast. Her brother-in-law would be pleased to know she had had a son. But twins—that was different! He would kill both babies and perhaps cast her out.

She finished washing them, then untied the shoulders of her tunic and let it fall. She picked up one baby and held him to her breast, and the child sucked hungrily. After a few minutes she lay the now-satisfied infant down on its belly and picked up the second baby to let him feed at her other breast. She looked down at the sweet, innocent child, then over at his brother on the blanket. They were tiny and red and wrinkled, but they were obviously healthy. They had all their limbs, had both suckled at her breasts with an eager appetite. Tiny hands pinched at her skin as the second boy continued to feed, and her eyes teared more. It seemed cruel and unfair that her precious babies should be destroyed, that she should have nothing to show for all she had just suffered, nothing to hold or love after all the months of carrying these tiny bits of life.

She lay the second baby down and rose, walking away

from the rocks and looking in the direction in which her people had gone. She realized that none knew what had just happened here. They only knew she had stopped to have her baby. Her heart raced with an idea that was both wonderful and heartbreaking. She could return with one baby. There was a good chance her brother-in-law would let her keep a son. She would have a baby to love and hold, a son to grow into a great warrior, and for now a child to take away her loneliness.

It was the only answer to her dilemma. She must keep one baby and leave the other behind, or both babies would be destroyed. Her young mind whirled with the torment of indecision. She could only hope the baby she must choose to abandon would die quickly, before some animal found it. She bent down to the blanket and studied her tiny sons closely, trying to determine which was the bigger, healthier child. She picked them up in her arms, holding them both close for a moment, finally deciding the child in her left arm was heavier and cried louder. She had no other way of determining which might be stronger.

She choked back tears as she tenderly kissed the baby in her right arm. She laid both babies back on the blanket then and rose, tying her canteen back onto her horse. She took a cradleboard from her supplies, something she had already made for the coming baby. She knelt to the blanket again and swaddled the slightly bigger baby into the deerskin casing of the cradleboard, lacing the skin securely so that the baby was tightly bound. She walked back to the horse and hung the cradleboard on the animal's side.

Quickly wiping at more tears, she returned to the blanket, lifting the second baby and folding the blanket so that the soiled section would be away from him. She held her chin high for a moment, asking the spirits to bless him and take him quickly to the great beyond with the least amount of suffering as possible.

"I am sorry, little one," she said as she laid the child back into the blanket and wrapped the blanket around the tiny life form. "I must choose, or lose you both. Always I will remember you, but no one will ever know my son was a twin. Soon you will join Many Horses in the Land Above and ride free.'' She leaned down and kissed the baby's cheek. The tiny boy made a little "o" with his mouth and reached toward her.

Through misty eyes Slow Woman wrapped him more tightly so that he could not move his arms and legs. She gently laid him up against the rock that was farthest under the overhanging flat boulder so that the sun would not reach him. He made a small gurgling sound as she rose, and she knew that the baby's last uttering would haunt her the rest of her life.

She turned, refusing to look back as she took up the reins of her horse and led it away, following the trail of her brethren. She felt weak and dizzy and knew she did not have the strength to climb up on the horse. She only hoped she would have the strength to get far away from the baby she had left behind before she could hear it begin to cry.

Vivian Morrow lay in the bed of the lumbering, canvas-topped freight wagon that her husband had rigged into living quarters for them both. Every jolt of the wagon disturbed her much-needed sleep and reawakened her sorrow. This unbearably hot desert was no place for a nineteen-year-old woman who had just lost a baby, but she knew that if she could just get through this desolate country and make it to California, it would be beautiful there, just like Lester had promised.

She loved her husband dearly, and she knew he shared her sorrow over losing the baby. But Lester Morrow had a dream: to get his wagons full of freight to the West Coast, set up a supply business there, and perhaps run supply trains back into the desert forts of Arizona and New Mexico with fresh farm products from California, as well as other valuables. The government had already contracted with him, and Lester was sure he could make his plan work and become a wealthy merchant in California.

Vivian had loved Lester since she first met him back in

12

Houston when she was sixteen. They had married just before this journey, knowing that once Lester reached California, he might never make it back to Texas. He was starting a new life, and they wanted to do it together. Vivian had confidence in Lester, who was fifteen years her senior, and who had driven freight supply wagons for another company all over Texas and was familiar with this land.

Lester's company consisted of twelve huge freight wagons, each one pulled by teams of eight oxen. The supplies inside had been purchased with money Lester had saved diligently, as well as through a loan from a trusting merchant/banker in San Antonio. Both the government and the merchant were confident Lester would manage this journey and would be successful in his venture. He was a big, hard-working man who was known for his honesty and his knowledge of the freighting business.

Once they reached California, Vivian would settle there; but the trip seemed to last an eternity. The wagons were heavily loaded, and the oxen moved at a snail's pace. Besides the heat and Vivian's grief, there was always fear of Indian attack. All day today the train of wagons had been following the trail of migrating Comanche. Lester had said they were Comanche because the long fringes that decorated the sides of their moccasins left little sweeping marks beside the footprints.

"Looks like a whole migrating tribe with women and children along," Lester had told her that morning. "It's no war party. But don't you worry. We're well-armed. And as long as we're behind them, they don't know we're here. They're probably on their way into the mountains to hunt."

Sometimes she wanted to hate him for bringing her, but she knew this was the only way they could be together; and she didn't have the heart to ask Lester to give up his dream and stay in Houston. She knew her feelings were scrambled right now. She had suspected she was pregnant when they left Houston, but she didn't want to tell Lester

13

and postpone the journey he had spent months preparing for; and whenever she looked into his tender, blue eyes and felt his lanky but strong arms around her, his big hands touching her face, all feelings of animosity left her. She realized losing the baby was not his fault, and she told herself she could have more children once she reached California and had gotten settled.

It was getting very dark now, and Vivian heard Lester's familiar whistle, heard him ordering the men to circle the wagons. Bullwhackers snapped their whips and shouted and whistled, while oxen snorted and the cattle that had been herded along bawled as riders began corraling them inside the circle that the wagons were forming.

Vivian was the only woman among a company of twenty-three men, most of them trusting friends of Lester Morrow, and most of whom had investments in Lester's dream. They were sturdy men, familiar with driving teams of oxen and good with their guns. Vivian was seldom afraid of attacks from outsiders because these men were well-armed. But she was terribly lonely, homesick for Houston and her family there, aching for the company of another woman. Most of all, she felt empty—empty of the baby she had hoped to give Lester, the baby she had hoped to hold to her breast, the baby she had planned to love and keep her company during the long periods when Lester would have to be gone because of his freighting business.

Soon the wagons were circled and the general din of making camp commenced. Men shouted back and forth, some unyoking oxen while others began a camp fire using buffalo chips and dry mesquite. Others assigned the job of cook would be opening their bins of flour and bacon and beans and the like. Vivian sat up and brushed her hair, then picked up her Bible, her main source of comfort on this long, lonely journey. She thought if not for Lester and her Bible, she would go insane in this desolate country.

She opened the Good Book to her favorite passage, Ruth 1:16–17. "And Ruth said, 'Entreat me not to leave thee,'" she read softly, "'or to return from following after thee; for

14

whither thou goest, I will go; and where thou lodgest, I will lodge: thy people shall be my people, and thy God my God: Where thou diest, will I die, and there will I be buried: the Lord do so to me, and more also, if aught but death part thee and me.'"

Lester was at the back of the wagon then, and she looked up from her reading. "I want you to eat something this time, and no arguments," he told her with his heavy drawl. His square chin was peppered with whiskers from two days of hard work without a shave, and his dusty clothes were damp with perspiration; but he was still the handsome, brawny man she had married.

"I'll try," she answered, setting aside her Bible. She reached out to him and he helped her down from the wagon.

"How are you feeling today?"

"Better," she answered, forcing back the tears of depression that were on the verge of falling. Lester was such a strong, able man. She hated showing weakness in front of him, even though he would understand.

He slipped an arm around her. "When we get to California, I'll build you a real fine home, Viv; and we'll eat your fine home cooking." He gave her a squeeze. "And you'll have lots more babies."

They walked toward the growing camp fire, where one of the cooks was already stirring a pot of beans. "Beans again," someone was grumbling.

"Just pretend you're eatin' steak and potatoes," the cook answered. "Use your imagination."

Vivian smiled at the remark.

"Soon as we're in higher country we'll slaughter one of the cattle and have a feast," Lester told them.

"Sounds good to me," another answered.

Vivian frowned then at the sound of a strange crying. Lester left her for a moment to help a bullwhacker with an ox that was thrashing its head while the man tried to get its yoke off. Vivian strained to listen, sure she heard the strange cry again; but the noise of camp made it difficult to tell. She moved away from the camp fire, sure the sound was different from the bawling of a young calf. It sounded almost human.

She circled the wagons, alert for the odd little cry. There it was again! It actually sounded like a human baby crying! She put a hand to her chest, wondering if she was indeed going insane from the loss of her own child. The cry became stronger, and she started to move between two wagons to go outside the circle.

"Don't you be walking out there in the dark, Mrs. Morrow," a man called out, catching up to her. "Too dangerous."

She looked up at Stuart Jones, one of the wagon drivers. "But . . . I heard something." The cry came again. "There! Do you hear it, Stuart? It sounds like a baby crying!"

The man frowned, listening intently, trying to hear the sound above the bawling, shuffling cattle and oxen, and the noise of making camp. "Yes, ma'am, I believe I do hear something like that."

Vivian sighed with relief. "Good. At least I know I haven't lost my mind."

"That's something none of us are too sure of out here." The man grinned.

"Go and get Lester, will you?"

"Yes, ma'am, but you have to stay put."

"I will."

Stuart left, and a moment later Lester was at Vivian's side. "What's this about hearing a baby?"

"Listen, Lester. It's crying harder."

The man frowned, listening closely. He looked at Stuart. "Could there be Indians out there?"

"Could be. But they generally have ways of keeping their babies quiet. They'd never let one cry like that and give away their presence. And we could still see pretty good when we began to circle. There's no big rocks or mountains or brush around here that Indians could hide behind."

"Get a couple of rifles and a lamp and we'll check it

out," Lester told the man. Stuart obeyed, returning with the items. Lester turned to Vivian. "You stay here inside the circle." He left with Stuart, and Vivian waited with curious anticipation. It was nearly twenty minutes before the two men returned, Lester carrying a bundle in his arms, something wrapped in an Indian blanket. "This is the damnedest thing I ever saw," he told Vivian, stepping over the tongue of a wagon and closer to her. "It's a baby—an Indian baby."

Vivian put her hands to her mouth in surprise. Lester opened the blanket and Stuart held up a lamp to reveal the tiny bit of life, which was still squalling. "Laying out there all alone," the man told her. "All wrapped up and tucked away under a rock. I saw my sister's new baby right after it was born, and I swear this one looks just like it—I mean, it looks like it can't even be a day old yet."

Vivian's eyes teared. "Oh, the poor thing." She looked up at Lester. "Let me hold it. Did you look to see if it's a boy or a girl?"

"It's a boy." Lester eyed her warily. "Vivian, this is an Indian child, most likely Comanche. Some of these men would just as soon we left it. There's some reason it was abandoned, and maybe that's the way it's supposed to be."

Her eyes widened in shock. "Lester, it's just a little baby! You can't leave it out there to die and be eaten by buzzards! Whatever reason its mother left it there, we can't say it's right. The Indians' beliefs are far different from our own."

"Taking it away from where it was left could invite trouble for us."

"Lester." Her eyes teared, and the pleading loneliness in them tore at his heart. He sighed deeply, looking at Stuart. "You know more about the Comanche than I do. What do you think, Stuart?" He bent a finger and stuck a knuckle into the baby's mouth to make it stop crying.

"Well, he ain't deformed," Stuart answered. "The only other reason I can think of why he'd be abandoned is that he could have been a twin. Normally Comanche kill twin babies—figure them to be bad omens. Maybe the mother had them alone and didn't have the heart to see her babies

17

killed, so she picked one to keep and left the other one."

"Oh, the poor woman," Vivian spoke up. "How barbaric that she should have to make such a decision."

"Depends on how you look at things like this," Stuart answered. "I don't expect whites will ever fully understand the Indian's way of thinking—but then they'll never understand our way either. There *is* another possibility."

"What's that," Lester asked.

Stuart removed his hat and ran a hand through his hair. "Well, the kid could have white blood. Thing is, though, the Comanche don't always have a whole lot against a half-breed, especially if it's a boy baby. Now if it was a girl, I'd be more suspicious it was a breed. But being a boy—I don't know. Maybe some Comanche woman was attacked by white men and she's ashamed of the baby."

Lester looked down at the tiny bit of life. "Or maybe it's the other way around. Maybe a white woman was taken by Comanche men and—" He hesitated, wanting to spare his wife the horrors of such a situation.

"I'd be less likely to suspect the mother was white," Stuart answered. "There just aren't any white women this far west. Your wife might be setting a record herself. I doubt any other white women have been into this part of the country yet."

Vivian put a hand on Lester's arm. "Lester, it doesn't matter who mothered the child. The fact remains we can't just leave the baby to die. It would be unchristian. His cries would haunt me the rest of my life. I could never forgive myself."

"I'll let you two talk this out," Stuart told them, putting his hat back on. He set down the lamp and left, and Lester studied his wife's pretty face, loving the way her light hair fell around her soft cheeks, loving her soft brown eyes.

"We have to keep this baby," she was telling him. "We have a couple of milk cows along. I can help it live, I'm sure of it, Lester. Just as I'm sure this is some kind of gift from God to help me through the loneliness of this journey."

"And when we're in California? Then what?"

"Then we'll . . . we'll decide . . ."

"You'll be attached. In fact, you'll be attached the minute I put this child in your arms. I know you, Viv."

A tear slipped down her cheek. "But he's so little."

"Viv, he's an Indian. Do you know what that means? It means a damn hard life for him growing up among whites, no matter how much love you might give him. And we'll want kids of our own."

The remark hurt her, and he realized it as soon as he said it. "I'm sorry about the baby, Lester."

"Honey, I don't blame you for that. You'll have more. But taking in a strange Indian baby now—with you so worn out and half sick—having to set up a home in California and get back on your feet—"

"Lester, what else can we do?"

He looked down at the infant. "I don't know. Maybe we could find some Indian family along the way that would take the child."

"You heard Stuart, and you know how suspicious Indians are. If they know this baby was abandoned, they won't want near it. They would think it was bad luck. Maybe they would even kill it." She touched his hand. "Lester, you don't fool me. You brought this baby here because you didn't have the heart to leave it out there to die. You certainly aren't going to take it back there now. We've found it, and God expects us to care for it. It's our duty. If it's the right thing to do, then it will all work out as the Lord intends, Lester. Now give me the baby and have someone try to get a little milk out of one of the cows, if its calf hasn't taken it all."

He scowled, looking out over the camp. "The men won't like this."

"They'll get used to it, and they trust your judgment. You're good at handling them, Lester. You can make them understand." She swallowed back a lump in her throat. "Lester, I need this baby. I think that's why God put him here for us to find. I've been so depressed and homesick, more than you know. I just didn't want to burden you with it. Please, Lester, let me keep him and care for him. We can't leave him here to die. I promise that when this trip is over, I'll trust your judgment on what we should do with him."

He grinned slightly and shook his head. "You really think after caring for him for two or three months you'd be able to hand him over to Indians or some orphanage or something? No, ma'am. Once you hold this baby, he's yours for keeps."

"Ours, Lester, not just mine."

He frowned, looking down at the baby. "I've had too many bad experiences with Indians to take lightly to calling one of them my own."

"You have a big heart. He'll grow on you."

He sighed resignedly, handing the baby over. "You might as well name him," he told her.

She took the baby, the motherly instincts that had been stolen from her immediately returning in full force. "Oh, Lester, he's so pretty and looks so healthy. What if we name him after your brother who died last year?"

"Wade?" He studied the infant. "Seems kind of strange calling an Indian baby by a white man's name."

The child opened its eyes, and Vivian gasped. "Maybe not so strange after all," she answered. "Look, Lester! I swear his eyes are light."

The man picked up the lamp and held it closer. "I'll be damned," he muttered. "He's got blue eyes! He *is* a breed." He closed his eyes, realizing the gravity of the statement. "That's even worse than a full-blood, far as whites are concerned. That must be why he got left behind then. Still, it's not like Comanche to turn their back on a boy baby, half-breed or not. Maybe Stuart's first idea was closer. Maybe he's a twin."

"It doesn't matter. He's just an innocent baby, Lester—a human being, nothing more . . . and certainly nothing less; and I don't ever want you or anyone close to us calling him a breed." She held him closer. "He's a child of God, and God has given him to me."

Chapter Two

Early spring, 1860

Jennifer kept the hood of her cape drawn over her auburn hair, glad it was a cool day in St. Louis so that it didn't seem unusual to be wearing the hood. She didn't want to be recognized. Her Uncle John would be furious if he knew she had left the house alone, but he was preoccupied now with planning her aunt's funeral. She would have to hurry in order to get back to the house before he returned from the funeral home.

She forced back a renewed urge to cry at the thought of her Aunt Esther's death, only yesterday. Esther Andrews had been her only mother figure for eight years now, ever since Jennifer's parents had been killed in a riverboat explosion when Jennifer was ten. Jennifer's memory of that night was vague. She remembered the sensation of hot flames shooting out at her back, catching her hair on fire. The next thing she knew, she was in the river, so numb from shock she didn't even know her back had been badly burned.

"It was by God's mercy you were thrown into the river," her aunt had told her often. "That's what saved you, child, and saved your beautiful face."

The ends of Jennifer's hair had been burned, but the lovely, lustrous waves of her auburn mane had grown back, and her only scars from the fire were on her back and around her right ribs, places no one ever saw except her aunt. She shivered at the thought that Uncle John had also seen them. She had never liked or trusted the man, ever since the time she was twelve and he had insisted one day when Aunt Esther was gone that she let him see her scars. She had been too young to understand or to object, and her humiliation at dropping her dress and the feel of her uncle's hands touching her back had never left her.

Ever since then she had been afraid of the man, uncomfortable about the way he often looked at her, feeling fear and revulsion whenever he came into her room at night to "tuck her in." When she was younger she had let him touch her in ways that were too familiar, afraid of offending him or seeming ungrateful that he had taken her in after her parents died. But as she got older, womanly instincts began to tell her the man had no right to touch her at all. And she knew his reasons for not allowing her to see young men were not for her protection, but out of his own jealousy. The man wanted her for himself, and she suspected the only thing that had kept her uncle from more intimate advances was the presence of her aunt.

Now Aunt Esther was dead. Jennifer would be alone in the house with Uncle John, and she knew instinctively she was in danger. After a feigned period of mourning, the man would come for her. Jennifer had made up her mind she would not be there. She had to get away, and quickly. But leaving would take money, and there again her uncle had left her helpless. She was aware that her parents had had money. Uncle John had been appointed executor of her parents' estate, and Jennifer had slowly come to realize she would never see any of the money she surely had coming to her. Her uncle had kept her in the dark regarding just how much money there was. She didn't even know what attorney or bank had handled it, if, indeed, there was any left. Soon after her parents' deaths, Uncle John had built a new home and had begun wearing fancy suits. He had opened his own hardware business and had become a wealthy man. Jennifer had no doubt where he had gotten the money.

All Jennifer had left of her own were a few pieces of jewelry that had belonged to her mother. Her aunt had given them to her. She carried that jewelry now in her handbag, realizing it was her only hope of getting away from Uncle John—that, and the letter she had secretly sent in reply to a newspaper ad for a wife. A soldier at a place called Fort Stockton in west Texas had placed the ad.

"Wife wanted. Shortage of women in west Texas forces this lonely soldier to advertise. Will provide travel fare. Please send picture if possible. You need not feel obligated to marry but refund of travel fare will be required if marriage does not take place."

The thought of marrying a complete stranger was terrifying; but the thought of staying alone with her uncle was worse. Besides, she reasoned, the ad said she would not be obligated to marry the man, as long as she could reimburse him the cost of her trip. The trip would at least be an adventure, and she would be far away from her uncle's clutches.

She searched the signs along the street until she found the pawn shop. She stopped walking, again taking the soldier's letter from her handbag. The man had replied to her answer to his ad. She had picked up the letter three days ago at her uncle's post office box. She was glad her uncle had at least let her continue to get the mail by herself. Because their home was near the post office, Jennifer had been allowed to go there every day with her aunt to get the mail, something she treasured, since her uncle so seldom let her go out of the house. Since her aunt took ill, Jennifer had been going alone, and her uncle had said nothing. She thanked God for that, for she had been able to secretly reply to the soldier's ad, and now had heard from him without Uncle John's knowledge.

She scanned the letter again:

My dear Miss Andrews. Thank you for answering my ad. From your picture I can see you are a very pretty woman. I am happy to send you the three hundred dollars for travel fare. I have been building my savings over many years of working and from my soldier's pay. It is a lonely

23

life out here, and every day I risk my life fighting the hated Comanche, but someone has to do it. I have lived in Texas since I was fourteen. I am now thirty-four years old and have never been married. I would like to have a family before I am much older, which is why I am looking for a younger woman. I am pleased that you are only eighteen. Life is hard here at Fort Stockton, but you would be safe within the fort, and I will take good care of you. Please let me know when to expect you so that I can make myself presentable. I am enclosing a picture, which is about four years old. Thank you again, and I look forward to meeting you within the next couple of months. Sincerely, Sergeant Anthony Enders.

Jennifer studied the faded picture again. The man was neither handsome nor ugly. He was simply average-looking, with dark hair and eyes. She shivered at the thought of what she was doing, but there seemed to be no other choice. She had considered just selling the jewelry and boarding a coach or a riverboat for any destination she pleased; but she had no idea where she would go, and she felt a little more secure having a destination where someone would be looking for her, waiting for her. Besides, her uncle would never suspect she would head for a place like west Texas. It was the last place he would look. She realized that if selling the jewelry did not bring enough money to reimburse Sergeant Enders in case she chose not to marry the man, she might have to marry him whether she wanted to or not.

She folded the letter and put it back into her handbag. She decided that marrying a man who sincerely wanted a wife and children would be better than being molested and all but imprisoned by a lusting uncle. The sin and shame of it would destroy her. She looked up again at the pawn shop sign. If she did have to marry the soldier, perhaps he would at least be respectful and kind to her, not ugly and leering like Uncle John. Surely he would understand that she would need time and patience before consummating the marriage.

She walked into the pawn shop, realizing how desperate

she must be to be doing this. She knew nothing about Texas, except stories she had read about how wild it was, and big. There was still Indian trouble there, and she could only pray she would not run into any wild Comanche before reaching Fort Stockton. The stories she had read and heard about what Indians did to white captives made her chest feel tight with fear.

She had already considered just leaving Uncle John but staying in St. Louis and finding a job here; but she knew her uncle, with all his power and influence, would find a way to force her to come back. He seemed to have the attitude that he "owned" her and that she was obligated to please him for having taken her in all those years ago. He had stolen her inheritance, and he meant to take her along with it.

She approached a man behind the counter, hoping he didn't know John Andrews. "Help you, ma'am?" he asked.

Jennifer took two rings, a broach, and a pearl necklace from her handbag. "Yes," she answered, trying to keep her voice from shaking. "These things . . . belonged to my mother. I don't want to sell them, but I have no choice. I need the money. Could you tell me what they're worth?"

The man picked the items up one by one, studying them carefully. He glanced over his glasses at her, wondering why the very beautiful young lady with the exotic green eyes was selling her mother's jewelry. He had no doubt whatsoever that under the hood and cape there rested a woman of exquisite beauty, with a body to match the face. Jennifer dropped her eyes, keeping the hood drawn over her hair.

"Hmmm," the man finally muttered. "Looks like the real thing, all right. I've seen enough to know the difference." He set down the pearl necklace. "I'll give you two hundred dollars for all of it."

Jennifer frowned. "Two hundred! Surely it's worth more than that."

"Might be. But I don't know if I can get what it's worth, and I don't know that this is really yours to sell. I'm taking my own chances, lady. Two hundred."

Jennifer refused to allow the tears of anger to come. Oh, how she would miss Aunt Esther. She had never felt so alone and vulnerable, not even when she lost her parents. "I'll take it," she answered, unsure how to argue with a pawnbroker.

The man smiled with pleasure at knowing he had made a very good deal. "Three days," he told her. "If you don't reclaim this stuff in three days, I have a right to sell it. What's your name, lady? I'll tag the jewelry."

Jennifer swallowed back a lump in her throat. "Never mind. I won't be reclaiming it. Just give me the money, and I want most of it in coins. I don't trust greenbacks. I've heard people say that with this country on the brink of a war between the states, paper money might be worth nothing in a few months."

The man glowered at her slightly. He didn't much approve of women who could think for themselves. He shrugged. "If that's the way you want it." He walked away from the counter, returning with two hundred dollars, most in gold and silver coins, about fifty dollars in paper money. Jennifer dumped it all into her handbag.

"You better keep a tight hold on that thing, lady," the storekeeper told her.

"I will. Thank you." She quickly left, hoping the man didn't know who she was. Her mind swam with thoughts of how she could get away now without her uncle knowing it. She hurried through the streets to the crowded docks, clutching her handbag tightly. She knew it was safer to take a carriage, but she didn't want to spend one cent of her precious money. She realized it would not be enough to pay back her fare if she didn't want to marry Sergeant Enders, but perhaps he would take what she had and she could somehow work off the rest at the fort. She could only pray he was an understanding man. Whatever happened, at least she had enough money to get to Texas. The money the sergeant had wired would pay her fare, but she would have to spend some of her own money for food and lodging. Where she would go from Texas if she didn't marry the sergeant, she had no idea.

The docks were noisy with crowds of people, and the clatter of wagons and bellowing of cattle and oxen being loaded and unloaded from what seemed hundreds of steamboats. Jennifer watched the boats, seemingly hundreds of them docked, others steaming up and down the Mississippi, and more heading west on the Missouri. St. Louis was a primary junction for all rivers north, south, and west. This was where most people going west gathered, most of them taking the steamboats because the railroads went no farther than Kansas and were very expensive.

Black slaves loaded and unloaded cargo. Carriages clattered by, children laughed and cried, chickens in cages squawked and clucked. Jennifer watched a group of soldiers disembark one steamboat, and it reminded her how close the country was to splitting apart. It seemed another good reason to get away from St. Louis. Heaven only knew what could happen here. More soldiers were being pulled out of the west and brought back east in case of trouble, and she wondered if Sergeant Enders would be among them. What if she got all the way out to Fort Stockton, only to find he had been sent back east? Surely he was quite sure he would remain in Texas, since he had already sent the money.

She wondered if he sympathized with the North, or with the South. It mattered little to her, except that she thought slavery was wrong. At least that was one thing her uncle agreed with. For now, the slavery issue was the least of her worries. She only knew she could not spend many more nights under her uncle's roof. The maid always left at night, and there would be no one there but her and Uncle John—no one to hear her scream for help or to hear her tears of humiliation.

She hurried to an office that read TICKETS—NEW OR-LEANS. She went inside, again watching the crowds to be sure she saw no one she knew. Her uncle let her out of the house so little that she was not a familiar face in town. She asked about tickets to New Orleans and connections to a stage that could take her to Fort Stockton, Texas.

"Not many people headed that way these days," the man replied. "Seems like a lot of folks are coming back East because they think they're going to fight a war." He studied his connections. "Well, there's a boat out of New Orleans that goes through the Gulf of Mexico to Galveston. Then you can catch the San Antonio-San Diego stage line—goes all the way from Houston to southern California, right by Fort Stockton—barring Indian trouble, that is."

"That's what I want then."

The man scowled. "You sure about this, ma'am? I mean, you going alone?"

"Yes. And I'm sure. My . . . my brother is at Fort Stockton. Our mother has died, and I'm going out to be with him now."

The man sniffed, writing something down. "If you say so. That's pretty dangerous country once you leave San Antonio—lots of Comanche renegades in the area."

"I'll be all right. My brother is sending an escort to meet me in San Antonio," she lied.

The man did some figuring. "That trip runs three hundred twenty-five dollars—five fifty to go all the way to California."

Jennifer's heart fell. She would have to spend twenty-five dollars of her own money. "That . . . seems like a lot."

"Sorry, ma'am, but that's what it costs. The stage line jacks the fare up when there's Indian trouble—have to pay their drivers more for the risks they take. It's not so much when you figure how far you're going—including the steamboat trips. And the boat fare does include two meals a day. I can't guarantee how good the food is, though."

"What about the stage line?"

"Food? You'll have to buy your own at the stage stops."

Again the tears wanted to come. She would have to spend even more of her own money, leaving her little to offer Sergeant Enders if she chose not to marry him. "It doesn't matter," she told the man. "Just get me there."

His eyebrows arched. "To each his own. Name?"

She hesitated. Uncle John might check here once he knew she was missing. He could track her down if she used her own name. "Charlotte," she answered, "Charlotte Eyre." She spelled the last name for him. Having just finished Charlotte Bronte's novel, *Jane Eyre*, she quickly came up with the name from a mixture of the two. The man wrote down her name, and she began counting out the money. She used the paper money she had received after cashing in the bank draft Enders had sent her, as well as some of her own paper money. As long as it was still good for now, she decided to use that up first. "When would I leave?" she asked.

"Day after tomorrow, about 9 A.M."

"Fine." Her aunt's funeral was tomorrow. A lot of people would be in the house, cooking and such after the funeral. Aunt Esther had been a popular, well-liked woman. She had a lot of friends. Already Jennifer was thinking of how she might be able to talk one or two lady friends into staying over that night to "watch over" her "grieving" uncle.

The man handed her the tickets. She shoved them into her purse, her heart racing with her daring plan. She could only pray it would work. Now all she had to do was leave the house very early the morning of her departure. Uncle John was a heavy drinker, which she knew would work to her advantage. The day of the funeral he was certain to down a good deal of whiskey, which meant he would sleep late into the next morning. She would be headed down the Mississippi on the steamboat before he realized she was gone.

"You sure about this, son?" Lester Morrow watched his adopted son pace. He seemed always restless and unsettled, which Lester attributed to his Indian blood. Wade Morrow was twenty-six now, a tall, handsome young man with the dark skin, high cheekbones, and straight, black hair of an Indian; but the taller build and deep blue eyes of a white man.

"I'm sure. You need me to go to San Antonio anyway. I'll see what I can do about setting up a new connection there for the freight line, and on my way back I'm going to see what I can find out."

Lester's heart ached at the thought that he could actually lose this young man to that part of Wade Morrow that belonged to another world. He and Vivian had both dreaded this day, but they knew Wade had the right to find out whatever he could about his Indian family if that was what he wanted.

"I'd make the trip myself, but these bones are getting old. Coming here to Tucson is as far away as I like to get from your mother and brothers," Lester told Wade. "If we do expand the business, it will be up to you and Henry and Billy to keep it going and do the traveling." He eyed Wade closely. "If you're still a part of this family after you check things out in Texas."

Wade turned to face the white man he had called father—the only father he had ever known. They shared a hotel room in Yuma, having gone there on business. Lester Morrow's dream of a successful freighting business had come true. Morrow Freighting Services was the biggest of its kind in the Southwest, and Lester had built his wife the grand home he had promised her. Their wealth was considerable, and Wade had been allowed to be as much a part of that business as Vivian and Lester Morrow's blood sons. Since Wade had already been a part of the family when Henry and Billy were born, there was no animosity on the part of Wade's two white brothers toward him. They had grown up knowing Wade as a brother, and the loving atmosphere of the Morrow home, especially their Christian upbringing by Vivian Morrow, had kept the brothers close.

"I'll always be a part of this family, Pa," Wade answered. "I intend to come back. But I've been haunted by this curiosity about my Indian side for years, especially after you told me I might have been a twin."

Lester sighed, his heart heavy. "Wade, you might have

Comanche blood, but you don't know anything about them."

"I've learned a lot from the scouts I've ridden with all these years taking our freight wagons back and forth to El Paso. I know most of my experience has been with the Papago and Navajo—but I've also had some experience with the Apache, who aren't a lot different from the Comanche."

"The Comanche are even more bloodthirsty." Lester saw the hurt in Wade's eyes. "I know I'm talking about people of your own blood, but we have to be realistic, Wade. You can learn the Comanche tongue from the scouts, and listen all you want about their way of life and all—but to actually ride into one of their camps is different. Besides, most of them are on reservations now, and those that aren't are wilder and more vicious than ever. They're renegades, struggling to stay alive. To them you would probably be just as much an enemy as any white man. After twenty-six years, what difference does it make any more, Wade?"

Wade plunked down in a chair in the corner of the room, his long legs sprawling out in front of him. "It just does, that's all. I can at least *try* to find out something. It's like . . . there's this whole other side to me I don't know anything about."

Lester ran a hand through his hair, coming away from a window to sit down on the bed. "Maybe you're better off not knowing."

Their eyes held. "Maybe," Wade answered. "I'm a big boy now, Pa. I can handle it. And I'm sure I can handle the Comanche. I've learned a lot about them from old Gabe Sanders. I can speak their tongue pretty good and I have a pretty good idea about their customs." He took a thin paper from his pocket and a tobacco pouch from a nearby table and began rolling a cigarette.

Lester studied the young man lovingly. He had not thought he could love the Indian baby Vivian had insisted on keeping that night in Texas twenty-six years ago, but

31

the boy had turned out to be bright and handsome and loving. Vivian had loved him like her own almost instantly, and Lester had never been able to bring himself to give the boy away while he was still a baby. Soon it was too late to even consider such a thing, too late not only for Vivian, but for himself.

"There's something else to think about," he spoke up.

Wade lit the cigarette, taking a drag and leaning forward, his elbows on his knees. "What's that?"

"I don't like to hurt you, Wade, but you know how some whites have treated you. It hasn't been easy for you, I know that. We've never gone as far as Texas before with the freighting business. You could get treated even worse there, being part Comanche. The word Comanche leaves a pretty bitter taste in the mouth of most Texans—the words Comanche and hate mean the same thing. You being educated and raised by whites won't make any difference to most of them."

Wade looked down at the cigarette in his fingers. "I know that. I've been handling whites all my life. I'll be all right."

"I wish you'd wait for Henry or Billy to come along. I can send one of them when I get back."

"No. I want to make the San Antonio deal alone, Pa. I want to show you I can run this business as well as you or my brothers. As far as stopping off in west Texas on my way back, it's something I have to do, Pa." He met the man's eyes. "I guess with you knowing both sides of your own family, you can't completely understand why I have to do this. It's hell not knowing the truth about your past. And to think I could have a twin brother out there somewhere among the Comanche just makes it all the harder."

"And if you find him?"

Wade took another quiet drag on the cigarette. "I don't even know. I guess I'd just feel better meeting him— knowing he exists."

"It could be very dangerous. The Comanche consider twins a bad omen. By all rights you should have both been

32

destroyed at birth. You could not only be risking your life, but also that of the twin brother, if he even exists. After all the fighting between the Comanche and the Texas settlers, the man could have been killed off long ago. Or he could have died from natural causes before he even grew up. The Comanche lead a hard life, Wade. It's a miracle any of them survive to adulthood."

"I know. I might not find out anything at all, but I'll feel better trying."

Lester began pulling off his boots. "Things could work out the other way. You might be welcomed by them— might find out the life of the wild renegade suits you."

Wade laughed lightly. "Pa, I was raised differently. Oh, I like my freedom—like being out there in the mountains and the deserts riding guard with the freight wagons and all that—but I'm not about to paint my face and go raiding and killing innocent people."

"To the Comanche they aren't innocent. Those Indians have just as much reason to do what they do as the whites. It's a vicious circle—constant revenge. I don't know how or when it will ever really end." The man set aside his boots. "But I do know you have a restless spirit, son, and without any Indian upbringing, you've chosen to let your hair grow long."

"Just saves having to get haircuts all the time. When you're out there on the trail, why bother?"

"You prefer buckskins to cotton clothing. You like Indian jewelry—would rather be on a horse in the desert than in a carriage in town."

Wade rose, walking to a window. "So?"

"So you're more Indian in spirit than you realize. Sometimes I see it in very subtle ways—a look in your eyes, the way you let out a whoop if you're excited about something, the hard time we had keeping you in school because you could hardly bear to sit still for very long at a time. You love to hunt and you can ride better than any white man I know."

Wade frowned, turning to face the man. "Why don't you tell me what you're really trying to say?"

Lester rose, his eyes tearing slightly. "I'm trying to tell you that I'm afraid of losing you, Wade, to that other world that has a hold on you without your even knowing it. I'm afraid you'll like what you find, or that something you find out among the Comanche will turn you against the whites."

Wade shook his head, smiling softly. "Pa, you and Mother and my brothers are the only family I've ever known. I've been with you all my life, and around your friends. I know there are good white people, and living on this side of it I understand their feelings toward Indians. Hell, I've fought them myself out there on the trail more than once. I'm not going to turn against the people who raised me. Sure, there's a lot about me that's Indian. And that is all the more reason to find out the truth, if I can. Part of me hungers for something, Pa, something I can't even name."

Lester put a hand on his shoulder. "I know, son. I guess that's what frightens me. I see you riding off, never to return."

Wade studied his father's weathered, aging face. "That would never happen. You need me and my brothers now more than ever. I'll be back, Pa."

Lester smiled sadly. "Then I'll trust you on that one. This will upset your mother, you know. The last few years she's always worried this would happen."

"I know. I would have said something first, before we left, but I couldn't stand the thought of seeing that look in her eyes. She's the only thing that has kept me from this for a long time."

"So, you're going to let *me* be the one to have to tell her and see that look that will break my heart, is that it?"

Wade grinned. "Sorry, Pa."

Lester sat down on the bed. "Well, when it comes to your mother, I've been giving in and giving up for twenty-six years. That woman has a way of making a man do her bidding with saying hardly a word. In this case, she won't be able to sway either of us because the deed will be done. It's just that she'll be mighty unhappy for a while, and

I hate to see that sadness in her eyes. I hope that you'll at least wire us once in a while to let us know you're all right—what you've found out and if you're coming back, that kind of thing."

"You know I will."

"Unless the Indians cut the wires."

Wade grinned. He walked back to the window and looked down on the rugged town of Yuma. Beyond it lay desert and mountains. He put the cigarette back in his mouth. Yes, he thought, this was wild, hot country, not unlike west Texas would be. But he loved it—felt at home in it, unlike most whites. He supposed his father was right. He was much more Indian than he realized.

What his father didn't know was that it frightened him as much as it did his parents. Was there a part of him that thirsted for blood? He had heard some of the customary methods of torture the Comanche could visit upon their captives. Was it an inborn instinct? He wanted to understand the Comanche beliefs, to know why raiding and living the nomadic life, torture, and revenge seemed as natural to those wild men of the Texas Plains as farming and doing business was for white men.

Sometimes when he looked at himself in a mirror, he saw a painted face, saw that wild look staring back at him. Maybe that was the look his father had mentioned. Inside, his beliefs and customs, all were white—as were his blue eyes. But his skin and features were undoubtedly Indian. Who had been his father? Was he abandoned for his white blood, or because he had been a twin? Why? Why had he been left to die? And who was his mother? Was she still alive? He had not mentioned that to his father, because he knew it would hurt the man. But it was a natural curiosity to meet and know his blood mother, wild and uncaring as she might be. It just seemed that to find her would fill this strange void in his life. There were so many questions he would like answered.

"I'm going down to check my horse and make sure I've got enough supplies," he told his father then. "I want to leave plenty early. I'll wire you from San Antonio about the deal with the merchant there we've been corresponding with. Once that's settled I'll head back—maybe stop off at Fort Stockton. They're right in the middle of renegade country. Maybe I can get some information there on how to find some of the Comanche, other than the ones on reservations."

"I'll be here," Lester answered. "We'll have breakfast in the morning before you leave."

"Fine."

Their eyes held a moment longer, then Wade left. Lester stared at the door, his eyes tearing again. He trusted Wade to come back, if he was able. That was the man's biggest worry. A million things could go wrong for someone like Wade in a strange land.

"God be with you, son," he said softly.

Chapter Three

Jennifer stood over the grave, tears of grief, combined with fear of what she planned to do, flooding her eyes. Uncle John put an arm around her shoulders and she moved slightly away, crying even harder. John Andrews thought it was just her grief over losing Esther that made the girl withdraw. His own grief was gentled by the thought that now there would be only Jennifer in the house at night. Jennifer depended on him. She had no home but with him. And Jennifer was an exceedingly beautiful young woman. It mattered little to him that she was his niece. He had watched her and wanted her for years, and now that Esther was finally gone, and Jennifer was most vulnerable, he would take what he wanted, and soon. The thought of it had kept him awake the last three nights.

The preacher spoke his last words, and the crowd dispersed. Jennifer was obliged to climb into the Andrews carriage with John. She scooted as far from him as possible, then looked around to see several carriages following them, people who were coming to the house. She breathed a sigh of relief.

"Your aunt was a good woman," John spoke up. "I know it hurts, child, but the pain of grief subsides with time."

She looked at his heavy body and double chin. John Andrews was a big man, with icy blue eyes and lips that

37

were fat like the rest of his body. He smoked so many cigars that the scent of them clung to him even out of doors. "I am not a child," she answered. She turned away. "And I'll always miss Aunt Esther." *Your own grief doesn't seem too great*, she thought.

"I know you aren't a child," John replied. "It's just hard for me to realize how you've grown. But you aren't ready for the outside world yet, Jenny, and I want you to know my home will always be yours. Uncle John will always take care of you."

He reached over and patted her knee, squeezing it slightly. Jennifer drew even farther away, realizing how strong the man was and how helpless she would be against him if he ever threw his full weight on her.

The carriage passed the telegraph office, and Jennifer hoped Sergeant Enders would receive the wire she had sent telling him approximately when she would be arriving. They reached the house, and Jennifer immediately climbed down, not waiting for John's help. She greeted guests warmly, secretly thrilled at the presence of others. Just as she suspected, John was soon pouring drinks for some of the men and downing shots of whiskey himself.

People brought food, and many of the women gave Jennifer reassuring hugs and words. She wondered what all these people would think when she would later be discovered missing. When she was married and settled, then she would tell Uncle John where she was—not for his sake, but so that he would tell these other kind people and they wouldn't worry. Perhaps she would write a letter to Aunt Esther's good friend, Freida Karr, or to the maid, Mattie. She suspected Mattie would understand her real reasons for leaving, since Jennifer had caught John making passes at the poor woman a time or two.

People ate and visited, and Uncle John drank more. Jennifer was keenly aware that he kept watching her. She wanted to ask one of the women to stay the night, but realized that idea was not such a good one after all. There was a good possibility Uncle John would snore through the wee hours of the morning and never miss her, but if someone else was in the house, it might spoil her plans to run away. She could only hope that people would stay so late that John would become too inebriated to come for her.

The afternoon and evening seemed to drag. Jennifer changed from her black silk mourning dress to a soft gingham of dark and light green stripes. No one knew that her bags were already packed and hidden in her closet. The luggage belonged to Aunt Esther, but she knew her aunt wouldn't mind her using them now. She realized she was leaving behind a comfortable life, a closet full of beautiful clothes, and a lovely room. But none of those things were as important to her as getting away from John.

People finally began to disperse, giving Jennifer their last words of comfort, leaving behind more food than she and her uncle could ever eat quickly enough before it would spoil.

"Would you like me to stay over, Jenny?" Mattie asked as she removed her maid's cap.

Both women glanced into the parlor, where John Andrews sat sprawled in a huge leather chair, snoring.

"No," Jennifer answered. "I'll be all right."

"I don't like saying this, Jenny, but I don't trust that man. A woman like me—I've been around, you know? He doesn't scare me. But you're so young, and I've seen him look at you—"

Jennifer put a hand on her arm, studying Mattie's curly dark hair and kind brown eyes. Mattie was a middle-aged widow raising three children alone. She had been close to Esther, and had often shared conversation with both Esther and Jennifer. Jennifer knew she was a woman truly concerned, one who could be trusted.

"Thank you, Mattie, for noticing and caring." Jennifer swallowed back a lump in her throat and pulled the woman farther away. "He'll sleep hard through the night. After tomorrow it won't matter."

Mattie frowned. "What do you mean, Jenny?"

"I can't tell you. No one must know, because I don't intend for Uncle John to find me."

39

"Jenny! You're not running away!"

The words were whispered, but Jennifer put a hand to the woman's mouth. "I'll be all right. I've got it all figured out. I'll be safe, Mattie, and I promise to write you as soon as I can. But you mustn't tell Uncle John until I say it's all right to tell him where I am. I'm only telling you because I don't think it's fair to let you worry and think I've been kidnapped or something. You've been good to this family, and a good friend to Aunt Esther."

"She was a fine woman." Mattie put a hand to her hair. "Jenny, you don't know anything about the world out there."

"I know more than you think. Uncle John has taught me to be cautious and wary. And I read a lot. I have to get far away, Mattie, or he'll come after me, and legally he can make me come back with him. He's well respected, Mattie. If I tried to tell people I'm afraid of him, they'd laugh at me and never believe me. I don't have any choice."

The woman embraced her. "No, poor girl, I suppose you don't. If I didn't have a family of my own to tend to, I'd go with you a ways and help you."

"It's all right. I have it all planned. When I knew Aunt Esther was dying, I started then, knowing I would end up in this house alone with Uncle John. I've thought a lot about it, and I have money. I sold my mother's jewelry. I'll be fine, Mattie, really I will. Just please act surprised when Uncle John says I'm missing."

"Oh, you can depend on that, girl. I'll put on quite a show of being terribly worried and upset." She studied Jennifer lovingly, her eyes tearing. "You're stronger and braver than I thought, Jenny, doing something like this, when I know how much you must be hurting for Esther. Esther certainly deserved someone better than John Andrews, didn't she?"

"Yes, she certainly did."

Mattie sniffed. "After losing Esther . . . oh, Jenny, it will be so hard losing you, too. I'd quit myself, but I need the money. I'm looking, though. With Esther gone, I don't want to work in this house any longer. Nothing will be the same."

"For me either." Jennifer hugged her once more. "I'm not so brave, Mattie," she added, breaking into tears. "I'm scared to death. But I'm excited, too. And I know that whatever happens, it will be better than staying here."

"God be with you, Jenny." Mattie gave her a squeeze and patted her back. "I wish you would tell me what you have in mind."

"I would, Mattie, but the more you know, the more it's possible Uncle John would find out. You know how he can be—browbeating and threatening. He might not believe you when you tell him you don't know anything about it. At least if you tell him you knew, you can honestly say you have no idea where I've gone. I'll write you later. Just trust me, Mattie. I have it all worked out, and I'll be safe, I assure you."

Mattie sighed deeply. "I have a feeling Esther will be with you in spirit. I think that woman secretly lived in hell, Jenny. She's better off now, and she knows you'll be better off getting away from here. She'll be with you."

"Thank you, Mattie. That's a nice thought."

Both women wiped their eyes and walked toward the front door. "I'll be back in the morning, around nine."

Jenny nodded. "I'll be gone by then."

Their eyes held. "Something new and exciting awaits you, Jenny. I can feel it. You write me soon and let me know if you're all right—wherever you are."

"I will."

"God bless." Mattie kissed her cheek. "I'll miss you, Jenny."

"I'll miss you, too. Bye, Mattie."

"Good-bye, Jenny." The woman quickly left, breaking into tears again. Jenny closed the door and leaned against it, breathing deeply for courage, her heart pounding so hard she was afraid Uncle John would hear it and wake up. She slipped past the parlor, peeking inside to see him still snoring away in the chair. She hurried up the stairs to her room.

Sleep was impossible. Jennifer lay on her bed, not even

undressing. She wanted to be instantly dressed and ready at the crack of dawn. She had already arranged her bed covers around pillows so that when Uncle John looked in on her in the morning, he would think she was still in bed sleeping. That would give her a little more time.

For hours she lay listening to the faint sound of Uncle John's snoring downstairs, until finally she drifted off into a light sleep from pure exhaustion.

That sleep was soon interrupted by the instinctive realization that she no longer heard her uncle's snores. A subtle alarm stirred her awake, her subconscious mind telling her to get up. She sat up, listening, catching the sound of Uncle John's slow but heavy footsteps on the stairway. He had awakened and was coming up the stairs!

She quickly rose, praying he was still too groggy and drunk to understand anything that was happening. She hurried to the closet, stepping inside and softly closing the door.

"Jenny," she heard her uncle calling softly then. "You asleep, child?"

Jenny shook with dread, scrunching down into a corner of the walk-in closet and pulling a quilt over herself. She knew she had to be quiet, a difficult feat when what she really wanted to do was scream.

"Jenny?" John staggered into her room. "I know you're feeling bad, honey," he slurred. "Uncle John is here to make you feel better."

Jenny grimaced as the man walked past her closet. She realized what he intended and prayed he would not find her. She feared her plans would be foiled this moment, as soon as Uncle John discovered the fake body in bed.

"Come let Uncle John hold you, child," she heard the man saying.

She squeezed her eyes shut, struggling not to let out a sob of terror. She heard the squeak of her bed springs, heard a light grunt and laugh. For the next few minutes there was pure silence. Jenny sat quiet as a mouse, finally pulling the quilt from her head for fear of suffocating. It was then she heard the snoring. She waited in disbelief, listening intently. There it was again—the rhythmic sound she had always hated, but one that she now loved. He had instantly fallen back to sleep! Maybe he didn't even know he had come to her room.

After several minutes she slowly rose, carefully opening the door just to the point where she knew it would squeak if she opened it any further. In the soft moonlight she could make out the huge, grotesque figure of her uncle on her bed. She reached inside the closet and took out her carpetbags and cape, still wearing the soft green striped dress.

She hurried downstairs, where she brushed her hair and ate a biscuit, then put her head down on the kitchen table, waiting for the grandfather clock in the hallway to strike 5 A.M. She wanted to get on the boat early and get herself tucked away under the name of Charlotte Eyre. If she was lucky, Uncle John wouldn't wake up until the boat had already left the docks. Then she would be free.

She thought of Aunt Esther, and all the warm, fun times they had spent in this kitchen, but she would not allow the tears to come. For now there was no time for tears, and crying might wake up Uncle John. Her days of living under Aunt Esther's protective wing were gone. She had to look out for her own welfare now. After all, she was eighteen, a woman. She would be all right.

She fell into another light sleep, wondering what Texas was really like, wondering what Anthony Enders would be like, and if she would see any real Indians along the way.

He was called Wild Horse, and the name was respected by the Comanche, feared and hated by whites. Both factions believed that his mixed blood only made him meaner, more determined to show just how Indian he really was in spite of his blue eyes. At fifteen he had taken the test of manhood, suffering the exquisite tortures of Comanche men and women alike, proving he was as worthy a warrior as any full-blood.

Bloody raids against whites and Mexicans, and a reputation of having stolen more horses, killed more of the enemy, and captured an equal number for slavery and torture than any other warrior, had earned him leadership status among the People. Especially since he came of age during the time that whites began to gradually hunt down the Comanche and put them onto reservations. Wild Horse grew to become one of the most wanted Comanche leaders, hated and hunted by citizens and soldiers alike.

Now, with the white man close to war in the East, soldiers were being removed from the West. Wild Horse was smart and cunning. He still had not been caught, and when he realized only skeleton crews of soldiers were being left at the forts, his raiding intensified. No settler in outlying areas was safe, and the stagecoach ran intermittently, depending on where it was suspected Wild Horse might strike next.

Wild Horse was an angry man. He hated his white blood, and seemed to be always trying to prove it meant nothing to him and did not make him weak. And he hated the white man, who had tricked and lied to the Comanche for years. There had been times when the Comanche had tried to settle matters, but always something went wrong and blood was shed. Now, for fear of starving to death and being shot down to the last man, most Comanche had given up.

But not Wild Horse. He was vowed to never turn himself in, never to die on a reservation. He would die fighting. Those who felt the same way held out with him, renegades who kept to the hills, moving out to strike in unexpected places, leaving behind tortured, raped, mutilated bodies, burned homes and crops, taking male prisoners, from whom the Comanche believed they drew strength and power through torture. He did not understand that when whites found these nearly unrecognizable victims, their wrath knew no bounds. To Wild Horse and his people, torture and killing were as ingrained a part of their lives and beliefs as breathing.

Such behavior was expected by the Comanche. If their own were taken by enemy whites, the Indians expected

44

they would be treated the same way in return. Wild Horse and the others could not understand why, at treaty councils with the whites, when white prisoners were brought in, beaten, scarred, and noses burned off, the whites suddenly would not continue the talks. Always they turned on them, making demands that were not originally agreed upon, arresting men, women, and children on the spot. Instead of being happy to get back their captives and paying the Comanche in promised food and tobacco and the like, the whites would become angry and turn their guns on the Comanche. This perplexed and angered Wild Horse, who had vowed never to turn himself in to anyone and get caught in that same trap.

He sat on a rise now, watching a house burn. A woman who had already been raped lay dead, pinned to the ground with a lance. A little girl also lay dead, and a young boy of perhaps eight years sat in front of one of the other warriors, crying. He would be taken and kept, to grow into a man and be trained to hunt for the tribe, to be a slave and help any warrior or Comanche woman who needed it. His father hung from a fence, his arms lashed to the crossbars, his body bloody from torture. The Comanche men had not taken much strength from that one. The man had done too much screaming, shown too much weakness.

Now, horses loaded with food and supplies stolen from the settlers, Wild Horse and his renegades were ready to ride back to their hideaway in the Barrilla Mountains, where they would rest and make preparations for more raids. Wild Horse had no fear that the soldiers would find them. No one could hide like the Comanche, and the rock-hard ground and mountain streams made tracking next to impossible.

They rode off, taking the boy and a few stolen horses with them, leaving behind the dead settlers and their burning cabin.

Jennifer leaned on the railing of the steamboat. Her first few nights on the boat had been hard, filled with memories

45

of the last time she was on such a boat. She remembered the pain of the fire and the horror of realizing the boat had blown up and her parents were dead. But being away from John Andrews, being free and bravely striking out on her own helped to ease the bad memories. Her heaviest sorrow now was for Aunt Esther, but even that sadness was overwhelmed with the bigger worry that Uncle John might find a way to track her down.

After six days, she was certain the man had by now torn half of St. Louis apart looking for her. She hoped he had not questioned Mattie too harshly. But then Mattie was a smart, somewhat hardened woman herself. She was probably right when she said she could handle Uncle John. Jennifer hoped the woman would be able to find another job and get away from the man completely.

Would Uncle John check at the docks? If he did, he would not find anyone with her name registered for any trips. But would the ticket master who had sold her the tickets remember her by description? She hoped her cape and hood had kept her enough in the shadows that the man would not be sure. Even so, Uncle John would have to catch up to her first before he could do anything, and she had a good head start.

She determined that if she kept to herself and made no trouble, that even if she was hunted down by description, the authorities in other states would have no right to detain her on something that was only suspected, not proven. She was eighteen years old, and she had paid for this trip with honest money. She had Sergeant Enders's letter, proving that this trip was legitimate and that she was going to Texas to be married. She was old enough to make that decision, and no one could stop her.

The steamboat let out a long whistle, and Jennifer watched the passing scenery, feeling more and more at peace with every mile she put between herself and her uncle. She studied the lush green countryside, listened with new awareness to the songs of the birds, enjoyed the smell of budding spring flowers and blossoming trees. Leaving the only home she had known since losing her parents had not been hard, once Aunt Esther was gone. If the woman had lived, Jennifer reasoned she probably would never have left, at least not to go far. Eventually she would have been old enough that Uncle John could do nothing about her seeing other men. She would have married and would have wanted to establish a home not far from Aunt Esther.

But all that was changed. Now she would marry for very different reasons, and there would be no Aunt Esther to help her with her decisions. She was on her own.

With every passing day, Jennifer grew more confident. She had met a married couple and befriended the young woman, partly because she truly liked her, and partly to have someone to be with along the journey for protection. When she was with the Hartleys, no one bothered her. When she was alone, she was occasionally approached by men who realized she had no escort. She remained cool toward them, quickly telling them with her eyes and remarks that she was not interested. She kept her cabin door locked and reread *Jane Eyre*, taking strength from the bravery of the heroine.

She wondered sometimes about some of the men who approached her, especially the young ones. Uncle John had not allowed her to be courted, but she had talked to young men at church and certain gatherings, and she was as fascinated as anyone her age would be about the mysteries of man and woman. Uncle John had made Aunt Esther's gentle description of womanhood seem ugly, and now Jennifer was confused over whether being with a man should be beautiful or dreadful. Being married to a man like John, she wondered how Aunt Esther had managed to keep the beautiful part alive. Perhaps it had once been that way for her, before Uncle John started drinking so much and letting himself turn to fat.

She imagined that mating might be pleasant, if a woman could get over the humiliation of it—perhaps if it was done in complete darkness. But it seemed it could only be that way if the woman truly loved the man she took as a husband. That was how Aunt Esther had said it should be. Would she learn to love Sergeant Enders? Would he wait for that to happen before insisting on marrying her? Could she bring herself to marry the man out of pure obligation?

She tried not to dwell on such thoughts too intently. For now she had to think about surviving her trip, watching out for herself, being careful of how much money she spent. She would worry about Sergeant Enders when she arrived at Fort Stockton.

She left the Hartleys behind at New Orleans, which was their final destination. It had been pleasant meeting new people. Now she was on her own again. She picked up her bags and boarded the boat that would take her through the Gulf to Galveston, Texas. Still, no one had stopped her to ask questions, and every night she thanked God she still had not been caught. She thought again about Mattie. She would like to wire the woman, but Uncle John might intercept the message. She had to wait until she was at the fort.

She missed Mattie, missed the house, missed Aunt Esther. Some nights the tears would finally come, no matter how hard she fought them. Her whole life would be changed now and forever. There would be no going back. She was proud of how bravely and intelligently she had planned this trip. But she was also afraid of what lay waiting for her in a desolate land from which there would be no return. She wondered sometimes if a fate worse than Uncle John lay waiting for her—if she had naively planned this venture, only to be carried off and horribly abused by Comanche Indians.

"Damn Comanche are at it again in west Texas," she overheard one man telling another in the dining area of the steamboat. She ate quietly, keeping to herself but listening intently. The man talking about the Indians looked as wild as any she had ever seen, with his gray hair long and tied at his neck. He sported a beard and buckskins, and he clamped a pipe between his teeth as he talked. He wore a knife on a colorfully beaded belt around his waist.

Jennifer had seen men similarly attired in St. Louis, but she got out of the house so little that she had seen only one or two, and none quite as wild looking as this one. Because St. Louis was the primary center of trade and travel to the west, such men were often seen there; but Uncle John had kept her sheltered from such things. Jennifer found the man intriguing, wishing she could ask questions of him herself, find out if he knew about Fort Stockton and what it was like there. But to speak to him would be much too bold. The man sitting with him looked like some kind of businessman. She sipped her coffee quietly.

"You think you can safely get goods and supplies through west Texas," the businessman was asking.

"Oh, it can be done—with enough men. The biggest problem is a renegade called Wild Horse. He's a half-breed, which makes him even meaner. I've never seen him myself—just the results of his raids, and it ain't pretty, let me tell you. What them Comanche can do to captives is somethin' I wouldn't dare go into here where people might overhear me, expecially women."

Jennifer kept her eyes averted, but she sensed they were looking at her.

"Well, it would be very profitable for me if I could hook up with Morrow's Freighting Service," the businessman answered. "I'm meeting one of his sons in San Antonio. A line all the way from New Orleans to San Diego would be quite a venture."

"I've scouted for Morrow a time or two. He's so well known in southern Arizona and New Mexico that he doesn't have too much trouble with the Indians through there. But a freight line through west Texas would be new to the Comanche, and those renegades are starving and in need of a lot of things. A supply train would look mighty good to them." The scout puffed his pipe a moment longer. "Which son are you meetin'?"

"I have no idea. All I know is someone is supposed to meet me there."

"Well, don't be surprised if it's an Indian."

"An Indian!"

"Morrow's got an adopted son in his mid-twenties, I'd say. He's half Comanche. Morrow's wife found him as an abandoned baby years ago when Morrow first came west. She couldn't bring herself to let him die, so she took him in. He's pretty well respected by those that know Morrow, but he's had some pretty hard times, bein' part Indian. I ain't sure how he'll be accepted in Texas, even if there's nothin' Indian about him but his looks. Folks in Texas don't much care. To them a Comanche is a Comanche."

The businessman lit a cigar. "Interesting. I've never met any of the really wild Indians, the ones still living free under their old customs. Don't see many in settled places any more."

"Most of the Comanche are up in Indian Territory north of Texas. But there's plenty left like Wild Horse to keep givin' Texas problems. And, of course, farther north the Cheyenne and Sioux are givin' the people in the central plains a lot of trouble. The Apache ain't settled yet, either."

The businessman ordered more wine for them both. "Well, I'm not sure the perils involved warrant me getting involved with Morrow Freighting."

"It would be his problem, not yours. There's also the possibility of war back East. Somethin' like that could bring you a hefty profit." The scout laughed. "Listen to me. We meet over a card game and here I am pitchin' Morrow Freighting to you." He puffed his pipe. "I'll let Morrow's son finish that. I can tell you, though, that they're a good outfit. Lester Morrow is an honest, trustworthy man. If he says he can get your goods from New Orleans to San Diego, you can pretty well count on them gettin' there. I rode with them for a couple of years, but the half-breed son does most of the scouting now. His first name is Wade. Ridin' that country suits him, I guess. A friend of mine, Gabe Sanders, he's worked for them, too. Had to teach Wade Morrow Indian ways, the Apache and Comanche tongue—ain't that somethin'? The kid is half

Comanche and had to be taught their language and customs by a white man."

Both men chuckled. "Interesting," the businessman replied. "I kind of hope that is the son I meet."

Jennifer rose and left her table, and the two men watched after her. "Kind of strange, isn't it," the businessman said then. "I've been watching that young lady. Seems awfully young to be traveling alone, especially knowing this boat is headed for Texas. Doesn't seem like the kind of place a young lady would go by herself."

"I was thinkin' the same. I thought maybe she's one of them ladies you don't really call a lady, but there's somethin' about her that makes that hard to believe."

"I agree. She's a proper lady, all right, which makes her being here alone all the more curious." He sipped some wine. "Oh, well, I guess it isn't our business."

"Guess not."

Jennifer hurried on to her room, suspecting the men were talking about her. She wondered if she should have thought of some other way to leave Uncle John. It was too late now to wonder, and she had no money to go back and change directions. Besides, there was still a man waiting for her at Fort Stockton who had sent her a great deal of money to come to him.

She closed the door and walked to a window, looking out at the passing scenery. She thought about the conversation she had overheard, and the half-breed the men had discussed. What must it be like to be of mixed blood? She knew nothing about Indians, had still never even seen one. She was fascinated by men like the scout, who had been so many places and knew so many things. It was obvious the people in Texas were going to be quite different from any she had known before. Soon she would be in Galveston, and would board a stagecoach bound for Fort Stockton and a future husband she had yet to meet. He had lived in Texas most of his life and had fought Indians. What would such a man be like?

Chapter Four

Staff Sergeant Anthony Enders led his squad of ten men down the ridge to the smouldering ruins of another settlement that had been attacked by Comanche renegades. The men rode slowly, eyes constantly watching the surrounding hills, Spencer repeating rifles drawn and ready. Nostrils curled from the smell of burning debris and bodies, two of which Enders spotted lying in blackened heaps on what was left of the porch of one of the houses.

Corporal James Deaver, who rode beside Enders, curled his nose. "Jesus, you can't hardly tell if they're man or woman."

"A little bit of hair left out away from that one body. Must have been a woman," Enders answered, his eyes sparkling with hate. "I remember these people came here from Houston—wanted a lot more land. Wasn't much worth it, was it?"

"Guess not." Corporal Deaver took off his hat and wiped sweat from his brow with the sleeve of his blue shirt. His naturally short, rotund body seemed to sweat more easily in this desert, and he hated the constant danger of Indian attack; but being here was better than being in jail back in New Orleans for robbery and assault. He had got out of there just in time, before his hotel room had been ransacked by the law. He wondered if the old man he had bludgeoned could have died. If so, that was even more reason to keep himself buried in west Texas with these

53

other volunteers, most of whom had similiar backgrounds.

Men didn't generally volunteer for this kind of service unless they were running from something or had reached the end, with no other way of survival. Service in this desolate land was a good way to eat and get a little pay, and hide from a fate that could be a lot worse than eating dust and baking under the hot sun.

For the moment, enlisted men were all that was left at Fort Stockton, except for Captain Bradley Howell, their leader, and First Lieutenant Michael Brown, the only commissioned officers left at the fort. Anyone of any real intelligence and importance had been called back East, where war could break out at any time. Several of the volunteers at the fort had run off, deciding that if there was going to be war, they would fight for the South, not the Union. That was the general feeling of most people in Texas, firm believers in states' rights.

Deaver couldn't care less, and he was not about to quit or go back East and draw attention to himself. Neither was Enders, who was wanted under another name back in Houston for shooting a gambler with whom he had been playing cards. He had taken the dead man's winnings for himself.

Although Enders held rank over Deaver, the two were both enlisted men, and over the three years they had been stationed here, they had developed a friendship based on mutual hatred of what they were doing, and a mutual necessity to stay put because they had nowhere else to turn. They had come to confide in each other, and often drank together and shared jokes about their pasts.

Enders, lanky, close to six feet tall, was an average-looking man who Deaver figured was close to handsome when he was shaved and spruced up; but since they were down to a skeleton crew at the fort, the men had become careless in their appearance. There didn't seem to be anyone who much cared, and Captain Howell was not very good at enforcing rules. There were sixty men left at

54

the fort, just enough to form a platoon or four squads, whichever might be necessary, and still leave a few at the fort.

Today two squads were out scouring the outlying territory, checking on rumors that Wild Horse was again raiding settlers. Captain Howell's biggest dream was to capture the hated renegade and earn a promotion for it. But tracking and capturing Wild Horse was not easily accomplished, especially since their best Comanche scout had recently died after being shot by a private who had got into a scuffle with the man. Howell still had the private doing extra duty for the killing, even though it had been in self-defense.

"You think Wild Horse did this?" Deaver asked Enders.

Anthony Enders spit tobacco juice at the burning debris. "Wouldn't doubt it."

They circled the ruined cabins and barns, and one of the men along threw up at the sight. Four families had settled here, all related, with the last name Williams. Women's stripped and tortured bodies lay strewn about, children lay dead, and men were nailed or tied to fencing or buildings, obviously tortured.

"Wonder if they took any captives," Deaver spoke up then.

"Hard to tell," Enders answered. "I'm not sure how many were here in the first place. Order a burial detail. Have the men take turns digging while the others keep watch. These fires are pretty fresh. Hasn't been long since the Comanche were here."

Deaver nodded, giving a rather weak salute. He and Enders had become such good friends that it seemed silly to salute each other, but they had to show some resemblance of army protocol in order to keep the other men in line.

Corporal Deaver turned to give the orders, and Sergeant Enders pulled a flask of whiskey from his haversack, taking a long drink from it. He rode back to the ridge to have a look around but saw no sign of Indians. He thought how desolate this part of Texas was, and he missed the coast. But he was still afraid of going back there for fear of being discovered.

Besides, with so few men left at Fort Stockton, and only two commissioned officers, he kind of liked the little bit of power he enjoyed for now. He reasoned that having a woman around would make things all the more pleasant. Since the Indians had started causing trouble again, the whores seldom set up camp near the fort any more. Rough and wild as they were, not even those women wanted to risk suffering what the Comanche could do to a woman. There were a couple other wives at the fort, neither of them much to look at, and there was Alice Hart, whose husband, a sergeant major, had been killed by the Comanche two years ago. Alice was perhaps forty-five, a short, stout, bossy woman over whom none of the men had romantic feelings, other than the fact that she was a woman and had all the parts to please a man as long as it was dark at the time. But Alice had a personality and a warning look that kept them away. She stayed on at the fort, cooking and washing clothes for the men, only because her husband was buried nearby and she wouldn't leave him.

Enders grinned, spitting more tobacco juice. Soon his own loneliness and need of a woman would change. In another couple of weeks Jennifer Andrews would arrive, and from her picture, he imagined she would be the best looking thing that had hit Fort Stockton in a long time. She was young and surely still a virgin, and he relished the thought of marrying her quickly and having himself a dandy time bedding her.

Staff Sergeant Anthony Enders would have the best-looking woman for miles around, and she would belong strictly to him. He had literally paid for her, in his estimation. Three hundred dollars was a lot of money—especially to a man making twenty dollars a month. He had risked jail for that money—part of it left over from what he had taken from the gambler back in Houston. The rest had been "earned" through card games with other soldiers; and one hundred twenty-five of it was money he had found inside a burned-out settler's house after an Indian raid. He had never told anyone about his find, not even Jim Deaver. The people were dead, so who would know or care? There had been one hundred fifty dollars altogether. He still had the other twenty-five dollars, which he would keep to impress Jennifer.

Jennifer. He liked the name, liked the face, hoped she had a body to match what he had seen in the small picture she had sent. He hoped she would arrive safely. It would be a shame and a waste for the Comanche to get hold of her first, enjoying that virgin body before he could.

He wondered what she thought of him. She probably imagined a brave man devoted to helping settle the Indian problem, no matter how dangerous. He intended to feed that image once she arrived. He would clean up and put on a good appearance. She would never know he was really Art Clements, a drifter and a gambler, whose father had been a worthless alcoholic and whose mother was a whore.

He slugged down more whiskey. Art Clements had never had anything, including respect. Now, as Anthony Enders, having earned the stripes of a staff sergeant, having some money in his pocket, and with a beautiful new wife on his arm, people would look up to him. He would be important and respected. Once Jennifer arrived and they were married, he could collect the bonus the Texas government owed him for volunteering, and he could leave this hellhole, maybe take his new wife to California and start a whole new life.

Maybe Miss Jennifer Andrews would bring along some of her own money, which he could use to gamble with once he left this place. He missed the big games, hated gambling for pocket money at the fort. He reasoned he could put his new wife to work so that he wouldn't have to look for anything really steady. This could all work out to be the best decision he had ever made. Once she was his wife, she had to do whatever he bid her to do. A wife could be a burden, but only if a man let her be. Handled right, she could make a man's life mighty pleasant.

A horse rode up behind him, and he turned to see Deaver

57

coming. "It's a damn mess down there," he spoke up. "I need a swallow of that whiskey, friend. My stomach needs settling. Private Payne puked again."

Enders chuckled, handing the bottle to Deaver. "That's one of the nice things about being the one in charge. I can assign the really ugly duty to somebody else." He sighed deeply. "I was just sitting here thinking about Jennifer Andrews. I sure hope she gets through all right. I wish Captain Howell would let me take some men out to meet her stage, but the bastard insists he can't spare anybody."

"That's too bad." Deaver handed back the whiskey. "From her picture, she sure looks like a winner, Tony, you lucky bastard. Any time you decide to share her, you let me know."

Enders laughed. "Not this one. Sharing a whore and splitting the cost is one thing. But this one is going to belong to me alone. I just hope she's not so shy and proper that she makes me wait too long before marrying me. The woman ought to feel obligated to marry me right off, considering all that money I sent. I saved for years. It was every last cent I had."

Deaver laughed. "Saved for years? Tell that to the gambler you shot."

Enders joined in the laughter. "If she buys my story, she'll take pity on me and feel the only proper thing to do is make this poor, lonely, devoted man happy."

Deaver shook his head. "You were born without morals, Enders."

Enders chuckled. "Same as you, Deaver." He raised the whiskey flask and took one more drink, then handed it out, signaling for Deaver to do the same. "By the way, look around the burned building good, and when no one else is looking, check the pockets of the dead men. I found quite a bit of money a while back after one of these raids. That's how I had enough to send for a wife."

Deaver's eyebrows arched, and he handed back the bottle. "And you never told me?"

"Finders keepers. That's what I'm telling you now. You find anything, you can keep it."

Deaver dug into his pocket and pulled out a tiny gold locket and a watch and chain. "Glad to hear that, since I already looted a dead man and woman."

Enders gave him a sly smile. "And I thought I could trust you."

"Same as I can trust you, friend."

They both laughed again, and Enders put the whiskey back into his haversack.

"You going to try to pick up Wild Horse's tracks?" Deaver asked him.

Enders sobered, staring out at the horizon. "Not this time. I want to be close by and healthy when my new wife arrives. I'll tell Captain Howell last night's rain made it impossible to follow any tracks."

"You'd probably get a hell of a bonus if you brought in Wild Horse. Howell wants him bad—wants to be able to report to the president that he captured the bastard. It will go good for his record."

"Well, bonus or no bonus, I'm not going after him right now. If Howell's so almighty anxious for recognition and promotion, let him go after the man himself. He knows how dangerous it is. I'm sure as hell not going after him with only a squad. We'll finish burying these people and head back to the fort."

Deaver nodded. "I never had any real devotion to this damn army, and I hate it out here; but still, even I would like to see that bastard caught. These folks don't mean much to me one way or the other, but when a man sees what's down there, it makes him mighty mad. I can kill a man easy as the next over a bottle of whiskey or a wad of money; but to stretch it out like that, that's beyond even my understanding. Same with the women. Hell, any woman can be took whether she wants it or not. That's not so bad. I just don't know why they have to go and cut them up like that and take their hair."

Enders spit more tobacco juice, wondering if Jennifer Andrews would go down easy, or hard. "Soft talk, a couple of presents, and just the right touch will generally do," he answered.

Deaver grinned. "We'll see if that works for Miss Andrews."

A gleam came into Enders's eyes. "She'll be my wife. She won't have a whole lot of choice in the matter."

Deaver felt an ache, envying his friend. "Well, if this works out, I'm going to find out a way to get hold of some money and send for my own wife. Sometimes I feel just about crazy with the need of a woman." He turned his horse. "I'll see if they're about finished below."

The man rode off, and Enders continued to watch the horizon, his breathing quickening every time he thought about Jennifer coming soon. Soft talk, a couple of presents, and just the right touch, just like he said. That was all it took to get a woman in the mood. Maybe he'd buy the stolen locket from Deaver and give it to her as a gift when she arrived. She didn't have to know it came off a dead woman.

Jennifer stared at the lovely harbor of Galveston as the steamboat approached. She was surprised at the size of the town, thinking there couldn't possibly be anything resembling St. Louis in Texas, which she had pictured being totally desolate. But here it was lovely, with a sparkling harbor and lush green foliage along the coast; a good-sized city with a harbor filled with both passenger and supply boats.

As the boat came closer, she noticed several cargo ships being loaded with cotton bales by black slaves.

"They call her the Queen City," someone beside her spoke up.

Jennifer turned to see the scout who had been in the dining room two nights earlier. He smiled. "Had a feelin' you've never been to Texas before, ma'am. Just thought you might want to know a few things."

She felt her cheeks reddening slightly. She was full of questions, but it didn't seem proper to talk to a stranger, and she was afraid of being found out. "Thank you," she answered. "But I don't have any questions . . . except how long it will take to get to Fort Stockton."

"Fort Stockton! You goin' all the way there? That's Comanche country, ma'am." He pushed back his hat. "You better have an awful good reason for goin' there. Once you head out of San Antonio, you leave civilization and these pretty little towns behind. Why, the desert alone will be enough of a shock for you, let alone the Indian—"

He thought he caught a tear in her eye as she turned her crimson face away. Sandy Carter realized how confused and frightened this young girl must be—and also realized it was none of his business why she was going to Fort Stockton. "Uh, it will take a couple weeks to get to the fort," he finished. "You, uh, need any help, ma'am? My name's Sandy Carter. I've been all over Texas."

"No, thank you. I'm fine." *I miss Aunt Esther and St. Louis*, she wanted to cry. *I've come here to marry a man I've never even met, and I'm scared.*

"Well, if you're goin' to Fort Stockton, I reckon' we'll see more of each other. We'll probably be on the same coach to San Antonio. I'm headin' up to Austin from there."

Jennifer didn't answer, and the man left her side. Her mind whirled with his warnings as the boat docked at the harbor. She picked up her bags and disembarked the boat, going to a booth to find out about the coach she was to take to Houston and then on to San Antonio. She walked to where she had been directed to find a handsome Concord coach waiting. Someone was already inside.

"Got her all washed up, huh, Nick?"

Jennifer recognized the voice. Sandy Carter was speaking to the stage driver.

"Sure did," the driver answered. "She'll probably be so covered with dust you won't know what color she is by the time we get to San Antonio, but the stage company wants them washed down whenever possible. The inside's clean, too."

"For a couple of hours, you mean," Sandy answered. Both men laughed.

Jennifer wondered what kind of long, dusty ride she was

in for. The driver nodded to her and took her bags, throwing them up to a man on top of the coach. "There you go, ma'am." The driver, who looked even rougher than Sandy Carter, helped her board the coach. He turned to Sandy. "Perty woman."

"Goin' all the way to Fort Stockton," Sandy answered. Nick's eyes widened, and Sandy chuckled. "I managed to get that much out of her, but she's not real eager to talk. That's all I know."

The driver scowled. "Just what I need—a perty woman along through Indian country. Last thing I want is to be responsible for somethin' happenin' to somebody so young and sweet like that."

The man grumbled more as he turned and climbed into the driver's box. Inside Jennifer sat down next to a window, two other women and two men inside. She recognized one of the men as the nicely-dressed businessman from New Orleans who had been talking to Sandy in the dining room of the riverboat. He smiled and nodded to her.

Next to him sat a woman who made Jennifer's face redden. Her face was heavily painted, her eyelashes thick and dark, her dress cut so low Jennifer feared something would fall out. Her hat was huge and feathered, nearly touching the top of the coach. She also smiled. It was obvious to Jennifer what the woman was. Her aunt had once told her about women who sold themselves to men. Now, as Jennifer thought back on it, she remembered the sadness with which Aunt Esther had told her about such women, and Jennifer wondered if Uncle John had been to see women like that. The good citizens of St. Louis didn't want them around, and Jennifer had never seen one, since they kept a low profile. But she realized that in these frontier towns they were probably bolder, perhaps welcomed, expecially farther west, where women were a scarcity.

She shivered at the thought of sleeping with strangers for money, and she wondered why such things were so important to men. Sandy Carter climbed into the coach, his eyes showing obvious pleasure when they fell on the painted lady and her ample bosom. "Howdy, ma'am," he said with a wide grin.

"Hello yourself, mister," she answered with equal pleasure. Sandy looked at the businessman, who grinned with equal enthusiasm. "Hello again, Mr. Strong. Looks like we'll have more time to talk, since you're goin' to San Antonio to meet one of the Morrow boys."

"Yes, I suppose so." The businessman, who Jennifer now knew was a Mr. Strong, glanced at her and smiled warmly as Sandy settled in beside the painted woman. "You were on our steamboat," Strong commented. "You going to San Antonio, too, little lady?"

"Yes," she answered, glancing at Sandy.

Sandy realized she didn't care to say anything further, and he decided not to announce he already knew she was going all the way to Fort Stockton.

"Well, my name is Bill Strong. I'm a merchant from New Orleans." Strong turned to the well-endowed woman beside him. "And your name?"

She gave him a coy smile. "Betsy. Just Betsy. I'm only going as far as Houston. That's where I live . . . and do business." She turned to Sandy. "Your turn, honey."

Sandy laughed lightly. "Sandy Carter—goin' to San Antonio and then up to Austin. I'm from everywhere." He leaned forward slightly. "By the way, Mr. Strong, once we get to San Antonio, I can help you find the Morrow boy. I know them all. 'Course if it's Wade Morrow, you won't have any trouble spottin' that half-breed." He turned to Jennifer. "You gonna' tell us your name, ma'am?"

Jennifer swallowed, not wanting to appear rude. "Eyre. Charlotte Eyre," she replied. She did not offer an explanation of where she was headed. She looked at the woman who sat beside her.

"I'm Louanne James, and this is my husband, Robert," she spoke up with a strong southern accent, putting her hand on the arm of the young man beside her. "We live in Houston. We've just come from visiting relatives in Alabama."

63

The three across from them nodded, and outside a whip cracked and the driver shouted "Git up there!" The coach lurched and began rolling west. Within minutes it began rocking and swaying rythmically, the leather thorough-braces doing a fine job of absorbing the shocks of the bumpy road. Jennifer's stomach soon grew queazy from the suspended motion, and again the loneliness and silent terror swept through her, but she refused to show it. She watched out the window at the buildings of Galveston, which soon disappeared.

The stage rocked and swayed its way toward Houston, fifty miles from Galveston. Because the boat had arrived late, it was impossible to reach Houston the same day, and Jennifer was grateful when the coach finally came to a stop at a small depot twenty miles from their destination. It took her a while to walk without staggering once they disembarked.

The stage stop was nothing but a small building where they could eat, a small rooming house, and a saloon. Betsy, laughing and on the arm of Mr. Strong, headed for the saloon, followed by Sandy Carter. Mr. and Mrs. James headed for the rooming house, as disappointed as was Jennifer at the sight of the tiny, dirty rooms that held just one small cot. "I guess I take the floor," she heard Robert James telling his wife.

Jennifer had no appetite. She was too upset from the rocky ride, combined with her loneliness and fear, and the strange room in what seemed the middle of nowhere. She sat down on the cot, fighting a need to cry. She could hear laughter and piano music coming from the saloon, and although she did not approve of the kind of woman Betsy was, she did admire her bold courage and the way she nonchalantly accepted the trip. Jennifer little realized her own courage, mistaking her natural naivety for fear and inexperience for cowardice. She walked to a window at the sound of arguing below and saw two Mexicans in the light of a lamp, drinking and pushing each other around. A gun

64

went off, and Jennifer jumped, stepping back from the window. A moment later she heard laughter, and when she looked again, the Mexicans were gone.

She sighed and sank back down onto the cot, thinking of the stark contrast between this place and St. Louis. She lay back, too tired to bother undressing, and too afraid to do so anyway because of the kind of men who might be lurking about. She thought about Uncle John. Yes, even the danger at this desolate stage depot was better than lying awake every night wondering when Uncle John might decide to force himself upon her. Pure exhaustion helped her fall to sleep. It seemed much too soon when she jumped awake at a knock on her door.

"Miss Eyre, it's Robert James. The stage is leaving soon. You awake?"

She sat up. "Yes. I'll be right there." She hurried to a mirror, her eyes puffy from needing to sleep longer. "Oh, you look terrible, Jenny," she muttered. She poured some water from a pitcher into a pan and splashed some on her face, then dabbed it off with a towel. She poured more water into a glass and rinsed her mouth, spitting into the pan.

She took a brush then from one of her bags and quickly brushed her hair, then pulled back the sides and fastened it. She pinned on her straw shepherdess bonnet and pinched her cheeks for some color. She longed for a bath and other pleasant toiletries, but there was no time; nor would she have considered stripping naked in a place like this. She could only hope she had not picked up some kind of bugs from the cot. She shook out her sprigged yellow calico dress and quickly dabbed on some lilac water, then picked up her bags and her paisley shawl and went out of the room.

Mrs. James was exiting her own room next door. "There's a privy out back," the woman told her. "I'll go with you if you need to go and we can watch the door for each other."

"Thank you," Jennifer answered, grateful for the offer. She did not look forward to Mrs. James or even the harlot leaving the stage at Houston. From then on she would apparently be the only woman, with Sandy Carter and Bill Strong. Both men seemed pleasant and trustworthy, but it would be awkward being the only woman.

"Robert is getting us some biscuits and coffee from the little diner next door," Mrs. James told her as they headed outside. "We'll have to eat quickly. The driver wants to leave soon."

"I'm glad you woke me up," Jennifer told her. "I fell asleep so late I never would have waked in time on my own."

The women relieved themselves in the unpleasant privy, then quickly ate before again boarding the coach. They were soon on their way again, and shortly after noon they arrived at Houston. The foliage around Houston was thick and green, and the air hung heavy. "Built her on a swamp," Sandy had told Bill Strong on the way. "That's why they built Austin and picked it for the capitol—higher, drier ground. Too much dangerous weather around Houston because of the coast—and too many insects and disease because of the swamps. Folks in Houston was mighty unhappy when they moved the capitol to Austin, but Houston will hang on. It'll still grow."

Jennifer reluctantly bid the Jameses good-bye. Betsy gave Bill and Sandy both a big kiss before disembarking, and Sandy patted her bottom when she climbed out. Jennifer reddened when the man gave her another long kiss. "I'll look you up again when I'm by this way, honey," he told her. Jennifer realized they must have slept together, and she looked away. Bill Strong cleared his throat nervously and lit a cigar. Sandy climbed back inside and the coach was off again, headed for San Antonio.

Jennifer sat quietly as Strong and Carter rattled on about Texas and Indians and the impending war, both men agreeing Texas would surely take the southern side if war did take place. "They grow too much cotton here to have a choice," Sandy was saying. "Lots of slaves here in Texas. Besides, nobody believes more strongly in states' rights than Texans. We're a mighty independent lot—don't like bein' told what to do."

They rode on in awkward silence for a while, Jennifer aware that both men still wondered about her traveling alone. "You still determined to go to Fort Stockton," Sandy finally asked her.

She glanced at him. "Yes. I'm . . . getting married."

Bill Strong's eyes widened. "You're going to Fort Stockton?"

Jennifer only reddened more. Both men looked her over, appreciating her beauty, envying her future husband. "I'm sorry, ma'am," Sandy spoke up again, "but I can't imagine any man allowin' his bride-to-be to travel through that country alone."

Jennifer swallowed, feeling embarrassed. "We . . . have no choice. He can't leave his post, and I suppose he couldn't get permission for an escort."

"Well, there must be somebody from wherever you came from who could have come along to watch over you," Bill Strong put in.

She looked away. "No. I . . . have no family."

"Where'd you start from?" Sandy asked.

She hesitated. "St. Louis," she finally answered.

"There must be someone—" Strong spoke up.

"No," Jennifer interrupted. "I've been on my own for a while. My parents are dead, and all our relatives lived farther east."

"Well, you can't have been on your own for long," the man answered. "You seem very young. Did your parents die recently?"

"Yes," she answered quickly. "I only stayed around long enough to take care of their estate and other legal matters. I had already become engaged and already had plans for going to Fort Stockton, so I'm going through with those plans."

Both men were sure she wasn't telling the whole truth, but again it was obvious she didn't want to tell them all of it. "Well, I hope you get there with no trouble, Miss Eyre," Sandy told her. "If I was goin' that way myself, I'd make a special point of keepin' my eye out for you. I've had experience with Indian fightin' and the like. But I'm bound for Austin. Gonna' be scoutin' for a supply train headed for Indian Territory."

Jennifer relaxed more at the words. "Thank you for your kind offer, Mr. Carter. I'm sure I'll be all right. The driver seems confident, and he has a guard riding with him."

Sandy decided not to tell her that two men would be little help if Comanche chose to attack. There was no sense in scaring the woman half to death. She looked nervous and frightened enough as it was. The conversation turned back to Texas as the stage rocked like a huge rocking chair. Jennifer relaxed more, joining in general conversation, finally taking out *Jane Eyre* and picking up where she had left off reading it last. She let the book take her into another time and another place, let it remind her that everyone had problems, and that she was not the only woman who had been forced to make decisions about her lonely destiny.

For three days and two miserable nights spent at two more pitiful excuses for depots the stage bounced and rattled on. Jennifer was grateful to at least be able to finally take a bath at the last stop. Strong and Carter both carried a tin tub to her room and insisted she have the pleasure of bathing, carrying water up for her and promising to watch the door for her. By then she trusted them enough to take them up on their offer, and she relished the feeling of being clean again.

She wore a blue flowered calico dress and a straw hat as the stage entered San Antonio around noon the third day. San Antonio was a pretty town. The stage would stay here the rest of the day and through the night, and Jennifer was sure the accommodations here would be a little better. She longed for a decent meal, and decided that finding a pleasant diner would be her first stop.

The stage pulled to a halt, and Sandy looked out the window. "Well, Morrow must have got your wire," he told Bill Strong. "And he did send the half-breed son. That's him over there. He must have been watchin' for you."

Jennifer leaned out her own window to see the man Sandy had talked about at considerable length during their journey. She stared at a tall, dark, handsome man in buckskins. His black hair was long, tied at the back of his neck. He wore a headband and was leaning against a support post smoking a cigarette, while people moved out of the way when they walked around him, some casting looks of disapproval. Jennifer immediately felt sorry for him because of the way people seemed to be shunning him. From things Sandy had said, she realized this Wade Morrow must be a fine man, with a good education and a Christian upbringing. How difficult it must be to have two such radically different bloods running in the same body.

She realized then he was watching Sandy and Bill Strong climb out of the coach. His eyes darted for a moment to see her watching him out the window. She was startled at how blue those eyes were, how handsome was his face. She immediately dropped her eyes, embarrassed that he had caught her staring at him. She had no idea that Wade Morrow was wondering if she was the woman called Jennifer Andrews. Just that morning a couple of men had been asking about a young woman with that name, wanting to know if she had been seen around San Antonio.

"Might be using the name Charlotte Eyre," they had said.

Wade glanced at the doorway to the depot, where the two men also stood waiting and watching. He wondered what they wanted with the woman, and why she would be using two different names. He greeted Sandy Carter then, an old scouting friend he had not seen in a couple of years. He decided he couldn't let himself be concerned about the woman and her problems. Men like Wade Morrow didn't dare get involved in the affairs of strange whites, especially when those affairs involved a woman.

69

Chapter Five

Jennifer climbed out of the coach, glancing again at the tall, handsome Indian who was greeting Bill Strong and Sandy Carter.

"It's been a long time, Sandy," he said with a warm smile that showed white, even teeth. His blue eyes moved to Jennifer, who quickly looked away.

"What are you doing this far east, Wade," Sandy was asking as he shook the man's hand. "I've never known you to go any farther than El Paso."

"I'm taking a bigger hand in the business. And I have some personal things to tend to this time on my way back."

Jennifer waited for her bags and could not help overhearing the conversation.

"How are folks around San Antonio treatin' you?" Sandy asked.

"Well, I couldn't get a hotel, if that's what you mean. For some strange reason people around here don't take kindly to someone with Comanche blood. I ended up making my own camp outside of town last night."

Jennifer felt a swelling of anger at the comment, amazed at how prejudiced people could be. Wade Morrow was clean and handsome, and he was well-spoken, obviously educated; and he was part of a successful freighting empire. How appalling that no one would rent him a hotel room!

"Well, Mr. Morrow, I'm Bill Strong, and I've got nothing against someone with Comanche blood—except for the ones who attack the freight wagons and destroy my merchandise."

Jennifer knew they must be shaking hands, but she was afraid to look again.

"My father and brothers and I don't care for those Comanche either," Wade answered with a light laugh. "I'd like to buy you lunch, Mr. Strong, and we'll talk. I actually found a restaurant in this town that will serve me. By the way, Sandy, we could use another good scout. How about coming back to California with me?"

"Oh, I'll mosey that way in the next few months. Right now I'm headed up to Austin to scout for a wagon train into Indian Territory. But thanks for the offer. I'll check back with you."

The conversation continued as Jennifer picked up her bags. "Coach won't leave out till tomorrow mornin', ma'am," the driver, Nick, was telling her. "I've got a problem with a wheel hub. Check back here in the mornin'. It's possible I won't be able to get it fixed by then and you'll have to wait one more day."

"Well, I hope it won't be too long. I'm expected at Fort Stockton."

"I'll do my best, ma'am. The Whitney Hotel up the street—that's a proper place for a lady like you to stay. You want me to carry your bags there for you?"

"No. I can manage." Jennifer turned with the bags, absorbed in worry over having to spend money on a hotel. She didn't notice the two men who had been watching her from the boardwalk. She climbed the step to walk along the boardwalk to the hotel when one of the men suddenly grabbed her arms.

"Jennifer Andrews?" he asked quickly.

Jennifer was so startled that she turned at the name without thinking.

"Just as we thought," the other man said. He was a big, dark-haired man with a menacing look. He took hold of her other arm. "You're coming with us, Miss Andrews. Your uncle has been looking all over for you."

Jennifer's heart raced at the words. Uncle John! Somehow he had found her! She jerked at the men's hold. "You let go of me! You have no right forcing me to go anywhere with you!"

"You're coming with us whether you like it or not," the second man told her, pinching her arm tighter and grabbing one of her bags.

"I can go where I please!" Jennifer jerked harder as the men began leading her away, their grips painful on her arms. She began to fight harder, furious at being treated like someone's property, terrified of being returned to St. Louis and Uncle John. She began to scream for them to let her go, and suddenly the men stopped. Jennifer realized someone was standing in their path.

"You better stay out of it, Wade," she heard Sandy Carter's voice coming from somewhere.

"I believe the lady said to let go," came a deep voice.

Jennifer looked up to see Wade Morrow standing in front of her.

"Who the hell are you?"

"The question is, who the hell are you," Wade answered. "A man sees two men dragging a woman off against her will, it makes him wonder if she needs help."

"This isn't your business, redskin," one of them answered.

Wade realized he had already gone too far to turn back. Much as he had intended not to interfere, the struggles of this beautiful young woman disturbed him.

"It isn't anyone's business," Jennifer answered, tears in her eyes. "I'm eighteen years old, and I have a right to travel wherever I please!"

"This young lady has traveled a long way alone," she heard Sandy's voice then.

The scout was now standing beside Wade Morrow, and Jennifer was glad that poor Mr. Morrow wasn't standing against these men all alone. She didn't doubt that the man could probably handle them both, but she knew instinctively that the fact that he was Indian was going to cause a problem.

"What business do you men have forcin' her to go off with you?" Sandy asked.

"We've been hired by a local merchant who's good friends with a John Andrews from St. Louis. Andrews is this girl's uncle. She ran away from him without saying where she was going, and he wants her back home. She's too young to be traveling alone."

Jennifer jerked away. "I am *not* too young! I have my own money, a valid ticket, and a man waiting at Fort Stockton to marry me! I'm eighteen years old and I can make my own decisions and go where I please!"

Wade could not help admiring the young lady's spunky attitude. Her green eyes blazed, and her pretty lips were puckered almost provocatively. He wondered what it would be like to kiss those lips, then pushed the thought away, surprised at it, and realizing it was a pretty stupid thought. Even though it was obvious he had white blood himself, he had always considered white women off limits.

"The lady has a point," he told the men.

The bigger man gave Jennifer a light shove, letting go of her and standing nose to nose with Wade Morrow. "Mister, if another white man wants to question or challenge me, that's one thing. But no damn Indian gets in my way, especially in defense of a white girl!" With that, the man pulled a knife and slammed his fist against Wade's chest, the knife blade pointing at his throat. "Now get out of my way, redskin! This is no place for a Comanche breed to be strutting his feathers."

In an instant Wade's strong hand grabbed the man's wrist and squeezed hard. At the same time he brought a foot behind the man's heel, giving a quick kick to its most tender spot and making the man's leg buckle. Wade kept hold of his wrist, squeezing more as the man crumbled, and causing him to let go of the knife.

Wade released his hold, and the man remained bent over on his knees for a moment, holding his wrist. Wade leaned over and grabbed up the knife, and for a moment people watched with open mouths, thinking perhaps the Indian would ram it into the man before their eyes. People gasped when he gave the knife a toss so that it stuck into the ground right in front of the man.

"I'll defend whoever I please, mister," Wade snarled. "I'm not the one who was bringing harm to the girl. You were!"

"I suggest you let go of her, too," Sandy was telling the other man. "And I strongly suggest you don't pull that gun you're restin' your hand on. Me and Wade there have taken on a lot worse than you, mister, believe me."

"What's going on here!" A man wearing a badge approached then.

"That Indian is makin' trouble, sheriff," an outsider shouted.

"Get that redskin out of here," someone else shouted.

Jennifer felt sorry for Wade Morrow, embarrassed for him. But he seemed unaffected by the remarks. She wondered if he had heard them so often throughout his life that he was hardened by them. He could pretend they didn't bother him, but surely they did. She admired his strength, not just physically, but surely emotionally. He was a man in total control of himself.

"This man wasn't making trouble at all," she spoke up to the sheriff. "He was only trying to help me against these men here, who I don't even know, who were trying to drag me off with them."

"We've been paid to take this lady back to St. Louis," the smaller man spoke up. "You know us, Sheriff. I'm Johnny Collins, and that there is Fred Russell." He indicated the bigger man, who was just then getting to his feet, still rubbing his wrist. "We work for Don Bensen over at the hardware store. He's good friends with this girl's uncle, John Andrews. Andrews has been looking for her for weeks."

"Wait a minute! Wait a minute!" The sheriff waved him off. "All of you come over to my office so we can straighten this out." He pulled a gun, pointing it at Wade. "You, mister, hand over your gun and knife. You'll sit in a cell until this is settled."

"That's ridiculous," Bill Strong spoke up. "Mr. Morrow here is a prominent businessman. I'm from New Orleans—come here to meet with him on business. You've got no call to lock him up. All he did a moment ago was defend himself. That man there held a knife on him."

"Mister, around here no Indian goes up against a white man, whether it's self-defense or not. Breeds can't be trusted, and until this is settled, I'll feel better if he's behind bars where he can't turn on anybody."

"Why, I never—"

"It's all right, Mr. Strong. I'm sorry for the interruption," Wade told the man.

"Well, I can vouch for Wade myself," Sandy spoke up. "I've known him and his family for years. He's a fine, fair-minded young man, with more education than most folks in this town. It ain't necessary to lock him up."

Wade handed over his gun and knife. "No sense arguing with the man, Sandy. I didn't come here to make trouble." He glanced at the young woman, wondering if her name was Jennifer Andrews or Charlotte Eyre. Had she been traveling under a fake name? If so, she must have been pretty determined to get away from her uncle. He wondered why.

Jennifer in turn fought tears of embarrassment for being the cause of so much trouble. Her cheeks reddened at the stares of outsiders, and she felt devastated that it was because of her that poor Wade Morrow was being hauled off to jail. She wanted to argue with the sheriff about it, but at the moment she was so humiliated and ashamed that she was afraid if she opened her mouth she would burst into childlike tears, which would betray her efforts at proving how grown up she was.

Johnny Collins took her arm again, and she jerked it away. "Don't you touch me," she barked. "I am perfectly capable of walking to the sheriff's office on my own!" Oh, how the tears wanted to come. She clamped her mouth shut again, swallowing back a lump in her throat. She picked up her bags and walked briskly behind the others, holding her chin high, watching the dancing fringes of Wade Morrow's buckskins as he took big strides on long legs toward the jail. She thought him a man of amazing patience and tolerance to be putting up with such treatment.

Bill Strong and Sandy Carter walked beside her as they crossed the street, people shouting obscenities at Wade. "We'll go along with you, ma'am, help however we can," Sandy was telling her.

Jennifer only nodded, grateful for their help, glad they knew Wade Morrow and could vouch for him. They crowded into the small front office of the jail, and the sheriff waved his gun at Wade, indicating that he should proceed into a back room where the cells were, acting nervous and afraid of the big Indian.

"He should be allowed to stay out here and have his say," Sandy spoke up.

"Indians don't get any say around here. I'll decide what's to be done with him." The sheriff waved at Wade again to go into the back room, and a moment later Jennifer heard the slam of an iron door. "You just sit tight while I get this settled," the sheriff was saying. The man came back out, throwing some keys on his desk. "Ma'am, you sit down there," he told Jennifer, indicating the only other chair.

"I prefer to stand," Jennifer answered.

The sheriff sighed, glancing at Sandy and Bill Strong. "I'm Sheriff North for those of you who don't know." He looked at the two men who had grabbed Jennifer. "Finish your story, Johnny. It better be good."

"It's like I said, Sheriff. We were hired to take the girl back to St. Louis. Her uncle is a prominent businessman there—raised her like his own. The ungrateful child ran off on him and he wants her back where she'll be safe. Her uncle finally figured out she might be traveling under the name Charlotte Eyre, because somebody by that name boarded a steamboat at St. Louis, with a ticket for Texas. She'd been reading some book by an author with that name or something like that. Anyway, it doesn't matter. This is no place for a lady who doesn't know anything about the area. And she sure as hell shouldn't be traveling alone."

"I have every right to travel alone if I choose," Jennifer answered, finding her courage and her voice again. Anger and determination were winning out over tears. "I am Jennifer Andrews," she told the sheriff firmly. "I ran away because I knew my uncle would never agree to what I am doing. But I am eighteen. I have my own money and a valid ticket to Fort Stockton, where I intend to be married. Here." She opened her purse and dug out her letter from Sergeant Enders. "Here is the proof. I answered an ad from a Sergeant Enders for a wife, and he wrote back and sent me the money to come out here. It's my duty to own up to my end of the bargain. I will not go back to St. Louis! For personal reasons I do not care to disclose, I have chosen not to live with my uncle any longer. I am old enough to make my own decisions, and no one has any right forcing me to go back to St. Louis." She looked haughtily at Johnny Collins. "The author, by the way, is Charlotte Bronte, and the book is called *Jane Eyre*. But then you probably don't even know how to read. I'll bet that Indian man in there can read better than *you* can."

In his cell, Wade Morrow smiled at the remark. He was glad he had defended the spunky young lady, even if it had landed him in jail.

In the outer room the sheriff looked over the letter and her ticket, as well as the birth certificate Jennifer had wisely taken from her aunt's papers before leaving. The sheriff frowned. "You're marrying some sergeant from Fort Stockton that you've never even met?"

Jennifer reddened again, secretly feeling some fear and apprehension at the thought herself, but she refused to show it. "Yes. His ad stated that I could refuse him, but I will have to pay back the money he sent if I do. If anyone has rights to me at the moment, Sergeant Enders has more rights than my uncle. Three hundred dollars is a lot of money for an army man."

"Hmmm." The sheriff studied the letter again, then looked at Jennifer shrewdly. "It certainly is, ma'am, more than you realize. I have to wonder where he got that much money. You ought to be aware that often the men who volunteer for service in west Texas are only doing it to duck the law back East. You better be mighty careful and mighty sure before you go marrying this Sergeant Enders. Now I don't know what your problem is with your uncle, but it must be a plenty big one for you to be taking the chance on traveling alone in country like this just to get away from the man."

"She ought to go back," Fred Russell spoke up, still rubbing his wrist, "and that Indian in there out to be run out of town."

"I'll get to that," the sheriff answered. He studied the letter and birth certificate a little longer, then handed everything back to Jennifer. "Well, Miss Andrews, everything looks in order. You're right about having the right to go where you please. If you're foolish enough to ride into Indian country to marry a man you don't even know, we've no right to stop you."

"Fine," she answered, grabbing back her papers. "Thank you, Sheriff North. Now what about that man in the cell? All he did was help me, and what he did to Mr. Russell here was done in self-defense. If he was the horrible, murdering savage you seem to think he is capable of being, he would have used that knife on Mr. Russell." She turned her eyes to the big man who had hurt her arm. "And he would have had every right as far as I'm concerned."

"She's right there, Sheriff," Sandy spoke up. "Any man gets a knife rammed up against his throat has the right to use it on the man who threatened him. Russell here is lucky he's alive. I should say he's lucky it was Wade Morrow he picked on and not some other Comanche, or his guts would be layin' in the street right now. Fact is, if it was me he'd pulled that knife on, the same might be true."

The sheriff looked at Johnny Collins. "That true, Johnny? Fred here pulled a knife on Mr. Morrow?"

79

Johnny shoved his hands in his pockets, looking uncomfortable. "Only after Morrow threatened him."

"With a weapon?"

"Well, no, but—"

The sheriff waved him off, looking irritated. He moved his eyes to Fred Russell. "That was a pretty stupid thing to do, Fred, Indian or no Indian. Any man would react to something like that."

"That just shows you the kind of man Wade Morrow is," Sandy put in. "Why don't you let him out of that jail so he can settle his business with Mr. Strong here. That's the only reason he's in San Antonio anyway. Just let everybody be on their way. I'm headed for Austin, and Morrow will be heading back West soon—Strong here back to New Orleans and Miss Andrews to Fort Stockton. No real harm has been done. It's all just a big misunderstandin'."

Sheriff North took off his hat and rubbed at his forehead. "All right. Johnny, you and Fred get going, and I want no more trouble out of you. I see no reason to detain Miss Andrews and have no authority to force her to be sent back to St. Louis. Her reasons for leaving are her business, and this is Texas. A man or woman is free to do as he or she pleases here, so you two stay away from her. You can tell her uncle that she is safe and is heading for Fort Stockton to be married. If he wants to write her or wire her, he can contact her there."

"Thank you, Sheriff," Jennifer told him gratefully.

The sheriff turned to Sandy. "You accompany your Indian friend while he completes his business with Mr. Strong here. I'm giving you the job of seeing that Mr. Wade Morrow leaves San Antonio by tomorrow morning. Around here men like him cause trouble without even trying."

"I'll stick with him till mornin'," Sandy answered, nodding.

"I'm sorry about all this, Mr. Strong," the sheriff told the man. "If you haven't lived around here, you don't understand how folks feel about the Comanche—civilized or not."

Strong only scowled with irritation while the sheriff went into the back room to release Wade Morrow. By the time Wade came out, Collins and Russell were gone. Jennifer blinked back tears as Wade came into the room and the sheriff handed over his knife and gun.

"These better not get used while you're here," the man told Wade. "No hard feelings, I hope. I did that for your own protection."

Wade gave him a hard look, shoving the gun into its holster and the knife into a sheath on his weapons belt. "No hard feelings," he answered, a note of sarcasm in his voice.

"I'd lay low while I'm in town. Any more women yell for help, let somebody else help them. A man in your position ought to understand that, especially when it's a pretty young white woman that's involved."

Wade's blue eyes drilled into the man for a moment. He turned, glancing at Jennifer for only a moment, obviously wary of saying a word to her. He looked over at Sandy. "Let's get out of here. You still interested in a meal, Mr. Strong?"

"Of course I am. I'm not the horse's ass some men are in this town. Let's go, Mr. Morrow."

The men filed out, and Jennifer hurried after, calling out to Wade Morrow. The man turned, his eyes darting around warily before resting on Jennifer, who he considered the most beautiful young woman he had ever seen.

Jennifer felt the crimson coming to her cheeks again, Morrow's handsome, awesome presence making her suddenly nervous, and stirring feelings deep within her that she had never felt before. "I . . . thank you for stopping those men. And I'm sorry . . . for the trouble it caused you. It's all my fault."

"I knew the risk," he answered. His eyes moved over her as though he secretly knew how she looked under her

81

dress. He thought of telling her he was also going to Fort Stockton, but he supposed it would seem too forward, and she probably didn't care anyway. "Good luck with your plans to marry. I'd be real careful about that, and I'd give thought to going back to St. Louis or staying right here. That's dangerous country."

Jennifer stiffened. "I'm going, and that's that. I owe it to Sergeant Enders."

Their eyes held for a moment, and to her surprise she found herself wondering what it would be like to be married to a man like Wade Morrow—a handsome man, indeed, but also a man of courage and admirable patience and self-control. He would be kind to a frightened young woman; she felt it intuitively. She dropped her eyes, wondering if he could read her thoughts.

"Good-bye, Miss Andrews. I can't be seen standing here talking to you, and it's best for you if you in turn don't give me the time of day. People around here have a word for white women who defend Indian men."

She shot him a proud look. "I don't worry about such things, Mr. Morrow. I don't judge people on the same level as those around here might. You're a fine man, and I appreciate what you did. I couldn't let you leave without telling you, that's all." She twisted her gloves nervously. "Good-bye, Mr. Morrow. Good luck to you."

He nodded, a sparkle of humor and appreciation coming into his eyes. "Good-bye, Miss Andrews." He turned, and Jennifer watched him walk away, nodding to both Sandy and Bill Strong as all three men left. She returned to the sheriff's office to pick up her bags, then headed up the street to find a room for the night.

Wade lay wide awake, looking up at the stars and thinking of a pretty young girl with reddish hair and green eyes. "She really going all the way to Fort Stockton?" he asked Sandy.

The old scout chuckled, taking a long drag on a pipe

before answering. "Somehow I had a feelin' you was thinkin' about that perty young lady." Since Wade could not get a room in town, Sandy had decided to camp out with him to talk about the old days and find out how his old friend, Lester Morrow, was doing. "That's dangerous thinkin', boy."

"I gave up worrying about what's dangerous a long time ago. For me, *everything* is dangerous, so I might as well live my life the way I want and let the chips fall where they may. And you didn't answer my question."

Sandy sighed deeply. "Yeah, she's really going all the way. Me and Bill Strong had our eye on her most of the trip, wonderin' about her, kind of watchin' out for her without her knowin' it. She's a brave little gal, I'd say."

"Scared inside though. Anybody can see that," Wade answered. "My guess, though, is she's more afraid of that uncle of hers than she is of traveling into Comanche country to marry a complete stranger. I've got a good idea why, and it makes my blood boil."

"I guessed the same thing. That uncle is after her for more than just lookin' after a niece. Maybe he already abused her in some way. Whatever it is, she's mighty determined to get away from him. Makes a man feel a natural need to kind of look after her."

"That it does."

"My advice is you stay out of it," Sandy told him.

Wade kept his eye on one particularly bright star. It was a warm, calm Texas night. He liked sleeping under the stars, liked the wide open country. He wondered how much of that was due to the Indian in his blood. "Good advice," he answered. "But not many people head on west from San Antonio, especially women. I figure after a few miles she'll realize what desolate country she's headed into. I can't help thinking how that would surely terrify her, even though she'd never let it show." He shifted in his bedroll. "I'm headed for Fort Stockton myself."

"And you're thinkin' about hitchin' a ride on the same coach," Sandy finished for him.

"No. I don't like riding in those contraptions. I just figured maybe I'd ride along beside it at a distance, keep my eyes open for trouble."

"You ever been this much of a fool before?" Sandy asked him.

Wade grinned. "I don't think so. But then no woman has weighed on my mind like that one. I admire her courage."

"More than her courage."

Wade laughed lightly. "I suppose. But men like me aren't supposed to think such thoughts about white women, remember?"

"You said it, I didn't. That's not my personal opinion, mind you. You got a right to pursue any woman you please, far as I'm concerned. It's just that I like you, and I don't want to see trouble for you. Your pa would be tellin' you the same. He loves you and doesn't want to see you hurt."

"I know. But the days are long over when he could keep me under his protection." Wade sat up and rolled a cigarette. "At any rate, I'm not thinking forbidden thoughts, Sandy. I'm just thinking there ought to be someone along who might be able to help protect her if something went wrong. Long as I'm going in the same direction, where's the harm? She's getting married when she gets there anyway."

"Well, I seen how she looked at you when she followed you out of the sheriff's office. You tread lightly, Wade." He puffed his pipe another moment. "'Course, like you said, once you reach the fort you'll both be goin' your separate ways. I'm not so sure this idea you've got of findin' out about your real family is a very good one. You seem to be determined to look for trouble since last time I seen you."

Wade smoked deeply on the cigarette. "Like I said, trouble follows me whether I want it or not. I might as well walk up to it and call it out. I'm determined to see what I can find out, Sandy. I want to know why I was left behind. I could have a brother."

"A twin—which would mean your certain death, my boy."

"Maybe." Wade smoked quietly for a moment. "But I can't let that stop me." He kept watching the bright star. "At any rate, you be sure to come see Pa when you're through with your scouting job. He'll put you to work. We'll have a line going all the way to the Gulf by then, thanks to Mr. Strong. We'll need more help."

"I'll remember that." Sandy stretched. He felt sorry for Wade Morrow. He was a fine, honest young man who had not chosen his lot in life. He seemed to accept his situation with stoicism and composure, a man of two worlds and belonging to neither. Sandy figured there had to be a lot of hurt deep inside a young man like that. He vaguely remembered someone telling him about some situation with a white girl a few years back, but he couldn't remember the story and had a feeling he had better not ask. "We'd best get some sleep," he said aloud. "You're supposed to be out of here come mornin'."

"I will be," Wade answered. He took a last drag on his cigarette, thinking again about the brave and determined Jennifer Andrews, wondering what the man she was to marry might be like. He smashed out his cigarette, angry with himself for caring, doubly angry for bothering to interfere earlier. He thought he had learned his lesson a long time ago when it came to white women. He decided he had better stick to his plans of finding an Indian wife, perhaps among the Comanche when he visited the peaceful ones. This feeling Jennifer Andrews gave him was simply a natural manly instinct to protect a young lady in need and nothing more.

He lay back and closed his eyes, remembering another time, remembering Rebecca. A man didn't forget that kind of hurt; and he had to be careful not to let the same thing come at him again.

Chapter Six

Jennifer carefully counted her money—one hundred sixty dollars left. Apprehension was building in her soul since the sheriff's remarks, as well as Wade Morrow's, about being careful of marrying a stranger at Fort Stockton. She was well aware of the drawbacks to such a proposal, but she had pictured Sergeant Enders as a fine, brave man.

She wished she had more money left, and she was beginning to hate Uncle John even more for cheating her out of what should have been rightfully her property and money. If she chose not to marry Sergeant Enders, she would be stuck at Fort Stockton, which apparently was not a pleasant place, until she could earn back enough money to repay Enders. All she could do now was pray the man was all that she had expected him to be.

She realized it would all be easier if she could concentrate on Enders and keep her thoughts away from Wade Morrow. But it was Morrow's face that kept coming to mind, his voice, his enchanting eyes and warm smile. It was Wade Morrow who had come to her defense when he knew it was a foolish and risky thing to do. It seemed ridiculous to keep thinking about him, since she would never see him again; but she found herself wishing she could talk to him a little while—wishing he could explain more to her about places like west Texas and men like Sergeant Enders. He seemed like the kind of man who would patiently answer all her questions.

She put her money away and looked into a mirror, pinning on her straw bonnet. She wore a soft yellow gingham dress, wishing she could press it a little but not wanting to spend the money to pay someone to do it. The room had cost her three whole dollars. She had skipped breakfast, also to save money, and she realized her dress hung a little loose. She put a hand to her thin waist, reasoning she must be losing weight from skipping so many meals. She knew she would have to eat lunch before boarding the stagecoach. The driver had warned her that from here on the trip would not be comfortable and there would be few stops. The journey from Houston to San Antonio had been rocky and dusty enough, and she wondered how much worse it could get, and what kind of people she would be forced to sit next to.

She picked up her bags and took them to the lobby, where she left them while she went to a restaurant next door and ate a lunch of venison and eggs, with biscuits and a cup of stiff coffee, spending another dollar. She was glad that she at least felt full enough that she could probably refrain from eating again until the next day. Judging from the food and accommodations at the stop between Houston and San Antonio, she decided she was better off not eating anyway, and perhaps better off trying to sleep inside the coach or under the stars than in a vermin-infested cot. If the land west of San Antonio was even more desolate, what must the stage stops be like? The driver called such stops "home stations," but for Jennifer, there was certainly nothing "homey" about them.

She walked to a telegraph office, deciding to send a wire to Sergeant Enders and let him know she had got this far and should arrive in another five days. Her heart raced at meeting the man, wondering what he would expect of her, hoping she would not herself be greatly disappointed. Perhaps she was doing something very foolish, but at least it had given her a plausible reason to leave St. Louis and a story that the sheriff had believed.

In spite of apprehension at what might lie ahead, she felt freer than she had felt in years. Thank God she would not be forced to go back to Uncle John. She had not forgotten the night he came looking for her and crawled into her bed, the terror she felt while sitting in the corner of the closet praying he wouldn't wake up and discover she was not in the bed at all. His actions that night only verified what she had feared all along, and the thought of the huge, drunken man putting his hands on her was much more mortifying and sickening than marrying a strange soldier.

She exited the telegraph office, looking up and down the street for a moment, secretly hoping to get another look at Wade Morrow. Surely, though, the man was already gone. The sheriff had told him to be out of town by this morning, and it was already one o'clock. The memory of how he had been treated still riled her, and she could not help feeling a lingering guilt at being responsible for his embarrassment and trouble. She hoped he was able to finish his business with Bill Strong.

She smiled at the memory of how surprised she had been when she first heard him speak. With his dark skin and long, black hair, she had expected his words to come out in some kind of broken English, not to sound so well-spoken and educated. The man was totally intriguing. She had never met anyone like him, and she knew she would not soon forget the blue-eyed Indian who had come to her defense.

She returned to the hotel and retrieved her bags, then proceeded to the stage station, where Nick Elliott was throwing baggage to another man perched atop the coach. "So, you're gonna go on to Fort Stockton, are you," the man asked. He shook his head. "It's your life, lady, but I still say you ought to stay here or go back to Houston—or all the way home, for that matter."

"I am going on, Mr. Elliott. Please load my bags."

"Yes, ma'am. And call me Nick, remember? I'll be the driver the whole way—all the way to California. We'll

89

stop at a swing station about twenty miles west of here—that's a place where we change horses and people can get out to, uh, relieve themselves—but there's no restin' or eatin'."

Jennifer turned to board the coach. Nick took her arm to help her, and she climbed inside, sitting down in the only spot left to sit, which was next to a window. When she looked around at the other passengers, she was glad to be near a window so that she could look outside and have an excuse for not looking at the others—seven men—all of them staring at her appreciatively, some almost hungrily.

The smell inside the coach was not pleasant, as cigar and pipe smoke, as well as the odor of more than one unbathed body permeated the leather and wood confine. Jennifer was anxious for the coach to get moving so that at least some air would circulate through it. Two of the men were well dressed, perhaps businessmen headed for the biggest town west of here, which as far as she knew was a place called El Paso, about six or seven days away. She wondered if some or all of them were going all the way to California, but was not about to strike up a conversation with any of them. She nodded politely and immediately turned her attention out the window.

The men proceeded to carry on a conversation about a possible civil war, but Jennifer could feel their eyes turning to her as they spoke. She realized that from this point on it must be very unusual to see a woman on a stagecoach, heading into wilderness.

Several minutes later the coach finally got underway, bringing much-needed air inside. Nick snapped the whip and the horses took off as though they were in a race. The coach lurched and swayed on the thoroughbraces, bringing back the light nausea Jennifer had experienced on the first part of her journey, and the air that filtered inside was full of dust. Jennifer already wondered why she had bothered to wash and primp before leaving. The light scent of the lilac water she had splashed on was completely overwhelmed by the odor of cigars and sweat, and her face and clothes would not long stay clean.

"Did I hear Nick say you was goin' all the way to Fort Stockton," one of the men finally asked her. He sat right next to her, and she had been struggling to politely keep her leg from touching his, but to no avail. The coach was simply too crowded. She glanced at him, feeling awkward at the man being so close, embarrassed that he was surely enjoying it. He wore buckskins and a beard, and his face was so crusted and lined from the western sun that it was impossible to tell his age.

"Yes," she answered. "I'm to be married there." She hoped the news would dispel any lustful thoughts some of them might be having.

"Well, congratulations," another told her. "You're a brave and loyal woman to go out there alone for your man."

Jennifer decided not to explain that she didn't even know Sergeant Enders. They would only look at her with those strange, questioning eyes, their imaginations running wild. "Thank you," she answered politely.

"I'm Adam Hughes—on my way to San Diego on business." The man puffed on a pipe, and Jennifer noticed he at least looked clean and well dressed. She nodded to the man.

"Jennifer Andrews." She was glad to at least be able to use her real name. "I'm from St. Louis."

"Would you like us to put out our smokes, ma'am," the man beside her asked.

Jennifer put a hand to her stomach. "I . . . I would greatly appreciate it."

She could not help a smile then as those with pipes and cigars quickly leaned over and tossed or tamped out their smokes outside the window. "We'll keep the smoking to a minimum—mostly at swing stations," the man beside her said. "By the way, I'm Will Perry—headed to an army post in New Mexico to do some scoutin'."

"Thank you, Mr. Perry, for thinking about the smoke."

"I'm Lou Huston," a dusty, young man wearing knee-high boots and sitting across from her said then with a drawl. He tipped a wide-brimmed hat. "Me and my friend

Buck here are cowhands on a big ranch in Arizona. Headed back there after drivin' some cattle to San Antonio." The friend called Buck sat beside Lou, a middle-aged man with a mustache and gritty features that again made it impossible to be really sure of his age. He nodded to Jennifer and she gave him a weak smile.

"Name's Larry Buchanan," came a voice from the other end of the seat on which Jennifer sat. She leaned forward slightly to see a man in denim pants and a calico shirt, also wearing high, dusty boots. She wondered if anything in Texas remained clean for long, or if men and women alike just gave up trying to clean anything. "I'm a horse trader—headed for New Mexico."

"And I'm Hank Griffith," came the voice of the man between Buchanan and Will Perry, who sat beside Jennifer. "Me and my partner there, Sid Menden, are going to El Paso to open a tavern." Griffith was dressed in a neat but already-dusty suit, as was his partner, who sat directly across from Jennifer beside the cowhand Lou Huston. "We'll be traveling a lot of miles together. Might as well know each other's names. And don't you worry, ma'am. We'll all keep an eye out for you." *And on you*, most of them were thinking, but they politely kept their thoughts to themselves.

"I appreciate it," she answered. "But I'm sure I'll make it just fine to Fort Stockton. Thank you for putting out your smokes."

They all nodded and smiled, and Jennifer felt her cheeks reddening. She looked back out the window, and now that the men all knew each other's destinations and vocations, talk turned to ranching, running taverns, and the like, with occasional turns to talk of renegade Comanche and the uneasiness they felt about the trip. She knew they were thinking about the horrible things Comanche did to white women, and the thought was heavy on her own mind.

Wade kept scanning the wide horizon as he headed west, passing the first swing station of the stage line at a distance. He knew the stage was well behind him yet and would remain so, since it would stop at the swing station for fresh horses and sit out the night at the next home station. He was not concerned about too much danger until the coach would be a couple more days west. From then on would be the very real possibility of renegade attack, although it seemed the Indians usually saved their raids for settlements or bigger supply trains. One coach didn't net much in the way of food and needed supplies, and the big, lumbering horses that pulled the coaches were not of great interest to the Comanche, who rode swift ponies. Still, they were horses and could be traded.

On his way east Wade had seen little sign of Indians. Most were already on reservations farther north. What was left were adept at keeping themselves well hidden in the mountains. In the case of the Apache and Comanche, it was quite possible most of them could be in Mexico for now, continuing their ancient ritual of raiding and looting Mexican settlements.

When he thought of the inbred lifestyle of the Indians, he wondered if they would ever be able to some day live like the white man. "Civilizing" the native American seemed an insurmountable task. He knew that now, from his own deep instincts. Even though he had never known the Indian way of life, he had an independent spirit, a need to be free of too many restrictions, a restlessness that had made it difficult to sit through lessons, or to work within the confines of his father's store. He much preferred scouting for the supply trains and taking on the tasks that required traveling for long distances.

He hoped that on this trip back he would get some answers for himself. Perhaps his restlessness would be more curbed once he learned more about that mysterious half of his nature that had brought him so much hurt and ridicule as he was growing up. It was only a deep, keen pride that had helped him through the insults, and talks with his loving white parents, who had preached to him from infancy never to be ashamed, to be a proud and honest man who was strong on the inside as well as out.

And he knew through their strong religious beliefs that a greater Being loved him and his Indian relatives just as much as any other race.

A hawk flew overhead, carrying a mouse in its beak. It reminded Wade that in this lonely, desolate land the key word was survival, at any cost. That was all that was left for the renegades, but also for the border settlers, determined, stubborn people who insisted on settling the frontiers. It was an age-old cultural clash that might never be settled.

He looked back, still seeing no stage coach in the distance. He decided he would stay ahead of it, acting as a kind of silent scout. If he caught any sign of Indians, he would warn the drivers.

He nudged his horse forward, heading for the home station. He saw no reason not to follow basically the same route, since he and the coach were headed in the same direction. He could not quell the strong desire to keep Miss Jennifer Andrews from trouble, if possible. He still could not get over her courage in coming here, nor could he ignore the pity he felt for her having to go to such drastic measures just to get away from what must have been a lecherous uncle.

Although Jennifer Andrews' beauty and inner strength stirred forbidden desires in his soul and aroused manly instincts, he reasoned that his only interest was to protect a lovely and innocent young lady from the horrors of being captured by Comanche renegades. To allow any kind of romantic thoughts was forbidden to a man like himself. At eighteen years old he had experienced his first, very painful love for a settler's daughter in California. He would never forget Rebecca, but he knew there would be no more white women in his life, except for the whores, who seemed to think it was exciting to sleep with an Indian. But it wasn't that kind of physical satisfaction he wanted, not just a release of animal instincts. He wanted to feel love again, like what he had felt for Rebecca, and to feel that love returned, as she had loved him so sweetly.

When he thought about the lessons he had learned in

that area, he was still surprised at himself for defending Jennifer Andrews the way he had. He had been so determined to stay out of it. But there was something about her that he could not even name that had made him react. She was so small and pretty, and the two men who had been waiting for her seemed like vultures ready to swoop down and get her in their claws. He realized he was a lucky man. A man like himself getting involved in a white woman's affairs in Texas could have cost him a lot more than a few minutes in a jail cell.

He dismounted, taking his canteen from his gear and uncorking it to take a swallow. He poured some water into his hand several times, letting his horse drink from it. "We'll find more water at the home station," he told the big, buckskin gelding. "Maybe they'll at least let me water you there." He removed his leather hat and wiped sweat from his brow, then left the hat off and removed his buckskin shirt.

"Too hot for all these clothes," he told his horse. Again he wondered if this, too, was the Indian in him. He liked being free of too many clothes, hated when he had to wear regular trousers and shirts, and especially hated wearing suits and hard shoes. The sun was white and hot, but he liked the feel of it on his dark skin, and it didn't seem to damage his skin the way it did some white people.

He grinned then, realizing he had thought in terms of "white people," as though they were suddenly some kind of enemy. Their life was the only kind of life he had ever known, and he loved his white family and their white friends who had accepted him and liked him. He realized being out here alone in the country where he had been born was having an effect on him. On his way out here he had not given it a lot of thought because he had a job to do for his father. But now he was finally going to find out something about his past, if he was lucky, and going back to his roots was doing something to him, somehow bringing out certain instincts he usually tried to ignore.

He mounted up. "Let's go, boy," he said softly to his horse. He headed west at a gentle trot, then urged his horse into a faster lope, covering the next twenty miles in less than two hours. He decided he had better make the home station well ahead of the stage so he could water his horse and leave again before the stage arrived. That way he could continue to stay ahead of it and watch for trouble. After the incident in town the day before, he didn't want Jennifer Andrews to think he was following her.

Suddenly the big gelding that carried him spilled forward without warning, whinnying in one long screech as its right shoulder slammed to the ground, catching Wade's right ankle beneath it for just a moment before the rest of his body was pitched to the side. The force of the fall gave Wade enough momentum that his foot was torn from under the horse, and he rolled and tumbled for several feet before a large boulder stopped him with a jolt.

Wade lay still for a moment, taking a quick mental inventory of his physical condition and regaining his breath from the hard fall. He was an excellent horseman, another natural ability that came from being related to the best horsemen on the Plains. The fall surprised him, as he had never been thrown before, except by a few broncs he had broken for his father's horse trading business. The big buckskin was one of the family's best, most sure-footed mounts, but now the animal still lay on its side, snorting and whinnying as though in pain, its legs flailing, nostrils flaring, eyes rolling back as it strained to catch sight of its master.

Wade got to his knees, shaking off dust and gravel. He moved his arms, discovering his right shoulder was sore. He slowly got to his feet, his right ankle giving him fierce pain. He looked down at it, lifting his buckskin legging to see the skin scraped away from the outer ankle bone and blood seeping through the skin, which was caked with dirt and tiny, embedded stones. He gently flexed his foot, deciding nothing was broken but not doubting the ankle would be bruised and damn sore for a few days.

He limped over to the horse, noticing a small but deep hole in the hard-caked earth, one of those freak accidents of nature waiting to make trouble for horse and man.

"Damn," Wade muttered. It was something a horse might ride over a hundred times without hitting the hole just right. "I should have kept to the stage trail like I did on the way out here," he added, in the habit of talking to his horse as though it understood him.

He realized then that Miss Jennifer Andrews had again inadvertently gotten him into trouble. He had figured that it would be easier to spot robbers or Indians if he stayed off the beaten path and kept to the surrounding rocks and gulleys.

He knelt down beside the horse, reaching out to pet its head and neck, calming the animal with a gentle voice. "Let's have a look, boy," he told the animal, moving his hand down to its right leg. He grimaced, realizing he didn't have to feel the leg to know it was broken, much too badly to have any hope of healing. Besides, in this country, the slightest malady was cause to shoot a horse. There was no stall, no facilities or medicines out here to treat an animal, let alone scarcely a handful of grass to feed the animal.

Pain was so evident in the horse's eyes that it tore at Wade's heart. He sighed deeply, realizing in an instant what he had to do. It had all happened so fast that it seemed unreal. Wade rose and looked ahead, wondering how far it was yet to the home station. He turned and knelt beside the horse again, pulling his repeating rifle from its boot on the saddle. He had to yank hard, since the gun barrel was caught under the horse. With a heavy heart he cocked the rifle, a lump coming to his throat.

"I'm sorry, boy," he told the horse. "Pa will hate hearing about this. He's always figured you one of our best." He knelt down once more and petted the animal's neck, realizing it would be much more cruel to let the animal live. It didn't take a man who knew horses long to realize this one would never get up again. He took a deep breath, rising and aiming the rifle. With great effort he pulled the trigger. A hole opened up in the horse's skull, and the animal stopped its struggling.

Wade ignored the grief he was feeling, realizing time

was important. His only hope of survival now was to reach the home station, and reach it before the stage coach left in the morning. So far the coach was still behind him, but he had a few miles to cover on foot. He only hoped his ankle was not hurt too badly to walk the distance. Carrying his saddle and gear on his back would not help, especially in this heat.

With considerable effort he managed to get everything off the dead horse, then cursed the hole and his luck as he rose and rigged everything together in such a way that he could slip his arms through the rope ties and carry it all on his back. Sweat was already beginning to pour from his face and chest as he started out, limping toward the direction of the home station, refusing to look back at the dead horse that had become like a friend to him on this trip. He only hoped he could find another horse at the home station.

As the hot, dusty journey progressed, Jennifer soon realized that in spite of their dirty appearance, most men in these parts seemed to have a high respect for proper young women, and she soon lost her fear of the seven men with whom she shared the coach. So far they showed her nothing but politeness, in spite of the way some of them smelled; and they had saved their smoking for the swing station, just as they had promised. The only one who made her a little uncomfortable was the one called Buck, who seemed to stare at her more than the others.

Now the coach clattered toward the home station, as the sun began to sink behind western hills. The coach grew quiet for a while, as the monotonous swaying and rythmic clattering of wheels took their toll on tired passengers. Jennifer was amazed at the tenacity of old Nick Elliott, who could take no rest. All through the journey she could hear his "git up's", hear the snapping of his whip. Driving a stage could not be an easy task, and a driver was in for ten- to fourteen-hour stints with reins pulling at his calloused hands, the hot sun pouring down on him. She wondered if a statement one of the men had made earlier was true—that some drivers literally slept while driving, their keen alertness waking them whenever the horses strayed or danger lay ahead.

"These teams know this road backward and forward," Adam Hughes had said. But to Jennifer that fact didn't lessen the importance of the driver, who risked his hide daily against the elements, outlaws, and Indians, let alone possible breakdowns or trouble with one of the horses. The man who rode shotgun had an equally responsible job, for he would be the first to put his life on the line in case of trouble, and he had to stay awake and alert. She realized she didn't even know the name of the second man above, yet her very fate could depend on him.

It was 10 P.M. when the coach finally rattled in to the home station, which with disappointment Jennifer could see was nothing more than a log and sod shanty, with a corral of horses beside it. Smoke drifted from an iron stovepipe, and she could smell something that resembled food. She could only pray it would be edible.

"Let's go," came Nick's voice from outside. He opened the door, and Jennifer stepped out first, letting him take her arm as she climbed down. Every joint and muscle felt stiff and sore, and she wondered how she was going to survive four more days of this, let alone the dirty way stations and the questionable food she was forced to put into her stomach at ridiculous prices. "Privy's in the back," Nick was saying. "Might as well let the lady use it first."

"It's gettin' dark. I'm just gonna go behind the shed," Buck answered, heading in the direction of an outbuilding.

"Suit yourself," Nick answered. "There's food inside, but only three cots. You men decide among yourselves which two of you gets a cot, since the lady here will get one of them with no argument. The rest of you can sleep in bedrolls outside or on the floor inside, or in the coach, whatever you prefer."

"I can sleep in the coach," Jennifer spoke up quickly. "It isn't fair that I get all the privileges."

"Fair or not, that's the way it is for our lady passengers," Nick told her. "I won't have it no other way. Go on with you now."

Jennifer made her way past the crude building where she would spend the night, her heart sinking now with every mile, wondering what life was going to be like at the fort. Was everyone right when they told her it was no place for a woman? It seemed everyone she had told had got a look on his face as though she had announced her doom. The kindness and personality of Sergeant Anthony Enders was beginning to look more and more important to her finding any kind of happiness in this lonely land. Her courage was waning, but her determination made up for it.

Before entering the privy she scanned the horizon, seeing nothing for miles on end, except for low mountains to the distant west—mountains infested with savage renegades, according to the men on the coach. But then Wade Morrow was one of those dark-skinned people, and he wasn't savage at all. She wondered if stories about the Comanche could have been exaggerated. She went inside and quickly took care of her needs, not caring to spend any longer in the smelly outhouse than necessary. When she exited, she looked around again, trying to get a grasp on reality, for she had never seen such country and had no idea it could be so big. Somewhere out there lay Fort Stockton and a stranger she had promised to marry. Never had she felt so alone.

She moved her eyes in a circle, looking east then. For a moment she thought she saw the figure of a man walking, so far away she couldn't begin to guess the distance. The figure disappeared into what she figured must be a dip between hills, although from here the land looked perfectly flat. She decided perhaps she hadn't seen him at all, that her eyes were playing tricks on her.

The sky was getting darker, and after hearing tales of Comanche raids she decided she didn't like being even this far from other people. She hurried back to the cabin, realizing that in spite of its primitive lodgings, it at least made her feel safer.

Chapter Seven

Jennifer managed to choke down a piece of tough venison and two eggs that were, surprisingly, cooked just right. She caught sight of mold on her hard biscuit and took only one bite, washing the food down with the strongest coffee she had ever drunk. She felt like crying at having to spend over a dollar on such an unsatisfying meal, but she had no choice. She only hoped it would be enough to tide her over until the next evening's course, since she was not about to dish out more money on breakfast in the morning if the food was going to be as bad as this.

The air inside the small cabin was stuffy, and the food lay in her stomach like a rock. She walked back outside to get a breath of fresh air, and noticed the men were all watching something and talking among themselves. She turned her eyes to the same direction, again seeing a figure walking; and she realized what she had seen earlier had not been a mirage after all. He was a tall man, and it looked as though he was carrying a saddle and all his gear. He walked with a limp, and as he came closer she could see he wore buckskin leggings but no shirt, and his hair was long and dark, pulled back behind his neck. Her heart raced unexpectedly when she realized the man was Wade Morrow.

"It's a damn Indian," Larry Buchanan, the horsetrader, remarked.

"What the hell," Hank Griffith muttered. "Hey, Nick, get out here," he shouted louder. Will Perry walked to the cabin to get the driver outside, and Jennifer hung back near the door, watching in curiosity. Nick came outside, and as the figure came even closer in the deep dusk light he recognized the man.

"It's that Wade Morrow—the one that had a run-in with some folks back in San Antonio over—" He didn't finish, and Jennifer realized the man had quickly decided not to bring her name into the picture.

"Wade Morrow? That's a white man's name, but that's no white man," Buck spoke up. "That's a damn Indian—has the look of Comanche about him at that."

Again Jennifer felt sorrow at the words, realizing Wade was close enough to have heard the remark. The man kept his eyes on Nick Elliott as he came even closer. He nodded. "Mr. Elliott."

Nick nodded. "Looks like you had a run-in with some bad luck, mister."

"You might say that." Wade unloaded his gear, and Jennifer dropped her eyes, feeling awkward at setting eyes on a man's bare chest. But she could not help glancing at him again in fascination, thinking how muscled and broad-shouldered the man was. "My horse took a bad fall, broke its right leg pretty bad. I had to shoot him. That was about four miles back," Wade explained.

"He talks like a regular white man," Buck spoke up in a near sneer.

Wade met his eyes, holding them proudly before looking back at Nick. "I was on my way to Fort Stockton," he told the man. Jennifer felt her heart pound even harder at the words. "I need a horse, but the ones they keep at these stations aren't much fit for riding. I figured I'd find something better at the fort, so I walked here hoping I'd catch you before you leave out again. I'd like to ride along, if it's all right. I can pay."

"We can't have an Indian riding our coach," Buck argued, stepping closer. "Think of the young lady we've got along. She doesn't want a damn redskin in the same coach with her."

Jennifer thought to speak up, then decided against it. If Nick had kept her name out of it to begin with, he apparently had good reason.

"I'll ride on top," Wade was saying, casting angry looks at Buck. He looked back at Nick. "I'm good with a rifle, and I've scouted for my father's supply trains for years in country just like this. I can be a big help in case of trouble."

Nick scratched at his beard. "Well, that's a thought."

"He's an Indian," Lou Huston broke in, walking closer himself. "You can't trust an Indian, Nick. Hell, he might have others waitin' for us farther ahead—him ready to kill us all right on the spot and take that pretty little woman over there off with him."

Wade rolled his eyes and turned away for a moment. It was obvious he was fighting to control his temper, and Jennifer stepped farther into the shadow of the doorway, afraid her presence might only embarrass him more.

"Mister, I'm as civilized as you are," Wade was telling Buck and Lou then. "Probably more. You ever been to college in the East?"

"What?"

"Well I have. I was raised in an atmosphere as white as your own, and my white adoptive father owns the biggest supply business between here and San Diego. I'm on my way back from doing business for him in San Antonio." He looked at Nick. "You've heard of Lester Morrow—Morrow Freighting Services?"

Nick nodded. "I have. I know all about it from last night."

"What about last night?" Buck had his hands on his hips in an authoritative gesture. "You said somethin' about him havin' a run-in with some folks in San Antonio. Anybody knows Indians are trouble, Nick." He raised his eyes to meet Wade's blue ones. "Breeds are even worse."

Jennifer was amazed at Wade's continued ability to refrain from punching the cowhand.

"This one is all right," Nick answered the man. "The trouble was made by somebody else, not by him. And I might add he had every reason and opportunity to kill the man that gave him the trouble, but he didn't do it. Hell, Buck, you can tell from the way he talks he ain't like no ordinary Indian, and I know about his pa—one of the most honest, successful men in California."

"I won't travel with an Indian," Buck complained, turning his back on Wade. The others all stood and stared.

"I'm not too crazy about it myself," his friend Lou put in.

"All right now, look," Nick said, turning to face them all. "This man is educated and he's part owner of a wealthy trading line. He's as civilized as any of you, and by God if he says he's good with a gun, I reckon he is. If he rode shotgun for his pa and has scouted for him, he's a damn good man to have along, Indian or not. The rest of you better think about the fact that we're ridin' into more dangerous country now, and we've got a woman along to boot. The more men we've got, the better."

"And if Indians attack us, is he gonna' really draw a bead on them—his own kin," Buck said sarcastically.

"Of course I would," Wade answered for himself. "I might be part Comanche, but my eyes are blue, mister, and those Indians don't know me from Adam. I'd be in just as much danger as the rest of you. Besides, I'm only going as far as Fort Stockton. That's only three more days, four at the most. If the rest of you are going farther, you'll be rid of me. And I'll ride up top where you don't have to associate with me, if that's so hard for you to stomach."

"He seems all right to me," Adam Hughes spoke up. "Nick is right. We can use an extra man where we're headed. It's obvious he's no ordinary Indian. Let him hitch a ride with us. I don't mind."

"Well, he ought to put a shirt on," Lou sneered. "That right there is a sign of his Indian blood, wantin' to walk around half-naked."

"Mister, if you had just walked four miles in this heat carrying all your gear, you might have stripped all the way." Wade reached into a leather pouch on his gear and pulled out several bills. "Tell me the fare and I'll pay you now," he told Nick. "I've got to eat something and get off this ankle. It's swollen pretty bad."

"Horse fall on it?" Nick asked.

Wade counted out a few of the bills. "Yes. First time that's ever happened to me."

"I reckon so, considerin' what good horsemen the Comanche are," Buck answered. "Must have been your white side that got throwed."

Some of the others chuckled lightly, but Wade did not smile. He held his eyes steadily on Buck, and Buck swallowed at the look there. "Must have been," Wade answered. He looked back at Nick. "How much?"

"Well, I reckon from here thirty would do it."

Wade counted out the money, shoving it into Nick's hand. "Thanks."

"You put on a shirt," Buck warned. "We've got a lady along on this trip. And you better stay away from her."

"I'll remember that," Wade answered sarcastically. He bent down and picked up his gear. "I'll camp out tonight beside the cabin. And since I upset everyone so much, I'll fix my own food at my own camp fire. I wouldn't want to go inside and shock everyone."

He limped away, and Buck continued to grumble about having an Indian along. "Awe, forget it, Buck," Lou told him. "He'll be up top anyway. We ain't got any choice but to go along. We'll be rid of him in a few days."

The others mumbled among themselves, some seeming just curious and undecided, Adam Hughes speaking up in Wade's defense. Jennifer watched Wade walk to the side of the cabin, feeling sorry for the way he had been treated and for the fact that he had lost his horse and hurt his ankle. Wade glanced at her as he walked past, and their eyes held for a moment before he looked away and disappeared around the end of the cabin.

Nick walked in her direction, seeing the pity in her eyes. "He needs help," she said when he got close. "He's hurt, Nick."

He frowned, putting a finger to his lips. "You stay out of it, little missy. It's best for you that way. You've got to travel inside the coach with the others. They get wind that you know Wade Morrow or see you talkin' to him or helpin' him, it won't be easy for you to travel with them, understand? I understand how you feel, after the way he stuck up for you, but you gotta' do like I say and stay away from him."

"I think it's horrible the way they talk to him," Jennifer pouted. "He's just a man, Nick, a very fine one at that."

"Hush. I know it, and you know it, ma'am. But he's a breed, and in these parts he's dirt to some men. That's just the way it is, Miss Andrews, and you've got to understand that. It's real important that you do. Even Morrow understands it. Now you get on back inside."

Jennifer frowned and reluctantly walked back into the stuffy, smelly cabin, sitting down wearily on one of the cots. She inspected it with a frown, seeing no bugs. There was nothing to do but lie down and hope to get some rest, but she knew that the heat and her upset stomach, combined with thoughts of Wade Morrow would not let sleep come easily. It seemed ironic that the man should again walk into her little world, as though he was being led to her by some strange twist of fate.

She wished she could tell this story to Mattie. How the woman would enjoy hearing of this adventure; but hearing the story and experiencing it were two different matters. The experience of actually traveling in this country and heading for an unknown fate bore no romantic excitement. She was miserable and tired, and her tender heart ached for Wade Morrow, who was so verbally abused and who must be in physical pain.

She lay back on the cot, aching everywhere, longing for a bath, missing the cool comforts of Aunt Esther's lovely home in St. Louis, but not missing Uncle John one bit. She finally dozed off lightly, unaware of the looks the men who worked inside gave her. It had been a long time since they had been around a pretty woman, and in these parts a man got hungry for feminine comforts. But looking and daydreaming were all they would do. Hank Griffith and Larry Buchanan came inside then, having won a coin toss to see who would get to use the cots. They, too, drank in the sight of Jennifer curled up on the cot, but each man went to his own bed without a word.

Outside Buck grumbled that he was going to sleep with one eye open, not trusting the "Breed." Nick and the man who rode shotgun, Ernie Peters, bedded down around a camp fire they built with Will Perry, Buck and Lou, and Sid Menden; while Adam Hughes decided to sleep inside the coach. One of the two men who ran the home station took his position on the porch of the cabin, rifle in hand, preparing to keep watch the first half of the night. His partner would replace him in a few hours. Inside his partner finished cleaning up from the meal and took his own cot, falling asleep with dreams of crawling into the cot beside Jennifer.

Wade Morrow had his own fire going, and no one joined him. He didn't mind. He was used to such treatment, although never had he been treated as badly as he had been here in Texas. He heated some smoked antelope and beans, discovering that the pain in his ankle had cut his appetite. He couldn't eat as much as he thought. He swallowed some of his own coffee, then wet some rags with water from his canteen and wrapped them around his sore ankle, grimacing as he did so. He stretched out on his bedroll then, resting the ankle and finding some relief in the cool rags.

He rolled and lit a cigarette, thinking the same thoughts Jennifer had been thinking earlier—that it seemed as though fate was intent on crossing their paths. He only wished he knew if that was good or bad. The only thing he did know was that Nick had cleverly not brought up Jennifer Andrews's name from the incident in San Antonio, and Wade knew why. In that case, he was not about to talk to the woman or cause any further trouble. Apparently none of the men along had witnessed the incident, which was fine with him. At least now he would be able to continue watching out for the woman without anyone knowing she was the only one on this trip that he cared about.

The night's desert air grew suddenly chilly, and he sat up and finally pulled on his buckskin shirt.

*   *   *

Jennifer awoke to the buzzing of mosquitoes. She slapped at one, then sat up, realizing it wasn't just the mosquitoes that had awakened her. All three men inside the cabin were snoring loudly. She felt overwhelmed by the closeness of the room, as well as feeling the call of nature. Another mosquito buzzed at her ear and she rose, walking quietly to the door, her feet making no sound on the earth floor of the cabin.

She cautiously opened the door to see the man who was supposedly keeping guard sitting in a chair asleep, also snoring. She stepped outside, taking a deep breath of clean, cool air. At a nearby camp fire she saw the others sleeping, and she had a suspicion that the only man among them who would truly be alert in case of danger was Wade Morrow, although she could not see him. He was camped around the side of the cabin—alone.

She left the porch of the cabin and walked around it, spotting the privy easily in the moonlight. She felt a hint of apprehension, walking alone in the dark, yet the knowledge that Wade Morrow was nearby gave her a sense of safety. She tapped on the privy door, and when no one answered she went inside and took care of urgent matters quickly, anxious to get back out into the fresh air. She wondered if she might not have been better off sleeping under the stars where at least she could breathe.

She headed back toward the cabin, then hesitated, feeling wide-awake and hating the thought of going back into the stuffy room with snoring men. She could not help wondering if Wade Morrow was all right, and youthful curiosity and a generous heart gave her the courage to walk to the corner at the back of the cabin. She put a hand to her heart, wondering if she was being sinfully forward and foolish as she peeked around the corner to get a look at the mysterious half-breed.

He lay on his bedroll, his right ankle wrapped in something. At first he looked asleep, but suddenly his eyes shot open and Jennifer froze in place. Their eyes held as he sat up. "Something wrong?" he asked quietly.

She shook her head. "I . . . I just wondered if you were all right. I couldn't sleep—mosquitoes. And it's so hot inside." She rubbed her arms, shivering a little. "I didn't think it would be so cold out here—"

He put a finger to his lips, signalling her to stop talking. He threw off a blanket and rose, limping closer. He took her arm and led her behind the cabin, and in the moonlight he seemed as big and fierce as a wilder Indian. For just a brief moment she wondered if men like Buck were right—that this man could turn wild and do something horrible to her; but just as quickly she brushed away the thought as ridiculous.

"You shouldn't be talking to me," he whispered, leaning closer to her. "It's best that way. You'd better get back inside."

"I think it's silly that I can't speak to you," she protested, keeping her own voice to a whisper. "You did a very kind thing for me back in San Antonio, Mr. Morrow. Now you're hurt, and I just wondered if there is anything I can do."

"No. I've been dressing my own wounds for years. Besides, this one isn't that bad. I'll be fine in a couple of days."

Jennifer felt a pull at her insides, realizing with confused thoughts that when he leaned close to her she felt a terrible attraction to him. She little realized what Wade Morrow was feeling, that he was thinking about how much she reminded him of a young girl he had loved once.

"I . . . I just wanted to thank you again, Mr. Morrow—and to tell you I hope you realize I don't feel and think like the others. I think it's terrible the way they talk to you."

He suddenly straightened, sighing deeply. "Please go back inside before someone sees us. I don't want you to be insulted. You have enough hardships ahead."

She tilted her head to look up at him. "Do you think I'm being terribly foolish to answer that sergeant's ad?"

"It's not for me to say; but I'd think about going back to St. Louis if I were you."

"No!" She answered almost too loudly, and he put a hand to her mouth. His touch sent shivers through her. "I'll never go back," she whispered when he took his hand away.

"That's your decision. Right now you've got to get back inside that cabin or there's going to be big trouble."

She scratched at a mosquito bite on her cheek. "It's so uncomfortable in there, and the mosquitoes are eating me up."

He touched her arm lightly. "Wait here." He left her for a moment, going back around the corner to his gear. He returned with a small, flat tin container. "Put some of this on your face," he whispered. "It will keep the mosquitoes from biting."

"What is it?"

"I'm not even sure. It's a salve Indians make from the roots of something. An old scout gave some to me a while back. It doesn't smell too great, but you can wash it off in the morning. If someone asks about it you can tell them it's something you bought in St. Louis."

"What about you? If I take it you won't have any."

"Mosquitoes like white people better than Indians. They don't bother me much."

"Is that true? Mosquitoes don't bite Indians?"

He flashed a handsome grin in the moonlight and struggled not to laugh out loud. "I don't have the slightest idea. All I know is they don't bother me much. Besides, that salve helps keep your skin soft. Out here somebody like you needs that a lot worse than I do."

She wrapped her hands around the small tin. "Thank you," she whispered.

He stepped back. "Good night, Miss Andrews. And remember to keep away from me tomorrow."

Without a sound he slipped back around the corner. Jennifer stood holding the salve, feeling warm and special. She did not understand the feelings Wade Morrow stirred in her, except that she hated leaving him. She felt as though she could sit and talk to him all night. She had so many questions, and she felt so safe when he was near. She was glad he was also going to Fort Stockton, and she wondered what his reason was.

She walked back around the other end of the cabin and to the door, where the guard still sat asleep. She went

110

inside, where the snoring continued. She made her way to her cot and quietly opened the tin, applying some of the salve to her face. It didn't have a truly distinct odor, yet it didn't smell good either. She lay down, thinking about Wade Morrow and what a strange and different kind of man he was from anyone she had ever met. She soon noticed the mosquitoes were not lighting on her any more, and finally she could sleep. Her last thought was of Wade Morrow's kindness in giving her the salve.

Jennifer washed as best she could in a small back room of the cabin. With so many men around she felt self-conscious about removing any clothes, even though she was out of sight. She sensed their underlying efforts at self-control, kindness, and respect but at the same time realized what every man with whom she traveled must realize— that they could take advantage of her any time they chose. The least excuse she gave them to consider her less than proper could mean big trouble for her, and in spite of her inexperience with men she understood why she could not converse with Wade Morrow.

She smiled, though, at the thought of her secret—that he had helped her back in San Antonio, and that last night she had talked to him and he had given her the salve. She studied her face in an old, yellowing mirror and smiled. While in the outer room the others complained of nagging mosquito bites, she didn't have any, except two she had gotten before applying the salve.

She brushed her hair and pinned it into a bun at the base of her neck, then put on her straw hat again. She looked down at her dress, which she had been careful to keep smoothed out beneath her when she slept. It wasn't too terribly wrinkled, but she was not happy with not being able to wash better and change. She reasoned that by the time she reached the fort, Sergeant Enders might find her so soiled and worn out that he wouldn't want her for a wife after all.

She re-entered the main room, where most of the men

111

were hungrily cramming eggs and greasy ham into their bellies. "Have a seat, miss," one of the men who ran the home station told her.

"No, thank you. I'm not eating."

"You gotta' eat, Miss Andrews," Buck told her.

"I'll be fine." She turned and checked her bag before tying the leather straps, and the men looked around at each other, suspecting her reason for not eating.

"I don't know about the rest of you, but I'm stuffed," Adam Hughes spoke up. He rose, adjusting his satin vest and wiping his mouth with a checkered cloth napkin. "I hate to waste these biscuits, though, seeing as how they're fresh made. Any of you men want them?" He gave them a wink, and they all gave various excuses for not wanting another bite.

"Fact is, I can't finish my biscuit, either," Hank Griffith spoke up. "Miss Andrews, I don't suppose you'd at least eat our biscuits for us, would you? They're fresh made, and it's a shame to let them go to waste, especially since we already paid for them. We'd feel a lot better if you'd eat a little something."

Jennifer was not quite sure if they suspected her monetary situation, but her stomach was growling, and she was grateful for their kindness. She only wished they could show the same kindness to Wade Morrow. "Well," she answered, "if you insist, I suppose I could eat at least one."

"Good, good," Hughes answered with a grin. He offered her his chair, and the cook brought her a cup of coffee.

"On the house," the man told her. "It's my payment for havin' such a pretty woman to look at these past hours."

She reddened as she took the coffee. "Thank you." She ate quickly as most of the men left, while a couple more finished their breakfast. Outside Nick and Ernie were whistling and cursing as they hitched a new team of horses to the coach. Jennifer gulped down her coffee, then picked up her bag and went outside. A couple of the men were helping Nick with the horses, while on top of the coach Wade Morrow was retying some of the luggage. He glanced at Jennifer, giving no sign of recognition.

"Hand up your bag, ma'am," he told her.

"Wait a minute," Buck spoke up, walking up and taking Jennifer's bag from her. "Don't even hand him your bag, ma'am. His hand might touch yours, and you don't want to be touchin' no Indian."

Anger welled up in Jennifer's soul like a volcano, but when she glanced up at Wade, she knew by his eyes she should not object. It took great effort on her part not to tell Buck exactly what she thought of him as she let go of her bag. He handed it up to Wade.

"Tie it on good, Indian, or it will be your ass if the lady's baggage gets lost or damaged. And remember what we told you about keeping your eyes off her."

Wade said nothing as he tied on the bag, and Jennifer's heart ached for him. Buck grinned as he watched Wade, and Lou came to stand beside him. "Is it true you really went to college, Indian?" Lou asked then.

"Leave the man alone," Adam Hughes spoke up.

"Mind your own business," Buck answered. "Me and Lou have good reason to hate men like this one. His relatives have caused a lot of bloodshed along the borders, and I don't think it's right for anybody with red skin to be allowed to go to schools meant for whites." He looked back up at Wade. "What the hell did they teach you, Indian? How to use a knife and fork? They teach you it ain't proper to go around naked, eatin' dogs and rapin' white women?"

"That's enough!" Nick himself came storming up to Buck then. "This man is paying his way, and he's not done anything to any of you. I'm the one who decides who can and cannot use this coach, mister, and if you don't lay off Wade Morrow, I'll leave *you* behind, not him!"

Wade was climbing down as Nick glowered at Buck. He stepped up beside Nick, keeping steady, cool eyes on Buck and Lou as he spoke. "One thing I learned is how ignorant some white men can be," Wade said. "How they don't know anything about judging a man by his real worth instead of his skin. You dumb bastards are about to go to war, about to tear apart your own country because of

Negro slaves. What is it about some of you that you can't accept a man with skin darker than your own? Most white men have a system of judging people I'll never understand. Maybe it's because they're just plain ignorant."

Buck's face darkened. "You saying I'm ignorant, Indian?"

"I have a name. It's Wade Morrow. And as far as you being ignorant, I don't have to say it. You do a good enough job showing it all by yourself."

"Why, you—" Buck raised a fist, but before he could swing it, Wade had hold of his wrist. In a flash Wade's big fist was in Buck's stomach with a thud. The man grunted and bent over, and Wade's fist came up into his face. The man sprawled onto his back, his lips and nose bloodied. Jennifer felt sick at the sight, but at the same time she felt like cheering.

Lou had just watched in surprise. He looked ready to defend his friend, but fear was evident in his eyes as he summed up Wade's size and realized Wade was ready and almost anxious for a fight. "I normally have a lot of patience," Wade told the man, his voice a near growl. "I know my place, mister, or at least what others think my place should be. But even I have a breaking point. We aren't in any town now. We're on our own out here, and I don't have to listen to your insults. I've paid my way and I'll be riding up top, helping protect your worthless hides. You've got no cause to give me trouble."

Lou swallowed, and the others watched in confusion, most of them agreeing inwardly that Wade Morrow had every right to hit Buck; but also seeing through their eyes a "savage Indian" whom they did not want to cross. Lou stepped back, leaning down to help his friend, while Wade turned to remount the coach.

"Don't even think about it," he heard Nick saying. "You'd never come out of it alive."

Wade turned to see Buck's pistol pulled from its holster. The others stepped even farther back, and Jennifer watched in wide-eyed terror. Wade slowly stepped to the ground again. "Cock it, and a knife will be in your heart before you can pull the trigger," he told the man. "You

114

want to see the Indian in me, this is a good way to find out, but you'll never live to tell about it."

"Leave it be, Buck," Lou told the man. "He's travelin' up top and gettin' off in a couple of days. It's not worth the risk."

"Listen to your friend, Buck," Wade told the man, his hand on the handle of a huge knife at his waist.

Buck slowly put back the gun. Wade glanced at Jennifer before turning to climb back up to the top of the coach.

"It ain't right," Buck complained, getting to his knees and spitting blood. "Lettin' a Comanche ride a coach."

"I told you that's up to me," Nick told him. "These other men don't seem to mind that much." He looked at Jennifer. "What about you, ma'am? Does it upset you to have Mr. Morrow along?"

Their eyes held, and Jennifer swallowed. She wanted to shout that she thought Wade Morrow a better man than all of them. "No," she answered. "As long as he stays up top." How she hated saying it. She felt like a traitor, but she knew she must lie, not just for her sake, but for Wade's. "I don't believe a man should be punished for the color of his skin. He's done nothing wrong. I think we should all get inside and be on our way. We're wasting time. I'm anxious to get to Fort Stockton."

With that she climbed into the coach, taking her same position as the day before.

"The lady is right. Now all of you board up and let's get going," Nick told them.

The men climbed inside. Buck plunked down, holding a handkerchief to his mouth and nose. "Damn savage," he muttered. "I won't forget this."

"I suggest you do," Adam Hughes told him, brushing some dust from his suit. "You pushed the man too far, and for no good reason. He seems well spoken and intelligent to me, and I personally don't blame him for hitting you. Any man would have."

Jennifer felt like thanking the man for his remark.

"Who asked you," Buck grumbled, rubbing at his stomach.

"I agree with Hughes," Sid Menden put in. "You had

115

no call to insult him that way."

"He was looking at Miss Andrews," Buck argued, his voice muffled by the handkerchief.

"For God's sake he was only taking her bag," Hank Griffith put in. "You weren't upset, were you, Miss Andrews?"

"No. Not at all."

"There, you see? We need the man, Buck. Anyone can see he knows how to handle himself. Leave him alone and he'll leave you alone."

"If his father owns Morrow Freighting Services, Mr. Morrow is actually rather wealthy," Hughes said. "Or at least he will be some day when his father passes on."

"It ain't right, an Indian bein' rich," Lou said. "It ain't fair."

"A lot of things in life aren't fair," Hughes replied.

Jennifer thought how true the statement was. She should herself be wealthy, but it had all been stolen from her by Uncle John.

The coach lurched forward as the horses got underway. Jennifer turned her attention out the window again, looking out at the desolate land ahead. Today she felt no fear. She knew these men better now, and her belly was full with the biscuits they had so kindly given her; but that was not the reason she felt better today. The real reason was that Wade Morrow was along. She touched her cheek, her skin feeling better after the long ride the day before in the hot, dusty air. The salve had helped it, just like Wade said it would. She glanced around at the men, seeing mosquito bites on all their faces, and she smiled to herself.

Chapter Eight

The coach clattered on, swaying relentlessly as the rutted road caused wheels to move over ridges and bounce through holes. Before the day was over a violent thunderstorm hit. Jennifer was forced to close the leather window shield, but rain still dripped inside onto her dress. Will Perry, who again sat beside her, offered to change places with her for the time being so that she wouldn't have to sit with rain blowing in on her. They shifted seats, but not without embarrassment to Jennifer and pleasure for the men, who had to hang on to her to keep her from falling into laps as she tried to move around while the coach bounced and swayed.

Jennifer settled in between Will Perry, the scout, and Hank Griffith, the man who was going to El Paso to open a tavern. Buck still sat dabbing at his nose and mouth. The bleeding had stopped, but his upper lip was badly swollen and scabbed, and a purple bruise was forming at the side of his nose, down over his mouth. He had not failed to curse Wade Morrow throughout the day, until Adam Hughes finally told him to shut up or he'd give the young man another bruise, even if it meant ruining his fancy suit. When two more of the men agreed that they were tired of hearing Buck complain, the man finally quieted, but sat in a sulk.

To her irritation, Jennifer noticed Buck seemed to stare at her even more today than he had yesterday. She thought how strange it was that this young man who had warned Wade Morrow not to even look at her was now staring at her himself, in a way that made her much more uncomfortable than Wade Morrow ever had.

She felt sorry for Wade, who had to stay up top through the storm. She knew it must be miserable up there, as the rain came down in a torrent. Again, the stamina of men like Wade, and Nick Elliott, who continued to drive the horses through the awful downpour, amazed her.

The coach splattered through mud holes, the mud sometimes getting flung right into the coach, peppering the men who sat by the two rear windows. The coach finally slowed, but the rain continued to come down. Then the vehicle stopped, and Ernie Peters opened one of the doors. He stood there in a poncho, rain pouring off his leather hat.

"Watch your feet," he shouted above the storm. "Swollen stream up ahead. We're gonna try to get through it, then up to higher ground. The Indian is gonna help lead the team through the stream. There's an old, abandoned farm up ahead where Nick says he thinks he can get the whole team inside the barn. The roof probably leaks by now, but it will be better than bein' out in this. Nick can't hardly see where he's goin'—says he'll have to stop till the rain lets up."

The man closed the door without waiting for a reply from anyone. Jennifer felt a growing apprehension as the coach moved forward again. If Ernie had said to watch their feet, that must mean the stream was so deep that water could come into the coach. She wondered if they could be swept away.

"That's the trouble out here," Will spoke up. "It gets so dry your own bones feel brittle; then when the rain comes, it comes all at once, so fast that the ground can't soak it up fast enough. Just once I'd like to see a gentle rainfall in these parts." He pulled back the leather window cover and grunted. "Brace yourselves, folks."

The stream was so swollen that Jennifer could hear its

swiftly moving waters above the sound of the pouring rain.

"I'll bet this is normally just a shallow creek, maybe completely dried up most of the time," Lou said. He leaned around Sid Menden to look out Sid's window. "Jesus," he muttered.

It seemed the coach suddenly dropped, and immediately water began pouring under the doors. Jennifer tried to pull up her dress and her feet, but the hem of her dress was already soaked. She felt sorry for Wade, who must be standing in the swirling cold waters. What he was doing had to be dangerous. Not only could he be swept away by the waters, but he was trying to lead a team of six powerful horses, who could trample him under the water if he wasn't careful.

She realized then that ever since first meeting Wade Morrow, her thoughts had been mostly of him. She had hardly thought about Sergeant Enders at all, and the trip had become so unusual and full of so many surprises that at times she almost forgot her real purpose for being here. Whenever she reminded herself of it, her heart raced and her stomach ached.

The coach creaked and shifted, feeling for a moment as though it might be swept downstream. Will and Hank each grabbed one of Jennifer's arms, and for the moment she didn't mind, sure she would be washed out of the coach any moment if not for their grasp. The water swirled nearly to the seats before they felt the coach rising again. The brown, muddy water began to drain from the carriage, and again it was moving. Adam Hughes pulled aside the leather curtain at his window to see Wade Morrow just then climbing aboard while the coach was already in motion. Jennifer could see his buckskin clothing was drenched. A moccasined foot disappeared above, and Adam leaned out the window.

"We're in the clear," he said, "and from the looks of that stream, we're damn lucky." He closed the leather curtain. "Well, we can thank the Indian for that one. I don't think

119

Nick could have managed the team through that alone. I've always heard the Indians have a way with horses."

"They've got their own way about a lot of things," Buck answered, "and they ain't all good."

"Well, right now you owe your hide to this Indian, cowboy," Larry Buchanan told him. "Mr. Hughes is right. I'm a horse trader, and I've seen first hand the special way Indians have with them."

The coach rattled and splattered its way for another mile before slowing again. Will looked out, muttering that a barn was just ahead. Moments later everything darkened as the coach was drawn inside the deserted building.

"Let's get out and stretch our legs," Sid Menden said. He opened the door and climbed out, followed by Will, who then helped Jennifer climb down. Her dress and petticoats, drenched by muddy water, suddenly felt as though they weighed fifty pounds, and the damp conditions gave her a chill.

"You best put on somethin' drier, Miss Andrews," Nick told her. "You can change on the other side of the coach. Me and the others will stay on this side." He looked up as Jennifer reddened at the suggestion. "Throw down her bags, Wade."

Jennifer looked up to see a soaked Wade Morrow remove some canvas from the baggage. "You've got two bags, ma'am," Wade called down. "Which one do you want?"

"The blue flowered one," Jennifer answered, while Buck watched with a scowl. Jennifer looked at Nick. "What about you and Ernie and Mr. Morrow?"

"No sense us changin' right now. Soon as the rain lets up a little we'll be leavin' out and get wet all over again."

Wade handed down the bag, and Jennifer was careful not to look up at him. She let Nick take the bag. She walked around the other side of the coach.

"You better come down, Indian," Buck called out then, "unless you plan to be lookin' over the side."

"Shut up, cowboy," Will Perry told him. "I wasn't

120

much for havin' the man along myself, but he got us across that stream and he seems pretty decent to me. We might be stuck here a while, and I don't feel like listenin' to your insults the whole time."

Wade climbed down, and Buck sat down on a small stack of hay.

"You men feed a little of that hay to the horses, will you," Nick asked the others. "Me and Wade and Ernie need a smoke. Just make sure you feed the animals from this side till Miss Andrews is finished."

The passengers obeyed, and on the other side of the coach Jennifer quickly changed. Some of the men watched her dress and petticoats fall to the ground beneath the coach, but Wade made a point not to even look in that direction. He laid back and quietly smoked a cigarette, feeling cold and uncomfortable, wondering if he was being a fool to try this late in life to find remnants of a family. Since his birth the Comanche had been decimated by white encroachment, famine, and white man's diseases. It was highly unlikely anyone who might know anything about him was even still alive. Yet this strange hunger to know for certain still clawed at him.

Jennifer appeared then, holding her wet clothes over one arm, wearing a soft green, cotton dress and a paisley shawl. "What should I do with these," she asked Nick, indicating her wet clothes. "I can't put them into my bag this way."

"We'll just roll them up and tie them on. At the next home station you can wash them and hang them out to dry overnight." He rose and took them from her, and Jennifer thanked him. Ernie climbed up top and tied everything back on, and Adam Hughes walked over to Wade to thank him for helping with the horses.

"We could have all been washed away back there," he told the man.

"I just want to do my share," Wade answered. "I've done that more than once, driving teams for my father's freighting business. Had a brother get stepped on and pulled under once, but he lived."

"Brother? You mean a son of the white man who adopted you, don't you," Lou Huston said with a note of sarcasm. "Your pa let you call him brother?"

"What's the story, anyway," Buck spoke up, lighting a pipe. "Your white pa your *real* pa? He have himself a good time with some Comanche squaw and then feel guilty about it?" He snickered after saying the words, and Lou joined him.

Wade cast a look at them that wiped the smiles from their faces. "My white parents found me as an abandoned newborn twenty-six years ago," he answered calmly, realizing the others were also wondering. "Since they weren't prejudiced ignorants like the two of you, they kept me, realizing all life is worth something. Being the good, Christian people they are, they raised me like their own, and when they had their own children, their sons were taught to consider me just as much a brother as a blood brother; I feel the same way about them. I have two brothers—Henry and Billy. When my father is gone we'll all share an equal partnership in the business."

"Your pa must be crazy to let an Indian in on all that wealth," Buck sneered. "I ain't never heard of an Indian who knew what to do with money except to spend it on guns to kill whites, and on whiskey to get him all tanked up for a raid."

Wade slowly stood up, while everyone watched with apprehension. He took a long drag on his cigarette, then took it from his mouth as he stepped closer to Buck. "I told you I had a breaking point, mister. What I did earlier was nothing. Insult my father again, and you'll not be able to walk the next time I light into you. There's no law in these parts. You remember that."

Buck moved his eyes to Jennifer, giving her a chill with the way he looked at her. "I'll remember it," he answered, looking back at Wade. "Same goes for you."

"Then we might as well finish it right now."

Buck just stared at him, then grinned, trying to look

122

unafraid but fooling no one. "There will be a better time," he answered.

"Sure there will—when you've got about six more men behind you. That's the way cowards operate," Wade answered. "It's happened to me before. I've seen it all, cowboy, and I can handle anything you want to throw at me, which I know would be anything you can think of except to fight like a man."

Buck's eyes narrowed. "I'm not fighting you in this condition."

"You won't fight me at all. You're all mouth, cowboy. Shooting a man down when he's not looking is more your style. You just remember I have eyes in the back of my head."

Buck rose, his face dark with anger. "My ma was killed by Comanche! You want to know what they did to her?"

"You don't have to tell me, especially not in front of the lady over there. But I didn't have anything to do with that, mister. I've never even *lived* among them!"

"An Indian is an Indian," Buck sneered. He sat back down, turning away.

"Let it go, Wade," Nick said then. "There's some folks that ain't ever gonna change their minds about some things. I expect you've learned that."

Wade turned and left, walking to the entrance to the barn and smoking while he watched the rain quietly. The men looked at each other, some of them feeling sorry for the man, others figuring harsh words were probably common to him and that since he was half Indian, and therefore only half human, it probably didn't bother him all that much.

A few minutes later the rain began to lighten. Everyone boarded, taking their original seats, and Wade climbed up top while Ernie took his position next to Nick, rifle in hand. Nick pushed off the brake, and the coach again broke away, heading west.

* * *

The sun came out, and mixed with the heavy rain and wet ground it caused the air to become so humid that Jennifer was sure she could see steam coming from the earth. She soon rid herself of her shawl, and her hair became so limp that, combined with the constant swaying of the coach, it began to come loose from its bun. Soon everyone was sweating.

Nick drove the team hard, and by the time they reached the next home station, night was falling, and everyone was damp and hot and irritable. Jennifer was disappointed to see that this station was no better than the last. Everyone disembarked the coach, and Wade quickly disappeared into a nearby ravine, emerging several minutes later wearing dry boots and denim pants, and a dry buckskin shirt. His still-damp hair was brushed back and tied neatly at the back of his neck.

"There's a pretty decent stream over there if the lady would like to wash a little and wash her muddy clothes," Jennifer heard him telling Nick. The words warmed her heart, for she knew that although he couldn't give her the time of day directly, he was thinking of her comfort.

"I hate for her to go over there alone," Nick answered.

Wade looked around. The land was getting more hilly, with more ravines and rocks and brush, more places for Indians or lowlife to hide. "I know," he answered. "The only ones I'd trust are you or Ernie—or maybe that Adam Hughes. Any of them, I suppose, except Buck or Lou."

"You help Ernie with the team. I'll go with her," Nick answered. He walked over to Jennifer, explaining the situation. "I'll be sittin' at the top of the bank lookin' the other way," he explained. "You have a problem, you just yell."

With crimson cheeks she agreed, eager to wash both herself and her hair and clothes. Wade handed down her bags, and she walked to the ravine, followed by Nick, who carried a lantern, since it was nearly completely dark. Buck watched jealously, angry that he wasn't trusted to guard the woman, even angrier that the Indian had been the one to say who should be with her.

He'd like to get his own dirty hands on her, I'll bet, he thought silently. He thought how pleasant it would be to win Miss Jennifer Andrews for himself and watch the anger and jealousy in Wade Morrow's eyes and the eyes of all the others. He had been wondering about the woman who put on such an air of being proper. What kind of woman would come out here to marry a complete stranger? What was she running from? Maybe she even had a husband someplace else, or a stained reputation. Maybe she had done something criminal. Whatever it was, he reasoned that no proper lady would be out here traveling to a place like Fort Stockton.

By the time Jennifer returned, the horses had been corralled and most of the men were eating. Much as she hated to spend the money, she could not ignore her hunger. She entered the crude cabin, where this time there were four cots besides those for the two men who manned the station. Again she felt Buck's eyes on her more than the others. It was hot and stuffy inside the cabin, and she dreaded sleeping through another night like last night. She wanted to sleep out under the stars, but that would not seem ladylike, and it looked as though it might rain again.

The men made room for her at the wooden table, and the cook dished up a bowl of stew that to her surprise was quite tasty. The biscuits were fresh and soft, and she didn't feel quite so bad about spending another dollar for the meal. She swallowed some strong coffee while the men talked about the storm and who would sleep inside tonight. The door opened then, and Wade stepped inside.

The cook scowled at him. "I don't serve Indians," he said.

Nick walked in behind Wade. "You can serve this one, Dennis. He's right civilized, and he's paid his fair share. He also got my team through a flooded stream today. He deserves a good meal."

The cook grunted. "If you say so."

Two of the passengers rose and excused themselves to let

Wade sit down. Then Buck and Lou also rose, saying they wouldn't sit at the same table with an Indian. They stormed out, and everyone else finished their meals, while Wade silently ate his own bowl of stew and ate the biscuits as though he was famished.

Jennifer rose from the table, and all the men remaining rose with her as she excused herself. "You'd best stay close," Nick warned her. "We're getting into more dangerous country."

"I'm just going out back for a moment," she answered, meaning the privy. "I'll be right back." She left eagerly, embarrassed to talk about such things around so many men, wondering when she would ever have true privacy again or enjoy the company of another woman.

Inside the cabin Wade finished his stew, then rolled and lit a cigarette. "I didn't want to say anything while the woman was in here," he said then, "but I smell something in the air."

Nick looked at him with a frown. "What do you mean?"

"I mean literally." He looked at the cook. "Any settlements near here?"

"About two miles off—a little farm. I've told the folks there before that they're riskin' an awful lot settlin' this close to the Comanche Trace, but they're convinced there won't be no more trouble because most of the Comanche are in Indian Territory now. I told them there have been rumors of a band of renegades out here, led by some half-breed called Wild Horse."

The room quieted for a moment at the mention of half-breed. Wade felt an odd premonition that he could not name. He sighed deeply. "Well, I was out looking around a while ago, and I smelled something—smoke—and not just from burning buildings—more like burning flesh. Much as all of you hate the Indian in me, one thing I inherited was a good sense of smell—and hearing. I put my ear to the ground, and I could swear I heard the sound of a lot of horses. I don't want to alarm you too much, but I'd keep an extra watch tonight. I've scouted enough to feel it in my blood when there's danger near, and I feel it tonight."

They all looked at each other, fear on their faces.

"My main concern is the woman," Wade continued. "I hope I'm wrong about the whole thing, but if we do get attacked and things get bad for us, somebody better shoot her. I imagine most of you know what would happen to her. She'd be better off dead."

Nick nodded and a couple of the others cleared their throats nervously.

"I suggest no one mentions this to her," Wade continued. "No sense getting her frightened for nothing. She can't do anything about it either way, so why worry her?"

"I agree," Nick answered. "Don't even mention it to Buck. He's got a big mouth."

Wade's face darkened at the words, but he didn't say anything.

Outside, Jennifer exited the privy, then gasped when suddenly someone stepped in front of her from beside the outhouse. "Hello there, Miss Andrews," came Buck's drawled words.

Jennifer frowned. She didn't like the man one whit, especially the way he had treated Wade. She did not reply, but turned and headed for the cabin. Buck grabbed her arm. "Hey, Miss Stuck up, no woman walks away from me."

"Let go of me," she growled in a low whisper, smelling whiskey on his breath.

"Not till you tell me the truth—why you're runnin' to some god-awful fort to marry a stranger. I think you're hidin' somethin' from us, lady, and I don't think you're all that prim and proper." He grabbed her other arm and jerked her close, her back to him. He wrapped both arms around her, across her breasts. "I think underneath all that proper behavior is a woman who loves bein' around all these men—temptin' us—" He nuzzled her neck, and she turned her head away. "Makin' us crazy. And you've been

127

watchin' me, lady. I've noticed."

"I've looked at you with contempt for your ignorance and stupidity," she sneered. She brought up her foot, ramming her heel hard into the instep of his right foot. He let out a yelp but refused to let go of her. Instead he dragged her to the ground, rolling on top of her so that she lay facedown and helpless in the dirt, struggling to get up while he kept his weight on her. She knew she should scream, but she also knew that would bring the others running, and the one most likely to light into Buck would be Wade Morrow. She dreaded getting him into more trouble.

"Come on, lady, you want me and you know it. You can't tell me you ain't ever been with a man before. I know the look. No proper lady comes out here to go to bed with a stranger. Now we're both lonely, and we both have a need. We can get it over with real quick, and nobody needs to know the difference."

Terror and revulsion welled up in her throat, and still she hated to scream and cause a commotion. She would be humiliated, and there would be more trouble among the other men. She thought what a hypocrite Buck was, to be telling Wade Morrow to keep his eyes off her, when all the time it was Buck who was the dangerous one. She squirmed more, and when she felt a hand pushing up her skirt and moving under it to her bottom, she could no longer hold back.

"No," she screamed. "Help! Help!"

Buck immediately jumped up, actually surprised. He was convinced she wouldn't put up a fuss. "You damn bitch," he hissed. "Who are you savin' yourself for, huh? Hughes, maybe? Maybe it's the big, buck Indian you want, you little whore!"

His words cut deep as she struggled to her knees. She heard Buck running off. Tears of humiliation and shock overwhelmed her. She could hear men running, heard voices, felt someone helping her up.

"What happened?" Adam Hughes was asking her.

"Keep an eye out," Nick said. "Could be Indians nearby."

"Buck," Jennifer answered, shaking and crying. She put a hand to her face, brushing at gravel that was caked into it. "Buck . . . attacked me," she said in one deep sob.

"Buck!" She wasn't sure whose voice it was. "Where is he now?"

"Must have run off," someone else said.

"I'll find the bastard." The words were low and cold, and this time she recognized the voice. It belonged to Wade Morrow.

"We all will," someone else said. She heard them running about, heard someone yell that he had located Buck.

"I . . . don't want . . . to cause trouble," she sobbed to Adam Hughes as the man led her back to the cabin.

"You didn't cause it. Buck did," the man answered.

Jennifer cringed as she heard the sounds of shouts and fists then. "Let him have it, Indian," someone shouted. Her heart ached with sorrow and fear for Wade Morrow. Again he was fighting a white man in her defense. Hughes led her inside the cabin and she sank down on one of the cots while the man got a pan of water and a rag for her to wash the dirt from her face.

"Hold it! Hold it," she heard someone outside shout. "You're killin' him!"

"Get hold of him! Get him off there. He's had enough," someone else yelled.

"I think we all should have a turn at him," came another voice. "He's caused trouble this whole trip."

"He won't be causin' any more," she heard Nick say then. "He won't even get up for a while. Somebody throw some water on him and lay him out for the night. I don't want him inside the cabin near Miss Andrews. Lou, you're his friend. You take care of him."

"That damn Indian had no right—"

"He had every right!" The voice came from Larry Buchanan. "If Morrow hadn't done it, the rest of us would have."

The voices came closer then, and a moment later several of them entered the cabin, slowing down and lowering their voices when they spotted Jennifer. She looked down. "You all right, ma'am?" Nick asked her.

"Yes," she answered in a near whisper. She dabbed at the dirt on her face, feeling Wade Morrow's presence as the men brought him inside and sat him down to the table.

"Soak your knuckles in a pan of water," Nick was saying. "I hope you'll be able to use a gun if the need arises."

"I'll manage," came Wade's panting reply. "Just get me the water."

Jennifer choked back tears, feeling like a sideshow in a circus as some of the men turned to look at her. The life she had led in St. Louis, Aunt Esther and the lovely home she had had there all seemed like another life now, a distant dream. She hated Uncle John even more for causing her to be in this godforsaken, dangerous land. Would her husband-to-be attack her this way on their wedding night, insisting on his husbandly privileges without even getting to know her first?

She shook as she washed, and Nick chased out most of the men. The room grew suddenly silent, as Wade sat soaking his knuckles, and Nick himself finally left to check on Buck. Only the cook was left inside, and he was turned away, washing a pan. Jennifer raised her eyes to see Wade looking at her with deep concern and a trace of his anger with Buck still showing. She knew in that instant that this was a man who would protect his woman at all costs, a man who would be patient and kind, a man who was brave and skilled. The feelings she was having at the moment surprised her, and she dropped her eyes.

"You all right?" he asked then. "Did he hurt you?"

She swallowed, shaking her head. "I just . . . scraped my face in the dirt." Her voice was a near whisper. "Thank you," she added. "You shouldn't have."

"He had it coming. I needed to light into him for more reasons than what he just did. That's the only way to shut the mouth of a man like that." He sighed deeply, thinking how there could be Comanche raiders nearby. They might all be dead by morning. He felt a keen disappointment that he would never get to know Miss Jennifer Andrews better. If the raiders didn't finish them all off, the fact still remained Miss Andrews was headed for Fort Stockton to be married; and that even if she wasn't, a man like himself could never get close to her, for her own sake as well as his own. Besides, why would such a lovely young lady from a fancy place like St. Louis give a half-breed a second thought; but then Rebecca had. Still, look what it had cost both of them.

He took his hands from the water, drying them long enough to roll and light a cigarette. He glanced at Jennifer again, hoping no renegades would come. He could not imagine having to put a bullet into that pretty head. What a terrible shame and waste that would be.

Chapter Nine

Those who knew raiding Comanche could be nearby slept restlessly, including Wade. Dawn broke peacefully, a mockingbird sitting in a nearby cactus plant giving out a variety of cheerful calls. In the distant foothills to the west, an abundant array of wildflowers bloomed.

Wade rose, aching from the fight and from lack of sleep; but his ankle felt better. With the eyes of a hawk he again scanned the horizon, listening intently, sniffing the air, his senses as alive as that of a wolf. He caught the lingering smell of smoke, but could see nothing. The night before it had been too dark to see the lay of the land. As morning broke he could see that they were in hillier land. The gradual slopes created enough of a barrier so that a settlement, or Indians, just over the next hill would not be seen. It was ideal country for raiders.

Soon everyone was up and ready to go, after eating a breakfast of ham and eggs. This time Wade was invited to join them, but he noticed Jennifer did not eat. She packed her bag and said she would wait outside.

Nick finished his own coffee and leaned over to Wade. "What do you think . . . about your suspicions?" he asked him. "I figured if there's Comanche out there, they would have attacked us this mornin'."

"Maybe. Then again maybe they're waiting until we leave. We'd be a lot more vulnerable away from this cabin."

"You still think they're out there then?"

Wade swallowed a piece of ham. "That's my guess. I could be wrong."

Nick sighed. "I have to decide whether to keep goin'," he said, rubbing his whiskered chin. "Thing is, the farther we go, the closer we'll be to Fort Stockton and Fort Davis, and the less likely the Comanche will attack. Besides that, there's plenty of men along who know how to use a rifle. Raidin' Comanche don't usually ride in very big packs. These are the independent ones—the ones who refuse to stay on the reservation. They act pretty much on their own. You can't never tell what they'll do. Thing is, they've got a lot stronger since that young half-breed has got them stirred up, that there Wild Horse. I wish I knew if this was part of Wild Horse's band."

"You think we should keep going then?"

"I don't think we have a whole lot of choice. I've got a schedule to keep, and we drive these coaches through anything. I've drove through this country plenty of time. There's always the threat of attack. If I stopped or turned back every time there was this kind of danger, the stage line would fold. Them Indians have to see we don't scare easy. Besides, they don't usually attack stagecoaches. There's not that much on a coach that they need. They're more likely to wait for a supply train to come along."

"Whatever you think. I'll help however I can till you reach Fort Stockton."

"Well, this strip between here and El Paso has always been dangerous. That's why they brought in soldiers, except that now with the threat of war back East, they've left hardly enough men at the forts to do any good for the border settlers. The Comanche know our defenses are weakened, and they're takin' advantage of it while they can."

Nick rubbed at his eyes and sighed, rising from the table. "It's the same old story," he continued. "The government says they'll send help, but they never follow through, and they ain't got no idea of the troubles out here. You can't hardly blame some of these people out here for the way

134

they feel about the Comanche, Wade. There ain't hardly a person in Texas who ain't lost loved ones or neighbors or whatever to them savages."

"I know that. But maybe if some of the treaty promises were kept, things would be better."

"Maybe. But the biggest problem is a whole passel of Comanche chiefs can sign a treaty—but it don't mean nothin' to the young warriors. By Comanche law, anybody that don't sign don't have to abide by the treaty. They're a real independent people. One man can't speak for another. This Wild Horse, though, he seems to have more control than some Comanche chiefs do. He's led most of the bloody raids that have been goin' on in these parts." Nick put on his hat. "We'd better get started." Their eyes held, both men knowing the danger that lay ahead. "You know what to do with the woman if things should get bad."

Wade felt a tightness in his chest. "I know."

Both men left the cabin. Wade glanced at Jennifer before he climbed to the top of the coach again. He saw the hint of a grateful smile, and he didn't mind his sore knuckles. Lou and Hank Griffith were helping Buck walk. Wade climbed up and watched, feeling a deep satisfaction at having had the opportunity to land his fists into the man.

Buck groaned as he managed to climb into the coach, his head hanging and his clothes torn and dirty. Everyone else climbed in after him. Jennifer could feel no pity for the man as he sat holding his ribs, his face a bruised mess. It was difficult to even look at him without feeling ill. He glanced at her, his eyes ugly and threatening.

"Keep your eyes off the woman," Will told him.

Jennifer looked out the window, glad the man was suffering. She would not forget last night for a long time, her face forced into the dirt, Buck's weight on top of her. She wondered what kind of hell her uncle might have put her through by now if she had stayed in St. Louis. Her right cheek was red and scraped and still stung this morning, but not nearly as badly as it might have if she had not had Wade Morrow's wonderful salve to put on it.

135

Adam Hughes had accompanied her and kept watch while she washed and changed at the stream this morning, so that she wouldn't have to wear the dirty, torn dress from the night before.

Today she wore a blue and white serpentine-striped cotton dress with a deep lace yoke and short, gathered sleeves. Two rows of ruffles decorated the hemline, and a blue sash at her tiny waist was tied into a bow at the back. Her stomach ached for food, but she was determined to go without until supper time. Her straw bonnet was pinned neatly into her auburn hair, which was rolled and pinned in a circular design around her head.

She wished there had been a way to press the dress, but realized with a resigned grin that it mattered little in this country whether or not one's dress was slightly wrinkled. She also had no idea just how neatly she had managed to pin her hair, since all she had was a small personal mirror to use. She only hoped nothing would happen to this dress, since the one that had got muddied was washed and dried now, but terribly wrinkled; and now yesterday's dress was torn and dirty. She had three more dresses along, but only one of them was nice enough to wear for her first meeting with Sergeant Enders. She wanted to look as good as possible, but her heart was growing more apprehensive and despondent with every passing mile. Her experience the night before with Buck did not help her fear of marrying a stranger.

Again, without effort, she found her thoughts turning to Wade Morrow, and the way he had looked at her the night before, after the fight. He had seemed almost possessive, had beaten Buck nearly to death because the man had touched her. But it was more than just the fight. Although they hardly knew each other, and to be close was forbidden, she felt a kindred spirit with the man, a special attraction to him that could not be denied; and she was sure he felt the same way about her. Still, it seemed pointless to dwell on it, for the only thing they would ever have in common was this journey. Fort Stockton lay ahead—and a new life for Jennifer Andrews.

With the snap of a whip and a shout, the stage lurched forward, Buck groaning and whining about "getting" Wade Morrow, the other men rather quiet. Will leaned forward and looked through her window, as though expecting to see something in particular, then leaned back, his hand resting on a pistol he wore at his waist. He glanced at Adam Hughes, both men exchanging a worried look before Hughes looked at Jennifer and put on a reassuring smile.

"Just a couple more days and you'll be delivered safely to your soldier at Fort Stockton," the man told her.

"Yes. That will be a relief," she answered.

"Sure will," Will muttered. "For more reasons than one."

The ride grew hot and monotonous, and Buck slept off and on, occasionally taking a swallow of whiskey offered him by his friend, Lou, supposedly to help relieve his pain. It was not until after they left the next swing station that he seemed slightly more recovered, his eyes resting on Jennifer more often, the whiskey giving him more courage and less pain.

"This is all your fault," he finally grumbled threateningly to Jennifer.

"Shut up," Hughes told him.

Buck kept staring at Jennifer. "She asked for it, flauntin' herself in front of us like she does."

"I said to shut up."

Jennifer reddened deeply, and Hughes grasped Buck's arm. "She hasn't done a thing wrong."

"She doesn't have to. It's all in the way she looks, those pretty eyes, the way those dresses fit—"

Hank Griffith reached over then and grabbed Buck's shirt. "One more word and I'll add another bruise to them you've already got." His fist was clenched, and Buck was not so drunk that he didn't realize how much another blow would hurt, or that he was in no condition to fight back. He glowered at Hank for a moment, then leaned back, pulling his hat over his face.

Hank returned to his seat, and Jennifer wished she could find a hole to crawl into. She was suddenly self-conscious of her whole body, but also angry that just being a woman minding her own business seemed like some kind of crime to men like Buck. What were the others really thinking? She felt more lonely than ever, and she thought about the times when she would sit and embroider and talk with Aunt Esther, or help Mattie in the kitchen. Would life ever be that good again?

She had no more time to ponder her fate, for just then the coach took a lurch forward and Nick began shouting "Git! Git up there!"

"What the—" Sid Menden frowned, looking out the window.

"I know these coaches make good time, but I've never known one to go this fast," Adam Hughes said. "This is downright dangerous!"

"Must be a reason," Will put in. He took Jennifer's arm. "Move over, Miss. Let me sit by the window."

"What the hell for," Buck asked.

"Shut up," Will answered. "And you'd better not be too sore to use that gun." He leaned out the window as far as he could, looking back. He moved back inside then, just as Jennifer heard an odd crack and a pinging sound at the back of the coach.

"That was a gunshot!" Hank exclaimed.

"There's a band of renegades chasin' us," Will said calmly. He put a hand on Jennifer's shoulder. "You'd better get down on the floor, Miss Andrews. It will be less dangerous, and if they get close, they won't see there's a woman in here."

"Jesus Christ," Lou muttered, taking out his gun.

There came another ping, and then Jennifer could hear fire being returned from above. Wade Morrow was up there, with little protection. There came more shots, and she knew Wade and Ernie were shooting at the renegades. The Indians must be getting closer! Her heart raced almost painfully, her mind already filling with tales of the

138

horrible things Comanche did to white women. Was this to be her fate then, to be raped and murdered and scalped, to come into this land and just disappear like the wind?

She got on her knees, kneeling in the narrow aisle between several pairs of booted feet. "Sons of bitches," Buck was saying. "That goddamn Wade Morrow probably knew about this all along."

"Like hell! He's up there risking his life for us, you damn fool," Adam answered.

The gunfire grew thicker then, and Jennifer stayed bent over, having no idea which man was shooting which time. She grimaced as someone stepped on her heel in an effort to get a better window position. The coach bounced and lurched dangerously, swaying back and forth, sometimes seeming to be traveling on two wheels instead of four.

"The horses are gonna' wear out pretty quick at this pace," Will shouted above the thunder of hooves.

"If the coach doesn't fall apart first," Hank answered.

"They're already slowing," Adam put in. "Those bastards are catching up! This team can't outrun Indians, especially not Comanche. They're the best riders on the Plains."

"Oh, my God," Larry Buchanan muttered. "There's more up ahead. We're riding right into them!"

"Jesus, I don't want to be taken alive by those bastards," Buck almost whined. "Maybe they'd leave us alone if we gave them the woman."

There was a sudden silence, and Jennifer felt sick to her stomach.

"You bastard," Will growled. "If we didn't need every man right now, I'd blow your brains out!"

Jennifer could hear war whoops then, and the coach careened dangerously as above Nick tried to take a turn off the road in an effort to go around the Indians ahead. But the team was lathered and frightened now, and Nick could not control them. They headed back toward the road, leading the coach to a rock and smashing the right wheels into the boulder, causing the coach to collapse on the right side and roll. It tore away from the team at the hitch.

Jennifer felt bodies falling against her. For a moment she couldn't breathe, as she was nearly crushed against the right door. The stage was surrounded by war whoops and gunfire then, and she wanted to scream with fear and dread, but she told herself to remain calm.

Outside Wade had jumped from the coach just as it went over. His head hit a rock, and he lay unconscious for several minutes while the renegades shot Nick Elliott full of arrows. Ernie Peters lay crushed under the coach, and one warrior rode up to him and quickly took his scalp. More Indians were swarming over the coach then, some falling away as men inside who could manage to get into position to shoot fired at them through the windows.

More warriors leaped onto the coach, stabbing through the windows with lances until the firing stopped. They ripped open the door then, pulling men out and running them through with lances one at a time, taking scalps, slitting throats, ripping clothes and boots from the dead bodies.

Jennifer was so filled with horror that she could not scream as she felt the weight on top of her getting lighter and heard begging screams from the men. She realized what must be happening, and that any moment the warriors would reach her own body.

"No! No," she heard Buck scream then. "Take the woman! Take the woman!"

In spite of his hideous, cowardly actions, Jennifer still could not help feeling sorry for the man as his screams continued. Surely he was being killed slowly. She vaguely remembered reading somewhere once that when the Comanche found a cowardly captive, they took delight in killing him slowly. It seemed the article had said that they respected bravery, and she knew that was her only hope, a very faint one at that. But how was she going to keep from screaming when she felt a savage hand on her arm?

She did not have long to wonder. Pure shock and terror were all that kept the screams from coming when she was viciously jerked from the carriage. She felt a sharp pain in her ribs and right shoulder, realizing only then that she must have been injured when all the bodies fell on her. For the moment those injuries seemed minor compared to the horror she saw when two painted warriors pulled her from the coach.

Bodies lay strewn everywhere. Several were Indians; the rest were the nine men she had come to know, except that most were nearly unrecognizable because they were so bloody and cut up. It was mainly the clothing she recognized. Buck was tumbling around several feet away, screaming as he was jabbed repeatedly with lances.

The two men who had pulled Jennifer from the coach dragged her then toward several others, all of them hooting and hollering at the sight of her. One grasped her hair, yanking hard on it, ripping off her hat and tearing the hair from its pins until it fell long. She forced herself not to scream, having no idea if it would do any good to try to act unafraid. Inside she wanted to die, and she prayed that if she was going to, it would be quickly.

As gunfire and shouting rang in her ears, and her stomach churned so that she was sure she would vomit any moment, she wondered vaguely what had happened to poor Wade Morrow. The Indians ripped at her dress, tearing it away and holding it up like a prize; they began tossing her back and forth, tearing off her petticoats. She heard a gunshot, and pain ripped through her left thigh, making her crumple to the ground. She knew she had been shot, but now it all seemed to be happening in a kind of strange nightmare, but not really to her.

Her abductors were laughing now, apparently thinking it was funny that she had been shot. She smelled smoke and realized they must have set fire to the coach. None of it mattered now. She was rolled onto her back and someone grabbed her hair. Was she going to be scalped alive, allowed to lay bleeding while they all raped her?

In the distance Wade regained consciousness. He lay still for a moment, opening his eyes to see the destruction. He realized he had not been touched yet only because he had lain still. Perhaps they had thought him already dead. Or, because of his dark skin, maybe in the confusion they had mistaken him for one of their own.

Whatever the reason, he was the only one left, or at least he thought at first that he was. He heard a man's screams then, and he saw Buck being tortured in the distance. Several Indians were dancing around another body. He watched for a moment, realizing with an aching heart that it was Jennifer. He could see her white bloomers and chemise, but she was making no sound.

He had clung to his rifle when he leaped from the coach, and now it lay nearby. He realized most of the Indians' attention was on the two remaining captives. He cautiously reached out for his rifle. He would surely die today, but he vowed at that moment that whatever it took, he would get to Jennifer Andrews first and kill her quickly.

He grasped the rifle then and rose up, firing the repeater several times and eliminating four of the Indians who were prepared to strip and rape Jennifer. The rest of them turned in surprise, and Wade fired again, saving his last bullet for Jennifer, who lay with blood soaking one leg and running down her face. She stared at him strangely, and Wade knew she was in shock.

One of the warriors raised a rifle and aimed it at Wade, but another put out a hand to stop him from firing. He said something in the Comanche tongue that sounded to Wade like "Strong Spirit."

All of those around Jennifer suddenly quieted, staring at Wade as though he were some kind of ghost. "Wild Horse," one of them muttered in the Comanche tongue. As Wade came closer, they all stepped back as though afraid. In the distance Buck's screams had finally ceased. He lay in a bloody heap as the rest of the raiders walked back to the coach to loot what they could. They hesitated when they saw how their friends were watching a tall man with a rifle. They frowned, coming closer. The man looked like one of them, yet he wore the pants and boots of a white man.

"Stay back! We go," one of them was saying to Wade then in the Comanche tongue.

Wade was fairly sure what the man had said, and he was

confused by their abrupt change in behavior. They could easily shoot him down and finish having their way with Jennifer, but they were backing off. Several of them scrambled to pick up their dead comrades, for whenever possible the Comanche took their dead with them after a battle. A few others grabbed some of the baggage and a bottle of whiskey that lay unbroken. Those who had tortured Buck came closer, looking shocked when they saw Wade, behaving in the same manner as the others had. They quickly mounted their ponies, one of them staring at Wade and repeating the name "Wild Horse," another saying "Bad Spirit."

"Tell Wild Horse! Tell Wild Horse," said another, as he turned his horse and rode off so fast that he disappeared in seconds.

One of the warriors again raised a rifle to Wade, but another knocked it away. "No," he shouted in the clipped tongue of the Comanche. "If you kill him, you kill Wild Horse! We must tell him what we have seen!"

They turned and rode off, and seconds later they were all gone. The air hung suddenly silent and heavy, the smell of blood and opened bodies stinging Wade's nostrils. He looked around at the ugly remains, still in a mild form of shock himself, realizing that he was related to the people who had done this. Why had the warriors stared at him that way? Why had they been afraid of him? Some had said Wild Horse's name, as though they were looking at the man when they looked at Wade. Why was he a "strong spirit" or a "bad spirit?" An odd intuition moved through him, one he did not want to name or think about for the moment.

You might have been a twin, his father had told him. Someone had said Wild Horse was a half-breed with blue eyes. "It couldn't be," he muttered. For the moment it didn't matter. He set down his rifle and walked over to Jennifer, who watched him in wide-eyed terror as he came closer. He realized he must look like all the others to her at the moment. She clawed at him and fought him when he bent down to help her, and he had to force her arms behind

143

her back as he knelt to his knees and pulled her tight against him.

"It's all right, Miss Andrews," he told her firmly. "It's all right. They've gone and we're both still alive. I'm going to help you."

She kept struggling, uttering little grunts of terror, but he hung on tightly, holding her close and repeating her name until finally she quieted. He closed his eyes, secretly thanking God that she had not been raped or fully scalped. He gently released her, laying her against a clump of grass. A deep cut could be seen along the hairline of her forehead, where a warrior had started to scalp her but had stopped, probably when he had seen Wade. Whatever the reason for the spell he had had over the Comanche raiders, he was glad for it. It had saved both his and Jennifer's lives.

"You lie still. I'm going to help you," he told Jennifer, his heart aching for her condition and the terror she must be feeling. He scanned her body quickly, studying the wound on her thigh and deciding it looked more like a bullet wound than lance or knife. He did not relish the thought that the bullet would have to be removed.

He leaned over her again, gently putting a hand to her face. "I'm going to move you to the shade of that rock over there," he told her, indicating a large boulder a few feet away. "Then I'll try to find my canteen and whatever else I can find to wash and bandage your wounds. Don't be afraid, Miss Andrews. The cut on your scalp will heal and you'll look as beautiful as ever. And I'll take care of that leg. You're going to be all right. I won't leave you. I'll get you to Fort Stockton if I have to carry you all the way."

He gave her a reassuring smile, but his own head ached fiercely and was bleeding from the blow he had taken when he jumped from the coach. Jennifer just stared at him as he reached for one of her petticoats that lay nearby and ripped it, gently tying a piece of it around her leg. She cried out then as the pain of the wound hit her.

Wade knew that as her shock slowly wore off, the pain would get worse. He hoped there was some whiskey left somewhere that he could use for her to drink and to pour

144

on the wound when he took out the bullet. The coach snapped and popped as flames enveloped it, and he knew there was no hope of salvaging anything that might have been left on top or inside.

"This bandage is just temporary because of the bleeding," he told Jennifer. "I have to find supplies before I can help you any more." He pressed another piece of petticoat to her head. "This one is slowing. I'll wash it good—try to keep the cut nice and clean so it doesn't leave much of a scar."

Jennifer still did not speak. She kept her eyes on him like a trusting little girl as he picked her up in his arms and carried her to a grassier spot, laying her in the shadow of the boulder. "Just lie still," he repeated.

He rose, turning to watch the coach continue to burn. Luckily a good share of the baggage that had been on top of the coach, including his saddle and gear, had spilled far enough away not to be harmed by the fire. He quickly took inventory of the rest of the bodies. He did not have to kneel down and check any of them to see if they were dead. He was only glad they had died quickly. He felt an ache in his heart at the sight of Nick's arrow-riddled body. Nick Elliott had been a good man.

He felt equal sorrow at the sight of Ernie lying under the burning coach. The man's eyes were still open, and his shirt and hair were on fire. Flames began to eat into his face then, and Wade turned away, torn with confusion over his own identity. If he had been raised by the Comanche, would he have done things like this?

He thought he saw movement then from Buck's body in the distance. With a pain in his stomach he hurried over to the man's naked body, feeling nauseous at the nearly unrecognizable body that was covered with what seemed hundreds of stabs. He stared at Wade, and Wade wasn't sure the man even knew who he was.

"Kill . . . me," he begged. "You . . . stinking . . . savage! Kill me . . . and get it . . . over with!"

His body began to shake violently, and Wade knew there was no hope for him. Whether Buck knew it was

Wade Morrow, or thought he was just another one of the renegades, he would never know. In spite of how he had felt about the man, he could not leave him in such misery. He pulled his pistol from its holster at his side and aimed it, thinking how he had done this to his horse not long ago. It seemed strange how quickly life could be snuffed out of man and animal alike. One moment his horse had been healthy and strong, the next it was down and dying. It had been the same for these men, with whom only hours ago he had shared breakfast.

"God forgive me," he said softly, as he pulled the trigger and put a bullet in Buck's head. The man lay still.

Wade turned away, holstering his gun and blinking back tears. He hurried to where baggage lay strewn. There was no time for mourning these men or contemplating life and death. There was only Jennifer Andrews, lying wounded, depending on him alone for help. He had to find whatever supplies he could to aid her. Once he had tended to her, he had to decide how he was going to get her to Fort Stockton. He could only hope that whatever the reason was that the Comanche had left him alive, they would stick to it and not come back.

Back where he had left her, Jennifer lay staring at a blue sky, trying to gather her thoughts. Everything hurt, especially her leg, which felt on fire. Had she been dreaming when she thought the raiders had ridden away; when she had seen Wade Morrow alive and bending over her, telling her he would help her? How could either of them have survived this terrible thing? She had to know if it was real, if the Indians were truly gone and Wade Morrow was still alive.

She looked around as best she could from where she lay. All she saw was the mutilated body of Adam Hughes. Poor Mr. Hughes! He had been kind to her. Never had she known such horror. She finally found her voice, uttering a pitiful cry of despair before calling Wade's name. She must have only dreamed he had lived. She put a hand to a wetness at her face and removed it to see blood on her fingers. Had she been scalped? She vaguely remembered

146

one of the raiders grasping her hair and putting a knife to her forehead. No!

Again she screamed Wade's name. Was she left here alone then? Were they coming back to finish her off later? Was this where her life would end? Mattie. What would Mattie think? She would never know what had happened to her.

Suddenly a tall, dark man stood over her, and the horror of her attack revisited her. It was one of them! "No," she screamed, over and over. He came closer, putting his arms around her and pulling her up slightly, holding her close.

"It's all right," he was saying. "It's me—Wade Morrow, remember? They've left, Jennifer. We'll be all right. I'm going to help you."

He had spoken her first name as though it was perfectly natural. She felt the choking sobs come then, and she could not stop them. Thank God she was still alive, and so was Wade Morrow. She let him hold her, needing to be held. She couldn't care less that it was the half-breed man who did the holding. His voice sounded wonderful. His arms felt wonderful, strong, and sure. If anyone could help her and get her to safety, Wade Morrow could.

147

Chapter Ten

Jennifer came to later that evening. Her memory of the first few hours after the attack was filled only with pain, and Wade Morrow's consoling touch and voice. She was in too much shock and too sick and weak to be modest. She didn't care that he slit open one side of her bloomers with his knife so that he could tend to the wound in her thigh. She only wanted the terrible burning pain to stop.

She remembered choking down a liquid that seemed to set her insides on fire, but Wade had told her she must drink it to help the pain. She remembered him saying something about taking out a bullet and that he was sorry to hurt her. She remembered screaming and begging him to stop when something dug at her leg, and she remembered she could not move then. He had tied her hands and her legs to something so that she wouldn't thrash around, and he sat on the wounded leg so she would keep it still.

There had been moments when in her pain and delirium she thought the Indians were torturing her, and moments when she thought it was Buck holding her down. Then there was nothing—only a blessed sleep, or had she been unconscious? She was not sure as she lay quietly now next to a fire. She had no idea where she was, only that her leg still hurt, but not as badly as before. She also knew instinctively that Wade Morrow was somewhere nearby, that he had made the fire, and that she was safe.

She was so weary she could not muster the strength to

call out his name. She just lay staring at the flames for several minutes, trying to gather her thoughts. Dead, all dead! Adam Hughes, Buck, Lou, Sid Menden, Larry Buchanan, Hank, Will. She vaguely remembered seeing Nick's body shot full of arrows. She couldn't remember seeing Ernie Peters at all, and she felt nauseous when she remembered seeing the raiders torturing Buck.

She shuddered at the remembered screams, the blood, the horror; at the memory of savages grabbing her, ripping at her clothes, pushing her around, shooting her, and holding her down to scalp her. She wasn't quite sure what had happened after that. It seemed that suddenly Wade Morrow was standing there, and the Indians let go of her and backed away. She could not imagine why. How could so many warriors be afraid of one man? Whatever the reason, she was still alive, and so was Wade.

After that there had been only Wade Morrow, his voice, his arms, his touch. She moved one hand to feel herself, to be sure she was really alive. She realized then that she wore only her chemise and remnants of bloomers. Under the blanket that covered her she moved a hand over her left hip, which was mostly bare; down to her thigh, where she felt bandages. Humiliation overwhelmed her then as she realized Wade Morrow had seen her bare leg and most of her hip—had seen her in only her underwear, her bare arms and shoulders exposed. How could she face him! She wondered if he had seen the scars on her back from the riverboat fire.

Her feelings were a mixture of gratefulness and humiliation. He couldn't help seeing her the way he had. He'd had no choice. He was only trying to help her. Yet he was a man, and a near stranger at that. Had he taken privileges with her she didn't know about? Had he looked at more than was necessary? She wished she could crawl away somewhere and just reappear in some civilized town, mended and healthy, never having to look into Wade Morrow's eyes again.

He suddenly appeared at the fire and she quickly closed her eyes, wanting him to think she was still asleep, or passed out, whatever she had been. She couldn't face him yet. She heard a sizzling sound and knew he was cooking something over a fire. Then she felt him come closer. In the next moment a big hand touched her face, smoothing back her hair.

"Come on, Jenny, wake up," he said softly. "Don't you die on me."

The words sent a rush of emotions through her, in spite of her pain. He had called her Jenny, with such intimacy and tenderness. He seemed to care so much, and she felt cruel not letting him know she was better. She felt him pulling the blanket away from her leg then, and she squeezed her eyes tighter, feeling the hotness at her face as it grew red with embarrassment. He placed his big hands on her leg, one just below and one just above the wound, on the side of her hip.

"At least there doesn't seem to be any infection yet," he muttered.

Tears of shame and embarrassment that he was looking at her engulfed her then, compounded by her pain and exhaustion. She choked in a sob and he quickly put back the blanket.

"Jenny?" He touched her face again. "Don't cry, Jenny. The Comanche are gone. I don't think they're coming back. I found a place for us to camp where you wouldn't have to wake up tomorrow and see the bodies. You in a lot of pain?"

"You shouldn't . . . see me this way," she sobbed, putting a hand to her face. She realized then her head was bandaged. "Oh, God," she moaned. "What did . . . they do to me. My . . . hair! They took my hair!"

He grasped her hand and squeezed it. "No they didn't. They only started to. All you've got is a cut along the hairline. It will heal. The biggest danger is your leg, Jenny. Can you move it at all?"

She clung to his hand, suddenly comforted, losing some of her embarrassment. After all, he was only trying to help her. "I . . . don't know," she answered, holding his hand tightly. "I'm afraid . . . to try."

151

"Then don't. Not tonight. Just lie real still." He touched her cheek with the back of his hand. "I took a bullet out of your leg, Jenny. I hated hurting you that way, but it had to be done. There's no reason for you to be embarrassed about anything. You needed help."

She shook in another sob and his heart ached for her. It was difficult to ignore the feelings he had for this young woman who must be so alone in the world. What must her uncle be like that she had to come out here and expose herself to these horrors? Where had she got the burn scars on her back? And if she was this bashful about letting him help her, how could she possibly submit herself to marrying a total stranger?

Already he had feelings of jealousy for the mysterious Sergeant Enders, who was waiting for this woman to come to him. He admired Jennifer Andrews's courage. She probably didn't even remember gritting her teeth and trying not to cry out when he cut into her leg—and what a slender, beautiful leg it was. He felt like a fiend, thinking about what he had seen—her round, firm hip; thinking about how velvety her skin was, how small and vulnerable she was, how pretty were her green eyes, cascading auburn hair, and her full lips.

He moved away from her then, gently letting go of her hand. "I want you to try to eat something," he told her. How he hated himself for feeling the way he did. It was wrong, and could lead nowhere. Why and when he had felt compelled to call her Jenny, he wasn't even sure. It just seemed to come naturally. Why was he constantly forced to be a part of this young woman's life?

This entire event had thrown a whole new kink in his plans to try to find some Indian relatives. After what he had witnessed, he wasn't sure he wanted to know anything more about them; yet he had a keen desire to understand the reasons behind such hideous raiding. Still, could he go riding into a renegade camp and expect to live through it?

He knelt down to turn the rabbit meat he was cooking in a pan, glad to have found enough supplies left to survive for a few days. He at least had his gun and ammunition.

He had killed the rabbit earlier, while Jennifer slept.

He gazed into the darkness beyond the camp fire. Were some of the renegades out there, watching, studying him? He was greatly disturbed by how they had reacted to him, mentioning the name of their own leader, Wild Horse. Wild Horse was a half-breed, just like himself. Was that all there was to it? Had they spared his life just because he had Comanche blood? Or was it something more? He knew deep inside that somehow he had to meet the one called Wild Horse, no matter what the danger. If he simply went on home now, this incident would haunt him the rest of his life.

He looked back at Jennifer, who lay crying quietly and wiping at tears with her blanket. Meeting her had interrupted his plans and his thoughts. It wasn't just that he had to help her and get her to Fort Stockton. After all, he was going there himself. The problem was he would be alone with her for the next few days, close to her, feeding her, dressing her. He would get to know her better than he wanted to know her, for to allow himself to get too close to her could mean disaster for him, both physically and emotionally. What would the soldiers at Fort Stockton think when he came walking in with her, knowing she had been alone with him for several days? He knew how men like that thought. It might even make trouble between her and the man she was supposed to marry.

He reasoned that if Sergeant Enders was any kind of a real man, he would understand; but when it came to Indians and white women, few white men had any room for understanding. They always thought the worst. Trouble was, he wouldn't mind the worst being true. Ever since the night Jennifer had daringly spoken to him back at the first home station, he had not been able to get her off his mind. Now this.

"I . . . need water," she spoke up.

Wade quickly retrieved his canteen and came to her side. He knelt down and helped support her head, holding the canteen to her lips. She gulped the water eagerly.

"Not too much at once," he told her. "It's always like

this with a bullet wound. Makes a person mighty thirsty."

She swallowed gratefully, then looked up at him. "Have you ever been shot?"

He thought of Rebecca. "More than once," he answered. He gently laid her back down. "When you drive supply trains through Indian and outlaw country, it's almost a sure bet you're going to take a bullet. So far I've just been lucky nothing vital was ever hit."

He walked back to the camp fire, and she watched him, thinking again what a skilled, brave man he was. She realized he could look just as wild and fierce as the warriors who had attacked them earlier, and it seemed so strange that he was as civilized and soft-spoken as any white man.

"Where are we?" she asked.

He sat down across the fire from her. "About two days from Fort Stockton." He began rolling a cigarette. "It will be that long before the soldiers there realize something must have happened to the coach. They might even give it another two days to arrive before they send out patrols. The forts out here are short on men, and if they know there are raiders on the loose again, they'll be extra careful about sending out small patrols that could get wiped out." He lit the cigarette with a small stick from the fire and took a deep drag.

"What does all that . . . mean? We . . . have to wait here for . . . four or five days? What if . . . the Indians . . . come back?"

"I don't think they will." He met her eyes, taking the cigarette from his mouth. "For some reason they let us live. I just hope they decide to leave it that way." He looked around. "As far as just waiting here, I'm not sure. If we wait for them to come to us, you're talking four to six days for a patrol to find us, and another two or three days getting you to the fort. I hate to take that long getting you to a decent bed and out of the elements, let alone worrying about infection. I just wish I had a horse, but the stage team ran off, or else the Indians stole them. I'm not sure which. Either way, I need to get you to the fort."

154

"But how? I . . . can't walk."

He smoked another moment. "I don't know yet. I'll carry you if I have to."

Her eyes teared with gratefulness and admiration. "I'm . . . sorry. Without me . . . you could probably make it fine . . . on your own."

He met her eyes. "It's not your fault. I'm just glad I came around when I did and prevented them from hurting you more."

She felt the color coming back to her face, realizing he must know what they intended to do to her. "I don't understand . . . why they do . . . such horrible things. We didn't . . . do anything to . . . them. It must . . . seem so strange to you . . . having Comanche blood."

"It does. Puts me in an awkward position. That's part of the reason I'm out here. I intend to find out more about my Indian side." He laughed lightly but sarcastically. "I got a good lesson today, didn't I?"

She closed her eyes, a dull pain moving through her leg. "I don't . . . understand this land . . . the Indians, the prejudice. It's all so . . . wild and different." *"Like you,"* she felt like adding. "Nothing . . . is the way I . . . had pictured it. I don't know . . . what to think now about . . . Fort Stockton and . . . Sergeant Enders. I just . . . hurt everywhere . . . and I'm scared."

He came around the fire, spreading out his bedroll. "You don't have to be afraid. I might look like one of them, but you know by now I'm here to help you, not hurt you. In a minute we'll eat some fresh rabbit."

"I . . . don't know if I . . . can eat. My head hurts . . . and I feel kind of sick."

"Probably all that whiskey I made you drink. But you couldn't have stood the pain without it."

"I've never . . . drunk whiskey . . . before."

He smiled a warm, handsome smile. "Well, you got a good introduction."

"I don't think . . . I want any more."

He laughed lightly and leaned toward the fire to again turn the rabbit. It was then she noticed traces of a bruise at

155

the left side of his forehead. "You're hurt," she said in concern.

He put a hand to the spot. "Just a bad bump. The biggest share of it is under my hair. Quite an egg. I jumped from the coach as it was going over and my head hit a rock. I think that's what saved me at first. I was unconscious for a few minutes, and the raiders must have thought I was already wounded, or dead."

"How about . . . your ankle?"

"It's a lot better." He came to her side again. "You want to try to sit up a little?"

"I don't know." She tried on her own and grimaced with pain in her ribs and shoulder. "Oh . . . I forgot," she moaned, sweat breaking out on her face.

He threw his cigarette aside. "You shouldn't try to do it alone."

"My side . . . and my shoulder. When the coach . . . overturned . . . everyone fell on top of me." The pain made her feel short of breath, bringing on a panic she would not normally feel if not still somewhat in shock. She grasped his arm, telling him she felt like she couldn't breathe, but in the next moment his big hands were pressed at either side of her face, his deep, calm voice telling her to relax. Her fear suddenly left her again. He was so calm and sure in spite of the horror of the day, and she knew from what he had already done that he would not leave her even if the Indians came back.

"I should have thought of other injuries," he fretted. He pulled the blanket to her waist, and she closed her eyes against her embarrassment as his strong but gentle hands moved over her ribs carefully. She realized he could break her in half, could do whatever he wanted with her, yet she was not afraid of him. "You probably have a couple of cracked ribs," he was saying. "I'll wrap you tight. That will help the pain." He checked her shoulder and she grimaced at the pain there. "I'll see what I can do about this, too. Probably just badly bruised. If something was broken you wouldn't be able to move your arm at all. It didn't help being dragged out of the coach like that."

He left her for a moment, coming back with some torn strips of petticoat. "I'm sorry to have to rip up your own clothes, but they were all I could find for bandages. You have two or three dresses left and a couple of petticoats."

She thought how strange it seemed that he had searched through her intimate things, that now he was pushing up her chemise to wrap her bare ribs with the cloth. He was careful not to expose her breasts, but her shame knew no bounds. Still, it was lessened by his seemingly genuine concern, and his expert attention to her injuries. He reached under her to grasp the cloth, wrapping it around and around. By the time he was through, breathing was not as painful. He wrapped her right arm to her side so that it could not move around too much.

"This will help the pain in your shoulder until it's better," he told her. "Now you just lie still while I feed you a little meat and some strong coffee. Then I want you to try to sleep again. Don't be afraid of one thing."

Her eyes teared again. "Thank you," she said in a near whisper. "Promise me . . . something."

"What's that?"

"If they . . . come back." She swallowed. "You won't let them . . . get to me . . . even if you have to kill me before they can?"

Their eyes held, and he wanted so much to hold her. *I'd never let them touch you,* he wanted to tell her. *I don't want any man but me to touch you.* "I won't let them get to you," he said aloud. "That's a promise. Earlier today, when I came to—" He searched her eyes. "My intentions were to shoot you then. But for some reason they let you go and ran off. I'm glad." He smiled almost bashfully then. "It sure would have been a waste. You're quite a woman."

She looked at the fire. "I don't know about that. It probably . . . wasn't very smart of me . . . to come out here." She looked at him again, alarm in her eyes. "My baggage! My handbag! Did you find it?"

He reached over toward his gear and retrieved her purse, handing it over to her. "Don't worry. The money is still in it."

She closed her eyes and clutched the drawstring, beaded bag. "Thank goodness. I have . . . little enough left . . ."

"You figuring on reimbursing that Sergeant Enders if you don't marry him?" *You shouldn't marry him*, he wanted to add. *It isn't right, something as pretty and cultured as you, living the miserable life of a soldier's wife in west Texas.*

She met his eyes, surprised at the realization that she was apprehensive now about marrying Sergeant Enders, yet she would marry someone like Wade Morrow without knowing him any better than she already did, and in spite of his bloodlines. Somehow she knew she could trust him, that he would be kind to her. But it was not Wade Morrow she had come out here to marry.

"Yes," she answered his original question. "I don't have enough left, but maybe . . . I can work it off. If I'm lucky . . . Sergeant Enders will be a fine . . . man . . . and it will be no problem."

She closed her eyes, trying to quell her fear of meeting her intended. What would he think of all of this? And what would he think if he knew of her attraction to Wade Morrow? She wanted to ask Wade what he thought of the whole thing, but it seemed ridiculous to get him involved. There were so many things she wanted to tell him, wanted to ask. Little did she know it was the same for him. "I can't eat," she told him then. "Maybe in the morning. I just . . . I want to sleep."

Wade sighed. "All right, but just tonight. You never ate breakfast this morning, and you're so slender that one good west wind could blow you clear back to San Antonio. I didn't go through all this and get you fixed up just to have you die of starvation."

She put a hand to her aching head. "Where are the others? Are we very far from the coach?"

"About a quarter of a mile—not far enough. I found a spot just over a little hill from the site so you won't have to see anything come light. I'll rig up some kind of travois tomorrow if I can use some things off the coach. I found enough of my own gear and a few other things to get us by.

158

I found both your bags, although some things were spilled out of them. A few items were looted, and I don't know what happened to the horses. I don't relish going back there in the morning and looking at all those bodies again." He poked at the fire. "I wanted to bury them, but there was no time. I had to tend to you. And in the morning we've got to get out of here. I'm sorry to leave the bodies, but we can't sit around here. Wolves and vultures and coyotes will come snooping around, and like I said, I've got to get you to the fort."

She rubbed at her eyes, the horror of the day taking its toll again on her emotions as a painful lump swelled in her throat. She felt so useless, such a burden to Wade Morrow, who would probably much prefer making his way to the fort alone. Without her along, such a journey would not be difficult for a man like him. All of this was like a horrible nightmare that would not end.

"What's a . . . travois?" she asked, sniffing back more tears.

He turned the rabbit once more, then took a piece from the pan and put it into a tin plate. "It's a contraption the Indians use—a piece of hide stretched between two poles and tied to a horse. They load their supplies on it and drag them along that way." He bit into the rabbit.

"But . . . we don't have a horse," she answered, wiping tears from her eyes.

He swallowed the rabbit. "I'll pull it myself."

She frowned. "Oh, but . . . you mustn't. It would be . . . too heavy!"

"I'll manage. I don't have much choice. Maybe we'll get lucky and come across the horses."

She didn't know what to say. A simple thank you didn't seem right. One thing she did know was that from this moment on she would never again pretend she didn't know him or was not interested in him as a fellow human being. She felt ashamed that she had ignored him earlier on the trip, even though he had himself insisted on it. He was a fine man, educated, kind, giving, honest. It was ridiculous that he was forbidden to associate with certain

159

people. She was proud to know him, grateful for the help he had been to her since that day in San Antonio when he defended her.

She gradually fell into an exhausted sleep, vaguely thinking how she would be spending the night alone with this half-breed who looked hardly different from the Indians who had abused her; yet she was not afraid. Somewhere in the night she was aware that she was shaking and crying, and that he came to lie down beside her, covering both of them with two more blankets.

"Don't be afraid," he had told her. "I'm just lying close to you to keep you warmer." She was pulled into strong, warm arms, and she nestled against him, the shaking subsiding. It was the last thing she remembered before waking up to the smell of coffee the next morning.

She looked around but did not see Wade. With great pain and effort she managed to sit up, using her left arm for support. She looked around more, seeing Wade nowhere about. It looked as though there was fresh wood on the fire, and with coffee steaming, she knew he had to be nearby. Perhaps he had gone back to the stagecoach to build the travois he had told her about.

She remembered him sleeping next to her in the night, holding her, keeping her warm. How strange it seemed that she didn't even mind. She looked down at her chemise, realizing how much of her bosom was revealed by the cotton lace undergarment, and she wondered with both shame and fascination if he had noticed. Her emotions were torn, and she attributed it to her condition. She was simply too dependent on Wade Morrow for the moment. These feelings would go away in time.

She had a great need to urinate, and the last thing she wanted was for Wade to have to help her with such a thing. Since he was gone she decided to fend for herself and get it over with before he returned. She pulled the blanket away to look at her bandaged leg, and she gasped at the size of the bandage and the bloodstain that showed through it. Her leg looked scarlet above the bandage, and she wondered with dread if it would get infected like Wade was worried about. She had heard of people having their legs cut off because of infection. She could not imagine anything more horrible.

She realized her bloomers were cut open at the side all the way to the elastic waist. The entire left side of her bottom showed. Again the humiliation returned. She was more determined than ever to take care of private things on her own, no matter how much it hurt. She rolled to her right side, grimacing at the pain in her shoulder. Supporting herself with her left hand and arm, she managed to get up on her right knee. She cried out then as she used her left knee for support while she got her right foot under her, then raised herself to a standing position with her right leg.

The moment she stepped on her left leg to walk, she almost fell because of the pain. She grimaced, forcing herself to continue, limping to a clump of cacti, the only thing she could find to provide at least limited privacy. With her left hand she managed to pull down her bloomers. The cactus near her had only knobs toward its bottom arms, no needles. She grasped one arm and used it to support herself as she squatted, keeping her left leg out straight. She felt ridiculously awkward, and she prayed Wade Morrow would not come along until she was finished. With her left hand she tore a bottom ruffle from the already-ripped left leg of her bloomers and used it to clean herself, then grunted with pain as she rose and pulled her bloomers back up, realizing they covered only half of her.

She turned to limp back to her bedroll when she saw him—a painted Indian on a horse, sitting on a nearby ridge watching her. Her heart raced, and it took her a moment to find her voice. "Wade," she finally screamed. "Wade! Wade!" She realized she should have said "Mr. Morrow," but using his first name came as easily to her as using hers had come to him. After what they had been through, it hardly seemed important.

She stood shaking, screaming his name over and over, then turned when she heard him call back to her. He came

161

running from over the ridge behind her, rifle in hand. He reached her in seconds, panting. "What is it?"

She turned and pointed to the opposite ridge, but the figure was gone. "Up there," she said frantically. "I saw an Indian . . . on a horse! He . . . was watching me."

He left her, hurrying up the hill, and Jennifer waited, her heart pounding, fearing a band of raiders would come over the ridge any moment and murder him. Moments later he returned, leading a sleek, spotted horse behind him. It sported a saddle and bridle, although not like any Jennifer had ever seen. An Indian blanket was under the saddle. Wade walked straight to Jennifer, looking confused.

"He left this horse," he told her, "as though he knew we would need it."

She held his eyes, her own still showing terror. "Why?"

He frowned. "I don't know. All I know is they seem awfully eager to keep me alive." His eyes fell to the enticing whites of her exposed bosom before meeting her eyes again, and she realized she was standing there in her underwear, her left leg and hip showing clear to the waist. "What the hell are you doing up on that leg?" he asked gruffly.

"I . . ." She reddened deeply, putting a hand over her breasts. "I had to do something . . . you weren't here."

He realized what she meant and he felt sorry for the devastated look on her face. He let go of the pony and in the next moment she was in his arms. "Don't ever do that again. It won't take much to get your leg bleeding again. I've had a hell of a time keeping that from happening. I can help you, Jenny. I told you before not to be afraid or be bashful around me."

He picked her up and carried her back to her bedroll, setting her down on it. She pulled a blanket across the front of herself as he checked her leg. "It's bleeding again, damn it. I don't want you doing another thing without my help. I'm going to get the travois I was working on. I'll tie the pony. At least now we have something to pull the travois. If this bleeding doesn't slow by the time I get back,

I'll rewrap your leg before we leave."

He met her eyes, and it was her first chance to study him closely in the daylight, now that she was free to set eyes on him all she wanted. His eyes were bluer than she thought, intensely handsome when set against the dark skin. His features were as perfect as a man's features could be, with high cheekbones and dark hair and full lips. She thought again about how he had held her the night before, and she wondered if he was thinking the same thing as his eyes suddenly took on a look of near worship. He looked as though he wanted to say something, but he suddenly turned away. He glanced at the ridge again, but no one was there.

"I'll go get the travois," he told her. "That Indian apparently didn't mean any harm, so I think you're all right. I'll be right back."

She wanted to cry out to him, to beg him to come back and hold her just for a moment, for the incident had terrified her all over again. She realized she would be entirely dependent on him for the next several days, and that was not going to help her avoid the growing emotional feelings she had for the half-breed man who was supposedly forbidden to someone like herself. She was not supposed to feel this way. She should be thinking about Sergeant Anthony Enders. But then maybe she would never reach Fort Stockton.

Chapter Eleven

Jennifer lay on the travois, thinking how strange her journey had become. It seemed as though she had known Wade Morrow for a very long time. She was fast losing her modesty and embarrassment around him because she had no choice. At noon he had cooked for her, carried her in his arms to a place where she could relieve herself, had come back for her and carried her again to the travois, then changed the bandage on her leg. He tended the wound with the same concern and personal detachment as a doctor might.

By evening Wade guessed they had traveled perhaps fifteen miles. He was taking a more direct route to the fort than the stage trail, hoping to get there more quickly, but in some ways Jennifer didn't want to get there at all. She felt safe and protected with Wade, but she had no idea what to expect from Sergeant Anthony Enders, and suddenly the thought of Wade delivering her at the fort and then going his own way made her sad.

Wade found a stream that still rushed with water because of the recent rain. He commented how lucky they were to have found it, since in these parts water did not come easily. "You want to wash?" he asked her. "I'll wash your hair for you if you like. I can take that bandage off your head. The cut would probably heal better now if we let air get to it."

"Oh, I would love to wash my hair," she answered,

managing to sit up. "I'd like a real bath, that's what I'd really like. But if I could wash my neck and arms and maybe change my—" She reddened then, realizing there was no place in this open land to hide while she did such things. "I'd like to put on some clean clothes and a dress."

He untied her bags from their gear. "You find what you need and I'll carry you to the stream. If you want different bloomers, I'll have to cut one leg off so I can keep changing the bandage on that wound. I hate to keep cutting up your clothes, but it's important to keep that wound clean and tended. The last thing you want is infection."

She kept her eyes averted, digging out clean underwear and a plain gray cotton dress. "I hope I'm able to buy some clothes at the fort, or at least send for some."

"They usually have quite a few supplies. You probably won't be the only woman there."

"Oh, I hope you're right. I'd be so lonely without a woman to talk to."

He met her eyes, studying her quietly for a moment. "If, uh, if things don't work out for you there, you don't have to stay, you know. The stage runs through there every week."

She looked down at a bar of soap she had retrieved from her bag. "You think I'm crazy, don't you?"

He came closer. "Not crazy—just ignorant of what it's like out here—and what most men at those forts are like." He sighed and gave her a smile. "But maybe it will all work out. I hope it does."

She met his eyes. *I would rather stay with you*, she felt like saying. How she wished she understood men better, wished she could be sure what he was really thinking and feeling inside. Could he read her own thoughts? He had taken a towel from his own gear and he picked her up. She wanted to put her arms around his neck, to cling to him and beg him not to take her to the fort. When he held her this way, she could catch his masculine scent, was too close to his full lips, too overwhelmed by his strength and

166

closeness. Was it her wounds and dependency that made her feel this way?

"I'm sorry I pretended not to know you and couldn't talk to you earlier," she told him. "I didn't like doing that, but you and Nick insisted."

"It was best."

"I don't care any more. It was rude and wrong. I'm not made that way, and I don't care what it costs me, I'll never behave that way again, not after what you've done for me."

He stopped near the stream, still holding her. He looked down at her, thinking how light and pretty she was, how close her lips were to his own. She was young and ignorant enough of life out here that she found nothing wrong with being friends with a half-breed. In fact, he was sure he had caught something more than gratefulness in those green eyes; but he didn't dare allow himself the luxury of contemplating anything romantic with this lovely creature. It would mean hell for them both. He told himself she was just feeling afraid now, and she needed him. In three or four more days they would make the fort, and that would be the end of this strange encounter.

He set her down then, irritated at the feelings the thought of her being with another man brought him. He knew what men at those forts were like. It was highly unlikely her Sergeant Enders would be patient and kind with her. In one night he would destroy her sweet innocence, and her trust. The thought of some man rushing her and being cruel to her tore at his insides, but he kept reminding himself it was not his business. Still, whenever he stole glances at the milky white mounds of her full, firm breasts that peeked from the ruffled bodice of her camisole, the thought of another man ravishing such beauty and being cruel about it tore at his guts like a knife.

"I appreciate your kindness," he told her, "but once we reach the fort, I wouldn't display too much affection if I were you. We simply survived a raid and you had no choice but to let me help you. In fact, you'd be best to act as though you're glad to finally get there and not have to be

167

alone any more with a half-breed man."

"I'll do no such thing." She looked at him with a scowl. "I can't be that cruel and ungrateful, and I won't lie. Now please help me wash my hair."

He sighed deeply, setting her on her feet. She set down her clothes, finding it strange that she felt less uncomfortable in front of Wade Morrow in only her underwear than she had felt fully clothed in front of Uncle John.

Wade spread a blanket near the edge of the stream. He picked her up again and lay her down on her back, her head at the edge of the water. "Just put your head back and I'll take off this bandage and wash your hair," he told her. He wondered if she had any idea what torture this was for him, her lying back, her head arched back in the same way it would be if she lay beneath a man, taking him inside herself. He took off the bandage to see the cut at her head was already healing. He soaped her hair, enjoying the exquisite pleasure of tangling his fingers in the thick mane. He dipped her head into the water and rinsed it as best he could, and she screamed lightly at how cold it was. He squeezed the water from it as she sat up then, and he put a towel around it.

"The cut is healing," he told her. "I don't think it will leave much of a scar. You want me to unwrap that arm and shoulder?"

"I think you'll have to, so I can wash better."

"Just don't get water on that leg. Can you manage all this alone?"

She felt the crimson coming to her cheeks then. Seeing her partially clad and wounded was one thing. But much as she needed the help, she could not imagine letting him see her naked. Still, the thought made her realize that she had a terrible desire to please this man, a longing to be touched by him in special ways. But she had no idea how he really felt, or what he would think of her if he knew her thoughts.

"I'll be fine," she answered, as he unwrapped her shoulder. "You . . . you promise to stay turned away, don't you?"

168

He laughed. "I promise. I'll go make a fire."

"I'm sorry. I didn't mean that I don't trust you."

"I know what you meant." He frowned again at the scars on her back. "You mind my asking what happened to your back?"

She reddened more, taking the towel from her hair and holding it over the front of her chemise. "My parents were killed when a steamboat exploded. I was with them. It all happened so fast that I don't remember much about it. One minute we were standing on the deck, and the next thing I knew I was in the water and someone was helping me into a boat. I don't even remember getting burned, except the pain of it later, after the shock wore off."

He sat down beside her on the blanket. "I'm sorry. How old were you?"

She met his eyes. "Ten." *Please hold me again,* she wanted to tell him. "My uncle, John Andrews, took me in." She looked away then. "He stole everything from me—everything that should have been mine. My father was in the merchant business. He was quite wealthy, but I never saw any of it. In fact, I had to sell some of my mother's jewelry to have enough extra money for this trip. I was hoping to have enough to pay back Sergeant Enders if I decide not to marry him, but I'll only have about half what I need."

"Why did you leave St. Louis in the first place? Even if your uncle stole everything, you surely could have found some kind of work there. Did you hate him so much that you couldn't live in the same town with him?"

She looked down at her bandaged leg. "It wasn't that. I could have overcome the loss of my property and such. It was Uncle John himself I had to get away from. He . . . he used to scare me . . . the way he would . . . look at me. I never worried about it until my Aunt Esther died. She was a saint. I loved her very much." Her eyes teared. "But I knew that once she was dead, I wouldn't be safe in the same house with Uncle John. I also knew I wasn't safe anyplace else in town. You have to understand, my uncle is a very wealthy, prominent man in St. Louis. Wherever I went, he

169

would have found some way to make me come back home. I couldn't have complained to anyone about him, because no one would believe he was anything but a fine, upstanding citizen." She shivered. "But I know different." She met his eyes. "You saw how far his power reaches. Somehow he figured out my fake name and sent those men for me in San Antonio."

His blue eyes were full of sympathy. "I think I understand."

Wade put a hand on her arm. "I'm sorry. Seems like sometimes the wealthy men in this world get away with murder. My pa is wealthy, but he isn't like that at all. He's the finest man I know."

She met his eyes, her own showing tears. "It shows in you," she told him. "Why did you defend me that day, Wade? You must have known it would only get you in trouble."

He shrugged. "I had every intention of staying out of it. But the way those men were dragging you off—I don't know. Nobody else was doing anything, so I figured I would. Besides, you remind me of someone."

"I do? Who is that?"

His eyes softened, and she saw there a look of affection that stirred her deeply. "It was a long time ago," he answered. He rose then. "You get washed. Yell if you need me." He bent down and picked up her clean bloomers, taking out his knife and slitting off the left leg near the crotch. "Sorry about that," he said, putting back his knife and walking off.

Jennifer realized he did not want to talk any further about whoever she reminded him of. But she knew without asking it was someone he had loved. So, she must have been white! He had loved a white girl once, and something terrible had happened, she was sure. Her curiosity ran wild, and her heart ached for him—such a fine, brave man, treated so cruelly for no reason other than he looked Indian. It infuriated her.

With great effort she managed to get off her underwear and wash, having no fear that Wade Morrow would stand

170

and gawk at her, or come and attack her while she was in such a compromising situation. She bathed under her arms and around her neck, careful to keep from getting the strips that were wrapped around her ribs wet. She washed private places and pulled on the clean underwear, stepping gingerly on the injured leg, and grimacing with the pain in her shoulder. By the time she slipped her dress over her head she felt weak and light-headed, and her stomach churned. Her leg felt on fire, and she sank onto the blanket, calling for Wade.

In a moment he was at her side, pulling her dress the rest of the way on and buttoning it for her. "I'm sorry to be such a nuisance," she told him, taking deep breaths against the pain.

"I probably shouldn't have let you do this at all," he answered. He worked his way up the front of the dress, unable to keep his knuckles from touching her breasts as he carefully closed each button. The urge to gently cup those breasts in his hands brought near pain to his insides.

Jennifer reddened deeply, at the same time feeling a rush of desire sweep through her at the light, teasing brush of a man's hands against forbidden territory. "I need to comb my hair," she said, keeping her eyes averted.

"I'll do it for you. I don't want you to do anything the rest of tonight but eat something and rest." He finished buttoning the dress, then pushed up the skirt of her dress to check the bandage on her leg. "A little new blood. I don't want you on your feet any more tonight. Come on. I'll come back for the rest of your things and I'll comb your hair." He picked her up again. "I hope you don't mind beans and biscuits tonight."

"Anything would be fine. And I'm the one who should be doing the cooking."

"I've been camping out most of my life. Doesn't bother me a bit to do the cooking." He carried her to a bedroll he had made up for her near the camp fire, setting her down. He rose, looking around, suddenly seeming to take on the cunning of an animal.

"Do you think they're out there watching us," Jennifer

asked, feeling sick again at the memory of the raid.

"I don't think—I know they are. For some reason they're still leaving us alone."

"Why?"

He shook his head. "I'm not sure, but I have my suspicions." He walked on long, powerful legs back to the stream. She could not get over how such a big man who hardly knew her was being so kind and attentive. He could have his way with her and kill her, and it would be blamed on the Indians. No one would ever know the difference. How strange that he looked so much like those who had murdered all those poor men on the coach and nearly murdered her, yet was so different.

Her eyes teared again at the thought of Nick and Adam and Will and the others. She rummaged through her bag to find her book of *Jane Eyre*, thinking that if she read for a little while, it would help her forget the bad memories and her pain. But she could not concentrate. Wade returned with her things and sat down to jam open a can of beans with his knife.

"I'm glad those Comanche fled too soon to find all the food," he told her, dumping the beans into a small black frying pan sitting on the fire. "We'll eat, then I'll wash up myself. I could use a shave, too." He glanced at her, his eyes falling to the book. "So, that's where Charlotte Eyre came from," he said with a soft smile.

"Yes. I love this story."

"I've read it."

"You have!"

He laughed harder. "Don't look so surprised. I told you I've had some schooling. I've even studied Shakespeare. How do you like that?"

She smiled. "Do you remember any of it?"

"Sure I do, especially a sonnet I used to read over and over."

"Which one? I don't believe you."

He grinned, beginning to look embarrassed. "You don't want to hear it."

"Oh, but I do. Please recite it. It will help me forget

172

some of the ugly memories of the last two days."

He shrugged, looking at the flames of the fire. "Well, let me see. It starts out, Live with me, and be my love, And we will all the pleasures prove that hills and valleys, dales and fields, and all the craggy mountains yields. There will we sit upon the rocks, and see the shepherds feed their flocks, by shallow rivers, by whose falls melodious birds sing madrigals."

He stirred at the beans, staring absently at them as his voice lowered, taking on an almost sorrowful tone. "There will I make thee a bed of roses, with a thousand fragrant posies . . ." He paused. "I forget a little bit of it right there. Something about myrtle and a belt of straw and ivy buds."

He was silent again for a moment, as dusk brought on the sound of thousands of crickets. "And if these pleasures may thee move," he continued then, "Then live with me . . ." He stared at the dancing flames of the fire. "And be my love."

A cool, soft night breeze brushed Jennifer's face as she watched him, realizing sadly he was thinking of someone special. Was it the woman she reminded him of? "That was beautiful," she finally spoke up, suddenly forgetting her pain and the ugly horror of the raid.

The sonnet had brought forth a picture of mountains and roses . . . and love. What an unusual man he was, to be so skilled and strong and wild-looking, yet to be able to quote Shakespeare. Her heart swelled with a feeling she knew bordered on love. Was it so foolish and impossible to feel this way so quickly? "Who was she, Wade—the woman I remind you of. I have a feeling you think of her when you think of that sonnet."

He kept staring at the fire. "Her name was Rebecca." He sighed deeply and cleared his throat. "Like I said, it was a long time ago." He stirred the beans. "Find your comb and I'll get the tangles out of your hair."

How she wished he would tell her more about Rebecca. She retrieved her comb and handed it to him. He smiled almost nervously when he looked at her, and she was sure she detected a watery look to his eyes. She said nothing as she turned around. A wonderful warmth moved through her when his fingers moved into her hair to grasp it while he began gingerly pulling a comb through it. She winced at the tugs, but knew it was necessary.

"Why are you going to Fort Stockton?" she asked, deciding she had to quickly change the conversation and get him talking about something else.

"Personal reasons," he answered. "But then I know you're dying of curiosity, and I guess we've been through enough together that we can share a few personal things. After all, you told me about your parents and your uncle." He thought how beautiful and shiny her hair was, in spite of the primitive conditions for taking care of it. "Of course I intend to buy a horse when I get there. But my main reason for going is to find out the situation with the Comanche, where the renegades generally hole up, that sort of thing."

"Why do you want to know?"

He managed to get the comb to the end of one section of hair and started on another. "Well, I am going to try to find some long-lost relatives, if that's possible. I've never known my Indian side, or if I might have brothers and sisters—a mother."

She turned, interrupting the combing. Her eyes were wide with concern. "You mean, you intend to ride right into a Comanche camp?"

"Something like that."

"But, you can't! It would be suicide. You've already seen what they can do!"

"They spared me, remember? That gives me all the more reason to follow through with my plans. There is something going on that I need to know about. I already know they don't want to harm me, for some strange reason. Turn your head back around, and don't concern yourself with my problems. You have enough of your own."

She obeyed, and he began combing her hair again. "But I care," she replied. "I would worry about you."

174

"Worry about yourself. Besides, I couldn't bring myself to change my mind now for any reason—not after those Indians stared at me yesterday like I was a ghost and kept muttering the name Wild Horse. Wild Horse is the leader and instigator of most of the raiding that goes on around here, so I'm told. I'm also told he's a half-breed—with blue eyes. If you were me, wouldn't that get your juices going to find out what this is all about? I have a past I don't know anything about, Jenny, a side of me that belongs to the people who raided that stage coach yesterday. I'm ridiculed and condemned for being Indian, when I've never even lived like one and know very little about that side of myself. It's time I got some questions answered."

"But what does it matter any more?"

"It matters because I was abandoned by my Indian mother. Contrary to what most white men believe, Indians *do* have feelings, Jenny—and children, especially boy children, are of primary importance to them. They are loved very much, and an Indian mother wouldn't leave a baby behind without damn good reason."

Jennifer's heart felt heavy with the realization of how determined he was. As soon as they reached Fort Stockton, he would leave, probably to die. The thought of it made her want to weep. "Maybe . . . maybe it was a white woman who had you . . . a captive," she said cautiously.

"I've thought of that." He stopped combing for a moment. "But twenty-six years ago there were very few white women this far west. Most came no farther than San Antonio or Austin. It's more likely I'm the product of some white trader or hunter and a Comanche woman. Back then most captive women were Mexican or women from enemy tribes, like the Apache." He began combing her hair again.

"I don't know anything about any of them," Jennifer admitted. "Back East we hear all kinds of stories, mostly bad, about all Indians. But there is a lot of sympathy for them there, I suppose because they have already gotten rid of all their Indians and aren't in any danger any more. I

175

have to admit, after yesterday, I'll have trouble sympathizing with them myself for a while. I can't understand that kind of brutality."

"Well, it isn't easy for me, either. But I can probably understand it better than most of my white friends, because I've experienced my own persecution, felt the white man's hatred. There's a part of me that sometimes wants to be as vicious as I can with some people—men like Buck, for instance. That fight I had with him—it wasn't just because of what he did to you, although that was initially the reason. When I saw you that way, I was never so angry. But once I lit into him, I started thinking about all his insults and how he seemed to represent everything I hated. If Hughes and the others hadn't pulled me off him, I might have used my knife on him."

He sighed, stopping the combing again and sitting down beside her. "That scared me a little once I started thinking about it," he admitted. "For a moment there, I was no different from those renegades yesterday."

She looked at him sympathetically. "You could never be like that, Wade."

He shook his head. "I don't know. I only know it would help me understand that side of myself if I could find out more about my past and the Comanche way of life. I especially want to understand the brutality." He got back to his knees and started combing the last section of hair. "This is kind of crazy, isn't it—telling all these things to a young woman from St. Louis I barely know, and who knows next to nothing about Indians and this land. You're easy to talk to, Jenny. You're a brave and resourceful young lady, and I admire you very much."

His conversation and the fact that he was sharing personal feelings with her set her heart to racing, and helped her forget her aching leg and shoulder. "You can tell me anything you want. I like talking to someone so different. When I left St. Louis, I knew it would be an adventure. I just didn't know it would be quite *this* adventurous. I would have settled for less."

They both laughed lightly. She still wanted to know

about the woman called Rebecca, but she suspected she had better not mention her. "Is life at the fort really as bad as that sheriff and Nick and some of the others hinted it would be?" she asked then.

"Oh, not as bad as it used to be." He stopped to stir the beans, then began pulling the comb back through her now-untangled hair. "But to someone from St. Louis's wealthier section, it won't be any picnic, Jenny. Like I said, nobody can make you stay."

"But I don't like breaking my word. The understanding is that I will reimburse Sergeant Enders if we don't marry, and I don't have enough money for that."

"Well, you could stall for a while—tell him you need time to get to know him better, work as a laundress to earn your keep until you decide. There is nothing that says you have to marry him right away. And while you're waiting, you'd be earning a little money. You could even give him just part of what you would owe and go on to a bigger town and get a job—send him the rest." He touched her shoulder and turned her to face him. "If worse comes to worst, I'll give you the money myself. I have plenty."

"Oh, no, I would never expect that! I can take care of myself."

He frowned, looking her over. "Well, I guess you have done a good job of that, except for yesterday. And if Enders is a decent man, you might do all right. It's just that out here a man gets lonely. That could put a strain on his patience, if you know what I mean."

She looked away and then his hand was on her arm. "I don't want you to get hurt, Jenny." She met his eyes again, and for a moment she thought he might kiss her. He was so close, and she was sure it was desire she saw in his eyes. Was she reading him wrong? What did she know of men? What did she even know when it came to what men to trust? She tried to remember just when he had started calling her Jenny, and she had started calling him Wade; tried to remember just when she suddenly felt close to him, able to tell him anything and knowing he would understand.

"I'm scared, Wade."

The words tore at his heart. He gave her a reassuring smile, taking her chin in his hand. "Don't be. No one can force you to do anything. Besides, I won't let anything happen to you. I've kept that promise so far, haven't I?"

She nodded, unable then to resist the urge to hug him tightly around the neck. "Thank you," she told him, the tears coming.

He knew in that moment that with the right words and touches he could probably lay her back and enjoy tasting her mouth, could take a great deal of pleasure in her, and she would let him. But he was not about to go through that kind of hurt again—not like Rebecca. With great effort he grasped her arms and gently pushed her away.

"Lord, woman, don't ever let any white men see you doing that," he tried to joke. "You lie back and rest now. I'll have something for us to eat real quick. Then I'm going to take my own bath."

Jennifer reddened deeply, sure he must think her foolish and forward, sure she probably misinterpreted the feelings she thought she had read in his eyes. She reminded herself of his position. He was determined not to get too involved with a white woman. He was simply giving aid to her injuries and seeing that she got safely to Fort Stockton, nothing more. She felt like a stupid child, lost in a world of unreality.

Chapter Twelve

Jennifer woke up in a sweat, realizing through blurred vision it was barely dawn. The fire was nothing more than the soft red glow of dying embers. She started to move, but her leg hurt more this morning than it ever had yet, and she cried out.

Wade, who again lay beside her, quickly turned, rubbing at his eyes and sitting up. Lying next to her in order to keep her warm through the chilly desert nights had cost him considerable sleep, as he lay fighting forbidden desires.

"My leg . . . hurts bad," she told him.

Wade reached out and touched her face. "My God, you're burning up." He quickly rose and searched out dried grass and a few buffalo chips, throwing them on the fire; then he tore out a few mesquite shrubs to build the fire more. There was little else to use for fuel, since they were in nearly treeless country.

As he rummaged then through his supplies for clean bandages and whiskey, he realized in the back of his mind that he could no longer hear the ripple of the nearby stream. He knew it had only appeared because of the rain, and that it would not take much more than another day for it to disappear altogether. He quickly untethered the Indian pony so mysteriously given to him, and led it to what was left of the stream, tethering it there to drink in case they had trouble finding water once they left this spot.

He filled two extra canteens that he had retrieved from the debris around the stagecoach, then hurried back over to Jennifer, who was trying to sit up.

"Stay down," he told her. She protested weakly as he quickly removed her dress. "I can't work on you with this thing on, and you don't want to keep it on while you're sweating like this, do you?" he told her gently. "You have few enough dresses left. I'll wrap you up in blankets."

"My leg," she moaned. "It's . . . infected . . . isn't it?"

"Most likely. I'm going to take a look." She felt her dress come off, felt a blanket coming around her. She protested that she was too hot, but he insisted she stay covered against the still-chilly air.

She groaned as he quickly slid his hunting knife up under the bandages on her leg and sliced through them. He began pulling them away as gently as he could, wincing when some of them stuck to the wound from blood and pus.

"Don't . . . cut off my leg," she cried. "Promise me. Just . . . let me die."

"You aren't going to die, and I'm not going to cut your leg off," he answered calmly. "Hang on. This is going to sting."

She screamed as he poured whiskey into the wound. From then on the day became vague and confused, as she lay in near delirium from fever and pain. The only thing that was real and comforting was the knowledge that Wade Morrow was there with her, holding her, bathing her in cool water, talking soothingly to her. She thought she heard him say something about cauterizing the wound. She scrambled to remember what that meant, finally realizing he meant to burn the tissue around the infection.

Someone was screaming for him not to do it. Was it her own voice? "I've got no choice now," he was saying. His voice was close to her ear, his strong arms around her. "I've been trying to avoid it, Jenny, but I can't now. You don't want to die or lose your leg, do you?"

Memories of the pain of her burns from the riverboat fire

terrified her. Was that how it would feel? "Just let me die," she muttered.

"You don't know what you're saying," he told her. "It will be over before you know it."

Was that a kiss she felt at her cheek? She was too hot and in too much pain to be sure. He lay her back, and her mind floated, first to the awful explosion and fire that had taken her parents from her. Then she saw her Uncle John, huge and looming, leering at her, his hands grabbing for her and holding her down. Or was it Buck?

She struggled, hearing the war whoops of Indians then, seeing their painted faces, screaming as they tore her from the coach. There were dead, bloody bodies all around, men screaming for her to help them—Adam Hughes, Will Perry. She struggled again, but then came the gunshot to her leg, or was it a flaming lance? She screamed with the horrible pain. The savages were holding her down, burning her!

She opened her eyes to see one of them bent over her now. He was saying something about it being "all over." What did he mean? Was he going to kill her now? She saw dark skin and a buckskin shirt and long, dark hair. Would he rape her now? Her body was engulfed with shaking then, and the last thing she remembered was the dark savage bending over her.

Anthony Enders rubbed at his clean-shaven face, wincing at several cuts. He shaved so few times now that whenever a razor met his skin, it was a painful operation. He stood back from the mirror, studying himself, considering himself reasonably handsome. He slicked back his dark hair with a scented oil another soldier had told him women loved to smell.

He straightened his blue uniform, feeling almost uncomfortable being so clean. He was not used to it; but if it meant getting his new wife into bed sooner, it was worth the effort. He had already talked Captain Howell into allowing him to use a small cabin within the fort grounds as his "honeymoon" quarters. The cabin had been left empty when another commissioned officer and his wife had gone back East with the many others who were preparing for a possible war between the states.

Enders could care less at the moment whether or not there would be a war, or what the government was going to do about the renegade Comanche. The only thing that mattered was that Jennifer Andrews was due to arrive today on the stagecoach. In two days the traveling preacher who always came to the fort the end of each month would arrive and he and Miss Andrews would be married.

Two days was plenty of time for the woman to get to know him. After all, what did she need to know? He was a man and he was lonely, or so he would tell her. Once she was his wife, it wouldn't make much difference what she thought of him or how he treated her. She wouldn't have any choice then. He hoped the preacher would arrive earlier than expected, or that perhaps Miss Andrews was so lonely herself and would be so impressed by him that she would allow consummation of their pact before the preacher even arrived.

He grinned at the thought, painful needs moving through him. He put on his hat and picked up the locket again, thinking what an impression he would make on her when he gave it to her as a gift. If it would soften her up, it was worth the five dollars he had paid Deaver for it. He put it in his breast pocket.

His chest puffed proudly, he marched out of the barracks, where a few men marched in a lazy drill while others swept off boardwalks and more were busily painting the officers' quarters, where he knew Captain Howell would be drinking with First Lt. Michael Brown, both men the only two commissioned officers left at the fort. Howell was frustrated at not being able to capture any of the Comanche renegades so far, who had been creating havoc for surrounding settlers. With war looking more and more likely back East, Howell wanted to impress his superiors, hoping to earn a promotion and be sent east himself, where his wife waited for him.

Howell and Brown both hated being stationed in west Texas, and they spent a good deal of time drinking and planning ways they could capture the renegades, especially the one called Wild Horse. They had come close once, when they had convinced the man to come to the fort for gifts of food and clothing and tobacco, as well as the promise to set aside some land in west Texas where they could live freely, in exchange for the return of white captives and a promise to stop the raiding.

Wild Horse had shown up, bringing only one white captive, a woman who had obviously been badly abused. For once Howell and the others, including Enders, had got a good look at the notorious renegade, all of them amazed at his handsome features and deep blue eyes. The man had brought along his own wife and son, hoping, Enders figured, that this time the white man would keep his word and follow through with his promise.

Enders didn't much care one way or another what happened to the Comanche. He would just as soon kill them all anyway, for he had seen the damage they could do. As far as he was concerned, there was nothing human about them. He considered it a good lesson to the man when area Texans who attended the peace council forgot all about any promises the minute they set eyes on the white woman captive. One of them opened fire, and all hell broke loose. The woman captive was immediately killed by Wild Horse, and stray bullets cut down Wild Horse's wife and son. Several other Indians were killed, but most of them got away, skilled horsemen and fighters that they were.

Since then Wild Horse had been more vicious than ever. Enders considered real peace an impossible task out here, since the whites had never kept one promise they had made to the Comanche, and the hatred between Texans and the Indians was too volatile to ever allow a reckoning. The Texans wanted one thing—for all Comanche to be dead or permanently planted in Indian Territory to the north. That was fine with Enders, since he, too, was a Texan and

183

was raised with hatred for all Comanche.

The U. S. Army's biggest problem was that the government, fearing they would be labeled heartless murderers, refused to allow its soldiers to hunt down and massacre Indians. If local volunteers wanted to do so, that was fine. But the army's duty was to patrol the area and defend settlers if necessary, pursuing raiders only after an act of violence had been committed. But Comanche could not be chased and caught. They were too clever. And since the army could not set out and hunt them aggressively, attacking and destroying Indian strongholds wherever found, there could be no end to Comanche aggression.

Enders figured the Comanche must be laughing at army strategy. In the meantime, local Texans were furious with the U. S. government's attitude, and they continued to wage their own war against the Indians. Their anger at how Washington was handling the Indian situation was just one more reason why Enders was certain that if a civil war should occur, Texas would stand for the southern cause, which was much more than the slavery issue. It was an issue of states' rights.

At least for the moment there was so much confusion due to a possible civil war, and the Indian trouble here, that no one would be concerned with checking out the backgrounds of any of the army's enlisted men. His real identity was safe, and in two more years his voluntary duty would be over. He would take his pretty new wife to California and return to his gambling ways. If Jennifer Andrews didn't like his gambling, he would get rid of her. She would have served her purpose by then—to provide sexual satisfaction for a lonely soldier until his service was up.

He had often contemplated deserting, once he realized the miserable mess he had got himself into by volunteering, but he didn't care to suffer the consequences if he was caught. He had seen two men shot for deserting; another hung by the wrists right now from a pole in the center of the parade grounds, his back bloody and torn from forty lashes with the whip. He had tried to desert. Enders watched as men cut him down and carted him off. He normally would have been left there until dark, but Miss Andrews was due to arrive today, and Captain Howell thought it only proper that the woman shouldn't have to see the ugly sight.

"Hey, look at you," Corporal Deaver spoke up then, coming close to his friend. "I haven't seen you this spruced up since I've known you, sir." The two men saluted gratuitously, both knowing it wasn't really necessary between them. "You sure look ready to meet your bride-to-be."

"I'm ready in more ways than one," Enders answered. Both men laughed. "I just hope that preacher shows up like usual," Enders added. "I don't aim to give Miss Andrews too much time to think about this. I'm in bad need of a woman."

Other soldiers looked at each other after seeing Enders spiffed up. They joked about "poor Miss Andrews," who didn't know what she was in for, and made dirty gestures with their hands, some of them daydreaming about having a woman in their own beds. A few restrained from the dirty bantering, feeling a little sorry for the woman, who surely didn't know the kind of conditions under which she would be living here, or the danger of the land and its wild occupants. They had little doubt that Sergeant Enders would be anything but kind and patient with his new wife, but they reasoned it was not their business.

Alice Hart watched from her cabin, to the south of the parade grounds. She busily scrubbed long underwear against a washboard, a daily project that helped her earn her keep at the fort. Ever since her husband, a Sergeant Major, had been killed three years ago by the Comanche, she had stayed on, for the moment the only woman on the grounds, since three other wives had left to go back East because of the danger, the boredom of fort life, the hard work.

But Alice stayed on, refusing to leave her husband's grave. She had loved him dearly, a big, rather homely, but honest man who had been totally dedicated to the U. S.

Army. Alice was not much to look at herself, a short, stout woman with graying hair and lines of hard living on her forty-five-year-old face. Her biggest regret was never having been able to give her husband any other children besides their daughter Anna, who had died ten years ago at the age of sixteen. They had been stationed in Ohio then. Her husband had volunteered for service in the West after that, wanting to get away from familiar places, trying to put the hurt behind them.

Now her husband was gone, too. Alice resented the lazy, slovenly ways of the soldiers and officers who had been left here. She felt sorry for Miss Jennifer Andrews, who surely didn't know what she was in for. She had a keen dislike for Sergeant Enders, but she figured his marriage by mail was his business. If Miss Andrews was crazy enough to come to this godforsaken place to marry a stranger, there was nothing she could do about it.

The day stretched into dusk, as everyone waited with anticipation. But the stagecoach did not arrive. Alice came outside to take down uniforms from her clothesline, and she noticed Sergeant Enders pacing and cussing. His clean-shaven face began to again show the shadow of a beard, and by dark he was strutting and cursing and venting his anger and worry on his men. He finally stormed over to Captain Howell's office, and everyone could hear yelling from inside. Enders finally came back outside. "He says I have to give it another day," he growled at Corporal Deaver. "They could have just had mechanical trouble or a sickness or something."

"Don't be thinking the worst yet, sir," Deaver told him.

Enders kicked at a rock. "If some Comanche bastard has got his hands on her, I'll kill every Comanche I see again on sight—man, woman, child, whatever!"

"You think Howell will let you take out a platoon tomorrow to search if the stage doesn't show?" Deaver asked.

"He'll give it all day tomorrow yet. I probably won't be able to make a search until the morning after. She could already be in Wild Horse's hands, for all I know—dead or raped and tortured—who knows! All I know is the preacher will be here tomorrow or the day after, and my woman better be here, too."

Alice scowled, folding a pair of pants. Knowing Enders, she was sure he was not so much concerned about what might have happened to poor Miss Andrews as he was about the fact that he might not have a woman in his bed anytime soon after all. There was something about the man she didn't like or trust, and she had no doubt he was one of the many volunteers who came to places like this just to hide from the law.

She put the pants into a basket, hoping nothing terrible had happened to Miss Andrews. In spite of the rude awakening the poor girl would have when she got to Fort Stockton, Alice had looked forward to having another woman around. She just hoped everything would work out and Miss Andrews would stay. She picked up the basket and carried it inside, deciding she'd better say a prayer for the young woman from St. Louis for whom everyone at the fort was eagerly waiting.

Jennifer awoke to see Wade stirring something over the fire. It was dark. She lay there quietly, gathering her thoughts. The last thing she consciously remembered was waking up at dawn with terrible pain in her leg and feeling on fire. Wade had said something about infection and cauterizing.

She immediately moved her left arm down to her leg, thinking for a moment that perhaps it wouldn't even be there. Wade's alert senses caught the movement, even though his back was nearly completely turned to her. He turned to see her eyes were open, and he came to lean over her. "How do you feel?"

"What did you do to me?" she asked, her eyes wide.

He touched her face, relieved to find it was cooler. "Saved your life, I expect. I burned out the infection, Jenny. It was all I could do."

Her eyes teared and her lips puckered, as she felt under

the blanket with her hand. "I don't mean that," she said, her voice shaking. "My bloomers are gone!" She turned her face away, confused, in pain.

"Jenny, all I've done is help you. You've been lying here all day, delirious. You had a little accident, that's all. I cleaned you up and put a towel under you, that's all."

"Oh, my God," she sobbed. "I hate you! I hate this land and I hate Sergeant Enders . . . and I hate my Uncle John and the Comanche and most of all you! How do I know . . . you're even telling me the truth! And . . . who gave you the right to . . . burn my leg! I have enough scars!"

She heard a deep sigh. "I could get angry, but I know it's only pain talking, and you must be pretty scared right now—"

"Of course I'm scared," she nearly screamed through sobs, her face covered.

"Jenny, I didn't do anything wrong. As far as cauterizing that wound, it was that, or let you die a horrible, painful death. You're too young and beautiful and important to let that happen. And on a woman pretty as you, a few scars aren't going to have much affect, especially since they're in places nobody would see anyway—except maybe your husband."

"Sergeant Enders won't . . . he won't like my scars. He won't want me."

Wade scowled. "If he doesn't want you because of a few scars, then he's not much of a man. Besides, I have a feeling you'll be better off if he *doesn't* want you."

He returned to his camp fire, stirring a mixture of a few potatoes he had left with a couple turnips and some beans. It was true he had seen things he had no right seeing, but he'd had no choice. He couldn't help feeling some anger and disappointment that Jennifer thought the worst and that she seemed totally ungrateful for what he had done for her. He had sat here all day nursing her, waiting for her fever to break, and for her to come around. He told himself he couldn't really blame her for how she felt. She didn't know her own mind right now.

"If your fever stays down, we'll leave right away in the morning. I'll get you to Fort Stockton and you can marry your sergeant and be rid of me," he said then. He poured himself some coffee and walked off into the darkness.

Jennifer wiped at tears. She had caught the anger in his voice, and she realized she had surely hurt him. She didn't understand what made her feel that way and say such cruel things to him. She had accused him of the worst thing a man could do to a woman, and she knew better. She cried more at her own blunder, hating herself more than she hated this land or the Indians. This whole idea had been a terrible mistake, but there was no changing it now. They were only a day or two from the fort.

She remained turned away from the fire. Several minutes later she heard Wade's footsteps coming close again. "I'm . . . sorry," she sniffed. "I need something . . . to blow my nose."

She waited, hearing him walk somewhere. A moment later he shoved a bandana into her hand, saying nothing. She blew her nose and wiped at her eyes, just then realizing she felt better than she had since the raid. There was not nearly as much pain in her leg, and her shoulder was better. She felt more clear-headed, probably because since the raid this was the first time she had not waked up with a headache and infection.

She turned onto her back. Wade was stirring the food again. "I really am sorry," she repeated. "I just . . . got scared for a minute."

"You thought what every white woman would think of someone like me."

Her heart ached with a mixture of anger and sorrow. "That isn't true! It didn't . . . have anything to do with you . . . being Indian . . . if that's what you mean. It wouldn't have mattered . . . who you were! How do you think I feel . . . knowing you . . . anybody . . . would see me that way." She reddened deeply, turning her face away again the moment he met her eyes.

"Jenny, a man doesn't think much about it when he's worried the person he's helping is going to die on him.

189

Maybe I care about you. Did you ever think of that?"

"You're just helping me because you know it's the right thing to do. You'll be glad to deliver me at Fort Stockton and be rid of me."

"I won't be glad to deliver you there at all, especially not to some damn stranger whose idea of getting to know you before making you his wife is probably a hello and a quick marriage ceremony! The only reason I want to get you to the fort is so you can rest in a real bed. But I sure as hell don't like the thought of some lonely, woman-hungry soldier making it *his* bed!"

She lay quietly for a moment, wiping at her eyes again. "Why should you care about that," she finally spoke up, more calmly.

"Because I care about *you*. You're too good for some flea-bitten soldier in a place like Fort Stockton. I wouldn't be surprised if the man was nothing more than a damn thief, wanted back East someplace—maybe worse."

She finally turned back to see him poking at the fire. "What do you think I should do?"

"I don't know yet."

She watched him for a moment, a different feeling moving through her then at the thought of him seeing and touching her. He had saved her life, twice now. "I really am sorry, Wade . . . about what I said. I just hate feeling like a big burden."

"You aren't a burden." He finally met her eyes. "How do you feel?"

Their eyes held. "Better. Lots better. I'm even hungry." She kept watching his eyes, wondering just how much he really did care. More than he dared? Why did she hope that was true? "I care about you, too, Wade. Is it possible to become close friends in only four or five days?"

He turned back to the fire. "Sure it is." He put some food into a tin plate and came closer. "Can you sit up?"

"I think so."

He set the plate aside and reached out to help her, lifting her and helping scoot her back against his saddle. His hands had hold of her arms, and he was so close. She could feel his breath, catch his manly scent. Again their eyes held, and she could see he was struggling with emotions.

"Do you want to know the real reason I got mad?" she asked.

He searched the green eyes that tore at his heart and desires. "What's that?"

She swallowed. "The real reason is because . . . because I have feelings for you I'm not supposed to have," she answered boldly.

He immediately let go of her and handed her the plate of food. "Don't talk that way," he said, sounding angry again.

"Why not? It's true."

"You've come here to get married and that's that."

"I only agreed to meet the man—*then* decide. I didn't know I would meet somebody like you along the way."

"You just feel dependent on me, that's all. A few days after I've left you at the fort you won't think much of it. Now eat your food."

She wondered at the sudden, desperate feelings she had, as though it was important she let him know how she felt; an odd fear of losing him forever. "You said you cared about me," she spoke up, wondering where she found the courage. "Just how much *do* you care?"

He met her eyes, and his own narrowed with fury at his own forbidden feelings, fury at her for stirring them up. "Too much for your own good . . . or for mine, for that matter." He rose. "I'm glad you're better. Try to get back to sleep when you're through." He walked into the darkness beyond the camp fire.

"Where are you going?"

"Don't worry," came his voice. "I'll be close by."

"Stay and talk to me, Wade. Please don't embarrass me more by letting me speak my feelings and then walking away. It isn't fair." There was nothing but silence. "I want to at least remain friends," she said then. "Where is the law that says we can't be friends, or that I can't care about you? I said I was sorry."

She saw the glow of flint as he lit a cigarette. He

remained in the darkness. "It's an unwritten law, Jenny. I learned about it when I was eighteen."

She saw the end of the cigarette glow red. "It's something to do with Rebecca, isn't it?" she asked cautiously.

For several seconds there was only silence, before he finally answered. "She was the daughter of a settler who lived near San Diego—that's where my father's warehouses are. He sold produce to my father, and whenever he delivered it, he usually had Rebecca with him." He smoked quietly for a moment. "He always acted friendly to my pa—and to me. I never gave a thought to how he'd feel if I set eyes on Rebecca." She could hear the crunching of gravel then as he paced.

"Then one day I got a chance to talk to her alone, and I asked her to a dance. She said she couldn't—that her father wouldn't approve. I didn't understand at first, and then the reason came to me. But I could see Rebecca didn't feel that way at all. We started seeing each other secretly."

He sighed deeply and stopped pacing. "I loved her. I guess the knowledge that our love was forbidden made us feel more desperate. I met her in her pa's barn one night, and we made love. I had every intention of marrying her, and neither one of us thought of it as wrong or bad. But her pa caught us. He shot at me, hit me in the arm. Then he and his men grabbed me up—beat me nearly to death, took me to my pa's place and dumped me off like a sack of potatoes, warned my pa he'd kill me if he ever saw me on his property again. By the time I recovered, Rebecca's father had sent her to school in the East." He cleared his throat. "She, uh, she died there—pneumonia or something. I never got to see her again after that night."

Jennifer's heart went out to him. "I'm sorry. I truly am. That's so sad, and so unfair." She thought of the sonnet he had recited, *And if these pleasures may thee move, then live with me, and be my love.* Surely he thought of Rebecca when he thought of those words. And after such a horrible experience, it was no wonder he was seemingly determined not to be caught having even the slightest interest in a white woman.

He stepped into the firelight then, an oddly stricken look on his face. "Now maybe you understand better about a few things."

How handsome he was! And surely he was one of the loneliest men alive, a part of two worlds and belonging to neither. "The only thing I understand is that Rebecca's father was wrong—very wrong. And you're wrong to let what happened affect your whole life. You have every right to love whoever you want to love, to have a family, and settle like anybody else."

He shook his head, grinning bitterly. "You sound like my mother. You're both too soft-hearted and caring to really understand. Men like me don't have the same rights as white men, Jenny. That's just the way it is. I've learned to accept it. If I didn't, I'd be fighting someone every day. That gets old after a while. A man gets tired. I figure maybe it will help if I find out something about my Comanche side. Maybe I'll even find a wife among them."

She felt a rush of jealousy and near panic at the thought. He had become her defender, her friend, her doctor, her guide. She loved him. She was more sure of it than ever, and he had as much as admitted he had strong feelings for her.

"I don't have a father," she said quietly. "I don't have anyone who would care or interfere if . . . if I should dare to love someone like you." She was surprised she had had the courage to say it.

There came a long silence. "Get some rest," he finally said. "I can have you at the fort by the day after tomorrow."

She heard him walking farther off. "Wade?"

There came no reply. She lay back down, suddenly losing her appetite. Somewhere in the distance a wolf howled, and it seemed the howl matched the longing and loneliness in her soul. She realized then that she and Wade Morrow were more alike than he realized, neither of them

193

belonging to any one place or person, both of them feeling a little lost and lonely.

She closed her eyes and tried to sleep, but she knew it would not come easily to her now. New emotions had been stirred, and words had been said that could not be undone. How would she face him in the morning? What could she say? Could they still be at least good friends?

She wanted more than that, much more; and she was sure Wade Morrow was feeling the same way.

Chapter Thirteen

Jennifer awoke to see Wade sleeping on the other side of the nearly-dead camp fire. It was the first time since helping her that he had not slept near her to keep her warm, and she realized with embarrassment it was partly because of her accusations the evening before; or perhaps he was afraid to be too close to her now, after she had told him of her feelings. Was he afraid of his own emotions and desires, just as she was?

She felt almost sick at the memory of their verbal exchanges, angry with herself for saying cruel things at first, embarrassed at later all but admitting that she loved him. But hadn't he done the same? She wondered how she was going to face him today. They still had at least two days of travel ahead of them, with no one but each other to talk to. She realized that if they didn't air their feelings and get it over with, those two days would be miserable.

She breathed deeply for courage. If Wade Morrow didn't want to admit to his emotions, that was his problem. She was too tired and distraught to control her own. It seemed incredibly ridiculous, but in the few days since she had met him, Wade Morrow had become her whole world, and she had felt a strong attraction to him and had felt the hands of fate bringing them together since the day he stepped in on her behalf back in San Antonio. How many days ago had that been? Six? Seven? It seemed as though she had known him much longer, as though they were old friends. Was there really such a thing as love at first sight?

She drew the blanket away and looked at her leg. It was still bandaged, but looked less red and puffy. Her ribs still hurt, and her shoulder ached, but she could use her arm now. A rush of confused feelings consumed her when she again realized she was naked under the blanket from the waist down. Knowing now how he apparently felt about her, had he let his eyes linger longer than necessary on private places no one else had ever seen or touched?

The thought was at first humiliating, yet again, the thought of him touching her out of desire brought a terrible rush of passion. Her cheeks burned to think of it, and she felt like a fool thinking she could ever totally please such a man, so big and wild and different from anyone or anything she had ever known. She reminded herself she was out here to marry someone else, but the thought of Wade leaving her at the fort, of never seeing him again made her heart ache.

She managed to get to her feet, keeping a blanket wrapped around herself. She felt a little wobbly at first, and realized she had not eaten for over twenty-four hours, and even then she had not eaten much. She put a hand to her head and stumbled away from the camp site, heading for a small stand of scraggly bushes near the creek. She vaguely remembered that first night here, when Wade had washed her hair and combed it.

Again she tried to remember how many days had gone by. This was surely at least the third day since the raid. It was likely that by now Sergeant Enders was out looking for her. Perhaps he would show up soon with some men. If so, the time left with Wade was preciously short.

She noticed there was no water left in the creek, only damp earth. How strange this country was—flooded one day and dried out the next. She moved toward the bushes when she heard Wade's voice behind her. "You need any help?"

She felt her cheeks going hot again, and she kept her back to him, wondering how long he had been awake and watching her. "No," she said quietly. "I can manage." She started forward again when he told her to wait. A moment later a pair of bloomers came across her shoulder, held by a big, familiar hand. Still she kept her back to him.

"You might feel better with these on. If I have to check your wound this time I can just push one leg up."

She took them, saying nothing. She moved behind the bushes, thinking that if anything more happened to her clothes, she wouldn't have a thing left to wear when she reached the fort. She was glad her best dress, a mint green silk dress with a lace yoke, was still undamaged. She decided that today she would put the gray cotton dress back on, then remembered Wade putting it on her the day before, removing it again, both times his big hands coming daringly close to her breasts.

She moved behind the bushes to relieve herself, then pulled on the clean bloomers. She wished she could bathe again, but there was not enough water here, and now there were these new, awkward feelings around Wade. She wrapped the blanket around herself and took a deep breath, realizing she had to face the man sooner or later. She limped back to the campsite, where Wade was rekindling the fire. He said nothing at first, as he watched the flames begin to reawaken.

"I'm sorry about last night," he finally spoke up. "I said some things I had no business saying."

So did I, she wanted to reply. But she knew it would be a lie, and she was tired of lying, tired of living by the unwritten rule that Wade Morrow was forbidden to women like herself, forbidden to love and be loved, allowed into the white man's world only to do business but forbidden to become emotionally or socially involved.

Her heart pounded wildly as she drummed up the courage to say what must be said. She didn't care if he hit her or laughed at her or refused to talk to her for the rest of the journey. She was not going to let Wade Morrow go out of her life with these hurt feelings.

"I'm not sorry about any of it," she answered, also watching the fire. She was standing not far from him, and he remained in a stooped position, poking at the coals.

"I'm only sorry for getting angry and saying those cruel things when I first woke up. But I'm not sorry for the rest. You can think and do what you want, Wade Morrow; and you can think of me as . . . as too bold and too forward . . . maybe even bad, because I'm supposed to get married when I reach the fort. But right now all I can think about is you." The tears started to come then, which made her angry. She didn't want to cry, not right now. "I love you," she said then, surprised herself that she had managed to get the words out.

She swallowed back a lump in her throat and quickly wiped at her eyes. "There," she added. "I wanted to say it and now I have." She sniffed, then breathed deeply to control her tears. "I don't believe . . . in all these unwritten rules you talk about, Wade. Others out here can think and act however they want, but . . . nobody can make me do or say anything I *don't* want. That's why . . . I left St. Louis and . . . Uncle John . . . to make my own choices. You have that right, too, Wade. You shouldn't . . . let anyone tell you otherwise. And right or wrong . . . I love you. Let them hang me for it, if it's such a terrible crime. At least I'd die knowing I did what I knew in my heart was right."

She turned away and grimaced as she lowered herself to her bedroll. Her face felt so hot she worried she could have a fever again, but she knew it had nothing to do with that. She put a cool but shaking hand to her cheek, waiting for an angry response, or perhaps a cruel laugh; wondering if she would get the most dreaded response—total silence or a look of disgust and ridicule.

"You don't know what you're saying," he said then, his voice directly behind her. She almost jumped at the words, realizing he had walked up to her without her even knowing it, another sign of the Indian in him. "You're just feeling grateful—"

"I know exactly what I'm saying," she boldly interrupted. She awkwardly tried to get to her feet without losing her blanket, and he was compelled to take her arm and help her. His touch made her feel almost dizzy with love and desire. He immediately let go of her when she had her balance, and she raised her eyes to meet his, seeing a look of near sorrow in his own blue eyes.

"It doesn't have anything to do with being grateful," she told him, sensing the redness in her face but not caring. "Don't you think I'm old enough and intelligent enough to know the difference? Do you think I'd fall in love with just anybody who came along to help me?"

A smile wanted to come to his lips, but the gravity of the situation prevented it. "I suppose not." How he wanted to hold her, to touch her soft skin and secret places he was sure only he had set eyes on. Now he didn't want anyone else to ever see or touch those places. He didn't want to just wash and comb her hair, or wrap her wounds and bathe her fevers. He wanted to ravish her, to wrap his hands in that hair while he tasted her mouth and moved inside her virgin body. But she seemed too good and sweet and innocent to put up with the kind of life she would lead being married to a half-breed.

It was only then he had thought of the word married. Such a thing was ridiculous to think about this soon, impossible to dream it could ever be, even if he had known her much longer than these few days. He was letting his feelings run away with him, and he wondered just when he had lost control of himself like a stupid young boy. Was it when she had first got off the coach at San Antonio?

He turned away, running a hand through his hair, unable to look into those green eyes any longer without falling into them, never to return to his logical, practical self. "I never should have let on last night about how I felt," he told her. "I'm sorry about all of it. You're out here to marry someone else. It's probably just . . . just being thrown together like this . . . what we've been through and all—"

"It isn't just that, and you know it," she replied, braver now that she had spilled out her feelings. As long as she had gone this far, she was not going to let him lie his way out of it, just because he thought it was best for her. "You feel the same way I do. I know it."

"You don't know anything," he answered, now sounding angry again. He whirled, his eyes nearly blazing. "What the hell do you know—an eighteen-year-old, pampered city girl who up to now has never known anything but a sheltered life with a doting aunt! How many men have you dated, Jenny? What do you really *know* about men?"

He stepped closer, hating himself, his heart torn at the sad, pouting look on her face. It was obvious she was about ready to cry again. Good! Maybe he could shake her dangerous feelings. "And how do you know I don't find *all* white women fascinating? How do you know you aren't just one of many? Maybe it's like Buck said, little girl. Maybe men like me just pant after any woman with light skin and red or yellow hair! Maybe I *did* take advantage of things yesterday. God knows I could have, and you would have hardly known the difference!"

She drew in her breath, refusing to take her eyes off his, refusing to look frightened or to let him browbeat her into backing off. Her face felt on fire, but the thought of losing him outweighed any inhibitions. "I imagine I would have known the difference, all right," she answered, shocking him with her bold reply. "I've never been with a man, and I never even wanted to be with one till now. And you're a rotten liar, Wade Morrow. I'm the first woman with light skin you've ever had special feelings for since Rebecca—except maybe the kind of women a man *pays* for favors. I know about those things. I know more than you think. My Aunt Esther told me a *lot* of things, and one thing I've always been sure of is that when the right man came along, I'd know it. Up to now I figured running away from Uncle John would mean I'd never have that free choice; but I'm thinking maybe I still do. I love you, and you can't lie me out of it or *bully* me out of it!"

She finally dropped her eyes. "Right now I don't think I can stand on this leg another minute." She slowly lowered herself, and he reached out when she wavered, helping her the rest of the way to the ground.

She met his eyes then, seeing tears in them. "Damn

you," he whispered. In the next moment he met her mouth in a crushing kiss that sent her senses reeling. She moved her arms from under the blanket and wrapped them around his neck, the blanket falling away from her. His kiss lingered, hot and penetrating, as he sank down beside her, drawing her onto his lap, his left hand digging into her hair, his other hand moving up under her chemise, gently rubbing at her bare back while his tongue slaked into her mouth in a kiss that was leaving her breathless.

He finally left her mouth, moving his lips over her eyes, whispering her name, tasting hungrily at her lips again before trailing his own down over her throat while his right hand moved around to the front of her chemise, up over the gauze that still wrapped her ribs, his thumb rubbing daringly at the base of one breast, bringing a whimper of desire from her lips.

He could not resist the open invitation to take greater pleasures, and he met her mouth in another burning kiss while his thumb gently rubbed over a taut, virgin nipple.

Jennifer thought she might faint with ecstasy. In her wildest dreams she never thought she could enjoy such things so much, that she could really want a man to touch her, taste her, make a woman of her. Now she could not imagine that man being anyone but Wade Morrow.

He left her mouth, bending his head to kiss at the whites of her breasts. She was sure he would pull the chemise off her breast and taste the nipple that lay erect and waiting just under the soft cotton garment; but suddenly he drew his hand from under the chemise and simply pulled her into his arms, kissing her hair while she lay nestled in his arms.

"We've got to slow down, Jenny," he said, his voice husky with repressed desires. "We've got to think about this."

"There's nothing to think about," she said, her own voice weak. "I love you, and you love me. Tell me you don't love me, Wade."

He let out a long, shuddering sigh. "You know I love you," he groaned. "That's the hell of it."

201

She kissed at his neck. "There's nothing hellish about it. It's right, Wade, I know it is." Her eyes teared. "You were right—about me not knowing much about men. But I know this feeling I have for you is real—and I know now how it feels to want a man and not be afraid of it. I always thought I would be, but I wouldn't be afraid with you."

"Don't talk like that, Jenny. You have no idea what that kind of talk does to a man, and we can't—" He threw his head back, breathing deeply. He gently scooted her off his lap then and rose turning away from her, walking around the other side of the fire as though in pain. She thought about things her aunt had explained to her, and for a brief moment she did feel a note of apprehension. But she reasoned that when a woman felt that about a man the way she felt about Wade Morrow, it couldn't be as humiliating and mechanical as she sometimes had imagined it must be. When she had been in his arms, letting him touch her had seemed like the most natural thing in the world. Surely making love would be beautiful with someone like Wade.

"We can't let ourselves get carried away, Jenny." He finally finished what he started to say when he tore himself away from her.

"I already am carried away," she answered, afraid he would turn around and find an excuse to deny his feelings again. She drew the blanket back around her shoulders, on fire at the memory of his hand touching her breast, his lips branding her mouth. She touched her lips. "And so are you," she added quietly. He had touched her, kissed her! There was no going back as far as she was concerned, no changing this feeling.

He walked farther away, his hands on his hips, his hawk-like eyes scanning the horizon. "We have a lot of things to talk about," he said then. "For one thing, I'm still determined to find this Wild Horse and see if I can find out something about my past."

"Do what you have to do. It won't stop me from loving you."

He wanted her so bad he wondered if he would explode into a hundred pieces. He wished he could talk to his father about this. He had let it happen again. After eight years he had fallen for another white woman. But this one was free to love him back—except for the fact that she was on her way to Fort Stockton to marry someone else. He had no choice but to take her there. She still needed help and rest. Besides, he didn't have time to take her someplace else. By now her Sergeant Enders would realize something had happened to the coach and he would come searching. They could be found any time now. She could go on to some other town once they reached the fort and things were settled between her and the sergeant, but to let her go on from there alone or even escorted was too dangerous. Apparently the only thing keeping her alive was the fact that she was with him, and for some reason the Comanche had chosen to leave him unharmed.

He finally turned and met her eyes again, passion ripping through him at the sight of her sitting there, so small and pretty and trusting, the blanket wrapped around her temptingly, for they both knew that if he touched her again he would rip it away, and more. Never had he had to summon more self-restraint than this moment. He had to think of what was best for her.

"Jenny, I want you to listen to me," he said then, coming back to the fire. "By now the soldiers know something is wrong. There's probably a patrol out right now looking for the coach, and I don't doubt your Sergeant Enders is with them."

"He's not *my* Sergeant Enders."

"You know what I mean. The first thing I want you to remember when we're found is to treat me the way those men would *expect* you to treat me."

"You mean insult you—act as though I'm repulsed by you and I'm overjoyed that they came along?" She scowled. "I won't do it! I told you I'd never behave that way again! I love you, and if I—"

"Damn it, Jenny, *listen* to me," he interrupted. He came closer, grasping her arms and shaking her slightly. "It's just for a little while, and you'd be doing it for *me*, as much as for yourself."

Her eyes teared again. "Why? I don't care any more, Wade. Let them think what they want."

He closed his eyes and sighed, as though he was about to throw his hands in the air and give up. He sat down beside her but facing her, taking her hands. "Jenny, I'm not trying to get out of these feelings. They're there and we've both admitted it. When the time is right, we'll let others know. All I'm doing is buying both of us some time."

She searched his eyes. All she wanted was for him to kiss her again. "I don't understand," she answered.

He squeezed her hands. "Jenny, we aren't equipped to try to run away from this. You've got to get some bed rest and get your strength back. The closest place for that is the fort, and we're going to be found—maybe today, maybe tomorrow—but we *will* be found. And until we can both get away from that fort, those soldiers have to think there was nothing between us but a woman in trouble and an experienced scout helping and protecting her. Just finding us together and knowing I fixed that leg is going to be enough to live down. They're going to think and suggest all kinds of things. I want to set them straight right off, and you can help me if you behave the way I tell you. I'm going to have to leave you at that fort for a while, and I want you treated right while you're there."

"But what could they do, even if they knew? I don't mind insults, Wade."

He squeezed her hands tighter. "Jenny, please pay attention and do what I say. Damn it, those men are hungry enough for a woman as it is. The only way you'll be safe is to do like I say—and to let Sergeant Enders think you're at least considering marriage. If they think for one minute there is anything between us, they won't think of you as any better than the women who camp out around those forts to accept money for favors—the kind of women you mentioned yourself. I don't have to tell you what kind of danger that could mean for you."

She blushed and dropped her eyes, wondering how often he had visited such women, jealous of all of them. She realized what he was trying to tell her, what could happen to her if the men lost their respect for her. "They'd treat me like Buck did," she said quietly.

He put a hand to her hair and drew her head against his chest. "There is no doubt in my mind."

"What can we do? What about Sergeant Enders?"

He stroked her hair. "At first you'll have the excuse of your injuries. You'll tell him you want to be completely healed before marrying him. Then you can tell him you need more time, that you want to get to know him better—that the journey out here was so horrifying that you're very shaken and confused, and you're just not ready to marry. Hold him off for two or three weeks. By that time I should be back."

She grasped the front of his buckskin shirt. "And what if you don't make it back?"

They sat quietly rocking in each other's arms for a moment. "If that should happen, if I don't show up within three or four weeks, you'll pay the sergeant his investment and you'll either go on to El Paso or go back East, but only when the stage is running regularly again and it looks like the raiding has stopped."

"I don't have enough money to pay him."

"I have plenty of money. I'm a rich man, remember?" He tousled her hair. "I'll give you enough to pay him plus have enough extra to get you out of there."

"I couldn't take money from you."

"Why not? You said you loved me—" He grasped her arms and leaned her back, meeting her eyes. "And I love you," he said softly. "I don't think I actually said it yet." He leaned closer and kissed her, lightly, gently. "I'd just be doing something for the woman I love, and I'd rest easier once I leave the fort, knowing you'd be taken care of no matter what happens."

Her eyes teared more. "Please don't go, Wade."

He pulled her close again. "I have to. It might seem unnecessary, but it's something that has bothered me all my life, Jenny. I hope you can bring yourself to understand. Living the white man's way all my life doesn't erase what I am. I have this need to know about that part of me. I've come this far, and I can't stop now."

"Not even for me?"

He turned her face up to his. "I'll be a happier man, more at peace with myself this way—which will be better for you if and when we end up together. And even if I didn't go out there looking for my family, the fact remains we still have to behave the way I said when the soldiers come. If we try running away, they'll find us and accuse me of abducting you. I'd be hanged on the spot, and God knows what they'd do to you. It's better this way, Jenny. You lie low and do like I said. You've got to be convincing. Even when I'm finished with my own business, I can't just come to the fort and carry you off. You've got to do what I said and just tell the sergeant you've changed your mind— pay him off and be on your way. Somehow I'll get a message to you where to meet me."

She closed her eyes and hugged him. "It scares me, Wade."

He smiled through tears. "You're braver than you think. You've already proven that, Jenny. That's partly what I love about you." He rubbed a hand over her back. "I can't help thinking I'm not being fair to you. My head tells me to forget all of this and leave you at the fort to do what you came here to do; but wrong as it probably is, my heart tells me different. I can't bear the thought of leaving you at the fort and never seeing you again. Most of all I can't stand the thought of some other man touching you."

His lips caressed her hair, her cheek, came again to her mouth in a kiss sweet with passion and desire. He pulled away then, putting a hand to her cheek. "From here on we can't do this, Jenny, not in the bright daylight. We're wide open here. Soldiers with binoculars could spot us a mile away. I don't want to take the chance of being caught holding each other."

"I wouldn't care—"

He put his fingers to her lips. "Remember what I told you. Promise me, Jenny."

She closed her eyes and sighed. "I promise."

He reluctantly let go of her, moving away from her.

"We'd better eat something and get going. We lost a day's travel yesterday."

"I could stay out here with you forever."

He grinned. "You'd tire of putting up with the dangers and the elements soon enough, let alone what this land can do to a pretty young woman's skin. Much as I hate to face what's ahead, we've got no choice. We might as well resign ourselves to it right now."

He dug through his supplies to see what food was left, feeling crazy with the need of her, wondering how he was going to get through the night knowing she was willing, that she wanted him as much as he wanted her. It didn't seem right to steal what was most valuable to her—not this way—not now. She was too special.

And yet what more was there than to love the woman? Where was the wrong when they had found something special, and when this might be all they would ever have together? He wondered when he had become such a weak fool. He had always prided himself on his strength and determination, his ability to hold back and do what was proper in any situation. But no woman had come along to make him feel this warm and alive and loved in years—not since Rebecca. He knew Jenny was the kind of woman his father would approve of, someone who didn't see others through the eyes of prejudice, but saw a man for his worth alone. His father would like that.

Jennifer watched him, loving everything about him, thinking that there couldn't possibly be another man to match his looks or his strength or his skills. She would have him for her own, no matter what it took. He had said he could not touch her again, not in the daylight. But what about tonight? She wondered if he was thinking the same thing—how would they get through the night? Once they reached the fort, he would go away, perhaps never to return. Could she let him go without letting him be the man who made a woman of her? How could it be anyone else? And how could it be wrong when she loved him so much and intended to be with him forever, if he wanted the same thing, and she was sure he did.

They both moved as though in a trance, hardly aware of cleaning up and eating. He tied her onto the travois, then leaned down to kiss her lightly before mounting the Indian pony and setting out. She watched the campsite until it was out of sight, thinking how that place would always be special to her, even though she would never see it again. She had found something here in Texas, something she had never planned to find.

She felt a little sorry for Sergeant Enders, but, after all, he didn't even know her, and he would get his money back. He was the one who had said in his ad that there was no obligation except the refund of his expenses.

"Sir, you've got to let me search for that coach," Enders begged Captain Howell. "It's two days overdue now. Please, sir, I've got to know what happened. She could be a captive."

Howell rubbed at bloodshot eyes, his head aching from too much bourbon last night, and from lost sleep over his own wife, who he was almost certain had found a new love back in Ohio.

"Believe me, Enders, no woman is worth risking your life for. They just turn around and spit in your face." The man rose and paced. "I'm sorry. I've got my own problems. We're supposed to be out here to protect the settlers and travelers, and I can understand your concern." He sighed deeply, walking to look out a window. "If Washington would let us handle the Indians the right way, we wouldn't have these problems, would we?"

"Does that mean I can take out a patrol?"

Howell turned to look at him. "Fifteen men—no more. That's all we can spare. You have four days—tops."

"Yes, sir. Four days. Thank you, sir."

Enders hurried out and began rounding up men and supplies, barking orders impatiently. His frustration knew no bounds. By all rights he should have had a woman in his bed the last two nights, and every part of him ached for it. Now the preacher was gone again and wouldn't be back for another thirty days. If he did find his bride-to-be, how was he going to keep himself from satisfying his needs until the preacher returned? He wondered just how "proper" she really was. Maybe, if he handled her just right, they wouldn't have need of a preacher, except to make things legal. He could care less about what was legal and what wasn't. He only knew Miss Jennifer Andrews had teased his desires long enough.

Chapter Fourteen

The day grew more windy as the travois on which Jennifer lay was dragged across the hardened earth, bouncing over patches of curly mesquite and buffalo grass. The land seemed so desolate, Jennifer could not imagine why anyone would want to come here and try to farm and settle. She could not even imagine why the Indians stayed, fighting and risking their lives to keep this place for themselves.

The land stretched out in a huge, flat plateau, with mountains bordering the western edge, mountains that seemed to just hang in the air, always the same distance away in spite of the fact that for four days they had been heading west. Jennifer was beginning to understand distance in this land, realizing certain things she saw were much farther away than she first imagined.

"Those mountains are a good fifty miles off," Wade had told her earlier, "maybe more."

It seemed incredible. Back East there were few places where one could see more than a mile ahead, with hills and thick woods creating barriers a person didn't find here in west Texas. No one back home could have prepared her for this land of wide horizons and little water, thorny plants and air so dry that whenever she blew her nose it bled. She could not have conceived of such country in her wildest imagination.

By afternoon the wind grew worse, kicking up a cruel,

stinging sand. She felt sorry for Wade, who plodded on until the wind grew to a near roar, and the dust was so thick a person could see only a few feet ahead. Jennifer knew it was a little easier for her, since she lay with her back to the wind. She covered her face with a blanket and could barely discern words Wade shouted back to her then.

"I'm going . . . reach . . . ridge up ahead. Looks like . . ."

She couldn't hear the rest. She simply trusted him to do what was best, and her heart ached for him as he headed the Indian pony into the blinding sand. She soon sensed that they were climbing. It was close to an hour later that there came a sudden relief from the horrible, blowing dirt, although Jennifer could still hear the wind howling. The travois stopped moving, and she took the blanket from her face to breathe clean, cooler air.

She slowly sat up, throwing off her blanket and shaking sand from it. She wore the gray dress. Wade decided she had better put it on again, since soldiers could come along at any time. "Wade, where are we?"

He dismounted, taking off a wide-brimmed, leather hat he had put on to help protect his eyes and hair. He brushed dirt from his clothes. His face was caked with it, little lighter-colored lines showing at the creases near his eyes, where dirt had not been able to penetrate while he squinted against the wind.

He grinned. "I'll bet I'm a sight." He looked around as Jennifer laughed lightly. "I was hoping I could get here. When the wind first kicked up I had a feeling a sandstorm was coming, so I looked for possible shelter and headed straight for it. I saw another plateau, kind of a shelf of land with a ridge of limestone along its wall. Most walls like that have several cave-like holes in them. I finally spotted this one, but I wasn't sure I'd still be able to find it once the sand got so thick I couldn't see ahead any more. I just kept coming in this direction."

Jennifer realized he had dragged the travois into a cave-like cutout in rock. She looked past the opening at the dark blizzard outside. "I've never seen anything like this."

Wade began unloading their gear. "I have, more times

than I can remember. I can see now that west Texas isn't much different from Arizona or New Mexico. Back East you have your snow blizzards. Here we have dirt blizzards." He unloaded the spotted Indian horse. "We might as well settle here for the night. It's already late afternoon, and it looks like that wind is going to blow pretty good for a while longer."

Jennifer lay back against the travois. "Oh, what I wouldn't give for a bath."

"You and me both. Actually it's mostly our faces and hair that need washing. All the water we have left is in three canteens, and in this country you don't waste water. Something could happen to prevent us from getting to the fort as soon as we think we will—like this sandstorm and that infection you had. You never know when you'll need every last drop of water just to stay alive."

"You mean I can't even wash my face?"

He grinned. "Sometimes these limestone ledges collect and drip water. I'm going to see if I can locate any leaks." He grabbed a leather waterbag from his gear, its contents gone due to bathing Jennifer's fever and infection. He headed toward the entrance of the cave-like hole when a figure loomed there, bringing a gasp from Jennifer. Wade was as startled as she. He threw down the leather pouch and grabbed for his rifle, but the figure raised his arms, displaying no weapons, but rather two leather pouches that looked full of water.

"Wade," Jennifer exclaimed, her eyes wide with fear when she realized the figure was an Indian man. Beneath the dirt that caked his face, she could see that it was painted. His hair hung loose and long, and his body was nearly naked except for a loincloth and apron.

"Just stay put," Wade answered, taking his hand away from his rifle. The figure came closer, and he handed out the water to Wade, who took it cautiously.

"Strong spirit," the Indian man told him in the Comanche tongue. "You come soon to Wild Horse." He moved his eyes and waved his arm to indicate a north-west direction. "White man call it Comanche Hills. Wild

213

Horse says you come."

Wade glanced at Jennifer, who had no idea what was being said. He set down the water bags and used his own limited Comanche along with sign language to indicate he first had to take the woman to Fort Stockton. The Indian frowned, then nodded.

"You take woman. Do not tell soldiers about Wild Horse. You come alone."

Wade nodded. "You have my promise."

The Indian looked him over as though almost afraid of him.

"Thank you," Wade told him then. "For the horse, and the water. Why are you doing this?"

"You are strong spirit—shadow of Wild Horse. He must see for himself." The man abruptly turned and disappeared into the blinding dust storm. Wade hurried to the cave entrance but could see nothing.

"Wade, what did he want?" Jennifer asked.

He turned, looking grave. "For some reason they're still helping us. I knew someone was close. I could feel it, but I couldn't see him. I don't know how he found us in this storm, or where he got that water, but I think he's the same one who left the horse for us."

"What did he say to you?"

He met her eyes, coming closer and kneeling beside her. "He said Wild Horse wants to meet with me, at a place called Comanche Hills. He said I am a shadow of Wild Horse, and that Wild Horse wants to see for himself."

She put a hand on his arm. "Wade, what do you think it all means?"

He frowned, rising again, walking back to the cave entrance, standing there silently for several seconds. "My white father and mother tell me I could have been a twin," he said reflectively. "The Comanche kill twin babies. They think they're a bad omen, something like that. My pa says my mother might have abandoned one baby in order to keep at least one. Maybe she was alone when she had them and she never told the others there was a twin."

He turned to face her, confusion and a strange longing

in his eyes. "Jenny, the man said I was a shadow of Wild Horse. When they saw me the day of the raid, they all stepped back like they were frightened of me, and they called me Wild Horse. The only sense I can make of that is that he could be my own brother, sorry as I am to think it. They say Wild Horse is a half-breed, with blue eyes. I'd like to think it's all just a coincidence, but when that Indian said I was a shadow of Wild Horse, and that Wild Horse needed to see me for himself—" He closed his eyes. "Good God," he said, his voice a near whisper. "It's as though I'm being led through all this by some power I can't even understand. I never thought I'd come across something like this."

Her heart raced with fear for him. "If he is your brother, what would that mean for you? Wade, if they kill twins, then you could be risking your life by going to Wild Horse. Maybe the man wants you dead."

He rubbed a hand over his eyes. "Jenny, I have to know." He looked at her then, his eyes bloodshot from the storm, but also showing a mixture of joy and dread. "I hope you can understand that."

Her eyes teared. "I think I can. I want to understand, Wade, but I don't want to lose you."

He came back over to her, kneeling down and picking up one of the water bags. "At least now we can wash," he told her. He met her eyes, both of them feeling the urgency and danger of both their situations. "Jenny, I don't want the soldiers to know what I'm up to, if at all possible. It's possible some of them have seen Wild Horse, and if I look so much like him, there's going to be some real confusion when we're first found. I might have to explain why I'm out here in the first place. However it goes, I don't want them to know where Wild Horse is hiding out, understand? I promised that Indian I would come alone, as soon as I get you to the fort. I promised I wouldn't bring any soldiers."

She nodded. "I won't say anything."

"I might just tell them I'm going to the reservation farther north to see what I can find out. I don't want to mention Comanche Hills." He turned away, retrieving a pan from his gear. "Here," he said, pouring some water into it. "I'll find some soap and a towel. I don't know if there are any clean ones left."

"Right now anything will do," she answered, grateful for the water, in spite of how she felt about the wilder Comanche. Seeing the one who had just appeared at the cave like a ghost had brought back the ugly memories of the day of the raid, the way they had cruelly tossed her around and had shot her and meant to scalp and probably rape her. Why? Now that she knew and loved Wade Morrow, she wished even more that she could understand.

It was then that a new worry moved through her. Was it possible that if Wade did go to his people and found a brother there, the Indian in him would take over? Was it possible he could want to stay with them, ride with them? Did they have any kind of special power that could influence Wade to turn to his Comanche side?

She watched him as he unwound a beaded leather strip that had held his hair in one tail at the neck. He shook out the long, dark, straight hair, then removed his shirt, revealing dark skin and a muscular torso. Yes, he was very Indian. But he was surely much too educated and refined to join his wilder relatives. After all, he had never lived that way, and he had a white family that he loved waiting for him, as well as a freighting empire of which he stood to inherit a one-third share.

He handed her a towel and soap, and she dipped her hands into the pan, rinsing her face, her emotions a torrent of confusion. She still found it amazing that he looked so Indian but was so white in his beliefs and habits and speech, except for his keener skills at scouting and hunting. She thought of the night Buck attacked her, how viciously Wade had beat him. Was that the Indian vengeance in him?

"I'm going to take the horse into a cutout near this one. He'll stay put as long as this storm rages," he told her. "I'll leave him a pan of water. This place isn't big enough for the three of us, and you don't need to be putting up with the smell of a horse. I'll be right back."

He untied the travois, on which she still sat, and unloaded their gear, then led the horse out into the dusty wind, carrying a pan and one of the water pouches. Moments later he returned, still carrying what was left of the pouch of water. She watched him cup water into his hands and wash off his face. He grabbed a towel and dried himself.

He turned then, and their eyes met. She realized his thoughts must be the same as her own. This could be their last night together. He could die once he went off to find Wild Horse. A heavy, worried silence hung in the air while he moved away and brushed out his hair. He waited for her to finish washing, then came closer again, shirtless, his weapons removed, his hair hanging loose over powerful shoulders. He knelt down beside her, reaching out to unbutton the top buttons of her dress.

"You can't wash good without taking this off," he told her.

Their eyes held. "I know." She swallowed, her face flushing as he moved his hands down the buttons, and the painful desires she had felt earlier in the day for him returned when the backs of his hands touched her breasts as he unbuttoned the dress. She remembered the aching need he had awakened in her when he had touched her bare breast earlier, when he had invaded her mouth savagely so that she lost all control, all inhibitions.

He pulled the dress off her shoulders, seeing her taut nipples outlined through the thin cotton camisole. How he wanted to touch those breasts again, only this time he longed to draw the fruit of her breast into his mouth and claim that and more as his own.

She slipped her arms out of the dress, then reached around his neck. Both had known this moment would come; both knew without asking that it would be impossible to get through this night without acting on their needs and passion, for the feelings were too strong to deny. Both knew this might be all they ever had. The

217

urgency of the moment, magnified by the ghostly visit from the Comanche man, only brought forth an even greater need.

"I probably didn't get my face too clean," he told her. "I can't see what I'm doing and neither can you. We'll wash the dust off each other." He pulled her arms from around his neck and helped her out of her dress. He took off her shoes, and she sat there in her bloomers and camisole, realizing it didn't bother her now when he saw her this way.

She dipped her hands into the water and soaped them, rubbing them over his face and neck, then dipping one end of the towel into the water and wetting it. Neither of them spoke as she washed the dirt from him, soaping her hands again and running them over his arms and upper chest. This was only the second time she had seen him or any other man, for that matter, bare-chested. She felt both awkward and daring. He took hold of her wrists then and moved her hands down over his own nipples. It seemed strangely wicked to touch him there, even though a man didn't have breasts like a woman, and she sensed that it stimulated him.

He kept hold of her wrists then, pulling her hands away. "I've argued with myself all day, Jenny," he told her, his voice soft and strained. "I've reasoned that the best thing to do is leave you alone until we reach the fort and I settle what I came here to settle. But my love and desire for you are too damn strong."

He sighed deeply, letting go of her wrists and picking up the towel. He put the wet part of it to his face and began rinsing off the soap. He moved it to his neck, his arms, and she waited, not sure what to say.

"I don't want to hurt you or rob you of anything you feel is too important to give away too quickly," he told her, "especially to someone who is still hardly more than a stranger to you." He finished with the towel, still kneeling in front of her, clean and handsome, looking like a lost little boy.

She trembled with the ecstasy of what he was telling her, and she held his eyes boldly. "I . . . thought about the same thing today." The words were shaky, her love for him so strong that she wanted to cry. "You're the only one I would want to give myself to. And you aren't a stranger, Wade. I think some people you can know for just a little while and know almost everything about them, trust them, love them. And some, like my Uncle John, you can know all your life and never really know them at all, never be able to trust them. I know I can trust you. I know when you say you love me, you mean it. And when you promise to come back for me, I know you'll try."

She took the towel from him, looking down to rinse it out. "I don't want you to leave me at the fort and go to Wild Horse without first showing you you're the only man I want to belong to. I want to give you more reason than ever to come back, Wade."

She met his eyes again, passion ripping through her at the look in his eyes. His jaw flexed with repressed desires as he took the towel from her. He nodded, both of them knowing what must be. "Now I will wash you," he told her.

It seemed her veins ran with fire instead of blood. She closed her eyes, feeling the flush at her face as he reached down and pulled at the waist of her chemise, lifting it up and over her shoulders and off her arms. For the first time her naked breasts were exposed to his eyes, and her heart pounded wildly.

"My God, you're beautiful," he said in a husky voice.

She heard the splash of water, and in the next moment his soaped hands were moving over her own face and neck. She opened her eyes and met his own boldly as he bathed her and rinsed her. He soaped his hands again, this time moving them down to her breasts, hesitating a moment before rubbing over the nipples with the slippery soap, gently massaging, squeezing, toying with the pink fruits.

"I'm told the Indian man has a custom on his wedding night of rubbing down his bride with oil," he told her, dipping the towel into the water then to rinse off the soap from her. "I think it sounds like a fine custom. I imagine it's very relaxing."

He rubbed the towel over her, removing the soap from her breasts. Their eyes met again, and he came closer, covering her mouth, moaning with need and passion as he drew her against him, pressing her bare breasts against his own bare skin. The contact was all that was necessary to throw away all caution, all reason, all logical thought, which they both knew would happen anyway. Right or wrong, this was something they both had to do.

His kisses were hot and passionate, hungry and urgent. He moved his mouth to her throat, cupping a breast in his big, gentle hand. "Are you sure you're up to this?" he asked in a near whisper.

"I'll be all right."

"You aren't really well yet."

"It doesn't matter." She met his mouth with equal hunger. "I'd go through anything to belong to you, Wade," she whispered after another kiss. "I just want it to be you. I . . . don't want you to go away without this. I love you so much, Wade. Teach me all of it. Show me how to love you in more than words."

He pulled away slightly, his eyes on fire with desire, his nostrils slightly flared with passion. He reminded her of a wild warrior, yet she was not afraid of him. "I'll make up a bed for us."

He stood up and took some blankets from their gear. Jennifer pulled a blanket over her bare breasts, listening to the wind continue to howl outside while Wade used all the blankets he could find to build up a comfortable bed on top of some soft sand. He came back beside her, sitting down to remove his boots and socks, then rose to remove his denim pants.

Jennifer dropped her eyes, and he knew she was not ready to look at that hidden part of man she had never seen. He removed his pants, leaving on knee-length long johns. He leaned down and picked her up in strong arms, carrying her to the bed of blankets. He pulled away the blanket she held in front of her and lay her down onto the other blankets, stretching out beside her.

Resting on one elbow, he leaned over her, his dark hair brushing across her breasts. He grasped her own cascading mane of reddish hair in his hand and bent down to kiss her lightly. Her eyes were closed. "Look at me, Jenny," he told her.

She opened her eyes, feeling fire rip through her at their close nakedness, realizing that before he was through she would be completely naked and he would own every part of her.

"If you aren't sure, tell me so now."

She swallowed. "I'm sure." She felt faint, felt as though she was floating in a world of unreality. Was this really the Jennifer Andrews who had left St. Louis only three weeks ago, an innocent, frightened young woman who knew nothing about Texas and men like Wade Morrow? "I love you, Wade. That's all that matters."

He met her mouth again, one hand moving to again caress her breasts, teasing, toying, awakening virgin desires. She lay her head back and closed her eyes as his lips moved over her throat then, trailing down to one breast, finding for the first time the sweet fruit he had so longed to taste.

The feel of his warm lips and tongue at her breast brought gasps of sweet pleasure to her lips. She dug her fingers into his shoulder, arching up to him, wanting to give him pleasure. Her gasps became soft whimpers as his hand moved inside her bloomers while his lips lingered at her breasts. Suddenly he was touching her in a magic place that brought such exquisite pleasure to her insides that she felt light-headed. He moved his fingers in lovely, circular motions that made her forget the pain in her leg, made her want to give herself to him, boldly, willingly, brazenly.

"Oh, Wade," she moaned, as his lips kissed her flat belly. She felt him pulling off her bloomers, felt the thrill of letting him drink in the sight of her naked body, this time in heated desire and not because he had to help her. He kissed lightly the reddish hairs that hid that part of her he intended to possess, drawing a groan from her lips.

He moved his lips upward then, tasting her breasts again ever so gently before meeting her mouth in an invading kiss that left her helpless, while his hand searched secret places. She felt something push carefully inside of her as his fingers explored and lightly introduced her to what was to come. The touch made her feel wild with desire, making her return his kisses with wild, innocent passion.

Wade felt more alive and loved than he had in years. She was young and eager, reacting with all the innocence of a woman's desires being awakened for the first time. He wanted to please her, to let her feel everything, experience everything, enjoy everything. He hoped he would not hurt her too badly, but he knew what had to be done. His own passion ran wild at the feel of her satiny juices on his finger tips. He felt privileged that she had chosen him to make a woman of her, and he knew he would never love like this again.

She cried out then, gasping, arching up to him. He knew she had experienced her first climax, and he moved on top of her, unbuttoning his long johns. He kept his left hand under her neck, kissing her between words.

"Relax now, Jenny," he whispered, moving carefully between her legs. "Am I hurting your leg?"

"No," she lied. Her leg hurt, but she didn't care. Nothing mattered now, nothing but to please Wade Morrow. "What . . . happened to me?"

He grinned a little, kissing her hungrily again, running his tongue deep. He pressed his hardness against her belly. "You're just ready for a man now," he told her in a husky voice. He could hold himself back no longer. In one swift, urgent movement he pushed himself inside of her, moving a hand under her bottom as she screamed with the pain, but he was unable to stop in spite of those screams.

Moments later he could not hold back his own ecstasy, nor would he have tried. He knew that for her sake it was best it was over quickly. With a final, deep thrust, his life spilled into her; and at first he felt a sudden rush of guilt.

Would his love for her destroy her? Had he stolen something to which he had no right?

He let out a long, shuddering sigh, coming down on her, grasping her hair in his hands and letting her cry into his shoulder. "I'm sorry, Jenny," he groaned. "I shouldn't have done this."

"No, no," she wept. "Don't . . . be sorry. Don't ever be sorry." Her fingers still dug into his back as a myriad of emotions engulfed her. The pleasure had turned to shock, now mixed with the sweet satisfaction that the man of her own choosing had been her first. "It doesn't matter now . . . what happens," she told him. "Nothing can . . . change this."

"I hurt you," he said, kissing her hair, her eyes.

"I wanted the pain. I wanted it to be you." She finally met his eyes, loving him more than ever now, for they had been intimate, and she knew that even if something happened to him, she could not share this with another man for a long time to come. "Maybe . . . after a little while . . . we can do it again," she told him, wiping at some of her tears with her fingers.

He frowned. "You sure?"

"I'm sure that I love you." She sniffed. "I'm sure I want it to be nice for me before you go away. I mean . . . the pain must get better, or women wouldn't keep . . . having babies, would they?"

He grinned. "Yes, the pain goes away." He kissed her eyes. "And I want it to be as enjoyable for you as it was for me."

For a moment she was jealous of any other women he might have touched, even Rebecca. "Then promise me we'll do it again," she whispered.

He stroked her hair. "Before this night is over you'll be solidly branded, Jennifer Andrews. And as soon as I can get you away from Fort Stockton, I'll change your last name legally, if you'll agree to marry me."

She smiled through misty eyes. "It's a little late for me to change my mind, I think."

He laughed lightly. "I suppose so."

She reached behind her and pulled a blanket over them. "Do you think God led us to this place, Wade, so we could do this before we reach the fort?"

"Maybe. And maybe He meant for us to resist the temptation."

She nestled against him. "I like to think He approves. In my mind and heart you're already my husband. I think God knows how we feel. I don't think He cares much about a piece of paper—just what's in the heart."

"Well, I think you're right, and in a sense this *is* legal anyway. This is the way the Indians marry, and I'm part Indian."

She smiled, kissing his chest. "Then we've been married Indian style." The thought reminded her that in a few days he would be more Indian than he had ever been in his life. Could she truly trust him to return for her? She looked into his striking blue eyes, seeing only love and near worship. "You've got to come back for me, Wade."

He searched her eyes, thinking how they reminded him of the sea. "Nothing short of death will keep me from it."

The word death stung deep. She leaned up and met his mouth, kissing him desperately. "I want to do it again," she said boldly. "Was it all right? Did I please you?"

"Oh, yes, *bil nashdehi*. You please me very much."

She ran her fingers lightly over his lips. "What did you say?"

"*Bil nashdehi* is Apache for 'my wife.' I'm afraid I know the Apache tongue better than the Comanche."

"You had better be careful when you go to see Wild Horse and not use any Apache. Aren't the Comanche and the Apache bitter enemies?"

He frowned. "Oh, yes. The Comanche chased the Apache right out of west Texas. They're the fiercest warriors of all the plains Indians." He spoke the words with feigned bragging pride, but she sensed it was not all fake. Somewhere deep inside part of him truly did feel pride at the statement. Could that part be kept tamed once he found his people?

She touched his hair, noticing how dark and straight it

224

was, noticing how lily white her hand looked next to his face. "I love you, Wade Morrow. You won't ever forget that, will you?"

He took hold of her hand, looking at it, also seeing the stark contrast. "I feel honored, Jenny. How could I forget such a thing? I haven't felt this way since Rebecca." He kissed her hand. "I can't wait for my family to meet you. They'll love you, and you'll love them."

"I just hope the day comes soon when I *can* meet them."

He kissed her eyes. "It will, Jenny, I promise." His lips moved to her mouth again, and the talking ceased. Outside the wind continued to howl, drowning out the sounds of passion inside the cave, while a lone Indian made his way back to Comanche Hills to tell Wild Horse that his shadow would come to him soon. Several miles southwest of the Indian, a patrol of soldiers under Sergeant Anthony Enders made its way against the raging dust storm along the stage trail.

"Shouldn't we stop, Tony?" Corporal Deaver yelled out to his friend.

"Hell no! Not till I find my woman," Enders shouted back. "The telegram said the coach made it past the second home station. That's only another day away. Whatever happened to it, we should come to it by sometime tomorrow morning if we can make it a little farther tonight!"

They rode on, eyes stinging, nostrils filled with dirt, while Sergeant Enders's betrothed gave her heart and body willingly and in sweet love to another man.

Chapter Fifteen

Jennifer opened her eyes, realizing it was the quiet that woke her. The howling wind had finally ceased blowing sometime during the night. She lay still, watching the dawning light filter into the crude cave-like shelter Wade had found. She lay with her back to Wade, his love for her making her less conscious of the scars on her back, which didn't seem to bother him. Never had she felt so beautiful, so loved and protected.

But she could not help wondering if this sweet joy could really last. They could reach the fort by tonight, and then he would go away; and she still had Sergeant Enders to face. Once the soldiers found them, her most difficult task would be pretending to detest Wade. She understood why she must do it, but the thought of it made her sick. She wanted to shout to the whole world that she loved him, that he was the finest, bravest, most intelligent man she had ever known. Why did people have to be so cruel?

She touched the powerful arm that was fastened around her, studying the dark skin, kissing his arm. Wade stirred, pressing against her and reminding her of what she had done through the night. She was not quite sure how many times she had given herself to him; she only knew that his promise had been right. In spite of lingering pain and soreness, she could tell that being with a man only got better and better. She never dreamed pleasing a man could bring so much pleasure in return. Uncle John's attitude and threats had made it all seem so ugly and frightening, but Wade Morrow had removed those barriers. He had touched her so magically that she had been surprised at her own flagrant wantonness, never dreaming she could be so bold with a man. With the morning light came the realization of what she had done, as though she was just now waking up from a strange, wonderful dream.

Wade pulled her hair away from her neck and kissed her there. "Good morning," he said softly.

Jennifer kept her back to him, answering sleepily.

"You okay?" he asked.

She sighed deeply. "Just terribly tired. And my leg hurts."

He sat up. "I'd better take a look at it and change the dressing." He started to rise, but she turned to him, pulling at his arm.

"Not yet," she told him. Their eyes held in understanding, both of them realizing this could be their last moment to lie in each other's arms. He pulled her close, and she kissed his chest. "You don't think I'm bad, do you?" she asked. "I mean . . . I never thought I could do what I did . . . not this way. But I love you so much, and I'm so afraid of something happening to you."

He stroked her hair. "And I love you. Don't ever doubt it, Jenny. How could I think you're bad when I know you love me. I feel like the luckiest man alive." He kissed her forehead. "Besides, a man knows when it's a woman's first time. To think you gave me the privilege of being your first man only tells me how special I am to you." He moved his lips to her eyes. "You belong to me now, Jenny. Don't ever forget it. Your Uncle John can't come for you, and Sergeant Enders can't claim you. You belong to Wade Morrow. You just remember that if anyone else tries to tell you differently."

She ran a hand along his strong arm. "I'll never love another man the way I love you," she told him. "If something happens . . . I'll never forget you, and I won't want another man for a long, long time. Maybe never."

He took hold of her hand. "You're young. You'll want

228

another some day—a home and children. Just don't take another man for any reason but love, Jenny."

She met his eyes. "I just want you," she whispered, her eyes tearing. "What will I do if something happens—"

He put his fingers to her lips. "Nothing is going to happen. God brought us together. I can't believe He means for it to end here." He moved a big hand to her belly, massaging it. "I hope I didn't do you any damage."

She smiled. "I'll be all right." She put a hand to her face. "I must look terrible. And my hair—"

"You look beautiful." He leaned down and kissed her cheek. Their eyes held, and they both knew they had to use this one last moment to unite their bodies once more. He moved on top of her, bending his head to kiss her neck, her shoulder, both her breasts.

She closed her eyes and returned his rhythmic movements, as he rose to his knees, grasping her bottom and drinking in her nakedness as he pulled her to him in a conquering gesture that brought out all his deeper masculine feelings of dominance, though he knew he could never force this on any woman. This one wanted him, and he could think of nothing more pleasant than making Jennifer Andrews his legal wife, of building her a fine home in San Diego, of seeing her belly swollen with his child.

His life spilled into her, and he hoped it would not take hold just yet, almost hating himself at the realization that he could die and leave her pregnant. He had wanted her so badly the night before that he had given little thought to the possible consequences, other than emotional, and he doubted Jenny had either. Still, there was no sense asking her about her last time of month. It would only worry her. If his seed took hold in her belly, there was nothing that could be done about it now. He simply had to do all he could to get back to her, and pray God would protect her.

He pulled away from her and lay back down beside her for a moment, and Jenny suddenly burst into tears, hugging him around the neck. "Oh, Wade, I love you, I love you," she sobbed. "I don't want to leave this place."

He held her close. "Neither do I, but we don't have any choice." He kissed her hair, wishing he could have been stronger about the whole thing. It had really been up to him to resist the temptation. She was too young and innocent and trusting to know or care. If only she didn't tear at his heart the way she did. If only she hadn't been so beautiful, so loving, so brave, so vulnerable.

"Everything is going to be all right," he reassured her. "In a month or so we'll be together again and I'll take you to California with me. We'll get married and spend the rest of our lives together." He kissed her tears. "Please don't cry, Jenny. You've got to be braver now than you've ever been yet."

She sniffed, wiping at her eyes, angry with herself for the easy, babyish tears. It seemed that they came too readily, her emotions torn and confused, exhaustion making it difficult to be strong. So much had happened over the last few days, she wondered sometimes if she knew what she was doing at all. But when she looked into Wade's eyes, she knew one thing for certain. She loved him, and nothing would change that.

"I'm sorry for crying," she told him. "I must seem like such a child to you. I don't know what's wrong with me."

"You just need a good, long rest," Wade told her. "I understand." He sat up slightly, gently stroking her hair back from her face, wondering if any man had ever loved a woman as much as he loved her. "We'll get washed and get you dressed," he told her then, as reluctant as she was to leave the warm love nest they had shared. But the morning sun had brought back the reality of their situation, and they had to leave.

He rose and stretched and she drank in the sight of his handsome nakedness in full light, feeling a secret thrill at knowing she belonged to a man of such strength and skill. She wondered if it was supposed to be wrong to take pleasure in watching him, to feel desire at the sight of him. Wasn't all this just a part of loving him? Surely it was, for when he pulled the blanket away from her and helped her wash, she saw only a look of near worship in his eyes as he gazed lovingly over her nakedness.

They both washed, and before Jenny dressed Wade changed the bandage on her leg, which was still tender when she tried to stand on it. Her heart fell at the sight of the new scar she would carry, but she knew it wouldn't matter to Wade. And if something happened to him, the injury on her leg would always remind her of Wade Morrow, his kindness and patience and gentle care.

She realized now that her night of ecstasy had taxed her physically more than she had realized at first. She felt totally spent. Everything ached, and she had little energy. Wade had to help her dress, and he made her sit down while he brushed her hair, careful not to pull too hard close to the still-healing cut along her scalp, where the skin was pink and puffy near the scab line.

They ate only jerked meat and drank some water, since there was nothing in the area to use for a fire. "You'll eat better at the fort tonight," he told her, again wrapping his sleek, shiny hair into a tail at his neck with a strip of beaded rawhide. He pulled on the denim pants, but put on a pair of moccasins instead of leather boots. He pulled a clean, blue calico shirt over his head and put on a silver and turquoise necklace.

"You look better than I do," Jennifer told him.

Wade laughed lightly. "I doubt that. I never saw a prettier woman in my life than the one who got off that coach in San Antonio."

"Well that woman was a far cry from this one." She put a hand to her hair. "I'll look better for you in a couple of weeks."

He knelt in front of her, putting a hand to her cheek. "Do you think I care about how you look?" He leaned forward and kissed her lips. "God knows we both need a genuine bath and a decent meal. Right now it doesn't matter. All that matters is that your leg is going to be all right, that we're both alive and we both finally admitted our feelings. I'm a happy man, Jenny, and I'm not going to let anything keep me from you."

He kissed her again and rose to finish packing the

travois. He walked outside to retrieve the Indian pony, letting it stop to graze for a moment on a small cluster of buffalo grass. He looked to the south, half expecting to see soldiers coming, wondering if they had found the coach yet, wondering jealously and protectively what Sergeant Anthony Enders was like.

He led the pony into the cave and tied the travois onto it, while Jenny watched quietly, studying his every move, wanting to remember everything about this man she loved, this man who had stolen her virginity in a night of passion she would never forget. He came to her then, picking her up in his arms. "Time to go."

"Just a little longer," she asked, her eyes tearing.

"Some things can't be put off, *bil nashdehi*. This isn't the end. It's just the beginning. Don't forget that."

She put her arms around his neck and they kissed one last, delicious, hungry kiss before he finally tore his lips from hers and lay her on the travois. She could see tears in his own eyes, and she knew this was as hard for him as it was for her.

There was nothing more to be said. He tied her securely onto the travois and turned the horse to lead it outside, checking around the cave to be sure no evidence of their lovemaking was left behind, in case soldiers should track them to this point. A sudden pain engulfed his heart at the memory of the sweet night he had shared here with Jennifer Andrews. It was done now. She belonged to him. Wrong as it probably was, there was no changing it, and he would kill any man who tried to bring his Jenny any shame or harm for loving a half-breed.

He led the horse outside, then mounted up. "Remember what I said to do when we run across soldiers," he told her, looking straight ahead.

"I'll remember," she answered in a small voice that made his chest hurt more.

"Your injuries will give you an excuse to hold Enders off for a while," he said, getting the horse into motion. "You can't turn him down right away or he'll be suspicious. I put four hundred dollars in your handbag so you can pay him off later on. Then just wait for me. If I don't show up in a month or so, wire my father in San Diego—Lester Morrow, of Morrow Freighting Services. I've been thinking about what to do, and I know one thing for certain—I don't want you getting on any stagecoaches. I have some brothers on their way out here, headed for Galveston to pick up some freight from New Orleans. I wired them from San Antonio. My father will be sure to get word to them to stop at Fort Stockton and pick you up."

He let go of the horse's reins and let it amble on its own while he rolled a cigarette. "You explain everything to them," he continued. "Once they understand how important you are to me, they'll see that you get safely out of Fort Stockton. If I . . ." He stopped and lit the cigarette. "If I don't make it back at all, I can guarantee that if you go back to San Diego with my brothers, my father and mother will make a home for you until you can manage on your own—or until you meet someone else and settle."

"Don't talk that way, Wade." She swallowed back a lump in her throat. "I'll do like you said." There was a moment of silence. "Thank you . . . for the money, for everything you've done. I love you, Wade. I can't say it enough, since I have so little time left to say it."

He took a long drag on the cigarette, and she could not see the tears in his eyes. "I love you, too." He watched the mountains ahead. "I'd give you every last dime to my name if it means keeping Sergeant Anthony Enders away from you and keeping you safe."

She watched the wall of limestone where they had spent the night, as the travois was dragged farther and farther from it. She finally could no longer see the little opening to the shelter where Wade Morrow had made a woman of her, but she knew it would forever remain vivid in her memory.

"Oh, my God," Deaver muttered when they came upon the scene. He curled his nose at the stench, as did the others, as they slowly came to a halt near the overturned stagecoach. Enders ordered everyone to dismount and make a search to find evidence of a woman being aboard, but it took only a moment to spot the ripped, blue and white dress lying not far from the coach.

One of the men held it up, and Enders dismounted, walking up to the man, his eyes blazing with anger and revenge. He grabbed the dress from the man, holding it in a shaking hand. "Sons of bitches," he finally shouted. "Damn them! Damn them all!" He threw down the dress, walking away with clenched fists.

"What a shame," someone muttered.

"This one over here looks like old Nick, the driver that's come through the fort so many times," someone else spoke up, covering his mouth then with a neckerchief. He stood near a body riddled with arrows.

"There's another one here under the coach, mostly burned up," someone else spoke up.

"What a mess," came another voice.

"Get out the damn shovels and start digging," Enders ordered angrily. "And dig fast! We've got to get back to the fort and report this, maybe convince Howell to go after the bastards that did this! My God, I don't see a woman's body anyplace. She could still be alive, still be with them!" He stormed up to the coach and kicked at its charred remains. "Check inside the coach," he added. "Count the bodies, and try to find some identification."

"Good God, it looks like this one was tortured first," someone shouted, standing near Buck's body in the distance. "He must have a hundred stab wounds." He pushed the stiffened body over on its back. "Somebody finally put a bullet in his head and put him out of his misery."

"I wonder what happened to the horses," said another.

"Comanche probably took them—maybe for food. Them team horses ain't much good to the Comanche for ridin'. They prefer somethin' smaller and quicker."

"Quit gabbing and get the bodies buried," Enders repeated. He walked back to his horse, raging inside that his pleasure had been stolen from him, wasted on Comanche renegades.

"What if you do find her?" Deaver asked him, coming up to him from behind. "You know what shape she'd be in by then, Tony. She'd be no use to you."

Enders took a flask of whiskey from his supplies and swallowed some. "I'd at least have the pleasure of stealing her back," he snarled, "and killing some of the bastards who took her!" He swallowed more whiskey.

"Then what?"

"Hell, I don't know. I'd send her back to where she came from, I reckon. Maybe answer one of those other women who wrote me. What pisses me off is this one was the prettiest, if you can go by her picture."

"And how in hell are you going to afford to bring another woman out?"

Enders sighed, shoving the flask back into his gear. "How the hell do I know? I'll get the money somehow. Help me look around. Maybe they left behind all her belongings—maybe her handbag. Hell, the woman was supposed to be prepared to pay me back if she didn't marry me. She must have had money with her. I at least ought to get back my investment if I've lost the merchandise."

They both walked to the coach, inspecting the blackened remains, digging through baggage left scattered on the ground. After several minutes of rummaging, Enders realized there were no woman's items among the scattered remains.

"Something's not right," he told Deaver, scanning the horizon then.

"What do you mean?"

Enders looked at the man, feeling much smarter than the corporal, to whom it seemed he had to explain everything. "First off, Johnson over there said somebody put that one man out of his misery. That's not like the Comanche. They would have let him die slow. And second, why didn't they take any of these clothes? Some of them would have been useful to renegades, and so would the bags—something to carry things in. And look at that body over there, the well-dressed one," he added, pointing to Adam Hughes, who lay with his eyes still wide and staring, but partly picked at by buzzards. "He's still wearing a fancy watch in his vest. There's no way the Comanche would have left something like that behind."

He walked over to the dead body and ripped the watch from it, stuffing it into his own pocket. He looked around more. "The bodies and baggage have hardly been looted at all, Jim," Enders added to the corporal. "It doesn't make any sense. And what really doesn't make sense is the fact that there's no sign of a woman's baggage. We know she was on this coach because they left that dress and part of a petticoat behind. But where's her baggage, her handbag? They wouldn't stop to pick up just her things. Indian women don't have any use for corsets and bloomers and such. And the way white women are treated by the Comanche, they sure as hell don't have any need of their own things any longer. If she hasn't been raped or beat to death by now, she's slave to some damn warrior, and she's wearing a Comanche woman's tunic."

He took off his hat and ran a hand through his hair. "It just doesn't make sense."

Deaver scratched his beard. "Maybe she survived. Maybe she's out there walking around in a daze, trying to find the fort."

Enders turned to look at him, wanting to laugh at the idea, but not so sure he couldn't be right. "Doesn't seem possible. You've seen the rest of these bodies. They didn't intend to leave anyone alive." He looked back out over the horizon. "And yet they didn't loot anything either. Why?"

"Maybe something or someone scared them off before they finished. Maybe whoever it was helped the woman after he chased off the Comanche."

Enders put his hat back on, contemplating Deaver's suggestion, surprised at the man's ability to think of it. "Let's look around a little more," he said. "That sandstorm didn't blow through here. Maybe we can find some kind of unusual tracks or something."

Both men began searching, while the rest of the men, already bone weary from riding most of the night, their faces crusted with dirt from the sandstorm the day before, began digging shallow graves for the mutilated bodies.

"Look here," Enders shouted to Deaver, who had walked in another direction. The heavy rain that had fallen before the attack had left the ground soft, and Wade's boot prints, now hardened into the soil, were easy to spot. Deaver came running over, and both men inspected the prints. "A big man," Enders said thoughtfully. "And the prints are deep. He was either heavy set, or maybe carrying something." They looked at each other.

"Maybe carrying the woman," Deaver said.

Enders rose and began following the footsteps to nearly a quarter of a mile from the site of the massacre and over a ridge. Deaver followed, and both men found an abandoned campsite, where the cold coals of a small fire were evident.

"Look here," Enders said. "There's still a flattened spot where someone slept." His eyes widened when he spotted something white and red. He hurried over to pick up some torn material that looked like it came from a slip. It was stained with dried blood. "My God! Maybe she *is* alive, but hurt! Maybe somebody *did* find her and help her."

"Not till the Indians had had their way with her, I'll bet."

Enders threw down the bloodstained material. "And if they did, whoever found her probably figured her for fair game. A big man with a small, hurt woman at his mercy. God only knows what has happened here!"

"But if it was just one man, how the hell could he have scared off the Comanche? That must be what he did, or the woman wouldn't have been left alive. She'd have been killed or carried off."

Enders rubbed at the back of his neck. "I don't know. It doesn't make any sense. Besides that, it must have been a white man. He was wearing regular boots, not moccasins. Let's see what else we can find. See if these tracks lead anyplace."

237

Both men began searching again, until Deaver shouted to his friend to come and look. He pointed out the definite marks of something being dragged. "Looks almost like the marks left by an Indian travois. There are boot prints all around, but up ahead are the prints of a horse. Looks like it was dragging the travois, and I'll be damned if it isn't an Indian pony—no shoes. Can you beat that?"

Enders shook his head. "I don't understand any of this." He moved his eyes forward in the direction of the horse and travois. "The tracks lead northwest, the straightest line toward the fort. Whoever it is, maybe they decided to get to the fort as fast as they could, maybe because the woman was hurt bad. Maybe he found her bags and such for her. The fact still remains that if her bags were intact and the rest of the baggage wasn't looted, why? How could one man scare off a whole pack of renegade Indians?"

"I've never seen anything like this," Deaver told him.

"Neither have I. But as long as those tracks head toward the fort, we're going to follow them, and we're going to ride hard and fast. I don't care how tired the men are. I intend to find out what happened to Jennifer Andrews. We're only about a day and a half from the fort, if we go at full gait. One man dragging a travois with a wounded woman on it couldn't have made very good time. Maybe we'll even come across them before they reach the fort. That sandstorm farther north we came through must have held them up, let alone if the woman's wounded. Maybe the man is wounded, too."

"You think she'd be safe, traveling out here all alone with a stranger?"

Their eyes held. "If the Comanche got to her first, she's no good to any man. He can have her, for all I care. I just want to know what happened." Enders looked off into the horizon again. "But if she was untouched, she was my property. If some stranger took advantage of her, I'll personally kill the son of a bitch."

He stormed back to the site of the raid, barking at the rest of the men to hurry it up.

*   *   *

John Andrews paced and stewed, then poured himself another drink. "Who the hell do they think they are down there, refusing to send my niece back to me," he grumbled. The young man who worked for him at one of his warehouses and who had brought him the telegram waited nervously.

"I've always heard Texans are a strange lot," he spoke up.

Andrews read the telegram again, sent to him by a good friend of his who had gone to San Antonio three years earlier to set up a merchandise store there.

SHERIFF OF SAN ANTONIO REFUSED TO GIVE YOUR NIECE OVER TO MY MEN. SAYS SHE IS OF AGE—HAD VALID TICKET TO FORT STOCKTON—MARRYING A SERGEANT AT THE FORT. LET ME KNOW IF ANYTHING ELSE I CAN DO. DON.

Andrews wadded up the note and threw it to the floor. Jennifer, running off to a place like Texas to marry a lousy army sergeant! What had possessed her to run off like that, to desert him after losing Esther, and after all he had done for her! The ungrateful little brat! This was the thanks he got for taking in his brother's little girl.

"You can leave," he barked at the young man who still waited for his instructions. He left quickly, and Andrews threw his glass of whiskey at the fireplace, shattering it. For months, years, he had dreamed of the day when he could climb into Jennifer's bed. With Esther gone, it would have been so easy—Jennifer would have been lonely and distraught. He would have consoled her. Just the right words and touch to a young innocent like that, and she would have been putty in his hands. He cursed himself for getting so drunk after Esther's funeral. He had not even realized until he woke up the next morning that Jenny had not even been in her bed. Had he frightened her away when he crawled in beside her? Or had she never been there at all? If he had stayed sober, he could have handled her, he was sure.

"I won't leave it like this," he grumbled. "That girl

belongs here with me, her uncle, her only family, not with some loser in west Texas! I'll wire the commander of that fort and tell him she does not have permission to marry that sergeant. I'll threaten to complain all the way to the top if they allow this marriage to take place!"

What angered him the most was the thought of Jennifer giving herself to a man who was hardly more than a stranger. He stormed out of the house and headed for the telegraph office on his own, deciding that even if Jennifer was already married to the sergeant, he would offer the man a bundle of money to have the marriage annulled and send her back to St. Louis. He knew the kind of men who were stationed in such desolate places. Worthless, all of them, as far as he was concerned. Let the man get his jollies. Maybe by the time he got the offer of money, he would be tired of Jennifer anyway and gladly send her back. She would return home sorry and devastated, a used, embarrassed, divorced woman and more vulnerable than ever.

He adjusted his tie as he lumbered on fat legs down the street, reasoning that even if his pretty niece had been with another man, that wouldn't change her looks or how she would feel in bed. In fact, she might be easier than ever, once she had known man. He would take her in, comfort her, offer her a home again. After experiencing the deprivations of fort life in west Texas and the abuse of a strange soldier, St. Louis and his fine home would look good to her. She would have to be grateful . . . very grateful.

Chapter Sixteen

"Can't see the tracks any more, Tony," Deaver spoke up. "Sandstorm wiped them out."

"I can see that for myself," Enders answered irritably. "I'm wondering if they lost their sense of direction in the storm, how in hell they protected themselves from it."

"Hell of a way for a woman from the East to be introduced to west Texas. After that Indian raid and this sandstorm, if she really is still alive, I expect she's more than ready to go back home."

Enders adjusted his hat. "Well, I'm going to do my best to convince her otherwise."

Behind him soldiers sat nearly asleep in their saddles, having ridden hard all day.

"We can't be more than a day's ride from the fort," Enders was saying. "We'll keep going till past dark, then make camp and rest. However far they got, they'll have to do the same tonight. Maybe we'll catch up with them in the morning."

Earlier in the day they had found signs of another camp, near a dried up stream bed. More bloodied bandages had been left behind, as well as a pair of woman's bloomers, one leg slit open nearly to the waistline, the material badly bloodstained. Enders was more concerned about the fact that the bloomers had been removed than by the fact that whoever had worn them had been badly wounded. Some stranger was traveling with the woman he was supposed to

241

marry, and the man had apparently seen things only Anthony Enders should see. His small, suspicious mind was already at work, wondering if the bloomers had been removed out of necessity, or for some more devious reason.

"Let's go," he told the others. "We can cover more ground yet tonight."

They headed out, amid groans and complaints from the other men, passing a high plateau, braced by a wall of limestone. Unknowingly they passed another abandoned campsite, a cave-like shelter in the stone wall, where Anthony Enders's betrothed had given herself to another man.

"We should make the fort by noon tomorrow," Wade said. He had managed to get a fire going with some dried mesquite and some buffalo chips he had picked up as they traveled that day. "I thought we were a little closer than we are." Jennifer watched him set a pot of coffee on the fire. "This is the last of my roasted coffee beans, and they're getting stale at that. I hope we can stand this stuff." He pulled more jerked meat from his supplies. "Sure wish I could have spotted a rabbit or a prairie chicken or something today. You need better nourishment than this."

"I'll survive," she answered, taking the meat from him and watching him lovingly. "Some day we'll have a home of our own, and I'll make you fine meals of turkey or venison, with whipped potatoes and home-grown vegetables and apple pie. How does that sound?"

He grinned as he chewed on a piece of the jerked meat. "Damn good," he answered. "I can't wait." He met her eyes. "You'll get along well with my mother. She's a great cook, and she's a generous, loving person, like you."

Their eyes held, both of them wondering what lay ahead. "Tell me more about your folks," she asked.

He laid aside the meat, deciding to wait until the coffee was done before finishing it. "They went out to California from Houston." He drank some water from a canteen, then handed it over to her and began rolling a cigarette. "My mother came from a fairly wealthy family who had moved to Houston from Louisiana, and my pa had worked for her father. He wanted to make a good life for my mother like what she was used to. He had this big idea about how profitable it might be to set up a supply business out west. That was back in the thirties."

He leaned forward and drew a small burning branch of mesquite from the fire, holding its flaming end to his cigarette to light it. "Pa said that back then he was one of very few people who believed this area would grow, or that some day California would be a part of the United States. He ended up being right on both counts." He took a long drag on the cigarette. "I know when you're out in these parts, it still seems wild and unsettled and raw. But there are lots of places out here that are really growing fast, the eastern cities of Texas, and places like Denver, Colorado and Salt Lake City, Utah and Los Angeles, which isn't far from where my folks live in San Diego."

He lay back against his saddle, and Jennifer enjoyed watching him, feeling a rich satisfaction that this man belonged to her, that she had learned how to please him in the night, and he had taught her the joys of being a woman. Now she knew what love was, and it was wonderful.

"At any rate," he was saying, "my pa's idea turned out to be a good one. He was one of the first big suppliers to the Southwest, and now he's going to run his route all the way to Galveston, 'into home country,' he puts it. He'll set up a warehouse and pick up supplies shipped through the Gulf from New Orleans. That's what I had to see that businessman in San Antonio about."

"Tell me about when they found you."

He looked up at the stars, taking another drag on the cigarette. "My mother had just lost a baby, so they tell me. She wasn't well, and she was pretty depressed. They came through this country with a huge supply train of wagons, and my poor mother was the only woman along. She was lonely, and the trip was hard on her. Then one night she

243

heard my crying and sent Pa out to investigate. He found me all wrapped up in an Indian blanket. They realized I had been abandoned. My pa never said, but I expect most of the men on that train would just as soon have left me there. My pa said that at first even he considered it, not because he's hard-hearted, but because he figured there was some good reason my Indian mother had left me behind. Whites don't like to go messing with Indian custom. It was obvious I wasn't wanted, and that was all my mother needed to know to feel sorry for me and take me in. Pa says it took her all of two minutes to love me like her own. He thought maybe he should turn me over to some reservation or something later on, but then he got hooked, too, and they kept me and raised me."

Jennifer sighed, lying back on her own bedroll. "They must be fine people."

"They are. After they had children of their own, they taught my brothers to love and accept me as they would any brother. We've always got along. As I got older, I began using my inborn Indian instincts to scout for my pa's wagon trains, except for the two years I spent back East studying English literature and business at the University of Pennsylvania. All that was after the fiasco with Rebecca. I thought about staying there and getting a law degree, but I missed the outdoors and the weather out here too much. I can't stand the cold and humidity back East. I need the dry air and wide open spaces." He grinned. "Pa says that's the Indian in me, too."

She lay on her side and watched him. "Did it bother you a lot, knowing you were abandoned and unwanted?"

He smoked quietly a moment before answering. "Sometimes," he finally answered. "I prefer to think maybe I was a twin with an Indian mother. But then even if my real mother was white, to want to save at least one of the babies would have taken great courage, because if she got found out, she could be punished, maybe even killed, for keeping a child that would be considered a bad spirit. I figure if it happened that way, she must have loved her babies very much, whether she was Indian or white. It would have had to be a terrible decision for her, choosing one. I figure she did the best she could and probably secretly pined for the baby she left behind. At least I like to think of it that way."

"It's so sad to think of having to choose," Jennifer said quietly. "I can't imagine having to make a decision like that."

"Well, I could be completely wrong about the whole thing. But with all this talk about me being a shadow of the one called Wild Horse, I'm thinking maybe I'm not so wrong after all. I know too much now not to want to know more, Jenny. That's why I have to go and meet with this Wild Horse. I'm not afraid now. They've let me live for a reason."

"Maybe this Wild Horse means to kill you himself."

He met her eyes, seeing the fear and dread in them. "Maybe. I'll just have to face that when I come to it. I can handle myself, Jenny. I'm going to come back for you no matter what."

Her eyes teared. "I wish we could make love again."

"You're too exhausted. Besides, like I said, we can't be seen even embracing. Soldiers could be anywhere now. They could be watching this camp even now with a spyglass. God knows I'd like nothing more than to make love to you once more before we reach that fort, but we can't Jenny."

A painful lump rose in her throat. "I love you, Wade," she said softly. "I miss you already."

He held her eyes lovingly. "I miss you, too." His eyes drank in her beauty. "I'll never forget last night, Jenny. The thought of you is what will keep me fighting and alive while I'm gone. I love you, and nothing that happens can change that. We might as well get it all said tonight, because I expect it will be our last chance. You remember what I said about wiring my family if anything goes wrong."

"I'll remember. And I'll always remember last night, too. I don't care how wrong it might have been. In my heart it was right." She blinked back tears and turned onto

245

her back, looking up at the stars.

"What about you," he asked, wanting to keep her talking so she wouldn't cry. "Do you remember much about your folks?"

She thought for a moment, realizing she was only eighteen but felt as though she had lived through enough that she should be much older. "I don't remember a lot about my father, except that he was completely opposite from my Uncle John. He was thin and had a mustache, and he was kinder, more soft-spoken. He owned three big merchandise stores in St. Louis. My mother was pretty, and she was a quiet woman. She was always there for me."

She kept her eyes on a falling star, and a light breeze kept the mosquitoes away as she talked. "After the explosion and fire on the riverboat, it took me a long time to realize it was true that my mother and father were never coming back. I don't think I could have stood the pain of my injuries and the pain in my heart if not for Aunt Esther. She came as close to being a mother to me after that as anyone possibly could."

She could not help the tears then, realizing there had been no time to cry over Aunt Esther. How she had loved her!

Wade waited, staring at the glowing end of his cigarette, wanting to go to her and hold her but afraid of being spotted by soldiers. He suspected she needed a good cry by now, but it tore at his heart. He wondered how many more tears she would shed in the future for loving a half-breed.

"I don't know how someone . . . like Aunt Esther . . . ended up with a man like Uncle John," she sniffed.

"Maybe when she was young, she saw him differently," Wade said. "Sometimes people just change. Maybe he was good to her in the early years."

She sighed deeply, wiping at her eyes. "All of that life seems like such a long time ago now. It's as though Aunt Esther has been dead for years rather than just weeks. Sometimes I feel like I've moved into another life and body, like the Jennifer Andrews who lived back in St. Louis was somebody else, not me. I could never go back there now, Wade, or go back to the old Jenny. Does that make any sense?"

"Sure it does."

She turned her head to look at him, wiping at another tear. "What about you? What about when you go out there among your people? Do you think it's possible you'll learn something about their world and their life that will make you want to stay? Maybe you'll feel you can never come back to this life, or back to being the old Wade Morrow."

He met her eyes, tossing a stub of cigarette into the fire. "I'll have you to come back to," he answered. "Nothing is strong enough to keep me from that, Jenny. Don't you ever forget it."

She smiled through her tears. "I won't." She sniffed. "Can't you at least kiss me, Wade?"

She saw the pain in his eyes. "Don't you think I want to? Don't make it harder on me, Jenny. We just can't take the chance. When we're found, or when we show up at that fort, you'll understand what I'm talking about. Believe me, I've been the brunt of suspicion and racism all my life. I know the initial problems we'll have when we're first found."

She couldn't help another tear. "Oh, Wade, how do you put up with it? It's so unfair."

"Sometimes I don't put up with it. That day in San Antonio, I wanted nothing more than to take the knife that man pulled on me and shove it right into his gizzard. And that night Buck attacked you, I wanted to kill him, not just for that, but because of his insults to me. The only thing that holds me back is remembering what my pa taught me—that people act that way out of ignorance, that I'm just smarter and more educated than they are—that I'm just as good as they are, if not better."

He grinned a little. " 'That's not being conceited or too proud, son,' he would say. 'That's just fact. Don't let them bring you down to their level. Don't let them prove to others that they're right—that just because you're Indian you're a fighter and a killer. Stand up for your rights, and defend yourself when you have to, but don't spend your life with a chip on your shoulder and a knife in your hand.'"

He smiled more, obvious love in his eyes for his father. "I expect he's right, and I've tried to follow what he said. But I let the insults go only so far, and when another man comes after me physically, he'd better look out."

"Like Buck?"

He raised up and reached out to pull back the lid on the coffeepot to see if it was boiling yet. "Like Buck," he answered quietly. "I'll tell you a little secret, Jenny." He looked at her then. "Much as I hated that man, even I couldn't stand to see him suffer. After the Indians rode off, he was still alive."

Their eyes met. "You killed him," she said quietly, more of a statement than a question.

He nodded. "He looked up at me and begged me to do it. I'm not even sure he knew who I was. Maybe he even thought I was one of them. I just . . . I don't know. For some reason I need you to know I did it out of mercy, not hate."

She sat up herself, picking up the meat. "I wouldn't have thought anything different."

Their eyes held another moment, each of them wanting to hold and be held, each of them feeling the dread of having to pretend they didn't care about each other once they reached the fort, feeling the dread of separation.

"I love you, Wade," she told him. "I still feel like I can't say it enough."

She was sure she saw tears in his eyes when he turned back to the coffee. "I love you, too. Might as well say it as often as I can myself."

Jennifer watched the receding southeast horizon, her heart heavy, since Wade was certain they would reach the fort today. If only he could have held her last night. If only she could have felt one more kiss, or even held his hand while she slept. She ached for him, and she realized that although she didn't want him to leave once they arrived at the fort, if she couldn't even touch him, it would be easier to bear with him gone than when he was so near.

She slept off and on, weary from the horrors and ordeals through which she had suffered, her body exhausted from fighting the infection. She had not realized until she spent her last energy making love to Wade Morrow just how weak and weary she really was, and lack of proper food had only made things worse. Using her physical condition for an excuse to put off Sergeant Enders would be no lie on her part, certainly not for the next couple of weeks. She was sure she could probably do nothing but sleep for at least that long.

Toward noon she fell into another fitful nap, the warm sun keeping her eyes closed, the dull dragging sound of the travois lulling her to sleep in spite of the bouncy ride over rocks and holes. She was not sure how long she slept when she awoke and saw them, several riders approaching from the south. "Wade," she called out. "Someone is coming!"

She prayed it was not Indians. Wade halted the horse and turned in the saddle to watch for a moment. "Soldiers," he said, a degree of disappointment and apprehension in his voice. "Let me do the talking."

Jennifer's heart raced. Would Sergeant Enders be among them? What was he like, and what would he think of all this? What would he expect of her? A terrible dread moved through her, for now she really would have to totally ignore Wade, act as though she was glad the soldiers had come. He came around to the travois, and she looked up at him, her eyes wet with tears. "I love you, Wade."

He held her eyes a moment and just nodded, then walked farther out, rifle in hand. Jennifer kept her eyes on him for as long as she could, wanting to remember everything about him, the broad shoulders and slim hips, the way his denim pants fit his long legs, his shining, dark hair. There was an air of power and beauty and near grace about him that reminded her of some sleek, wild animal.

The soldiers came closer, sabers clanking, saddles squeaking, horses snorting. "It's a damn Indian," some-

249

one shouted. "An Indian's got her!"

Someone fired a pistol before Wade or Jennifer even knew one had been drawn. The bullet whizzed past Wade's left arm, jerking through his outer flesh and his buckskin shirt just enough to cause him to whirl and fall.

Jennifer screamed, so shocked at first by the sudden attack that it took her a moment to gather her thoughts. By then the troops had them surrounded. One heavyset man had dismounted and kicked away Wade's rifle, and another kicked Wade in the jaw when he tried to rise.

"Wait! Stop," Jennifer screamed. "It isn't what you think!"

Wade rolled and came to his knees, seeing another soldier approach. In pain and anger he waited for the foot to come up. When it did, he grabbed it and pushed up, making the soldier fall flat on his back. Wade quickly rose, seeing another man approach from his left side. He kicked out, slamming a foot across the side of the man's head and sending him reeling. He whirled then, facing a man who looked like some kind of officer. "I'm no damn Indian," he growled. "Not the kind you think!"

The officer and another man had guns raised, ready to shoot, when the officer reached out and pushed down the other man's gun hand. A couple of other men helped up those Wade had flattened, while the officer stared wide-eyed at Wade, as did some of the others now. Wade noticed the man who had prevented him from being shot wore a sergeant's stripes, and he wondered if this was the mysterious Sergeant Enders Jennifer had come here to marry. His heart raged with jealousy and anger.

"What is wrong with you?" Jennifer screamed. "Can't you see this man has been helping me? What kind of men are you?"

"Kill him, Tony," the heavyset man said. "It's Wild Horse, sure as we're standing here! You'll be famous!"

"I'm not Wild Horse," Wade growled, wiping blood from his lip. "My name is Wade Morrow, and I'm from San Diego. I was out here on personal business when my horse took lame. I hitched a ride on the stagecoach, and it was attacked by Indians. This woman and I survived. She was hurt and I helped her, that's all there is to it. I've been trying to reach the fort."

He brushed dirt from his clothes, blood staining his left arm. Jennifer longed to go to him and help him, but she forced herself to remember what he had told her.

The sergeant stepped closer to Wade, studying him as though he were a ghost. "Look out, Tony," the heavyset man spoke up. "He'll kill you."

Jennifer watched the sergeant, realizing Tony was short for Anthony. Was this her Sergeant Enders? If it was, she already despised him for his behavior. "He won't kill anyone," she answered. "He's telling the truth. Can't you see that he helped me? We've been trying to reach the fort, but a bad infection in my leg and a sandstorm slowed us down."

The sergeant's eyes moved to look at her. In spite of her disheveled condition, Anthony Enders thought her the prettiest thing he had seen in a long time. "You Jennifer Andrews?"

"Yes," she answered. "And this man's name is Wade Morrow. I'm not exactly pleased to have to travel with someone who's part Indian, but he saved my life, more than once. This is not the way I expected soldiers to act."

Enders removed his hat, running a hand through his hair. "I'm sorry, Miss Andrews. I'm Sergeant Enders. I've been worried sick about you. Out here, when we see an Indian, we tend to get riled real quick."

"It seems to me you could be a little more professional about it. If this man had anything wrong in mind, would he be traveling right toward an army fort?"

Enders swallowed, realizing he had got off on a bad foot with his intended. "No, ma'am, I guess not." He moved his eyes to Wade, too engrossed in the man's likeness to Wild Horse to give even Jennifer the attention she deserved at the moment. "But this case is different, Miss Andrews," he said, looking Wade over. "You've got to understand that this man looks exactly like a notorious renegade leader we've been trying to catch for a long time." He put his hat back on his head. "Mister, you've got some explaining to do. It's a damn good thing you speak English. That's the only thing that saved your life just now. Wild Horse doesn't speak any English." He walked closer and took away Wade's pistol and knife. "I want some answers."

The man Wade had kicked groaned and held his jaw. Blood still ran from Wade's arm, and from a cut lip.

"It's like I told you—I was on the stagecoach when it was raided. For some reason, when the Indians saw me, they drew back and left. That was before they had had a chance to harm the woman, except that she was hurt when the coach overturned, and the Indians had tossed her around and shot her in the leg. When they saw me they let her go and rode off, didn't even loot the coach. I took a bullet out of Miss Andrews's leg and made up a travois— headed northwest to take a more direct route to the fort. That's all there is to it."

Jennifer watched anxiously, remembering Wade had told her not to do too much talking. She trembled with fear for him and apprehension about Enders as the sergeant circled Wade while the others stared and held their guns on Wade.

"I've never seen anything like it, Tony," the heavyset man spoke up. "You sure Wild Horse can't speak English? Maybe this is some kind of joke."

Wade held Enders's eyes. "Would this Wild Horse be carrying a white man's wallet, with considerable money, and papers proving who he is? Would he even come near an army fort? Would he help a white woman rather than kill her or ride off with her?"

Enders scowled. "Where'd you get the Indian pony?"

Wade sighed. "The Indians left it for me."

"Left it for you?" Enders laughed. "What the hell for?"

"I don't know. Maybe because I look like this Wild Horse. When they saw me, they reacted a lot like you, except they seemed a lot more afraid. They rode off and left us this pony, as though they wanted me to live. From then on they left us alone. I don't know what's going on myself, except that I must look so much like this Wild Horse that they thought I was something special. One called me a strong spirit. Whatever their reason, my presence saved my life and Miss Andrews's. She was hurt bad, so I've been nursing her the whole way here. When I boarded the coach I intended to come to Fort Stockton to buy another horse and be on my way."

Enders rubbed at a chin that sported the stubble of a three-day beard. "Well, it's sure easy to see why the Comanche scattered when they saw you. You could be Wild Horse's twin."

The words struck deep. Enders was the first person besides himself to make the suggestion. "You've got no right to take my weapons," he told Enders. "I've done nothing wrong. In fact, if you're Sergeant Anthony Enders, I've done you a favor. This woman told me she was on her way to Fort Stockton to marry a Sergeant Enders. If not for me, she never would have made it."

Enders moved his eyes from Wade to Jennifer, sensing something was wrong but not quite sure what it was. He didn't want to believe the worst, for Miss Andrews looked too young and pretty for that. After all, she was an inexperienced innocent from St. Louis. Surely she wouldn't even want to be friends with a half-breed, let alone anything else. From what he could see of her, bundled and tied to the travois, she was a fine-looking woman, and it peeved him that this Wade Morrow had apparently got quite a look at her before he had. He looked back at Wade, his dark eyes holding contempt and suspicion.

"I reckon' I *should* be grateful," he told Wade. "But first maybe you can explain the lady's bloomers I found farther back at one of your camps."

Wade's jaw flexed in anger, and Jennifer spoke up before he could. "For heaven's sake I had to change them," she said boldly. "Couldn't you see they were ripped and covered with blood from my wound? Mr. Morrow understood that I would feel better if I could change my clothes and wash, so he let me. I had enough strength to do

253

it on my own, but it wasn't easy. I put up with the pain because I couldn't have him help me do such a thing. It was bad enough I had to let him tend to my wound, but I had no choice. Mr. Morrow turned his back and was a perfect gentleman the whole time."

Enders's eyes moved to her. "What about the dress the Indians tore off you?"

Her face reddened, more with anger than embarrassment. "What about it?"

"Well—" The man fumbled a little, now getting embarrassed himself. "Well, hell, you must have been half dressed when this half-breed helped you."

Jennifer scowled, her eyes blazing. "Yes, I was," she said, spitting the words. "I was also half *dead!* I hardly think either of us was worried about how I was dressed at the time, Mr. Enders! And for you to bring up such a thing is ludicrous and rude! It has taken me all of five minutes to figure out the man I came out here to marry is short-tempered, prejudiced, suspicious, and unmannerly," she added, "let alone the fact that he seems more concerned with how I was dressed than he is with the fact that if not for Mr. Morrow I could have been killed!"

The rest of the men struggled not to chuckle as Enders's face grew redder. Jennifer hoped she had not said too much, but she was too angry to care.

"It would have been nice if you had asked by now how I am, Mr. Enders," she added. "But I will tell you anyway. I am in a great deal of pain. I'm tired and dirty and hungry, and I would appreciate it if you would get me to the fort where I can rest in a real bed. And I think you owe Mr. Morrow here a deep apology. The least you can do for him is see that he gets a decent meal and a horse and a few supplies at the fort so that he can be on his way. I have delayed him from his own business long enough."

Enders felt the hidden laughter of his men. Jennifer Andrews was pretty, all right, but he was not going to be ordered around by her, not now, and not when she was his wife. Once he got that ring on her finger, she'd tone down soon enough. For the moment, he had little choice but to behave as she expected, if he ever wanted to get under her skirt. Still, he didn't like looking like a fool in front of his men.

He sighed, again removing his hat. "I'm sorry, Miss Andrews. There's a lot about this land and the feelings of soldiers for Indians that you don't understand yet. I assure you, my reaction was only out of my concern for you. I'm pleased to meet you, and we'll get you to the fort right away. But you have to understand that I can't give back Mr. Morrow's weapons until I take him to my commanding officer and he answers a few questions."

"Do what you have to do, but you should tend that wound on his arm."

"We'll take care of that at the fort," he answered, keeping his eyes on Wade again. "It's only about another hour north of here. Mount up, Morrow."

Wade held his eyes a moment, knowing already deep inside that if this man laid a hand on Jennifer wrongly, he would kill him. Already the two men had a strong dislike for each other.

Enders looked around at the rest of the men. "What the hell are you looking at," he growled. "Mount up!"

They all returned sheepishly to their horses. Wade turned, his eyes meeting Jennifer's for just a moment. He gave her a look that told her she had done all right. He mounted the pony then, and Enders walked up to the travois, holding the reins of his own horse and kneeling down beside her.

"I truly am sorry we got off to a bad start here, Miss Andrews. I didn't mean to act as though I'm not grateful that you're all right. When I first found that coach, I thought I'd go crazy wondering what might have happened to you. Then we couldn't find any of your things, and we figured maybe you survived. We found the travois tracks and followed them."

He tried to take her hand, but Jennifer pulled hers away, wondering how she could have been so foolish as to write to a stranger and offer to be his wife. After being with Wade, she could not imagine letting this man touch her, even if he were decent, which she sensed he was not. She realized that for now she had to keep him at bay and let him think she was still interested, like Wade had told her. If she turned him down too quickly, he might suspect something, and he seemed to be suspicious enough as it was.

"Well, I am very glad to be found. I must admit I was frightened having to travel with Mr. Morrow. He is not exactly the one I would have picked. I have no great fondness for men of Indian blood, Mr. Enders," she said rather haughtily, "especially after what happened to the coach and all those poor men with whom I had been traveling. It was so horrible." She let her eyes tear, which was easy to do. "I just want to get to the fort and rest, Mr. Enders. Is there a woman there with whom I can stay while I heal?"

"Yes, ma'am, a Mrs. Hart. She's a widow woman. She'll take care of you." He frowned, putting a hand to her hair to look at the healing cut along her forehead. She hated the touch but said nothing. "What the hell? Did they try to scalp you?"

"Yes. They stopped when they saw Mr. Morrow."

He shook his head. "You're a lucky woman, Miss Andrews." He glanced up at Wade, whose back was to him. "You're even luckier that Mr. Morrow turned out to be an honorable man. Most breeds are worse than their full-blood brothers, believe me."

Jennifer did not respond to the remark, but she knew Wade must have heard it, and she ached for him. Enders rose and mounted his horse. "Let's go," he yelled out. "You ride easy there, Morrow. That's my future wife you're hauling."

Wade said nothing, but Jennifer knew what he must be thinking, and she prayed there would be no trouble.

Chapter Seventeen

Jennifer felt everyone staring at her for the rest of the journey, and was grateful they were only a few hours from the fort. She felt like a sideshow, Sergeant Enders riding right beside her, sitting in a cocky pose, trying to make an impression on her with his authority over the other men. She wondered if it was just because she cared so much for Wade that she found herself disliking Enders, or if she would have felt the same way meeting him for the first time, even without already loving someone else.

She reasoned she would probably feel about the same. No matter how attentive the sergeant tried to be, there was something about him that did not ring true. Perhaps if she were the same naive Jennifer who first left St. Louis, she would be more impressed with the man; but now she could not help wondering if he could be one of those who had volunteered for duty out here because he was hiding from the law.

She argued with herself that it was wrong to be so suspicious, and she reminded herself that the poor sergeant had been waiting excitedly for weeks for her to come to him. It wasn't his fault that he must think she should have eyes only for him, that once she was healed she would agree to marry him. She had to let him think that for now, to keep his thoughts off Wade, and to keep him at bay until Wade could come for her.

"You'll be well taken care of at the fort, Jennifer. Do you

mind if I call you Jennifer? Considering the reason you came out here, I should think we can at least call each other by our first names. You can call me Tony."

Jennifer wondered what must be going through Wade's mind. He said nothing, but she knew he would like nothing better than to knock Sergeant Enders from his mount and declare his love for her.

"Call me Jennifer if you like," she answered. "But it will take me a little while to call you by your first name, Sergeant Enders."

His eyes lingered on her strangely, and she pulled the blanket to her neck, wincing when the travois bounced over a rock.

"I have to say, Jennifer, that you're even prettier than your picture. If you're this pretty after what you've been through, you must be very beautiful when you're up and well."

She wished he would stop looking at her, wished the soldiers riding behind the travois would also stop staring. "Thank you, Sergeant Enders," she answered.

"Fort's in sight, Sergeant," Deaver said then.

Enders rode up beside Wade. "You mind yourself, mister, till my commanding officer talks with you. I'm still not convinced you didn't have something to do with that raid."

"Don't be an idiot," Wade answered with disgust. "My story is the same as Miss Andrews's. You calling your bride-to-be a liar?"

"No. I'm only saying maybe it was all planned, but that you called off those Comanche wolves because of the woman. Maybe you had intentions for her yourself, except that she got hurt, and you had just enough feelings for her that it bothered you. I know how men like you pant after white women."

Wade halted the horse, and Jennifer's heart raced with worry for him. "If you weren't such an ignorant fool, mister, and if you didn't have all those men there to back you up, I'd show you what men like me can do to men like you. My father's supply business happens to have a contract with the government to supply you bastards with food and other necessities. One more insult from you, and there's going to be a problem that will be pinpointed directly to you and your commanding officer. I don't think you want to answer for that, or to show your new wife what an irresponsible fool you are. The fact that that woman is alive is proof enough of my side of this mess."

Wade started riding again, and Jennifer suppressed a smile. Enders rode on ahead and didn't say another word. Minutes later she spotted some buildings and heard someone shouting marching orders. A dog barked and someone yelled that Enders was back with an Indian man dragging a travois with a white woman on it. Men gathered and stared, few of them looking as spiffy and regimented as Jennifer had imagined. She felt like pulling the blanket completely over her face so they would stop staring.

"Somebody get Alice," Enders was ordering. "A couple of you men untie that travois and unload it except for the lady. Carry it over to Alice's place and tell Alice to do whatever she can for Miss Andrews. I'm taking Morrow to Captain Howell."

Men began unloading the travois, and then Jennifer saw Wade bending over her. "Get away from the woman and come with me, Morrow," Enders was saying.

"I have a right to get my tobacco. I need a smoke," Wade answered, his eyes on Jennifer. She knew it was only an excuse for one last look. Oh, what pain it was not to reach up and hug him, not to feel his lips on hers one more time, not to be able to tell him she loved him, to tell him goodbye. He gave her a soft smile, and she ached to be able to help him bandage his arm and wash the cut on his face where he had been kicked. No, right now she couldn't like Sergeant Enders one tiny bit.

"I'm all right," he told her quietly as he took a tobacco pouch from his gear. He understood her concern. "Remember what I told you." He left her then, and she watched him walk away, her heart aching with love. She prayed he wouldn't come across any serious trouble with the commander.

Moments later men were lifting the travois and carrying her. A neat, whitewashed cabin came into sight, and a stout, graying woman was hurrying toward her. "Oh, you poor child," the woman was saying. "Take her inside and put her on the bed. A couple of you bring over an extra cot. I'll use that while she's mending. My bed is much more comfortable than those army cots."

"Yes, ma'am," someone answered. Others carried her inside and held the travois near the bed while Jennifer managed to move herself from it to the bed.

"You men get out of here now," the woman ordered. "This poor girl needs a bath and a good rest."

The men fumbled with good-byes and last stares, one of them muttering about what a "lucky bastard" Sergeant Enders was. Jennifer looked around the small cabin, which consisted of just two rooms, one large one that contained a wood-burning, potbelly stove, a sewing machine, a small fireplace with the painting of a pretty young woman hanging over it as well as an army sword and hat with a feathered plume in it. There was also a frayed pink velvet loveseat near the fireplace, as well as a high-back, stuffed chair, a table and two wooden chairs, and a wooden rocker. The room was not very big, and the furniture took up most of the space; yet everything looked neat and tidy, and there were braided rugs on the swept wooden floor. A wardrobe stood in one corner, and a man's shaving table in another, although it was closed and was decorated with a small cactus plant. She couldn't see into the other room, except that she could see a pantry and realized it was the kitchen.

"I'm Alice Hart," the woman said then, coming to her side. "And you must be Jennifer Andrews, the woman Sergeant Enders has been waiting for."

Jennifer took a good look at the woman for the first time, seeing lines of age and experience, but kind, blue eyes. Her hair was pinned into a bun, but a few strands hung loose, as though she had had a busy day. Her dress was a plain black cotton, and she wore a white apron.

"Yes," Jennifer answered. *I don't want to be here*, she felt like screaming. *I just want to go away with Wade Morrow.*

"Whatever happened, child!" The woman put a hand to her forehead, studying the still-healing cut there. Jennifer explained the raid and how Wade Morrow had saved her life. "I know he's part Indian, and people around here hate men like him, but he saved my life not just from the Comanche but from infection, too. Sergeant Enders and the others treated him terribly. They won't bring him more harm, will they, Mrs. Hart?"

The woman folded her arms, studying Jennifer closely. "I don't expect so, but that's not for you to worry about any more. You're here and you're safe, and when you're healed you can get to know Sergeant Enders. When the preacher comes back by the first of next month, we'll have us a wedding. Right now let's get you bathed. I'll take a look at that leg myself and put some clean bandages on it."

Jennifer felt self-conscious, even though Alice Hart was a woman. She didn't like imposing on strangers. How she wished it could be Wade who bathed her, Wade who changed her bandages, Wade who could sleep with her tonight in this bed.

Alice walked outside, telling Jennifer she would put a kettle of water over a fire she had going outside. "Too hot to be lighting the wood stove or the fireplace," she called out. "You get undressed."

Jennifer sat up, wishing she knew what was happening to Wade, wondering if she would get to see him at all before he left. She began unbuttoning her dress. "What about your husband?" she asked Alice when the woman returned. "He might come home—" She vaguely remembered then that Sergeant Enders had said something about Mrs. Hart being a widow, and she reddened at realizing her error.

"My husband is dead," the woman was already saying. "He was killed three years ago by the Comanche. He was one of the first men picked by the colonel who originally ran this fort. The colonel was commissioned personally by Jefferson Davis, so my husband was among the first to come to Texas as part of the cavalry Davis personally trained and sent here to fight the Comanche. Those were fine men, not the riffraff you see here now. All the best men have been sent back East because of the trouble there. A lot of them were Southern boys, who left to join the Confederate cause."

She walked into the kitchen, returning with a huge tin tub that seemed too big for her to carry. She set it down in front of the fireplace and looked up at the picture and sword that hung there. "My husband would be on the side of the Union if he were still alive, even though we were from Tennessee. He wouldn't want to see this country divide itself." She sighed. "That's his sword up there," she said with a note of melancholy. "He was a fine, brave man; killed by the Comanche." The last words were repeated bitterly, and Jennifer wondered if the woman hated the Indians as much as most of the soldiers seemed to hate them. It made her feel more lonely and out of place. How could she ever hope to share her feelings for Wade with such a woman?

Alice sighed deeply. "I've stayed on here at the fort to be near my husband's grave," she added. "I do laundry and mending for the other men to earn my keep. I just can't bring myself to leave."

"Who is the girl in the painting?" Jennifer asked cautiously.

Alice turned, tears in her eyes. "She was our daughter. She died ten years ago of pneumonia. She was only sixteen." She walked closer to Jennifer. "That's part of the reason I don't mind having you here at all, Miss Andrews. You remind me of our daughter, and I'm happy to tend to you."

The remark made Jennifer feel a little more welcome. "Please call me Jenny," she answered. "And I'm really sorry to put you out this way."

"It's no bother at all." The woman finally smiled a

genuinely warm smile. "In fact, it's a joy having another woman around. I'm glad Sergeant Enders has two years to go before he can leave here." She sat down on the bed beside her. "You just remember that you don't *have* to marry that man, Jenny," she said, putting an arm around her shoulders. "You've been through so much, and I'm sure this place is nothing like you pictured it. Don't throw yourself into marriage with a near stranger unless you're really sure about it. God knows the ordeal you have been through is excuse enough to wait a while."

Jennifer met her eyes. "Don't you like the sergeant?"

A look of disgust moved into the woman's eyes. "It's probably not my place to say—not right now anyway. He's certainly not the soldier my husband was. Not many of the men here are. But I suppose it's up to you to decide. It's not my business. You give yourself some time to get to know him, then we'll talk about it some more."

The woman rose to go back outside and see how the water was doing. Jennifer turned, trying to see through lace curtains toward a building where Wade had been taken. A few soldiers milled about, and she felt a knot in her stomach. How she wished he could come to her, or that she could be over there with him. She *should* be there, she reasoned, to verify his story and stand up for him. How she hated all this pretending.

She finished unbuttoning her dress, remembering when she had let Wade do it, remembering the feel of his hands at her breasts, his lips covering her own; remembering the strength of his arms, the comfort of his words of love, the ecstasy of taking him inside herself. Maybe she would never know those things again.

The thought, added to the realization she would have to put up with Enders for the next few weeks, brought a rush of tears to her aching, battered body and soul. She turned and nearly collapsed onto the bed, and Alice returned to find her sobbing into a pillow. The woman's heart ached for her, realizing her loneliness, the fear and shock she must have suffered and still be suffering, let alone her pain. She thought she understood all the reasons for

Jennifer Andrews's pitiful tears, never suspecting she was really weeping for Wade Morrow.

Wade sat in Captain Howell's office, his big frame seeming to fill the room. First Lieutenant Michael Brown, a slender, blond-haired man who appeared only to be in his twenties, stood in one corner watching the questioning closely, rifle in hand. Sergeant Enders leaned against a wall watching, arms folded, a sneering look in his eyes.

Captain Howell sat behind his desk, studying Wade. Wade guessed the man was no more than thirty, but his thin, reddish hair was already receding. A neatly-trimmed, red beard covered his round face, and his pale blue eyes studied Wade intently.

"The resemblance is astounding," Howell told Wade then. "You can't blame us for holding you for a few questions, Mr. Morrow. If you didn't speak such good English and know so much about San Diego and your father's business and all, it would be hard to believe you weren't Wild Horse. But then Wild Horse can't speak English, and he wouldn't come near an army fort."

His eyes moved over Wade suspiciously. "I'll question Miss Andrews before you leave. If she verifies you didn't offend her in any way, you're free to go."

Wade glowered at the man. "If this was a white man sitting in this chair, you wouldn't think you had to verify his story. Fact is, Captain, she was probably a lot safer with me than she would have been with most white men I know. The woman has been through quite an ordeal. If you insist on questioning her, go easy on her, and don't embarrass her."

"Why did it take you so long to get here?" Enders asked. "Seems to me like you could have made it in a couple of days."

Wade turned his blue eyes to the man, giving Enders a chill at the look of murder in them. "I told you she got a bad infection. I had to burn it out. We lost a whole day just waiting until she was well enough to be moved again.

Then the sandstorm held us up for another day."

"And how did you protect yourselves from the sandstorm?"

Wade knew what he was after, and he was not about to give Enders one inch of room toward suggesting something went on between himself and Jennifer. "I dragged the travois up against a rock formation where most of the sand blew over us. It was the best I could do."

"You seem awfully clean for having been through a dust storm."

"She washed her face and I washed mine. Is there a law that says half-breeds can't clean up, or that people traveling with them can't?"

"Let it go, Enders," the captain said then, his eyes on Wade. "It's obvious the man helped your intended. Just be glad she's safe and mending."

"How do I know the Comanche didn't rape her," Enders sneered. "Maybe she doesn't want me to know and she made this one promise not to tell. Maybe while she was delirious he took his own turn."

Wade leaped from the chair, knocking it over. Enders pulled a pistol but Lieutenant Brown quickly stepped between the two men, brandishing his rifle at Wade, who stood with fists clenched.

"If that woman had gone through something like that, would she be as recovered as she already is?" Wade growled at Enders. "She doesn't mean anything to me except a poor woman who needed help, mister, but by God, if you suggest something like that to her face, I'll *kill* you, you filthy-minded bastard!"

"I agree the remark was uncalled-for," the captain spoke up. "Sit down, Mr. Morrow." He looked at Enders as Lieutenant Brown gave Wade a light shove with the rifle. Wade cast him a belligerent look, then backed away and picked up his chair. "Sergeant, I want no more remarks like that one," Howell told Enders. "It's bad enough that you let your men beat Mr. Morrow before you even knew what had happened. I'm tempted to reprimand you for that."

"What was I supposed to think? He looks every bit Comanche except for those eyes, let alone the fact that he looks like Wild Horse. Hell, Captain, nobody wants to capture Wild Horse more than you do. I figured for a minute there we had him."

"Watch how you talk to me, Sergeant," the captain warned. "And I don't want another word out of you." His eyes moved back to Wade, who sat back down into the chair but looked ready to leap out of it again. "The sergeant has a point, Morrow. And right now, you remind me of how Wild Horse looked when he turned himself in once—all jumpy, his eyes darting around like a caged animal. We were going to send him and his people to the Clear Fork reservation. Someone made the mistake of trying to handcuff the man, and he figured he'd been tricked and was going to be killed. All hell broke loose. Before it was over, Wild Horse got away again, with several of his men, but his wife and small son were killed. He's been on a rampage ever since."

Wade held the man's eyes. He could just imagine what had happened, and although he was not sure yet about this man called Wild Horse, he felt sorry for his loss, and felt a strange kinship with him. He understood what it was like to be an Indian in the white man's world. "Can you blame him?" he asked.

The captain sighed. "I suppose not. But you can't blame our side either. The Comanche have done some god-awful things to Texas settlers, Mr. Morrow; the Texans retaliate just as viciously. We do what we can to protect both sides, but with so many men sent back East, I just don't have enough to go galavanting all over such big country to find a handful of renegades." He leaned forward, his elbows on his desk. "Tell me something, Morrow. You said you were headed back to San Diego. You also said you've done a lot of scouting for your father. Back there when the coach was raided, you said those Comanche rode off when they saw you, then left you a horse. Surely now you know why they did that."

266

Wade shrugged. "Because I look like this Wild Horse, I suppose."

"Doesn't that make you wonder? You said you were found by Lester Morrow as an abandoned baby. Don't you wonder why you were abandoned?"

Wade told himself to be careful. The last thing he wanted was for this man to know why he was here. He had promised Wild Horse he would bring no soldiers. "Sometimes," he answered.

"For God's sake, man, you must have been a twin," Howell told him. "I know for a fact that Wild Horse's mother was Comanche. She was raped by white men. No one will ever know which one was the father. They were later murdered by the Comanche. At any rate, maybe the woman had twins. Maybe she didn't have the heart to see them both killed, so she kept one. Wild Horse could be your own blood brother. Doesn't that make you curious? Don't you want to meet him?"

Wade rolled another cigarette. "It's a little late for that, don't you think?"

Howell leaned back in his chair. "We could kill two birds with one stone here, Morrow. You could scout for my men, help us find Wild Horse. Hell, the man has probably heard about you by now anyway. You could scout him out without the danger of them killing you. They obviously don't want to do that. You could find him—find out if he's your brother—then you could report back to us and tell us where he is so we can capture him and end this bloodshed."

Wade licked the cigarette paper and sealed it. "You mean you want me to turn in my own brother, if that should turn out to be the case."

Howell sighed. "Well, if you're so unconcerned about even finding out, why should you care if he gets caught? You said yourself that after all these years you'd have no feelings for the man."

Wade struck a match and lit the cigarette. "I didn't say that at all. I said it was a little late to be worried about finding any Indian relatives. That doesn't mean I wouldn't have any feelings for them if I did." He took a long drag on the cigarette. "I've never lived among them. I understand them hardly any better than you do, Captain. Our worlds are as different as night and day, so how would it benefit me to go looking for them?"

The captain shrugged. "You could meet your real mother. I expect any man would want that." The man noticed the flash of interest and nostalgia in Wade's eyes. The man was not able to hide the look in time. Howell grinned. "Wild Horse's mother is still alive, Morrow. Her name is Slow Woman, and she's up in Indian Territory, a Comanche reservation just north of the Red River. Personally, if I had never known my real mother, I would jump at any chance I had to find her, if it was possible she was still alive. In fact, I almost admire any old Comanche who has survived this long. Between the army and the Texas Rangers, white man's diseases, the dramatic loss of wild game for food—it's a miracle there are any Comanche left. There are just a few hundred now. Used to be thousands. You pass up this chance to find out about your Comanche relatives, you might never get another opportunity to find them alive."

Wade smoked quietly. "Maybe not," he finally answered. "I might give consideration to finding them, but if I did, it would be a personal thing. I wouldn't go inviting the whole damn army to join me. Why should I have a hand in helping kill off my own blood, especially if, as you say, there are so few of them left?"

"I'm not talking about killing them off. I'm talking about helping them survive, Morrow. Ones like Wild Horse have to be convinced to go to the reservations. They'll be well cared for."

Wade could not help snickering at the words. "I know about reservations, Captain."

The man put up his hands. "All right. I know conditions are bad. But the odds of survival are a lot better than living the way Wild Horse lives."

Their eyes held. "Maybe he'd rather die young and free than as a shriveled up old reservation Indian, with no pride left."

The captain nodded. "Maybe. And maybe you understand the man better than you think. Maybe you also have enough Indian in you that you don't really want to see your race die out completely. Maybe you'd like to see the children live; maybe you'd like to know the language and the culture will be preserved, and that you had a hand in keeping your own people from complete extinction. You think about it long enough, and you might even realize it's your duty to help end the bloodshed and save what's left of the Comanche. You're in the best position to help, Morrow. You *are* Comanche, yet you understand the white man. You can work both sides. Why don't you stay on a while, scout out Wild Horse for us. Maybe you could convince him to go to the reservation, convince him there would not be a repeat of the last time he turned himself in."

Wade rose. "It's a little late for that, too, isn't it? He's already lost his wife and son. Fact is, if he's my brother, *I've* lost a sister-in-law and nephew I'll never know now, thanks to the army. No, thanks, Captain. Oh, I might see about visiting the reservation and finding this Wild Horse's mother, just to see if I can find out if she ever had twins. I'll admit the idea of finding my mother interests me. But that's as far as I go. I'm not going to turn in any Comanche to you people."

"You'd be helping them, Morrow," Howell answered, also rising. "You think about that."

Wade took another drag on his cigarette. "Right now I just want to get word back to my father in California that I'm all right and then be on my way. I have money to buy a good horse, if you'll have someone show me where I can get one. Then I'll gather my gear and be on my way. I would like permission to say good-bye to Miss Andrews and give her my wishes for a quick recovery."

"I'll tell her for you," Enders sneered, hot with jealousy

over the thought of the half-breed seeing Jennifer Andrews's naked leg, nursing her, befriending her, touching her in any way.

"Considering what Morrow did for the woman, Enders, I believe he's perfectly proper to want to tell the woman good-bye." He turned to the lieutenant. "Take Mr. Morrow out to the corral and let him pick out a horse, Lieutenant Brown. Then take him over to the supply house and let him stock up on whatever he needs. I will go and have a short talk with Miss Andrews." He looked at Wade. "After I've asked the lady a few questions, you can come over to Mrs. Hart's place and have a word with Miss Andrews, but only if she is willing. The woman has been through quite enough. Perhaps she won't want to see you at all."

Wade felt a painful ache for Jenny. If the man knew just how much she would want to see Wade Morrow, life would be hell for her here. "Thank you, Captain," he said aloud, keeping his cigarette between his lips. "And I want my weapons back."

Howell picked up Wade's knife and pistol from his desk and handed them out. Wade, his top lip puffy and scabbed at the left corner and a bruise on his left cheek, took the weapons, casting a look of hatred and disgust toward Enders. He shoved his gun into its holster and the knife into its sheath, sorely tempted to use one or the other on Enders. Howell handed him his rifle, and Wade reached out and took it without taking his eyes from the sergeant.

"You remember what Captain Howell said about what Miss Andrews has been through," he told Enders. "She's nothing special to me and wouldn't be even if I wanted it that way. She's a nice lady and damn proper. She doesn't know much about life out here, and she's been through hell. When a man nurses a person back from death, he can't help but take an interest." He took his cigarette from his mouth and smashed it in an ashtray on Howell's desk. "She only turned to me for help because she didn't have any choice. You remember that, Enders. And you give her some time to heal and get her senses together."

"I don't need you to tell me how to treat my woman."

Wade's eyes narrowed, and he stepped closer. "She's not your woman *yet*, Enders. It's *her* choice, and I'm telling you she's a fine lady, and what she decides is her right. If she decides to marry you, you'd better treat her the way she *deserves* to be treated."

"And what would *you* do about it? You're leaving, remember?"

Wade smiled a little. "Well, now, you never know. I just might come back sometime to see how Miss Andrews, or Mrs. Enders, is doing, seeing as how I had a hand in her still being alive and all. I sure as hell hope she tells me she's happy and well cared for." He turned to Howell. "Sorry I can't take you up on your offer, Captain. I have my own plans."

Wade turned and walked out, and Enders glowered at the captain. "I don't trust him, Sir. Why did you tell him he could go over and see my woman?"

The captain gave him a look of irritation. "Because, like he said, she's not your woman yet. And after what he did for her, he has every right. It's not her fault it was Morrow who ended up having to help her. I'm sure it was a terrible experience for her and she would not have chosen a half-breed to have to travel with. At the same time, I'm sure she's mannerly enough to appreciate Morrow wanting to tell her good-bye and give her his best wishes." The man moved his eyes to the doorway. "I'm more concerned with this revelation of finding a half-breed who looks just like Wild Horse. I can't believe he'll just go his merry way without finding out if Wild Horse could be his brother. You wire ahead to the Comanche reservation at the Red River and tell them to be on the lookout for a half-breed named Wade Morrow who looks like Wild Horse—tell them he might try to visit Slow Woman. If he does, I want to know about it. From then on I want him tracked. He just might lead us right to Wild Horse."

Enders nodded, leaving quickly. He hardly knew Wade Morrow, but he would like nothing more than to see the man dead. He would be glad when he was finally gone. He hoped he *would* look for Wild Horse. The crazy Indian would probably kill Morrow, if Morrow really was a twin. The Comanche did not allow such a thing. Wild Horse would surely have Wade killed, slowly tortured, most likely, so that Wild Horse could draw from his brother all the strength and spirit he would believe had been robbed from him for being a twin. Enders knew the Comanche well enough to understand that much about them.

He glanced over at Alice's cabin. Jennifer Andrews would be in there now, probably taking a bath. She was naked. How he'd like to take a peek at what would belong to him—soon, very soon—before the preacher even came, if he could talk her into it. The thought of a pretty woman just beyond those walls, one that was going to be his wife, made him ache. He almost wished he could prove there *had* been something between her and Wade Morrow. Then she'd be considered a worthless slut, and no one would blame him for taking her whether she wanted him or not. After that she was anybody's toy, for all he cared. He was not about to marry a woman who would let a half-breed lay his hands on her.

Chapter Eighteen

Jennifer settled into the luxury of a real bed. Although it was no more than a homemade frame with a woven rope support under a feather mattress, it felt wonderful compared to the hard ground or a bouncing travois. She only wished that being here didn't mean having to be separated from Wade. The two hours since she had watched him walk off with the soldiers seemed an eternity, and she wondered how she was going to survive the next month or so without him.

She had already told Captain Howell her story, which matched Wade's. She was glad the captain believed her, and she hoped her eyes did not give away her special feelings for Wade. Now she waited anxiously, struggling to hide her excitement and joy at the news that the captain was allowing Wade to come and see her once more before leaving.

Someone tapped lightly on the door then, and her heart raced. She prayed it was Wade and not Sergeant Enders. She tried to reason that Enders probably had every right to be upset and suspicious. After all, it was his intended wife who had been hurt and missing and in the hands of a half-breed stranger. Still, it was more than the way the man had behaved today that brought an almost instant dislike.

Alice came from the kitchen to open the door, gasping slightly at first. "Oh, it's you," she said, a note of bitterness in her voice. Jennifer felt a surge of love and joy when she heard Wade's voice.

"I'm Wade Morrow. I'd like to say good-bye to Miss Andrews, if I may."

Alice looked him over with a scowl. "I know who you are, but it seems sacrilegious to allow a Comanche man into my home. Comanche killed my husband."

Jennifer could not quite see Wade, but she saw his hand move as he raised it to remove his hat. She saw the fringe on the sleeve of his buckskin shirt, and just that much made her heart flutter.

"I'm sorry about that, ma'am, but I've never been a part of those Comanche. I'm afraid I can't help how I look, but I assure you I'm as civil as the next man. Now I went through a lot to save Miss Andrews's life and get her to this fort. I think I have a right to have a few words with her before I'm on my way."

Alice sighed, glancing over at Jennifer. "You want to see Mr. Morrow?"

Jennifer struggled not to appear too excited. "Yes, of course. It would be only proper, Mrs. Hart. The man did save my life. I'm sorry to put you out this way."

The woman softened when she looked at Jennifer. "I told you it's no bother. I'll enjoy having you around, dear, and please call me Alice."

Jennifer gave her her best, most gracious smile. "And you call me Jenny. Please let Mr. Morrow come in for a moment. He really is a fine man, Alice."

The woman glanced back at Wade. "Well, you do speak well. There sure doesn't seem to be anything Comanche about the way you talk and act." She looked at Jennifer again. "I've got laundry to tend to out back. Is it all right to leave you alone with him?"

Jennifer smiled again, wanting to roll her eyes and scream at the woman to let the man inside. "Alice, I was alone with him for five days, and he was with me and those who traveled with me for nearly three days before that. He was a tremendous help to the stage driver, and he saved my life twice. I hardly think I'm in any danger, certainly not here in the middle of an army fort."

"Well . . ." The woman looked back at Wade, then

stood aside. "Come on in. There's a chair there beside the bed."

Wade came inside, his commanding presence seeming to fill the little room. Jennifer struggled to appear only casually friendly, putting out her hand. Wade came over to the bed and took her hand, squeezing it gently, and Jennifer knew by his eyes he wanted nothing more than to crawl into bed beside her and hold her.

"Hello, Mr. Morrow," she said softly. "I'm glad you came by before leaving."

"I'll be right out back," Alice told Jennifer. "You yell if you need anything."

Jennifer almost laughed at what the woman meant by the remark. Alice nearly stomped through the room on her way out. As soon as she was gone, Jennifer leaned forward and felt the wonderful comfort of Wade Morrow's strong arms around her.

"Oh, Wade! Thank God I got to see you once more alone." She felt his lips at her neck.

"Jenny," he said softly. He breathed deeply of her fresh-bathed scent, gathered her still-damp hair in one hand. "I've been going crazy wanting to hold you," he groaned.

She turned her face and met his mouth in a long, hot, hungry kiss that left her flushed and trembling. Then she saw the cut on his lip. "Oh. Wade, what have they done to you?"

"We have to be careful," he said softly. "Mrs. Hart could come back." He pulled away from her. "Don't worry about me. I'm all right."

"I hate this pretending, Wade."

"I know. But at least you're safe now, and there's a woman here to talk to and take care of you. You'll be all right now." A look of anger suddenly came into his eyes. "I wanted the chance to tell you to be damn careful around that Sergeant Enders. Don't go off alone with him. For the next two or three weeks insist on visiting with him here with Mrs. Hart around. I don't like the man and I don't trust him."

"I know. I feel the same way. It isn't just because of how

he treated you." She closed her eyes. "Oh, Wade, what if I had never met you? I would never have been strong enough to face all this."

"Yes, you would have." He squeezed her hands lovingly. "You're a strong, brave woman, Jenny, and that's what I love about you. I'm so damn sorry it has to be this way, but I've got to find out about this Wild Horse. All these men here, they tell me I look enough like him to be his twin. And I understand better now why the man keeps raiding and killing. He turned himself in once. Someone started shooting, and before it was over, his wife and young son were dead. The man must be full of hatred and sorrow, Jenny."

"Oh, Wade, how awful!"

He studied her lovingly, hating to leave her, but unable to resist the chance to find out about his Indian blood. "The Captain says Wild Horse's mother's name is Slow Woman, and she's on a reservation up north of the Red River. I've got to go and see her, Jenny. I've got to ask her if Wild Horse was a twin. She could be my own mother."

Jennifer kept hold of his hands. "I understand. To come this far, to be this close to finding out something about your Comanche blood—I'd never forgive myself if I kept you from knowing the truth, if it's so important to you. But it scares me. It could mean terrible trouble for you. You might be in great danger."

He sighed. "I don't know. Surely there's a way to reason with Wild Horse if he truly is my brother. All I know is I've heard too much now to be able to just leave this place and never meet the man. But when I promised to go out to him, you and I hadn't . . ." He squeezed her hands again, love and near sorrow coming into his eyes. "I'm so damn sorry, Jenny. I had no right doing what I did, not knowing how all this would turn out."

Her eyes lit up with love. "I wouldn't have had it any other way. I love you, Wade. I'll say it again while I have the chance."

"And I love you," he whispered. He looked back toward the kitchen, then leaned forward and kissed her once more, putting a hand to the back of her neck and lightly running his tongue around her mouth, wanting to savor the taste of her, remember the smell of her.

He left her mouth reluctantly. "I can't stay too long or it will look bad," he told her. "You remember what I said. If I don't get back, and there's too much trouble, you wire my father in San Diego. My brothers, at least one of them, will be coming through this way, probably by the end of the month. My father will know how to get hold of them. Maybe they'll even come here to the fort. They'll help you if you ask. Don't be afraid to tell them about you and me. My folks will gladly help you out. But for the next few weeks you're going to have to stall Enders. You've got lots of excuses—your wounds, the shock of what you've been through, no preacher—and you've got enough money to pay him off."

"Thanks to you," she said lovingly. "Wade, if you . . . if you don't come back . . ." Her eyes teared. "I'll love you forever. I'll never forget you, and I'll never love anybody else the same."

"Don't cry." He quickly wiped at a tear with his thumb. "You can't cry, Jenny, at least not right after seeing me." He smiled for her, wanting to cry himself. "I *will* be back, Jenny. You just think of it that way. I don't break promises."

She sniffed and breathed deeply, too tired and too frightened and too much in love to have the strength to fight the tears. "Oh, Wade, I'm sorry," she squeaked, taking more deep breaths and wiping at tears.

He rose, glancing back toward the kitchen again and then moving to sit on the edge of the bed, taking her face firmly in his hands. "Jenny, it's going to be all right. I'll take care of things as fast as I can. Then I'll find an excuse to come back here and you'll know I'm all right. When that happens, you pay off Enders and take the next stage out of here. I'll follow the stage and pick you up after you're a few miles from the fort. But if I *don't* show up here, do what I told you. Wire my father. Don't get on any stagecoach unless you know I'm out there to watch over you and pick you up."

He leaned forward again and lightly kissed her eyes. "We'll be married and we'll go to California. You'll love California, and my parents will love you. You'll see, Jenny. It's all going to work out."

She grasped his wrists, feeling a soothing strength and comfort with his big, strong hands at her face. "Be careful, Wade," she sniffed.

He wiped at more tears with his thumbs. "You know I will. I'm not exactly inexperienced at survival or at Indian fighting, you know." He gave her his most reassuring smile, and she thought how handsome that smile was. "Bye, Jenny," he said softly. He kissed her once more, lightly, lovingly. "I'll be back."

She just watched him, wanting to remember every feature, drinking in the handsome blue eyes and the fine nose and perfectly-etched lips, the high cheekbones and the proud look of him. How strange that there was another man who looked just like this one, but who was so drastically different, wild and vicious, a man who plundered and raped and murdered. Was there a gentle side to the one called Wild Horse? She prayed there was, for Wade's sake.

"I wish I could just hold you forever," she said softly.

She saw the pain in his eyes as he took his hands away from her face and rose. "For your sake, I can't stay any longer." Their eyes held for a few more seconds, each having so much more they wanted to say, each longing to be held by the other. Would the day ever really come that they could go to California together, settle together, have children? Oh, how she loved him! His Indian blood meant nothing to her. How strange that she could feel this way, after what the Comanche renegades had done to her.

"I'll pray for you," she told him. "Do any of the soldiers know what you're going to do?"

"No, but I think the captain suspects. I'm heading due west when I leave. I'll veer north after I'm sure no one is trailing me. Enders and Captain Howell would both like to get the capture of Wild Horse under their belts. I don't

278

intend to be responsible for that. I'm not here to judge or capture the man—just to find out if he's my brother."

He sighed deeply, looking suddenly like a little boy having to be taken from his mother for the first time. "Damn, I hate to leave you, Jenny," he said in a near whisper.

The door to the kitchen squeaked open then and he backed farther away while Jennifer quickly wiped away more tears and put on a smile. "Good-bye, Mr. Morrow," she said then, "and good luck to you. I hope you make it safely to California."

He nodded. "Good-bye, Miss Andrews. I hope things turn out well with you and Sergeant Enders." She saw the flash of jealous protection move through his eyes at the words.

"I'm sure they will," Jennifer answered, telling him with her eyes that Anthony Enders would never touch her.

Alice came into the room, and Wade glanced at her as he headed for the door. "Thank you for allowing me into your home," he told the woman. He took some money from a deerskin pouch tied to his gunbelt. "Here is fifty dollars for your trouble."

The woman stared at the money wide-eyed, then looked at Jennifer and up to Wade. "Is it true then—you were raised by a white man, a wealthy man in the freighting business?"

Wade grinned. "It's true."

Jennifer's heart swelled with love when he cast Alice a smile that Jennifer knew was winning the woman over. He had a warmth about him that belied his appearance. Alice looked at the money again and slowly took it. "Jennifer says you went to college, back East?"

"Yes, ma'am—the University of Pennsylvania."

Alice shook her head. "Strangest thing I've ever seen—a Comanche Indian talking English good as any white man, throwing money around." She looked down at the money and back to Wade. "It's Sergeant Enders's place to do this, although I never would have asked. In fact, this is too much."

"It's not too much if you promise to take as good care of Miss Andrews as possible, and to give her the womanly friendship she needs. She doesn't know anyone here, and she's been through a lot. As far as Sergeant Enders, I don't want her to be any more in debt to him than necessary. She's a fine lady. If she marries Enders, it should be by choice, not out of obligation."

Jennifer noticed a hint of a smile on Alice's lips. "Well, I have to agree with you there, seeing as how I'm not real fond of Sergeant Enders. I sure never thought I'd let a man like you into my house, but the way you talk and all—" She shook her head. "Sure is strange. Good-bye, Mr. Morrow, and thank you for the money. Lord knows a laundress in a place like this makes hardly enough to stay alive. I only stay on here because I want to be near my husband's grave. I just wonder what he'd say about somebody like you."

"I'm sure I would have been proud to know him, ma'am. You take good care of Miss Andrews now. I just might check back with you some day to see how things turned out." He gave her a wink, and Jennifer realized he knew it was possible either he or Jennifer might need the woman's friendship later on. He was doing his best to win her over. Jennifer loved him for it, and for the moment his efforts at erasing the woman's prejudiced image of him helped her bear the thought of his leaving.

Now Alice smiled fully. "Well, she'll be took good care of, all right. She's just about the age my own daughter was when she—" Her smile faded. "When she died. It warms my heart to have Jenny here. A woman gets pretty lonely out here."

"I imagine so." Wade nodded to her, then turned to Jennifer, holding her eyes for a moment. He did not have to say a word for her to know what he was thinking. "Good-bye again, Miss Andrews."

"Good-bye, Mr. Morrow. Godspeed."

He forced a smile, glancing at Alice once more before leaving. The woman watched after him for a moment before closing the door. She turned to Jennifer. "If that isn't the strangest thing—talking to a Comanche man like he was just like anybody else.''

"He *is* just like anybody else," Jennifer answered, reminding herself not to sound too melancholy when she talked about Wade. "In fact, he's a better man than some I know. I will be forever indebted to him, Alice, Indian or not.''

Alice looked down at the money, shaking her head again. Jennifer heard the sound of a horse riding off, and her heart tightened. "I'm awfully tired," she said then, unable to look at Alice for fear the woman would see her misty eyes.

She turned to her side, and Alice left the room. Jennifer finally released the tears of terror and loneliness that wanted to come. Wade! She might never see him again. It was all like some strange dream, but then she moved a hand to her belly, where a dull ache remained from giving herself to Wade Morrow in passion and wild desire. No, it was not a dream at all. It was very, very real, and it seemed at the moment that if Wade didn't come back, there would be nothing left to live for.

Enders entered the command post, in response to Lieutenant Brown's message that the captain wanted to see him. He was irritated by the command, always hating having to answer to others. His most satisfactory moments were when he was in the field, when he was the one in charge with no one standing over him.

His irritation was only enhanced by the frustration of still not being able to see Jennifer Andrews. What right did the woman have to keep turning him away? "Still not feeling well," Alice kept telling him every time he came to the door. He hated that old biddy anyway, and he suspected she was deliberately keeping him away, maybe trying to convince Jennifer that she shouldn't marry him. It had been three frustrating days now since Jennifer came to the fort, and all he had seen of her was the frazzled, wounded young woman who had come here on a travois.

Why did she keep putting him off? Whatever the reason, he was going to see her this afternoon if he had to barge in and break down Alice's door.

He entered the Captain's quarters and saluted, then took a chair when the Captain told him, "At ease. Have a seat, Enders."

Tony removed his hat and ran a hand through his thinning, but dark and wavy hair. "What did you want, Sir?"

Howell handed out a piece of paper. "I got a telegram today—from a John Andrews in St. Louis. Took it a couple of days to get here through all the relay stations."

Enders took the telegram and read it.

"MY NIECE, JENNIFER ANDREWS, HEADED FOR YOUR FORT TO MARRY A SGT. ANTHONY ENDERS. NO PERMISSION. SHE IS MY CHARGE. PLEASE ESCORT HER TO NEAREST SAFE STAGE STATION AND HIRE SOMEONE TO BRING HER BACK. MONEY NO OBJECT. IF SHE HAS ALREADY MARRIED MR. ENDERS, INFORM ENDERS I WILL PAY WHATEVER HE ASKS TO ANNUL THE MARRIAGE AND SEND MY NIECE BACK TO ME."

The message followed with a name and address. Enders frowned. "No wonder it took so long to get here. The man *must* have money to send a telegraph this length."

"What do you think," Howell asked the man. "I don't feel this is my business, Enders. I'm in charge of you men when it comes to army matters, not your personal lives. The woman is of age. I can't forbid you to marry her, if it works out that way. I just wanted you to know it's your decision. You ought to have a talk with her, though—find out what this is all about."

Enders nodded. "Yes, sir, I will. She ought to be well enough today for a visit. I don't know anything about her past or why she answered my letter in the first place. I'll, uh, I'll try to do what's right."

"Fine. I don't want any part of it. Just don't let her run around here a free woman too long, Enders. Creates too much unrest among the men. She's a pretty woman.''

Tony grinned. ''She *is* pretty, all right. Don't worry, I'll take care of this.'' He rose and saluted and the captain dismissed him. Tony hurried out, his mind racing. ''Money no object,'' Jennifer's uncle had said. He also said he would pay whatever Enders asked for an annulment. It would obviously be more profitable to marry Jennifer, then contact the man. He could rake it in on both ends—have the pleasure of bedding Jennifer Andrews, then make a bundle of money divorcing her and sending her back to her uncle.

He folded the telegram and rammed it into his pocket. He would talk to her, try to find out her background. But he would not tell her about the telegram. Why should he? It would only make her suspicious of his intentions in marrying her. She was better off not knowing.

He grinned. Placing that ad could be the smartest thing he'd ever done, and the most profitable. He hurried back to his quarters to bathe and shave. He would visit Miss Andrews today, whether she and Alice liked it or not. After all, the woman had come here to marry him, hadn't she? It was time they got to know each other.

Jennifer lay listening to the sounds of camp. Men were drilling and horses trotted back and forth. Sabers clanked as a patrol made its way past Alice's cabin to ride out and check on settlements that bordered the Comanche Trace. She hoped Sergeant Enders would be among them, which would give her more time to put off seeing him, but then she heard booted footsteps on the wooden porch of the cabin. Her heart sank when someone knocked.

She knew who it would be, and she also knew she couldn't say no again. She didn't like the idea of lying in bed while she talked to a stranger, but she figured that if she remained bedridden, he would better believe her story about not being healed enough yet to go walking. And, after all, her leg really wasn't healed yet. Walking to the privy out back with Alice's help was about all she could do. The pain seemed to come and go, and she realized that while she was with Wade, just his presence had made her feel better.

Alice came in from the kitchen and glanced at her as the knock came again. "I imagine it's Sergeant Enders. Should I let him in this time?" the woman asked Jennifer.

Jennifer looked down at herself, making sure her robe was wrapped appropriately around her. Alice had helped her wash and had brushed out her hair this morning. "I suppose I should talk to him," she answered, touching the sides of her hair to be sure no strands had fallen from the combs that held it away from her face. "Do I look presentable?"

Alice smiled. "You look beautiful." She leaned over the foot of the bed. "You just do what you feel is right. Go ahead and get to know Sergeant Enders, but then you do what's best. And you take all the time you need. He can't force you into anything, and I enjoy having you with me."

Jennifer smiled. She had quickly grown to like Alice, discovering that under her crusty surface lay a woman of warmth and love, a very lonely and sometimes bitter woman to whom life had dealt some hard blows, but whose kind and generous spirit would not allow her to be as mean as she sometimes pretended to be.

The woman opened the door, and Jennifer heard Enders again announce himself and ask if he could see Jennifer.

"She's some better today. She says she'll see you," Alice answered.

Jennifer's heart pounded with dread as the man entered. He wore a clean uniform and was clean-shaven, his hair plastered to the sides of his head with some kind of sweet-smelling oil. He smiled, his teeth slightly yellow, and Jennifer suspected he didn't think to take much care of his mouth. She thought of Wade again, and how he liked to clean his teeth with baking soda and always kept peppermint in his supplies. When he kissed her, his breath was always sweet, but Sergeant Enders did not look like the kind of man who had sweet breath, although he was relatively handsome for his thirty-five years. She guessed he would be even more handsome if he knew how to properly groom himself. Her immediate impression was that he had done a quick job of "surface cleaning" for her sake.

His eyes lit up as he came closer, still grinning. He carried a bouquet of wildflowers in his hand, then handed them out to her. "These are for you, Jennifer. Lots of them grow out back of the officers' barracks."

She reached out to take the flowers. "Thank you, Sergeant Enders."

"Tony. Remember?"

"Yes. Tony. You, uh, you might as well call me Jenny, although it still seems a little strange to me to be using first names."

He nodded, reaching out and bringing the chair beside her bed a little closer before sitting down. She hoped he did not intend to stay too long. His eyes moved over her in a way that made her feel as though she was lying there naked, and a chill moved through her at the thought of letting this man do to her the things Wade had done.

"I'm sorry I couldn't see you sooner," she told him, unsure how to start a conversation. "I needed lots of rest. That first day I slept all that afternoon and all night and until nearly noon the second day. I guess the exhaustion and all the horror of what had happened caught up with me."

He nodded again. "I suppose." He looked her over again, making her feel like a piece of merchandise whose value was being determined. "It's true then that the, uh, the Comanche didn't—I mean, that Mr. Morrow scared them off before—"

"They didn't touch me wrongly," Jennifer answered for him. "Is that so important, Sergeant Enders?"

"Tony."

She looked down at the flowers.

"No, I guess not. I mean, I was just asking on your account—wanting to understand what all you've been through."

"They killed the driver and caused the coach to

overturn," she told the man without looking at him. She kept her voice steady, wanting to scream at him to leave. "They killed everyone else. Mr. Morrow was thrown from the coach when it overturned and he hit his head. Apparently they thought he was hurt or dead. They left him there. I came last. I had a couple of cracked ribs and a sprained shoulder from the accident—from peoples' bodies falling on me."

She hesitated, thinking about the men she had come to know on that short journey, feeling sorry for the good ones, like Adam Hughes, and Nick. "The Indians hauled me out, tossed me around and tore my dress. Then one of them deliberately shot me in the leg. The only thing I remember after that is Indians all around me, then suddenly they were gone, and then blackness. I woke up hours later beside a camp fire. Mr. Morrow was there. I remembered screaming before that, feeling horrible pain—yet I wasn't really in this world. When I came around I learned he had taken a bullet out of my leg." She looked at Enders. "From then on he took care of me, burned out an infection—saved my life, and my leg. It's badly scarred, Sar—I mean, Tony. You should know that."

He could hardly conceal his lust. "Oh, that would never bother me," he answered.

"My back is also scarred," she added. "My parents were killed eight years ago in a steamboat explosion. I escaped, but my back was burned."

He shook his head, grinning. "Jennifer, you're just about the prettiest thing I've ever set eyes on. If you have scars, they sure aren't anyplace anybody would notice. Far as me—I mean, if we married, I'd see them. But it wouldn't matter. You seem like a fine lady, and I'd be proud and honored to call you my wife. You have no idea how happy I was to see how much prettier you are than the picture you sent." Jennifer kept looking at the flowers, blushing slightly, wishing he would just go away. "Tell me, after your folks died, who raised you?" he asked cautiously.

"My aunt and uncle. My aunt died recently, and I felt

like a burden to my uncle. He's a busy man. I decided it was time I struck out on my own."

"Clear out here to a place like this? To marry a stranger?" he asked suspiciously. "How come? Why didn't you stay in St. Louis?"

She shrugged, scrambling to think. He might think her too desperate if she told him the truth; and he might think she had used him. Maybe he would even send her back! "I just . . . I had read and heard so much about the West," she answered. "I told my uncle I wanted to come out here. He said it was too dangerous and wouldn't help me, so I answered your ad. My uncle was a little angry, but he couldn't do anything about it, since I'm eighteen. He tried to stop me back in San Antonio, sent some men to bring me back. But the sheriff there said I had a valid ticket and a legitimate reason for coming here, and that I was old enough to make up my own mind. So, here I am." She finally met his dark eyes, seeing a mixture of hunger and suspicion there. "See all I went through to get out here?" she said then, wanting him to forget about her uncle. "I must say I certainly didn't expect all this adventure, if you want to call it that; nor was I prepared for just how big and dry and desolate this country really is. Staying here will take a lot of consideration, Tony. But I do have the money to reimburse you, if things don't work out."

He thought about her story about her uncle. It sounded reasonable, and he decided not to ask any more questions about her past. It might scare her off. Whatever had happened, what did he care now anyway? He could talk her into marrying him, have a good time in bed with her, then collect from dear Uncle John. He wondered what she would think of her uncle's offer, and he wondered with his own hungry needs why her uncle was ready to pay anything to get her back. Maybe it had been more than her just wanting to see the West and not wanting to be a burden to her uncle. Maybe she was running from him.

"Don't be worried about reimbursing me," he told her. "We'll be married when the preacher comes around the end of the month. That will give us plenty of time to get to

287

know each other. I won't be needing any money from you."

She watched him, wishing she could tell what he was really thinking. She wanted to ask him about his own past, but it was too soon, and she didn't dare show too much interest too fast. "I'm still very tired, Tony. Could you come back tomorrow?" she asked, wishing he would quit looking at her like a hungry man eyeing a steak.

"Sure. Uh, I have a present for you." He reached into his shirt pocket and took out the gold locket he had stolen from the dead woman. He handed it out to her. "It's real gold," he told her.

Jennifer took it, studying it, recognizing that it was not "real" gold at all. She had lived among finer things long enough to know real gold jewelry. She wondered if Enders knew it wasn't really gold and thought her an ignorant woman who could be easily fooled, or if he really believed it was gold. It was actually quite lovely, with a little flower design on the heart-shaped locket. When she held it, she felt an odd presence, as though it had been made for someone special, but not for her. She didn't know whether to admit she knew it wasn't gold, or if that might hurt his feelings.

"Thank you," she told him. "It's very pretty." She met his eyes. "You shouldn't be giving this to me yet."

"Oh, I want you to have it," he answered, hoping to impress her, determined to at least get a kiss out of her before too many more days. "It's yours, whether things work out or not," he told her. "But I hope they do, Jennifer. A man gets lonely out here, and you're a lot more than I expected. I'm, uh, I'm sorry about showing such a temper when we first found you. You can imagine how I felt, seeing that worthless half-breed with you. But he's gone now, and you won't have to put up with that humiliation any more. Must have been awful for you, with only him to turn to. I guess he's on his way to California now. That *is* where he was headed, isn't it?"

Jennifer kept her eyes averted so he wouldn't see her anger at his remark. She thought for a moment before answering, wondering why he had asked the question. Why would he be concerned about where Wade was going?

"Of course it is," she answered. "That's where he lives and where his father conducts his business. He was anxious to find a good horse and be on his way. I felt bad that I slowed him up so much. It *was* rather humiliating to have to travel with him, but I had little choice, and he was kind to me and saved my life, Tony. You shouldn't say too much against the man, even though he is part Indian." She closed her eyes. "I don't want to talk about it any more. I would rather try to forget."

"Sure you would. I'm sorry, Jennifer." He rose. "I'll come back tomorrow and we'll talk more. Everything will be all right now, you'll see." She kept her eyes averted. "Well, I'll be going now. You rest and mend. I want you to get all well before the preacher comes, and I can't wait to show you off to the other men." He leaned down and patted her arm, and she could hardly stand his touch. "I'll see you tomorrow."

"Yes," she answered, still staring at the flowers, the locket in her hand. "Thank you for the necklace and the flowers."

"I only wish I could do more." The man walked to the door and said good-bye again before leaving.

Jennifer stared at the locket. Was Anthony Enders as fake as this gift he had given her? She had no doubt he was, and when he left there remained a lingering odor of tobacco and liquor. "Oh, Wade," she whispered. "Where are you? Please, please be all right. And please come back soon." She called for Alice to bring some kind of vase for the flowers, which were already wilting.

Chapter Nineteen

The land was high but mostly flat, except for the hills to the north where Wade was headed. The fort was three days behind him, but he knew he could reach it in two if he had not lost a day heading west rather than north. He breathed deeply of the crisp air. It was early, the sun barely peeking over the eastern horizon.

He liked this time of day, all life awakening, birds singing here and there. He rolled and lit a cigarette, his belly already full, for he had risen even earlier than normal in order to get underway at first light. He would reach Comanche Hills in just a couple of hours, and he had no idea what this day might hold for him.

He wondered if that was why he felt especially alive this morning, why the sky seemed a brighter blue and gold, why he enjoyed looking at the blooming cacti and scattered wildflowers, even the scrubby brush that surrounded him. Perhaps today he would die.

In the distance a small antelope bounded across the high plateau, and he thought what an intricate web nature wove, each form of life dependent on another. He reasoned the Indian fit perfectly into that web, until the white man came along. The Indian breathed, ate, worshipped, and migrated with Nature, and they had got along just fine before the whites came along and killed off most of the game; before the whites tried changing their religion; before the whites brought the diseases that decimated whole tribes; before the whites forced the Indians onto small pieces of land where they felt smothered and where many died from sheer homesickness.

A great part of him understood the Indian's need to migrate with the seasons and the buffalo. He understood that a reservation was like a prison to an Indian. Several thousand acres sounded like a lot of land to a white man, but not to an Indian. He had learned that much from the Indians he did know, and from scouts. But he realized it wasn't just that. He felt it—in his soul. He couldn't always understand some of the Comanche practices, especially murder and torture, but he understood the spirit of freedom.

He turned to saddle his horse, a sturdy gelding with a shining chestnut coat and black mane and tail and black coloring from knee to hoof, looking like stockings. He had no name when Wade purchased the animal, and Wade simply called him "Red." It was a good horse, and fast. He wondered if he would end up needing that speed to get away from the Comanche. So far he had not been bothered, but he knew he was being watched.

He was close now, close to the mysterious Wild Horse. It gave him a strange feeling to think he could have a renegade brother. It was as though God had led him to this place at this time; as though all this was meant to happen, for he had never felt such a strong desire to find his connection to the Comanche as he had the past few months.

He was not really completely surprised at this turn of events, for all his life he had felt a connection to some unknown source. He had wanted this moment, even if it meant his death. At least he would know the truth about himself. The only thing that didn't fit, the only thing that did surprise him, was finding Jennifer Andrews. The last thing that had been on his mind when he came here was falling in love, especially with a white woman! He could only pray this encounter would not end as disastrously as had his love for Rebecca.

He prayed inwardly and constantly that no harm would

ome to Jennifer, feeling guilty for having left her at the fort; but he could not turn away from this man called Wild Horse, nor could he have brought Jennifer into this situation. He reminded himself she was strong and resourceful, and she loved him. She would find a way to stay safe and wait for him. She had money, and she knew who to contact for help. He was comforted in knowing without any doubt that his father and mother would see that Jennifer was cared for. There was no reason why she should have to submit herself to Sergeant Enders in any way.

He yanked the cinch tighter at the thought of Enders. He hardly knew the man, but he despised him. The thought of Enders putting his hands on Jenny brought a boiling rage to his soul, and it only made him more anxious to get this mission over with as soon as possible. He would meet this Wild Horse and see the resemblance for himself. Then he would find Slow Woman and get the truth from her.

He took a last swig of stiff coffee and threw the rest onto the coals of his camp fire. The liquid made a soft sizzling sound, and a puff of steam rose from the remnants of the fire. He stuffed the tin cup into his gear and tied everything onto the horse, then walked over to where the Indian pony was tied. He had brought the horse along to return to the Comanche, hoping the gesture would be appreciated, and hoping to express his own gratefulness for being able to use the animal. He took hold of the rope tied to the animal's rawhide bridle and led it to Red, then mounted up, keeping hold of the Indian pony.

He took another appreciative look at the wide open land around him. He realized that although he had not been through Texas before, he felt at home here, felt a kinship with this land. This was Comanche country, and he reasoned it always would be, even if the whites managed to finally keep the Indians out forever one day. In spirit this land would always belong to the Comanche.

He rode north, toward Comanche Hills, leading the Indian pony behind him. He couldn't help wondering if he would ever see Jenny again. He longed to hold her once more. Surely the next time they made love would be the most satisfying experience of his life, for she would be healed, both from her wounds and from her first encounter with man. It would be more enjoyable for her, and her response to him, her desire and womanly needs would be even more powerful and demanding.

He would gladly meet that demand. He could imagine nothing more gratifying than seeing the intense pleasure on her face at taking a man with sheer desire and wantonness, feeling no more pain, but only pleasure. He had awakened her to womanhood, and it gave him a feeling of power and accomplishment, mixed with a love so strong that it made him feel more alive, more aware of every nerve end, every breath he took. She was his woman, and no matter what the odds against their relationship, he was not going to lose this one.

After an hour's ride the land grew more hilly, rising and falling like a stationary sea. Soon he had to force himself to stop thinking about Jenny and stay alert, for he spotted two Comanche braves on a rise to his left. He gave no indication that he saw them. He kept riding forward until three more appeared on his right.

"Appears we have an escort now, Red," he said softly to his horse. He could not help the pounding of his heart at the anticipation of meeting Wild Horse and knowing the man could be his blood brother. If it was true, he wasn't sure how to feel about his real father. He supposed the man deserved the death he suffered for raping Slow Woman. Trouble was, there had been more than one. He would never know any of them. He supposed he could feel neither hatred nor love, for his father was nonexistent, a stranger without a name. It gave him a lonely feeling, and he was glad Lester and Vivian Morrow had come along and had taken him in. Les Morrow was as fine a man as any boy could ask to have for a father, and in spite of his real beginnings, Wade knew he was loved by the parents who had raised him, just as much as if he had come from their own blood.

Now he sensed the Indians on each side of him coming closer, as well as sensing more coming up from behind. He kept his horse at a slow trot, waiting for them to show him what to do next. One thing he knew about the Comanche was that the last thing he should do was show any kind of fear. Actually, he didn't feel any, in spite of knowing the atrocities they were capable of committing, especially against a captive. He was too full of a need to know the truth to be concerned about his own hide for the moment; and, after all, they had let him live after the raid, and they were the ones who had invited him here. Coming here could hardly be considered an intrusion.

Another brave rode closer, riding right beside him then. Wade turned to see the same man who had brought him water at the cave. He suspected it was the same man who had left the Indian pony for him. He halted his horse and held out the rope to the pony. The man took it and Wade gave a sign of "thank you." The man nodded, then pointed to a distant hill, where at least twenty warriors were now gathered. The Indian motioned for Wade to follow him, and they rode toward the waiting Comanche, Wade wondering if he should be saying his last prayers.

As they came closer, one man rode out ahead of the others. Even from this distance Wade began to see the resemblance, and his blood chilled at the reality of the situation. He had worn buckskins today, had left his own hair straight and loose, with a red bandana tied around his forehead. He figured he looked as Indian as any of those riding beside him, and for the first time he felt a certain pride in the look and feel of it that he had never felt before. His blood rushed faster, he sat a little straighter; and for a moment he realized as he kept his eyes on the man who waited for him that there, but for the grace of God, sat Wade Morrow. It was chilling to think that the only reason he was riding into the Comanche world from a world entirely different could be because of one quick and painful decision a Comanche woman made twenty-six years ago. How strange was fate.

Those who rode beside him left him then, and he

continued forward until he was within a few feet of the man he knew now had to be Wild Horse, for if not for the difference in their horses, and the fact that Wild Horse wore nothing but a loincloth and a hairpipe breastplate, Wade would have thought he was looking into a mirror.

Wild Horse fit his name. In spite of his blue eyes, he was every bit the wild looking warrior Wade had imagined. Black and white striped paint adorned his cheeks, and additional hair had been braided into the ends of his own hair to create a length that nearly reached his saddle. Wade was aware that the Comanche often used the hair cut off by others in mourning to tie into their own hair and make it longer.

A wind rose, as though God himself was touching this event. It made tiny bells on Wild Horse's moccasins tinkle, and a strand of hair found its way across Wade's face. He pushed it back, waiting for Wild Horse to make the first move or say the first word. For the moment, his shock was obvious. He stared at Wade as though he were a ghost, with the same disbelief Wade had seen on the faces of the other warriors the day of the raid.

"Bad spirit," someone nearby murmured in the Comanche tongue.

"*Strong* spirit," another said.

Wade didn't know whether to be overjoyed, or if he should turn and ride out of here as fast as he could ride. A thousand feelings moved through him. It would be ridiculous to think there was a possibility this man was not his brother. He wanted to embrace him, but the look in Wild Horse's eyes did not show him any welcome.

"So, it is true," the man finally said in the Comanche tongue. His blue eyes moved over Wade, then met his eyes again. "What are you called?"

"I carry a white man's name—Wade Morrow."

Wild Horse nodded. "And why have you come here to destroy me, Wade Morrow?"

Wade frowned. "Destroy you? I have only come to find my brother. I did not even know I had a brother, until now. I was taken in by whites twenty-six summers ago, and I have never known my own people. I came here to find people of my own blood, to learn why the Comanche abandoned me."

Wild Horse's eyes narrowed to hateful slits. "Now you know. And now *I* know that my mother betrayed her people. We should both have been destroyed."

"Why?"

"Twin spirits are a bad sign. Twin spirits can never be strong, for they must share their strength. One robs from the other."

"I am no less strong because of you, and you are no less strong because of me."

"It is a bad sign. Now my people wonder about my power. Now they wonder if I am strong and wise enough to lead them. They have seen my shadow. They know there are two of me. This will bring bad things to them, they fear, and I fear. There is only one thing to be done now. One of us must die!"

A mixture of sadness and keen alertness moved through Wade at the words. "No, Wild Horse. We are brothers. All my life I have dreamed of finding family among the Comanche. They are as much my people as yours."

Wild Horse kept a proud posture. A flicker of affection showed in his eyes, and Wade was sure that for a moment he caught a look of deep sorrow there. "Comanche law is Comanche law," the man said then. "It is not something that is changed because of blood or feelings. Twin spirits are bad medicine. It is true the Comanche are also your people, but we cannot both belong to them, nor they to us. It must be decided which one of us is the strongest, which one can belong to the people and which one cannot. It is the way."

Wade felt a creeping dread. This man was a vicious fighter, more experienced at the Indian way of fighting than Wade. "And how do we decide?"

Their eyes held. "It is between you and me. The others will bring you no harm. Only you and I can decide, and it must be done finally and quickly. We fight, Wade Morrow, until one of us dies."

Wade breathed deeply to stay calm, wondering how he could get through to this man. "You are my brother. I will not fight you."

"You must!" Wild Horse's eyes blazed. "I will be a broken man, a man of no respect, a man of shame, if you go on existing as my shadow, if you go on robbing me of my strength and power."

"I'm not robbing you of anything! I want to know you, Wild Horse. I want to talk to you, learn the Comanche way."

Wild Horse shook his head. "One of us must die."

Wade felt his anger at the primitive idea rising. He told himself to stay calm, told himself he had come here to understand. "I won't fight you," he repeated. "Kill me if you must, but I won't fight my brother."

Wild Horse jerked at his horse's reins, causing the animal to turn in a restless circle. The anger on the man's face was enough to cower any man, but Wade sat firm on his horse, refusing to flinch.

"I cannot just kill you," Wild Horse growled. "It would prove nothing. It must be a test of strength. You must fight me!"

"I will not!"

Wild Horse rode close to him, whipping out a knife and slamming it flat against Wade's chest, its tip close to Wade's throat. "Then I will *make* you fight me," he sneered. "I will bring you pain until you hate me and want me dead!"

Wade met his eyes. "It isn't right, Wild Horse."

"It is the *law!*"

The tip of the knife cut into Wade's skin, drawing blood. Wade quickly reasoned that if he was going to be forced into fighting this man, this was not the time or place. One false move now would bring Wild Horse's blade across his throat. He did not relish fighting the man at all, but such a fight, if it had to be, must not take place until he had found his real mother.

"There are some things about the Comanche I will

298

never understand," he told Wild Horse, "even though our blood is the same. One of them is the belief that twin babies must die. But if you say we must fight to the death, I respect that belief, Wild Horse, because we are brothers, and because I did not come here to bring you shame or to take power from you. Let me go for now, long enough to find Slow Woman, your mother—*our* mother. I want to speak with her. I want to know if it is true she had twin boys and abandoned one and kept the other. I have a right to meet my own mother, Wild Horse. Is there a Comanche law against that?"

The man slowly withdrew the knife, and blood trickled down Wade's throat. "No." He grinned a little. "So, I will see how brave and honest you are, Wade Morrow. I will let you go and see our mother first, to be sure what we feel and see with our eyes is true. I will see if you are brave enough to return to a certain death. I will see if you are honest enough to keep your word. We will watch you, Wade Morrow. We will know if you try to flee, and we will find you. If you run like a coward, it will be bad for you."

Wade nodded. "I won't run. I am no coward. I am the brother of Wild Horse."

Again he caught a flicker of feelings, but Wild Horse was too steeped in Comanche custom to ever allow feelings to overcome "the way." Wade felt torn. He did not have the heart to try to kill his own brother, but neither did he care to bring the man shame or to destroy his spirit. He had no idea what he was going to do. It just didn't seem right to raise a hand against the man, even though Wild Horse was determined that was how it must be. If he continued to refuse to fight, he suspected Wild Horse would keep his promise to bring him enough pain to make him hate him. All he could do was try to appeal to their brotherhood, but he suspected that was a very faint hope. Devotion to Comanche law was too strong in Wild Horse's soul.

"Go and find our mother. She dwells with the Comanche north of the Red River—the Comanche who have given up their spirits and have chosen to live the lives of old women on the white man's reservation! I do not accept such a life!"

"I know that you tried once, Wild Horse. I know that you lost a wife and son. I am deeply sorry."

Pain moved into the man's eyes. "Being sorry does not bring them back. The only thing that takes away the sorrow is revenge! Ever since, I have made the whites pay: white women for my woman, white children for my son, white men for their treachery! Blood for blood! It is the way! We who choose not to live on the reservation are hungry and hunted, but at least we are free. This is Comanche country. The *tejanos* refuse to understand that. They insist on learning the hard way. They are fools!"

"They are also great in number, Wild Horse. Fools that they are, they will still win, and your people will keep dying. You only make things worse for yourselves. If you keep this up, some day there will *be* no Comanche to occupy this land!"

The man grinned a little. "Spoken like a white man. The white man's way is deep in your soul, Wade Morrow. That is why it will be easy for me to kill you."

Wade held his eyes. "Maybe. First I will find Slow Woman and learn the truth."

Wild Horse pulled his horse back. "Go then! I will be waiting for you."

"There is someone else I must also see before I come back."

A sneer moved across Wild Horse's face. "The white woman."

Wade frowned. "How did you know?"

"Two Hawks told me about the woman in the cave, when he brought you water. We knew there was a white woman on the white man's coach. We know that you helped her. Again your white ways show. No Comanche man would care about a white woman, except to bring her shame and death."

Wade shook his head. "It doesn't have to be that way, Wild Horse. My own white parents loved me as much as

300

any Comanche would have. They are good people, and the white woman who waits for me at Fort Stockton is also good. Not all whites hate the Comanche."

"It matters not how good some might be. They do not belong here. And their kind has betrayed and murdered us, they have starved us, shamed us, stolen our land from us. I see no good or bad white people, Wade Morrow. I see only the enemy."

Wade could see he was getting nowhere. He backed his horse slightly. "I go to find Slow Woman now. Then I will see the white woman once more before coming back to find you."

"You will not find us, Wade Morrow. We will find you."

Wade watched him sadly. "Yes, I suppose you will."

Wild Horse rode closer again, reaching out and grasping Wade's wrist in a grip that told Wade his life would definitely be on the line when and if he fought this man. "It is the way," the man repeated. "You want to learn about being Indian. Then learn that there are times when you must not feel. You must only act. In our world, Wade Morrow, we know only survival . . . and revenge!"

Wade opened his hand to grip the man's wrist in return, wondering if this was to be the only chance he would have to touch his brother in peace. Wild Horse suddenly let go, yanking his wrist from Wade's hold, then turned his horse and rode back to the others. He let out a call that seemed more like a wild animal than human. In seconds the entire group of braves disappeared over the ridge.

Wade looked down at his wrist, which still had white marks on it from Wild Horse's fierce grip. He kicked at Red's sides and headed north, toward the Red River.

Jennifer sipped some tea, looking again at the mantle clock above the stone fireplace in Alice's little cabin. Crutches, which Anthony Enders had ordered made for her, sat leaning against the fireplace. Across from her Alice looked up from some mending and grinned. "You waiting anxiously for Sergeant Enders to come, or wishing that clock would stop so he never comes at all?"

Jennifer grinned a little and met the woman's fading blue eyes, wondering what she would think if she knew her thoughts had been of Wade Morrow, not Anthony Enders. "I think I wish it would stop."

Alice chuckled. "Still not too fond of the man, hmmm?"

Jennifer sighed. "No. Something about him doesn't ring true, Alice. He says he's from Houston, that his parents died when he was about fourteen, and he's been on his own, working at odd jobs and such, ever since. Then he joined the army, supposedly because he wanted to help protect Texas settlers."

Alice let out a snicker and shook her head. "Joined the army to get away from the law, more than likely, like a lot of others out here. They don't fool me one bit."

Alice looked down at her teacup. "It isn't just his rather vague past that bothers me, Alice. It's the feeling I get around him. He frightens me. On the outside he behaves himself. He's kind and attentive and all; but I sense a mean streak under all those manners. I can't marry a man I'm afraid of, let alone the fact that he isn't . . . well, he isn't very clean."

Alice's eyes still showed some humor, but also concern. "I didn't figure a pretty young lady like you would go for a man like Sergeant Enders. And you can bet that a man who's been out here as long as he has isn't going to be patient and kind on his wedding night. I hate to embarrass you, dear, but those are the facts." She frowned. "Why don't you just pay him off right now and tell him to forget the whole thing? Soon as you're completely well and it's safe to go, you could go back to San Antonio or maybe Houston or New Orleans—maybe up to Austin. A young, educated lady like yourself could tutor some rich folks' kids, something like that. You'd do all right. There's no sense taking this thing with the sergeant any farther."

Jennifer leaned back in the wooden rocker in which she sat, closing her eyes for a moment. How could she tell Alice the real reason she had to keep up the pretense? "It's only been nine days, Alice. And part of those I couldn't even see Tony. I suppose I have to make it look as though I'm giving him a chance. I keep hoping each time he comes that I'll find something about him that I like." She met the woman's eyes. "Besides, I still have some healing to do, like you said; and where I go from here will take some deep thought. On top of that I can't leave right now anyway. Things are too dangerous out there." She grinned. "And how can I leave you here all alone now that I've met you? You said you were glad to have a woman's company, and I've grown to like you very much. Maybe I'll just stay on here a while and work as a laundress."

Alice smiled again. "Well, I'd like that just fine. But it wouldn't work. If you stayed on here a free woman, those men out there would kill each other off trying to be the man you pick. After a month or so you've got to make up your mind or get out of here. Believe me, a pretty, single woman in a place like this only spells trouble. It's not even allowed. Only wives can live here, and even they have to work as cooks or laundresses. Now there's no wives left. Most went back East with men who got sent back, the rest got out because it's too dangerous around here for women now that the army is so thinned out." She cut off a piece of thread from a shirt she was mending. "Those damn Comanche seem to know when the army has pulled out again. Soon as they see an opening, they come sneaking back down here from up by the Red River and start their raiding and murdering all over again."

Jennifer sipped some more tea. Would Wade find his brother and mother? Would he become like them? "Why do they do it, Alice?"

The woman laughed in a short, bitter grunt. "Because they're Comanche. It's in their blood, like breathing and eating. They've been nomads and plunderers for so many centuries, they don't know how else to live. They don't understand settling in one place, farming, having only one wife. They're like animals. They move with the seasons and the buffalo. You can't tame a Comanche any more than you can tame a bobcat."

Jennifer lowered the teacup. "But look at Wade Morrow. He's more civil than some white men I know. He's kind and intelligent, highly educated."

"He's also only half Comanche. But then he wasn't raised among them. I'm saying the ones that have lived the Comanche way all their lives can't be changed. They are what they are. The only hope of changing that is to take all the newborn babies from them and raise them among whites from infancy. But even then, there's going to be a restless spirit there that will show. Take the bobcat again. Raise one from a kitten and it will be pretty tame. But the time will come when you hang out some meat to smoke, and it will come up missing; then maybe your neighbor's small dog will come up missing, or a small child will be found mauled. There's a wild instinct bred into that bobcat that will come out, in spite of how it was raised. It's the same with Indians."

Jennifer thought for a moment. "Perhaps. But I don't think that would happen with a man like Mr. Morrow. Maybe it's because he's already half white and was raised by whites. All I know is he could never turn on those who raised him, or become wild and vicious. He's much too good, a very kind and gentle man, although he is brave and skilled when it's called for—but only in self-defense, never deliberately."

She ran a finger around the edge of her cup, not even realizing the strangely soft, melancholy way she had spoken the words. Alice watched her for a moment. This was not the first time she had sensed that Jennifer Andrews had special feelings for Wade Morrow. Alice couldn't help agreeing the man seemed well-spoken, and he was amazingly handsome in spite of his Indian blood, but still, he was part Comanche. Maybe this young woman from St. Louis still didn't understand how people out here felt about such a thing.

"You be careful defending that half-breed, especially around Tony Enders. I agree he seemed pretty decent, and he did save your life. But he's Indian, Jenny, and it's not good for a white woman to be defending a man like that."

Jennifer looked over at her, frowning. "A man like what? He's just a man, Alice, that's all."

The woman scowled. "Not in Texas. In Texas he's Comanche. You've got a lot to learn. I just don't want you to learn the hard way. Besides, it doesn't make any difference now. The man is gone."

The pain moved through Jennifer's heart again. Gone! Little did Alice know how that word pierced her chest like a knife. She didn't even know if he was alive or dead, and she wouldn't know for weeks. How she longed to share her pain and agony with someone, to talk to someone about her love for Wade, talk to someone about her first experience with man. But she certainly couldn't talk to Alice. She was alone in this, as she had been alone in everything else she had done since Aunt Esther died.

She rose from her chair and grabbed the crutches. "I think I'll write a letter home," she said then. "I promised my uncle's maid I would write her and let her know I'm all right. We were good friends."

"You'd better tell your uncle, too. He must be worried. You should at least tell him you haven't married yet. You ought to consider going back to him, Jennifer. I'm sure he doesn't think of you as a burden, and you have surely seen all you want to see of this West you thought would be so exciting."

Jennifer limped out to a small table beside the bed, sitting down in a chair near it and taking up a quill pen. "I'll write him, too," she lied. She had no intentions of contacting her uncle until she was well on her way to California with Wade. He apparently had given up on her, since there had been no word since the two men he had hired tried to grab her in San Antonio. She hoped she was rid of the man for good. Mattie, however, deserved to know what was going on. She would write Mattie and tell her not to tell her uncle yet that she had arrived at the fort and that she might not marry the sergeant.

She wondered if she should tell the woman about Wade. Perhaps for now she would just tell her she had met another man, who was in the freighting business. After all, that's what Wade was in her eyes—just a man like any other, except that she was desperately in love with him. She didn't see the dark skin that surrounded those blue eyes. She didn't care that he wore his hair longer than white men. She only cared that he might still be alive, and would be coming for her.

Dear Mattie, she began writing. *"You will not believe the things that have happened to me since leaving St. Louis. I will tell you only some of them, as I do not want you to worry or be alarmed. I am fine now, and I am at Fort Stockton. I am trusting in our friendship when I ask that you do not show this letter to Uncle John, or tell him any of its details or that I got here all right. When the time is right to tell him, I will let you know.*

"West Texas is more wild and desolate than I could ever have imagined, yet there is something about this land that grows on a person and begins to hold him or her here, even against their will . . .

Chapter Twenty

"Wild Horse! He has come back!"

Wade glanced at the Indian woman who spoke the words. He said nothing as others began staring when he rode past them toward a trading post. One woman ran out into a field, where a Comanche man was walking behind a plow, trying his luck at farming. It looked to Wade as though he was not being very successful, and he doubted the man's heart was in the work. He was already aware that most Comanche still refused to farm at all, calling it womanly to do such work, and feeling it was wrong to tear a plow into the earth. For centuries they had survived on what Mother Nature had provided freely. All of this work was the white man's way, and they could not understand why the white man had to make everything so difficult.

Wade couldn't help but understand that attitude himself at times; but he also understood that the country was filling up with too many people for all of them to subsist strictly on what Mother Nature provided in animals and wild roots and berries. Now man must begin helping the process through farming and raising cattle. It was a situation that could not help but bring conflict with people of an entirely different culture.

Now he was himself caught up between these two worlds, and he felt as though he was being crushed between two stones. Wild Horse had been heavy on his mind these last five days. He wanted to be friends with the man, not kill him. He knew now that convincing the man that neither of them had to die was going to be the most difficult task he might ever accomplish, if, in fact, he could accomplish it at all. He knew that if push came to shove, he would have to defend himself, but he was not sure he could literally land a knife into Wild Horse's heart and end his own brother's life. Just the thought of it filled him with sick remorse.

A few young braves came running, hope in their eyes, and Wade realized they thought a beloved leader had returned to stay with them for a while. Perhaps he had brought news of a great new uprising. Perhaps he would tell them they could go back to their homeland. More women, a few children, and old people began walking in his direction, and he wondered if his own mother could be among them.

He drew his horse to a halt in front of the trading post, and a white man wearing an apron came out, being herded along by two women who were gabbing rapidly that Wild Horse was here.

"He wouldn't come here," the man was saying irritably. "He knows soldiers are lookin' for him. They'd drag him back to Texas and the citizens there would have him hanged. Why, he'd no more—"

The man looked up at Wade then as he wiped his hands on the apron. His eyes widened. "Wild Horse! What the hell are you—" He stopped and began speaking in the Comanche tongue then. "What are you doing here!"

"You don't need to speak to me in Comanche," Wade answered in English. "I'm not Wild Horse. My name is Wade Morrow, and I believe Wild Horse could be my twin brother. I've come here to find Slow Woman. Do you know where I can find her?"

The man's eyes widened, and some of the Indian women gasped at the fact that this man was using the white man's tongue. Wild Horse spoke only Comanche. Now they began to notice little differences. He did not ride an Indian pony. The horse looked like the kind the bluecoats used, and his gear was white man's gear. His pistol and rifle looked like fancier models than any Indian could afford, although they could have been stolen in a raid.

"Mister, you better come inside and explain yourself better," the man answered. "I'm a trader here—name's Jake Owen." The man told the others in the Comanche tongue that Wade was not Wild Horse, that he might be the man's twin brother. Immediately there was a sound of gasps, and faces took on a frightened look. Again Wade heard the words "bad spirit" and "strong spirit," as well as "bad medicine." Most of those who had been staring at him scattered, as though they might die if they looked upon him any longer.

Wade dismounted and followed Owen inside the trading post, and more Comanche immediately vacated the building. A rather bitter grin moved across Wade's lips. "I feel like the black plague," he said with a note of sarcasm.

"In their minds you're worse than that. Have a seat," Owen answered, pulling a chair away from a table. "Want some whiskey?"

"I could use a shot."

Owen retrieved a bottle of good bourbon, which he reserved only for himself. He decided maybe he couldn't fool this Wade Morrow with the watered-down liquor he usually sold to the Indians. He poured Wade a glass and listened to the man's story, all the while finding it incredulous how much he looked like Wild Horse.

"Well, if that ain't the damnedest thing I've ever heard," he said when Wade finished. "I've never seen the like." He poured himself another shot of whiskey. "You know you're a dead man if you go back to Wild Horse, don't you?"

Wade sighed. "Maybe. I can handle myself pretty good."

"Maybe so. But if you end up havin' to fight Wild Horse, mister, you'd better understand that if you don't dredge up a true killer instinct, there's no way you'll win. You've got to be just as vicious as he is. You've got to understand that kind of hate, understand the Comanche way, and you can't hesitate or let emotions get involved for one

309

second, 'cause that's when Wild Horse will slide his knife right through your innards. You remember that. When it comes to somethin' like that, there's no room for compassion."

Wade stared at his empty glass. "I'm beginning to understand it, but I don't like it." Owen started to pour him another glass, but Wade waved his hand over the top of it. "No more. I want my wits about me when I talk to Slow Woman. Where can I find her?"

Owen shook his head, setting the bottle back down. "I'll take you to her, but you won't get much of a visit. She's dying—mostly from old age, I guess."

Wade frowned, his heart feeling heavier with every new revelation.

"She can't be more than forty, but for these people that's old," Owen continued, "especially the ones who have lived through the events of the past twenty years. They've been raked with white man's diseases, starved, hunted, driven out of their homeland, butchered, burned out, lied to, you name it. I'm no Indian lover myself, and I'm just as much against what these people have done to the poor settlers as the next man. But I understand some of the reasons, and I understand a little bit about the nature of the Comanche. Most folks don't try to understand. They just figure anybody who doesn't live and believe like they do is wrong. And a lot of them figure any man with skin a shade too dark is fair game, like rabbits, figure they're worthless and can never learn another way. I've seen some of them around here try, but it's hard for them. Now you, you're livin' proof that a Comanche man can be as civil as any white."

Wade hardly heard the man's words. Slow Woman was dying. And she was only forty? That meant she was only fourteen when she gave birth. He imagined a mere child going through that hell alone, left with the awful decision of choosing which baby to keep, and his heart ached for her.

It hurt to realize that if she was his mother, there was little time left now to get to know her. This trip was becoming more and more of a disaster—except for Jennifer. Right now the thought of her was like a cool drink of water in the middle of a desert, his only comfort when he went to sleep at night. Somehow he had to survive all of this and get back to her.

"I'd like to talk to Slow Woman now, if I could," he told Owen.

"Sure." The man slugged down the whiskey and rose, picking up the bottle to cork it and put it back in its hiding place so no Indians would find the "good stuff." He took off his apron, which was bloody from killing chickens that morning. Wade could smell the odor of a man who had cleaned the innards out of an animal without washing afterward, and he had never stopped being amazed sometimes at what the white man considered "civil."

For the moment, Jake Owen's physical appearance meant little. There was no time to contemplate the strange, unsolvable difference between the races. Today he was himself Indian, and his chest actually hurt him as he followed Owen through the sorry-looking village of Comanche, who were no more than refugees chased from their homeland. A few gaunt-looking children stared at him with wide, dark eyes until their mothers jerked them aside and ordered them not to look upon the "evil spirit." Dogs ran about, most of them looking hungry, and a few smoky fires burned here and there, while horses grazed nearby, flies eating at them without mercy.

Again he thought about how one woman's choice had meant the difference between his being raised by Lester Morrow, or living here in filth and poverty. Owen approached a tipi and shook at a bell that hung near the entrance to announce his presence. A middle-aged Comanche man stepped in front of its entrance, arms folded. He gave Wade a long, hard look.

"So," he said gruffly in English, "it is true, what the people came to tell me. You look like Wild Horse."

"I want to talk to Slow Woman," Wade answered. "Is she your sister?"

311

The man nodded. "She is dying," he said flatly. "I do not think it would be good for Slow Woman to see this bad spirit who accuses her of betraying the Comanche way. You must go."

Wade stood his ground. "You must be my uncle. What are you called?" He saw the same flicker of affection in the man's eyes as he had seen briefly in Wild Horse's.

"I am Aguila. Now go away from here!"

"No," Wade answered sternly, pushing Jake Owen aside and stepping closer. "I have come to see the woman who could be my mother. I have that right. And I have the right to know the truth. So does Wild Horse. How can we know whether or not we must fight this out if we aren't certain of the truth?"

"My sister would not disobey Comanche law."

"For God's sake," Wade growled, *"look* at me! Can't you see what the truth must be? I'm your nephew!" He knew the importance of the relationship between uncle and nephew in the Indian culture. He realized then that he could actually touch this man more easily than he could touch his own brother. Aguila's eyes softened a little as he moved them over Wade.

"Why would my sister allow this?"

"Maybe because she was nothing more than a frightened *child* when all this happened! Maybe because a woman's love for the life she has carried in her womb is much stronger than Comanche law! Can you tell me that no Comanche woman has ever wept when her twin babies have been killed?"

Aguila glanced at Owen, who simply shrugged. He didn't like to get involved in the personal affairs of the Comanche. It was bad business, and he knew it was dangerous for Wade Morrow.

"I have a right to see my own mother, Aguila," Wade was saying then. "And I'll do it, even if I have to fight you to get to her."

Aguila shook his head slowly. "I would not fight you. That is for Wild Horse. And if you should be my nephew, I could not lay a hand on you."

"Then let me see Slow Woman. I promised Wild Horse I would discover the truth, and I would go to him with it. I cannot go back to him unless I know for certain, and I do not intend to break my word. He is your nephew. Surely you understand how important this is to him."

Aguila stepped aside. "All right, you can see her. Just do not raise your voice to her. She does not have long left to live." He searched Wade's eyes. "She has never been a happy woman. She never got over the shame of what the white men did to her, and she never took a husband. Wild Horse was all she lived for." His eyes showed more sadness. "Sometimes the sorrow deep inside can slowly kill as surely as disease or hunger. Perhaps all these years she has carried a sorrow for the child she left behind."

Wade felt his throat tighten. He did not answer. He pulled aside the entrance flap to the tipi and ducked inside, where he saw the small, frail form of a woman lying on a mat. Although it was hot and muggy outside, the tipi was surprisingly cool because of the relief from the sun. The bottom of the buffalo skins that formed the structure were rolled up about eighteen inches and tied, in order to let air flow through it; also letting in enough daylight to make it bright and pleasant inside.

Wade approached the woman on the mat, noticing she looked terribly thin. Her tunic, clean but worn, looked too big for her as it draped loosely over her bony ribs and gave outline to her protruding hip bones. It was too warm to use a blanket, and her legs were exposed, spindly-looking, the knees bony. Her breathing came in short, agonizing gasps, and Wade guessed she had pneumonia. Although she was only forty, her hair showed shocks of gray. But the face he looked upon when he knelt beside her still carried a lingering, youthful beauty.

"Slow Woman," he spoke up softly in the Comanche tongue.

She slowly opened her eyes, which had a glazed look to them. She studied him a moment, then smiled softly. "Wild Horse," she whispered. "My son." She put a weak hand on his arm. "You have come . . . to see me . . . before

313

I die." Alarm came into her eyes then. "You should not! The bluecoats . . . will kill you."

Wade took hold of her hand, afraid to squeeze too tightly for fear of breaking it. He leaned a little closer. "Look at me," he said softly. "I am not Wild Horse. I am called Wade Morrow, and I have come here to learn the truth." He watched joy turn to terror, then to an awful sorrow as he explained his beginnings and why he had come to see her.

"No," she groaned. "It . . . cannot be!"

"Tell me, Slow Woman. I must know!"

She let out an odd cry, like a wounded animal. Aguila ducked inside at the sound, hesitating when he saw how Slow Woman was looking at Wade. "I thought . . . you must have died . . . out there," she croaked in a raspy voice. "All these . . . years . . . wondering . . . what had happened . . . to the little son I . . . left behind." Her eyes teared, and Aguila watched in agony, torn between his love for his sister, and his disappointment that she had kept a twin son and had never told the truth.

"My God," Wade whispered.

She pulled her hand away and scooted farther back with all the strength she could muster. "I did . . . a bad thing . . . and I have been punished with a sad . . . heart. Now . . . I will die . . . and so will you . . . my son. You . . . should never . . . have come!"

She began coughing then, a wrenching gagging that made her spit blood. Again Wade reached out to her, refusing to let go of her arms when she tried weakly and vainly to get away. Wade pulled her gently back to the mat where she had been lying. He kept hold of her arms and leaned over her.

"If coming here means my death, then so be it," he told her. "I would not trade this moment for life, my mother. And you didn't do a bad thing. The custom of killing twin babies is *wrong*, Slow Woman. You knew it in your heart. And you gave me life by not telling anyone that I existed. I am glad to have found you. All my life I have wondered about myself, wondered where the Comanche side of me belonged, whether I had family here. Now I know—I have a mother and an uncle, and I have a brother."

She shook her head, tears flowing out of her weary eyes. "He will . . . kill you. He has no . . . choice. One spirit . . . cannot share two . . . bodies."

"Before he knew I existed, Wild Horse did just fine. Learning he has a brother doesn't change anything."

"Yes . . . it does," she whispered. "He has not . . . had a happy life." She gasped for breath. "He lost one wife . . . and a son to . . . white man's disease. He lost . . . another wife . . . another son . . . to . . . white man's treachery. He has . . . watched his people give up . . . and grow weak . . . and leave their homeland. Now alone . . . he tries to keep fighting . . . the white man. Now he will know . . . that all this has come upon him . . . because he was born under a bad omen. He will not . . . be strong enough . . . to defeat the white man . . . until he has killed you . . . and takes your strength and . . . spirit . . . into his own heart. It is . . . the way."

"Slow Woman!" Aguila came closer. "What have you done! You have destroyed us!"

"She's done nothing," Wade answered angrily, looking up at the man. "She was only a mother who loved her sons, and she was hardly more than a child!"

"Go," Slow Woman said weakly. "Go . . . and let me . . . die."

Wade looked down at her. "No. I will stay with you for a while."

"No. Go to Wild Horse. Do . . . what must be . . . done."

Wade studied her, wanting to remember every feature, a chill moving through him at the realization that he was touching his real mother, something he had once never thought possible. He looked back at Aguila. "Is there a doctor around here—a *real* doctor—a white man's doctor?"

"She will not let a white man touch her. Even if she would, there is not one for many miles, two days at the least. She will not even live that long. I have heard that kind of breathing before. I know what it brings."

315

Wade looked down at Slow Woman. "Then I will stay until her death. I will hold her and look at her and talk to her. She is my mother." He saw deep affection in her eyes, as her joy at knowing the other son had lived overcame the terror of what she had done. "This is all I will have of her," Wade continued, touching her hair. "I will not leave."

Her eyes teared more, and she reached up with a shaking hand to touch his face. "I am . . . sorry . . . I left you to die. And yet . . . now I am sorry . . . you lived . . . for now you must die . . . all over again."

"If I do, it will have been worth it," he answered. He drew her close, and she was too sick and weak to push away from him. He sat down and drew her into his arms, and she rested her head against his chest. Wade felt torn with emotion, wishing his white mother could be here. She would have understood this. She would have wanted to meet Slow Woman. Vivian Morrow's love was all the motherly love he had ever known; yet he knew that this frail woman had also loved him all his life, but secretly.

Aguila left, and a moment later a naked little girl snuck inside from under the rolled-up buffalo robes. She was perhaps three. She toddled up to Slow Woman, who still rested in Wade's arms, seeming to be asleep. She stared at Wade a moment, then touched Slow Woman's hair. "Father's sister," she said in the Comanche tongue. She patted the woman's head.

Wade watched her, realizing she had to be his cousin. The affection she showed the woman, and the protective defense Aguila had shown her earlier, as well as the fact that Aguila had taken care of the woman all these years and had been a father to Wild Horse, only verified that the Comanche were as capable of feelings and family closeness as any white family. Wild Horse's own rage and revenge were because he had lost wives and sons to the white man. This was the first time Wade had heard there had been yet another wife and son whose deaths could be attributed to whites. Surely Wild Horse felt a deep hurt. Surely he had had strong feelings for the women he had called wife, and for the sons they had given him.

The little girl put a small, chubby hand to his face then, smiling a wide, pretty smile. "Wild Horse," she said. She leaned forward, touching her cheek to his, and he didn't bother trying to explain who he was. She turned then and leaned down to crawl back out, her little bare bottom disappearing last.

He looked down at his mother, feeling a sudden peace unlike any he had ever before experienced. Somehow, knowing this was the woman who had given him birth, knowing this was where his life began, helped ease the lonely feeling of never belonging anywhere. He realized he could not stay with them, but a part of him would always belong here.

"Looks like Alice will have her vegetables again this year," Enders told Jennifer. They walked beside a flower and vegetable garden behind Alice's cabin, flowers and roses beginning to green up and pop open; tiny green shoots sprouting from seeds for peppers and beans. Jennifer still used her crutches, although she was sure she could get along without them now. It had been two weeks since Wade left, but she was stretching out her excuse of not being fully healed as long as she could, in order to keep Tony Enders from pushing her too hard too soon. He had already brought up the subject of marriage several times, and she knew that soon he would begin demanding answers from her.

"Yes," she answered. "Alice told me how much she enjoys gardening." She kept her eyes averted, never able to look Enders straight in the eyes for fear he would see the dislike she held for him. She studied the garden, deciding Alice must have a very green thumb to be able to make anything grow out here, but thanks to the fort's location close to Comanche Springs, there was enough water for a garden.

Enders had told her the area where the fort was located had once been a primary gathering point for the Comanche, because of the plentiful supply of water. She thought to herself how angry she would be if someone stole such a precious gift of nature away from her, especially in this arid land. In some ways she could understand the vicious Comanche retaliation.

She had learned, however, that men like Tony Enders had no interest or desire in understanding anything the Comanche did. To them the Comanche were evil, vicious, brutal animals, and she supposed in some respects they could be exactly that. After all, she had been the brunt of that brutality herself. Yet, after knowing Wade, she realized there had to be something more to the Indians than what the white man usually saw. Surely within their own families there was love and compassion.

She reasoned that if Tony Enders would show just a little compassion himself, a little courtesy and gentleness when the subject of the Comanche arose, she could like him a little more. But to him they were "murdering savages," and the country, especially Texans, would be better off if they were all dead.

Jennifer had come to realize that it wasn't just Enders's attitude toward Indians that upset her. She felt instinctively that he had the same attitude toward most things, and that if she was his wife, he would show her hardly any more compassion than he would show a Comanche. She could tell by snide remarks and his general attitude and manners that he considered women inferior, something put on earth for man's satisfaction and that was all.

Oh, Wade, where are you? she thought. *Please be all right. Please get back here soon.*

"The, uh, the preacher will be here in less than two weeks," Enders was saying.

How she dreaded this conversation. They had had it too many times already. "I see," she answered.

Enders stopped walking. "I don't think you see at all," he said. He put a hand on her arm and moved in front of her. "I want to marry you, Jenny, but you haven't given me the slightest hint either way. This isn't easy for me, you know, having to look at you, think of you as my wife. I mean, out here a man gets damn lonely, and . . . my God, woman, if we're going to be married, why do we have to wait for everything. The least you could do is . . . well . . ."

Before Jennifer realized what he was going to do he jerked her close, clamping his arms around her waist and pressing her tight to him while he planted his mouth over hers. She could smell whiskey and tobacco, and the kiss was not warm and sweet like Wade's kisses. It was cold, and so rough that he hurt her mouth. Jennifer twisted in his arms, losing hold of one crutch, but managing to whack his left leg with the other.

Enders grunted and let loose of her enough that she managed to step back from him, stumbling slightly. She wiped at her mouth savagely, tears of anger stinging her eyes. "How dare you," she almost screamed.

He rubbed at his leg a moment, looking at her darkly while she limped over to pick up her other crutch. He grabbed her shoulder and jerked her back around to look at him. "What do you mean, how dare I? My God, woman, you came here to marry me."

"I came here to see if I might *want* to marry you." She told herself to calm down, that she might have to leave this place too soon if she wasn't careful. "You must give me more time, Tony." She pulled away again, shaking, longing for Wade. How could the touch of one man be so wonderful, and the touch of another be so repulsive?

"You've had two weeks," he complained. "Besides, what's a kiss? It's not as though I did anything to offend you. For God's sake, you came out here with at least a *pretty* good idea of marrying me, didn't you? I mean, how in hell can you know if you might like to be my wife if we don't kiss?"

"Watch your language," she answered, her voice shaking. She walked a little farther away from him, scrambling to think of the right things to say without giving him too much hope. "If I want a kiss, you'll know it. Right now, I'm still full of bad memories."

Enders frowned, wondering if he'd have a problem once

319

she was his wife. He reminded himself she was a virgin and he had to be careful, but that only made him more anxious than ever. The thought of breaking her in made his desires soar, and he could hardly stand the thought of waiting another two weeks. Maybe if he just took her and had it over with she would find out how good it felt and wouldn't be so cold and elusive. Then again, maybe it was more than that. Maybe she had lied about what the Comanche did to her. If she had, she certainly had no right to put him off. She wouldn't even be worth marrying if that were true, except he'd marry her anyway in order to soak her uncle for all he could.

"What bad memories?" he asked. "You told me the Comanche never touched you."

"They didn't." She kept her eyes averted, hating talking to him about something so intimate, hating the realization that the man was itching to get into her bed. "They didn't need to," she added. "Just knowing what they intended was bad enough—being tossed around like that, tearing at me . . . shooting me and trying to scalp me alive." She turned and met his eyes, her own blazing now. "Don't you think that's enough horror to try to get over? They didn't have to do more than that. What they did do was enough to give me nightmares for a long time to come! I'm sorry, Tony. If I had arrived here my normal self, without these memories, without these wounds, it would have been easier to try to get to know and to marry a stranger. But it's all different now, and I need more time. You said yourself it will be two more weeks before the preacher arrives."

He held her eyes, his own showing a pompous pride. "You didn't have to wipe your mouth like I had the plague."

She reddened slightly. "I'm sorry. It was just a reaction, from being so startled. I'm . . . I'm not used to men," she said, hoping that would pacify him.

He nodded, studying her closely. "What about that big half-breed who brought you here? You exposed your whole leg to him. More than that. He wrapped your ribs, didn't he?"

She turned away, appalled by the inflection in his words. "For heaven's sake, Tony, I was wounded. I could have died."

"Fact remains that SOB saw more than I ever have. And I can't believe he didn't try something with you. Those Indians pant after white women like a bear after honey."

She faced him again. "I thought in time you would show your true self. Now I am beginning to see the real Anthony Enders, and it's disgusting," she said sternly. "You can believe what you want, but if you want to marry me, such remarks will do nothing but turn me away. Do you really think you can talk to me that way and then expect me to fall in love with you?"

He sighed deeply, realizing if he wasn't careful he would lose her *and* her uncle's money. He was angry with himself for letting his terrible desire for her and his jealousy of the half-breed get in the way of his careful handling of her. She was driving him crazy with want. How did a man get to a woman like this? Most women he'd known were easy, but then most of them had been whores to begin with. This one was different, prim and proper, and too damn cold.

"I don't know what I thought," he answered. "I just meant . . . well, I guess I just want you so bad myself that I can't stand the thought of anybody else looking at you. Is that so terrible, Jenny? I mean, I already know I love you, and waiting like this, wondering if you'll marry me, it's driving me crazy. It makes me do and say the wrong things. I'm sorry. I'm real sorry."

Jennifer reminded herself that for the moment she had to keep going along with him. She all but hated the man, but she didn't dare tell him so—not yet. It galled her to realize the things he was imagining with her and the Comanche, or how his dirty mind was working on her and Wade. And she knew now what he would do to her if he should get any idea of what had really happened between her and Wade. It had been beautiful, sacred. But someone like Tony Enders would make it into something ugly and sinful.

"All right," she managed to say. "I . . . accept your apology. But I don't think I want to walk with you any more today. You can come for supper, day after tomorrow. I need tomorrow to think about things. I need a day away from you."

Bitch, he thought. He wanted to shout it at her. "Sure," he answered aloud. "I'm . . . I'm real sorry we've got off to a bad start. And I'm sorry I haven't realized how bad your experience with the Comanche affected you. Out here, we get kind of hardened to such things. We forget what it's like for somebody who doesn't understand this country. After you've been out here a while, you tend to get kind of hard and unmannerly. I, uh, I haven't been around a proper lady in a long time. I really am sorry, Jenny."

She wished she could believe he meant it. At the same time, she knew the incident and her explanation of why she needed more time had bought her just that—more time. She hobbled closer to him, telling herself that for Wade's sake she had to keep up the pretense. She leaned up and kissed his cheek, even though she would much rather have struck him.

"I'm sorry, too," she told him. "I'm sorry this whole thing became so difficult. I really did come out here to be married, Tony. A lot of things just got in the way." She sighed and stepped back. "I'm going inside now. You don't need to walk me. I'll see you day after tomorrow."

He nodded, hating her, wanting her, wondering what was true and what wasn't. He watched her for a moment, envisioning the body under the dress, then turned and stomped away, imagining shoving himself inside her while at the same time his hands were wrapped around her pretty, slender throat. He headed for his own barracks when Captain Howell stepped outside his quarters and called him over.

Tony hurried over to the man, saluting when he came closer. "Yes, sir."

"I just thought I'd tell you, Enders, the Indian agent up by the Red River wired me that Wade Morrow did indeed go there. He heard about it from some of the Comanche and went to investigate. Morrow found his mother. She died while he was with her. He didn't say where he was going from there, but some of the Comanche say he intends to find Wild Horse—they say Wild Horse wants to kill him because he's a twin. You know how the Comanche are about those things."

Enders grinned. "Looks like Wade Morrow could lead us right to Wild Horse." Inside he was more joyful over the fact that Wade Morrow would surely die. There was no way he could defeat Wild Horse. Big and experienced as he was, he was surely no match for Wild Horse's savagery. He had not been able to make himself believe there had not been something between Wade Morrow and Jennifer, or that at least Wade Morrow would have liked it that way. Even though the man was supposedly no threat, the thought of him dead gave Tony Enders great pleasure. He would tell Jenny about it and see how she reacted. He would know by the look on her face if she had feelings for the half-breed.

"I'm having Morrow followed," Howell was saying. "Apache scouts will trail him but stay well behind him so he doesn't spot them. If he leads them to Wild Horse, they'll come and tell us, and Wild Horse will be ours. We ought to both earn a promotion out of that. You'll be making more money then, Enders. That will help, with a new wife and all."

Her uncle's money will help a lot more, Enders thought. "Yes, sir. How long ago was this?"

Howell put a pipe into his mouth and puffed it a moment before answering. "About five days. The agent didn't know about it till after Wild Horse's mother was dead. That's when some of the Indians told him another man had been there who was Wild Horse's brother. He had already left by then, but the Apaches will be able to track him. They'd like nothing better themselves than to help catch a wanted Comanche leader. We'll get him, Enders.

We'll get him. And if Wild Horse doesn't kill Morrow, we'll have him arrested, too, for consorting with a Comanche renegade. The man lied to us about going back to California. He knew all along he was going to find Wild Horse, and he could have led us to him." He clamped the pipe into his mouth again. "Well, stay alert and ready, Enders. Those Apache scouts could show up any time."

The man saluted Enders, then turned and re-entered his quarters. Enders almost laughed out loud. Wade Morrow would pay for setting eyes on Jennifer Andrews. And he would pay for lying about where he was going when he left the fort. The man knew all along he intended to go and find Wild Horse's mother and Wild Horse himself. He wondered if Jennifer had also known what Morrow was going to do. If she did, then she was protecting the man—even protecting Wild Horse! There would be only one reason she would do that. He'd find out, one way or another.

Chapter Twenty-One

"I don't know what to do, Alice," Jennifer told the woman. They sat at the kitchen table, and a coyote yipped somewhere in the distance. The night hung dark and heavy, thick clouds hiding the moon. Jennifer rose and walked to the back door, looking through the screen into nothingness. "Tony kissed me today, against my will, I might add. I . . . didn't enjoy it at all. I don't think I could bring myself even to like him, let alone love him."

"Then it's decided. You aren't going to marry him," the woman answered. She set down a cup of coffee. "It's that simple. You'll stay on here with me until you're completely healed and think you're ready for the hardship of a journey back to San Antonio. I'll talk to Captain Howell about it myself. If you stay inside most of the time, there shouldn't be any big problems with the other men; and if you help me with my work, you'll be earning your keep. You said you had the money to pay back Sergeant Enders, didn't you?"

"Yes." *Thanks to Wade Morrow*, Jennifer thought. "It just seems . . . I don't know. Maybe it's still too soon. I mean, it's not too soon for me to know in my own heart. But maybe it's too soon to tell the sergeant. I told him today to give me more time. He seemed . . . genuinely apologetic, when he realized how upset I was. But he made some rude remarks . . : about Wade Morrow seeing things he hadn't seen himself yet. It was very embarrassing, and it only tells me where his mind is. I'm worried how he'd treat me once I was his wife. I don't think he'd be very patient."

"Of course he wouldn't. It's hard enough on a young woman when she loves the man, and you sure don't love Tony Enders. I wouldn't wait more than another week to give him a flat no. Frankly, I don't understand why you don't do it right now and get it over with."

Jennifer sighed. "I suppose I should. I'm so confused. I feel a little guilty for building up Tony's hopes."

"Don't ever feel guilty where that one is concerned. My husband never liked that man, and he was always a good judge of character. If you don't marry the man, he'll live. He'll just place another ad. I hate to put it so bluntly, but personally I think he just wants a woman in his bed at night—one who is clean and won't give him a disease, if he doesn't already have one."

Jennifer shivered, rubbing the backs of her arms. "I guess that's about as blunt as you can get," she said with an embarrassed smile.

"Well, I'm a lot older than you, child. I know a little bit more about men."

Jennifer wondered what the woman would think if she knew just how much Jennifer did know—and who had taught her. Outside one guard called out to another. Jennifer had met few of the men. Tony didn't want them gawking at her; but she had felt their eyes on her when she was outside helping Alice with laundry, or when she walked with Tony.

She had also met a Corporal James Deaver, who Tony described as a good friend, but who Jennifer disliked even more than Tony. The man was about Tony's age, but shorter and heavyset. His uniform never seemed to fit quite right or look neat, and Jennifer didn't like the way the man looked at her.

She could already understand to some extent why it was hard for a woman to stay here. Fort life was boring enough for the men, but for the women, who had to stay behind when the men went out on patrol, it surely became almost unbearable. How Alice stood it once the other women had left, she could not imagine. Perhaps that was why the woman didn't seem to mind being kept busy from morning till night doing laundry and mending; and Jennifer could understand the woman's wanting to stay near her husband's grave. If something happened to Wade . . .

The pain moved through her again. Wade. Where was he now? Would that night in the cave, when he had so gently made a woman of her, be their only time together? "I think I'll turn in," she told Alice then. "And I insist on taking the cot. I changed the bedclothes today while you were scrubbing clothes outside. I want you to take back your bed, Alice."

"Nonsense. You aren't healed enough yet. The bed is much more comfortable."

"That's why I want you to have it. I know your back has been bothering you, and you work so hard. You deserve the bed. I'm healed enough to sleep on the cot, and I intend to start helping you with more of the laundry tomorrow. I insist."

"I'm not sure you're ready."

"If I get tired, I'll let you know. I want to do more, Alice. And I promise to make up my mind soon and be out of your hair."

Alice rose, putting a hand on her arm. "I don't think of it that way at all, and you know it. Jenny, is there something else wrong, something you aren't telling me? So many times I've seen you staring off into the horizon, looking so lost and lonely. Is it the loss of your aunt, or did something more happen when you were attacked than you're telling me? You can confide in me, Jenny."

Jennifer studied the woman's kind eyes, the lines of age and wisdom around them. How she wished she could tell her the truth, tell her she was in love with Wade Morrow. "I guess it's just a combination of all of it," she answered. "Losing my aunt, running away from Uncle John, the rude awakening I got when I came out here." She sighed and turned away. "Now I've got Tony Enders to contend with."

327

"Well, I wouldn't worry about that last problem. You're free to make your own decision there. It's just too bad your uncle was the kind of man he was. I'd like to give him a good tongue lashing and let everybody in St. Louis know what kind of man he really is."

"I never told Tony the whole truth about it. I just couldn't bring myself to share something so personal and embarrassing. He would have made it more dirty in his mind."

"He probably would. You go on to bed now. I'll be retiring myself in a few minutes." Alice put an arm around her shoulders and squeezed. "I've learned, child, that things always have a way of working out. You're a brave and resourceful young lady. In a week or two you'll leave here and go back to Houston or San Antonio and teach or find some other honorable way to fend for yourself, and somebody pretty as you will find a man you can love and be married in no time. Then life will be good for you and you'll forget these terrible things that have happened to you."

Jennifer gave her a smile, touching the woman's wrinkled hand. "I suppose you're right. I can hardly believe it has only been six weeks since I first left St. Louis. Sometimes it seems like years ago. I feel like a completely different person."

"I know how that can be. And sometimes something that happened years ago seems like yesterday. I still half expect my Ben to come walking through the door at the end of the day, or to hear my daughter calling for me." Alice's eyes teared. "I'll miss you terribly when you go, Jenny. But I want you to do what's best for yourself. Don't let anyone steer your course for you, child."

Jennifer nodded, giving the woman a half-hearted smile before leaving the room. She went to the main room and closed the curtains, then undressed for bed. She lay down on the cot and immediately wondered how Alice had managed to sleep on it. Minutes later Alice retired to her own bed, giving Jennifer a last good night.

Alice blew out the lamp near her bed, leaving one

lantern dimly lit on the kitchen table so that the house was lit up just enough for each of them to see her way around if she woke up in the middle of the night. Jennifer knew her problem would not be waking up, but getting to sleep.

It seemed only minutes until Alice was snoring as loudly as a man. Jennifer grinned at the sound, glad the woman was finally sleeping comfortably, but wondering how she was going to get to sleep herself with the steady, irritating sound. She wished she could stop thinking and worrying about Wade, but that was impossible.

The night was too warm, which only added to her wakefulness. Finally she rose, pulling on a robe and going into the kitchen. She longed for a cup of tea, but it was too hot to light the kitchen stove. She moved to the back door and quietly opened it. She could still see the soft red glow of embers from the fire outside that Alice had made to cook supper. Jennifer picked up a kettle of water, deciding that since the fire was behind the cabin, no one would spot her outside in her robe. She could set the kettle on the coals long enough to heat it for tea.

She carried the kettle out, using only one crutch to give her a little support while she carried the kettle in her other hand. She set it directly on the coals to heat faster. She grasped the crutch and rose, standing and watching the kettle for a moment.

It was then she sensed another presence, although she could see nothing. Her blood ran cold. Was it Tony, or worse, some Comanche renegade set to pounce on her and drag her off? Either way, it was someone the guards had not noticed, so it was most likely Tony. He could go where he pleased with no questions asked.

She turned to walk back to the cabin, wondering if she could make it in time, since she couldn't run. She thought about screaming out for Alice as she came closer to the door, but then she heard the voice.

"Jenny," it said softly. "It's me—Wade."

She recognized the voice, especially the gentle way he spoke her name. It came from the darkness to her right. She walked in that direction, and suddenly he loomed in front of her, a commanding figure that would have frightened the wits out of her if she didn't already know him.

"Wade," she whispered. She let go of the crutch and in the next moment she was in his arms, relishing a welcome, reassuring, warm embrace that both of them needed. Oh, how wonderful those arms felt, how overjoyed she was that he was all right!

"Jenny," he whispered, his lips at her neck, moving over her cheek to cover her mouth in a sweet, warm, wonderful kiss, so different from Tony Enders. He pressed her close, but gently, fearing he would hurt her ribs. She reached around his neck, her feet coming off the ground.

He left her mouth then and just held her for a moment. "Oh, Wade, thank God," she whispered. "I've been so worried, so confused."

He pulled back just slightly, keeping hold of her. "Is Alice asleep?"

"Yes."

"I don't want any of them to know I'm here," he whispered.

"But how did you get this far without being spotted?"

Her eyes were adjusted to the darkness now, and she could see his smile. "I'm an Indian, remember?"

She smiled in return. "Oh, yes," she answered, touching his face. "I remember everything about you. Is it over, Wade? Should I leave now?"

His smile faded. "Not yet. I have to go back to Wild Horse."

"Back? Why? Didn't you already see him? And did you find your mother? Are you really Wild Horse's twin?"

He sighed deeply, embracing her closer again so that her head rested against his chest. "Yes," he answered. "Wild Horse is my brother. I found my mother on a reservation up by the Red River. She died just a couple of days after I got there. She had already been sick with pneumonia."

"Oh, Wade." She hugged him and looked up at him. "I'm so sorry."

He put a hand to her hair. "I have to go and tell Wild

Horse, Jenny. I have to see him once more. I promised him I'd come back and tell him what Slow Woman said about our birth."

She wished she could see his eyes better, for she knew that they would tell her if there was danger. "What will happen? You said Comanches never allow twin babies to live. What about the ones who *do* survive?"

He leaned down and kissed her eyes. "Let's just say Wild Horse isn't too enthusiastic about this. But he's my brother, Jenny. I think I can work it out. In the meantime you just remember what I told you about contacting my family."

"Wade, he wants to kill you, doesn't he," she whimpered.

"It's not as bad as you think. I have to want to fight him in return, or it would bring him no honor. I don't intend to fight him. Besides, I saw a flicker of affection in those wild eyes of his. I think I can convince him it's wrong. It's going to work out, Jenny."

She hugged him closer again. "Oh, Wade, I feel only danger and death. Please don't go. I don't want to live without you. These last two weeks have been unbearable, waiting and wondering."

"I'm sorry, but I have to do it, Jenny." He tangled his fingers into her long, loose hair. "How are they treating you here? What has happened with Enders?"

"I've managed to keep him at a distance," she answered, relishing the feel of his powerful chest against her. She decided not to tell him about the kiss. She didn't want him to worry about anything right now but getting things settled with his brother. If she told him the truth about Enders, he might do something foolish, like make his presence known.

"He's getting anxious for an answer from me, though," she continued. "So far I have managed to convince him that I need more time to recover from my experience and from my wounds. I don't need my crutches so much any more, but I don't want him to know that. I keep using them."

The moon appeared from behind a cloud, and she studied his eyes in its light. "I can't put him off more than a couple more weeks, Wade. Then I'll have to leave, whether you show up or not. I hope someone from your family or at least some men who work for them will be in the area by then. I don't want to go off on another stagecoach. If we would be attacked again, there would be no Wade Morrow along to save me."

He put his hands to her face. "I'll find a way to get back here," he told her softly. "That's a promise. And within a week or so, my brothers or someone from my father's company will have to be coming through here. You can feel free to tell them the truth, and they'll help you. Once you have them behind you, Enders nor anyone else can hurt you."

"All I care about is that you make it back," she whispered.

He leaned down and kissed her again, gently, suggestively. Each knew the other longed to do more, but they would not get the opportunity now, and it was torture for them both. He ran one hand gently over her throat and down to a soft breast, cupping it lightly in his big hand, feeling the firm nipple through the soft, flannel gown.

The touch brought a whimper from her lips, and his kiss became more heated. He moved both arms back around her, pressing his hardness against her belly.

They were lost in each other for a moment, each feeling desperate to mate again, to share their love in the most fulfilling way, for she was healed now, and she knew instinctively that the next time Wade Morrow surged inside of her, it would be the most glorious experience of her life. The next time there would be no pain, only ecstasy. To have him this close, to feel his arms around her, his mouth smothering her own, yet being unable to do more, was torture for them both.

"God, Jenny," he groaned, trembling. "I need you so."

"And I need you," she whispered in return.

"I'm so sorry. It's a matter of honor. All of this means too much to me, and I gave Wild Horse my word I would come in person." He pulled away again. "It's something I have to do, Jenny."

She reached up and touched his hair. "I know."

He embraced her again, grasping her hair and pressing her head against his chest. "I need to know, Jenny," he whispered. "You aren't . . . I need to know when your last time of month was. I'm worried I might have got you pregnant."

She was glad for the darkness, for the remark brought a flush to her cheeks. She didn't know a lot about such things herself, except she remembered that when she had her first frightening experience with a period, Aunt Esther had explained to her that it meant she could have babies, but that a period meant a woman was not pregnant.

"The week after you left," she answered shyly. She felt him sigh as though greatly relieved.

"Good," he answered. "It would be bad enough if something happened, without me leaving you pregnant by a half-breed."

"Oh, Wade, don't say it that way. I would have gladly had the baby, and I would have loved it more than my own life. In a way I wish it *had* happened, so I would know I will always have something of you if you don't make it back."

He kissed her hair. "I *will* come back, Jenny. You're all I thought about while I was gone. The next time I come back, it will be for good." He stroked her hair, loving the feel of it. "If you have to leave, then do what's best for your own safety. Don't let Enders push you. If you can leave with my brothers, all the better. If I haven't come back by the time they show up, go with them anyway. You know I'll find you. Promise me."

"I promise."

He kissed her hair. "You sure Enders hasn't been a problem? Are they treating you all right?"

"Everything is fine," she lied. "And I have Alice. She has become a good friend. She's very kind, and she treats me like a daughter." She looked up at him. "I'll be all right, Wade. It's you I'm worried about."

333

He leaned down and kissed her once more. "I have to go," he said then. "I was lucky the clouds have been hiding the moon tonight, or I never would have made it this far without being spotted. I'm camped about two miles from here with a Comanche man named Aguila. He's my uncle, my mother's brother. He decided to come back with me. He wants a hand in whatever happens. Uncles have very close relationships with their nephews in the Indian culture. Aguila raised Wild Horse."

"Will he help you?"

Wade sighed. "I don't know. He has taught me a lot about the Comanche on the way here, but he doesn't seem to hold the fondness for me that he does for Wild Horse. To him I am a stranger, almost an enemy, because I have disrupted Wild Horse's leadership and credibility. Being a twin has caused him to lose face with those who follow him."

"But how can it be settled?"

"I don't know yet." How could he tell her it was Comanche law that he and Wild Horse must fight to the death? It would only give her nightmares. She was well enough aware of the danger. To spell it out would be torture for her. "But I'll find a way," he added, hoping against hope he was right. He couldn't help wondering if he was making the biggest mistake of his life, for he loved Jennifer Andrews more than he had loved any other woman since Rebecca. But the need to settle things with Wild Horse was a matter of honor now, something he knew would haunt him forever if he turned his back on all of it now. Besides, he suspected Wild Horse would hunt him down before he would let him out of Texas, and he didn't want Jennifer to be with him when that happened. Better to settle it while Jenny was safe.

"I have to go," he said then. "I'm damn sorry, Jenny. I love you even more for understanding."

"Just come back, Wade," she pleaded, reaching up to meet his mouth again. The sweet, hot kiss lingered as tears stung Jennifer's eyes. How painful it was to see him so briefly and have to let him go again. "I love you. I love you," she whispered frantically when his lips left her own.

He gently and reluctantly pushed her away. "You'd better get back inside." He touched her hair, her face. "I love you, too, Jenny. God be with you."

"And with you." She took his hand and kissed his palm, and he could feel her wet tears against his skin.

"I'm sorry, Jenny."

"You mustn't be," she whispered. "A man has to do what he knows is right."

He squeezed her hand lightly, then wiped gently at her tears with his other hand. "And I'll do right by you when I come back. That's a promise." He leaned down and kissed her once more, quickly this time, wanting one last taste of her. "Good-bye," he said, the word filled with pain.

He suddenly disappeared into the darkness. Jenny wanted to call after him, but she feared she might be heard. She stood there feeling numb. Quickly his visit in the night seemed like a strange dream. She limped back to the fire, using her robe to shield her hand from the heat as she grasped the handle of the now-steaming kettle. She struggled into the house with it, her stomach and chest aching with sorrow and a terrible longing to be with Wade.

He was going back to Wild Horse. Did that mean certain death? She couldn't let herself think it. She had to hope he was right that it could be worked out. She set the kettle on the stove, then sat down to the table, too shaken, too full of desperate, reawakened love now to bother fixing the tea. In one sense she almost wished he had not come at all until everything was over, but he realized she had to know he was all right—and he had been worried about her, worried he had got her pregnant.

She put a hand to her belly, remembering with sweet ecstasy what he had done to her, almost wishing his life *had* taken hold, married or not. In their hearts they were as married as anyone with a license. "Wade," she whispered.

Enders concentrated to understand the Apache scout. The dark, wild-looking Indian stood in Howell's office, explaining what he and the Apache man who scouted with him had discovered.

"Tracks come this way," the man told Howell. "They make camp. Do not understand."

"Don't understand what?" Howell asked the man.

"Two men—Wild Horse's brother and Aguila. They leave together—come close to fort—maybe two miles. One set of tracks come from camp to fort. Other man stay at camp. Now both men gone."

Howell leaned closer, and Enders unfolded his arms, his mind whirling.

"Are you saying one of them came to the fort?" Howell asked.

The Indian nodded.

"But we've not seen hide nor hair of either man," Howell told him.

The Indian shrugged. "Tracks come this way—to small white cabin. I follow. Two women there, washing clothes. Old one, she scream when she see me. Young one just stare. Old one, she calm down—she know who I am then—see me here before when I scout for her husband, she say. Then I come here to you."

Enders frowned. "A set of tracks led to Alice Hart's cabin?"

The Indian nodded again, and Enders looked at Howell. "What the hell could that mean?"

Howell scowled at him. "I don't know, but I'd have a talk with Jennifer Andrews, if I were you."

"Jenny?" Enders was having trouble believing what had to be the truth.

"Face it, Enders," Howell told him. "Morrow saved Miss Andrews's life, traveled alone with her, and nursed her for five days. He seemed awfully defensive of her when he was here. I didn't want to think anything about it then, for your sake. But the fact remains that someone went to that cabin last night, and one of those two men is Wade Morrow. Now which one would have any logical reason to go there? And who would he want to see? Certainly not Alice Hart." He sighed irritably. "You and Lieutenant Brown get a patrol together—fast!" He looked at the Apache man. "Both men kept going then?"

"Go back north. We must hurry to keep up now if we want to catch Wild Horse."

"I agree." Howell looked at Enders. "Get going. There's no time to lose."

Enders saluted. "Yes, sir." He quickly left, his mind racing with the possibilities of why Wade Morrow would pay Jennifer Andrews a visit in the middle of the night. No one had seen him, and he had obviously deliberately hidden his presence. Why? The only explanation was that there was something between him and Jenny after all. Maybe that was why she had been so cold, why she wouldn't give him any straight answers. If it was true, she'd pay, and pay dearly for putting on such airs! Any white woman who would have any affection for an Indian, especially a half-breed, was no lady at all, and sure couldn't expect to be treated like one.

The thought brought a thousand possibilities. He could blackmail her into marrying him, threaten to expose her sordid secret to everyone and risk her coming to insults and bodily harm. Or he could take her himself whether she liked it or not. It would serve her right. He had to think about this, if his anger and damaged pride didn't get in the way of being rational. He had intended to confront her with the news that Wade Morrow was apparently searching for his brother—that he would most certainly be killed. He was sure he would know by the look on her face if she cared.

Now there would not be time. But he would find the time when he got back, and by then Wade Morrow would most likely be dead. He would have a lot more to discuss with her then, and there would be no Wade Morrow to come to her defense. Jennifer Andrews would be on her own, and she had better have some good answers for him when he returned. He only wished there was time to talk to her before he left.

The bitch! She had been lying to him, holding out on him, pretending to be so proper. He'd show her what he thought of her when he got back! He'd get more out of her than the $300 she owed him!

Chapter Twenty-Two

Jennifer watched from the doorway of Alice's cabin as more than half the men at the fort mounted their horses and formed themselves into three rows. She sensed the urgent excitement of men who had been bored and restless finally having something to do, and she heard the name Wild Horse being passed among them.

She felt a growing dread, wondering what was happening and if Wade would somehow get involved and get hurt. She knew this sudden call to arms had to have something to do with the Indian scout who had wandered into Alice's backyard earlier. He had frightened Jennifer at first, but Alice had staunchly challenged the man and learned the reason for his presence. He had said only that he was tracking someone, and Jennifer feared it was Wade. Now, suddenly, the fort was a bustle of whinnying horses and clanking sabers, some men complaining, others laughing, most apparently looking forward to whatever adventure lay ahead.

Sergeant Enders rode through the parade ground shouting orders. He glanced at Jennifer, and his look gave her a strange chill. Was Wade in danger? Did Tony know he had come to see her? She saw Alice then, walking hurriedly back to the cabin, after going to see the commander. A strange, worried expression showed on her face as she came closer.

"Get inside," she told Jennifer.

Jennifer's heartbeat quickened at the words, which were spoken gravely. She glanced at Enders once more, wondering why he didn't come over to her and tell her where he was going and how long he might be. Again he cast her a dark scowl. She turned and followed Alice inside, closing the door.

"Alice, what's happening? What's wrong?"

The woman turned, her eyes showing near shock, and a deep disappointment. "That scout was following Wade Morrow, Jenny, and the tracks led right to my back door."

Jennifer could not control the flush that came to her cheeks. She turned away, struggling to find the right words.

"He came here last night, didn't he? Why, Jenny? What haven't you told me?"

Jennifer swallowed back a lump in her throat. She felt as though her whole body was suddenly bathed in perspiration. She was not worried so much for herself now, but for Wade. "Where are those soldiers going?" she asked.

"You answer my question first."

Jennifer breathed deeply for self-control, then turned, holding her chin proudly. "I'm in love with Wade Morrow, and I will be damned if I will show any shame in it, or let you or anyone else do the same! He's one of the finest people I've ever known—strong, brave, educated, more civil than some of the white men I traveled with on that coach—certainly more of a gentleman than Tony Enders has ever been!"

Alice closed her eyes, giving off a deep sigh. She shook her head and slowly sat down in her rocker beside the fireplace. "You should have told me, Jenny."

"Why? So that you could throw me out sooner?"

Alice looked up at her. "No. So that we could talk about it. You aren't from around here, Jenny, so you don't understand the gravity of what you just told me—how dangerous that makes things for you. Now Tony Enders and Captain Howell both suspect."

"I don't care. It's time people knew. I've hated pretending, hated acting as though I would be appalled at

Wade Morrow's touch. On the journey here I saw him insulted and ridiculed—and for what? Just because his skin is dark, just because he has high cheekbones and long hair! No one cares that he is college educated, that he is a wealthy man who will one day inherit one of the richest freighting enterprises in the Southwest! But that isn't why I love him. I love him for the man he is inside, Alice, for his kindness and generosity and warmth and courage."

She turned and walked to the window, watching the bustling soldiers outside. "Wade could have left me to die out there," she continued, "or he could have done what the Comanche intended to do to me. I would have been helpless. But he risked his life to save me, and he stayed with me, doctored me, sat with me, encouraged me. He even gave me money so that I could pay off Tony Enders and still have enough to get by on until he could get back to me. He told me how to contact his family in case something happened to him, told me they would take care of me. I believe him, because I know by the kind of person Wade Morrow is that his white parents must be wonderful people."

She kept her back to Alice, brushing at tears. It felt good to admit her feelings. She had wanted to shout her love for Wade Morrow for over two weeks now. She was glad it was in the open, no matter how dangerous it was for her.

"You and Tony Enders and everyone else can think what you want," she said firmly. "I know Indians killed your husband, but that's no more reason to hate all Indians than it is to hate all white men when just one of them kills someone you love. The Comanche are what they are, and nothing can be done about it. Wade has discovered he's Wild Horse's brother, but just because he's related to the man doesn't mean he's like him. He's just Wade Morrow, a fine man."

She heard Alice's rocker creak. "You knew he was going to find Wild Horse, and his own mother, didn't you? You knew he would try to come back here and see you."

"Yes." Jennifer remained turned away. "And you haven't answered my question about the soldiers."

341

Alice rose wearily. "Captain Howell suspected what Mr. Morrow would do once the man knew he could be Wild Horse's twin. Howell left word at the reservation to let him know if Mr. Morrow showed up there. When he did, the Captain ordered him to be followed when he left, hoping the man would lead the scouts to Wild Horse. He left with a Comanche man, and one of them came here last night. Howell has no doubt it was Wade Morrow. The Apache scouts are out tracking again, sure that now Mr. Morrow and the Comanche man will go to Wild Horse. Those soldiers out there are preparing to follow. There is nothing Howell wants more than to capture Wild Horse." She looked up at her daughter's picture. "I hope your Wade Morrow doesn't get caught in the cross fire. Even if he lives, he's in trouble either way. Howell is furious that the man lied to him and refused to help him find Wild Horse. And when Wild Horse sees the soldiers, he'll think Mr. Morrow brought them deliberately. The man has no friends on either side, Jenny. It looks bad for him."

Jennifer's throat ached with a need to cry. Wade! Alice was right. He was surrounded by enemies. "All he wanted to do was find someone of his own blood," she said quietly, her voice shaking. "He knew . . . Wild Horse might be his brother. How could he tell Captain Howell where he was going? He didn't want to bring harm to his own brother. And he had a *right* to find the woman who might be his mother. He *did* find her. She died only a couple of days later." She turned to Alice, a tear slipping down her cheek. "This is a very personal thing for him, Alice. Captain Howell has no business getting involved!"

Alice rubbed at her eyes and faced her. "You might be glad that he *does* get involved, Jenny. If Wade Morrow goes back to Wild Horse alone, it will mean certain death."

"What do you mean?"

"I mean I've been out here long enough and heard enough stories from my husband to know quite a bit about the Comanche. Twins cannot be allowed to live. Now that they are grown men, Wild Horse will want Wade Morrow dead. There will be no room for compassion or brotherly love. It won't matter to Wild Horse. Maybe your Mr. Morrow thinks he can reason with the man, but he can't. A born and bred Comanche will follow the law at all costs, personal and physical. That's the way they are. They're superstitious, and twenty-odd years of believing in bad omens and such won't change overnight. Wade Morrow won't be able to change it either, and unless he's damn good at handling himself, he'll die."

Jennifer struggled to control an urge to scream. Alice's words cut like a knife. "What if . . . what if he *refuses* to fight Wild Horse," she asked.

Alice shook her head. "You have a lot to learn, Jenny. I hate to tell you these things, but you should know. Wild Horse will find a way to *make* him fight. He'll goad him and torture him until Wade Morrow is mad enough to kill him. Wild Horse won't want it to be easy. It will be a test of strength and skill—which one of them has the strongest spirit. Wild Horse believes that once he kills his brother, he will be even stronger. That's what he wants, so that he can be even more successful in fighting for his land."

Jennifer just stared at her, her face pale. "What should I do?" she asked weakly. "I . . . have to believe Wade will survive. I have to wait for him."

Alice came closer and put a hand on her arm. "There's no use waiting, Jenny."

"I have to!" Her voice broke. "Nothing will matter . . . if something happens to Wade. Nothing!"

Alice's eyes showed surprise. "You really *do* love him, don't you?"

Jennifer took a handkerchief from a pocket on her blue calico dress. She wiped her eyes. "Is that so hard to believe? Is it so wrong?"

Alice sighed. "Maybe not. I'll agree Mr. Morrow was well-spoken, and he did save your life. I can't imagine in my own mind loving an Indian, but you don't come from the same background as army people, or people who have lived in Texas all their lives. People in St. Louis don't know anything about Indian trouble. I'm not con-

343

demning or judging you, Jenny. I've just come to care very much about you, and I think you're asking for more than you can handle when you admit to loving an Indian man. Perhaps if you had more time to think about it, if you hadn't been hurt and confused—"

"It had nothing to do with that. How can I make you understand? I simply love the man. I was attracted to him before I was ever hurt and stranded with him."

Alice put a hand to her waist. "Come and sit down." She led Jennifer to the rocker and sat down across from her. "If Wade Morrow told you to contact his family, then I think you had better do so right away."

"His brothers or some of his father's men are supposed to come through here soon. They're on their way to Galveston to pick up some supplies from New Orleans." Jennifer blew her nose. "Wade said they would help me if I explained."

"Then you'd better go with them when they come through. Pay off Enders and just tell him you've decided against marrying him. Give him a little extra. Maybe that will pacify him. Even so, the men around here will lose their respect for you, Jenny. If Mr. Morrow hadn't come here to see you last night, you wouldn't have been involved at all. He must not have known he was being followed."

"He never would have wanted this. That's why he came at night. He didn't want anyone to see me with him. Oh, Alice, I don't want him to die!" The tears came harder then. Now nothing mattered but that Wade would come back to her.

"Tell me how to get hold of Mr. Morrow's family, Jennifer. I'll send a wire for you so you don't have to go out there and be stared at by the other men. Maybe by the time some of his family gets here, you'll know what has happened to Mr. Morrow." Jennifer only cried harder, and Alice put a hand on her shoulder. "I don't understand all of this, Jenny; but I do understand how it feels to be in love. Lord knows it's the most wonderful and sometimes the most painful thing there is for someone young as you. When you get older, you'll look back on all of this and realize life goes on. You'll love again, child. Maybe it's better this way. Life for a white woman with an Indian man is not an easy one."

"I don't care," Jennifer sobbed. "I would put up with anything to be with him. And . . . once we were with his family in California . . . it would be easier. He has friends there . . . a family who loves him."

Alice touched her hair. "You talked that seriously? You talked about marriage?"

"Yes." Jennifer realized she could not tell the woman just how far things had gone between her and Wade. How could she explain it, especially since she had been with Wade such a short time. She looked over at Alice, her eyes swollen and red. "He loves me, Alice, and I love him. There was nothing ugly or wrong about it. I don't see him as an Indian at all. He's just a man, a good man who deserves to be loved like any other."

Alice shook her head. "I don't know about that, Jenny. I only know loving an Indian man will only bring you trouble." The woman rose. "I'll get some paper and you can tell me how to wire his family."

Jennifer watched her walk away, feeling the woman's disapproval, although she knew Alice still cared about her. The woman surely thought she was just young and foolish and didn't know her own mind. But she did. She loved Wade Morrow, and nothing anyone said was going to change that! She didn't care what problems this was going to bring her. She only prayed that Wade would not get hurt, either by the soldiers or by the Indians. She wished there were some way to warn him, but she was helpless. She could only sit and wait.

The Comanche scout rode hard into camp, his long hair and his horse's tail flying in the wind. He rode directly to Wild Horse's tipi, which had been offered him by Bright Flower, a widowed Comanche woman who gladly accommodated the handsome Comanche leader in any way he needed. There were some now who doubted Wild

Horse's wisdom and power, although he had always proved himself a great warrior. But now they knew he shared his spirit with another. He had been born under a bad omen, and only his death or the death of his brother would bring renewed strength to the Comanche nation. Surely then the others could come here from the Red River and be strong again.

"He comes," the scout said, dismounting before his horse even came to a halt. "Aguila comes with him."

Wild Horse's nostrils flared with excitement. "Aguila! He promised to stay with Slow Woman until—" His eyes suddenly changed from a man thirsty for a fight to a man who felt great sorrow. He turned away. "So . . . my mother must be dead." He breathed deeply. "This is what this brother of mine has done. He brings death. He makes my people doubt me."

"You do not know yet that he is your brother."

Wild Horse turned to look at the man, his eyes watery but blazing with hatred. "I know without asking. There is no other reason Aguila would come. The man called Wade Morrow is his nephew. He would want to be here when we fight." The man walked a few yards away. "Only the two of them?" he asked.

"I think so. They are perhaps one day away. By sunrise they will reach our village."

Wild Horse stared out over a sea of rolling hills dotted with red rocks and cacti. "I do not trust him. He said he would go and see the white woman first. Aguila would never go to that fort with him. Wade Morrow could have told the soldiers what he is doing. He could be leading them to us."

"There were no soldiers with him."

"Maybe not. But they might follow. If my brother is the coward I think he is, he will bring the soldiers to save him. He will show up thinking that proves he has kept his word and that he is not afraid of me. But then soldiers will come, to rescue him and to capture me." The man turned. "Tell the women and children we will move our camp. We will circle around." He waved his arm in the general direction from which Wade would be coming. "If after a day's ride we see no soldiers, we will know we have not been betrayed. Then we will find Wade Morrow, rather than to let him find us first. If we *do* see soldiers, we will lie in waiting for them. We will surround them and kill them!" A look of sweet victory came into his eyes. "Then *I* will find and kill Wade Morrow!"

The man walked back to his tipi, ordering Bright Flower to prepare his mount.

Morning broke bright and clear. Wade opened his eyes to see Aguila putting dry mesquite on the smouldering embers of their camp fire. He studied the man a moment. Aguila was his uncle, but he had shown Wade no particular affection. Wade realized the man's heart would have to be with Wild Horse, the man he raised from a small boy.

Aguila had at least shared with Wade some of the Comanche beliefs, some of their sorrows and losses, how they felt about reservation life, how the white man's president had never delivered all the things that had been promised to them. They were dying of starvation, disease, and broken hearts. Only those like Wild Horse, who dared to defy the orders of the white man's government, still lived like the free Comanche. But, Aguila admitted, he realized their days were numbered. It was only a matter of time before Wild Horse would also have to give up, or die.

"Perhaps our luck will change when he kills you," the man had said matter-of-factly. It was then Wade realized he would get no help from his uncle. It was up to him to try to change Wild Horse's mind, but his hopes looked dimmer each day.

Aguila turned to see him watching. "We will drink more of the white man's coffee this morning," the man said. "There is some left. I like coffee, but we seldom see it on the reservation. We see mostly bad whiskey and rotten meat."

Wade threw off his blanket. "I'm sorry, Aguila. If you

347

could convince Wild Horse to forget about this ridiculous idea that I must die, I could get the Comanche all the supplies they need. My white father owns a supply business. All I have to do is ask, and he would take wagonloads of supplies up to the Red River, if Wild Horse would just give up fighting and go back to the reservation."

Aguila rose. "You do not understand. Our pride and honor has been too much destroyed for the white man to make it better now. And it should not be you who should bring the things promised. It is the duty of your white man's government." His dark eyes fell on Wade. "Besides, Wild Horse and the others would never accept gifts from a bad spirit."

Wade scowled and got up, frustrated at how difficult it was to get through to people of his own blood. "I give up," he muttered. He walked away to relieve himself, then stretched, flexing his muscles, wondering if he would die today, wondering what would happen to his precious Jennifer if he did. Was he wrong to be doing this?

He turned then to see Aguila watching the eastern horizon and seeming to be listening intently for something. Suddenly he got down on the ground, lying flat out on his stomach and putting his ear to the ground. He looked at Wade then with a strange, astonished look, then slowly rose. He walked to his gear and whipped out his rifle, cocking it and pointing it at Wade before Wade realized what he intended to do with it.

"You brought soldiers!"

Wade frowned. "I did no such thing, Aguila. I came back from that fort alone."

"Soldiers are coming—many of them!"

Wade looked in the general direction Aguila had looked. He saw nothing.

"You said once you were a scout yourself. Put your ear to the ground, Wade Morrow. Tell me you do not hear many horses. Strain your ears. Tell me you do not hear distant voices, men shouting orders!"

Wade walked closer, his own pistol and rifle lying near

his bedroll. Aguila quickly walked to his gear and kicked the weapons away. "Listen!"

Wade watched him closely as he got to the ground and put his ear to the hard, dry earth. What his keen ears picked up gave him chills. He reasoned Aguila sensed the presence before he did because the Comanche were accustomed to being hunted, accustomed to listening for such things. He got to his feet, concentrating on listening intently. It was then he heard the voices, barely discernible because of several hills that rose and fell between them and the soldiers. He looked at Aguila.

"I don't understand. I swear to you I brought no soldiers," he told the man. His thoughts immediately turned to Jennifer. If soldiers were following him, somehow they must have found out about his going to Fort Stockton the night before. Had he been followed? And had he and Aguila been followed since then, with the hope they would lead the soldiers to Wild Horse?

"Get our things together, Wade Morrow. We must find Wild Horse—quickly!"

Wade met his eyes boldly. "I brought no soldiers, Aguila. Someone must have suspected what I was up to—maybe had us followed this way from the reservation. I would not betray my brother, or you."

"We will see who has been betrayed!" The man held the rifle on Wade, while with his left hand he reached down and dumped the coffee out over the fire. "Hurry!" He picked up Wade's pistol and rifle then, holding them while Wade prepared their mounts. Wade considered jumping the man, but that would prove nothing. It would only make him look more guilty. This was something to be settled with Wild Horse.

Both men mounted up, Aguila telling Wade to ride ahead of him. Wade's stomach growled with hunger as he rode forward, and he wished he had at least gotten a swallow of coffee, realizing breakfast might have been his last meal. He cursed his predicament. If soldiers were following, they knew Wade had lied about going back to California. As a citizen, he had a right to do what he pleased, but there would be no love lost when it came to Captain Howell's attitude toward him. His prospects with Wild Horse looked even worse, and now Jennifer might be in trouble. That was the worst part.

"Stop," Aguila said then. The man halted his own horse and listened. Then his eyes lit up. "Do you hear it? Gunfire! Fighting! War whoops! Wild Horse has found the soldiers!"

"Or the soldiers have found him," Wade answered.

"No. He knew you might bring soldiers. He must have circled behind us. Go back, over the hills to the east!"

Wade reluctantly obeyed. He felt the noose tightening around his neck. If he survived an encounter with Wild Horse, the U. S. Army would be after his hide if Wild Horse had set up some kind of ambush. Wild Horse thought Wade had brought the soldiers. The soldiers would think he led them into a trap for Wild Horse. Either way, he was a dead man.

Chapter Twenty-Three

Gunfire roared and war whoops pierced the air as Wade and Aguila rode hard toward the sound of battle. They came upon a rise to see what Wade guessed to be about thirty soldiers, trapped in a gully, Comanche warriors firing on them from both sides. Several soldiers already lay dead. Wade spotted Wild Horse sitting and watching from the top of a rock-studded hill, and he headed for the man at a hard gallop, ignoring the fact that Aguila held a rifle on him.

Wild Horse saw Wade coming, and he turned his horse to face the man, his eyes blazing. "So, you thought me a fool, brother!"

"I thought no such thing! Stop the slaughter, Wild Horse."

"It is *you* who should be slaughtered, for bringing them!"

"I did *not* bring them! Commander Howell must have had me followed, maybe all the way from the Red River."

A proud, arrogant look spread across Wild Horse's face as he looked at the melee below. "I will win even more victories after you are dead and my spirit is whole," he told him.

"Call off your warriors, Wild Horse, before those soldiers are all dead."

Wild Horse gave him a look of evil joy while Aguila rode up beside them both. "Do you think I *care* if they all die?" Wild Horse continued. "This is why you cannot win a battle against me, my brother. You do not *hate* enough! You have not *lost* enough! You care too much for people who do not deserve to live."

"Not all those men down there deserve to die, any more than all *Comanche* deserve to die!"

Wild Horse raised his eyebrows. "Only *some* Comanche? Am *I* one who deserves to die?"

Their eyes held challengingly. "I don't know yet," Wade answered. "I only know for certain now that you are my brother, and because you are, I have no wish to fight you *or* kill you!"

The right side of Wild Horse's mouth curled into a wicked smile. "You will—in time." In an instant, without warning, he lashed out with his war club, landing it across the side of Wade's head in a stunning blow that knocked him from his horse. He landed facedown, and before he could move he felt a heavy foot pushing down on the back of his head so that he nearly smothered in the dirt, while someone jerked his arms behind him, tying the wrists painfully tight with rawhide.

"This is so you do not think about riding down there to help your white soldier friends," Wild Horse sneered. It was he who bound Wade's wrists while Aguila kept his foot shoved against his head. When Wild Horse finished tying him, Aguila finally took his foot away, and both men helped Wade to his feet.

"Get back on your horse and watch," Wild Horse sneered, giving Wade a shove. "Learn the ways of the Indian!" He held Wade's arm for support while Wade spit dirt and shook it from his hair and eyes so that he could see his stirrup. He turned to Wild Horse before mounting up, blood streaming from a gash on his left cheekbone, where Wild Horse's war club had slammed into him.

"I am enough Indian not to break my word," he sneered. "Why would I have gone through all this when I could have walked away from it, if it didn't mean so much to me to find you! Why would I bring soldiers to destroy my only brother!"

Again he saw the tiny flicker of feeling in Wild Horse's eyes, but it quickly vanished.

"Perhaps you did not bring them, but that does not change what must be between you and me. I could let you go down there and help the soldiers, or even fight on the Comanche side, if you should choose to do so. But you could be killed by another man's bullet. I do not want someone else to kill you, or for you to die from a bullet. It must be by my own hands. Get on your horse. When this is over, you will come back to our camp. There I will find a way to make you fight me, to make you *hate* me!"

Wade's eyes drilled into Wild Horse's. *"Damn you,"* he sneered.

Wild Horse only grinned, then laughed. "That is better, my brother. Perhaps the fight will be more of a challenge for me than I expect."

With Aguila's help Wade mounted his horse, feeling warm blood trickle down past his throat. With an aching heart he watched the slaughter below, more worried about Jennifer now than the soldiers. They would find a way to blame her for this, blame both of them. Her name would be smeared, and God only knew how safe she would be. Somehow he had to survive this. He had to get back to her.

Below, Enders and Deaver lay side by side, each man taking careful aim from behind a small rock that gave them little protection. "Damn bastards," Deaver almost screamed. "We're all gonna' die, and it's all the fault of that Wade Morrow." He looked at Enders, his eyes blazing. "And that damn bitch who came out here to marry you, puttin' on airs, all the time panting after an Indian man!"

"Shut up and reload," Enders growled in return, his own fury with Jennifer knowing no bounds.

Deaver kept cursing and moaning while he reloaded his rifle. He aimed it farther up the hill, then noticed a familiar horse and rider. "Look! Look up there," he shouted to Enders. "That's a damn army chestnut if I ever saw one. Why would an army horse be up there? It's Wade Morrow, that's who it is! That's the horse he bought at the fort! Look at him, just sittin' there watchin' us get slaughtered!"

Tony looked up, studying the figure, which was too far away to shoot. "Bastard," he sneered. "If I get out of this, Jennifer Andrews will pay!"

"I get my turn at the slut," Deaver growled.

Suddenly Tony's body jerked back and slumped down, falling over onto its back. Deaver stared at a gaping hole in the man's head, then screamed his name, grabbing his shirt. "Tony!" He jerked the body up but knew instantly it was lifeless.

James Deaver was not a man to have deep feelings about anyone, but Tony Enders had been an interesting friend and had helped relieve the boredom at the fort. He would miss him. His sorrow was quickly replaced by anger as he looked at his dead friend, anger at Tony for bringing Jennifer Andrews to Fort Stockton. It seemed her presence had taken away from their friendship, and had brought only bad luck.

He did not stop to reason any of it, to realize that it was not Jennifer's fault that she happened to be on the same coach as Wade Morrow, or that the coach had been attacked and she had been left with no one to help her but the half-breed. In Deaver's mind, Anthony Enders was dead because of Jennifer Andrews; this slaughter of his friend was partly her fault.

He hated her, hated the way she had pretended to be so proper. God only knew what had gone on between her and Wade Morrow before they arrived at the fort, but he had a damn good idea.

He slowly lowered Tony's body, and a bullet hit the dirt next to him, startling him into action. He quickly returned to his post and began firing again, pretending each man was Wade Morrow, and thinking gleefully that with Tony dead, and Jennifer Andrews a "soiled" woman, she was now fair game for everyone. He would make damn sure the woman paid for Tony's death, and that she learned what happened to white women who consorted with Indians.

The bugler sounded the call for retreat. Deaver quickly grabbed a roll of money he knew Tony had in his pants pocket. "Sorry, friend, but you won't need this any more," he muttered. He quickly joined what was left of the platoon in hurriedly mounting up, some taking on an extra man because some of the horses had been killed. They all rode off at a hard gallop, realizing the danger of riding with their backs to the Indians, but knowing it was fruitless to keep fighting. They would die to the last man if they didn't get out. Deaver felt bullets and arrows whizzing past him, but he rode hard, leaving his dead friend behind.

From above Wild Horse watched, eyes glittering with victory. "So," he said, turning to Wade. "When you were free, things did not go so well for us; but now that you are my prisoner, we have a victory." Sorrow suddenly filled his eyes. "But I take no joy in it. Our mother is dead, isn't she?"

Wade frowned. "How did you know?"

"Aguila would not have left her otherwise." Wade detected more emotion in the man's eyes in that one brief moment than he had seen yet. "And you have learned the truth?"

Wade held his eyes. "We are twins. Slow Woman loved both her babies. She didn't want to see them both die, so she kept one, praying the other would not suffer too long before it died."

Wild Horse shook his head. "She was young and foolish. She broke Comanche law."

"It was her *wish* that we both should live. Will you go against your own mother's heart?"

"*She* went against Comanche law! I honor her as my mother, but I do not honor any wishes that bring harm to me or my people!" He turned his eyes back to the fleeing soldiers. "Look at them run. You are my captive, and we have won this battle. It is a good sign. It will be even better for us once you are dead. Come. We will go below and see what weapons and other supplies were left behind."

He grabbed the reins of Wade's horse and led it down the hill. Wade watched sadly as the warriors began looting the bodies and taking scalps. His eyes fell on one man in particular, an ugly bullet hole in his forehead. The face was distorted because of the wound, but Wade was certain it was Anthony Enders.

He stared at the man with mixed feelings, sorry for the slaughter, but relieved that at least the man could no longer make trouble for Jennifer. Still, he knew that did not mean she was out of danger, and his own chances of getting back to her were getting dimmer. He could only pray for her safety, and that she would get hold of his father and brothers. He knew they would take care of her; and he also knew he might never get the chance to do it himself.

"I'm tellin' you I *saw* the man, just sittin' up there watchin' us. He must have known what was comin', or he would have warned us instead of sneakin' in here a couple of nights ago and out again without a word! That bastard had already reached Wild Horse. He had to know Wild Horse planned to circle around and attack us. It's Wade Morrow's fault my best friend is dead!"

Corporal Deaver stood in Captain Howell's office, putting on a fine show of anger and sorrow over Tony Enders's death. Howell turned his eyes to Jennifer, who had been half-dragged to his office by Lieutenant Brown, whose grip on her upper arm had left a bruise that still hurt her. The three men, as well as another sergeant and another lieutenant all stared at Jennifer as though she were dirt, and she felt her cheeks tingle with her own fury at how she had been treated and the accusations Deaver was making against Wade.

"If he had known, he would have warned you," she said calmly and firmly to Howell.

"I brought you over here because I want the truth this time," the man growled. "What were Wade Morrow's plans? Did he come to see you personally the other night? What did he tell you?"

Jennifer couldn't help feeling sorry for the tattered men

who had ridden into the fort only thirty minutes or so earlier. They had been gone two nights. With what Jennifer had just heard, she knew Wade was with Wild Horse, and she knew the hope of his surviving that was not very strong.

"If Wade was sitting and watching," she told Howell, "then I'm certain he was being held against his will. Wild Horse wants him dead." She wondered how she was managing to keep from screaming and weeping. Wade! He was in Wild Horse's hands! He would never have sat and watched the massacre of the soldiers.

"Wild Horse is his brother," Deaver sneered. "He made an agreement to help the man. Comanche blood runs thick!"

Jennifer moved her eyes to meet his boldly, ignoring the contempt she saw there. "Not when the Comanche involved are twins," she answered. "You know that as well as anyone." She looked back at Howell. "Wade's only intention in coming here in the first place was just as he had told you—he was looking for his roots among the Comanche. He has that right. He never wanted any trouble for the Comanche or for you and your men. He would no more have led your men into a trap than he would have helped capture Wild Horse. His mission was very personal. If anyone has been betrayed, it's Wade—by you, *and* by Wild Horse. As far as why he came to see me in the night, he was trying to protect me from the ridicule of ignorant, prejudiced men who he knew might turn on me if they knew about us." She kept her voice strong. "I love Wade Morrow, Captain Howell. He's a fine, educated, successful man, very generous, very caring."

Deaver let out a hiss of disgust, and one of the other men snickered, while the rest just glared at Jennifer in disbelief at her words.

"Right now it's quite possible that he's dead, or being tortured and goaded into fighting Wild Horse," Jennifer went on, keeping her eyes on Howell. "Alice told me how it will be for him, and I believe her. I think you know yourself what will happen. Surely you understand

Comanche ways. Wild Horse wants Wade dead, and it must be by his own hands. Wade doesn't want to fight him, but Wild Horse will find a way to *make* him fight. As far as the attack on your men, Wild Horse must have suspected you might have Wade followed, or perhaps he didn't trust Wade. Maybe *he* thought Wade would bring soldiers, the same as you're thinking he helped Wild Horse. Wade has been caught in the middle, Captain. He's an innocent man."

The tears finally made their way into her eyes, one trickling down her cheek. She quickly wiped it away. "Can't you . . . can't you go after Wild Horse, take more men and follow him? Can't you seek out his camp? Alice said it's the soldiers' duty to pursue the Comanche."

"We don't have enough men left," the captain answered. "With the time it took getting back here to regroup, we'll never find Wild Horse now. He can make himself disappear like the wind." He studied the very beautiful Jennifer Andrews, finding her love for Wade Morrow incredible, but finding his own feelings mixed. She seemed very sincere in her love, and he had to agree Wade Morrow was a well-spoken man who had seemed quite civilized. Still, he was an Indian. He sighed deeply, ordering Deaver and the others to leave.

"I say Wade Morrow ought to be hanged if he shows up here again," Deaver grumbled. "I wouldn't doubt the shot that killed Tony Enders came from his own gun! Who would have better reason to kill Tony than Morrow? Tony wanted to marry the man's . . ." He turned ugly eyes on Jennifer. "Woman," he finished, a distinct dirty suggestion in the way he said it.

Jennifer faced him. "Wade would never deliberately murder any man," she told Deaver, her voice rising. "I daresay he's a thousand times more civilized than *you* will ever be, Corporal Deaver, with your slovenly ways and your ignorant attitude! How far did *you* go in school, Corporal. Can you even read? How about your background? Why did *you* volunteer for duty in this desolate place? Could it be you're running from the *law*, Corporal?"

"I told you to leave, Deaver," Howell spoke up.

Deaver kept his eyes on Jennifer, and what she saw there gave her chills. "Sure," he answered with a sneer. "I'll leave. But ask Miss Andrews why she's sheddin' tears for a half-breed, when she's just found out that the man she was supposed to marry is dead, layin' out there, probably bein' butchered up by the Comanche. For all she knows her civilized Mr. Morrow is wearin' Tony's scalp on his belt right now!"

"That's enough, Corporal," Howell shouted. "Get out now or I'll have you arrested and whipped for insubordination!"

It was all Jennifer could do to keep from lashing out at Deaver for his crude remark. The man turned and saluted Howell, then stormed out with the others. The door closed, and Jennifer was suddenly alone with Captain Howell. She turned her eyes to meet his own.

"I never held any special feelings for Sergeant Enders," she told the man. "I answered his letter sincerely, and I had every intention of getting to know him and marrying him. But my coming here was always with the understanding that it would be my decision. I found the man crude and unclean. I found nothing about him to love. I would have felt exactly the same way whether or not I had ever met Wade Morrow. I am sincerely sorry he is dead, Captain, but I don't mourn him any more deeply than the others. I'm sorry about *all* of them. I truly am. But I swear to you Wade would never have had a hand in leading you and your men into a trap." She glanced at a dirty rag that was tied around the Captain's upper left arm, which showed fresh bloodstains. "You should let Alice and me tend to your arm."

The man sighed, running a hand through his hair. "I'll be all right. We have a medic, although I'm not so sure he's an honest-to-God doctor. I never sent him to you because you were apparently healing fine and you had Alice. I

359

figured at that time the last thing you needed was another strange man tending to you."

He sat down wearily in his chair. "Sit down, Miss Andrews." Jennifer obeyed. "My biggest problem now is what to do with you," the man continued. "With the men knowing about you and Wade Morrow, you can't stay here. Not only are you single and attractive, but you've lost the respect the men held for you. I hate to be so blunt, and I'm not saying it's my own opinion. But those men out there are damn mad, and they're blaming part of this on you." He leaned forward. "I lost twelve men, Miss Andrews, with ten more wounded, a couple of them not expected to live. Only eight of us came out unscathed or with minor injuries. In their minds, all this stemmed from Wade Morrow coming here."

"That's ridiculous," she answered firmly. "Who gave the order that Wade be followed in the first place?" She could tell by the look on his face Howell was the culprit. "If Wade had been left alone to tend to his own personal business, none of this would have happened," she told the man. "This is *your* fault, Captain, not Wade's!"

"I have a duty to hunt down and capture Wild Horse," he said, irritation in his voice. "The man has bloodied the whole Texas frontier."

"I am aware of that! But what you do out of duty shouldn't be blamed on an innocent man!"

Their eyes met challengingly. Howell leaned back in his chair then. "All I'm telling you is how the *men* see it. They know I ordered Morrow to be followed. They knew my intentions. But they think Morrow betrayed them— betrayed *me*. Nothing I can say will change their minds."

Her eyes teared more. Wade! What was happening to him? "I'm sure it won't," she said, a note of defeat in her voice. She dabbed lightly at tears with her handkerchief. "The day you and your men rode out after Wade, I wired Wade's family in California. If none of the lines have been cut, they should have gotten word by now. Wade's white brothers, or at least some of his father's men are headed

360

this way to—'' Her voice choked, and she took a deep breath to stay in control. "To bring some freight wagons to Galveston and pick up some merchandise from a merchant in New Orleans. Wade . . .'' Oh, how it hurt to even say his name. "Wade told me that if I got word to them, they would come by here and take me with them . . . that I could go back to California with them and his . . . parents . . . would help me. I have nowhere else to turn. For personal reasons I will not go back to my uncle.''

"Did Sergeant Enders tell you about your uncle's telegram forbidding him to marry you?''

Jennifer frowned. "No.''

"The man wanted me to send you back. He said if you were already married he would pay Enders any sum of money for an annulment. I told Enders it was his business. I have better things to do than worry about young women who have run away from home. I don't know your reason for doing what you did, Miss Andrews, and I wasn't going to make you leave. But things have changed now.'' He rubbed at his arm. "I'll let you stay on until some of Mr. Morrow's men come for you. If they don't show up within another week, two at the most, you've got to leave. Where you go is your business, but I'll play hell keeping trouble away until then.''

"But it's dangerous right now. The stagecoach isn't even running on a regular schedule. Wade told me I'm supposed to wait for him to come for me, or his family.'' Her voice choked again.

"If what Alice says and what I know about the Comanche is true, Miss Andrews, I doubt that the man is coming back. I'm sorry, but everything else aside, even if Mr. Morrow tried to befriend Wild Horse, and even if he *did* help lead those soldiers into a trap, maybe to show Wild Horse his loyalty, it won't likely change Wild Horse's determination to kill the man. Unless Wade Morrow is awfully good at hand-to-hand combat with a Comanche man, I would forget about your feelings for him and get on with your life.''

361

He said the words matter-of-factly, as though it would be a simple thing to do, as though Wade were just a passing acquaintance. How little he knew! They had shared more than friendship, more than just words of love. She had been a part of him, and he a part of her. She had given herself to Wade Morrow in rapture, and he had tenderly made a woman of her, taking her into the depths of passion and fulfilling their love in the most intimate, most wonderful way a woman could experience. Now she was supposed to just forget about the man?

She rose wearily from the chair. "I will leave as soon as it is safe," she told Howell, her voice dull. "I am hoping Wade's family will come through soon. I will relieve you of the terrible burden I impose on you, Captain."

She walked out without another word, holding her head proudly as she walked back to Alice's cabin, while she felt a hundred pairs of eyes on her. How she made it to the cabin, she wasn't sure, but once there she collapsed into tears on the cot. Wade! Oh, to hear his voice again, to feel his arms around her. All she had left was the memory of that last stolen kiss, deep in the night.

She felt a hand on her shoulder then. "I'm going to see if I can help the doctor," Alice told her. "They blame Mr. Morrow, don't they?"

"Yes," Jennifer sobbed. "It was awful, Alice, the things Jim Deaver said. Tony's dead, but Wade is the one . . . I mourn for. Deaver saw him . . . with Wild Horse. Oh, Alice, I know he was being held against his will. I know he didn't have anything to do with Howell's men . . . or Tony . . . getting killed. He's going to die. He's going to die, and I'll never see him again."

"I'm sorry, Jenny." The woman touched her hair. "I'm going to see what I can do. You had better stay right here. Don't go out alone. We'll talk when I get back."

Jennifer heard the woman leave, and the tears came even harder. Even Alice didn't fully understand her agony; even Alice, who had lost a husband, didn't realize her own loss seemed just as great, for in her heart, and in body, Wade

Morrow *had* been her husband; but for such a short, sweet time. She was alone again, more alone than she had ever been before.

Wade could no longer feel his hands, numb from the tight rawhide bindings around his wrists. His stomach ached from hunger and his mouth was like sandpaper from lack of water. Wild Horse led his horse and the other warriors followed. They had ridden all day after the battle and into part of the night. The rest of the night had been spent on the cold ground without food or water or a blanket, and Wade realized he was being treated no differently than any other Comanche captive. Wild Horse was determined to make Wade hate him, and he was doing a good job of it.

Now they approached a camp bigger than Wade had expected to see. There were a few women present, and a smattering of children; but mostly it seemed that between the forty or so warriors who rode with Wild Horse and the ten or fifteen who waited at the campsite, Wild Horse's following was made up of men, hardly one over the age of thirty. They were young, angry, frustrated men who could not bring themselves to settle into the sedantary life on a reservation. All they needed was someone like Wild Horse to keep their blood hot.

Once inside the village, women and children and more men gathered around Wade. Wild Horse pushed him from his horse, and without the use of his hands, Wade fell hard onto his shoulder. The others stayed back from him as though afraid to touch him.

"Let him eat and drink," Wild Horse told Aguila. "I want him to be strong. I will give him a day to recover before I begin to teach him about pain!" The man turned to the others as Aguila helped Wade up and finally cut the ties at his wrists. "We have won a great victory against the bluecoats," Wild Horse was shouting. "Here you see my brother weak and beaten—my captive! Here is proof I have the stronger spirit! Soon I will let you decide how he will suffer. He will not fight me, but I will make him *want* to fight me, and you will help. Then I will defeat this evil spirit, and we will be even stronger!"

The man held up his lance, the others held up fists and weapons, yipping and howling, some of them dancing.

"Tonight we hold a victory dance," Wild Horse told them "Build a fire!"

There was more shouting and celebrating. Warriors held up soldiers' jackets and held up lances with fresh scalps attached to them. Wild Horse walked up to Wade, meeting his eyes. "My dead wives and children celebrate tonight. I can feel it—here." He put a fist to his heart. "When white men are killed, they rejoice—up there." He pointed to the sky. "They see. They know I avenge their deaths, and the deaths of so many others."

"You can't keep this up, Wild Horse," Wade told him.

"When you die, there will be no end to my victories."

"That's a false belief—a superstition that makes no sense. We're two different people, Wild Horse. In the white man's world twins don't bring bad luck."

"The white man does not have to struggle as we do. He does not understand what life is like for the Comanche. His strength is not tested as ours is, except when we capture one and draw strength from the brave ones who do not cry out under our torture. How brave are you, my brother? How *white* are you? I will soon know."

Wade rubbed at his cold, tingling hands. He could feel a tightness at the side of his face and neck, where blood had dried from the wound on his cheek.

"I don't know if I'm stronger or more skilled or braver than you, Wild Horse. I don't even *want* to know. I just want to *talk* to you, to *understand* you."

"All you need to understand is that one of us must die. Why is that so difficult for you to master? Do you fear death?"

Wade shook his head. "I don't fear death, Wild Horse. I fear losing the only blood brother I have. We're *brothers!* Doesn't that mean *anything* to you?"

Their eyes held. "If you were not a twin, I would welcome you," Wild Horse answered, a sudden look of near sorrow in his eyes. "I would thank the spirits that I had found you. But you are a curse, Wade Morrow, a curse on my soul, my spirit. When you truly understand the Comanche way, you will understand why I cannot let you live, and you will not think so badly of me."

The man turned and walked away, putting an arm around an older but attractive Comanche woman who had approached to look at Wade. She smiled and patted Wild Horse's chest. "I have captured my other spirit," he told the woman proudly.

"You are a brave man," the woman answered.

Wild Horse moved a hand to her waist as they walked and gave her an affectionate hug. A little boy ran past him and Wild Horse moved to scoop the child up in his arms, holding him up and calling him a little warrior. The child giggled, and Wild Horse gave him a hug before setting him on his feet.

Wade watched in astonishment, seeing the affection the man was capable of feeling and showing; understanding it even better when he realized that much of what Wild Horse did was in revenge for losing his wives and sons. He was surely a lonely, hurting man. That much Wade could understand. But how the man could be so affectionate toward others, and so bitterly hateful of his own brother still made no sense to him.

"Come," Aguila told him. "I give you food and water. Wild Horse wants you strong. Soon you will need that strength. Soon he will turn the women on you. They are very good at bringing pain without killing a man. For tonight, when you are through eating, you will be allowed to sleep without binding, but you will be closely watched. Tomorrow you will again be bound."

"Aguila," Wade spoke up. The man turned. "Can't you stop this? You're my *uncle*."

"I told you before, it is the way. I raised Wild Horse from a small child. I taught him the ways of the Comanche. If he learned from me, what makes you think *I* would go against Comanche law? I care very much for Wild Horse. He is like my own son. I want him to be happy—strong. I want these people to look to him with the same respect they had before. You are not my nephew. You are half of Wild Horse. I want him to be whole."

Wade followed the man to the tipi of a woman Aguila apparently knew. Aguila asked the woman for food and she said she would oblige, but she pointed to Wade, saying she did not want "that evil spirit" inside her tipi. Wade sat down outside, deciding to take one moment at a time and enjoy for this moment a much-needed rest. He closed his eyes, putting his hands to his head and thinking of Jennifer.

Jennifer. His heart ached at the thought of her waiting for him, and what it would be like for her to finally realize he was not coming back. He shook away the thought, looking at his hands then, making them into fists as he felt the life coming back into them.

God, how he hated the thought of trying to kill his own brother; but he knew the same thought didn't bother Wild Horse in the least. In the end, perhaps he would have no choice after all, and with the thought of Jennifer waiting for him, perhaps he could find the extra determination and skill he would need to kill Wild Horse; but to do so would go against every Christian teaching in which he believed.

He looked up to see a little girl staring at him. Her face was dirty and sunburned, and her dark hair was greased; but there was no mistaking her features were white, apparently a captive. She looked no older than eight or nine.

"Who are you?" he asked.

She skittered away as though terrified of something, and Wade reasoned she probably was not allowed to talk to anyone else brought back to camp. He wondered what she had seen and suffered, and who she was. Most likely her parents were both dead by Comanche hands. The sight of her made Wade more determined to survive whatever lay ahead. Maybe he could find a way to get the little girl back to her own people.

He looked down at his own hands, also Comanche. It seemed amazing how radically different the lives of two men could be when they had been born to the same mother. He deliberately pushed away thoughts of the poor little captive, and of Jenny. He didn't dare let the ache of it get hold of him right now. For the moment the only thing to think about was survival.

Chapter Twenty-Four

Jennifer salted the pot of near-boiling water, preparing to drop in the small cuttings of dough to make dumplings. Alice loved dumplings, and Jennifer wanted to do something for her, as well as keep herself occupied. It helped pass the aching hours of suspense over Wade.

Another day had passed since Captain Howell had returned with the remnants of his platoon. Alice was at one of the barracks still helping doctor some of the injured men. It was an unusually cool morning for west Texas this time of year, and Jennifer had taken the opportunity to build a fire in Alice's indoor cook stove. Alice continued to warn her not to go out, except to use the privy, hoping that in a few days the animosity toward Jennifer would wane.

Jennifer dropped in the dumplings, then walked into the larger room of the cabin to pick up some mending, thinking to help Alice with her usual work while the woman had to be with the wounded men. Someone tapped on the door then, a gentle knock that held no threat. Jennifer's first thought was of Wade. Could he have survived? Had he come for her? She set down the mending and went to the door, opening it cautiously.

The door was barely ajar when it was suddenly pushed open so violently that it knocked Jennifer backward. She gasped and her eyes widened as she stumbled against the fireplace and Corporal James Deaver came inside, slamming shut the door. Jennifer knew instinctively he had come to do more than talk. She quickly grabbed up an iron fireplace poker and backed farther away, stumbling against a rocker. "Get out of here," she demanded.

Deaver just grinned. "You owe me, woman. You owed Tony, my best friend, and now he's dead. You're nothin' but a buck-lovin' white squaw, and there's only one thing women like you are good for."

Jennifer swung the poker, but Deaver only ducked, then came up and grabbed it out of her hand, slinging it across the room where it knocked a pitcher off a table and broke it. Jennifer ran toward the kitchen, but Deaver was on her in a flash, tackling her to the floor and putting his weight on her. He grasped both her slender wrists in one strong hand, hovering over her with a leering, whiskey-stenched grin.

"You want to know the truth, bitch? Tony suspected you were worthless all along! He was only going to marry you for the pleasure of getting inside you, and then he was going to have the marriage annulled and collect a bundle from that uncle of yours in St. Louis. Is that where it started, pretty lady? Your uncle already been under your skirts?"

Jennifer started to scream, but a fist slammed across the side of her face, and for a moment everything went black. Somewhere in the darkness she could hear Deaver's voice.

"That locket Tony gave you," he sneered. "It came off a dead settler woman. That's how much Tony thought of you, little lady. You were just somethin' with all the right parts to make a man feel good in bed." She felt a hand grasping at her breasts. "Now I'm going to take up where Tony left off. I'm going to do what he *should* have done in the first place—take you off that high and mighty pedestal you tried to put yourself on!"

Jennifer's vision began to clear. She could see Deaver's face close to hers, felt his hand moving up under her skirt to grope at her bloomers. He was trying to rip them off. With all the strength she could muster, she slammed her head forward into the man's nose. She heard a crack, and the man screamed, leaping away from her.

"My nose! You goddamn bitch!"

Jennifer ran into the kitchen, but just as she reached the backdoor a strong hand gripped her arm and jerked her away, shoving her hard so that she fell across the table and landed on the other side of it. Her ribs, still not totally healed, flamed with renewed pain, as did her leg, which looked healed but was still very tender. She ignored the pain.

She scrambled to think. She had to get to the door; she had to find a way to hurt Deaver enough to get past him. He stood on the other side of the table as she slowly got to her feet. His nose looked crooked and was bleeding, and with his leering grin and face red from anticipated ecstasy, he had the look of an ugly monster.

"If you touch me, Captain Howell will punish you," she screamed at him.

"It would be worth a lashing to get inside of you, slut! Loose woman like you, I'll bet you're damn good. Wade Morrow liked it, didn't he? Did you enjoy havin' a half-breed bastard panting over you?"

The ugly words made Jennifer's stomach turn. The left side of her face felt numb, and she could taste blood in her mouth. She glanced briefly at the boiling water on the stove, then made her way around the other side of the table as though to run back into the main room.

Deaver followed her movement, making ready to grab her, when she suddenly darted around the other way. There was no time to think, or to worry about doing any harm to herself. She grabbed up the pot of water and threw it. Horrible screams tore at her ears as she charged out the backdoor then, her hands already blistered, bringing back horrible memories of how it felt to be burned. Now confused, overcome by pain and the sound of Deaver's blood-chilling screaming, she ran blindly, screaming herself, until someone caught her. She pushed and fought at him until the man shook her to her senses.

"Miss Andrews, it's me, Lieutenant Brown. What the hell is going on?"

Her breathing came in short, terrified gasps. Her hair

was tumbled from its bun, and the left side of her face was already turning purple. She held out her blistered, shaking hands while Brown kept hold of her arms. "Deaver," she gasped. "He . . . broke into the house . . . attacked me . . . tried to . . ." She jerked away, looking down at her hands. "I threw . . . boiling water at him."

She heard Brown ordering someone to go and help Deaver. He took her arm then. "Come to the Captain's office with me."

She looked up at the young man, tears on her bruised face. "I didn't . . . do anything. He . . . broke in . . . beat me. I haven't done anything wrong, Lieutenant Brown. Why is everyone . . . treating me this way?"

"Not everyone." He put a hand to her waist. "Come on. I'm not too happy about all this myself, but I don't go along with what Deaver did." He led her to Howell's office, where he sat the shaken, hurt Jennifer down while Howell demanded to know what had happened. Brown quickly explained while Jennifer rocked in the chair, hurting everywhere, her face and head, her ribs, her leg, most of all her hands. Someone came inside then.

"Deaver's a mess," the man said. "His face and shoulders mostly—burned pretty bad. He's already blistered up something awful."

"It will save him a whipping," Howell answered angrily. "I daresay he has already received enough punishment for attacking Miss Andrews."

There was an odd moment of silence. "Deaver says she invited him," the extra man said then.

Revulsion engulfed Jennifer. "That's not true," she said, near hysteria. She stood up, looking like a mad woman, holding out her own burned hands. "Does this look like I *invited* him? He knocked at the door, and when I opened it a little he pushed his way in and attacked me! How dare you say he was *invited!* Damn you! Damn *all* of you for your filthy minds and ignorant prejudice!"

The words were nearly screamed, and the third man backed out. "Go and get Alice," Howell called after him. "And get some ointment for Miss Andrews's hands."

"Water," she said, her voice weaker again. She sat back down. "I want cold . . . water . . . in a pan. I've been burned . . . before. I remember . . . my aunt discovered cold, wet rags . . . made it feel better."

"Get her some water," Howell told Brown.

Brown quickly left, and Howell sighed deeply. "I was afraid of this," he said wearily. "Miss Andrews, you're getting on the next coach that comes through here, no matter which direction it's traveling. I want you off these premises. I'm sorry to sound so cold and rude, but having you here is no good for my men."

She raised her green eyes to meet his brown ones, realizing the man was nearly as prejudiced as the rest. He simply had been trying to be more of a gentleman about it. "I want to wait . . . for Wade's men."

"That could be another week, maybe longer, for all we know. I can't let you stay here that long. You can contact them from the next town—whether that is San Antonio or El Paso depends on which stage comes through next. If they show up here, we'll tell them where you can be found."

"Wild Horse is out there raiding! I've already suffered one attack." Her eyes teared more. "You know what they do to white women! If Wade is . . ." The word stuck in her throat, for she didn't want to believe it. "If he's dead, I'll mean nothing to them. I was only safe because of Wade."

"Wild Horse has likely ridden well out of range. He won't want to be found for a while."

"That's a lie, and you know it! With his victory over your men, he'll be out raiding stronger than ever."

The man rose, scooting back his chair. "All I know is I've lost a lot of men and I have to answer for that. I'm stuck in this godforsaken place even longer now because of what happened. There will be no promotions for me, Miss Andrews! And with you around, I'll have even more explaining to do if we keep having problems between you and the men, let alone explaining what you're doing here in the first place! You're getting on the next stage, and that's that. Don't make me embarrass you more by having you dragged aboard kicking and screaming!"

Jennifer rose, facing him boldly. "You're a kind, generous man, Captain Howell, a real gentleman." Brown came in with the water, and Alice followed close behind.

"Jenny! What happened?" Alice asked with concern.

Jennifer still looked at Howell. "Army hospitality and chivalry," she answered the woman. "I'll get on that stage, Captain," she added. "Quietly and willingly. Whatever happens, it will be better than staying on here. It's obvious most of your men are no more civil than the Comanche." She turned to Alice. "I'm sorry about the cabin and the . . . dumplings." Her throat ached terribly. "I'll help you clean up the mess and pay you for any damages."

She ignored the water and walked past Alice and outside, feeling hard as stone. There was no one to help her or care about her now, not until she could somehow find Wade's family. She was on her own, but that was how she had started out from St. Louis. She refused to feel shame in loving Wade Morrow, and she refused to show any. She held her head erect as she walked back to the cabin while she felt men staring at her. From one of the barracks she could hear Jim Deaver's screams of pain. She shivered at the sound, but felt no remorse.

Jennifer hurriedly packed her bags. A coach had come sooner than expected, only the next day after Captain Howell had said she must leave. It carried a long-overdue payroll for the soldiers at the fort.

"The whores from San Antonio will show up any time, no doubt," Alice said with a note of disgust. She folded one of Jennifer's dresses. "Those women smell a payroll fifty miles away—or rather their pimp does." She turned to Jennifer, who was folding a petticoat gingerly, her hands wrapped in gauze. "Here, let me do that. Your hands must hurt you."

Jennifer stood back, her emotions mixed. She had liked Alice, and she knew the woman cared about her. But her attitude had changed slightly, and now Jennifer felt awkward living in the woman's house. She was almost relieved to be leaving, if it were not for wanting to stay and wait for someone from Wade's family.

"Aren't the . . . those women . . . aren't they afraid of Indian attack?"

Alice grunted a laugh. "The men who bring them out here sell guns and whiskey to the Indians in return for safe passage. They ought to be hanged, far as I'm concerned. They know good and well the guns are used against their own people, but they don't care. The almighty dollar is all that matters to them. They follow the pay wagons, and their women take advantage of lonely soldiers, bleed them of practically their whole month's pay." She sighed and straightened, looking at Jennifer. "I'm sorry you have to go, Jenny—sorry about all of this. It would have been nice having you around the fort, married to one of the men, although Lord knows it couldn't have been Sergeant Enders."

Their eyes held. Jennifer felt cold now, void of emotion. Personal pride and her refusal to show shame in her love for Wade had brought on a new strength and determination not to let the insults and the fact that she was being banished from the fort get to her. She would not weep. She would not hang her head; and she would not put up an argument and be dragged forcefully, as Howell had threatened to do.

"I'm sorry, too, Alice. I appreciate all you've done for me, and I'm terribly sorry about the mess from yesterday. If it weren't for my hands, I would have cleaned it up myself."

Alice's eyes seemed to tear. "Deaver got what he deserved." She studied Jennifer's bruised face and bandaged hands. "I'll say one thing, Jenny. I still think you were just being young and impetuous and a little ignorant in loving that Wade Morrow. But you're a brave and resourceful young lady, and I sincerely wish you God's blessings, wherever you end up." She put her hands on Jennifer's arms. "Some day you'll find a nice young man

375

and settle and have children, and all this will seem like a strange dream.''

"No, it won't, Alice. It will always remain all too real. I will never forget Wade Morrow, and for the moment I refuse to believe he's even dead. I feel him with me, and I know he feels me with him. He'll do whatever he can to survive, so that he can come back to me.''

The woman shook her head. "When you're young, it's easy to believe in the impossible; but I do care for you, Jenny, and if Wade Morrow is the only one who can make you happy, then I hope he does survive.''

Someone knocked at the door, and Alice opened it to see Captain Howell standing there. "The stage driver wants to get going,'' he told the woman. "Is Miss Andrews ready?''

"You've given her precious little time, but she's about ready. You're wrong to make her leave this soon, Captain. She's in a lot of pain.''

"Her hands will heal just as well sitting on a stagecoach as sitting here causing unrest among my men.''

Alice glowered at him. "She'll be out in a minute.'' She closed the door on him and turned to Jennifer. "I'd argue more with him and tell him what I really think of him, but I'm being allowed to stay on here only through his permission. If I put up too much of a fuss, he'll make me leave, too.''

Jennifer gingerly closed the corded latch to one of her bags, using her burned fingers awkwardly. "I don't know how you stand it. You should get back to civilization, Alice, get out of this place. Maybe *you* would find another man yourself.''

The woman laughed lightly. "Me? No, I'm used to it here. And once this thing back East over states' rights is settled, things will liven up around here again. More men will be sent out, and some will bring their wives with them.''

"Maybe.'' Jennifer walked over to a mirror to check her straw hat. Her lustrous hair was pulled back at the sides with attractive combs. She wore a pink calico dress with just one thin petticoat. It was too warm again to wear too many layers. The dress had three-quarter-length sleeves and a lightly scooped bodice, and her straw hat was adorned with pink silk flowers. She winced as she pulled on a pair of white gloves to hide the gauze on her hands. "I wish there was a way to cover the bruise on my face."

"Yes, it's too bad. But otherwise you look lovely, Jenny."

Jennifer met her eyes. "I'll miss you, Alice, and I won't forget you. I'll write and let you know what happens to me."

The woman smiled softly. "I'd like that."

Jennifer walked to the bed and picked up her purse. "I'd like to pay you something."

"Mr. Morrow already did that, remember? He gave me more than was necessary. I don't need any more from you. You keep what you have. You might need it."

Jennifer sighed. "Yes, I suppose I will." She walked up to Alice and embraced her. "Good-bye, Alice. God be with you."

"You're the one He needs to protect," the woman answered, giving her a tight hug. She pulled away, dabbing at her eyes. "Do you want your crutches?"

"No. I couldn't hang onto them anyway with these hands. I can get along fine without them now."

Alice nodded quietly. "I'll carry your bags for you. Lord knows that would be painful, too." She turned and picked them up. There was nothing left to be said, and the driver was waiting. Jennifer followed her out, ignoring the fact that half the men at the fort were standing around watching her, wanting to be sure that she got on the stage, no doubt.

"It's about time, lady," the driver told her as he took the bags. Jennifer could see he was no Nick Elliott.

"She's no lady," one of the soldiers called out. "She's an Indian lover, a white squaw."

Jennifer held herself proudly as she turned to Alice. She hugged the woman once more and climbed into the coach, refusing to cry—not here, not now. She sat down across from two men. Another sat in her same seat. She knew they had heard the remark by the way they looked at her now, and she knew that this journey was going to be miserable, both physically and emotionally. She said nothing to the men, deciding there would be no use in trying to explain what they had heard. None of it would make sense to them, and they would keep their opinion no matter what she said. There were no Adam Hugheses or Frank Griffiths among these men.

She settled into a corner, looking out the window at Alice as the driver threw her baggage up top. The man riding shotgun caught them, and the driver climbed aboard. Alice dabbed at tears and waved, and Jennifer waved back as she heard the snap of a whip. The coach lurched away.

Wade gritted his teeth, refusing to cry out, determined to show Wild Horse he was a man of as much courage and stamina as his twin brother. The Comanche women danced around him, while he stood helplessly with his arms tied above his head to a pole, wearing nothing but his long johns.

The women jabbed and poked at him with blunt poles, some with knives tied to the ends of them, their points exposed just far enough to draw pain and blood, but not long enough to cause serious injury. The blunt poles were jabbed mercilessly at his privates, the sharp poles all over his body except his face. It was obvious this was an enjoyable game for the women, and for Wild Horse, who sat nearby with Aguila, radiant in the captivity and humiliation of his "other spirit," feeling stronger with every jab and poke. He suddenly barked an order to the women, and they drew back, standing silently while Wild Horse approached Wade.

"Maybe now, my brother, you hate me enough to fight me," he sneered.

Wade breathed deeply against the pain. "Why can't you respect my own beliefs, my *brother*," he sneered. "I believe

378

it is *wrong* to kill your own brother, just as strongly as you believe one of us must die at the other's hands. If you . . . wish to torture me . . . then you will torture me to death before I will fight you. Death by torture would not serve your purpose, and even if . . . you torture me more to make me fight you . . . I would be too weak and beaten to make it a worthy battle. Either way . . . you will not make me give in . . . nor will you hear me cry out, like I know you're hoping for."

Wild Horse's eyes blazed with indignation and frustration. He pulled out a knife and held it under one of Wade's eyes "I *will* find a way, Wade Morrow. You have not yet seen or felt the worst!"

For a moment Wade thought the man was going to gouge out his eye, but he suddenly reached up with the knife and cut the rawhide strips that held his arms to the pole. Wade slumped to the ground and Wild Horse backed away. The women approached with their sticks and poles.

"Leave him," Wild Horse ordered. "Let him rest again. I do not want him too weak. In another day we will begin again." He turned and walked away, and the women gathered around Wade shouting insults and making jokes about him.

Wade curled up on the ground, his arms screaming with pain from being over his head for so long. He decided there wasn't one inch on his body that did not hurt. He erased some of the pain by shutting out the women's voices and Wild Horse's threats, turning his thoughts to Jennifer, and how nice it would be to lie in her arms now, to have her soothingly tend to his wounds and tell him she loved him. "Jenny," he whispered.

The coach rocked rhythmically, reminding Jennifer of another journey, a fateful one that had led her into Wade Morrow's arms. Now she was headed even farther west, toward a town called El Paso, moving through not only Comanche country, but headed into Apache country—not that it mattered to anyone what happened to her.

She gazed out at far horizons, more mountainous country ahead. Somewhere out there Wade could be suffering. Perhaps he was being tortured, or had fought Wild Horse and was badly hurt. His last visit seemed so long ago, so unreal. She knew Alice was probably right. Some day all these things would seem like a strange dream, if she survived at all. But right now it was painfully real. She felt like a deserter. What if Wade was alive? What if he lived through some terrible torture and made it back to Fort Stockton, only to discover she was gone? Would she be able to get hold of his family and make contact with them?

She jumped when someone touched her shoulder. "You feelin' a little lonely right now, missy," the man next to her asked. "Name's Jason."

Jennifer glared at him. "Get your hand off my shoulder!"

The man grinned, pulling his hand away. "Looks like some Joe clobbered you good. What'd you do to make the man so mad, hmmm?"

She turned to look back out the window. "None of your business."

This time the man laughed, and the two sitting across from him grinned. All three men looked like drifters, with unshaven faces and soiled clothes. "You hear that, boys? It's none of our business." They all chuckled, and the man beside her sidled closer. "We heard what that man said back at the fort," he told her. "Some Indian buck get his hands on you, did he; made you his squaw? You have a soldier boyfriend that got all heated up about it?" He inched a hand toward her knee.

Jennifer quietly grasped an extra hat pin that she had pinned into her cloth purse. While all eyes were on her face and breasts, she pulled out the pin and suddenly jabbed it into the back of Jason's hand. The man cried out and jumped away from her, rubbing gingerly at the painful, bleeding wound.

"You goddamn bitch," he snarled.

Jennifer's fury knew no bounds. She faced all three men

380

boldly. "The last man who touched me wrongly is lying near death back at Fort Stockton with third degree burns over his face and upper body. *I* put them there, with boiling water!" She pulled off a glove, revealing the gauze on her hands. "I got burned myself," she said, holding out the hand. She reached into her handbag then. "I am carrying a pistol in this bag," she lied. "The next man who touches me wrongly will get more than just burned!"

They all glanced at the handbag, deciding maybe they had better believe her. Jason scooted even farther away, and the other two men leaned back in their seats.

"Don't get all lathered up, lady," one of them told her. "We didn't do nothin'."

"Then I would suggest you keep it that way and mind your own business," Jennifer told him. She looked back out the window, keeping her hand in the purse in spite of the pain it brought her. She wanted them to think her finger was on a trigger ready to pull.

She realized more than ever that in this land it was survival of the fittest, and maybe the meanest. She didn't want to be so cold and callous, for it was not her nature. But out here there seemed to be no room for kindness and friendliness and trust. She decided that for this trip to be bearable, she had to get on a coach with passengers who didn't know anything about her brand as an Indian "squaw." These men could be put off only so long before they realized she was lying about having a gun. Even if they didn't touch her, she was not about to finish this long journey with their sinister eyes drilling into her the whole way. She determined she would get off at the next home station and wait for another coach, no matter how crude the station, and no matter how long the wait.

Chapter Twenty-Five

Jennifer soaked her bandaged hands in a bucket of cool water. The wet gauze felt better than dry, and the cool water soothed her pain. It was all she could do to lift her clothes at the outhouse or carry a bag. She was glad that at least this home station was shaded by a few cottonwood trees, and a stream flowed nearby. The building was as much a shack as the first ones she had encountered on her earlier journey, but the bedding seemed cleaner, and the lone man who worked here, Seth Tyler, had a Comanche wife.

She was grateful that the driver had said nothing about what he had heard about her while they were stopped there, for she sensed that even though Tyler had an Indian wife, he would frown on a white woman being with an Indian. The other three men who had been on the stage also said nothing. Whether it was because they were afraid of her retribution, or because Seth had a Comanche wife, she couldn't be sure. She only knew that at least now no one on the next stage would look at her as a branded woman.

"I've changed my mind," she had told Seth. "I've decided I want to go back to San Antonio." When he had asked why she was on the stage at all, she told him she had come to Texas in reply to a soldier's ad for a wife, but that he turned out to be a brutal man, who had left the bruise on her face. "I picked up a pan of hot water and threw it at him," she had told him. "I didn't do him much harm, but I burned my hands. Needless to say, I decided not to stay at the fort a moment longer. I thought I might go farther west, but I think I prefer the Gulf Coast."

Seth, an ageing, bearded man who looked more like he belonged in the mountains hunting bear than running a way station, had listened nonchalantly, seeming not to care one way or the other. "It's your business," he had told her.

She appreciated his disinterest, at the moment preferring an uncaring attitude as opposed to staring, accusing eyes and ugly remarks. The driver of the coach on which she had arrived had whistled and shouted orders to the horses that morning and the coach had clattered off without her. Now it was late afternoon, and the air hung heavy and quiet, with only the occasional noise of one or two birds, here and there the croak of a frog along the creek bed. Tufts of fuzz from the cottonwood trees floated in the air, some of them getting caught in her hair.

Jennifer sat alone near the creek, holding her hands in the bucket and feeling strangely at peace. For the first time in several days she was not under the scrutiny of judgmental eyes. She was just Jennifer Andrews again, a woman traveling to San Antonio when the next stage going east came along. There was no more explaining to do. Seth had assured her that the next stage coming through was not one that would stop at Fort Stockton.

Seth was reasonably personable, although his Comanche wife was silent, seeming sometimes bashful, other times looking at her as though she was the woman's mortal enemy. Watching her made Jennifer think of Wade, and brought back aching memories, especially when she set eyes on the woman's son by Seth, a dark, handsome little four-year-old with eyes as black as any Comanche, but who had sandy-colored hair.

She wondered what kind of emotional problems lay ahead for the child, who would apparently not have the advantages Wade had had. And she thought what a loving and understanding father Wade would have been to a child of his own. Maybe some day people's prejudice against someone with Indian blood would disappear, and they would be accepted like any other human being. When she watched the Comanche woman with the boy, quietly disciplining him in the Comanche tongue, never losing her temper with him, occasionally picking him up and giving him a hug, she could see the same motherly love as with any white mother.

Surely, even though he had been raised differently, Wild Horse had the same human emotions and deep feelings that Wade possessed. Maybe Wade had found a way to reach the man and was still all right. She had to hope, or lose her mind in this remote, lonely land. She wished she could talk to the Comanche woman about Wade and Wild Horse and get her opinion, but the woman spoke very little English.

The day had been long and hot. It was only the second day after leaving Fort Stockton, which was now just a day's ride away; yet it seemed like hundreds of miles. She missed Alice and was sorry for how lonely the woman surely was. But who was she to say what she would do herself if she could be near Wade's grave. Was there a grave, or perhaps just a mutilated body left for the buzzards? She could not forget what had been done to some of the passengers on the first stagecoach she had taken. To think of Wade suffering only made her lonely heart ache more.

She heard the sound of horses then, and she sat up straighter, expecting perhaps soldiers or travelers. Instead, eight Indians were approaching from the north. Her first thought was to hope Wade might be among them, but as they came closer she realized they were wilder looking, their faces and horses painted. She rose from where she sat by the creek and ran to the station, hurrying inside. "Indians are coming," she told Seth.

He looked up at her from where he sat brushing a pair of boots. He seemed totally unconcerned, twitching his gray mustache when a fly buzzed near his nose. He rose, a tall, lanky man whose head seemed to nearly touch the low ceiling of the small enclosure. "Don't worry," he told her. "They're probably some of my wife's relatives. She's got a couple brothers who ride with Wild Horse."

"Wild Horse!" Ugly memories came rushing back, and she moved farther toward the back of the small room.

"They won't bring you any harm, long as you're with me. How do you think I've survived out here, bein' a white man? They trust me—consider me a friend."

By the time he finished the Indians had burst into the little cabin without so much as a knock. They looked around uneasily, as though they didn't like being inside the enclosure. One of them rested his eyes on Jennifer, and she gasped, recognizing him as the man who had brought the water to her and Wade at the cave. She stared at him and he at her as one of the others began conversing with the Comanche woman in their own tongue. She smiled and said something back, handing him some bread. Another was saying something to Seth.

"Rest easy," Seth told Jennifer. "They just want some food and some tobacco. Fast Horse and Two Hawks, they came to see their sister." He indicated the one Jennifer recognized when he mentioned Two Hawks.

Heart racing, Jennifer moved a little closer. "Seth," she said, her eyes on Two Hawks. "Would you . . . would you ask this one . . . Two Hawks . . . if he knows anything about a man named Wade Morrow? If he doesn't understand the name, tell him the one who is Wild Horse's brother."

Seth scratched his thinning hair. "Now what would a pretty little thing like you know about Wild Horse or any brother he might have—which he doesn't?"

"Just ask him—please. Ask him if Wade Morrow is still alive."

Seth shrugged and spoke to Two Hawks in his own tongue. Jennifer watched the Indian as Seth talked. Two Hawks's face was covered with tiny pitted scars, and she guessed he had had smallpox at one time. She had heard of waves of smallpox and cholera wiping out whole tribes. The man's dark skin and hair were greased with something that did not smell too pleasant. Two Hawks gave a short, grunting reply to Seth, and Seth turned to Jennifer. "He says yes, the man called Wade Morrow still lives."

Jennifer felt faint with relief. She closed her eyes and breathed deeply, tears coming to her eyes. "Ask him when they're going to let him go."

Seth relayed the message, and Jennifer could tell by the look in Two Hawks's eyes and his inflections and almost angry reply what the answer was.

"He says Wild Horse will never let him go—says one of them has to die—they have to fight. What's goin' on here?"

Jennifer faced him. "I met a man on the way to Fort Stockton. He's a half-breed. He was on his way to find some of his family. The soldiers told him he looked like Wild Horse. He went to find the man, but people told me that if they should happen to be twins, Wild Horse would not allow him to live. But Wade doesn't want to kill his own brother. The last we knew, he was with Wild Horse. I feared he was dead by now."

Seth eyed her closely. "Sounds like you took a personal interest."

"I did," she answered without a flinch. She looked at Two Hawks. "And now that I know he's still alive . . ."

"It won't be for long if what you say is true. Comanches kill twin babies. It's bad luck to let them grow into adults. I reckon Wild Horse is pretty upset by it. Your Wade Morrow is probably in pretty sorry shape by now."

Two Hawks spoke up to Seth, finally taking his eyes from Jennifer. He rattled on, waving his arms, pointing at Jennifer.

"No, no, no," Seth answered, shaking his head and trying to wave the man off. Two Hawks seemed to become more angry. He said something to Seth's wife, and the woman started yelling at her husband and waving her arms, nodding toward Jennifer. Seth turned back to Two Hawks, who drew a knife. Jennifer gasped and shrank back, while Two Hawks barked at Seth again. Seth sighed, glancing at Jennifer. "He wants to take you off with him—to Wild Horse's camp."

Jennifer's eyes widened, as a mixture of emotions swept through her. The thought of going off with Comanche men, of being taken to their most notorious leader, knowing what usually happened to white women, made her feel faint with fear. She felt numb and sick, remembering the awful day of the raid on the stagecoach

"Why?" she asked, her voice thin with fear.

"He ain't sayin' why, lady. But I've got a good idea. Are you that Wade Morrow's woman?"

Her cheeks felt hot. "Woman?"

"You know what I mean. It's just us now. Might as well get this straight. Two Hawks says you're Morrow's woman. That true?"

She raised her chin slightly. "Yes," she answered. "Now tell me why Two Hawks wants to take me to Wild Horse. Will they let me help Wade?"

The man looked away from her almost sheepishly. "Not exactly."

Two Hawks barked at the man again, waving the knife.

"I think he's got an idea how to help Wild Horse make Wade Morrow fight him." He glanced at Jennifer. "My guess is he figures Wild Horse can use you for bait. If torture won't make Wade Morrow fight, maybe the threat of harm comin' to you will."

Her eyes widened. Seth didn't have to explain to her what the statement meant. "You . . . you aren't going to let them take me!"

The man turned away. "Ma'am, there's eight Comanche out there. Only thing that keeps me alive is I'm married to Two Hawks's sister, but if I help in breaking Comanche law, I'm a dead man, sister or no sister. For me, the Comanche come first, and I don't hardly know you. If I refuse, Two Hawks will shove that knife through my gut and take you anyway. I see no reason to die over it."

Never had Jennifer felt such terror, or such utter devastation at a man's cowardliness; and never had it been driven home so painfully that she was utterly alone.

"Do you realize . . . wnat will happen to me if . . . if Wade should lose?"

"He *will* lose. That's not my business. It's not my fault you picked my station to hole up in. Maybe you'll get lucky." He turned to meet her eyes, his own looking sad but resolute. "Maybe this Wade Morrow will strike up some kind of deal with Wild Horse for your safety."

Her eyes teared more as she trembled with anger and fear. "And I'm supposed to believe Wild Horse's word can be trusted?"

The man nodded. "If Wade Morrow can get him to make certain promises, he'll keep them. He's a lot of things you don't understand, but he speaks the truth and he keeps his word."

She swallowed back a lump in her throat. "Well, that's a comfort, isn't it? That makes it all easier for you."

He shook his head. "I'm sorry. Maybe by God's grace your Wade Morrow will defeat Wild Horse." He looked at Two Hawks and said something in the Comanche tongue.

Two Hawks shoved his knife into its sheath, and the Comanche woman grinned. Two Hawks said something excitely to the others, and they all seemed to become more excited. Two Hawks appeared to be feeling quite proud, and Jennifer knew with dread that it was because he would be bringing Wade Morrow's "woman" to Wild Horse. She was so full of ugly memories and terror that she hardly felt it when Two Hawks marched over and pulled her hands behind her, binding her wrists tightly with rawhide strips. He touched the gauze on her hands, and she grunted with pain. Two Hawks said something to Seth.

"He wants to know what's wrong with your hands— where you got the bruise on your face," Seth interpreted. "That true about the soldier you were supposed to marry gettin' rough with you?"

She looked at him with angry eyes. "No. The truth is another man at the fort attacked me, because I happen to love a man who is part Indian. I fought back. It *is* true that I threw boiling water at him and burned my hands. He got burned much worse. He might not even live."

Seth explained, and Two Hawks grinned and said something to the others, grasping Jennifer's hair and yanking slightly on her head. The others grinned in return, all muttering something, nodding their heads as though to approve.

"They think you're a brave woman," Seth told her. "They like brave captives."

"So I've heard," she said dully. She told herself she had to remember that, sensing that to fight them would only make matters worse for her. She was in enough pain already. Somehow she had to survive long enough to see Wade once more. God only knew what Wild Horse would do to her to make Wade fight him.

Two Hawks ripped the straw hat from her head and pushed her forward. She knew it was ridiculous to worry about bringing her bags. Where she was going, she was not likely to return. She wondered if Seth would give her clothes to his Comanche wife, and keep all her money for himself, knowing she would never come back to reclaim it.

"I'll report this to Captain Howell at Fort Stockton," the man told her before she went through the door. "That's the best I can do."

She glared at the man. "See that the money I had with me is given to the men from Morrow Freighting. They'll be coming through this way soon, and most of the money belongs to Wade. Tell them what happened. I take it I can trust you to do that much," she sneered.

The man nodded. "Like I say, that's all I can do. I can't stop this, Miss Andrews."

She looked him over scathingly. "Of course you can't."

Two Hawks grasped her arm and pulled her outside, half dragging her to his horse. Her leg was still too sore to walk fast. He grasped her about the waist and plunked her on his horse, mounting up behind her and grasping the reins. Her ears hurt and her blood chilled when he let out a victorious war whoop. He and four others rode off, leaving the other three behind to collect their food and tobacco. Two Hawks obviously did not want to wait. He was

390

anxious to bring his "prize" to Wild Horse and win the man's praise.

It was a hellish journey for Jennifer, who was not accustomed to riding. Two Hawks rode well into the night, and the other Indians from the way station caught up with him before Two Hawks stopped for the night. The man grabbed her down from the horse and finally cut the bindings at her wrists. He took her arm and led her a few feet away from where the others proceeded to make camp.

To Jennifer's shock, Two Hawks pulled aside his loincloth and relieved himself. At his first move Jennifer thought the worst, then turned away when she realized what he was doing. In the next moment he tapped her on the shoulder, making motions to indicate that she should take care of her own necessities. To her relief he walked off and left her there alone. She quickly answered nature's call, terrified they would all come back and take advantage of her; but nothing happened.

She stood there a moment then, considering trying to run off; but she decided it would be fruitless. She was in desolate, unfamiliar country, and there was no way she was going to outsmart any Comanche warrior in his own home territory. She would be caught, and perhaps receive much worse treatment than she was getting now. She returned to camp, deciding that no matter what happened, at least she would get to see Wade again.

She sat down wearily in some grass, a few feet back from the campsite, wanting to draw as little attention as possible. Two Hawks brought her a piece of dried meat and a canteen, and she ate quickly, surprised she was being fed at all. From tales she had heard of other captives, she decided she was being treated better than most. So far the worst had been the painful wrist bindings and the long, arduous ride on horseback. Her thighs and bottom burned, and she was sure she was getting blisters. But most of her pain was from the injuries James Deaver had inflicted rather than Two Hawks.

She drank down some water, not caring for the moment that Two Hawks's own lips, or perhaps one of the other's, had drunk from the same vessel. She needed the water badly. When she was through, Two Hawks came over and grabbed her wrists, pulling out her hands and unwrapping the gauze on them. She wondered if he was going to find some way to torture her with the burns, but he searched through a beaded parfleche and drew out a leather pouch. He dipped his fingers into it, gathering some kind of a crude-looking salve. He began applying it to her burns, and to her amazement a good deal of the pain vanished.

"I wonder why you're doing this," she said, knowing he didn't understand her. "You're saving me for Wild Horse, aren't you? You'll let him decide what to do with me."

Two Hawks met her eyes, and she wished she could read his thoughts through his wild, dark eyes. It seemed strange to think what he and the others would probably normally do to her, for so many other white women had died so violently by some of these men. Yet she knew the same men were capable of caring for their own women and children, caring so much that losing them brought this awful revenge.

And then there was Wade, a perfect example of how people of the same race can be radically different. Wade could be so gentle and loving. Surely men like Two Hawks could also be that way, but making war and seeking revenge and conquering the land and any strangers who came into it were all part of daily life for these people.

"You humiliate and torture and kill your enemy because that's the code by which you live, isn't it? It's all you've ever known. You think nothing of it because that is how it has always been for you and your ancestors."

Two Hawks just scowled and finished applying the salve. To her disappointment, he retied her wrists, which were already raw. He spread out a blanket and indicated she should lie down on it. She accepted the invitation

392

gratefully. It would not be a comfortable night's sleep, but for the moment she was too weary to care that her bed was nothing but a thin blanket on the cold, hard ground. How she managed to drift off to sleep, she wasn't sure; but when she awoke at dawn, someone had covered her with another blanket.

Jennifer's heart raced when she saw the village ahead. She immediately began searching for Wade, dread and disappointment filling her when she saw him nowhere in sight. Was he already dead? Had something happened that Two Hawks didn't know about? And if he was dead, what would happen to her?

Someone began drumming, and war whoops filled the air as Two Hawks came closer. He joined in the shouting, and Jennifer cringed at his wild voice near her ear, his fierce strength bumping against her. Someone came out of a tipi, and Jennifer gasped. "Wade!" she cried at first glance.

Two Hawks dismounted and jerked her down from the horse, dragging her over to the man who she at first thought was her beloved. Upon a closer look, she realized there was a wildness about this man's countenance that Wade did not possess. Two Hawks spoke to him in the Comanche tongue, and she realized with a sinking heart that she was looking into the eyes of the infamous Wild Horse. It seemed incredible he could be such a replica of Wade, yet be so different. His eyes moved over her appreciatively as Two Hawks carried on in the strange tongue that made them all seem even more fearsome. Jennifer supposed he was telling Wild Horse who she was and how he had found her. A look of great joy and victory began to spread over Wild Horse's face as he slowly walked around her, while the camp quieted slightly, women and children staring at Jennifer.

Wild Horse touched the bruise on her face, then picked up her wrists and studied her hands. Finally he turned to Two Hawks and put a hand on his shoulder, saying something that was unmistakably some sort of praise. He barked something at a woman standing nearby and she hurried off, leading a fine-looking gray gelding when she returned. She handed the reins to Wild Horse, and he in turn handed them over to Two Hawks. Jennifer realized Wild Horse was apparently giving the man a gift for bringing him such a prize.

Wild Horse turned his eyes to her, a sly grin moving across his face. She met his gaze boldly, thinking with chilling reality that here, but for a young girl's choice so many years ago, could be Wade; while this man might have been raised by Lester Morrow and know nothing of this strange, aboriginal life.

"Where is your brother?" she asked, keeping her voice steady and demanding. "Where is Wade Morrow?"

His eyes lit up at the name, and she knew that he understood what she had asked. His nostrils flared as he looked at her almost challengingly. He suddenly grabbed the hair at the back of her head and pushed her along with him then, leading her to a tipi, pushing down on her head so that she bent to go inside. Her first thought was that he intended to immediately humiliate her in the worst way, but as soon as she was inside the tipi she saw a man lying on his back, his arms extended past his head and his wrists tied to a stake. His body was covered with bruises and wounds, and when their eyes met, her heart went out to him.

"Wade!" she cried.

She rushed to him, and he opened his eyes. They widened in horror. "Jenny! What are you—" He looked past her at Wild Horse. "What is she doing here?" he growled in the Comanche tongue.

"I think you know, my brother."

Wade's eyes filled with fury, and he jerked on his bindings.

"Oh, Wade, I thought you were dead," Jennifer groaned, touching his wounds gently. "What have they done to you?"

"It's what they intend to do to *you* I'm worried about,"

394

he said angrily. "How in God's name did they get hold of you?"

"I was at a stage station. It's a long story, Wade. Two Hawks saw me there. He recognized me. The station attendant just let him take me away with him."

Wade looked up at Wild Horse. "Take her back!"

Wild Horse just grinned wickedly. "She is much too valuable, my brother. I have already given Two Hawks my best horse for this fine prize." The man walked over and jerked Jennifer up, clamping a strong arm around her chest and whipping out a knife. He held it at her throat, then trailed it down over one breast. "If you will not fight me for your own honor and for Comanche law," he sneered, "perhaps you will fight me for your *woman!*"

He shoved the knife back into its sheath, keeping a firm grip on a terrified Jennifer while he pushed his other hand into her hair, gripping it so tightly it made her wince. "She is a fine-looking woman, young and strong. I think perhaps I would not kill her. It would be much more enjoyable to make her a slave in my tipi, don't you think?"

"Let her go," Wade growled, yanking on the ties again.

Wild Horse threw back his head and laughed. He let go of Jennifer and shoved her aside so hard that she fell. "Tomorrow, my brother. You have had two days of rest and food. Tomorrow you will fight me, because tonight I will claim your woman. I will be no kinder to her than I would be to any other white captive." He looked down his nose at Wade challengingly. "And if I get tired of her, I will turn her over to the others. If she lives through that, the women can play games with her, like they did with you. Now I will let you have a last moment alone with her."

The man turned to leave. "Wait," Wade growled. Wild Horse turned. "I'll fight you, you bastard, but only if you leave her untouched, and only if you promise she goes free even if I lose! And not just Jennifer. That little white girl captive. Let her go with Jennifer!"

Their eyes held. "So quickly you decide to fight me now. The woman means that much to you."

"Enough to die for! Enough to kill my own brother over! You'll not lay a hand on her! I wouldn't be fighting for my life. I'd be fighting for hers! And for the little girl, too!"

Wild Horse glanced at Jennifer, then back at Wade. "I agree to only part of your demand. Whether you win or lose, she and the child go free; but only if you fight to the death. The fight is all I want, Wade Morrow, not your woman." He puffed his chest proudly. "As for tonight, I cannot make any promises. You will give me a better battle if you truly hate me, my brother, and now that I know how much you care for the white woman, I can think of only one way to make you hate me so much."

Wade's eyes blazed. "How do I know you'll keep your word to let her go once the fight is over?"

Wild Horse held his chin proudly. "When I give my word, I keep it. You should know that much about the Comanche."

"I want your promise that you won't just turn her and the child out to die. I want them taken somewhere where they'll get help. And I want you to tell your people that if *I* win, neither Jennifer nor the girl *nor* I have to worry about the rest of your people turning on us. You tell them you've given your word."

Wild Horse grinned again. "You will *not* win, my brother, but I will tell them. Even if you *should* win, they would not turn on you. They would see you as the stronger spirit, and they would respect you for it." He glanced at Jennifer once more before meeting Wade's eyes again. "I will leave her here until sunset. Tonight she sleeps in my tipi."

"Like hell she will," Wade growled, yanking on his ties again. "Right now, Wild Horse. We'll fight right now!"

Wild Horse just laughed. "Finally I see in your eyes a desire to kill. Finally I see hate in your eyes. I will let you think about it, and wonder about it, my brother, through the night. It will give you more strength, more hate. It will be a good fight."

The man ducked outside, and Jennifer collapsed beside

Wade and put her head on his chest. "Oh, Wade, what's happening?"

"Jenny," he groaned. He breathed deeply of the scent of her hair. "If I don't fight him, he'll have you treated like any other white woman captive. And tonight . . . he's taking you to his tipi." He drew his lips back in a sneer, looking as wild and fearful as any other warrior. "Bastard," he growled, yanking at his bindings again. "My God, the son of a bitch has finally found the one thing that can make me hate him. I never wanted you to get involved in this, Jenny. *Damn* him! Damn all of them!"

Jennifer sat up, touching his face. "Oh, Wade, look at you! You *can't* fight him! Not like this!"

"I don't have any choice. I only have until tomorrow morning to decide, but I've already decided. He said you can stay here until dark, then he's taking you away, and I have to just lie here . . ." He closed his eyes, gritting his teeth as he jerked on the ties again. "My God, Jenny. All I can do is hope he's bluffing about you."

Jennifer breathed deeply for control, a sick terror engulfing her. She forced herself not to show it. "I'll survive, Wade. Somehow we'll *both* survive this and we'll be together. We'll find a way to put all of this behind us. We have to." Tears made white streaks down her dirty cheeks. "I'm not afraid of anything now that I know you're alive. Oh, Wade, look at you!" She touched his wounds lightly. "Look what he's done to you. I don't understand any of this. It's so wrong."

"He at least promised that if I lose, you'll go free," he said, panting from his struggles. "If I win, we are both to be allowed to leave unharmed."

"If you lose, I would want to die anyway, Wade."

"No, Jenny. I wouldn't want that." His eyes studied her, love and passion flaring in them, quickly replaced by renewed anger and fierce possessiveness. "What happened to you! Did Two Hawks or Wild Horse put that bruise on your face? Why were you at a stage station instead of the fort?"

She put a hand to the bruise. "No Indian gave me this. It was Tony's friend, Corporal Deaver."

"My God, Jenny, your hands! What happened to your hands?"

She touched his hair. "None of it matters, as long as you're alive and I've gotten to see you one more time." Her eyes teared more.

Two Comanche men came inside then. One walked over and cut the bindings on Wade's wrists. Wincing with pain, Wade sat up.

"Wild Horse said to free you so you can touch your woman," the man told him. "But if you try to escape, it is she who will suffer, not you. He says to touch her all you want and enjoy what he will be enjoying tonight when he comes for her." The man stepped back, a victorious grin on his face. "There will be many braves sitting outside this tipi through the night. They will know if you try to escape."

Wade looked up at the man with angry eyes. "You tell Wild Horse his brother is not a coward who runs from a fight. You tell him I'm *braver* than he is, because *I* would never use a *woman* to get what I want! No matter how much I might come to hate him, I would not abuse *his* woman! You tell him that!"

The man nodded and left. Wade looked at Jenny, then embraced her. How wonderful it felt to see her again, hold her again. He had no choice now. He would die before he would let this woman he loved so much be treated like a common Comanche captive. He could only pray that his last words about it being cowardly to use a woman would have some effect on Wild Horse. The thought of the man touching Jennifer brought an unbearable rage to his soul.

Chapter Twenty-Six

Wade leaned against a backrest made of a piece of deer hide stretched over cottonwood poles. Jennifer leaned into his shoulder, relishing the feel of his strong arm around her.

"There must be something I can do about your wounds, Wade," she said, pain in her voice.

"Not with those hands. I'm all right. The Comanche women are very good at inflicting pain without any dangerous injuries." He spoke the words bitterly. "I'll tell you one thing. There are a couple of other men I'd like to kill besides Wild Horse, including Captain Howell."

"It doesn't matter now. All that matters is that you win that fight tomorrow." She straightened. "It isn't fair. Look at you. Every time Wild Horse strikes you it's going to bring you terrible pain. That gives him an advantage."

He put a hand to her bruised face. "My own advantage will be you. He said he'll let you go if I lose. That may be so, but if I don't fight him at all, I have no doubt he'll keep his word tomorrow about turning you over to the others. One thing I've learned about the man is you can't argue with him, and he always does exactly what he says he's going to do. My biggest worry is tonight." He was so full of rage and a need to protect her that his eyes were bloodshot. "He wants me to hate him, Jenny."

Their eyes held, both knowing what Wild Horse intended to do. Wade moved a hand behind her neck. She could feel his own power, in spite of what he had been through; and she knew what was going through his mind.

"Maybe what you told him about it being cowardly to use a woman will make him think twice," she told him, trying to keep her voice steady. "He and the others seem to consider me quite brave for fighting the man who attacked me at the fort. Maybe I'll be able to somehow make an impression on him, if I act brave and defiant."

A faint grin passed over his lips, but his eyes were watery. "You're some woman, Jennifer Andrews. Look at what you've been through. You should be sniveling and cowering and begging." He touched her hair. "My God, I'm so sorry, Jenny. I never dreamed you would get dragged into this. I never should have come back here."

She held her chin stiffly, refusing to make this all worse for him by weeping and showing her terror. "You did what you thought was the right thing, Wade. I know you love me. My being here isn't your fault. It's Captain Howell's and James Deaver's fault."

She looked down at the soiled skirt of her dress, thinking how prim and proper she looked when she first left the fort. Her hat was gone. Her hair hung in a tangle. Her face was dirty and tear-stained and her dress was wrinkled and grass-stained. "Strangely enough," she said quietly, meeting his eyes again, "I feel kind of hardened, a little numb. I'm not afraid any more, Wade. I guess anger has taken over. And it isn't even Wild Horse with whom I'm most angry. It's men like Tony, and the Captain; and ones like that man at the stage station, people who have shown me in no uncertain terms that a person is really on his own in this life. I feel so lucky to have found you, and I can't believe God will take you away from me. You're going to win tomorrow, Wade—for me. We'll both survive this."

He sighed deeply, taking hold of her wrist and bringing a burned hand to his lips to kiss it. "I'd love to see Deaver right now. I'll bet he's a sight. The bastard deserves every bit of pain he suffers." His grip tightened on her wrist at the thought of another man daring to touch her. Then he gently began rubbing the raw skin where Two Hawks's bindings had hurt her. "I never should have let myself love you in the first place. I should have been stronger." He met her eyes. "And once it went so far, I should never have come here to Wild Horse. I was just so sure I could find a way to get through to him."

Her own eyes teared. "Don't be sorry, not for wanting to know your own brother, and certainly not for loving me. Never be sorry for that. I'm not. We're going to be together, Wade. We'll go to California, like we planned. There is only one thing that can stop us now, and that's Wild Horse. You can't let him stop us, Wade."

He turned away, putting a hand to his own sore ribs. "He's my brother, Jenny. I know what I have to do now. But it's the one thing I wanted to avoid." He closed his eyes and sighed deeply. "With my real mother dead, Wild Horse is all that is left, besides Aguila. I thought I could learn to understand him, bring him around to my way of thinking. I've had a lot of experience with Indians. I could even have found a closeness with the Comanche, maybe even lived among them for a while, learned a lot more. They would have accepted me, and Wild Horse would have welcomed me, if he had been anything but a twin."

He slowly got to his feet, flexing his arms, rubbing at his ribs. He put his head back as though in agony, and Jennifer knew it was emotional agony. "I understand them, Jenny—their frustration, their vengeance, their sorrows. In my own way I have suffered much of the same. But this one thing Wild Horse just won't give on."

He looked at her, kneeling back down beside her. He leaned forward and kissed her cheek. "I was hoping you would be able to wait at the fort for my brothers. If you get out of this, I still want you to contact my family." He touched her hair adoringly. "Jenny, there's a little white girl here—a captive. I saw her once, but she was afraid and ran away from me."

Jennifer's eyes widened. "Oh, the poor child!"

"I managed to make Wild Horse agree that when this is over and he lets you go, you are to be allowed to take the little girl with you. See if she has any relatives around. If not, promise me you'll take her to my folks when you go to them. They'll take care of her. I know my mother. She'll treat the girl like she was her own daughter."

"Of course I'll take her! I just hope Wild Horse keeps his promise to let us go."

He studied her lovingly, but with great sorrow. "He'll keep it. I only wish I could have convinced him not to . . ." He closed his eyes and turned his face away. "Jenny, if Wild Horse . . ." He trembled slightly at the thought of it. "I just hope you can forgive me for getting you into all of this," he said in a near whisper. "We both know what Wild Horse intends to do. I tried to talk him into fighting me right now and getting it over with, but he refused."

He met her eyes again, wondering if after tonight, they would still hold the love for him he saw in them now. "Once Wild Horse lets you and the little girl go, promise me you'll go to my parents, at least for a while, Jenny. My mother is a wonderful woman. She can help you." He pulled her close. "I can't tell you enough how sorry I am for all of this. I love you so much."

She touched his hair. "I love you, too; and I told you not to be sorry. You did what you thought was right. You didn't know Howell would send me away."

He pulled back, running a thumb over the dirt on her face. "You look so tired, Jenny, and I know you're in pain. Come and lie down with me. I can hold you for what little time is left." He moved over to a blanket spread out on straw and put up an arm, moving it round her as she stretched out beside him.

Jenny's throat ached with a need to cry, both with joy that she had found him alive, and sorrow that tomorrow he could die. She refused to think about what could happen to her in just a little while. All that mattered was that she was here with Wade, and this could be their last moment together.

She nestled into his shoulder, finding peace and comfort as his arms came around her. Both were too tired and in too much pain to think about doing anything more. It was simply understood that under different conditions, they would like nothing more than to again consummate their love, again share their bodies in the ecstasy they had known in that little cave, while outside the sand blew in a furious storm.

How long they lay there, touching, petting, talking softly, neither was sure. They only knew the precious moment suddenly ended when Wild Horse threw back the robe at the tipi entrance and ducked inside. He grinned at the sight of them lying together before Wade had a chance to quickly sit up.

"She comes with me now," Wild Horse told him. "Aguila will bring you food and water. My woman will feed your woman."

Wade slowly rose, matching Wild Horse in size. "Just make sure the Comanche women don't abuse her." Two more warriors came inside then, wielding lances.

Wild Horse cast Jennifer an arrogant look, then met Wade's eyes. "I am the one you should worry about, my brother. She is fine looking and brave, something rare in white women. I find her appealing, and I have no patience with captives."

Wade grabbed at the man's vest, but the other two warriors shoved lances flat-side against Wade, pushing him back. Wild Horse looked at Wade with smouldering eyes. "Tomorrow, my brother. I can see you are finally ready."

"You have no right touching my woman. My agreeing to fight should be enough for you!"

"But not for you, my brother," Wild Horse sneered.

"My woman wishes me to tell you that she thinks using her to get your way makes you weak in her eyes! She will be ashamed to have to give herself to a coward!"

Wild Horse turned his eyes back to Jennifer, raking them over her. He looked back at Wade. "I do not listen to women." He motioned to the other two men, who immediately wrestled Wade to the ground to tie his wrists to the stake again.

"Fight me *now*, Wild Horse," Wade growled. "Right

now!" He struggled against the other two men, and Jennifer screamed when he managed to break free. He leaped to his feet, charging into Wild Horse and pushing him out the tipi entrance with such force that it pulled the structure away from some of its supports.

Wild Horse sprawled onto his back outside, but before Wade could do any damage, six more warriors were on him, wrestling him back to the ground.

Jennifer stumbled out of the tipi and groaned Wade's name as three Comanche men sat on him while he lay face down in the dirt and another warrior tied his wrists tightly behind his back. Jennifer knew the ordeal had to be painful for Wade's already-battered body. She gasped when Wild Horse grabbed her then, yanking her close, her back to him. He held her in a strong grip while the other men helped Wade back to his feet. Wade glared at Wild Horse with as much fury in his eyes as Jennifer had ever seen in any warrior.

Wild Horse grasped one of her breasts, and Jennifer turned her eyes from Wade. "I like the look in your eyes, my brother," he told Wade, rubbing at her breast. "But we will not fight yet. It is as I told you. You will think about your woman this night, and by tomorrow, you will be the warrior I want you to be."

He turned and dragged Jennifer away with him. Wade screamed out Comanche words at Wild Horse, and Jennifer needed no interpretation to know he was calling the man every bad name he could think of in the Comanche tongue. Apparently it amused Wild Horse, who only laughed.

Wade fought violently as the other warriors dragged him back into the tipi to again tie him to a stake, while women secured the supports that had been damaged. Wild Horse pushed Jennifer inside a nearby dwelling where a middle-aged Comanche woman and a boy of perhaps seven or eight looked up at her. Wild Horse shoved Jennifer down, and the woman pushed a plate of wild meat and some kind of boiled roots in front of her. It was then

Jennifer noticed another man sitting inside the tipi. She looked down at the food, but had no appetite.

"Wild Horse's woman will consider it an insult if you do not eat," the other man told her.

Jennifer looked over at him in surprise. "You speak English?"

"Yes. I am Aguila."

Her eyes turned to pleading. "Can't you do something about this?"

He shook his head. "It is the way. Eat so you will stay strong. No harm will come to you."

Jennifer turned fiery eyes to Wild Horse. "That is not the impression *he* just gave me!"

Aguila grinned and said something to Wild Horse. Wild Horse looked Jennifer over, replying to Aguila while he kept his eyes on her own.

"Wild Horse says to tell you it is for your man's own good. He must be angry. He must hate. He must think Wild Horse will abuse his woman tonight. He says to tell you that if you truly love Wade Morrow, you should not be angry with him. He was only putting on a show for Wade Morrow's sake. His hatred will give him strength. This is the way Wild Horse wants it. He does not want an easy victory."

Jennifer watched Wild Horse, realizing he was only using psychology on Wade. The realization that he meant her no harm gave her at least a little better appetite. She did not remove her eyes from his. "Then tell him I am grateful," she answered. "Because he has no idea the harm he has done to himself. Wade Morrow will kill him tomorrow."

Aguila grinned at her bold statement, and he interpreted it to Wild Horse. Wild Horse's eyes sparkled, and he actually laughed. He said something to Aguila, then lay against a backrest.

"He says you are brave for a white woman," Aguila told her. "He says that if his brother had to pick a white woman, he picked a good one."

Jennifer gave Wild Horse a scathing look. "I don't care what he thinks." She bit into the meat, which tasted better than she thought it would. The young boy came over to Wild Horse, showing him a small spear. Wild Horse looked at it, unwinding some of the rawhide binding that held the tip to the pole and saying something to the boy. Jennifer was shocked at the sudden gentleness in his voice as he talked to the youngster and seemed to be teaching him something about the proper way to secure the weapon.

"He is Gentle Wind's son," Aguila explained, indicating the Indian woman who had given Jennifer the food. "Gentle Wind gives comfort to Wild Horse, feeds him, takes him to her bed. Wild Horse has adopted her son, whose father was killed by soldiers. He cares very much for the child."

Jennifer looked at Wild Horse and the boy again, finding the contrast between Wild Horse's vicious side and this loving side incredible. It seemed a waste and a shame that the man could not have seen his way to be friends with his own brother.

"I will tell you something, white woman," Aguila told her. "My heart lies with Wild Horse, because I raised him like my own. But Wade Morrow is also my nephew. I will mourn Wild Horse if he should not win the fight, but I will honor Wade Morrow. I did not have the chance to teach him the Comanche way like Wild Horse, so I feel it is my duty to do one small thing to help him, even though I do not wish anything to happen to Wild Horse."

"And what can you do," Jennifer asked, turning her eyes back to Aguila.

"I can give you some advice. If Wade Morrow is to have any hope of winning tomorrow, he must be full of hate. He must erase any remaining feelings he might still have for Wild Horse. You can help. Tomorrow when Wild Horse takes you before Wade Morrow, you must make Wade Morrow think the worst. Do you know what I mean?"

Jennifer's cheeks flushed, but she realized the man was

406

right. "Yes," she answered. "I know what you mean." Their eyes held. "Thank you, Aguila."

The man nodded, then rose and left. Jennifer ate more of the meat, not knowing or caring what it was. She simply had a feeling it would not be wise to insult Gentle Winds.

She contemplated what she must do in the morning. Aguila was right. Wade had to think Wild Horse had abused her. When this was over, if Wade was the victor, she would tell him his uncle had tried to help him. Perhaps it would be a small consolation, but it was something.

It was nearly dark when the train of ten huge freight wagons hauled into Fort Stockton, three men leading a small remuda of riding horses and extra mules behind it. Dust billowed as the lead wagon drew to a halt just outside fort grounds, and a handsome, tall, sandy-haired young man jumped down, followed by a somewhat shorter young man who closely resembled the first.

Both men wore dusty, knee-high boots and denim pants, the taller one wearing a blue calico shirt, the other a red shirt with a leather vest. They sported pistols, slung low on their hips, and sweat ringed their wide-brimmed hats, their faces tanned dark by months of traveling under the hot, Southwest sun.

The entourage they brought along was impressive— sturdy freight wagons in excellent repair, each wagon pulled by a team of several oxen, some by mules. Three men rode on each wagon, one to drive, the other two riding shotgun to protect their goods against Indians and outlaws, except that for now the wagons were empty. With the men who herded the remuda, as well as two men who handled the cook wagon, the company consisted of thirty-six men, ten freight wagons, the cook wagon, and nearly a hundred animals.

The two men apparently in charge headed into the fort, stopping a lieutenant to ask where they might find the commanding officer.

"That would be Captain Howell," the soldier answered.

"I'm Lieutenant Brown. What do you want to see the Captain about?"

"Has there been a Wade Morrow through here?" the tall one answered. "I'm Bill Morrow and this is my brother Henry. Wade Morrow is our brother."

Brown's eyebrows arched. He noticed immediately that the men, obviously carrying no Indian blood, called Wade Morrow brother, not half brother or step brother. He glanced over at the impressive display of freight wagons, where strong, rugged-looking men milled about, sporting pistols and rifles. He looked back at Bill and Henry Morrow.

"You mean, this Wade Morrow really *is* rich? I mean, you two the sons of a Lester Morrow? Is that part of his freighting company?"

"Our pa is Lester Morrow," Henry answered. "We're on our way to pick up some goods in Galveston. We've never taken the line this far east before. Wade set it up with a Bill Strong back in San Antonio. We'll probably be coming through here a lot on our way to and from Galveston. We're based in San Diego."

"Part of the reason we want to talk to your captain is to talk about supplying the army forts here in west Texas," Bill put in. "But right now we're mainly concerned about Wade. You talk like you've seen him. He all right?"

Brown swallowed. "I think you'd better talk to Captain Howell about that. I'll take you over."

Bill looked at Henry, seeing equal curiosity and worry in his brother's eyes. They followed Brown to the captain's quarters, both noticing a strange look on Howell's face when the lieutenant introduced them. Howell immediately appeared to be nervous. "Well, what can I do for you gentlemen?" he asked.

"You can tell us where we might be able to find our brother, Wade Morrow. We're a little worried about him, and so are our folks. He came out here to set up a business deal for our pa, then was supposed to come this way and find some of the Comanche who might be left in these parts. Wade is half Comanche. Our folks found him abandoned as a little baby and raised him."

Howell cleared his throat. "I, uh, I saw your freight wagons out my window. That's quite a setup. Your, uh, your father does well then, I take it."

"He owns the biggest freighting business in the Southwest," Bill answered. "We wanted to talk to you about supplying Fort Stockton through a government contract. We already supply several forts in Arizona and New Mexico." He frowned. "You and the lieutenant both seemed surprised to learn about our pa's freighting business. Or is it that you're more surprised that Wade Morrow was telling you the truth that he owns a share of the business?" He was beginning to bristle. "I suppose you didn't believe him because he's Indian."

"Where's our brother, Captain Howell?" Henry asked.

Howell sighed, sitting down in a chair behind his desk and indicating for Bill and Henry to take seats in chairs across from him. He surmised the two young men couldn't be over twenty-five, yet they seemed able and sure. If their father had put them in charge of such a big enterprise as what he had seen outside, the man must trust these young men to do the job right. Both men had a rugged, experienced look about them, and Howell guessed they could not be easily fooled.

"You men didn't get a telegram somewhere along the line?" Howell asked.

Bill shifted in his chair. "No. Were we supposed to?"

Howell cleared his throat. "Well, I thought someone wired your father in San Diego to, uh, to be sure to get hold of you and be sure you stopped here on your way to Galveston. There has been a lot of Indian trouble. Maybe the message didn't get through."

"What message?" Henry demanded.

Howell rubbed his eyes. "It's a rather long story, gentlemen," he told them. "Your brother was through here. His horse broke a leg and he had to shoot it. He hitched a ride on the San Antonio—San Diego stage line intending to come here and purchase another horse. The stage was attacked by Comanche renegades. They killed every last passenger and the drivers, but Wade Morrow and a young white woman were spared. The woman was badly hurt and Morrow took a bullet out of her leg and nursed her other wounds, which were several. He saved her life. She was coming here to marry a Sergeant Enders when the accident happened. Once your brother arrived here, we all understood why he had been spared—why the renegades ran like they had seen a ghost when they saw him after attacking the coach."

The captain ran a hand through his hair, his nervousness evident. "I've seen the leader of the renegades—a half-breed called Wild Horse. Wade Morrow is his spitting image. Morrow bought a horse and left here to find the man, figuring he must be a brother."

The captain went on to tell the story, while Bill and Henry listened curiously, a growing anger showing in their eyes.

"You had no right having Wade followed," Bill told the man. "And Wade would never deliberately lead your men into a trap. He wouldn't have had anything to do with that. Maybe this Wild Horse was following *him!*"

"Well, now that I see the kind of background from which the man comes, I have to agree he doesn't seem like the kind of man who would do such a thing. But the man *is* part Comanche. You have to understand what that means out here. If you knew some of the things the Comanche have done, you'd hate them as much as most Texans and most soldiers do."

"So, you didn't believe him and you judged him just because of how he looks," Bill said with slight sneer. "Wade's a good man, Captain, as civil as the next, educated, generous, and smart. You just left him there with this Wild Horse then, knowing he could have been a captive, knowing Wild Horse likely wants him dead?" The man rose, leaning over the captain's desk. "We know about the Comanche, Captain. We haven't had a lot of experience with them, but in our business you stay on top of these things. We know the kinds of awful torture they can put a man through. Our brother could be *dead.*"

410

"That was his decision. He didn't have to go hack to them," the captain answered defensively.

"Why did he come back here after he left the reservation?" Henry asked. "You said you had him followed by Apache scouts. They tracked him here and then out toward Comanche Hills, where your soldiers were attacked. I know damn well he didn't come back here just to lead soldiers into a trap. He had some other reason for coming back here. You're leaving something out, Captain, and you haven't told us what the telegram we were supposed to get was all about."

Bill stepped hack and began rolling a cigarette. "Why don't you tell us the *whole* story?"

Howell swallowed again, realizing that Lester Morrow could quite possibly have enough pull with the army to foil Howell's own attempts at promotion. Howell had already had trouble with deserters, let alone the massacre of so many men after he had led them straight into a trap. Morrow supplied several army posts and must have connections in Washington. He rubbed his temple, feeling a headache coming and longing for a drink.

"Your brother came back to see Miss Andrews. That's the young woman on the coach whose life he saved. They apparently . . . well, they didn't let on to us, but Miss Andrews finally admitted to me that she and your brother had fallen in love. She had decided she was not going to marry Sergeant Enders. But it wouldn't have mattered. He was killed in the Comanche attack."

Henry looked at his brother, then back to the captain. "You said the injured woman on the stage was white."

"Yes," Howell answered.

Henry and Bill looked at each other again, both grinning a little. "It's about time Wade found himself another woman," Henry said. His grin faded. "It's just too bad Wade had this trouble with Wild Horse. You think he's still alive?"

Bill sighed. "I don't know, but we're damn well going to find out." He looked at the captain while he lit the cigarette he had rolled. "Where is Miss Andrews?" he

411

asked after taking a drag. "We'd like to meet her."

Howell seemed to pale slightly. "Well, uh, she's the one who sent the telegram. It seems your brother wanted you to pick her up on your way to Galveston and take her back to San Diego with you, in case he didn't make it back from Wild Horse's camp. You apparently never got the message."

Bill watched him carefully, keeping the cigarette between his lips. "Apparently not," he said with a hint of sarcasm. "Well, at least we're here and can still take her with us."

Howell reddened slightly. "Yes. Well, uh, she . . . she isn't here."

"Where is she?" Henry asked.

Howell straightened. "Look, there is something you both have to understand—"

Someone knocked on the door, and Howell looked up irritably as a second lieutenant stepped inside with a staff sergeant. "Sir? Sergeant Steen here says he still has the message for the Morrow brothers, the one she sent them before she left. Maybe they'd like to take a look at it."

Bill turned and rose, reaching out to take the telegram, scowling even more as he read it. He turned to Howell, removing the cigarette from his mouth. "Where did Miss Andrews go? And why did she leave at all after sending this telegram? Why didn't she wait for us?" He handed the telegram over to Henry while the lieutenant left and closed the door. "What the hell is going on?" Bill nearly growled. "According to that message, Miss Andrews said she would be waiting here at the fort for us—that Wade wanted her to go with us if something happened to him. Why isn't she here!"

Howell gripped the arms of his chair. "Look, Morrow, I have a responsibility to this fort and my men—a responsibility to keep things in order! Ever since your brother came through here, I've had nothing but trouble. Do you know how men in these parts look upon a white woman who consorts with an Indian, let alone a *Comanche*? Miss Andrews might have been a perfectly proper young lady, but not in the eyes of men in west Texas!"

"Just say it out, Howell," Henry said. "What happened to Miss Andrews? If this message is true, Wade would have wanted us to look after her."

Howell rose. "I sent her away."

"What!" Bill, who was still standing, threw down his cigarette and stepped on the stub. "What the hell for? Didn't she tell you she wanted to wait here until we showed up?"

"I did it for her own good," Howell answered, raising his voice slightly. "One of my men attacked her. She managed to fight him off. In fact, she threw a pot of boiling water on him. He's lying in his quarters right now in grievous pain, close to death."

"*Grievous* pain? What about Miss *Andrews?*"

"She got hurt also—burned her hands. But I knew it was dangerous for her to stay here because of the label my men had put on her. I had every right to send her away. It was for her own protection. I can't watch every man every second of the day, Mr. Morrow!"

"You could have given some kind of order that any man who brings her harm will pay with a lashing and extra duty," Bill answered. "Where did you send her?"

Howell seemed to pale even more. "She boarded a stage to El Paso, but I have received word that for some reason she got off at the next home station to wait for a stage going to San Antonio."

"She probably figured she'd find us easier in San Antonio," Henry put in. "She still at the home station? We'll send some men back to get her."

Howell sighed deeply. "I'm afraid some renegades came and took her away—some of Wild Horse's men."

The room hung silent for a moment. "Just . . . took her away, huh," Bill finally spoke up. "Nobody knows why? Nobody tried to stop them?"

"There is just one man running the station, and he has a Comanche wife. The man wouldn't last two minutes if he tried to argue with renegades who come through there.

413

Why should he die for one white woman he doesn't even know?"

Bill's face darkened with rage, and he trembled to stay in control. "Yes. Why *should* he? Of course *Wade* was ready to die for her when that stage was attacked! Maybe that tells you a little bit about the kind of man our brother is. And what about *you?* You aren't going to send out a detail to try to find the poor woman, *or* Wade?"

Howell's cheeks colored. "To begin with, it isn't my fault Miss Andrews was foolish enough to get off that stage; and I only learned a short time ago through a message from the home station what happened. Be that as it may, I simply don't have enough men to go galavanting all over west Texas trying to find two people who are probably already dead!"

"You're a *coward*— and in your mind an Indian man and a white "squaw" aren't worth losing lives over, isn't that it, Howell?" Bill raged. "Well, let me tell you something. I've got enough experienced men out there to be a big help to you. Put them with twenty or so of your soldiers, and you've got over fifty men! You know damn well Wild Horse has to be someplace in Comanche Hills. My brother and that woman could still be alive. Maybe they need our help. My pa would expect us to try to find Wade; and by God, if you don't help, my pa will also have a few things to report about you to men in Washington who can make or break you! You'll sit out here in this godforsaken fort the rest of your life, and you won't be wearing a captain's decorations and be in charge either!"

Howell drew in his breath as though someone had hit him. "You can't threaten me, Morrow!"

"Can't I? You'd be surprised who my pa knows, Howell!" Bill leaned over the desk, glaring at the captain. "I have a suggestion, Howell, and you'd be wise to take me up on it. I'm offering you over thirty men—all hard-bitten, experienced Indian fighters. I suggest we pool our resources and see if we can rout out Wild Horse and find my brother. We're going, whether you join us or not; but my father would look a lot more favorably on you if you

414

helped us—and you just *might* get lucky and get credit for capturing Wild Horse! I'm not sure my brother would approve of that, but if it's the only way we can save him and Miss Andrews, we have to do it. Maybe if we can at least find this Wild Horse we can learn if Wade and Miss Andrews are still *alive!*"

Howell sighed deeply, running a hand through his hair again, obviously shaken. "All right," he finally said. "Our best bet is to go north and hope we find some sign of Comanche. Believe me, when they don't want to be found, it's like looking for a needle in a haystack. What about your appointment in Galveston? Don't you have to be there by a certain date? What about your business?"

"Our pa would consider this a lot more important," Henry answered. "How soon can you have some men ready?"

"It's too late to try to leave yet tonight," Howell answered. "We'll leave at dawn."

Bill moved away from his desk, adjusting his hat. "My men will be ready at first light." He looked at Howell with smouldering dark eyes. "One thing you better understand, Howell—Wade Morrow is worth more than all your men put together. He's as much a brother to us as if we carried the same blood, and he means a lot to our ma—pa, too. You better hope he's all right, and that Miss Morrow is, too."

Both men turned and left, and Howell plunked down into his chair with a deep sigh. He quickly grabbed up his log book, opening it to the present date.

Visited by Bill and Henry Morrow, he wrote. *Part owners of Morrow Freighting. Because of the fine reputation of this company, and the fact that Mr. Lester Morrow carries government contracts with the army leaves me reponsible to help Bill and Henry Morrow find their step brother, Wade Morrow, who has been captured by Wild Horse. I cannot in good conscience withdraw my help in this mission, in spite of the fact that it will be dangerous and I am*

short of men. But duty calls. It is my hope to also
capture Wild Horse and rid this area of the Texas
frontier of the terror and bloodshed for which he is
responsible.

He sat back and read the report, deciding it made him sound like a dedicated officer. He closed the book, deciding the Morrow brothers might be doing him a favor. If he could capture Wild Horse, he might finally earn himself a promotion that would send him back East. Either way, *not* helping Bill and Wade Morrow could quite possibly erase all hope of ever getting out of Texas.

"Damn troublemakers," he muttered. He barked orders for Lieutenant Brown to come in, giving the man instructions to prepare twenty-five men to be ready to leave in the morning.

Chapter Twenty-Seven

No night had ever seemed longer for Jennifer. She could not forget what Aguila had told her. If Wade was to have any chance against Wild Horse, he had to have that extra bit of hate to goad him on. She had to convince him Wild Horse had raped her. She dreaded what was to come, dreaded watching the fight, yet knew it would be almost harder to sit inside somewhere and not watch at all. She sensed that for an Indian man, it was a matter of pride and honor that his woman watch him in battle; and white as Wade was in his beliefs and actions, it was obvious he carried that same deep pride.

She lay on a mat, while outside were the sounds of insects, and the occasional call of a wolf. Wild Horse lay sprawled on a mat not far away. Watching him by the dim light of a dying fire made her miss Wade, for in sleep, one could hardly tell the difference between the two men. But she could not watch Wild Horse lovingly, only with near hate, and with distrust. Her mind raced with the possible ways of making him change his mind about the fight. Deep in sleep as he was, she could easily kill him; but she was not sure Wade would want her to do that. Maybe somewhere deep inside he *needed* to do it himself. She was surprised she could even consider murdering someone, and she realized then the extent of her love for Wade.

She lay back again, finally falling into a light sleep. She was not sure how long she had lain there before someone jerked her from her mat and slapped her hard before she realized what was happening. The blow sent her sprawling, and she let out a startled scream.

"It is time to take my brother's woman," Wild Horse shouted loudly in the Comanche tongue, deliberately raising his voice so that Wade would hear him.

Jennifer had no idea what he had said. She watched Wild Horse in shocked wonder, unsure of his intentions, surprised he had awakened at this late hour just to abuse her. Had he ever really been asleep? Had he caught her watching him and somehow been angered by it?

She gave another frightened startled scream when Wild Horse yanked her to her feet again and began tearing away her clothes. The woman with whom he lived sat back smiling, and her son just stared as though watching a sideshow.

"Stop it! Stop it," Jennifer could not help yelling as the man ripped open the bodice of her dress and tore at the skirt. He hit her again, and she heard Wade yelling her name as she again fell down. She felt Wild Horse grab at her bloomers, and in an instant they were ripped off. She grabbed frantically at what was left of the skirt of her dress and pulled it over her knees, curling away from him. "Stay away from me," she screamed.

She heard Wade call for her again, and Wild Horse grinned. He reached down and dragged a kicking, screaming Jennifer to his mat, pinning her there, letting her scream at him and fight him until she went limp from an exhaustion that came easily because of her weakened condition. Her sobs met Wade's ears, and the whole village could hear him growling and shouting obscenities at Wild Horse.

Suddenly Wild Horse released his painful grip on Jennifer's wrists. She looked up at his grinning face as he slowly moved off her. He nodded to her and backed away, sitting down beside a small fire inside the tipi. He kept watching her, still smiling, while Wade continued to call for her. She realized then that what had just happened had

418

all been done to rile Wade. If he was to think Wild Horse had raped her, he had to hear her screams.

She watched Wild Horse in surprise and wonder, putting her hand to the sting at her face and realizing that Wild Horse had not hit her nearly as hard as he could have. She jumped then when Wild Horse suddenly let out a war whoop and growled like a man who had just enjoyed something delightful. Jennifer hung her head when she heard Wade's agonizing cries. Wild Horse had not touched her, but come morning, Wade would be thoroughly convinced otherwise.

Time moved even slower then. Jennifer turned and crawled back to her own bedroll, aching to go to Wade, to tell him she was all right. But she knew that was the worst thing she could do now. She knew instinctively that Wild Horse would not bother her the rest of the night, and she finally managed to get a few hours sleep before she was awakened by the first hint of light from a rising sun.

Aguila came into the tipi, and Jennifer struggled to keep the front of her torn dress from falling away from her breasts. Aguila took a look at her, then moved his eyes to Wild Horse, who still sat by the fire and had apparently not gone back to sleep. The two men exchanged words, and Aguila gave Jennifer a look of approval.

Jennifer could hear the general commotion then of an awakening camp. Wild Horse drank some water, then said something to Gentle Winds. The woman retrieved a small tin and set it in front of him, and he began painting his face black. When finished, he tied his long, black hair into a tail at the back of his neck, then rose and stripped to only his loincloth. He picked up Jennifer's bloomers then and came over to her, grasping her arm, holding her eyes as she slowly rose. The time had come.

Jennifer's heart pounded as she allowed Wild Horse to drag her outside. She decided that if Wade was to be thoroughly convinced she had been abused, she would feign a struggle yet this morning. Wild Horse shouted orders to two other men, and they went inside Wade's tipi.

419

Others began to gather then, some laughing, some letting out war whoops, eager for the fight that would finally take place.

Wade was brought out of the tipi. He still wore only his knee-length long johns. It took four men to hold him back as Wild Horse dragged Jennifer closer to Wade, then held out her bloomers. Jennifer hung her head as though in shame.

"Your woman now belongs to Wild Horse," the man told Wade. He threw her bloomers into a camp fire. "She will not need them."

If ever a man could make the sounds of a wild animal in the heat of battle, it was Wade Morrow at that moment. Wild Horse grinned as Wade struggled to get away from those who held him. Aguila came up and took Jennifer away, and she felt sick to her stomach at the thought of what was to come. In minutes Wade could be dead, and she would not even be allowed one last kiss or touch.

She followed Aguila to an open area where the fight was apparently supposed to take place. Men continued to hold Wade while Wild Horse picked up two small hatchets. He handed one out to Wade.

"Now, my brother, you are strong enough and angry enough to fight me fairly. You have no feelings left for me, because I have enjoyed your woman."

Wade moved his eyes to Jennifer. She raised her own to meet his, seeing the pain there. "I'll never be able to forget, as long as he's alive," she told Wade, hoping the words would put even more hatred into his heart.

Wade looked back at Wild Horse, and for the first time Wild Horse wondered if he had gone too far. The others let go of Wade, and Wade promptly grasped the hatchet Wild Horse offered him.

"I hope you feel this is a good day to die, my brother," he told Wild Horse, "because after this morning, you will no longer walk this earth!"

Wild Horse crouched for battle, and Wade did the same, the two men circling, getting a good grip on their hatchets, challenging each other at first only with their eyes. Jennifer could not imagine how Wade could be in any condition to fight, with numerous cuts and bruises still showing on his body, his wrists raw and bleeding from tugging at his ties. She saw something in him now that had not been there before, an innate viciousness, a keen instinct for survival, and a deep desire to kill.

Wade ducked back when Wild Horse took the first swing, more of a teasing gesture. He grinned, waving the hatchet while beckoning Wade with his other hand to come closer. Wade seemed to be gauging his brother, as he continued to circle, his hair long and loose, looking as much the warrior as any man there.

Jennifer put a hand to her stomach, watching in terror while she held the bodice of her dress over herself with her other hand. She wished there were something more she could do; to make Wade think the worst of his brother would have to remain her only contribution to his winning this battle.

Wade suddenly darted forward, managing to lightly slice his hatchet across Wild Horse's belly just before the man could dart away quickly enough. The unexpectedly aggressive and surprisingly quick move caused Wild Horse to lose his grin. Now his teeth gritted with determination, his eyes smouldering, while blood made its way in several streams down the front of him.

Jennifer felt ill at the sight, shuddering at the thought of Wade being sliced to ribbons. The warriors surrounding the sight were becoming more and more frenzied now, all of them rooting for Wild Horse, Jennifer was certain. Wild Horse, spurred by the urgings of the others, began swinging viciously at Wade, several quick, relentless lashes that kept Wade backing up. Jennifer was forced to move with the crowd as they broke apart to let the two men through. She watched in dread and terror, expecting Wild Horse's hatchet to open up Wade's skin at any moment.

Wild Horse swung again. As soon as his arm came around, Wade suddenly charged into him, pinning his arm against his chest and knocking the man to the ground.

He raised his hatchet, but Wild Horse managed to push Wade off with the arm Wade had pinned against him. When he did so, his hatchet came across Wade's shoulder. Jennifer gasped as blood immediately began pouring from the gash.

Wade stumbled backward but managed to get to his feet at the same time as Wild Horse. Both men circled again, both now covered with not only their own, but each other's blood; both looking as wild and ferocious as a grizzly might look after feasting on a deer. This time it was Wade who made a gesture with his left hand, grinning, telling Wild Horse to come closer.

Jennifer prayed that if Wade was going to win, the fight would be over soon, before he bled to death. There would be no winners if he managed to kill Wild Horse and ended up dying himself. Wild Horse jumped closer and swung again, but Wade caught his wrist, his own hatchet raised. Wild Horse quickly grabbed Wade's hatchet arm, and the two men pushed against each other, each trying to bring down his hatchet.

The viewing warriors were frenzied now, hardly noticing Jennifer. They spread out to give the fighters more room as the conflict suddenly turned into a test of strength, each man pushing at the other. Wild Horse finally managed to swing out a foot and catch it behind Wade's knee, bringing him down. Jennifer whimpered Wade's name as Wild Horse landed on top of him, both men still pushing at each other's arms.

Wade arched up, suddenly rolling Wild Horse over onto his back. Now it was Wade who was on top. He had managed to flatten Wild Horse's right arm to the ground, and he dug his thumb into the man's wrist in such a way that it hit a nerve that made Wild Horse unwillingly open his hand. Wade leaped off the man, grasping up the hatchet before Wild Horse could get it back. Wild Horse jumped to his feet, his eyes wide with astonishment.

Now it was Wade who was grinning. He kept his eyes on Wild Horse while he crouched to toss the man's hatchet aside. It slithered through the dirt, and one of the other warriors picked it up. Wade knew the man would not give it back to Wild Horse. It would not be honorable. Wild Horse had lost his weapon to his opponent.

Wild Horse scowled, his eyes slithers of hatred. He pulled out his hunting knife then, getting a good grip on it. The two men circled again, Wild Horse jabbing out with his knife threateningly, but unable to get close enough to do any damage because Wade still wielded a hatchet. Wade swung his weapon several times, and this time it was Wild Horse who kept jumping back.

Finally, after Wade swung from left to right, Wild Horse slammed into him, and again both men fell to the ground. Wade managed to get a grip on Wild Horse's knife arm before the man could shove the big blade into his side. Only the tip of it entered Wade's flesh. Jennifer watched in terror, knowing that the moment Wade lost his grip, the blade would sink deep, for Wild Horse would use every ounce of strength he had to ram it hard.

Again the conflict turned into more of a wrestling match, as both men pushed against each other, Wild Horse on top of Wade. With a sudden burst of strength, as though he knew it was now or never, life or death, Wade managed to arch violently, pushing Wild Horse's knife arm even farther away and rearing up so that they rolled over. Wade quickly scooted forward on Wild Horse's body, bringing up a knee and pressing it against his chest with all the strength he could muster, while each man still held the other's weapons arms.

Wade pushed hard with his knee so that he could see Wild Horse was unable to breathe. He jammed the knee harder, and Jennifer felt ill at the sound of a crack. She knew it was either a rib or the man's breast bone. Wild Horse's eyes got bigger as he struggled to breathe. It finally became too difficult to hang onto his knife. His hand went limp, and Wade yanked the knife from his hand and leaped to his feet.

Wild Horse rolled over, panting for breath, holding his chest while Wade stood back waiting for him to get up again. Now Wild Horse was weaponless. As Wild Horse struggled to regain his breath and get to his feet, Wade realized that technically he had already won the battle. He would have kept his personal vow not to kill his own brother, if not for what he thought the man had done to Jennifer; and he knew that this would be no satisfactory end for Wild Horse. In spite of what the man had done to both him and Jennifer, Wade understood the reasoning behind it, and he respected his brother's Comanche pride, for he felt it himself now. Wild Horse would rather die than live on in shame.

Wild Horse got to his feet then, taking deep breaths, glaring at Wade. Both men were covered with blood and dirt, and at the moment Jennifer's heart ached for both of them, two men who should have been able to share the bond of brotherhood; one man who did not want to kill his brother, the other deliberately making his brother believe a lie so that he would hate enough to kill. Wild Horse began to speak, and Jennifer could only guess what he might be saying. A look of resignation showed in his eyes.

"So, my brother," he was saying to Wade, the word panted. "You have taken both my weapons. I . . . misjudged your skill and strength. A woman . . . can give a man much power . . . fill a man with much hatred and vengeance. Now you understand . . . my own vengeance for what happened to my wives . . . my sons. Now you understand . . . the Comanche heart!"

Wade hesitated, and Jennifer could see by his eyes that he was touched by whatever Wild Horse had said. She had not missed the note of near affection in Wild Horse's tone of voice.

Wade was himself confused and surprised by his brother's sudden look of compassion. "Why?" he asked. "Why did you have to hurt Jennifer?"

Wild Horse's eyes narrowed. "Because one of us must *die!* That is the one thing . . . you must understand above all others. If you do not end this fight . . . I will keep you and your woman here . . . and she will continue to share my bed. Perhaps the next time . . . I will let you *watch!*" A proud sneer returned to the man's face.

The words brought Wade back to reality, brought back the hatred that had made him gladly battle his brother. He tossed aside the hatchet. There was now only the knife between them.

"So, my brother," Wild Horse said, his grin returning, "you are at least an honorable man. You give me . . . a better chance."

"You have *no* chance, my *brother!*" Wade sneered. He moved the knife to his right hand and lunged at Wild Horse, slamming his left arm against the man's already-cracked breast bone, while he tried to shove the knife into Wild Horse's groin; but with a strength surprising for his condition, Wild Horse managed to again grab Wade's right arm. It all happened then in a matter of seconds. Because of the way Wade charged into him, Wild Horse was already stumbling backward. At the same time he shoved Wade's arm to the right. Gravity forbade either man to stay on his feet. As they went down, Wild Horse lost his grip on Wade's arm, which Wade curled around the man in an automatic reaction to break their fall.

They landed with a thud and a grunt from Wild Horse, whose eyes suddenly widened. His face quickly paled, and it took a moment for Wade to realize the man had fallen onto his own knife, still in Wade's hand. The point of its wicked, eight-inch blade could be seen protruding from Wild Horse's stomach, while Wade's right hand was pinned under the man's back.

The circle of cheering warriors quieted. They moved back, and Jennifer stared as both men stayed on the ground, seeming suddenly frozen in time. At first she wasn't even sure just what had happened.

Wild Horse just stared at Wade, managing to reach up then and touch Wade's face with his right hand. "So . . . my brother," he said in a whisper. "It is . . . done. You should . . . know . . . I did not touch . . . your woman. I only wanted you . . . to think it. She knew . . . it had to be so . . . for your sake. But I . . . did not think

. . . it would help you this much. It is . . . good. The spirits . . . smile upon us both now. I go . . . to my death . . . a happy man."

He grasped at Wade's hair, a soft grin on his face that finally faded into death. His hand dropped, and Wade stayed bent over him for a moment, then rolled the man slightly to his side and yanked out the knife. His eyes teared, and he closed them, bending his head to touch his cheek to Wild Horse's.

"Damn you," he whispered. "It didn't . . . have to be, my brother," he choked out. "It . . . didn't have to be. Why couldn't I make you understand that?"

He raised up slightly, touching the man's face and closing his eyelids. He threw back his head and let out a long, piercing cry like a wounded animal, and the others watched in shock and sorrow. Wild Horse was dead. Wade wept over the body for several minutes, and Jennifer could not help her own tears, her heart aching for him. He finally rose, staring down at the bloody knife still in his hand. He turned to Aguila, whose own face was wet with tears. Wade stumbled over to the man, holding out the knife.

"You take it," he told the man in English. "He was like a son to you. I am not, and I cannot take the man's place. These people belong to you now. They have lost their leader. It is your decision what they must do."

Aguila slowly took the knife, his jaws flexing with a need to weep openly. He nodded and turned sadly away. Wade turned and slowly walked toward Jennifer, holding his chin proudly, keeping his eyes steadily on her own he came closer. "He told me . . . he never touched you," he said, his voice gruff.

She dropped her eyes, her throat aching. "I didn't want you to die," she answered, wondering if he was angry with her. She felt his hand at her face then, and he drew her closer, wrapping her in his arms, neither of them caring that he was covered with blood.

"It's all right," he told her. "It had to be. I understand that now." He hugged her closer. "I feel strangely at peace

426

now, Jenny. I know I belong to a fierce, proud people. I know part of me belongs here, and I understand the wildness I sometimes feel inside me."

She put a hand to his chest. "Let me tend to your wounds, Wade, before you bleed to death."

He kept his arms around her shoulders, turning to look back once more at Wild Horse's body, his wounds and suffering of the last few days leaving him in a kind of weary stupor. "I look at him . . . and it's like seeing myself lying there . . . as though I killed myself, Jenny. In a way . . . maybe I did. I killed . . . the Comanche in me. I just . . . want to go home now . . . and take you with me . . . if you'll come."

She took his hand and kissed it. "You know that I'll come. We made it through this horror, Wade. Now we can face anything together. Nothing can stop us from loving each other and being together."

He put his arm back around her shoulders for support, and she moved an arm around his waist, helping him to Wild Horse's tipi so she could dress his wounds. A weeping Gentle Winds ran to Wild Horse's body, letting out a pitiful cry of mourning.

Wade and Jennifer walked behind those who carried the stretcher that held Wild Horse's body. It was wrapped tightly in a buffalo robe, his favorite possessions and weapons positioned around him. Behind Wade and Jennifer the rest of the warriors and the few women and children who had been with Wild Horse's camp followed in a funeral procession.

Aguila and the three other men who carried the stretcher raised it up, placing in on four poles fashioned from thick cottonwood branches strong enough to last well after Wild Horse's body would wither enough that wild animals would no longer be interested in it. The poles were secured in the ground, and they held the stretcher high in the air.

Wild Horse's people had picked a place higher in the

hills but in a spot surrounded by tangled vines and cottonwoods, a place where their leader's body would not be found and looted by soldiers or other whites. The women began keening their death chants, and Wade stood staring at the stretcher, wondering at times if any of this was real. His shoulder ached but the wound had done no paralyzing damage. All his other wounds were superficial. He felt like one mass of cuts and bruises, but his injuries gave him no concern for the moment.

He had killed his own brother. He wondered how he would ever explain to his parents in California why this had to be. His Christian upbringing tangled with the Comanche spirit he had come to understand, and somehow he sensed God would not be angry with him for what he had done. He had killed other men, but for reasons of self-defense, which was his reason for killing Wild Horse. But this was different. This was his brother, and he knew he was right in what he had told Jennifer earlier. In killing Wild Horse he had put an end to that part of him that had haunted him all his life, a strange inner force that had tried to claim him.

Jennifer held back, knowing this was a traumatic moment for Wade. He had said little while she dressed his wounds, and he had finally fallen into an exhausted, much-needed sleep. At dawn he had joined the other warriors in fashioning a platform for Wild Horse, then had come to get the body, which the women had annointed with special herbs and carefully wrapped.

Jennifer sat down in the grass, her own emotions mixed, thinking what an interesting person Wild Horse might have been to know, if he would have befriended Wade. She wished she knew how to comfort Wade, but he had to find his own way. This was a very personal trauma for him, and he had to come to grips with it on his own terms. She was only glad that he truly did seem more at peace now, in spite of his grief over killing his brother.

Wade went to his knees, and she could see his shoulders shaking. She closed her eyes, her own tears coming then. Suddenly she felt a hand on her shoulder. She wiped at her eyes, turning to see a young white girl standing near her. Her face was dirty and badly sunburned, her legs and arms showing sores from mosquito bites. Her dark hair was greased and braided. She sat down in the grass beside Jennifer, who just stared at her a moment, realizing this must be the young white captive girl Wade had told her about.

"Wild Horse is dead now," the little girl said in a small voice. "The wife of the man who captured me pushed me away and would not let me come back into her tipi. I think she thinks I am bad luck now." The child spoke with amazing calmness and obvious intelligence. She looked up at Jennifer. "They killed all my family—my grandmother, my mother and father, my brothers. There's nobody left. What should I do?"

Jennifer's heart went out to her. "Dear God," she muttered. She moved an arm around the girl's shoulders, wondering if she had ever even had the chance to cry yet. "I know how it feels to lose your whole family and feel alone," she answered. She touched the girl's hair, overwhelmed with grief and pity. "Wild Horse agreed we would not be harmed if Wade won this battle," she told the child. "We will leave here soon. You will come with us. What is your name?"

"Kathleen. Kathleen Williams."

Jennifer gave her a hug. "Mr. Morrow has a fine home in California, Kathleen. White people raised him, and they're very kind, Christian people. Would you like to come with us to California?"

"Are there Indians there?"

Jennifer smiled through her tears. "None that would bring you any more harm."

"What about him?" She pointed. "Mr. Morrow. He looks like an Indian, and he fought like one."

"He only did what he had to do. He isn't like the others, Kathleen. I know him well. He's a good man. Maybe he would even let you live with us—be our daughter, although at my age, you would seem more like a sister."

The girl's eyes teared a little. "My mother was pretty like

429

you, but she was older." She frowned. "Why did they do that? Why did they kill my family?"

Jennifer sighed, pulling her close so she could rest her head against her shoulder. Today Jennifer wore an Indian woman's tunic, which Aguila had brought over to Wild Horse's tipi for her because of her torn dress. Gentle Winds had not come back to the tipi.

"It's very hard to explain, Kathleen," she answered. "Many of them have broken hearts, and they feel desperate, because they have lost so much. Some day, when Mr. Morrow is over his grief, you should ask him. I think he understands better than I do. He told me something Wild Horse said to him. He said, 'Now you understand my own vengeance for what happened to my wives and my sons. Now you understand the Comanche heart.' I think perhaps he does. He is the one who can answer your questions."

She held the child close, glad for the chance to help at least one unfortunate captive. She glanced at Wade, who had stripped off the deerskin shirt he wore, one that had belonged to Wild Horse. To her shock he pulled his knife and deliberately cut his arm, drawing blood. Several others had done the same. She realized then it was a form of mourning, and for the moment he was as Comanche as the rest of them.

She closed her eyes and turned away from the pitiful sight. She knew there was a small part of him she would never understand. She could only accept it . . . and love him.

Chapter Twenty-Eight

The camp was quiet, and Jennifer saw neither hide nor hair of Gentle Winds, who apparently was refusing to come back to the tipi she had shared with Wild Horse, now that he was dead. It seemed to Jennifer that Wild Horse's death had quickly robbed most of the young warriors of their cockiness and fighting spirit. All day, since the funeral that morning, everything had been quiet. Jennifer felt no fear, realizing Wade was greatly honored by the Comanche. Wade had been in council with several of them and with Aguila most of the evening, not even taking time to eat.

Jennifer shared some fry-bread with Kathleen, her hands healed enough that they no longer gave her the excruciating surface pain that they had at first. Now they were just red and tender, and she could tell they would be slightly scarred, but she knew it wouldn't matter to Wade.

Earlier she and Kathleen had bathed in a nearby stream. It felt good to be clean again. Both she and the child wore Indian tunics, for they had no clothing of their own left intact. Jennifer guessed that other than being terrified and probably beaten and forced to help with chores, Kathleen had at least apparently not been sexually abused. She knew by the way the little girl was bouncing back to her natural sweet spirit that such a horror had not been visited upon her, and she thanked God the child had been spared.

Jennifer sat and talked with the girl, telling her about

her own past and how she met Wade, and Kathleen in turn told Jennifer about her family, at times struggling against tears. "My mother had a favorite locket," she told Jennifer. "It was gold, and shaped like a little heart. Sometimes I think I'd feel better if I could just have that locket. Pa bought it for her. It was nothing real expensive, just special."

Jennifer thought about the locket Tony had given her. Deaver had sneered that the man had stolen it off a dead settler. Could it have been Kathleen's mother? She wondered if the man at the stage station had disposed of her belongings, or if he was saving them. "We'll check at the fort and a couple other places," she promised the girl. "Maybe whoever found and buried your family kept some of their personal possessions for possible survivors."

The child seemed comforted by the promise. She finally fell asleep, and two hours later Wade ducked inside the tipi. Jennifer looked up, seeing the lingering sorrow in his eyes.

"I think Aguila and I have convinced them to go back to the reservation on the Red River. I'd like to go along with them, which means you would have to come, too. I won't let you out of my sight again. Do you mind?"

Their eyes held. "No," she said quietly. She watched him as he came near and sat down. He was such a magnificent specimen of man, especially tonight, for he wore only a loincloth since he had bathed earlier in the day. She checked the gauze she had wrapped around his wounded shoulder and was relieved the spot of blood there looked no bigger.

"Do you realize you have single-handedly ended some of the worst raiding in west Texas?" she asked. "Not that any of Texas's citizens will be grateful."

He sighed, staring at the small fire she had built. "If I did anything great, it was by accident. And it certainly isn't the way I would have chosen to do it." He talked quietly now, seeming tired, resigned.

Jennifer put a hand on his arm. "Do you want something to eat?"

He shook his head, glancing over at a still-sleeping Kathleen. "She's kind of latched onto you, hasn't she?"

"I suppose." She met his eyes. "I promised her she could come to California with us. She has no family left."

He smiled a little. "Wait till she meets Vivian Morrow. She'll adjust and be a happy little girl again in no time once she is under my mother's wing." He sighed deeply. "There sure isn't anyone around here I'd leave her with, not even at the fort." He turned to meet her eyes, reaching out to touch her face, which was still bruised. "You remind me of my white mother, wanting to take in an orphaned child, so full of love and compassion. When I think of what you've been through, all because of me—"

She put her fingers to his lips. "Willingly," she answered, "because I love you, Wade. None of it has been your fault. It's the fault of prejudiced people." She looked down at his bandaged arm from cutting himself in mourning. She had been grateful to find his gear remained intact, and she was able to find enough gauze to wrap his wounds.

"For a little while yesterday," she said, "when you were fighting—" She touched the wrapping on his arm lightly. "And this morning, when you did this, I was afraid perhaps you had become more Comanche than I could accept. But tonight you seem a little more like your old self. I could almost envision you taking over in Wild Horse's place." She met his eyes, breathing in his familiar scent. His hair hung straight and loose and shining. "But I know you could never be completely like him," she added. "Still, you will always be a great warrior in my eyes, Wade Morrow."

She saw the pride come into his blue eyes, and he drew in his breath, drinking in the sight of her glorious green eyes and cascading auburn hair. He put a hand to her hair.

"My God, Jenny, it's like I just realized you're really here, and you're all right and you're still mine. Is it true? He never touched you?"

She reddened slightly. "He slapped me around, tore my dress. He wanted you to think the worst, and I knew I had

433

to let you think it, too. I'm sorry, Wade."

"Don't be," he whispered. "It was that thought that saved my life."

Their eyes held, and in the next moment his mouth covered hers in their first kiss since the night he had come to the fort. But that night had been so different. Then she feared she would never see him again. Now the worry was over. They were safe and together. The burning kiss became more passionate, as both of them realized they had not enjoyed the luxury of intercourse since that night in the cave. How long ago was that? Three weeks, perhaps? They had both lost track of time.

Wade laid her back on a blanket that was spread over straw. Their wounds could not keep them from what they needed most. She needed to know he was truly alive, that the horror was over and Wade Morrow could truly belong to her. He was full of the feel of pride and power, possessed with a kind of fury at the thought of any other man touching her, needing to prove she was Wade Morrow's woman.

He moved on top of her, being careful to keep his greater weight off his wounded shoulder. But that was the least of his worries. The kisses grew hotter, heavier, hungrier. Suddenly he wanted, needed his woman, and he could tell she felt the same way. He untied her tunic at the shoulders, pulling down the front of it to touch her breasts almost worshipfully.

Jennifer drew in her breath when finally, she again experienced the glory of Wade Morrow's warm lips pulling at her breasts as though to take nourishment from them. She wrapped her fingers into his hair, glancing over to be sure Kathleen was still asleep. Wade smothered her in kisses, her breasts, her throat, her mouth again, back to her breasts, as though desperate for her. Her blood ran hot as she felt a big hand on her thigh, the scarred, still slightly-sore leg that this man had nursed and saved.

His hand moved under her tunic, where she wore nothing. In the next moment she gasped when his fingers touched her magically again, easily drawing forth the satiny moistness that assured him she wanted him just as badly as he wanted her. He untied and removed his loincloth, pushing up her tunic and moving between her legs.

It all happened quickly, uncontrollably. He was inside of her, and she knew in that moment that he had been right. Taking a man did get more enjoyable after the first time. This time she was healed, and her leg was also healed. She arched up to him as he raised up, grasping her bottom with big, strong hands, pushing hard while he looked down at her like a conquering warrior. He moved in ways that made her mad with desire, and in moments she felt the glorious climax. He sensed it, pushing deeper, holding out as long as he could endure, for his own ecstasy was beyond measure.

She felt his life surging into her, and she hoped it would take hold. He threw back his head and groaned with pleasure, waiting several seconds before leaning back down to kiss her hungrily again. "I don't want to stop yet, Jenny," he whispered. "I love the feel of being inside of you."

She felt him already swelling with the want of her, for they were starved for each other. "Then stay inside of me," she answered in a silken voice. "We have the rest of the night. We have forever now."

He grinned, moving his lips to her throat, lightly licking her skin. Jennifer closed her eyes, hoping Kathleen was a hard sleeper.

"Indians ahead, sir, moving kind of slow, mostly warriors, but I swear I saw that white woman, and a young white girl. The white woman was riding with one of the warriors—sits tall on his horse. I think it's Wild Horse."

The army scout had ridden up to Captain Howell with the news. Unwittingly, Howell and his men had intercepted what was left of Wild Horse's party, now headed for the Red River.

"If the white woman is still with them, it *must* be Wild

435

Horse," Howell answered, excitement in his voice. "They must not even know we're here! We'll circle ahead and trap them!"

"Wait a minute," Bill Morrow said, moving his horse in front of Howell's. "Which way were they headed?" he asked the scout.

"Almost directly north."

Bill moved his eyes to Howell. "That's the direction of the reservation. For all you know, that's where they're headed—*peacefully!* My brother could be with them. Even if he isn't, you know damn well that when attacked by surprise the Comanche usually kill their captives before they let the soldiers get them back. You'd be endangering Jennifer Andrews's life, and the life of the little girl if you attack them straight on. For all you know the man your scout thinks is Wild Horse could be Wade."

"This is an army matter, Mr. Morrow! Wild Horse could be down there, and I'm not going to let him get away from me this time!"

Bill surprised the man when he pulled a gun and pointed it at him. The rest of his thirty-plus men followed suit, literally surrounding the soldiers, every man appearing ready to shoot.

"Tell your men to hand over their weapons, Captain," Bill told the man.

Howell's eyes widened. "Are you crazy!"

"You're not going to attack them, Captain," Bill declared. "I won't have your men shooting at a man who could be my brother! Now those Indians out there are a lot more likely not to run if they see regular citizens approaching them. You show a blue coat, and they'll scatter like birds fresh kicked up. Let me and my brother and a few of my men ride in first, with white flags, kind of feel them out. If Wade has been with them, something could have happened we don't know about!"

"I'll have you hanged for this," Howell growled.

"You can't do a thing to me." Bill looked at his men. "Take their weapons, boys." He looked back at the captain as his men began taking guns from the soldiers.

436

"It's me and my brother who will be putting our lives on the line," he said. "If you hear shooting, my men will give you back your guns and you can come riding in. If they're peaceful and if my brother is with them, I'll send one of my men back to tell you. You can ride in—no guns! I know how trigger-happy soldiers get around Indians. I'm not about to let this turn into a needless slaughter. When you come in, you do it damn slow. I don't want them thinking we tricked them, or my brother and I will be the first ones they take aim at."

"This is preposterous," Howell roared. "You can't do this!"

"Well, I'm doing it." Bill looked around at his men, picking those he knew were the most experienced with Indians. "Pete, Justin, Nick—you three come with me. Get a petticoat or something from the woman's baggage and rip it up for white flags."

The one called Pete obeyed, opening one of Jennifer's carpetbags and pulling out her only remaining slip. They had gone to the stage station first to talk to the man called Seth, where they had picked up Jennifer's belongings. Bill wondered how Seth was feeling today. In his anger he had landed a hard fist into Seth's face, knocking the man clear across the room. He would much rather have killed him, but Howell would have arrested him and he wouldn't have been able to come here to try to help Wade.

Pete tore up the slip and handed pieces of it out to the others.

"Keep your rifles in their boots and hold the white cloth up high with one hand," Bill told them. "Let's go."

The men rode off, and Howell watched, his fury and humiliation knowing no bounds.

Wade spotted the five riders first. He raised his hand to halt the small, migrating band of Indians. Jennifer's heart quickened at the sight of someone approaching. She looked over at Kathleen, who rode in front of Aguila on the man's horse. "Don't be afraid, Kathy," she told the girl, giving her a reassuring smile. She kept her arms around Wade. *No,* she thought, *we don't have to be afraid. We have Wade.* She felt safe and protected, her blood still rushing warm at the thought of their heated lovemaking the night before. Still, what was this new trouble coming? Would her dream of being with Wade forever end after all?

One of the Comanche women uttered words of fright, and Wade sensed immediately that all of them, men and women alike, were thinking of fleeing at the sight of white men. "Wait," he called out to them. "Don't run! They're carrying white flags, a sign of peace." He turned to Jennifer. "Let me do the talking until we know who these men are." He headed his horse farther ahead, and the others watched warily. "I'll be damned," Wade muttered then.

"What is it?"

"I swear it looks like my brothers." He grinned more as they came closer, then he turned and hollered to Aguila. "It's all right. Tell the others not to be afraid. It's my white brothers. They mean no harm!" He laughed lightly. "Hang on!" he told Jennifer. He rode forward at a near gallop then, and Jennifer clung tightly to his waist.

Bill and Henry drew their horses to a halt, hardly recognizing Wade at first because of his near-nakedness and the wild look about him.

"Bill!" Wade called out. "You son of a bitch! *Now* you come! Where were you when I needed you?"

Wade rode up beside the man to whom he had spoken, grasping his wrist, and Bill clasped his own hand around Wade's wrist. "Wade? My God, what's happened to you? You look so wild I was about ready to shoot you." His eyes took a quick inventory. "Good Lord, man, you're a sight. What the hell did they do to you?"

Wade's smile faded slightly. "It's a long story."

Henry moved to the other side of Wade, and Wade turned and grasped the man's hand. "You're a damn good sight, Henry." He looked back at Bill. "Both of you. A damn good sight. Thank God I've still got a family."

Jennifer felt warmed immediately at the sight of Bill

and Henry Morrow. They were handsome, solid looking men with a warmth in their eyes she was sure showed the kind of man their father was. Bill looked at her then, and she was immediately self-conscious of how she must look. He only grinned, looking back at Wade.

"What the hell have you been up to, brother? Captain Howell tells us you went and lost your heart to a white woman. I take it this is her."

Wade grinned, twisting his body slightly to put a hand on Jennifer's arm. "You're right. This is Jennifer Andrews. I intend to make it Jennifer Morrow as soon as possible. We could write a book about what we've been through since we met a few weeks ago. Jennifer, these are my brothers, Bill and Henry."

Wade nodded to the other men, all men he knew from his father's company, while Jennifer nodded to his brothers. "I'm glad to finally meet you," she told them. "I'm sorry for the way I look. For a while I wasn't sure either Wade or I would ever see anyone from the civilized world again."

Bill put out his hand, and she reddened. "I'm sorry. My hands—" She looked down at their red, puffy condition.

"I'm the one who's sorry," Bill told her. "I forgot. Howell told us how they got burned." He looked at Wade. "She's beautiful, even without fancy clothes and hairdo. We're both glad for you, Wade, damn glad. Ma and Pa will be happy as hell to meet her."

"Hey, Miss Andrews, you'll be glad to know Bill gave that man at the stage station a good wallop for letting the Indians take you. And we got back all your things. They're over the other side of that hill, with the rest of our men and Captain Howell."

"Captain Howell!" Wade sobered. "He's with you?"

"Him and about twenty of his men," Bill answered. "We didn't know what we'd run into, Wade, so we brought a few soldiers along for extra guns. We figured we'd have to rescue you from Wild Horse."

Their eyes held, and Bill saw the sudden sorrow in Wade's. "Wild Horse is dead," he told Bill. "I killed him."

Bill sighed, and Jennifer was amazed and pleased at the look of true love and concern in the man's eyes for the Indian man he called brother. "I'm sorry, Wade. I know you wouldn't have wanted it."

"The man left me no choice. Some day when we've got more time, I'll explain. Right now I'm concerned about those soldiers. I've convinced Wild Horse's people to go back to the reservation. If they see soldiers, they'll think they've been tricked again and they'll scatter all to hell."

"I had the men take their guns. I figured you might be here—and I was afraid if you weren't, and Howell and his men went riding in shooting, those Indians would kill Miss Andrews. The scout said there was a little girl along, too, who looked white."

"Kathleen Williams," Jennifer told the man. "Wade and I are taking her with us to California. She was a captive, but they've let her go, and she has no family left."

Bill grinned. "Ma will like taking in another orphan. You know how she is."

"Yes," Wade answered softly, thinking of Slow Woman, remembering the feel of her in his arms. He loved Vivian Morrow all the more for being the mother he never would have had otherwise. He sighed deeply and met Bill's eyes. "Let me go and try to explain to Wild Horse's men before you ride back to Howell. I don't care if you and the others have to shoot those soldiers' horses from under them. Don't let them come this way! There's no use in it now. It's Wild Horse Howell wanted, and he's dead. Howell might as well go back to Fort Stockton."

"We'll go back and tell him." The man grinned, tears in his eyes. "Damn, it's good to see you, Wade. I was afraid we'd have to go back and tell the folks you were dead. It would have been hard on Pa, worse for Ma. I'm just sorry the way things had to turn out. It would have been nice for you if you could have been friends with your blood brother."

Wade's horse tossed its mane and whinnied. "I did find an uncle. And I have a cousin back at the reservation, a little girl. I've agreed to ride there with them. I'm hoping to convince all of them to stay there and stop the raiding, and I want to see the little girl once more."

"Sure, Wade," Bill answered. He glanced at Jennifer once more. "Welcome to the family, ma'am," he told her. "Anybody Wade loves, we all love."

Henry grinned and tipped his hat to Wade. He and Bill turned and rode off then with the others. Wade turned his horse and rode back to Aguila.

"They brought soldiers," he told the man in English so the others couldn't understand. He saw the alarm come into Aguila's eyes. "They only did it because they didn't know what they'd find. They're good men, Aguila. They can be trusted. I told them to tell Captain Howell to go back to Fort Stockton."

"Soldiers cannot be trusted," Aguila told him.

"My brothers won't let them come here. I'm going back myself to convince Howell to give it up. All he wanted was Wild Horse, and Wild Horse is dead. You keep going with the others. Jennifer and I will catch up. I give you my word, Aguila. The soldiers won't follow. My brothers have enough men along to force them to turn back."

Aguila nodded. "I will trust your word—no one else's." He shouted to the others to keep going. He turned his horse, but Jennifer called out to him. "Let us take Kathleen for now," she told the man. "If the soldiers see her, they'll be even more convinced that you are keeping your word and are returning to the reservation."

Aguila nodded, handing Kathleen over to Wade, who plunked her in front of him on his horse. "We'll see about borrowing an extra horse from my brothers or one of the soldiers," he told Jennifer. He gave Kathleen a light hug. "Don't worry, we won't leave you behind. You're staying right with us."

Kathleen leaned against Wade's chest, some of her childish joy of life returning with each passing day that she was cared for by this kind Indian man and Jennifer, who had become her very good friends.

Wade turned his horse and headed back over the hill where his brothers were already riding. He followed close

441

behind, and as they approached the soldiers, Howell watched in astonishment.

"Wild Horse," the man muttered.

"No. I expect it's Wade," one of the Morrow men told him. "Sit tight, Captain. I never heard no shooting."

Wade and his brothers came closer. "Wild Horse is dead," Bill called out to Howell. "You and your men can go back."

"Is that so!" Howell moved his eyes to Wade, his shock evident at Wade's battered condition. "What's going on here?"

"Get down," Wade told Jennifer. She slid off the horse and reached up for Kathleen. Wade rode closer to Howell. "My brother told you," Wade said, his anger immediately building at the sight of the captain. "Wild Horse is dead. I killed him myself. How else do you think I got these wounds?"

"How do I know that's true? Maybe you're protecting him while he gets away."

In an instant, and to everyone's surprise, including Jennifer's, Wade's knife was out and pressed against Howell's throat, Wade's other hand gripping the man's uniform at the scruff of his neck. "And maybe I've just about had my fill of you, Howell! You turned Jennifer out, knowing the danger she would be in! You can believe Wild Horse is dead because I'm *telling* you he's dead. I'm no liar, Howell!"

Howell's eyes widened in terror. At the moment Wade looked no less murderous than Wild Horse himself would have. "Those Indians over the hill are heading back to the reservation—*peacefully*," Wade growled. "Why start something that isn't necessary? Leave them alone, Howell! It's *over*! You've got no Wild Horse to tuck under your belt and earn a promotion. And even though I had to kill him myself, I'd sure as hell rather have it end for him that way than for him to be imprisoned and hanged by the likes of you!"

He shoved his knife back into its sheath but still had

442

hold of the back of Howell's uniform. With a strong arm he yanked hard, pulling Howell toward him so violently that the man fell from his horse. Jennifer gasped as Wade quickly dismounted himself, grabbing Howell up by the front of his uniform and landing a big fist into the man's face, sending him flying.

"That was for Jennifer," he told the man.

Howell rolled to his knees, spitting blood from his mouth, more trickling from his nose.

"Here's what you're going to do, Howell," Wade told him, while Howell's men watched in surprise. "You're going to leave those Indians alone, and you're going to leave me and my family alone! In return, you're welcome to report that Wild Horse is dead. You can say he was killed by me, because Wild Horse insisted one of us should die. You can report that once Wild Horse was dead, his followers decided to return to the reservation. Take all the credit yourself, if you want, even for the return of that little girl over there. She was one of Wild Horse's captives. Her name is Kathleen Williams. Her family is all dead, and Jenny and I are taking her to California with us."

He reached down and jerked Howell to his feet. "Tell whoever you answer to that you were the one who convinced Wild Horse's people to stop their raiding. *That* should win you a stripe or a star or whatever the hell you're after! Do whatever you want about reporting this, but just leave us alone and leave those people over the hill alone!"

Howell wiped blood from his nose. "Where is Wild Horse's body? The authorities won't believe me."

"Do you really think I'd tell any white man where he's buried so they can go and desecrate his grave? The fact that his people are returning to the reservation is proof enough the man is dead. If he wasn't, they would all still be out there raiding!"

Howell's face was beet red with embarrassment. "How dare you hit me in front of my men!"

"How dare *you* send Jennifer away! Do like I say, Howell, and *maybe* I can talk my white father out of having you drawn and quartered!"

Howell glowered at him. "Have your men give back my men's weapons!"

"Not until you all reach the fort. I gave those people my word that you wouldn't come after them."

Howell looked him over. "All right. You win, Morrow. I'll just be glad to be *rid* of you! The woman, too!" The man mounted his horse, taking a handkerchief from his pocket and holding it to his still-bleeding nose. "I'll say one thing, Morrow. The body of Wild Horse might be buried out there somewhere, but he's not dead! He's standing right in front of me!"

The man turned his horse and ordered his men to head back. The men who carried Jennifer's bags untied them and set them down on the ground. "You might need this stuff, ma'am," one of them told her. She looked up at him and thanked him, feeling none of the animosity and disrespect she had felt from Tony and the others for loving an Indian.

"I'll ride back with Henry," Bill told Wade. "We have plenty of extra horses with the remuda. The woman and little girl can share my horse."

"Thanks, Bill. We'll head north. Soon as we reach the reservation, we'll head back south and try to intercept you. You should be returning from Galveston by then. You'll be traveling slower because of the wagons."

"And we'll all head for California," Bill said with a wink. "I'll bet home sounds good to you."

"It does," Wade answered.

"Bill," Jennifer spoke up. "There's a woman back at the fort named Alice. Please tell her I'm all right—and Wade, too. Tell her we're going to be married and go to California. Tell her I'll always remember her, and I'll write her."

"Yes, ma'am," Bill replied, tipping his hat. "Be glad to." He mounted up behind Henry then, and Wade walked up to Henry, grasping his arm. "See you in about three weeks, little brother. Ride easy now. Don't lose your brother."

Henry laughed. "Sure!" He immediately took off at a gallop, Bill yelling and cussing at him until they were out of sight.

Jennifer smiled and knelt down to open one of her bags. She rummaged in one of the inside pockets, pulling out the locket. She held it out to Kathleen. The child's eyes widened, and she paled slightly. With a shaking hand she reached out and took the necklace.

"Is that the one?" Jennifer asked.

"Yes," Kathleen whispered. She closed it in her fist and held it against her heart. "How did you find it!"

"One of the soldiers back at the fort . . . saved it," she told the girl. "He thought someone might want it," she lied. How could she tell the child the man had ripped it off her mother's dead body, thinking it might be worth something? "He gave it to me for safe keeping. Now it's back where it belongs."

The girl's eyes teared. "Thank you, Jenny."

Jennifer embraced her for a moment, then rose and faced Wade, who pulled her into his arms. "Once we're on our way, I'll wire my uncle, and Mattie," she told him. "Mattie deserves to know I'm all right. My uncle doesn't, but I suppose it's only right he knows for certain what happened to me. Once we're married, he can't hurt us."

Wade kissed her hair. "No one can hurt us. No one. I'm never going to feel guilty for this, Jenny, and you're never going to hang your head in shame. I love you, more than my own life."

She looked up at him. "And I love you . . . so much."

Already they again longed to unite their bodies, but there was plenty of time for that now. They would go to California, and make a home there, for themselves and Kathleen. Their lips met in a sweet kiss, while Kathleen draped the locket around her neck.

Wade helped Jennifer mount up on Bill's horse then, handing Kathleen up to her. He tied Jennifer's bags onto the horse, then mounted his own horse with ease and grace.

They headed north, toward the Red River, neither of

them aware that for years neither settler nor Indian would venture into Comanche Hills, for many who dared to do so would tell tales of a ghostly Indian who rode those hills on moonlit nights, his hair flying back in the wind, his hatchet raised. He would let out bloodcurdling war cries, so they would report, and when he came close, they could see that his eyes were blue.

> *Entreat me not to leave thee, or to return from following after thee; for whither thou goest, I will go; and where thou lodgest, I will lodge: thy people shall be my people, and thy God my God . . .*

Author's Note

I hope you have enjoyed my story. For information about other books I have written, as well as a personal bio, please feel free to write me at 6013 North Coloma Road, Coloma, MI 49038-9309. Be sure to include a legal-size, self-addressed, STAMPED envelope. Thank you!